J. A. Cuddon was born in
College, Oxford, where,
work on the concept of evil and the devil in medieval
literature. He also represented the university at cricket, rugby and
hockey, though without gaining a 'blue'. For some ten years he wrote
only plays, before turning to other forms. Apart from numerous essays,
short stories, articles, contributions to encyclopedias, a dozen plays
and three libretti, he has published a number of novels, notably *A
Multitude of Sins, Testament of Iscariot, Acts of Darkness, The Six Wounds*
and *The Bride of Battersea*, which have been translated into several European languages, and two travel books, *The Owl's Watchsong: a Study of
Istanbul* and the *Companion Guide to Jugoslavia*, which have also been
translated. He has also written *A Dictionary of Literary Terms* (published
in the Penguin Reference series) which he began while on a fellowship
at Cambridge in 1968. In 1971 he received an award from the Gold-
smiths Company to make a study of medieval frescoes in Serbia and
Macedonia. In 1980 he published *A Dictionary of Sport and Games*, a two-
million word account of most of the sports and games of the world
since 5,200 B.C. This came out in paperback in 1981. A compulsive
traveller (with a special interest in the Balkans and the Near East), his
main recreations are going to the theatre, watching sport and pursuing
an amateur interest in zoology. He has edited *The Penguin Book of Horror
Stories* and is finishing a book about travels in the Balkans.

THE
PENGUIN
BOOK
OF
GHOST
STORIES

Edited by J. A. Cuddon

Penguin Books

PENGUIN BOOKS

Published by the Penguin Group
27 Wrights Lane, London W8 5TZ, England
Viking Penguin Inc., 40 West 23rd Street, New York, New York 10010, USA
Penguin Books Australia Ltd, Ringwood, Victoria, Australia
Penguin Books Canada Ltd, 2801 John Street, Markham, Ontario, Canada L3R 1B4
Penguin Books (NZ) Ltd, 182–190 Wairau Road, Auckland 10, New Zealand

Penguin Books Ltd, Registered Offices: Harmondsworth, Middlesex, England

This collection first published 1984
7 9 10 8 6

Introduction and selection copyright © J. A. Cuddon, 1984
All rights reserved

The acknowledgements on pages 9–10 constitute an extension of this copyright page

Typeset, printed and bound in Great Britain by
Hazell Watson & Viney Limited
Member of BPCC plc
Aylesbury, Bucks, England
Set in VIP Palatino

Contents

Contents

Who is the third who walks always beside you?
When I count there are only you and I together
But when I look ahead up the white road
There is always another one walking beside you
Gliding wrapt in a brown mantle, hooded
I do not know whether a man or a woman
But who is that on the other side of you?

T. S. Eliot: *The Waste Land*

Acknowledgements

For permission to reprint the stories specified we are indebted to:

Sheila Reeves for 'A Haunted Island' from *The Empty House* by Algernon Blackwood (1906); Edward Arnold (Publishers) Ltd for 'The Rose Garden' from *The Ghost Stories of M. R. James*, copyright 1931 by M. R. James; The National Trust, Macmillan (London) Ltd, and A. P. Watt Ltd for 'The Return of Imray' from *Life's Handicaps* by Rudyard Kipling, copyright 1891 by the National Trust for Places of Historical Interest and Natural Beauty; A. & C. Black (Publishers) Ltd for 'My Adventures in Norfolk' by A. J. Alan (*c.* 1924); The Executors of the Estate of H. G. Wells, and A. P. Watt Ltd for 'The Inexperienced Ghost' from *The Short Stories of H. G. Wells*, copyright 1927 by the Literary Executors of the Estate of H. G. Wells; The Executors of the Estate of E. F. Benson, and A. P. Watt Ltd for 'The Room in the Tower' from *The Room in the Tower and Other Stories* by E. F. Benson, copyright 1912 by the Executors of the Estate of E. F. Benson; Constable & Co. Ltd and Watkins/Loomis Agency, Inc., for 'Afterward' by Edith Wharton, copyright 1909 by the Century Company, renewal copyright 1937 by D. Appleton-Century Co., Inc.; Martin Secker & Warburg for 'The Wardrobe' from *Stories of a Lifetime* by Thomas Mann; A. D. Peters & Co. Ltd for 'The Buick Saloon' from *The Song in the House* by Ann Bridge (1936): David Higham Associates Ltd for 'The Tower' by Marghanita Laski; A. D. Peters & Co. Ltd and Don Congdon Associates, Inc., for 'The Wind' from *The October Country* by Ray Bradbury, copyright © Ray Bradbury, 1943, 1971; Hughes Massie for 'Exorcizing Baldassare' by Edward Hyams; Harold Ober Associates, Inc., for 'The Leaf-Sweeper' by Muriel Spark, copyright © Copyright Administration Ltd, 1966; Mr Fielden Hughes for his story 'Dear Ghost . . .', copyright © Fielden Hughes, 1965; Victor Gollancz and Brandt & Brandt, New York, for 'Sonata for Harp and Bicycle' from *A Bundle of Nerves* by Joan Aiken, copyright © Joan Aiken, 1976; Miss Elizabeth Walter for her story 'Come and Get Me' from *Come and Get Me*, copyright © Elizabeth Walter, 1973; The author and the Hogarth Press Ltd for 'Andrina' from *Andrina and Other Stories* by George Mackay Brown, copyright © George Mackay Brown, 1983; Jonathan Cape Ltd for 'The Axe' by Penelope Fitzgerald from *The Times Anthology of Ghost Stories*, copyright © Penelope Fitzgerald, 1975; A. D. Peters & Co. Ltd for 'The July Ghost' by A. S. Byatt, copyright © A. S. Byatt, 1982.

In spite of extensive inquiries over many months it has, unfortunately, not been possible to trace who holds the rights in A. M. Burrage's story 'One Who Saw' or Alain Danielou's story 'The Game of Dice'.

Publishing details for the remaining stories are as follows:

'The Beggarwoman of Locarno' (1810) is from *The Marquise of O and Other Stories* by Heinrich von Kleist, translated by David Luke and Nigel Reeves (Penguin Books, 1978), translation copyright © David Luke and Nigel Reeves, 1978; 'The Entail' is from *Tales of Hoffmann* by E. T. A. Hoffmann (1817), selected and translated by R. J. Hollingdale, with the assistance of Stella and Vernon Humphries and Sally Hayward (Penguin Books, 1982), translation copyright © Sally Hayward, 1982; 'Wandering Willie's Tale' is from *Redgauntlet* by Walter Scott (1824); 'The Queen of Spades' is from *The Queen of Spades and Other Stories* by Alexander Pushkin (1834), translated by Rosemary Edmonds (Penguin Books, 1958), translation copyright © Rosemary Edmonds, 1958, 1962; 'The Old Nurse's Story' by Elizabeth Gaskell was first published in *Household Words* magazine (1852); 'The Open Door' by Margaret Oliphant was first published in 1868; 'Mr Justice Harbottle' by Sheridan Le Fanu was first published in 1872; 'Le Horla' is from *Selected Short Stories* by Guy de Maupassant (1887), translated by Roger Colet (Penguin Books, 1971), translation copyright © Roger Colet, 1971; 'Sir Edmund Orme' by Henry James was first published in 1908; 'Angeline, or the Haunted House' by Emile Zola was first published in 1898, this translation copyright © Clive Smith, 1983; 'The Moonlit Road' by Ambrose Bierce was first published in 1894; 'Footsteps in the Snow' by Mario Soldati, translated by Gwyn Morris, is from *Italian Short Stories*, edited by Raleigh Trevelyan (Penguin Books, 1965), translation copyright © Penguin Books Ltd, 1965.

Introduction

'... it was but the breath of a whisper overheard. It was the hour when night visions breed disquiet, as men lie chained by sleep; fear took hold of me, a fit of trembling that filled my whole frame, and made every hair bristle. All at once a spirit came beside me and stopped; there it stood, no face I knew, yet I could see the form of it, and catch its voice, light as a rustling breeze.'

This is not an extract from a recently discovered tale by Edgar Allan Poe, nor an excerpt from a story by, say, C. R. Maturin or Arthur Machen, but a passage from the Book of Job (composed some time between the sixth and the fourth century B.C.) in Monsignor Ronald Knox's rendering. It continues magnificently with a series of momentous questions from the apparition which are uttered in a whisper. It is a comparatively early instance of a ghostly experience in recorded literature.

One might hazard a guess that ghost stories antedate literature and belong to a primordial world in 'the dark backward and abysm of time'. It is a fact that in primitive religion, mythology and ancient epic the interrelationship of the living and the dead, the natural and the supernatural, is commonplace. All societies which hold animistic beliefs have been (and are) disposed to believe in ghosts; and, as Sir James Frazer, E. B. Tylor (who first used the term 'animism') and others have shown, it is next to impossible to find societies which do not have such beliefs. Even when many members of a given society have rationalized them or repudiated them or merely allowed them to fall into desuetude the beliefs display a certain resilience, a tendency to linger on.

Such beliefs pervade pre-Christian literature in Europe and in the Near and Middle East. From the fourth century onwards, in the *Patrologia Latina*, in philosophical and moral treatises, in chronicles, in collections of legends, *exempla*, homilies and sermons, in theological handbooks, as well as in a wide range of other didactic literature, and in an extensive variety of literature designed primarily to divert and entertain, there are numerous references to ghosts and anecdotes about them.

From time to time official and surprisingly scientific investigations were made in cases of alleged visitation by ghosts. There were even periodic instances of poltergeists, about which much has been said and written in the twentieth century. The annals of the abbey of Fulda, for example, contain an account of a farm near Bingen which was haunted by an incendiary, stone-throwing poltergeist in A.D. 858. When subjected to the ritual of exorcism, he struck some bystander, called the priest by name and accused him of fornication. He also claimed to have taken cover under the priest's cassock when he sprinkled holy water. As in this case, many ghostly activities and pranks were associated with demonic agency. In the literature referred to above there are many hundreds of stories of devilry, and a very large number involving good spirits. For a thousand years and more the multifarious world of the supernatural was deemed to be contiguous to the natural order; cheek by jowl with it, so to speak. As it had been, in different modes and under other dispensations, in pre-Christian times.

Moreover, Christian precept, doctrine and belief, derived from the Old Testament, the gospels and the Acts, confirmed the existence of the supernatural order over and over again. The theological and philosophical works of the metaphysicians ratified the teaching of the Church. The Son of God Himself was the most illustrious ghost in history (to say nothing of the Holy Ghost). Christ was reported to have made no fewer than eleven appearances after the Resurrection. You could hardly believe in the Resurrection and not believe in ghosts.

The wonder is, perhaps, that the ghost[1] story as we understand it today (and have for close on two hundred years) – at its simplest, a work of fiction of indeterminate length about a place haunted by the spirit of a dead person (a spirit which may or may not 'materialize' in some shape or form) – did not appear sooner.

Until very early in the nineteenth century, most stories about ghosts were anecdotal (often with a basis of fact) and could not really be regarded as fiction in the way in which we now regard the ghost stories of, say, Henry James or E. F. Benson. However, here and there we find quite striking examples of stories which are very near to being fiction, or are so wrought that they approach that category. For instance there is Lucian's

1. The word *ghost* itself is an old one. The Old English form of it is *gast*, denoting a soul or spirit. Equivalents were Old Frisian *gast*, Old Swedish *gest* and Old High German *geist*.

tale of the haunted sandal in his satirical sketch of the pathological liar. In Petronius's *Satyricon* and Apuleius's *The Golden Ass* there are inset ghost stories which come near the modern form and idea. They are sophisticated and well constructed and are clearly intended to send a chill down the reader's spine.

The beguiling Pliny the Younger, too, shows an interest in the ghost story. Writing to Licinius Sura he says: '. . . I should very much like to know whether you think ghosts exist, and have a form of their own and some sort of supernatural power, or whether they lack substance and reality and take shape only from our fears.' He goes on to relate the experience of one Curtius Rufus (this story is also told by Tacitus in *Annals*, xɪ:21) who, when on duty in Africa, was one day walking up and down the colonnade of his house. During his perambulation there came an apparition: the figure of a woman of superhuman size and beauty. She claimed to be 'the spirit of Africa' who would foretell his future. Predictions promptly followed and proved true.

Rather more interesting is his tale of a haunted house in Athens. Here we find several of the standard constituents of the traditional ghost story. It was a large house with a sinister reputation for being dangerous to its occupants. At dead of night there could be heard the clanking of iron and the rattle of chains. Before the terrified inhabitants there would then appear the filthy and emaciated spectre of an old man with fetters on his legs and chains on his wrists. Those who tried to live in the house were so frightened they could not sleep. Lack of sleep, plus fear and anxiety, made them ill. So the house was deserted but was advertised for sale or to be let in case someone could be found who knew nothing of the ghost.

Eventually the philosopher Athenodorus, when visiting Athens, heard that the house was to let, but was at once suspicious of the low price. In due course he found out about the ghost and, being an inquisitive man, determined to rent the place. The spectre duly appeared and beckoned the philosopher to follow him. This he did. In the courtyard the ghost vanished. Athenodorus marked the spot and the next day advised the city magistrates to have the place dug up. 'There they found bones, twisted round with chains, which were left bare and corroded by the fetters when time and the action of the soil had rotted away the body.' The bones were formally buried, and thereafter the ghost was laid.

Pliny's other story, rather less detailed, concerns one of his freedmen.

Very different from these (and much more detailed) is a story related in the *Grettir* saga (anonymous and first written down *c.* 1200). The events are slightly reminiscent of those which befell Hrothgar at Heorot in *Beowulf* when first Grendel and then Grendel's dam beset the Geat stronghold.

Thorhall's farm was haunted by a dangerous and malevolent troll which did a great deal of damage. In desperation to protect his flocks and his men Thorhall hired the shepherd Glam, 'a huge unkempt man with a shock of hair and great grey staring eyes, uncanny to look on'. Glam was a success, but eventually the troll got the better of him and killed him. In due course the all-too-solid ghost of Glam began to haunt the farm, marauding and plundering. Thorhall hired another shepherd, Thorgaut, to guard the flocks, but he, too, met a bloody and terrible end.

Glam's depredations became worse. Eventually the warrior Grettir the Strong heard of the haunting of Thorhallstead and went to visit Thorhall. The farmer was enormously pleased to have the warrior's protection. The climax came with an epic wrestling match between Grettir and Glam. Grettir, almost at his last gasp, just had strength enough to draw his sword and 'behead' the dreadful ghost – but not before Glam had laid his 'weird' upon him. Ever after Grettir saw strange shapes in the dark and all sorts of horrors disturbed his sleep. 'And often he saw before him Glam's rolling glassy eyes.' It is characteristic of all epic (especially that in oral tradition), from *Gilgamesh* to the South Slav *narodne pesme*, that the men are ten or more feet tall; the ghosts are in the same heroic mould.

Much different is the scale of Chaucer, who includes two inset stories (both originally related by Cicero and Valerius) in 'The Nun's Priest's Tale'. They are part of Chauntecleer's long disquisition to Pertelote on dreams and in each case depend on the dream convention so popular in the Middle Ages. And they are tantalizing because they make one wonder what Chaucer might have made of a full-length ghost story (perhaps a comic one) from a pilgrim.

In the first, two companions arrive in a town where they have great difficulty in finding accommodation. In the end one dosses in an ox stall belonging to an inn; the other finds separate lodging. The latter dreams (twice) that he hears his friend calling for help, crying out that he is going to be murdered for his money. The third time he dreams that the bloody vision of his friend appears and explains that he *has* been murdered. The spectre enjoins his sleeping comrade to rise early the next morning and go to the west gate of the town:

'A carte ful of dong ther shaltow se,
In which my body is hid ful prively;
Do thilke carte arresten boldely . . .'

And so it turns out and the carter and innkeeper are tried and hanged.

In the second, two men are planning a sea voyage. During the night before embarkation one of them has a dream vision: a figure at his bedside warns him not to sail the next day, otherwise he will be drowned. He decides to trust the premonition, but his friend, derisive of the experience, sails; and, sure enough, the ship sinks and all are drowned.

The French chronicler Jean Froissart, a well-travelled man and an assiduous gatherer of information, was almost an exact contemporary of Chaucer. His *Chroniques*, which cover the period 1325–1400, contain two quite long and rather strange ghost stories. They are fashioned in such detail and with such skill (Froissart was a literary artist as much as he was an historian) that one might think that here is the 'modern' ghost story almost fledged; but it was to be still another four hundred years before that fledging took place.

'The Haunting of Sir Peter' occurs in Book III, which is devoted to the years 1386–8 (just when Chaucer was on course with *The Canterbury Tales*). Sir Peter of Béarn took to walking in his sleep and feared to sleep alone. When he rose at night to sleepwalk he armed himself and engaged in duels with an imaginary assailant, much to the alarm of his servants, who had orders to wake him.

His peculiar behaviour was associated with the pursuit and killing of a huge and dangerous bear which had killed and maimed several of his hounds. Having despatched the bear with his sword Sir Peter had returned to his castle in Biscay. As soon as his wife saw the dead bear she fainted and, shortly afterwards, on the pretext of making a pilgrimage with her children, took refuge with the king of Castile.

The reason for her fear was that her father had once hunted the same bear and had heard a disembodied voice saying: 'You hunt me though I mean you no harm. You will come to an evil end.' In fact he did come to such an end: the king had him beheaded. And now Sir Peter was haunted by a phantom assailant in the night . . .

Froissart's other story (which belongs to the same period) is more complex. It is called 'The Tale of the Familiar' and has some comic aspects. There are also elements of *diablerie* and suggestions that the haunting spirits were some form of poltergeist.

Pope Urban V gave a judgement in Avignon in favour of a priest's right to tithes in the domain of Raymond, Seigneur of Coresse. The seigneur refused to abide by the judgement and sent the cleric packing. On departure the priest gave a solemn warning: '. . . as soon as I can I shall send you a champion who will frighten you more than I do.' The baron scoffed at this, but, about three months later, strange disturbances began in his castle; there were loud knockings, bangs, bumps. His wife was terrified and so were the servants. However, the baron, who feared little or nothing, began to have conversations with one of the visitants who was named Orton. Eventually he persuaded Orton to leave the service of the priest and work on his behalf. Thereupon Orton became a kind of spook informant and spy, bringing to the baron details of events in various parts of Europe. It continued for five or six years.

The baron became increasingly curious to see the embodiment of his familiar. At last Orton agreed to materialize, but wouldn't divulge what form he would assume.

One morning the baron saw an enormous sow in his courtyard, but it was so thin it was nothing but skin and bones, with 'great long teats dangling under it and a long hungry-looking snout'. He ordered his dogs to drive it off. Too late he realized who the sow was. Orton never returned to the castle and the baron died within a year.

These few instances reveal some of the possibilities of the ghost story as envisaged by earlier writers; and they prefigure the fictional creations of the nineteenth and twentieth centuries.

During the Renaissance period, in Europe and England, and until near the end of the seventeenth century there was widespread and often erudite and scholarly interest in supernatural matters and the 'occult sciences' – especially in demonology, magic (usually black), witchcraft and necromancy. By the mid seventeenth century there was a copious literature on these subjects. It was a product of a continuous inquiry, as it were, into the preternatural, and much of that which, latterly, has tended to come under the heading of what the late Arthur Koestler preferred to name the 'paranormal'.

By *c.* 1650 that inquiry had been going on for hundreds of years, and if we look back no earlier than the eleventh century we find from then on a succession of formidable men who applied their keen intellects to a wide range of knowledge and speculation, sometimes to their peril and the danger of others. Such a man, for instance, was Michael Psellus, Professor of Philosophy at the University of Constantinople, who, among many *opera*, published in 1050 a learned treatise on demons (with special reference to their energy). And there were Peter Lombard (*c.* 1100–*c.* 1160), author of the famous *Liber Sententiarum*; Roger Bacon (1214?–94); John Bromyard, Chancellor of Cambridge University, who wrote *Summa Praedicantium* (1495), a major theological handbook; Cornelius Agrippa (1466–1535), author of *De Occulta Philosophia* (1529); Paracelsus (1493–1541), the founder of modern chemistry, who was expert in magic, alchemy and astrology; Girolamo Cardano (1500–1576), a renowned mathematician and master of the occult sciences; Robert Fludd (1574–1637), the physician and Rosicrucian; and those two notorious Dominican witch-hunters Sprenger and Kramer (authentic forerunners of Senator McCarthy's zealous hatchetmen) who compiled the sinister *Malleus Maleficarum* (1484). To these one might add Wyer, Bodin, Remigius and Del Rio, all of whom wrote on matters of demonology and magic, and Eloyer who compiled the celebrated *Histoire des spectres* (1605).

All these scholars (and many others) were interested in psychic phenomena and thus in ghosts. But it was the Tudor and Jacobean dramatists who perceived the rich possibilities of using ghosts as 'characters' in their plays. In doing so they were considerably influenced by Seneca's tragedies – for example *Agamemnon*, in which the ghost of Thyestes delivers the prologue, and *Thyestes*, with the prologue ghost of Tantalus. In his plays the revengers are sometimes urged on by the hallucination that they see the spirits of the dead.

There are literally scores of ghosts in the many hundreds of plays written and produced between *c.* 1580 and *c.* 1620. They are particularly prominent in chronicle and history plays, and in the tragedies and revenge tragedies. Some are malignant and vengeful (e.g. the ghost of Andrea and Revenge in Kyd's *The Spanish Tragedy*); some have an important part in the plot (e.g. the ghost of Hamlet's father); some have a premonitory role (e.g. the spectre of Caesar who appears to Brutus before Philippi); and some have walking-on parts, so to speak, to give the audience an additional shudder (e.g. the apparitions of Isabella and Brachiano in Webster's *The White Devil*). Thereafter the 'stage ghost' was to have a variable history. It never had a place in comedy, but it throve on melodrama in the nineteenth century and is by no means defunct today (cf. the important role of the gravedigger's boy in Edward Bond's *Lear*).

Stage spooks apart, ghosts virtually 'disappear' from European literature in the course of the first half of the seventeenth century and they do not reappear until the advent of the 'Gothic' story in the latter part of the eighteenth. However, they are mentioned with some frequency in works pertaining to supernatural matters[1] and there is little diminution of their presence and activity in oral tradition, in ballad and folklore, in folksong, in popular superstition, and also in the more durable form of stories and poems printed in broadsheets and chapbooks. Some of the best ghost stories have in fact lived in the predominantly bold and concise form of the traditional ballad (cf. 'The Wife of Usher's Well').

In 1706 Defoe published his celebrated 'A True Relation of the Apparition of one Mrs Veal'. This arose from a strange incident of a haunting in Canterbury which Defoe investigated personally by going to see Mrs Bargrave, the chief witness. As one might expect from Defoe, it is a vivid piece of writing. It is journalism rather than fiction, but one can see easily enough how it might have been made into a ghost story of the kind that became popular in the nineteenth century. Defoe wrote it plumb in the middle of the Augustan age – taken, narrowly, by Goldsmith to be the period of Queen Anne (1702–14) – the age of reason and neoclassicism when the prime literary and aesthetic virtues were good sense, order, harmony, restraint, elegance and decorum. Literate and educated people were disinclined to believe in ghosts. When such a matter was raised the attitude towards it would be one of urbane and mildly amused scepticism and condescension.

In the 1740s there began to develop a marked shift in sensibility. This was signalled by those who came to be called 'graveyard poets'. 'Graveyard poetry' displayed a preoccupation with death, suffering and the sepulchral. It also challenged rationalism and was fundamentally different in tone, mood and theme from anything that Pope and his fellow Augustans had

1. The Cambridge Platonist, Henry More, in *An Antidote Against Atheism* (1653), related 'strange and undeniable Stories of Apparitions, poltergeists, hags, and vampires'. One of these tales concerned 'The Devil of Mascon', a spirit which haunted a Huguenot minister's house in Burgundy for three months. Robert Boyle the chemist actually interviewed the minister in Geneva to establish the facts. A disciple of More, Joseph Glanvil, wrote *Defence of the Being of Witches and Apparitions* (1666) and in 1668 told the tale of the Drummer of Tedworth (it occurs in *A Blow at Modern Sadducism*), a soldier who was transported for an offence and whose drum was confiscated by one John Mompesson. Mompesson's house was subsequently haunted by a particularly rowdy and destructive ghost. Cotton Mather and John Aubrey also wrote accounts of ghosts, and in 1685 George Sinclair published *Satan's Invisible World Discovered: or A Choice Collection of Modern Relations, proving evidently against the Sadducees and Atheists of this present Age, that there are Devils, Spirits, Witches and Apparitions*. The Presbyterian divine Richard Baxter later weighed in with a book with an even more resounding title: *The Certainty of the World of Spirits. Fully evinced by unquestionable Histories of Apparitions and Witchcrafts, Operations, Voices, &c. Proving the Immortality of Souls, the Malice and Miseries of the Devils and the Damned, and the Blessedness of the Justified. Written for the Conviction of Sadducees and Infidels* (1691).

approved and advocated. The main poems were Edward Young's *Night Thoughts* (1742–5), Blair's *The Grave* (1743), and James Hervey's *Meditations among the Tombs* (1745–7). Some would add Gray's *Elegy*. There was also Thomas Warton's *On the Pleasures of Melancholy* (1747).

Such writings had a pronounced influence on the Gothic novel which was shortly to appear, and with it the ghost in fiction. They also had a profound effect on German writers of 'terror fiction' at the turn of the eighteenth century.

Most Gothic novels were tales of mystery and terror, intended to chill the spine and curdle the blood. They contain strong elements of the supernatural and the now traditional props of the haunted house (a site exploited *ad nauseam* in the cinema and in much third-rate fiction). They are often set in medieval castles which have secret passages, dungeons, perilous staircases, torture chambers, and a more than adequate complement of spooky happenings and spectres.

One of the earliest examples of the genre was Smollett's *Ferdinand Count Fathom* (1753), perhaps the first novel to propose terror and cruelty as its main themes. Much better known than this (and much more influential) was Horace Walpole's *The Castle of Otranto* (1764). He wrote this in his house at Strawberry Hill, Twickenham, where he had made his abode into a 'little Gothic castle'. Barely readable today merely for diversion, it is a tale of villainy, blood and passion, and includes a monstrous ghost. It was an immensely popular book and is believed to have gone through 115 editions since it first appeared.

In the next fifty years or so there came a succession of such novels of variable quality, not a few of which were dramatized (as was *The Castle of Otranto*). Some of the major examples of the genre were Thomas Leland's *Longsword* (1762), Clara Reeve's *The Old English Baron* (1778), William Beckford's *Vathek* (1786), Ann Radcliffe's *Mysteries of Udolpho* (1794), M. G. ('Monk') Lewis's *Ambrosio* and *The Monk* (1796), C. R. Maturin's *The Fatal Revenge* (1807) and *Melmoth the Wanderer* (1820), and Mary Shelley's *Frankenstein* (1818). William Godwin's *Caleb Williams* (1794) is often grouped under the Gothic heading, but it has a particular importance as an early instance of the propaganda novel and the novel of crime and detection.

During the same period German writers were developing their own brand of sensational and Gothic fiction, and this is of some importance because of the initial German contribution to the ghost story.

During the eighteenth century German literary circles displayed great interest in English literature: Klopstock, Gellert and Wieland, for instance,

were much influenced by Shakespeare, Milton and Richardson – and also
by Edward Young and James Hervey. Goethe even thought that Young
was on a par with Milton. There was a corresponding English interest in
German literature. They interacted. 'Monk' Lewis, for instance, was well
read in German literature, a talented translator, and was to influence
E. T. A. Hoffmann. Translation of German 'terror fiction' began in 1794
with the appearance of an English rendering of Benedikte Naubert's
Hermann von Unna. A series of translations followed. They included work
by Karl Grosse, Leonhard Wächter, C. H. Spiess and Heinrich Zschokke.
C. A. Vulpius's *Rinaldo Rinaldini* proved very popular. Ann Radcliffe was
influenced by Schiller's *Der Geisterseher* (1789); and Schiller's play *Die
Räuber* (1777–80), translated in 1792, was perhaps most important of
all.

But there was a major difference between German and English practitioners of Gothic: the German fictional heroes were 'political'. There was
overt social comment, and anti-clericalism was clearly voiced. Schiller,
especially, was an advocate of the individual against social convention
and taboo. The *Ritter- und Räuberroman* and the *Schauerroman* – counterparts
of English Gothic – were an aspect of the *Sturm und Drang* revolutionary
literary movement.

Elsewhere in Europe many people read such fiction and there was a big
demand for it. However, except in France, few writers were inspired to
emulate, develop or exploit the Gothic style and tradition. In France,
English Gothic novels were widely read and imitated. The influence of
these, plus that of the German Gothic and the *Schauerroman* and, more
particularly the tales of Hoffmann, was to be felt in French literature until
at least the 1880s. Charles Nodier, Balzac, Gérard de Nerval, Prosper
Mérimée, Théophile Gautier and Petrus Borel all experimented successfully with Gothic and horror themes in their *contes* and *nouvelles*. Later,
Barbey d'Aurevilly, Maupassant and Villiers de l'Isle-Adam – to name no
others – were to make notable and idiosyncratic contributions.

Gothic also travelled to America, where Isaac Mitchell (*c.* 1758–1811)
achieved some reputation with *The Asylum* (1811) and Charles Brockden
Brown (1771–1810), America's first man of letters, attained something
approaching fame with such Gothic romances as *Wieland* (1798), *Arthur
Mervyn* (1799), *Ormond* (1799) and *Edgar Huntly* (1799). The main influences on him were Richardson, Godwin and Ann Radcliffe. In turn, Brown
was to influence Hawthorne and Poe, and also several English writers,
notably, Keats, Sir Walter Scott, Hazlitt, Mary Shelley, and Shelley himself,
who, according to Peacock (and, in view of the closeness of their

friendship, Peacock would certainly have known), was deeply involved with Brown's work.

This kind of cross-pollination was to continue for a long time during the nineteenth century, and the Gothic type of tale, in various forms, was not only vigorously alive at the end of the century but was to receive further expression in the cinema (horror films continue to be very popular in the 1980s) and, from the 1950s onwards, in fictional horror stories.

Among British and German writers the influence has been diachronic. The Americans are best exemplified by Hawthorne, Poe and Ambrose Bierce in the nineteenth century; later, by H. P. Lovecraft, John Hawkes, James Purdy and Thomas Pynchon. Poe, at his worst (e.g. in 'Ligeia') or at his best (e.g. 'The Fall of the House of Usher'), remains the most widely known.

At the outset of the nineteenth century the then newly emergent form of the *Novelle*, as conceived by Goethe, coincided with the advent of the short story. The short story had been there, in embryo as it were, all along. It was what might be called an inherent form.

Its forefathers, however rude in some cases, were myth, legend, parable, fairy story, fable, exemplum and *Märchen* – to say nothing of the *lai*, the *fabliau*, many short Gothic tales, and even the ballad. The accounts of Cain and Abel, Ruth, Judith, Susannah, the Prodigal Son are all short stories; so are Chaucer's *Canterbury Tales* and the *novelle* of Boccaccio's *Decameron*. We have already seen some instances of inset and detachable short stories; others can be found in the *Mabinogion*, *Don Quixote*, *Zadig* (which contains a story of detection in which the exact methods of Sherlock Holmes are prefigured), and so forth.

Rather suddenly (and, perhaps, a little unexpectedly) we not only find the short story in a well-advanced state of development; we also find the ghost story – *as a short story* – in the work of Kleist and Hoffmann. But the ground had been prepared, if somewhat haphazardly. One might even go so far as to suggest that the 'atmosphere' in the opening years of the nineteenth century was right for the parturition of the ghost story.

One may adduce various possible causes and reasons for this state of readiness. For between forty and fifty years the Gothic tale (in its various forms) and terror fiction had helped to condition a reading public to the idea and use of supernatural and quasi-supernatural forces and agencies. It had also accustomed them to being frightened. But there were, I believe, a variety of other more specific influences which contributed to making people susceptible to and receptive of a new kind of ghost story. For example, there was a marked recrudescence of interest in the concept of evil (and in the operations of the devil himself). The Faust theme was revived (and was to be persistently attractive to writers and composers in the nineteenth century), and so was the disturbing legend of the Wandering Jew. There was a widespread study of folklore and ballads (this had been going on since the middle of the eighteenth century), both of which were a source of ghost lore and tales. In addition there was a sensational interest in the darker features of the Middle Ages (already manifest in Gothic tales), a growing curiosity about superstition, a renewal of interest in mysticism, and a noticeable preoccupation with the dual nature of man (hence a series of split-personality and *Doppelgänger* stories). The partial failure of orthodox Christian beliefs and practice may have encouraged superstition. Nor can we discount the effect of pseudo-magi such as Cagliostro and Saint-Germain. Finally, there were the influential writings of Johann Hamann, who vigorously supported the operations of intuition and instinct as opposed to reason, and the much more potent views of Swedenborg on psychic phenomena and the workings of the spirit.

It is noticeable, too, that major poets were attracted to the possibilities of magic and the supernatural in narrative: for example, Bürger's 'Lenore', Coleridge's 'Ancient Mariner' and 'Christabel', Keats's 'La Belle Dame sans Merci', 'Lamia' and 'Isabella'. Subsequently, supernatural narrative in verse (as well as prose) was to be prominent in English and European literature throughout the nineteenth century.

As far as the advent of the ghost story is concerned, it seems at any rate plausible that people were beginning to feel the need for something more sophisticated and, in a sense, realistic. After fifty years of Gothic extravagance there were signs that enough had been as good as a feast; at the very least that there was a need for some variety. In her inimitably droll manner Jane Austen had suggested as much in *Northanger Abbey* (1818), which was begun in 1798 and prepared for the press in 1803. In 1818, too, Peacock published *Nightmare Abbey*, which benevolently pokes fun at Gothic excesses and has a hilarious chapter on the subject of ghosts (plus a ghost of suitably bloody and spectral appearance). However, on the whole, terror fiction was taken rather seriously; partly, no doubt, because, as Jane Austen had implied, it had little or nothing to do with reality. In 1819 Leigh Hunt remarked in his introduction to *A Tale for a Chimney Corner*:

a man who does not contribute his quota of grim story nowadays, seems hardly to be free of the republic of letters. He is bound to wear a death's head as part of his insignia. If he does not frighten everybody, he is nobody. If he does not shock the ladies, what can be expected of him?

Moreover, the publication in 1818 of John Polidori's *The Vampyre* reflected a renewed interest in vampirism which grew steadily during the nineteenth century; not a few writers were attracted to it as a subject for their tales.

However right the atmosphere may have been, the fact remains that at the start of the century we find a most carefully wrought fictional ghost story: Heinrich von Kleist's 'Das Bettelweib von Locarno' ('The Beggarwoman of Locarno'), published in *Berliner Abendblätter* in 1810 and in *Erzählungen* in 1811. It is very short (some 800 words) but contains, in little, several of the constituents (foreshadowed by Pliny and Froissart) of a traditional ghost story in a highly concentrated form: the dwelling-place (in this instance a castle) which comes to be haunted (and is thus difficult to sell), the erring owner who is guilty of starting a chain of events, the terrified wife, the visitor who is afraid, the dog that senses the presence of preternatural forces, the themes of guilt and retribution . . . It is written beautifully and with the utmost economy. One is tempted to think that the story might have been a draft for something more ambitious. It is easy to see how and where Kleist might have amplified it. All the characters (including the dog) could have been developed; the basic events might have been elaborated; the suspense and tension could have been protracted. Much more might have been made of the conclusion, which is abrupt to the point of seeming impatience. Eight hundred words might easily have become eight thousand.

By contrast, a few years later (1817) there is E. T. A. Hoffmann's very long story 'Das Majorat' ('The Entail'), thirty times longer than Kleist's and (with the notable exception of Henry James's 'The Turn of the Screw') very probably the longest 'short' story in existence which involves a ghost.

Hoffmann has that strong sense of the past which was to become central to the evolution of the ghost story during the next hundred years, and he achieves much more than a tale about a haunted castle: he creates a microcosm which has deep roots in custom, attitude, taboo, social convention and family relationships. And he gives himself ample time and space in which to create and develop several characters. The build-up of a sombre and sinister atmosphere is gradual; so is the elaboration of tension and uncertainty. These are offset by an ironical tone and occasional moments of sardonic humour.

Had Kleist and Hoffmann been writing at a time when the ghost story was well established (in, say, the 1870s) and there were numerous precedents, their achievement would have been less remarkable. But they were pioneers who, starting from scratch, so to speak, produced two superlative ghost stories (though these were by no means their only excursions into the supernatural) and made a major contribution to the creation of the short story, then scarcely heard of. The odd part about it is that from then on and up to the present day German writers have made a minimal contribution to the genre of the ghost story, which has been dominated by British writers, especially the English. There have been some Americans of note, and a handful of Europeans (some of whom are represented in this anthology). But if you do a quantitative survey you find that something like 98 per cent of ghost stories are in English and about 70 per cent of those are by English writers. Why this should be is, in itself, an interesting question.

The first ghost story of importance by an American author was 'The Legend of Sleepy Hollow' by Washington Irving: a humorous tale and very well written. Like Hoffmann, Irving sees the need for space to develop character and prepare for his comic effects. It was published in *The Sketch Book* (1820), accompanied by 'The Spectre Bridegroom', a more sinister tale. Both show German influence, and the latter is set in Germany.

Sir Walter Scott's *Redgauntlet*, a novel published in 1824, contains one of the best ghost stories, 'Wandering Willie's Tale', which incorporates elements from legendry and shows a fine grasp of structure and logic in the combination of natural and supernatural events, greatly enriched by Scott's masterly use of border dialect, and also by a certain sardonic humour.

His other two ghost stories were 'The Tapestried Chamber' and 'My Aunt Margaret's Mirror' – both first published in *The Keepsake* (1828). He also wrote an essay *On the Supernatural in Fictitious Composition* (1827) which displays a very shrewd understanding of what can and cannot be done in the genre. Perhaps his most telling observation is: 'The supernatural . . . is peculiarly subject to be exhausted by coarse handling and repeated pressure. It is also of a character which is extremely difficult to sustain and of which a very small proportion may be said to be better than the whole.' Many a ghost story and many a horror story fail precisely because of 'coarse handling and repeated pressure', and because of attempts to sustain suspense for too long. Only a handful of writers have succeeded with the long ghost story and the long horror story. Even over a short distance the casualty rate is high, as is illustrated only too well by some of the work of, for instance, Edgar Allan Poe, F. Marion Crawford, W. W. Jacobs and H. P. Lovecraft.

It was in the 1830s that Edgar Allan Poe began to make his impact; his first collection of short stories – *Tales of the Grotesque and Arabesque* – appeared in 1840. His influence on the evolution of the short story (ghost, horror and suspense) was very considerable and, perhaps, not entirely for the good of some writers. It persisted through the nineteenth century in the work of the French Symbolists (Baudelaire published translations of Poe's tales in 1856 and 1857), of such English writers as Rossetti, Swinburne, Dowson and Stevenson, and, later, of such Americans as Ambrose Bierce, Hart Crane and H. P. Lovecraft. Poe, in his turn, had been influenced by Hoffmann. As a commercial writer he understood well what he was aiming at. In his piece 'How to Write a Blackwood Article', he advises a new contributor thus: 'Sensations are the great things after all. Should you ever be drowned or hung, be sure and make a note of your sensations – they will be worth to you ten guineas a sheet.'

It seems to me that Poe has been somewhat overrated, though it is almost certainly heresy to say so. Moreover, his best stories are not ghost stories; they are horror and suspense stories. And what is arguably his best ghost story – 'Ligeia' – is marred by those faults which remind one, not of the 'worst excesses of the French Revolution', but of the worst excesses of the Gothic novel.

A lesser contemporary talent was that of the English parson R. H. Barham, who made some contribution to the development of the ghost story in the 1830s. He was an accomplished versifier and a skilful and witty practitioner of light verse (his adroitness in securing clever rhymes is outstanding) and he wrote several good ghost stories in verse. He also wrote two long ones in prose: 'The Spectre of Tappington' and 'The Leech of Folkestone'. Much of his work was published in *Bentley's Miscellany* and reissued in 1840 in that collection which was to become popular for a hundred years and more: *The Ingoldsby Legends*.

In 1834 Alexander Pushkin published 'The Queen of Spades': the story of the young gambler and the aged countess who visits him after her murder. It differs from most other ghost stories of note since the spirit of the old noblewoman appears at the very end to resolve the plot and finally causes the young gambler to be deceived at a game of cards, the loss of which drives him insane. In Russian literature it is something of an 'odd one out', an isolated and brilliant phenomenon. Few Russian writers have composed ghost stories, though Gogol and Dostoyevsky, among others, made extensive use of supernatural elements. Gogol's grotesque horror fantasies (e.g. 'Viy') owed something to the influence of Hoffmann.

By 1840, Charles Dickens, still only in his late twenties, had become famous and his influence on the ghost story was to be of the utmost importance. He more than anyone associated such tales with Christmas. He was familiar with traditional customs (such as telling stories round the fireside) and with that folklore in which ghosts were linked with Christmas Eve. Moreover, he very much enjoyed writing about Christmas.

His earliest ghost stories were inset tales in *The Pickwick Papers* (1837). There followed *A Christmas Carol* (1843), in which Old Marley is the first of a series of apparitions. Then came a succession of Christmas books: *The Chimes* (1844), *The Cricket on the Hearth* (1845), *The Battle of Life* (1846), and *The Haunted Man* (1848). Of his later ghost stories the two best known were written for special Christmas issues of his magazine *All The Year Round*. They are usually known as 'The Trial for Murder' and 'No. 1 Branch Line: The Signalman'.

Dickens's contributions to the development of the ghost story is not confined to his own works. In 1851 he initiated a special supplement to his magazine *Household Words* to which he invited writers to submit seasonal offerings. The 1852 supplement, entitled *A Round of Christmas Stories by the Fire*, included Elizabeth Gaskell's splendid 'The Old Nurse's Story'. From 1854 the framework for the tales became more elaborate. In 1859 he closed *Household Words* and started *All The Year Round*. Again there were Christmas supplements with a common theme, and ghost stories were a popular feature.

In the 1860s and 1870s many ghost-story writers were women, among whom we should mention particularly Amelia Edwards (author of 'The Engineer' and 'The Phantom Coach'), Rosa Mulholland, Mrs Braddon, Mrs Riddell, and Mrs Oliphant, who wrote 'The Open Door' – one of the best of all ghost stories.

Thackeray tried his hand at the genre ('The Story of Mary Ancel') and Wilkie Collins was prolific. In 1856 he published *After Dark and Other Stories* (in 2 volumes), in 1859 *The Queen of Hearts* (in 3 volumes) and in 1879 *Little Novels*. Collins collaborated with Dickens and contributed to his magazines. Bulwer Lytton also wrote ghost stories, of which the best are 'The Haunters and the Haunted' (1859), commissioned by Dickens, and 'A Strange Story' (1861).

Ultimately more famous than these as a practitioner of the form was Sheridan Le Fanu, whom M. R. James considered 'in the first rank as a writer of ghost stories'. By the time Le Fanu died in 1873 the genre was fully established; it was to continue to burgeon for the next hundred years.

Le Fanu's first ghost stories date from between 1838 and 1840. In the next thirty years he wrote a great many, showing a particular gift for depicting states of guilt and fear. His ghosts are uncannily 'real' and convincing. Among the best known stories are 'Mr Justice Harbottle', 'Green Tea', 'The Familiar', 'Squire Toby's Will', 'The Drunkard's Dream', 'The Vision of Tom Chuff', 'Dickon the Devil', 'Strange Disturbances in Aungier Street' and 'Carmilla'. His 'psychic doctor' Hesselius, the protagonist in a number of stories (like serial detectives), was to be followed by Algernon Blackwood's John Silence and William Hope Hodgson's Carnacki – a psychic research investigator or parapsychologist.

During the second half of the nineteenth century there was a growing and increasingly widespread interest (it has continued unabated) in psychic phenomena, in psychotherapy and extreme psychological states, and in spiritualism. F. W. H. Myers, who was deeply interested in Mesmer's theories, helped to found the Society for Psychical Research. Drugs and their effects, duality and double identity, dreams, madness, diabolism, the diabolic pact, black magic and witchcraft also exercised people's curiosity. In view of all this activity and inquiry it is in no way surprising that ghosts should continue to fascinate.

Ghost stories proliferated: from the 1870s onwards there were scores of them. It is almost as if they were beginning to fulfil a kind of spiritual need; as if the possibility of ghosts was a reassurance of an after-life. Besides, ghosts were a link with the past, with tradition, between the living and the dead. Moreover, writers do not seem to have regarded their ghost stories (and other tales of the supernatural) as mere diversions and entertainment: they had serious intentions, including exploring states of consciousness, examining aspects of appearance and reality, investigating the meaning of existence. And they were not only looking into the 'dark backward'; they were looking in the dark present, the 'underside' of the mind where were the

> . . . cliffs of fall
> Frightful, sheer, no-man-fathomed.

Kipling and Stevenson made highly individual contributions. Kipling wrote a number of ghost stories published in 1887–8 in the *Civil and Military Gazette*. Later came 'The Return of Imray' (1891), 'The Phantom Rickshaw' (1895) and 'They' (1904). Two of Stevenson's best known are 'Thrawn Janet' (in *The Merry Men*, 1887) and the tale of 'Tod Lapraik' (in *Catriona,* 1893). In both he matched, magnificently, Walter Scott's use of dialect.

I mentioned earlier that few European writers had shown any interest in the ghost story; fortunately, de Maupassant was one of them. He wrote several memorable and frightening tales, including 'Le Horla' and 'Was it a Dream?' (1887), 'An Apparition' and 'Who Knows?' (1890). 'Le Horla' (*hors-là*, 'out there')[1] is the most famous of his psychological ghost stories.

A little later Emile Zola wrote 'Angeline' – so far as I know his only attempt at a ghost story. It derived from his so-called 'exile' in England in 1898–9 when he lived near Weybridge in Surrey. During a bicycle ride he discovered an abandoned house which had a legend to it. He transposed the setting to Orgeval and wrote the story in October 1898.

During the last twenty-odd years of the nineteenth century the Americans Ambrose Bierce and O. Henry (William Sidney Porter) were publishing their short ghost stories. Outstanding among Bierce's tales are 'The Middle Toe of the Right Foot' and 'An Occurrence at Owl Creek Bridge' (both of 1891) and 'The Moonlit Road' (1894); O. Henry is chiefly remembered for 'The Furnished Room' (1906).

At this period, too, Vernon Lee (Violet Paget) was making some idiosyncratic contributions. Her major collection, *Hauntings: Fantastic Stories*, published in 1890, included three of her best known: 'Amour Dure', 'Oke of Okehurst' and 'A Wicked Voice'. She was very considerably influenced by Nathaniel Hawthorne, more especially by his novel *The Marble Faun*. Her rather obsessive interest in the past was characteristic of some writers of the period. As she put it in her preface to *Hauntings*, a ghost story ought to consist of

the past, the more or less remote Past, of which the prose is clean obliterated by distance – that is the place to get our ghosts from. Indeed we live ourselves, we educated folk of modern times, on the borderland of the Past, in houses looking down on its troubadours' orchards and Greek folks' pillared courtyards; and a legion of ghosts, very vague and changeful, are perpetually to and fro, fetching and carrying for us between it and the present.

Few writers have possessed a keener, more delicately subtle and pervasive sense of the past than Henry James (who was also much affected by *The Marble Faun*), as he frequently revealed, not least in his unfinished novel *The Sense of the Past* (1917), which is concerned with a form of haunting about which perhaps nobody but James could have written.

He had begun writing ghost stories back in the 1860s when Dickens and Le Fanu were still alive, and forty-odd years later he was still experimenting. In his first two, 'The Romance of Certain Old Clothes'

---

1. It may be that he invented the word, basing it on *horzain* – a term used in Normandy to describe a stranger.

(1868) and 'De Grey: a Romance' (1868), Hawthorne's influen
apparent. Later, among others, came 'Owen Wingrave', 'Sir Edm
Orme', 'The Passionate Pilgrim', 'The Jolly Corner' (1908), and what m
people regard as his masterpiece in the genre – 'The Turn of the Screw
(1898).

James achieved his effects by hint and suggestion, by a kind of stealth.
The stories are more interesting than most because the situations he
invents and the characters he creates occupy one's full attention: the actual
ghost may be of subsidiary importance, a subfusc presence like Sir
Edmund.

In the late 1890s M. R. James began to write his celebrated *Ghost Stories
of an Antiquary* (first issued under that title in 1904). *More Ghost Stories of
an Antiquary* followed in 1911, and the collected stories were finally
published in 1931. They were written to be read aloud, usually to friends
at Christmas time. He has the distinction of being the most anthologized
of all writers of ghost stories, and he is very probably the only writer of
short stories to have concentrated exclusively on ghosts. Not that there are
a great many of them. But then James was also an outstanding bibliogra-
pher, iconographer and palaeographical scholar who produced a monu-
mental translation of the Apocryphal New Testament.

James was a student of the nineteenth-century ghost story (he must
have read hundreds) and shows a thoroughly 'professional' approach to
the craft of writing them. He worked out his own rules, which appear in
brief prefaces to his collections of tales. He liked a setting that was 'fairly
familiar' and characters and talk of the kind you might come across any
day. As he put it in his introduction to *Ghosts and Marvels*:

> Let us, then, be introduced to the actors in a placid way; let us see them going
> about their ordinary business, undisturbed by forebodings, pleased with their
> surroundings; and into this calm environment let the ominous thing put out its
> head, unobtrusively at first, and then more insistently, until it holds the stage.

In M. R. James everything is subordinate to the plot – and he was an
expert plotter. Nevertheless, there is a great deal of body to his stories. He
is very good indeed at evoking *locale* and atmosphere and in the
description of buildings. His massive erudition is kept under careful
control and is always functional. His characters are, in E. M. Forster's
terms, 'flat' rather than 'round' (this is true of most of the characters in
ghost stories), but not *quite* so flat and transparent as some have made out.
He has a knack for producing a personality quickly through description
and speech. Dialogue is one of his strong points. He had a good ear for the

spoken word (in fact he was a talented mimic) and he also had a good ear (and eye) for pastiche in Latin as well as English. Above all, he has the imponderable quality of style. His relaxed but elegant prose is continually pleasing.

James's best effects are achieved by meiosis and the quiet tone. He works away stealthily on the reader's nerves and can be genuinely frightening. It is hardly surprising that he is the only writer of ghost stories whose collected works have remained continuously in print. Like Henry James, but in a different way, he had a profound and sensitive awareness of the past and adapted a number of themes from legend, ballad and myth. As he put it himself: 'I have tried to make my ghosts act in a way not inconsistent with the rules of folklore.'

Everybody has his favourite M. R. James stories. Among the very well known are 'A School Story', 'Oh, Whistle, and I'll Come to You, My Lad', 'Casting the Runes', 'Martin's Close', 'The Ash-Tree', 'Lost Hearts' and 'The Mezzotint'.

Algernon Blackwood was an almost exact contemporary of M. R. James, though he lived some years longer. Unlike James he was seriously interested in psychic phenomena and wrote some powerful stories with supernatural themes. Particularly well known are 'Ancient Sorceries' and 'Secret Worship'. His first collection in this genre, *The Empty House and Other Ghost Stories* (1906), was followed by *John Silence, Physician Extraordinary* (1908). He remained interested in the occult for most of his life.

Another near-contemporary was William Hope Hodgson. His parapsychologist, Carnacki, differed from John Silence in that he used equipment and instruments to track down spirits. Some of the tales are ingenious (e.g. 'The Horse of the Invisible' and 'The Whistling Room'), but Hodgson was not a very good writer; he would *overdo* it.

Yet another long-lived contemporary was the prolific Arthur Machen, much influenced by Stevenson, who experimented with a variety of supernatural tales including 'The Great God Pan' and 'The Inmost Light' (1895), 'The Three Impostors' (1895) and 'The House of Souls' (1906).

The Benson brothers, A. C., E. F. and R. H. (sons of the Archbishop of Canterbury), all published stories about ghosts and the supernatural at the turn of the nineteenth century. A. C. Benson's work is seldom read now, but some of the tales of Robert Hugh Benson (a priest deeply interested in the occult, spiritualism and necromancy) have survived. E. F. Benson had a long and successful career as a novelist and short-story writer. He excelled at ghost stories and, like M. R. James, adhered to fairly definite rules. He is seldom less than competent, and at his best rivals masters of the form. For much of the twentieth century he has been a favourite among schoolboys. His first collection, *The Room in the Tower and Other Stories* (1912), was followed by *Visible and Invisible* (1923) and *Spook Stories* (1928).

Also of before the First World War are Robert Hichens's 'How Love Came to Professor Guildea' (1900), Oscar Wilde's delightful comic tale 'The Canterville Ghost' (a perennial favourite ever since), W. W. Jacobs's terrifying 'The Monkey's Paw' (1902) – a standby to anthologists for many years – Oliver Onions's 'The Beckoning Fair One' (1911), Saki's spoof ghost story 'The Open Window', and some of the tales in E. M. Forster's *The Celestial Omnibus* (1911). Edith Wharton's collected *Tales of Men and Ghosts* (1910) are cerebral stories very much in the manner of her close friend Henry James: the ghosts are projections of men's mental obsessions. Another collection – *Ghosts* – appeared in 1937. At her best (in, for instance, 'All Souls' ' and 'Afterward') she is as compulsively readable as Henry James and M. R. James.

Between the wars the ghost story continued to flourish, though not with the style, vigour, variety and originality of the years between, say, 1850 and 1910.

In the early days of broadcasting in the 1920s A. J. Alan (Leslie Harrison Lambert) made a very idiosyncratic contribution. He worked for the Foreign Office and made his broadcasts in evening dress (black or white tie as the time of day might require). He became a well-known raconteur of his own works, subsequently gathered in *Good Evening, Everyone* (1928) and *A. J. Alan's Second Book* (1933). His style was relaxed to the point of facetiousness and casualness (all most carefully contrived); the stories were neat, low-toned, disarmingly guileful. Among the better known are 'The Hair', 'The Diver' and 'My Adventure in Norfolk'.

L. P. Hartley wrote a number of ghost stories in the 1920s (*Night Fears and Other Stories* was published in 1924) and more were to come sporadically in the next forty years. In 1922 David Lindsay published *The Haunted Woman*, an unusual and now neglected novel. It is in the form of a ghost story but was before its time in that its main theme is the need for a revolution to effect equality between the sexes so that, as the heroine suggests, men exist as much for women as women for men.

At that time other distinguished contributions were being made by Hugh Walpole, Lord Dunsany, Cynthia Asquith (who was still writing and editing ghost stories in the 1950s), Margaret Irwin (author of the excellent 'The Earlier Service'), A. M. Burrage (who also wrote under the pseudonym Ex-Private X, the author of several good tales including 'Smee' and 'One Who Saw'), and H. G. Wells, whose ingenious *tour de force* 'The Inexperienced Ghost' combines the comic and the horrific. Wells also wrote 'The Moth' and 'The Red Room'.

Some were to follow rather sedulously in the steps of M. R. James, but it was complimentary 'imitation', and they were sufficiently good writers to avoid mere plagiarism or copying. Chief exponents of the Jamesian techniques were H. Russell Wakefield (*They Walk at Night*, 1928), W. F. Harvey (e.g. *Moods and Tenses*, 1933), A. N. L. Munby (*The Alabaster Hand*, 1949), and, more recently, William Croft Dickinson (*Dark Encounters*, 1963). In 1969 Kingsley Amis published *The Green Man*, a novel about a pub haunted by a seventeenth-century magician called Dr Thomas Underhill. This clever and very well written story is the most sustained 'imitation' of M. R. James.

From the inter-war period, again, I should mention H. P. Lovecraft, Machen's American disciple, a specialist in tales of horror who also wrote some ghost stories of variable quality. The skeletal shadow of Poe was inclined to lie somewhat broadly over him, and he was vulnerable (like some other writers) to that 'coarse handling and repeated pressure' which Scott had acutely perceived to be harmful to the supernatural tale.

On the other hand, Elizabeth Bowen during the same period (and later) wrote a number of ghost stories of notable merit. Some of the best were eventually collected in *The Demon Lover* (1945), which contains 'Pink May', 'The Cheery Soul', 'The Happy Autumn Fields', and the sinister and frightening title story which is set in wartime London.

Walter de la Mare was probably the most prolific English writer of ghost stories between the wars. To the art of this particular kind of fiction he brought a highly personal vision. Like Henry James, he explored the shifting and ill-defined frontiers which lie between what seems to be reality and those other zones so powerfully suggested by T. S. Eliot in, for instance, some of the choric passages of *Murder in the Cathedral*, and in that ghostly and haunted play *The Family Reunion*:

> . . . the world around the corner
> The wind's talk in the dry holly-tree
> The inclination of the moon
> The attraction of the dark passage
> The paw under the door.

> . . . the sobbing in the chimney,
> The evil in the dark closet.

De la Mare achieved his effects by stealth and quietness, by hint and suggestion, and excelled at the evocation of atmosphere. His ghosts are heard, not often seen. Among his better known stories are 'Seaton's Aunt', 'All Hallows', 'The Guardian' and 'Bad Company'. There were several collections including *The Riddle* (1923), *The Connoisseur* (1926), *On the Edge* (1930), *The Wind Blows Over* (1936) and *A Beginning and Other Stories* (1955).

De la Mare's settings and topography are predominantly pre-First World War; indeed there is a discernible tendency in ghost stories of the 1920s and 1930s (and thereafter) not to make much concession to change. Perhaps it was felt that technology (the car, radio, aeroplane, and the enormous increase in the supply of electricity) was somehow not compatible with ghostly circumstances, or even inimical to manifestations. However, a car and a lorry are of prime importance to A. J. Alan's 'My Adventure in Norfolk' (*c.* 1924), and late in the 1930s Ann Bridge wrote a delightful story about a haunted Buick saloon: witty, deft and poignant, it is also extremely plausible.

The First World War profoundly modified people's feelings in respect of death, ghosts and ghost stories. That cataclysm produced tens of thousands of 'ghosts': the missing, the believed killed in action, the 'walking wounded' of a spectral no-man's-land who were to haunt the memory of Europe for years. The Second World War vastly increased their ranks. Death was in ascendancy on a scale not witnessed since the great plagues of the fourteenth and fifteenth centuries. For many, a ghost story might have been a little too near the bone for diversion – or, after the actualities of fear and terror, too trivial. Nor can one here overlook the powerful influence of Freud and his followers, which caused people to consider the operations of the unconscious and to think differently about their inner fears and inhibitions.[1]

In the 1950s the phrase 'the novel is dead' became a boring cliché. If proliferation is a sign of incipient death there may have been some truth in it. People might just as easily have been saying, for different reasons, that the ghost story was dead. In the event the ghost story (like the novel) has shown no sign of lying down and surrendering its spirit. Although thus far nobody of the stature of Walter de la Mare, M. R. James, Henry James or Le Fanu has come forth, and few major writers have given the genre their full attention, hundreds of ghost stories have been published since the late 1950s. Able practitioners include Rosemary Timperley, James Turner, George Mackay Brown and Elizabeth Walter. Numerous

1. In 1918 Freud published his essay 'Das Unheimliche' ('The Uncanny') which has several fascinating observations on the ghost story.

writers have produced the occasional one (e.g. Ronald Blythe, William Sansom, Angus Wilson, William Trevor). Here and there a story stands comparison with those of past masters (for instance, Mario Soldati's sad and tender 'Footsteps in the Snow'); a lot are middling-good, but many are not much more than hack work. The few that I have chosen to represent their period range from Marghanita Laski's bleak and sinister 'The Tower' to the comic exuberance of Joan Aiken's 'Sonata for Harp and Bicycle'.

In making the whole selection I have been guided by fairly straightforward, self-imposed rules. I have taken a ghost story to be a piece of fiction in prose, of variable length (ranging from about 1,000 words to about 25,000 words), in which the spirit of a person (or the spirits of persons), no longer bound by natural laws, manifests itself, or seems to do so (either embodied in some form or disembodied), and 'haunts' a place, person or thing as a kind of 'presence'.

I have excluded stories which involve demonic pacts, *Doppelgänger* ('double-goers', 'double-walkers'), vampires, werewolves, succubae and poltergeists – and the numerous denizens of undiscovered or partly discovered countries which lie or are believed to lie beyond this world. I have also excluded tales of witchcraft, the prolepses of magic, and that wide variety of occult practices associated with such matters as Cumberlandism, spiritualism, exorcism, telekinesis, hylomancy and so forth.

From the outset I settled for a chronological representation covering the greater part of the last two hundred years. So I begin with Kleist's 'The Beggarwoman of Locarno' (1810) and end with A. S. Byatt's 'The July Ghost' (first broadcast in 1981).

At all stages I looked for originality of content and ideas and excellence of form and style (many a good ghost story has been ruined by poor writing), and I have tried to present a range of stories which vary in mood and tone as much as they do in technique and style. Thus at one extreme, for instance, we have Thomas Mann's rather Expressionistic and Kafkaesque 'The Wardrobe', at the other M. R. James's comparatively 'naturalistic' 'The Rose Garden'. I do not suppose there is much that will be new to the connoisseur, but there may well be some stories which are unfamiliar to the general reader – and it is the general reader whom I have had primarily in mind.

It will at once be apparent that a number of famous writers of ghost stories are not represented. They include Poe, Dickens, Wilkie Collins, Vernon Lee, Arthur Machen and Walter de la Mare. A main reason is that their stories (often the same ones) have quite often appeared in other anthologies. A number of famous ghost stories by other writers have similarly been excluded (e.g. 'The Canterville Ghost' by Wilde, 'An Occurrence at Owl Creek Bridge' by Ambrose Bierce and 'The Monkey's Paw' by W. W. Jacobs). This said, an explanation should be given for the inclusion of stories that have indeed appeared in other anthologies. The principal reasons are three: (1) they will stand reprinting; (2) they are necessary for balance and variety; (3) they are by authors who must appear in order that the selection should be regionally and chronologically representative.

Finally, when all is said and done, there is a limit, and it is the compiler's unenviable task to decide what must be omitted. It is axiomatic that no anthology is going to please everyone.

I remarked earlier that the ghost story has been dominated by British writers, particularly by the English. It is also worth noting that in oral tradition and popular belief there is a very extensive ghost lore in Britain which is being added to all the time. Not only that: there is a copious 'literature' on the subject which continues to burgeon. Since 1960 – to take a date arbitrarily – more than seventy books on matters to do with ghosts have been published in Britain. Thirty-six of them appeared in the 1970s. There are guidebooks to the ghosts of individual counties and regions, detailed studies of particular places and their spooks, historical surveys, case histories, ghost-hunters' manuals, and even maps showing the population density of ghosts.[1] From a perusal of these books I infer that murder, suicide and execution have been the main begetters of restless, haunting spirits and the stories that go with them.

In Greater London alone there are about a hundred tolerably well known ghost stories associated with particular people and places. If we consider England and Wales alone there are well over five hundred prominent ghosts with a definite identity whose collective spectral existence spans more than a thousand years. Apart from rural ghosts connected with

1. By contrast, the critical literature devoted to a massive quantity of fiction is negligible. There are a few short essays, including one by Virginia Woolf on Henry James's ghost stories, and Montague Summers's introduction to *The Supernatural Omnibus* (1931). Plus a handful of books: *The Supernatural in Modern English Fiction* (1917) by Dorothy Scarborough; *Wilkie Collins, Le Fanu and Others* (1931) by S. M. Ellis; *Supernatural Horror in Literature* (1945) by H. P. Lovecraft; *The Supernatural in Fiction* (1952) by Peter Penzoldt; *Night Visitors: The Rise and Fall of the English Ghost Story* (1977) by Julia Briggs – an excellent book and one which, unhappily, I discovered to late to benefit from in preparing this anthology; and *The Literature of Terror: A History of Gothic Fictions from 1765 to the Present Day* (1980) by David Punter. Biographies of individual authors naturally contain critical comments on their stories.

specific stretches of countryside there is a multitude that haunt castles, houses, theatres, inns, courtrooms, jails, railway stations, quays, streets, churches, farms, banks, warehouses – and where not? And, of course, graveyards and the sites where gibbets formerly stood.

As to personalities, we have not only monarchs and members of the nobility and aristocracy but large numbers of more or less illustrious spectres who would have entries in any reputable *Who Was Who*: Bishop Lancelot Andrewes, Fred Archer (the jockey), Thomas à Becket, Jeremy Bentham, Emily Brontë, Admiral John Byng, William Constable, Oliver Cromwell, Dickens (most appropriately), Disraeli, Sir Francis Drake, Sir Fulke Greville, Henry Irving, T. E. Lawrence, Ivor Novello, Alexander Pope, Amy Robsart and Dick Turpin – to name but a handful. One of the most venerable British ghosts is that of King Athelstan, whose haunting of Dacre Castle, Cumbria, dates from the middle of the tenth century; one of the more recent the phantom of the A23 at Pyecombe, Sussex, a female hitch-hiker killed in a motor-bike accident whose wraith was last sighted in 1972.

In the world of the supernatural inanimate objects, too, are capable of uncanny behaviour – for example the famous ghost train of Box Tunnel, Wiltshire, the phantom Spitfire of Biggin Hill, and the phantom fiddle of Poole, Dorset.

Horses and dogs are especially conspicuous in ghost lore. The horses, headless or otherwise, are nearly always associated with human ghosts. Dogs often have a more individual and separate existence, like the ubiquitous Black Shuck, the phantom hound sighted frequently in East Anglia and known in other regions as Shriker, Hooter, Guytrash, Boggle, Dobby, Barguest, Old Snarlyow and Shug Monkey.

My personal favourite non-human ghost is the 'Phantom Chicken of Highgate', the victim of an experiment in the theory of refrigeration conducted by Sir Francis Bacon in the winter of 1626. During a blizzard Sir Francis went out to the duckpond on top of Highgate Hill and stuffed frozen snow into the carcass of a freshly plucked chicken. The enterprise was too much for Bacon, then in his sixtieth year. He caught a cold, developed bronchitis, and died. The spectre of the luckless fowl, feather-less, squawking, and agitating the stubs of its wings, has ever since sporadically haunted Pond Square. Observers remark that it disappears through a brick wall.

The materials of legend, folklore and oral tradition have often been exploited by writers of ghost stories, and the common stock of such material goes on accumulating. In the course of their lives a surprising number of people have at least one experience of a sufficiently weird and uncanny nature to warrant its being ascribed to ghostly influence. Emotional, mental and spiritual stress – grief, loss, pain, guilt, extreme states of mind – make them particularly susceptible. The experiences may be 'imaginary' but they are none the less real for that. Ambrose Bierce was very likely right when he remarked that ghosts are 'the outward and visible sign of an inward fear'.

People go on reading ghost stories because, at a basic and perhaps somewhat childlike level, they rather enjoy being frightened. A really good ghost story *is* frightening. There's no doubt about that. It puts the wind up one. And in the corpus of such tales the absurd and the comic have their therapeutic place. What might be described as the 'anti-ghost' (by analogy with anti-hero), a spook endowed with the vocation of failure, is a necessary counterpart to the malevolent and tormented spirit – for instance, Wilde's Canterville ghost who, try as it might, simply couldn't put the wind up anyone; and that woebegone wraith, conceived by H. G. Wells, which, because of its inexperience, couldn't remember how to disappear. But *that* story has a very sinister conclusion.

Lastly I would like to thank a number of people who have been generous with their time and knowledge: Mr Tony Barham for suggesting several authors; Mr John Blanchard for very helpful advice on modern ghost stories; Mr Michael Charlesworth who supplied a lot of invaluable material and advice; Miss Geraldine Cooke, my patient and helpful editor; Mr Paul Craddock for advice on Slavonic literature; Mrs Peggy Dale for helpful suggestions; Mr C. R. Dale for helpful suggestions; Mr David Gledhill for advice on classical literature; Mr Harry Jackson for advice on German literature; Mr Paul Moreland for help on classical literature; Dr David Singmaster and Mrs Deborah Singmaster for numerous suggestions and the generous loan of a lot of books; Mr Clive Smith for his translation of Zola's 'Angeline'; Professor J. P. Stern of Cambridge University for advice on German literature; Dr William Thom for many suggestions and the loan of a large number of books; Mr Stewart Thompson for advice on German literature; Dr K. W. Ulyatt, Dr H. P. Upadhyay and Mr Clive Wilmer for helpful advice.

The Beggarwoman of Locarno

Heinrich von Kleist

In the foothills of the Alps, near Locarno in northern Italy, there used to stand an old castle belonging to an Italian marquis, which can now, when one comes from the direction of the St Gotthard Pass, be seen lying in ruins; a castle with high-ceilinged spacious rooms, in one of which the mistress of the house one day, having taken pity on an old sick woman who had turned up at the door begging, had allowed her to lie down on the floor on some straw they put there for her. The marquis, by chance, on his return from hunting, entered this room to place his gun there as usual, and angrily ordered the woman to get up from the corner in which she was lying and remove herself to behind the stove. As she rose, the woman's crutch slipped on the polished floor and she fell, dangerously injuring the lower part of her back, as a result, although she did manage with indescribable difficulty to get to her feet and to cross the room from one side to the other in the direction indicated, she collapsed moaning and gasping behind the stove and expired.

Several years later, when the marquis found himself in straitened financial circumstances owing to war and a series of bad harvests, he was visited by a Florentine knight, who wished to buy the castle from him because of its fine position. The marquis, who was eager to effect this transaction, told his wife to accommodate their guest in the above-mentioned room, which was standing empty and was very beautifully and sumptuously furnished. But in the middle of the night, to the consternation of the husband and wife, the gentleman came downstairs to them pale and distraught, assuring them on his solemn word that the room was haunted: for something that had been invisible to the eye had risen to its feet in the corner with a noise as if it had been lying on straw, and had then with audible steps, slowly and feebly, crossed the room from one side to the other and collapsed, moaning and gasping, behind the stove.

The marquis, filled with an alarm for which he himself could not account, dismissed his guest's fears with feigned laughter, and declared that to calm them he would at once get up and spend the remaining hours of darkness with him in his room, but the knight begged to be permitted to remain in the marquis's bedroom in an armchair, and when morning came he called for his carriage, took his leave, and departed.

This incident caused an extraordinary stir and, to the marquis's extreme vexation, deterred a number of purchasers; consequently, when his own servants began to repeat the strange and inexplicable rumour that a ghost was walking at midnight in that particular room, he resolved to take decisive steps to refute this report, by investigating the matter himself on the following night. Accordingly, when evening fell, he had his bed set up in the room in question and, without going to sleep, awaited midnight. But to his horror he did in fact, on the stroke of the witching hour, hear the inexplicable sounds: sounds as of someone rising from a bed of rustling straw, and crossing the room from one side to the other to collapse in moaning death-agony behind the stove. When he came down next morning the marquise asked him how his investigation had gone, whereupon he looked about him apprehensively and uncertainly, bolted the door, and assured her that the reports about the haunting were true. At this she was more terrified than ever before in her life, and begged him not to let the matter become generally known until he had once again, in cold blood, and in her presence, put it to the test. But sure enough, on the following night, both they and a loyal servant, whom they had asked to accompany them, heard the very same inexplicable, ghostly sounds; and it was only because of their urgent desire to get rid of the castle at all costs that they were able in their servant's presence to conceal the dread that seized them and to attribute the occurrence to some trivial and fortuitous cause which would no doubt come to light. When on the third evening the couple, determined to get to the bottom of the matter, again went upstairs with beating hearts to the guest-room, it chanced that the house dog, which had been unchained, met them at the door; whereupon, without any explicit discussion of why they did so, but perhaps instinctively desiring the company of some third living creature, they took the dog with them into the room. At about eleven o'clock they each sat down on a bed, two candles burning on the table, the marquise fully dressed, the marquis with a rapier and pistols, which he had taken out of the cupboard, laid in readiness beside him; and while they sat there trying as best they could to entertain each other with conversation, the dog lay down in the middle of the room with its head on its paws and went to sleep. Presently, at exactly midnight, the terrible sounds were to be heard again: someone visible to no human eye, someone on crutches rising and standing up in the corner of the room, the rustling of the straw, the tap, tap, of the advancing steps – and at the very first of these the dog, waking and starting to its feet with ears erect, began growling and barking exactly as if some person were walking towards it, and retreated backwards in the direction of the stove. At this sight the marquise, her hair standing on end, rushed from the room; and while her husband, snatching up his sword, shouted 'Who's there?', and on getting no answer lunged like a madman in all directions through the empty air, she called for her carriage, resolving to drive off at once to the town; but even before she had packed a few belongings together and gone clattering through the gate, she saw the whole castle burst into flames around her. The marquis, in a frenzy of horror, had seized a candle and, the house being panelled with wood throughout, had set fire to it at all four corners, weary of his life. In vain she sent in servants to rescue the unfortunate man; he had already perished miserably, and to this day his white bones, gathered together by the country people, still lie in that corner of the room in which he had ordered the beggarwoman of Locarno to rise from her bed.

The Entail

E. T. A. Hoffmann

Not far from the shore of the Baltic there stands Castle R., the ancestral seat of Baron von R. The district is wild and desolate; hardly anything grows, a blade of grass here and there in the bottomless quicksand; and, instead of a castle garden, a scanty pine-forest cleaves to the bare walls on the landward side – a place of eternal gloom in which there echoes only the croaking of ravens and the screams of storm-proclaiming seagulls. A quarter of an hour away – and nature is suddenly different: as if by magic one is transported to blossoming meadows and flourishing farmland and pasture. Here is the prosperous village and the spacious residence of the manager of the estate. At the head of a coppice of alder trees there can be seen the foundations of a large manor house one of the former owners intended to build. His successors, who made their home in Courland, neglected to continue it, and even Baron Roderich von R., who returned to live in the ancestral seat, did the same: the ancient, isolated castle appealed more to his dark, misanthropic nature. He restored the decaying structure as well as he could and shut himself up in it with a morose steward and a few servants. He was seldom seen in the village; he would walk and ride instead to the seashore, and people fancied they saw him addressing the waves and listening to the roaring and hissing of the surf, as if it bore the answering voice of the spirit of the sea. On the highest point of the watch-tower he had installed an observatory and fitted it out with telescopes and other astronomical apparatus; during the day he looked out to sea and watched the ships passing on the horizon like white seabirds; on starlit nights he practised his astronomy (the people regarded it as astrology), assisted by his ancient steward. He was in general suspected of knowledge of the so-called black arts, and it was rumoured that he had had to leave Courland because an unsuccessful operation of his in this realm had offended a high princely family in the most grievous way. The slightest allusion to his residence there filled him with horror; but whatever had disrupted his life, whatever had happened to him there, he ascribed to his forebears, who had wickedly abandoned the ancestral seat. To bind the head of the family at least to maintaining it in the future, he established it as an entail, and the crown confirmed it the more readily in that a wealthy and chivalrous family already drifting abroad would thereby be restored to the fatherland. Neither Roderich's son, Hubert, nor the present Lord of the Manor, also named Roderich, had wanted to live in the castle, and both had remained in Courland; it was presumed that, of a more cheerful disposition than the gloomy grandfather, they shunned the dreadful desolation of the spot.

Baron Roderich had allowed two old, unmarried and unprovided-for sisters of his father to dwell with him: they lived with an elderly maidservant in the warm little rooms of the adjoining wing and, except for them and the cook, who had a large room on the ground floor close to the kitchen, the only person who frequented the halls and galleries of the main building was an aged huntsman, who also acted as the castellan. The rest of the servants lived in the village with the estate manager. Only in late autumn, when the first snow started to fall and the wolf- and boar-hunts began, did the abandoned castle come to life: Baron Roderich arrived from Courland with his wife, relatives, friends, and numerous hunt-followers. The neighbouring nobility, and even hunt-loving friends from the nearby town, appeared, and the main building and adjoining wing were scarcely able to accommodate them all; fires crackled in every stove and hearth; from grey of dawn until late into the night the roasting-spits turned; upstairs, downstairs, ran the guests and servants; goblets were clashed together and hunting-songs resounded; there was music and dancing, jubilation and laughter everywhere – so that for over a month the castle was more like an inn on the highway than a manorial seat.

Baron Roderich devoted this time, so far as he could, to serious business: withdrawn from the social whirlpool, he attempted to run the estate. He had a complete account of income prepared, listened to any suggestions for improvements, heard the complaints of his tenants and endeavoured to put right any wrong or injustices. In this he was assisted by old Advocate V., who usually arrived at the estate at least a week before the baron did.

In the year 179– the time had come for Advocate V. to journey to Castle

R. Vigorous though he still was at seventy, he must have thought that a helping hand would be of use to him; and one day he said to me, as if joking: 'Cousin!' – so he called me, though I was his great-nephew, since I had been given his forenames – 'Cousin! I have been thinking you ought to get a little sea air into your lungs and come with me to Castle R. You can give me some help with my often wearisome business, and you might also try the wild hunting life, after you have spent one morning drafting a contract, you can spend the next looking into the gleaming eyes of a long-haired wolf or a savage-toothed boar – or even learn how to bag one.'

I had heard so many strange things about the hunting season at R. that I was highly delighted that this time my great-uncle wanted to take me with him. Already fairly well acquainted with the business he had to deal with, I promised to relieve him of all his cares and worries. The next day we were sitting in the carriage, enveloped in warm furs and driving to Castle R. through thick flurries of snow that heralded the coming of winter.

On the way, the old man recounted to me all manner of strange stories about the old Baron Roderich, who had established the entail and, ignoring his youthfulness, had appointed him his legal adviser and the executor of his will. He spoke of the rough, wild character of the old baron, which seemed to have been passed on to the whole family: even the present master, whom he had known as an almost effeminate youth, seemed to become rougher and wilder with each passing year. He instructed me that I would have to be alert and unconstrained if I was to find favour with the baron, and he referred finally to the living quarters in the castle which he had, once and for all, chosen for his own: they were warm and comfortable and so situated that we could withdraw from the uproar of the company whenever we wanted to. He had two small rooms, hung with warm wall coverings, next to the courtroom in the side wing opposite the wing in which the aged aunts lived.

At last, after a quick though arduous journey, we arrived at R. late in the night. We drove through the village. It was in fact already Sunday; at the inn there was music and dancing and jubilation, the estate manager's house also resounded with music and was illuminated from top to bottom, and the desolation into which we now drove was all the more dreary. The wind howled piercingly from the sea and, as if awoken by it from a deep magic sleep, the gloomy pine-trees groaned back with a muffled wail. The naked black walls of the castle towered up from the snow-covered ground; we stopped at the closed gate. We called, cracked the whip, hammered and knocked, but to no avail: everything seemed dead and there were no lights visible in any of the windows. The old man called in his penetrating voice: 'Franz! Franz! Where are you? The devil take it, move yourself! We are freezing out here! The snow is lashing our faces bloody! Move yourself, the devil take it!'

Then a yard-dog began to whine, a light moved along on the ground floor, keys clattered and the heavy gate creaked open. 'Ay, welcome, welcome, Herr Justitiarius, in this terrible weather!' cried old Franz, lifting his lantern, so that the light fell full on his shrivelled face, drawn strangely into a smile.

The carriage drove into the yard, we climbed down and I saw for the first time the old servant's strange figure, dressed in ancient hunting livery marvellously adorned with braid. Over his broad, white forehead there were a few grey hairs, the lower part of his face bore the robust tan of the huntsman, and though the drawn muscles made it seem almost a mask, the geniality which shone from his eyes and played about his mouth restored to his face its humanity.

'Now then, old Franz,' began my great-uncle, knocking the snow from his coat in the hallway, 'is everything ready, have the carpets in my rooms been beaten, have the beds been brought in, has everything been properly heated, yesterday and today?'

'No,' Franz replied calmly, 'no, worthy Herr Justitiarius, none of that has been done.'

'Good God!' my great-uncle exploded. 'I wrote to you in good time, I have come at the right date; what stupidity! Now my rooms will be ice-cold.'

'Yes, worthy Herr Justitiarius,' said Franz, carefully removing a glowing ember from the wick with the lamp-trimmer and extinguishing it with his foot. 'Yes, you see, but all that, and especially the heating, wouldn't have been much use, because the wind and snow are blowing right in, through the broken windows and . . .'

'What!' my great-uncle interposed. 'What! The windows are broken and you, the castellan, have done nothing about it?'

'Yes, worthy Herr Justitiarius,' the old man calmly continued, 'not much can be done with them because of all the rubbish and all the stones from the walls lying around the room.'

'How, in the name of Heaven, have rubbish and stones got into my room?' my great-uncle roared.

'Bless you, bless you, young sir,' cried the old man, bowing politely, as I sneezed; then, continuing immediately, he said: 'It's the stones and plaster from the middle wall, which fell in with the great shaking.'

'Have you had an earthquake?' my great-uncle exploded.

'No, not an earthquake, worthy Herr Justitiarius,' replied the old man with a smile, 'but three days ago the heavy ornamented ceiling of the courtroom fell down with a tremendous crash.'

My great-uncle was about to give vent to a mighty oath; but as he pulled his fur cap from his head, he suddenly stopped, turned to me and said, laughing loudly: 'Truly, cousin, we must keep our mouths shut, we mustn't ask any more, or we shall learn of some still worse catastrophe, or the whole castle will fall on our heads. But,' he continued, turning to the old man. 'Franz, couldn't you have had the wit to get another room ready for me? Couldn't you have some other hall fitted out for the court hearing?'

'That's already been done,' the old man said, motioning us to the stairs and beginning to climb them.

'Bless me if this isn't a strange fellow!' said my uncle as we followed the old man. We went on through long, high-ceilinged corridors, Franz's flickering light casting an uncanny glow into the deep gloom. Pillars, capitals and coloured archways appeared, as if hovering in the air, our giant shadows strode along beside us, and the curious pictures on the walls past which they flitted seemed to shudder and tremble, with their voices whispering in the booming echo of our steps: 'Do not wake us, do not wake the mad enchanted beings who sleep in these ancient stones.'

At length, after we had passed through a row of cold, gloomy apartments, Franz opened the door to a hall in which a brightly blazing hearth welcomed us. I was restored to good humour as soon as I entered, but my great-uncle stood in the middle of the hall, looked around him and said in a very serious, almost solemn tone; 'Is this to be the courtroom?'

Franz, holding his lamp high, so that on the wide, dark wall a bright spot as large as a door met one's eyes, said gloomily: 'A court has already been held here!'

'What is that you say?' cried my uncle, throwing off his coat and stepping up to the fire.

'Nothing, nothing,' Franz replied. He lit the lamps and opened the adjoining room, which had been made comfortable for our stay.

It was not long before a table was set before the fire; the old man brought an excellent repast and – what gave us both real pleasure – a splendid bowl of punch, brewed in the true northern manner, followed it. Fatigued by the journey, my great-uncle sought his bed as soon as he had eaten; but the novelty and strangeness of the accommodation, even the punch, had aroused my spirits too much for me to be able to think of sleeping. Franz cleared the table, adjusted the fire and, with a friendly bow, left me.

Now I was sitting alone in the baronial hall. The snow had begun to ease off, the storm to cease its blustering, the sky had grown lighter and the bright full-moon shone through the arched windows, illuminating all the gloomy corners of the room, into which the candle and the firelight could not penetrate, with a magical light. The walls and ceiling were decorated in an antiquated manner, the walls with heavy panelling, the ceiling with fantastic pictures and gaily coloured painted and gilded carvings. Out of the larger canvases, most of them depicting the confusion of bear- or wolf-hunts, there protruded the heads of men and animals, carved in wood and set on to the painted bodies, so that, especially in the flickering light of fire and moon, the whole assumed a gruesome reality. Between these paintings there hung lifesized portraits of knights striding out in hunting dress – probably the hunt-loving ancestors. Everything – paintings and carvings – bore the dark tinge of the long passage of time; the bright bare patch on the wall through which two doors led into the adjoining apartments was therefore all the more striking, and I soon realized that this patch must also have been a door, now walled up. Now, we all know what power the unusual has to grip the mind; even an idle imagination comes to life in a valley surrounded by strange cliffs, within the gloomy walls of a church; it anticipates experiences such as it has never had. If I add that I was then twenty years old and had drunk several glasses of strong punch, you will easily believe that my baronial hall filled me with strange sensations. Imagine the stillness of the night, in which the muffled murmur of the sea and the whistling of the wind sound like the notes of a mighty organ played by invisible spirits, the clouds flying past overhead seem to peer through the rattling windows like giants – I was indeed likely to have felt that a strange kingdom might now rise up visibly and tangibly before me. Yet this feeling was like the pleasurable chill one experiences at the vital telling of a ghost story; and it occurred to me that I had never been in a better mood to read a book which, like so many others at that time, I carried in my pocket. It was Schiller's *Ghost-Seer*. I sat and read and heated my imagination more and more. I had come to the gripping story of the wedding feast at the Count von V.'s – just as Jeronimo's bloodstained figure entered, the door leading to the hallway sprang open with a mighty crash. Terrified, I shot into the air, the book fell from my hands. But everything was still, and I was ashamed of my childish fears. The door might have been blown back by a draught. It was nothing – my over-excited imagination transformed everything into a ghost! Thus calmed, I picked the book up from the floor and threw myself back into the chair – something was walking quietly and slowly with measured tread across the hall, and there was a sighing and groaning, and in this sighing and groaning there lay an expression of the most profound human suffering, of the most inconsolable misery. Ha! a sick animal had been locked in on the ground floor – at night every distant noise seems close – who could be frightened by that? Thus I calmed myself again; but now there came a scraping, and louder, deeper sighs, as if emitted in the dread of death, and they came from behind the new wall.

'Yes, it is a poor animal locked up. I will call out, I will stamp on the floor, all will grow quiet' – was what I thought; but the blood was coursing through my veins, cold sweat stood on my forehead, and I sat frozen in my chair, incapable of standing, still less of calling out. The horrible scraping stopped at last, the footsteps again became audible; I seemed to come to life again, jumped up and took two steps forward – when an icy blast struck through the hall; in the same instant the moon threw a bright light on to the portrait of a very earnest-seeming man and, as if his voice were whispering through the roaring of the sea and the whistling of the night wind, I heard him say: 'No further, no further, or you will fall prey to the spirit world!'

Now the door slammed shut with the same heavy crash as before, I heard the footsteps in the hallway – they were going down the stairs – the door of the castle opened with a rattle and was closed again. Then it was as if a horse had been taken out of its stall and after a while led back in again – then everything was still! In the same instant, I perceived that my great-uncle in the adjoining apartment was sighing and groaning; this brought me to my senses; I grasped the lamp and hurried in. The old man seemed to be fighting an evil dream.

'Wake up, wake up!' I cried, taking him gently by the hand and letting the light of the candle fall on to his face. The old man woke with a muffled cry, and then looked at me in a kindly way and said: 'You did well, Cousin, to wake me up. I was having a really bad dream, and this room and that hall is to blame for it, for I was thinking of past times and of the many strange things that have taken place here. But now let us get back to sleep again!' And with that, the old man pulled the bedclothes about him and seemed to fall asleep immediately; but as I extinguished the candle and laid myself down in bed, I heard the old man quietly praying.

Work started the next morning: the estate manager arrived with the accounts, and people came to have disputes settled and affairs put in order. At noon, my great-uncle went with me to call on the two aged baronesses. Franz announced us; we had to wait a few moments and then were led into the sanctuary by a bent little old woman of sixty who called herself the chambermaid. There the old ladies, eccentrically attired in a fashion long outmoded, received us with amusing ceremoniousness, and I especially was the object of their wonderment when my great-uncle introduced me as a young attorney assisting him. It was obvious from their expression that they believed the wellbeing of R.'s inhabitants was endangered by my youth. The visit was very enjoyable, but the horror of the previous night still clung to me. I felt as if touched by some unknown power, or rather that I had already approached the circle to enter which means perdition. So it was that even the baronesses, with their strange, high-piled hair and their weird and wonderful clothes, seemed, not amusing, but quite dreadful and spectral. I wished I could read in their shrivelled faces and watery eyes, I wished I could hear in the bad French which came half through their pinched lips and half through their pointed noses, how the old ladies had got at least on to good terms with the uncanny beings which haunted the castle. My great-uncle, who was in a very merry mood, got the old ladies so entangled in his mad chatter that, had I been in a different mood, I would not have known how to control my laughter; but, as I have said, the baronesses remained spectral to me, and my great-uncle, who had thought the visit would give me especial pleasure, looked at me with amazement.

As soon as we were alone in our room, he burst out: 'Cousin, for Heaven's sake tell me what is the matter with you! You don't laugh, you say nothing, you eat nothing, you drink nothing! Are you ill? Are you in need of anything?'

I did not now hesitate to tell him all the horrific events of the previous night. I concealed nothing, and especially not that I had been drinking a lot of punch and reading Schiller's *Ghost-Seer*. 'I have to admit this,' I added, 'for it may be that it was my over-heated imagination that created all these apparitions.'

I thought my great-uncle would scoff at my ghost-seeing; instead of which, however, he grew very serious, gazed at the floor, then suddenly raised his head and, regarding me with a burning look, said: 'I do not know your book, Cousin, but you have neither it nor the spirit of the punch to thank for that ghost. You should know that I myself dreamt what happened to you. I was sitting, just like you (as it seemed to me) in the armchair by the fire, but what you only heard, I saw. Yes! I saw the gruesome fiend as he entered, as he crept to the walled-up door, how he scraped at the wall in despair until the blood spurted from under his torn nails, how he then went down the stairs, led the horse out of the stable and then brought it back. Did you hear the cock crow in the village? You woke me up just then, and I soon summoned up my resistance to that evil ghost.'

The old man fell silent and I did not like to question him: I knew he would explain everything to me if he thought fit. After a time, during which he was lost in his own thoughts, he continued: 'Cousin, have you the courage, now you know all the facts, to confront this ghost again, this time with me?'

I naturally declared I was quite capable of doing so. 'Then let us watch together tonight,' my great-uncle said. 'An inner voice tells me that, if I have the courage, the spirit must yield, and that it is no reckless undertaking but a religious work if I venture life and limb to banish an evil fiend which is expelling the sons from the seat of their ancestors. But do not let us think of danger: in such firmness of mind and devotion as exists within me, one is and remains a triumphant hero! Should it nonetheless be God's will that the evil power shall overcome me, then, you, Cousin, must proclaim that I fell in Christian battle with the spirit of Hell. Keep well away! – then nothing will happen to you!'

Evening came. Franz had cleared away the meal and brought in the punch, the moon shone full through the clouds, the sea thundered and the night wind howled and rattled the windows. In spite of our excitement, we forced ourselves to sit and talk. My uncle had laid his repeater-watch on the table. It struck twelve. With a fearful crash the door sprang open and, as on the previous night, soft slow steps passed across the hall, and there came the sound of groaning and sighing. My uncle had turned pale, but his eyes shone with an uncommon fire, he rose from his chair, and as he stood, a tall figure with his arm raised towards the middle of the room, he looked like a commanding hero. The sighing and groaning grew louder, and then, even more horribly than before, there began the scraping on the wall. My uncle strode firmly to the walled-up door. He halted before the spot where the scratching was growing more and more desperate and said in a solemn tone, such as I had never heard from him: 'Daniel, Daniel! what are you doing here at this hour?'

There was a terrifying scream and a heavy thud, as of a burden falling.

'Seek mercy before the throne of the Most High. There you should be! Away with you out of life, to which you can never again belong!' – so cried my uncle, in an even louder voice than before. And it was as if a gentle whimpering floated through the air and died away in the rising storm. Then my uncle went to the door and threw it shut, so that the sound echoed through the empty hallway. In his speech, in his bearing, there was something superhuman which filled me with awe. As he sat again in his chair, his gaze was as if transfigured; he folded his hands, he prayed silently. After a few minutes, he said in his gentle voice, which penetrated so deeply into my heart: 'Well, Cousin?'

Trembling with dread, horror and anxiety, with love and awe, I fell to my knees and moistened the proffered hand with hot tears. The old man embraced me in his arms, and as he pressed me warmly to his heart he said very gently: 'Now we can sleep in peace, dear Cousin!'

And so we did; and as nothing whatever uncanny occurred the following night, we recovered our former gaiety.

Some days later, the Baron at last arrived with the Baroness and numerous hunt followers, the invited guests collected and the castle now suddenly came to life in the fashion already described. As soon as he had arrived the Baron visited our apartments and seemed strangely surprised to find us there; he cast a baleful glance at the walled-up door and, turning away, passed a hand over his forehead as if to dispel some painful memory. My great-uncle mentioned the devastation of the courtroom and the adjoining apartments and the Baron exclaimed that Franz should have found us a better alternative; my great-uncle, he said, had only to ask if there was anything lacking for his comfort. The Baron maintained an attitude of a certain respect towards my uncle, as though he were an elder relative, but this was the only thing which in any way reconciled me to the man's generally rough and domineering manner. He seemed to regard me as no more than a clerk; the very first time I undertook a transaction he sought to find something wrong with it, and I was on the point of an angry retort when my uncle interposed and assured the Baron I had done all correctly. When we were alone, I complained bitterly about the Baron, whom I was coming to detest from the bottom of my soul.

'Believe me, Cousin,' replied the old man, 'the Baron, despite his unfriendliness, is the most excellent, good-natured man in the world. He had acquired this attitude, as I have already told you, only since he became the head of the house: before that he was a mild and modest man. But really, he is not as bad as you make out, and I would like to know why it is you dislike him so very much.'

As he said this, my uncle gave a mocking smile which sent the blood rushing to my face and made clear to me my innermost feelings: was it not obvious that this overwise unaccountable hatred originated in love, and specifically in love of one who seemed to me the most wonderful being that had ever walked the earth? This being was none other than the Baroness herself. Immediately I saw her, her dainty form enveloped in a Russian sable and her head in a veil, she affected me with an irresistible magic. Even though the aged aunts, in even stranger garb than I had seen them in before, were tripping at her side when she arrived, gabbling welcomes in French, as she gazed gently around her, nodding to this person or that in a friendly manner and speaking a few German words in her clear Courland dialect – that first impression already produced on me a strange effect, and I involuntarily associated it with that of the uncanny spectre, so that the Baroness was an angel of light before whom the powers of evil gave way. The lovely image remained in my mind's eye. She was then perhaps no more than nineteen years old; her face was angelic, and in her dark eyes there lay the indescribable magic of moonbeams suffused with melancholy yearning. Often she seemed lost in her own thoughts, and at such times dark clouds passed over her lovely brow: one might have thought that she was disturbed by painful memories, but to me it seemed rather that what was filling her mind was a presentiment of a future full of misfortune, and – I have no idea why – I connected this with the castle ghost.

The morning after the Baron's arrival everyone gathered for breakfast. My uncle introduced me to the Baroness; not surprisingly, I behaved in an indescribably foolish manner, became confused over the simplest questions the lady put to me and succeeded in giving the aged aunts the impression I was tongue-tied with awe, so that they found it necessary to come to my assistance and to assure the Baroness that in reality I was a *garçon très joli* and quite a gifted fellow. This annoyed me and, suddenly assuming control of myself, I spoke some witticism in much better French than the old ladies', whereupon they gazed at me with wide eyes and treated their long pointed noses to a good helping of snuff. From the look the Baroness then give me, I realized that the intended witticism had failed of its effect, a fact which irritated me still further, and I damned the old women to the depths of Hell.

The period of sheepish longing and childish infatuation had long since been teased out of me by my great-uncle, and it was clear to me that the Baroness had taken more powerful a hold on my inner feelings than any woman had ever done. I saw, I heard only her; I was aware how mad it would be of me to risk any flirtation with her, yet I could not gaze from a distance like a lovesick calf; what I could do, however, was to approach her more closely without allowing her to suspect my feelings, absorb the sweet poison of her eyes and her speech and then, far away from her, carry her image forever in my heart. The idea of this romantic, almost knightly form of love, as it occurred to me during a sleepless night, set me childishly haranguing myself with great pathos; at length I sighed very lamentably: 'Seraphine, O Seraphine!' so that I awoke my uncle, who called out to me: 'Cousin! Cousin! Stop fantasizing out loud! Do so by day, if you want to, but do let me get some sleep at night!'

I was not a little concerned that my uncle, who had already noted my excitement at the arrival of the Baroness, should have heard me utter her name; I expected him to engulf me in ridicule, but the following morning he said nothing, except, as we went into the courtroom: 'May God give us sound understanding and keep us from making poltroons of ourselves.'

Thereupon he took his place at the great table and said: 'Write very clearly, dear Cousin, so that I can read it without a hitch.'

The respect, even reverence, in which the Baron held my great-uncle was evident in everything he did. Even at table he occupied the envied place next to the Baroness; chance determined where I sat, though a couple of officers from the capital usually succeeded in requisitioning me in order to unburden themselves of all the latest news from there – a recitation attended by much drinking. Thus it happened that I sat for several days at the far end of the table from the Baroness, until at last chance brought me into her proximity. As we were going into the dining-room, a companion of the Baroness – a lady no longer exactly youthful but still presentable enough and not without wit – involved me in conversation; in accordance with etiquette, I had to offer her my arm, and I was overjoyed when she took her seat quite close to the Baroness, who nodded to her amiably. You can well imagine that all I said from then on was intended less for my companion than for the Baroness. It may be that my inner tension gave a particular animation to everything I said: suffice it to say that my companion became more and more attentive, and soon our conversation sent out sparks in the direction I desired. I noted in particular that my companion cast several significant glances at the Baroness, and that the latter was endeavouring to hear what we were saying, especially when the conversation turned to music and I spoke rapturously of the sacred art and revealed that, notwithstanding my dry and tedious profession, I was quite a competent pianist, could sing and had even composed several songs.

We had gone into the drawing-room to take coffee and liqueurs, and I found myself – I do not know how – standing before the Baroness, who was talking with my former companion. She turned to me at once and, speaking as though to an old acquaintance, repeated the questions she had asked on her arrival: whether I was enjoying my stay at the castle and so on. I assured her that in the first few days the dreariness of the region, even the ancient castle, had put me into a strange mood, but that this mood itself had conjured up many wonders and I only wished to be spared the wild hunts, to which I was not accustomed.

The Baroness smiled: 'I can imagine that cavorting through our forests would not be your idea of amusement,' she said. 'You are a musician and, if I am not completely mistaken, a poet too! I love both the arts passionately! I even play the harp a little, but I have to do without it here; my husband does not like me to bring it with me, and its gentle tones would certainly not go with the shouting and horn calls which is all that is allowed here! Oh my God, how I would like to hear some music here!'

I assured her I would do all I could to fulfil her wish: there must, I said, exist an instrument somewhere in the castle, even if only ancient piano. But Fräulein Adelheid (the Baroness's companion) laughed aloud and asked whether I realized that in all human memory there had been heard in the castle no instruments but croaking trumpets, lamenting horns and the squeaking fiddles, out-of-tune basses and bleating oboes of itinerant players. The Baroness held fast to her wish to hear music, however, and she and Adelheid exhausted themselves in suggestions as to how a tolerable piano might be procured. At that moment, the servant Franz passed through the hall.

'Here's the answer!' Fräulein Adelheid cried. 'Franz will know what to do!'

Franz came across to us and Adelheid made him understand what was wanted; the Baroness, with folded hands, her head inclined forwards, listened to the old man and a gentle smile lit her eyes: she was like a pretty child eager to get her hands on some desired toy. After he had stated in his roundabout way the many reasons it was a sheer impossibility to procure so rare an instrument at short notice, Franz finally stroked his beard and said with a self-satisfied smirk: 'But the estate manager's wife over in the village plays the clavichord uncommon well, or whatever they now call it with their outlandish names, and she sings to it so well and lamentably that your eyes water like with onions and you want to skip about with both legs.'

'And possesses a fortepiano?' Fräulein Adelheid interrupted.

'Oh, indeed,' the old man continued. 'It came direct from Dresden. It's a –'

'Splendid!' the Baroness interjected.

'– lovely instrument,' continued Franz, 'but a little feeble, for when the organist recently wanted to play on it the tune *In allen meinen Taten*, he smashed it to bits, so that –'

'Oh my God!' cried the two ladies.

'– it had to be sent at great expense to R. to be repaired,' Franz said.

'Is it back again then?' Fräulein Adelheid asked impatiently.

'Oh indeed, Miss, and the estate manager's wife will count it an honour.'

At this moment the Baron came by; he glanced at our group with a look of some annoyance and whispered mockingly to the Baroness: 'Is Franz having to offer his advice again?'

The Baroness blushed and dropped her gaze, and old Franz, breaking off startled, stood with head erect and arms down stiffly to his sides, in the posture of a soldier.

The aged aunts swam over to us and led the Baroness away. Fräulein Adelheid followed them. I was left standing as if bewitched. My delight that I would now be able to approach my idol fought with my annoyance at the behaviour of the Baron: if he was not a despot, would his grey-haired servant have behaved so slavishly?

'Do you hear, can you see?' cried my great-uncle, clapping me on the shoulder. We went out into our apartment.

'Don't throw yourself at the Baroness so,' he said as we went in. 'Where could it lead to? Leave it to the young dandies who like paying court and whom there is certainly no lack of.'

I explained how everything had happened and invited him to tell me now whether I had earned his reproaches; but he only replied 'Hmm, hmm,' put on his dressing-gown, lit his pipe and sat down in the armchair and talked about the previous day's hunt, teasing me about the shots I had missed. The castle had grown quiet, but the musicians with their fiddles, basses and oboes of whom Fräulein Adelheid had spoken had arrived; there was to be nothing less than a full-scale ball that night. My uncle, preferring sleep to such foolishness, remained in his room; but I had dressed myself for the ball when there was a light tap at the door, and Franz entered and informed me that the estate manager's wife's clavichord had been fetched by sleigh and taken to the Baroness; Fräulein Adelheid invited me to come at once. You can imagine how my heart beat, with what sweet trepidation I entered the room in which I found her. Fräulein Adelheid encountered me joyfully. The Baroness, already dressed for the ball, was sitting reflectively in front of the mysterious box in which there were slumbering the sounds I was supposed to awaken. As she stood, the radiance of her beauty made me gaze at her speechless.

'Now, Theodore' – she called everyone by his forename, after the pleasant practice of the north – 'the instrument has arrived; pray Heaven it may not be entirely unworthy of your skill!'

As I opened the lid, a number of broken strings sprang up at me; and when I struck a chord, it sounded as if all the remaining strings were out of tune.

'The organist has been at it again with his gentle touch,' Fräulein Adelheid laughed, but the Baroness, who was quite put out, said: 'What a misfortune! Again I shall find no pleasure or enjoyment here.'

I searched in the instrument's box and found a few rolls of strings but no tuning-key. Fresh complaints! Any key whose ward would fit the pegs could be used, I declared; whereupon the ladies ran hither and thither, and it was not long before a whole row of shining keys lay before me on the sounding-board. Now I really got busy. Fräulein Adelheid and the Baroness herself endeavoured to assist me, testing this or that peg. Then one of the keys fitted. 'It works, it works!' they cried happily.

Then the strings began to become entangled and we fought together to unravel them. At length, however, some of them agreed to stay in place, and from the discordant noise there gradually emerged clear, pure chords. 'Ah, success, success! The instrument is in tune!' cried the Baroness, looking at me with a lovely smile.

This activity together swiftly banished all constraint between us; now that the pianoforte was tolerably in tune, I gave expression to my feelings, not in passionate fantasias, but in those sweet *canzoni* which came to us from the south. To the sound of *Seza di te, Sentimi idol mio, Almen se non poss'io, morir me sento, Addio* and *Oh dio*, Seraphine's eyes grew more and more radiant. She had placed herself at the instrument close beside me; I felt her breath on my cheek and a white ribbon which had come adrift from her gown fell over my shoulder and fluttered there like love's messenger, moved by the music and by Seraphine's sighs. It was amazing that I kept my senses! Then Fräulein Adelheid jumped up from where she had been sitting in a corner of the room, knelt before the Baroness and, taking her hands and pressing them to her breast, begged her: 'O dear Baroness, dear Seraphine, now you must sing too!'

'What are you thinking of?' the Baroness replied. 'How can I raise my wretched voice before our virtuoso here?'

Like a bashful child, with downcast eyes and blushing furiously, she fought with desire and shyness. I implored her and did not give up until she tried a few notes on the instrument as an introduction to a Courland folk-song. Now she began, in a soft, bell-like voice, a song whose simple melody bore the character of those folk-songs in which we can recognize our higher poetic nature. A mysterious magic lies in the insignificant words of the text: they become hieroglyphics of the inexpressible with which our heart is filled. Who cannot recall those Spanish *canzoni* whose words say not much more than: 'I sailed on the sea with my sweetheart, the storm blew up and my sweetheart was afraid. No! – I shall not sail again with my sweetheart on the sea!'? Thus the Baroness's song said nothing more than: 'When I was young I danced with my sweetheart at a wedding, a flower fell from my hair, he picked it up and gave it to me and said: "When shall we go to a wedding again?"'

As I accompanied the song, as I stole the melodies of the other songs straight from the lips of the Baroness, I seemed to her and Fräulein Adelheid as the greatest *maestro* of music. They heaped praise upon me. Then the shriek of out-of-tune trumpets and horns announced it was time to gather for the ball.

'Now I have to go, alas!' cried the Baroness. I jumped up from the instrument. 'You have given me a marvellous hour. These were the happiest moments I have ever spent here in R.'

With these words the Baroness gave me her hand; and as, in an ecstasy of delight, I pressed it to my lips, I felt the racing pulse in her fingers. I do not know how I got to my uncle's room and then the ballroom. A Gascon fears the battle because every wound must be fatal to him – he is all heart! I compared myself to him: every touch was fatal. The Baroness's fingers had struck me like poisoned arrows, my blood burned in my veins! My uncle heard the whole story early next morning and suddenly became very serious: 'I would ask you, Cousin, to resist the stupidity which has you in its grip,' he said. 'What you are doing, harmless though it may seem, can have the most dreadful consequences; you are standing on thin ice, and it will break under you before you know it. I shall take good care to keep you firmly attached to my coat-tails, for I know you will deceive yourself you have done no more than catch a cold, when in reality a fever is consuming you, and you will take years to recover. The Devil take your music if you don't know anything better to do with it than entice impressionable women.'

'But,' I interrupted, 'is it in my mind then to flirt with the Baroness?'

'Fool!' cried my uncle, 'if I thought that, I would throw you through that window!'

The Baron interrupted this embarrassing conversation, and business then tore me out of my daydreams of love, in which I saw only Seraphine. In company, she said only a few friendly words to me now and then, but almost every evening a secret message came from Fräulein Adelheid, calling me to Seraphine.

Soon many other kinds of conversation mingled with the music, and many indications forced me to admit that the Baroness really did have some sort of mental disorder, as I had read in her look the first time I saw her. The harmful influence of the castle ghost came back to me: something dreadful had happened, or was to happen. I often felt moved to recount to Seraphine how I had encountered the invisible foe, and how my uncle had banished him for ever, yet an inexplicable shyness prevented me.

One day the Baroness was not at luncheon; she was said to be unwell and unable to leave her room. Asked whether the illness was serious, the Baron smiled disagreeably and said: 'Nothing more than slight catarrh caused by the raw sea air; it is hard on sweet voices and kind only to the harsh halloo of the hunt.'

He threw me a penetrating glance, and I realized that it was to me that he had been speaking. Fräulein Adelheid blushed scarlet and, staring down at her plate, murmured: 'And you will be seeing Seraphine again today, and again your sweet songs will console her injured heart.'

In that instant it seemed to me that I had entered into some forbidden relationship with the Baroness which could end only in something dreadful, in a crime. My great-uncle's warning lay heavily upon my heart. What should I do? See her no more? As long as I remained in the castle, that was impossible; and even if I was permitted to leave the castle and return to K., I was incapable of doing so. I felt only too well that I was not strong enough to shake myself out of the dream I was in. Adelheid almost seemed to me like a procuress, and I wanted to despise her – yet, on reflection, I was ashamed of my foolishness, for what had happened in those evening hours which could lead to any relationship with Seraphine other than that permitted by manners and decorum? Why should it occur to me that the Baroness felt anything for me? – and yet I was convinced I was in danger.

The table was cleared quickly: wolves had been spotted in the forest close to the castle. The idea of hunting appealed to me in my excited state of mind and I told my uncle I wanted to join in. He smiled happily and said: 'That's good. It will do you good to get out. I'll stay at home. You can take my gun and hunting-knife – it's a handy weapon in emergencies, provided you keep calm.'

The part of the forest in which the wolves were thought to lie was surrounded by the hunters. It was bitingly cold, the wind howled through the pines and drove the bright snowflakes against my face, so that, now dusk had fallen, I could scarcely see six paces in front of me. Quite numb, I left the spot appointed to me and sought cover deeper within the forest. There I leaned against a tree, the gun under my arm; I forgot the hunt; my thoughts bore me to Seraphine in her room. I heard the sound of distant firing; in the same instant there was a rustling in the thicket and not ten paces away there appeared a powerful wolf. I took aim, I fired – I missed, the animal sprang at me with blazing eyes and I would have been done for had I not had the presence of mind to draw the hunting-knife and stab it in the throat as it sprang. Its blood spurted over my hand and arm. One of the Baron's huntsmen, who was standing not far from me, came running up, and on his repeated hunting call the others gathered round us. The Baron hurried up to me: 'In Heaven's name, are you bleeding? You *are* bleeding! Are you wounded?'

I assured him I was not; then the Baron turned to the huntsman who had been standing closest to me and reproached him for failing to shoot after I had missed; the latter, however, maintained that he would probably have shot *me* instead, and the Baron, agreeing, conceded he should have taken more care of me himself. In the meantime the hunters had lifted the animal. It was the biggest of its kind seen for a long while, and there was general wonderment at my courage – though at the time I had given no thought to the danger I was in. The Baron was especially solicitous, and we went back to the castle arm in arm (one of the huntsmen had to carry my gun). He continued to speak about my heroic deed, so that in the end I too began to believe in it: I lost my self-consciousness, I had passed my examination and my anxieties had been wiped away. I felt I had acquired the right to try for Seraphine's favours. But then everyone knows what silly dreams an infatuated youth is capable of.

That evening, by the fire with the steaming bowl of punch, I was the hero of the day. Only the Baron had killed a wolf the equal of mine; the others had to content themselves with stories of other hunts and of dangers survived at other times. I now expected to amaze my uncle and recounted to him my adventure with great gusto and did not forget to emphasize the extreme savagery of the beast I had killed. My uncle, however, only laughed and said: 'God moves mightily in the weak!'

As I went along the corridor to the courtroom, tired of the drinking and the company, I saw a figure slip in before me with a lamp in its hand. Stepping into the room, I recognized Fräulein Adelheid.

'One has to wander around like a ghost, like a sleepwalker, if one is to find you, my brave wolf-hunter!' she whispered as she took me by the hand. The words 'sleepwalker' and 'ghost' weighed on my heart, spoken here in this spot: for a moment they brought to my mind the ghostly apparitions of those two gruesome nights; and, now as then, the sea-wind was growling like the deep notes of an organ, rattling and whistling shrilly through the windows, and the moonlight fell on to the wall where I had heard the scraping sounds. I thought I could see spots of blood upon it. Fräulein Adelheid must have felt the icy chill which shuddered through me.

'What is the matter?' she said softly. 'You are quite numb with cold. Now I will call you back to life. The Baroness can hardly wait to see you. She fears the wicked wolf has eaten you up. She is dreadfully worried. What have you done to Seraphine? I have never seen her like it before. Ha! Now your pulse is beginning to beat! How the dead man is suddenly awakened! Now, come along: we must go to our dear little Baroness!'

I allowed myself to be led away. Adelheid's manner of speaking of the Baroness seemed to me unworthy, especially the hint it contained of some secret understanding between us. As I entered her room, Seraphine came towards me with hurried steps and a gentle 'Ah!' Then she stopped, as if coming to her senses. I dared to take her hand and press it to my lips. She let her hand remain in mine as she said: 'But, dear God, is it your profession to take on wolves? Do you not know that the days of Orpheus are over and that the beasts have lost all respect for singers?'

This cheerful remark made clear the nature of the Baroness's interest in me and instantly restored me to discretion. I do not know how, but, instead of sitting at the instrument as usual, I placed myself next to the Baroness on the sofa. Her words: 'And how did you come to be in danger?' showed our mutual understanding that today it was to be not music but conversation. After I had related my adventure in the forest and referred to the lively interest evidenced by the Baron, hinting that I had not thought him capable of it, the Baroness began almost sadly: 'How violent and rough the Baron must seem to you! But, believe me, it is only while he is within these dark, inhospitable walls, only during these wild hunting trips in the dreary forest, that his nature, or at least his behaviour, changes. What puts him especially out of humour is the thought, which haunts him constantly, that something dreadful is going to happen here. That is why your adventure has shaken him so deeply. He will not allow the least of his servants to be exposed to the slightest danger, much less a newly found friend; and I knew for certain that Gottlieb, whom he blames for having left you unguarded, is to be punished with the most shameful punishment of having to follow the hunt in the rear, without knife or gun but armed only with a cudgel. Such hunts as we have here are never without danger, and the Baron constantly fears misfortune; yet he himself beckons on the evil demon. Many strange things are told of the ancestor who established the entail, and I know there is an evil family secret locked up in these walls, a dreadful ghost who drives the rightful owners away, so that they can endure this house only among a wild, noisy throng. But how lonely *I* am in this throng, and how troubled by the dread which seeps out of these walls! You, my dear friend, have with your music given me the first happy moments I have experienced here. How can I thank you?'

I kissed the hand she offered me and declared that I too had sensed the sinister atmosphere of the castle. The Baroness gazed fixedly at me as I went on to speak of the style of architecture, the decoration in the courtroom, the sighing of the wind, but – perhaps my tone and expression hinted that I meant something else – as I fell silent the Baroness cried vehemently: 'No, no! Something dreadful happened to you in that room, which I can never enter without a shudder. I beg you, tell me everything!'

Seraphine's face had grown deathly pale. I realized it would be better to tell her what had happened, rather than leave it to her imagination to conjure up some ghost which might be even more frightening than the one I had experienced. She listened to me with growing anxiety, and when I spoke of the scraping on the wall, she cried: 'That is dreadful! Yes, yes: there *is* some dreadful secret hidden in that horrible wall!'

When I then related how my uncle had banished the ghost, she sighed deeply, as if released from a heavy burden. Leaning back, she held both hands to her face. Only then did I notice that Adelheid had left us. My tale had been finished for some time and, as Seraphine was still silent, I quietly stood up, went over to the piano and endeavoured with music to lead her out of the gloom into which my story had plunged her. I intoned softly one of the holy *canzoni* of Abbé Steffani; and to the melancholy tones of *Ochi, perchè piangete*, Seraphine awoke from her dreams and smiled gently, shining teardrops in her eyes. How did it then happen that I found myself kneeling before her, that she bent down towards me, that I embraced her in my arms, that a long glowing kiss burnt my lips? How did it then happen that I did not lose my senses, that I felt how tenderly she pressed me to her, that I released her from my arms and, rising quickly, went back to the piano? Turning from me, the Baroness took a few steps towards the window; then she turned again and came up to me with an almost proud bearing which was not at all like her. Looking me in the eyes, she said: 'Your uncle is the worthiest old gentleman I know. He is the guardian angel of our family. May he include me in his prayers!'

I was unable to utter a word: the poison which I had imbibed from that kiss seethed and burned in my veins, in every nerve. Fräulein Adelheid came in, and the rage of the battle going on within me poured out in hot tears which I could not hold back! Adelheid gazed at me in amazement – I could have killed her. The Baroness gave me her hand and said with indescribable gentleness: 'Farewell, my dear friend. Farewell, and think that perhaps no one has understood your music better than I. Ah, those sounds will long echo in my heart!'

With a few disjointed words I compelled myself to leave. I ran to my room. My uncle had already gone to bed. I fell to my knees, I cried aloud, I called out the name of my beloved – in short, I abandoned myself to the foolishness of infatuated madness, and only the loud complaining of my uncle, awoken by my ravings – 'Cousin, I think you have gone mad, or are you wrestling with the wolf again? Get off to bed, if you please' – drove me to bed, where I lay with the firm intention of dreaming only of Seraphine. It must have already been past midnight when, still not asleep, I thought I heard distant voices, a running hither and thither and the opening and shutting of doors. I listened: footsteps were coming closer in the corridor, and there came a loud knock on the door.

'Who's there?' I cried. A voice outside said: 'Herr Justitiarius! Wake up, wake up!'

I recognized Franz's voice; as I asked 'Is the castle on fire?' my uncle awoke and cried: 'Where's the fire? Are there ghosts loose again!'

'Get up, Herr Justitiarius!' said Franz. 'The Baron is asking for you.'

'What does the Baron want,' my uncle asked, 'at this time of night?'

'Get up, sir!' Franz repeated. 'The Baroness is dying!'

I leaped out of bed with a cry of horror.

'Open the door for Franz,' my uncle cried to me. Half fainting, I tottered around the room, unable to find the door. My uncle had to help me; Franz entered, his face white, and lit the lamps. We had scarcely thrown on our clothes when the Baron was heard in the hall, calling: 'Can I talk to you, dear V.?'

'Why have you got dressed, Cousin? The Baron asked to see only me,' my uncle said as he went out.

'I must go down – I must see her and then die,' I murmured as though from the depths of pain.

'Indeed! You are right, Cousin,' my uncle said, slamming the door in my face so that its hinges rattled, and locking it from the outside.

Enraged by this, I wanted at first to run against the door; but, quickly coming to my senses, I resolved to await my uncle's return and then give him the slip. I heard him talking energetically with the Baron and I heard my name mentioned several times, though I could not understand anything else. My position was becoming worse with every second that passed. At last, I heard someone run up to the Baron and the Baron quickly walk away. My uncle came back into the room.

'She is dead!' I cried as I rushed towards him.

'And you are a fool,' he said calmly as he forced me into a chair.

'I must go down!' I cried. 'I must go down and see her, even if it costs me my life!'

'Do that, dear Cousin,' said my uncle, locking the door and putting the key into his pocket.

Now I flared into rage. I made a grab for the loaded gun and cried: 'Here, before your eyes, I shall put a bullet through my head if you do not open the door for me immediately!'

My uncle stepped in front of me and said, as he held me with his glance: 'Do you think, boy, that you can frighten me with your threats? Do you believe your life is of any worth to me if you are capable of throwing it away like a discarded toy? What business have you with the wife of the Baron? What right have you to push your way in where you do not belong and where no one wants you? Do you want to play the sighing lover in the hour of death?'

Devastated, I sank down into the chair. After a while, my uncle continued in a more gentle tone: 'And to set your mind at rest, there is probably nothing at all to worry about. Fräulein Adelheid is beside herself over nothing, as usual. If a drop of rain falls on her nose she cries: 'What dreadful weather!' Unfortunately, the alarm penetrated as far as the aunts, who have rushed along with unseemly wailing and a whole arsenal of strengthening drops, elixirs of life and I don't know what else! A bad bout of the vapours.'

He ceased, walked back and forth a little, then halted before me, laughed heartily and said: 'Cousin! Cousin! What foolishness! Satan is haunting this place in many ways; you have run into his clutches and he is now having a little game with you.'

He again paced back and forth, then he continued: 'There is no chance of sleep now. I shall smoke a pipe and thus pass the few hours of night and darkness left.'

With that, he took a clay pipe from the cupboard and, humming a tune, slowly and carefully filled it, then looked among a pile of papers until he found a sheet, tore and folded it to make a spill, and lit it. Puffing thick clouds of smoke, he said: 'Now then, Cousin, how was it with the wolf?'

My uncle's calmness had a strange effect upon me: it was as if I was no longer at Castle R. and the Baroness was far, far away. But the question my uncle put to me annoyed me.

'Do you find my hunting adventure so very funny,' I asked him, 'so suitable for mockery?'

'By no means,' he replied. 'Not at all. But you would not believe how comical a figure you cut when Almighty God for once lets something special happen to you. I had an academic friend, a quiet, sensible, contented sort of person. Fate implicated him – who had never given cause for such a thing – in a matter of honour, and he, whom most of us took for a weakling, behaved with such decisive courage that everyone marvelled at him. But from that time on, he was a changed man: from an industrious, sensible youth, he turned into a boastful and intolerable bully. He drank, he shouted and fought and was at last killed in a duel. You can make whatever you like of that story, Cousin. And now to return to the subject of the Baroness and her illness.'

Soft footsteps were heard in the hall, and a sound like a groan was borne through the air; 'She has gone!' was the thought which flashed through me. My uncle rose quickly and called: 'Franz, Franz!'

'Yes, dear Herr Justitiarius,' was the reply from outside.

'Franz,' my uncle continued, 'give the fire a poke, and if it can be done, would you make us a couple of cups of tea! It is devilish cold,' my uncle said, turning to me, 'and we would be better off outside by the fire.'

He opened the door and I followed him mechanically.

'What is going on downstairs?' he asked.

'Oh,' replied Franz, 'it really didn't amount to much. The Baroness is quite herself again and is blaming her fainting fit on a bad dream!'

I was about to shout for joy, but a glance from my uncle silenced me.

'Good,' he said. 'On the whole, I think it would be better if we were to lay our heads down for a couple of hours. Leave the tea for now, Franz.'

Franz left the hall, wishing us a peaceful night although the cocks were already beginning to crow.

'Cousin,' my uncle said, as he knocked his pipe out in the hearth, 'it is a good thing no misfortune happened to you with wolves or with loaded guns.'

I now understood everything and was ashamed I had given the old man reason to treat me like a naughty child.

'Be so good,' my uncle said next morning, 'dear Cousin, as to go downstairs and inquire how the Baroness is. You only need to ask Fräulein Adelheid, who will willingly give you a complete bulletin.'

You can imagine with what haste I hurried down; but as I was about to knock on the door of her antechamber, the Baron came out and bumped into me. He stood amazed and measured me with a penetrating glance.

'What do you want here?' he exclaimed.

Although my heart was beating wildly, I replied in a firm voice: 'On my uncle's instructions I am inquiring the state of health of your gracious wife.'

'Oh, it was nothing at all – one of her usual nervous attacks. She is sleeping quietly, and I know she will appear at table quite well again. Say that – tell him that.'

The Baron said this with a certain intensity which seemed to me to indicate he was more concerned about the Baroness than he wanted anyone to suspect. I turned to go, but the Baron suddenly grasped my arm and cried: 'I have something to say to you, young man!'

I thought I had before me an offended husband and feared a scene. I remembered the hunting-knife my uncle had presented to me and which I still carried in my pocket. I followed the Baron, determined to defend myself if need be; we entered his room, and he closed the door behind him. Now he paced rapidly back and forth with his arms folded; he halted before me and repeated: 'I have something to say to you, young man!'

With courage born of foolhardiness I replied: 'I hope it will be something I should like to hear.'

The Baron gazed at me in amazement, as if he did not understand me. Then he began marching up and down the room again. He took down a gun and examined it as if to see whether it was loaded. My blood tingled; I felt for my knife and stepped close to the Baron so as to make it impossible for him to take aim at me.

'A lovely weapon,' he said, replacing the gun in the corner. I took a few steps backwards and the Baron came over to me; when, clapping me on the shoulder a little more forcefully than necessary, he said: 'I must seem excited and disturbed to you, Theodore. After my night's vigil I am full of a thousand anxieties. My wife's attack was not serious, I realize that – but here in this castle, in which a dark spirit lurks, I feared something dreadful, and it is the first time she has been ill here. You – you alone are to blame.'

How that could possibly be the case I had not the slightest notion, I replied calmly.

'Oh,' continued the Baron, 'if only that damned box of misery belonging to the estate manager's wife had broken into a thousand pieces on the ice, if only you . . . but no – no! It has to be, it must be so, and I alone am to blame. As soon as you began to make music for my wife, I ought to have explained the whole thing, the whole matter of my wife's moods.'

I made as if to speak.

'Let me talk,' said the Baron. 'I must at the outset stop you from making any hasty judgement. You will take me for a rough Philistine. I am not so. But I am convinced that such music as moves everybody's soul, and certainly mine, must be forbidden here. My wife suffers from an excitability which must in the end undermine all her joy in living, and within these strange walls it is greatly stimulated. You will wonder why I do not spare her this dreadful place, this wild hunting life. But – you may call it weakness if you wish – I cannot leave her behind on her own. I would suffer a thousand anxieties and could concentrate on nothing. On the other hand, I feel that the regimen here ought to produce a strengthening effect. And now the sea breeze blustering its way through the trees, the bellowing of the hounds, the blaring of the horns, have to contend with a languishing strumming at the piano, such as no man ought to be able to play: you have set out methodically to torment my wife to death!'

The Baron spoke with a harsher voice and with wild, blazing eyes. My blood rose to my head, and I made a vehement movement with my hand. I made to speak, but he would not let me.

'I know what you want to say,' he went on, 'I know; and I repeat that you were on the way of killing my wife and, though I do not for a moment believe you intended to, you will understand that I must put a stop to it. In short: you have excited my wife with your playing and singing, and then, when she is floundering rudderless in an ocean of dream-like visions and forebodings which your music has conjured up, you thrust her further into the depths with tales of a ghost which is supposed to have haunted you. Your great-uncle has told me everything, but I would ask you to repeat to me all you saw, or did not see – or heard . . . or felt . . . or had a suspicion of.'

I pulled myself together and narrated calmly all that had happened. The Baron now and then interjected an expression of amazement. When I came to the point at which my uncle had banished the ghost, he clasped his hands together, raised them to Heaven and cried elatedly: 'Yes, he is the guardian spirit of our family! He shall rest in the grave of our ancestors!'

I had completed my story.

'Daniel, Daniel! What are you doing here at this hour?' murmured the Baron to himself, as he walked up and down the room with folded arms.

'Was there anything else, Baron?' I asked loudly, as I made as if to leave.

The Baron revived as if from a dream, grasped me amiably by the hand and said: 'Yes, dear friend. You must cure my wife, whom you treated so badly without meaning to. You are the only one who can do it.'

I felt myself blushing, and if I had been standing at a mirror I should certainly have seen in it a very childish, bewildered face. The Baron appeared to delight in my embarrassment and looked me in the eyes with an ironic smile.

'How on earth should I set about it?' I at last managed to stammer.

'Well,' the Baron said, 'you are not having to deal with a dangerous patient. I am now making a direct claim on your art. The Baroness is drawn into the magic of your music and to tear her away from it suddenly would be foolish and inhuman. Continue with the music. You will be welcome in my wife's apartments in the evenings. But you must gradually introduce more invigorating music; you must alternate the gay with the serious – and then, above all, you must often repeat the tale of the ghost. The Baroness will get used to it, then she will forget that it is lodged here in these walls, and the story will have no greater effect on her than any other fairy story. Do that, dear friend!'

With these words the Baron dismissed me. I was inwardly devastated, reduced to a mere child! I, who was mad enough to believe I could inspire jealousy in him! He had himself sent me to Seraphine, an instrument to be employed and then discarded! A few minutes before I had feared the Baron and the consciousness of guilt lay upon me, but this very guilt had made me feel that I was maturing to a man; now I saw only a foolish boy who in his folly had taken for gold the paper crown he had placed on his hot head. I hurried to my uncle, who was already waiting for me.

'Now then, Cousin, where have you been, where have you been?' he called to me.

'I have been talking to the Baron,' I replied quietly, incapable of looking at him.

'Good grief!' he said, as if amazed. 'Good grief! Yet I thought it must be something of the sort. The Baron has challenged you to a duel, eh, Cousin?'

The peal of laughter he emitted proved that he had completely seen through me again. I clenched my teeth: I did not want to utter a word, since I knew it would require no more to launch the thousand teasing quips already brimming on his lips.

The Baroness came to table in a morning gown whiter than newly fallen snow. She seemed tired, yet a sweet desire, a repressed ardour, shone from her eyes. She was more beautiful than ever. Who can number the follies of youth? I transferred the bitterness I felt towards the Baron to the Baroness; it all seemed to me a hopeless mystification. Like a sulky child, I avoided her and found a place at the end of the table between the two officers, with whom I began to drink and to talk loudly. A servant brought me a plate on which lay a few bonbons with the words: 'From Fräulein Adelheid'. I took them and saw that on one of them there had been scratched: 'and Seraphine!' My blood coursed through my veins. I looked towards Adelheid, who looked back at me with a sly expression, lifted her glass and nodded to me with a slight movement of her head. Almost involuntarily I murmured silently: 'Seraphine', took up my glass and emptied it in a draught. My glance flew across to her; she too had taken a drink at the same instant and was setting down her glass – her eyes met mine, and a malicious devil whispered in my ear: 'Unhappy man! She does love you!'

One of the guests rose and, in accordance with northern custom, proposed the health of the lady of the house. Glasses resounded in loud jubilation. Delight and despair – the wine flamed up within me, everything was going round, and I thought I should throw myself at her feet and breathe my last.

'What's the matter, dear friend?' – this question from my neighbour brought me to my senses. Seraphine had disappeared, the guests were rising from the table; I wanted to go, but Adelheid took hold of me; she spoke, but I understood nothing; she took me by the hands and, laughing loudly, shouted something into my ear. As if paralysed, I stood mute and motionless. Then, without thinking, I took a glass from Adelheid's hand and emptied it; I found myself alone at one of the windows; I staggered from the hall, down the stairs and into the forest. Snow was falling heavily, the trees were sighing in the storm; like a madman, I laughed and cried wildly: 'Hey! the Devil is having a game with you!'

Who knows how it would have ended if I had not suddenly heard my name being called loudly in the forest? The storm had eased off, the moon was shining through the clouds; I heard the hounds starting up and saw a dark figure approaching. It was the old huntsman.

'Herr Theodore!' he began. 'You got lost in the storm, I see. The Herr Justitiarius is waiting for you very impatiently!'

I followed him in silence and found my uncle working in the courtroom.

'You did well to go outside to cool down,' he cried to me. 'Don't drink quite so much; you are still too young to take it. It is not good for you.'

I sat at the desk and said nothing.

'But now tell me, dear Cousin, what did the Baron want you for?'

I told my uncle everything, and ended by saying that I did not intend to lend myself to the dubious cure the Baron had suggested.

'There would be no time for it, in any case,' my uncle said. 'We are leaving early tomorrow.'

So it happened, and I did not see Seraphine again.

Hardly had we arrived back home in K. when my great-uncle complained that he felt more than usually exhausted by the journey. His silence, broken only by violent outbursts of temper, presaged the return of his gout. One day I was called for urgently. I found that the old man had been smitten by a stroke and was lying speechless on his bed. A letter was crushed in his hand. I recognized the writing as that of the estate manager at R. and in my anguish I dared not take the letter from his grasp. I did not doubt that he was close to death; yet even before the doctor had arrived his pulse had begun to beat again and he had begun to recover. A few days later the doctor declared him to be out of danger.

The winter was more tenacious than ever, and a bitter, gloomy spring followed; his gout, rather than the attack he suffered, kept my uncle to his bed. He had now retired from business and all hope of ever returning to Castle R. had thus disappeared. I alone was permitted to care for him and to entertain him with conversation. At length, even his gaiety returned, and there was no lack of jokes and humour; but even when it came to tales of hunting and I expected my heroic deed with the wolf to be again the subject of banter, never, not even once, did he mention our visit to Castle R., and I too forbore to remind him of it. The concern I felt for my uncle had almost banished the memories of Seraphine; but one incident served to recall her, and in such a way that ice-cold shudders ran through me. When I opened the briefcase I had carried at Castle R. a dark lock of hair tied with a white ribbon fell out of the folded papers. I recognized it instantly as Seraphine's. But as I looked at the ribbon more closely, I saw upon it a drop of blood! Perhaps it was Adelheid who had sent me this memento, but where did the bloodstain come from? and why did it seem to me like a fearful warning? The ribbon was that which, when I had first drawn close to Seraphine, had fluttered around me, but it now seemed to possess some dark power and to have become a symbol of fatality.

At last the storms gave up their blustering, summer asserted its rights and by July it was the heat that had become unbearable. My uncle was visibly regaining his strength and, as was his custom, took himself off to a garden in the suburbs. One mild evening we were sitting together in the fragrant jasmine arbour; my uncle was unusually cheerful and in a gentle, almost mellow mood.

'Cousin,' he began, 'I don't know how it is, but today I feel a special wellbeing such as I haven't felt for years. I believe it is a forewarning of my death.'

I tried to turn him away from such gloomy thoughts.

'Let it be, Cousin,' he said. 'I shall not be remaining here below for much longer, and I therefore want to clear up a debt to you! Do you still think about the autumn at Castle R.?'

The question struck me like a bolt of lightning, but, before I could reply, he continued: 'Heaven willed that you should become entangled in the darkest secrets of that house. The time has come for you to learn everything. We have often spoken of things which you have guessed at rather than understood. They say that nature represents the cycle of human life symbolically in the changing seasons, but I think of it in a different way. The spring mists fall, the summer haze shimmers, and only in the clear ether of autumn can the distant landscape be seen clearly before the world is immersed in the night of winter. In the clear sight of old age the workings of the inscrutable power can be seen more clearly. The dark destiny of that house now stands clearly before my ancient eyes! Yet no tongue can express the heart of it. Listen, my son, to what I am going to tell you as to a remarkable story; keep within your soul the knowledge that the secrets into which you strayed – perhaps not accidentally – could have destroyed you! Yet – that is all in the past now!'

The story of Castle R. which my uncle now recounted I have carried so truly in my memory that I can almost repeat it in his own words (he spoke of himself in the third person).

One stormy autumn night in the year 1760, a tremendous crash, as if the whole rambling castle had collapsed in a thousand pieces, awoke the servants in Castle R. from a deep sleep. In a moment everyone was on his feet; lamps were lit; and, with fear and anxiety on his deathly pale countenance, the steward came panting up with the keys. In a silence like that of the grave, he moved through the passages, halls and rooms, but nowhere was there the slightest sign of damage. A dark foreboding seized him. He went up to the big hall, in one of the side rooms of which Baron Roderich von R. used to rest when engaged on his astronomy. Between the door of this room and another small room there was an entrance which led through a narrow passage directly to the observation tower. But as Daniel (as the steward was called) opened this heavy door, the storm, howling and roaring, hurled rubble and broken masonry at him, so that he recoiled in terror and, as he dropped the lamp to the floor, cried aloud: 'O Lord of Heaven! The Baron has been dashed to pieces!'

At that instant, the sound of wailing was heard from the Baron's bedroom: Daniel found the servants gathered around the body of their master. Fully clad, he was seated in his chair as if resting. As daylight came, they saw that the top of the tower had collapsed, stones had crashed through into the astronomy chamber, and the heavy timbers, exposed by the fall, had broken through the lower vaulting and torn away part of the castle wall and the passage. To step through the doorway from the hall was to risk falling eighty feet into the abyss.

The Baron had foreseen his death to the hour and had told his son, so Wolfgang, Baron R., the eldest son of the deceased and hence holder of the entail, arrived the following day from Vienna, where he had been on a visit. The steward had had the large hall hung in black, and the dead Baron lay on a bier in the dress in which he had been found, surrounded by silver candelabra with burning candles. Silently, Wolfgang went up to the hall and stood gazing into his father's colourless countenance. At length, with a convulsive movement, he murmured: 'Did the stars compel you to make miserable the son you loved?'

Stepping back a pace, he gazed heavenwards and said gently: 'Poor deluded old man! Your game is now finished! Now you may learn that what we have here has nothing to do with what is beyond the stars. What will or power can reach beyond the grave?'

He again fell silent – then he cried vehemently: 'No, not one atom of my earthly happiness, which you sought to destroy, shall I be robbed of now!'

With that, he drew a folded piece of paper from his pocket and held it to one of the candles: the paper flared up, and, as the reflection of the flame flickered on the face of the corpse, it seemed as though the muscles were moving and the dead man speaking soundlessly, so that the servants standing at a distance were overcome by dread. The Baron calmly trod out the last piece of paper smouldering on the floor, then gave his father a final look and hurried from the hall.

The following day, Daniel told the Baron of the destruction of the tower and of all that had happened on the night of his father's death, and said that the tower should be rebuilt immediately – or the whole castle would be in danger.

'Rebuild the tower?' the Baron exclaimed, his eyes blazing with anger. 'Never! The tower,' he continued more calmly, 'will not collapse further if there is no further cause. How if it was my father himself who destroyed the place where he carried on his uncanny astrology? How if he himself found certain contrivances which made it possible for him to destroy everything whenever he wanted to? Let it be as he wishes; and the rest of the castle can cave in too, for all I care. Do you think I intend to live here in this owl's nest? No, that wise ancestor who laid the foundations for a new house in the valley anticipated me and I shall follow him.'

'And so,' said Daniel dejectedly, 'all the old faithful servants will have to take up their staves and go.'

'That I will not be served by doddering old men goes without saying,' the Baron replied, 'but I will throw nobody out. You shall eat the bread of charity.'

'Shall I be treated so?' the steward exclaimed.

The Baron, who had been on the point of leaving the hall, wheeled round, his face red with anger, and strode up to the old man. 'You hypocritical rascal,' he cried, 'you who carried on those sinister activities up there with my father, to whose heart you clung like a vampire, you who perhaps used his madness to drive him to the devilish decisions which brought me to the edge of the abyss – you, I ought to fling you out like a mangy dog!'

The old man had dropped to his knees in terror at this dreadful outburst, and so what happened may have been an accident; in anger, the body often mechanically follows the thought, and as he concluded his tirade the Baron struck out with his foot and kicked the steward in the chest, so that he fell with a muffled cry. As he then rose with difficulty he emitted a sound like the whimper of a dying animal and pierced the Baron with a look of rage and despair. The bag of money which the Baron threw to him as he went out he left untouched on the floor.

In the meantime, relatives had gathered, and the old Baron was interred in the family vault in Castle R. church with great ceremony. As the guests went their own ways again, the new Lord of the Manor, abandoning his gloomy mood, seemed highly delighted with what he had inherited. With V., the old Baron's legal adviser, to whom he seemed to have given his trust immediately on meeting him and whom he had confirmed in his office, he drew up accounts of the estate's income and considered how much could be used for improvements and for building the new house. V. believed the late Baron could not possibly have spent all his annual income, so that, as there were only a few insignificant sums in bank-notes among the documents and as the cash found in an iron box was only just over a thousand thalers, there must be money hidden away. And who would know where it was if not the steward Daniel? The Baron was now worried that Daniel, whom he had seriously offended, would revenge himself by letting this hidden treasure rot away rather than disclose it. He recounted to V. all the circumstances of the case and ended by declaring his conviction that it had been Daniel who had nurtured in the late Baron an inexplicable horror of seeing his son in Castle R. The Justitiarius declared this conviction misguided: no human being in the world could sway the old Baron's mind in the slightest. He also undertook to discover from Daniel the secret of any money hidden away. This hardly needed doing, however, for scarcely had he begun: 'How is it, then, Daniel, that your former master left so little money in cash?' when Daniel replied, with an unpleasant smile: 'Do you mean the paltry few thalers you found in the box? The rest is in the vaulting next to my dear Master's bedroom! But the best of it,' he continued, his smile changing into a fearful grimace and his bloodshot eyes flashing, 'is that there are thousands of gold pieces lying buried under the rubble!'

The lawyer at once called on the Baron, and together they went into the bedroom, in one corner of which Daniel shifted the wall panelling and revealed a lock. The Baron gazed at it greedily and drew a large bundle of keys from his pocket and prepared to try them. Daniel stood very upright, looking down at him as he crouched at the lock. With a quivering voice, he then said: 'If I am a dog, your excellency – I have the loyalty of a dog!'

With that he handed to the Baron a shining steel key. The latter tore it from his hand and easily opened the door. They stepped into a low vault, in which there stood a large iron trunk with its lid open. On the sacks of money there lay a note in the familiar hand of the late Baron:

One hundred and fifty thousand Reichsthaler in old Frederichsdor saved from the income of the Castle R. estate and intended for the upkeep of the castle. Further, the Lord of the Manor who follows me in ownership shall use some of this money for the construction of a high lighthouse tower for the benefit of seafarers on the highest hill to the east of the old castle tower, which he will find collapsed in ruins, and shall have it lighted each and every night.

Michaelmas Night in the year 1760, at Castle R.
Roderich Baron von R.

Only after the Baron had raised the bags of money one after another and allowed them to drop back into the chest, delighting in the jingling of the gold, did he turn to the steward, thank him for the loyalty he had displayed and assure him it was only slanderous gossip that had led him to treat him so badly at the outset: not only should he stay in the castle, but he would retain his post of steward with double salary.

'I owe you full recompense,' he said. 'If you want gold, take one of these bags!'

The Baron indicated the chest and stood with downcast eyes. Suddenly the steward's face became a burning red, and he again emitted the dreadful sound as of a dying animal; as he did so he muttered between his teeth something that sounded like 'Blood for gold!'

The Baron, lost in gazing at the treasure, was oblivious to all else. Shaking in every limb, Daniel humbly approached him, kissed his hand and said in a tearful voice: 'Ah, my dear, gracious Master, what should a poor, childless old man like me do with gold? But the doubled salary – that I shall joyfully take, and will carry out my duties tirelessly!'

The Baron paid no particular attention to the old man's words, but let fall the heavy lid of the trunk, so that the vault resounded. Then, as he locked the chest and carefully withdrew the key, he said: 'That's good, that's good, old fellow! But,' he continued when they had regained the hall, 'you also mentioned a quantity of gold pieces lying buried under the ruined tower.'

The steward went silently to the doorway and opened it with effort. The storm drove a thick flurry of snow into the hall; a frightened raven fluttered up, cawing and croaking, beat against the window with its wings and, having found the open doorway, plunged into the abyss. The Baron stepped into the passageway but took only a single glance into the depths before starting back.

'Hideous sight! I am giddy,' he stammered as he sank into the lawyer's arms. Pulling himself together, he eyed the steward sharply: 'And down there?'

The steward had closed the door again. He now turned to the Baron and said, toying with the great key and smiling strangely: 'Down there lie thousands upon thousands, the lovely instruments of my late Master – telescopes, quadrants, globes, reflectors – everything lies in ruins among the stones and rubble!'

'But money, actual money!' the Baron interrupted. 'You spoke of gold pieces, did you not?'

'I meant only objects,' the steward replied. 'Things which cost thousands of gold pieces.' And he would say no more.

The Baron was delighted that he had suddenly acquired the means of executing his favourite plan of raising a splendid new house. The lawyer V. pointed out that the will of the departed provided only for the repair and renovation of the existing castle and that it would be difficult to equal the simple grandeur of the old building in any new one, but the Baron stuck to his intention and asserted that in any matter not covered by the entail the wishes of the dead would have to yield to those of the living. He would improve the ancient castle to the extent the climate, ground and surroundings permitted; and he added that he would shortly be bringing home as his wife a creature for whom no sacrifice could be too great.

The way in which the Baron spoke of this union led the lawyer to suppose it had probably already been sealed and cut short any further questions on his part; but he was consoled by the feeling that the Baron's desire for riches was fuelled by a wish to provide for his beloved rather than by simple greed – though the sight of the Baron gloating over the Friedrichsdor made it rather hard to sustain this feeling. 'The old scoundrel is certainly not telling the truth,' the Baron said. 'But next spring I will have that rubble cleared away under my own eyes.'

Builders came and the Baron discussed with them at length how best to proceed with the new building. He discarded plan after plan; no design was sufficiently grand for him. He began to draft plans himself: this occupation, which kept the sunniest images constantly before his mind, put him into a mood that often touched on exuberance and expressed itself in generous, even opulent hospitality. Even Daniel appeared mollified, though it was clear the Baron still mistrusted him. What appeared wonderful to everyone was that the steward seemed to grow younger every day: perhaps the grief for his late master was wearing off, perhaps it was because he was no longer obliged to spend cold, sleepless nights in the tower; but whatever the cause, he had changed from a tottery old man to a robust, red-cheeked fellow who walked vigorously and laughed loudly.

The gaiety of life at Castle R. was now disrupted by the arrival of the noteworthy figure of Baron Wolfgang's younger brother, Hubert. When the Baron saw him he went deathly white and exclaimed. 'Wretch! What do you want here?'

Hubert threw himself into his brother's arms, but the latter led him away into another room and shut the door. The two were together for several hours; then Hubert reappeared with a wild demeanour and called for his horses. The lawyer tried to detain him, for he feared a fatal outcome to this quarrel; then the Baron also appeared and called loudly: 'Stay here, Hubert! You will come to your senses.'

Hubert mastered himself, and as he threw his coat to a servant he took

V.'s hand and said with a mocking smile: 'The Lord of the Manor is, it seems, willing to have me.'

They went into a side room. V. said that whatever had arisen would only have been intensified if Hubert had left. Hubert took the tongs which stood by the hearth and poked the fire: 'You will note that I am a good-natured fellow and quite skilled in homely tasks,' he said. 'But Wolfgang is full of the most marvellous prejudices and inclined to be a skinflint.'

V. did not feel it advisable to pursue the subject further, as Wolfgang's behaviour indicated a man torn by emotions of every kind.

Late that evening he went to the Baron's apartment and found him pacing the room, his hands clenched behind his back. When he noticed the lawyer, he stopped and, looking him gloomily in the eyes, said in a broken voice: 'My brother is here. I know what you are going to say. But you know nothing about it. My wretched brother – I am right to call him so – crosses my path everywhere like an evil spirit and disturbs my peace. He has done everything possible to wreck my life. Since the promulgation of the entail he has pursued me with a deadly hatred. He begrudges me these possessions – though in his hands they would be dissipated like chaff. He is the maddest spendthrift there is. His debts more than exceed his share of his property in Courland, and now, pursued by creditors, he has come here for money.'

'And you, his brother, refuse him –' V. interrupted. The Baron took a step backwards. 'Yes!' he cried. 'I refuse him! I cannot and will not give away one thaler of the estate's income. But listen to the proposal I put to the madman a few hours ago and then judge me. Our possessions in Courland are, as you know, considerable; I agreed that he should have the half which falls to me. Hubert has a wife and children, and they are starving. I proposed that the property be administered, the money needed for his keep given to him from the revenues, creditors satisfied. But what does an ordered life matter to him, what do wife and child matter to him? Money, cash in large sums, is what he wants, so that he can recklessly squander it. Some devil has told him the secret of the hundred and fifty thousand thalers, of which he is demanding half. I must and I shall refuse him. And I now feel he is plotting my destruction.'

V. tried to talk the Baron out of his suspicions against his brother, but to no avail. He was authorized to deal with Hubert and his monetary needs, and he performed this task with all discretion; at last Hubert agreed: 'Let it be so, then. I will accept the Lord of the Manor's proposals, but on the condition that, since I am on the point of losing my good name and honour for ever through the harshness of my creditors, he give me a cash advance of a thousand Friedrichsdor and allow me to make my home with him, for a time at least, in his beautiful castle.'

'Never!' the Baron exploded when V. transmitted these proposals to him. 'Never will I agree to Hubert's spending even a minute in my house once I have brought my wife here. Go, dear friend, and tell that disturber of my peace that he shall have two thousand Friedrichsdor, but not as an advance; no, it is a gift, and then he must be gone – gone from here.'

V. now suddenly realized that the Baron had married without his father's knowledge, and he guessed that the dispute between the brothers must have its origin here. Hubert listened composedly to what he had to say and then replied gloomily: 'I will think about it. For the moment I will stay a few more days.'

V. tried to prove to him that the Baron was in fact doing all he could to recompense him for the injustice inherent in an entail, which so greatly favours the first-born; there was, indeed, something hateful in the whole conception. As if suffocating, Hubert tore open his jacket, placed a hand on his hip and spun round like a dancer. 'Bah!' he exclaimed. 'Hatefulness is born of hatred.' Then he laughed loudly and said: 'How graciously the Lord of the Manor throws his gold pieces to the beggar!'

V. now realized there was no question of a reconciliation between the brothers.

Hubert installed himself in the side wing and, to the Baron's annoyance, seemed ready for a long stay. He often had long conversations with the steward, and they even went hunting together; but apart from this he was seldom seen and he avoided meeting his brother. Altogether, V. felt he understood the dread the Baron had evidenced on beholding Hubert's arrival.

One day, when V. was alone in his study, Hubert entered and said, on an almost melancholy tone: 'I will accept the most recent proposals of my brother. Can you manage it so that I receive the two thousand Friedrichsdor today? I will then leave tonight – by horse – entirely alone.'

'With the money?' V. asked.

'Correct,' replied Hubert. 'I know what you are going to say. The weight! Make it out in notes to Isaac Lazarus in K. I will go straight to K. tonight. I am being driven from here: the old man has cursed this place with his evil spirits.'

'Are you speaking of your father, Herr Baron?' asked V., very seriously.

Hubert's lips trembled; he held firmly on to a chair so as not to fall, then cried: 'Today then, Herr Justitiarius!' and staggered from the room.

'He realizes he can do nothing once my mind is made up,' said the

Baron, as he made out the notes to Lazarus. He felt a load had been lifted from his shoulders and as he sat at supper that evening was happier than he had been for a long time. Hubert had sent his apologies, and all were glad he was not there.

V. resided in a somewhat distant room whose windows looked out on to the courtyard. During the night he was awoken by what seemed to him a distant, plaintive wailing. He listened, but there was no repetition, and he had to dismiss it as a trick of some dream. Nonetheless, so strong a feeling of horror and anxiety had overcome him that he could no longer stay in bed. He rose and went to the window. Before long the castle door opened and a figure holding a burning candle stepped out and crossed the yard. V. recognized the steward, Daniel, and watched as he opened the stable door, went into the stable and emerged again, leading a saddled horse. Now a second figure appeared out of the darkness: it was wrapped in a fur coat and wore a fox-fur cap; V. recognized Hubert. He spoke earnestly with Daniel for a few minutes, then again disappeared. Daniel led the horse back into the stable, locked it and returned across the yard the way he had come. It was evident that Hubert had intended to ride off but had for some reason changed his mind; it was also evident he was involved with the steward in some kind of conspiracy. V. could scarcely wait for morning to come to inform the Baron of what had occurred.

But next morning, at the hour when the Baron was accustomed to rise, V. heard a running hither and thither, the sound of doors opening and shutting, confused talking and shouting. He stepped out into the corridor, and everywhere there were servants running. At length he learned that the Baron was missing: they had sought for him for hours in vain. He was known to have gone to bed; he must therefore have got up again and have wandered off with the candelabra in his hand, for that also was missing. Driven by a dark foreboding, V. rushed to the fateful hall where, like his father, Wolfgang had made his bedroom. The door to the tower stood open; horror-struck, V. cried: 'There he lies, dashed to pieces!'

It was so. Snow had fallen, so that from above only one arm of the unfortunate man could be seen protruding from the stones. It was hours before workmen succeeded in climbing down and retrieving the body. In the convulsion of death, the Baron had clung to the silver candelabra, and the hand with which he still held it was the only part of his body uninjured: the rest had been shattered by the impact on the stones and rocks.

With a fury of despair in his countenance, Hubert rushed up to the body, which lay in the hall on a wide table just where the old Baron had lain a few weeks earlier. Crushed by the sight, he wailed: 'Brother! O my poor brother! No, this is not what I desired from the devils who were driving me!'

V. shuddered at this insidious language, for he believed he would have to proceed against Hubert as his brother's murderer. Hubert lay unconscious on the floor; he was put to bed, but recovered fairly quickly with a strengthening tonic. Pale and with grief in his eyes, he then went to V. in his room and said as he slowly lowered himself into a chair: 'I have wished my brother dead, because my father bestowed on him the best part of his estate through that evil entail. Now he has met his death in a dreadful way. I am Lord of the Manor. But my heart is crushed. I shall never be happy again. I confirm you in your office. You shall have the widest powers to administer the estate, on which I shall not be living.'

In a few hours Hubert was on his way back to K. It appeared that the unhappy Wolfgang had risen during the night, had probably made for the library, but, bemused by sleep, had mistaken the door. This explanation did not satisfy V. If the Baron could not sleep, he could not have been bemused by sleep and thus could not have mistaken the door. The tower doorway was, moreover, firmly locked and must have been difficult to open. He expressed his doubts to the assembled servants.

'Ah,' said Franz, the Baron's huntsman, 'my dear sir, indeed it never happened like that.'

'How else, then?' V. asked him.

Franz declined to speak in front of the others; he desired to say what he had to say in confidence. V. now learnt that the Baron had often spoken to Franz about the treasure which lay buried under the rubble and that, as if driven by an evil spirit, he often went at night to the doorway, to which Daniel must have given him the key, and looked down longingly into the depths for these supposed riches. What was probable was that, on that fateful night, the Baron had again made his way to the tower and had there been seized by a sudden dizziness and had thus fallen. Daniel, who also appeared very shaken by the Baron's death, proposed that the dangerous doorway be walled up, and this was done.

Baron Hubert von R., now Lord of the Manor, returned to Courland. V. received unrestricted authority for the administration of the estate: the building of the new house was discontinued and the old building put in as good condition as possible.

Many years passed. Late one autumn, Hubert again appeared at Castle R. and spent several days closeted with V. Then he returned to Courland;

on his journey through K. he deposited there his last will and testament. During his visit he had spoken much of forebodings of an early death, and these forebodings were fulfilled, for he died a year later. His son, also named Hubert, came quickly from Courland to take possession of his inheritance. His mother and sister followed him. The youth seemed from the first moment to combine all the evil qualities of his forebears: he wanted many changes on the spot, he threw the cook out of the house, he tried to thrash the coachman (but did not succeed, for the fellow was as strong as a tree) – in short, he was well on the way to making himself thoroughly unpopular when V. stepped in firmly to assure him that not so much as a chair should be moved before the reading of the will.

'You are subordinate here to the Lord of the Manor,' the Baron began. V. did not allow him to continue. 'No hastiness, Baron!' he said. 'You may not hold sway here before the will is read. For the moment I, and I alone, am master here and well know how to meet force with force. I have the power of my authority as executor of your father's will and am authorized by the power of the court to prohibit your stay in Castle R. I advise you to take yourself back to K.'

The decisive tone in which he spoke gave his words suitable weight, and the young Baron retreated with derisive laughter.

Three months passed, and the day arrived on which, according to the wishes of the late Baron, the will was to be opened at K., where it had been deposited. In addition to the court officials, the Baron and V., there was also in the courtroom a younger man, of noble appearance, whom V, had brought with him and whom everyone assumed to be V.'s clerk, as a sealed document was sticking out of his pocket. The Baron looked askance at him, as he did at almost everybody, and demanded that the tedious ceremony be disposed of quickly. He recognized the hand and seal of his late father, and as the clerk prepared to read the will aloud he gazed indifferently out of the window, an arm thrown carelessly over the back of his chair. After a brief preamble, the deceased Baron Hubert von R. declared that he had never possessed the entail as true Lord of the Manor, but had only administered it on behalf of the only son of the deceased Baron Wolfgang von R., named Roderich after his grandfather: it was to him, accordingly, that the inheritance fell. Detailed accounts of income and expenditure would be found at his estate. Wolfgang von R. – so Hubert recounted – had in Geneva made the acquaintanceship of Miss Julie de St Val and taken so passionate a liking to her that he had resolved never to be parted from her. She was very poor, and her family was of the people:

he could, therefore, never hope for the consent of old Roderich, whose whole endeavour had been to enhance the status of his house in every way; and when he had, in fact, disclosed to his father what his intention was, the old man had specifically declared that he had already chosen a bride for the Lord of the Manor of R. and that there could never be any question of another. Wolfgang had then, in the name of Born, married Julie; after a year she had borne him a son, and it was he who was now to become Lord of the Manor.

The Baron stared at the clerk as if thunderstruck. As the clerk finished reading the catastrophic document, V. arose, took the young man by the hand and said, as he bowed to those present: 'Here, my Lords, I have the honour to present to you Baron Roderich von R., Lord of the Manor of R.'

Hubert stared at the youth who, as if fallen from Heaven, had robbed him of everything. With rage in his burning eyes and clenched fists, he ran from the court without a word. Baron Roderich now handed over to the court the documents which proved he was who he claimed to be. V. perused them and said, as he put them back in order: 'Now God will help.'

At once on the following morning, Baron Hubert submitted a complaint to the authorities at K., in which he applied for immediate possession of the entail. Neither by testament, nor in any other way, his lawyer asserted, could the deceased Baron Hubert von R. dispose of it. On the death of the father, ownership passed automatically to the son; there was no need for any declaration of accession; the terms of the entail could not be waived. What reasons the deceased may have had for appointing a different Lord of the Manor were quite immaterial. It should also be noted that the former Baron had himself had a love affair in Switzerland, and his alleged brother's son was perhaps his own.

Though the probability that the facts asserted in the testament were accurate was very strong, and though the judges were particularly incensed that the son did not shrink from accusing his father of a crime, yet the son's view of the case was correct, and it was only the tireless efforts of V. which succeeded in having the transfer of the entail postponed to give him time to establish the legitimacy of the youthful Roderich.

He realized only too well how difficult it would be. He had been through all old Roderich's correspondence without finding any trace of a letter, or even a paragraph, connecting Wolfgang with Mlle de St Val. He was sitting in old Roderich's bedroom in Castle R. and working on a letter to a notary in Geneva, who had been recommended to him as sharp-witted and who was to produce notices for him which might clarify the case of the young Baron. It was midnight and the moon shone brightly into the adjoining hall, the door of which stood open. It seemed as if someone was slowly climbing the stairs, rattling and jingling keys. V. rose and went into the hall; now he heard someone approaching the door of the hall from the passageway. It was opened, and there entered a man with a deathly white face, dressed in night attire and holding a candelabra in one hand and a large bunch of keys in the other. V. at once recognized the steward and was on the point of calling out to him when he was gripped by an icy chill: in the whole attitude of the old man there was something sinister and ghostly. He realized he had a sleepwalker before him. The steward went with measured tread through the hall and up to the walled-up door which had formerly led to the tower; in front of it he stopped and emitted a howling sound which echoed so dreadfully throughout the hall that V. trembled in horror. Then, placing the candelabra on the floor and hanging the bundle of keys on his belt, Daniel began to scratch at the wall with his hands, so that blood was soon spurting out from under his nails, while groaning as if tormented by the pangs of death. Now he put his ear to the wall as if listening to something; then he motioned with his hand as if silencing someone, bent down, picked up the candelabra and paced quietly back to the door. V. followed him warily, lamp in hand. The steward went down the stairs, opened the main doors, proceeded to the stable and, to V.'s amazement, fetched saddle and harness and with great care saddled a horse. After brushing back a lock of hair from its forehead and patting it on the neck, he took it by the bridle and led it out. In the courtyard he stood still for a few seconds as if receiving orders, to which he responded with a nod of the head. Then he led the horse back into the stable, unsaddled it and tied it up. Now he took the candelabra, closed the stable door, returned to the castle and disappeared into his room, which he carefully bolted.

V. was deeply disturbed by this scene: a foreboding of some dreadful deed reared up before him like a black ghost.

Filled with a sense of the dangerous position his protégé was in, he believed he must employ what he had just seen to his own advantage. The following day, as dawn was breaking, Daniel came to his room to receive instruction about some domestic matter. V. seized him and made him sit down.

'Now listen, Daniel, my old friend!' he said. 'I have been wanting to ask you what you think about the muddle Hubert's strange will has got us into. Do you believe the boy is really Wolfgang's son, born in wedlock?'

Avoiding V.'s gaze, the steward said peevishly: 'He might be and he might not be. Why should I care? Let whoever wants be master here now.'

'But I mean,' continued V., drawing closer to the old man and laying a hand on his shoulder, 'as you had the old Baron's complete confidence, surely he didn't keep silent about his son's relationships? Did he tell you of the alliance Wolfgang had made against his wishes?'

'I can't remember anything of the sort,' replied the steward, yawning.

'You are tired, old fellow,' said V. 'Did you have a restless night?'

'Not that I know of,' replied the other coldly. 'But I will now go and prepare food.'

With this, he rose wearily from the chair, rubbing his back and yawning again.

'Just wait a moment,' said V., taking him by the hand and indicating that he wanted him to sit down. The steward remained standing, supporting himself on the desk. 'Why should I care about the will? Why should I care about the dispute over the entail?' he exclaimed.

'Let us not talk about that any more,' interrupted V., 'but about something completely different. You are being cantankerous, you are yawning, and I almost believe it really was you last night.'

'What was I last night?' asked the steward.

'Last night, at midnight,' continued V., 'as I was sitting in the old Baron's chambers next to the great hall, you came in through the door, quite stiff and pale, you walked to the walled-up door, scratched on the wall with both hands and moaned as if you were suffering great agony Are you a sleepwalker, Daniel?'

The steward dropped back into a chair which V. quickly pushed towards him. He made no sound, his face was hidden in shadow, but V heard him breathing and his teeth chattering.

'Yes,' continued V. after a short silence, 'it is a strange thing with sleepwalkers. The next day they don't remember the slightest thing.'

Daniel remained motionless.

'I have experienced something similar,' continued V. 'I had a friend who, as soon as the moon was full, regularly began nocturnal wanderings Many a time he would sit and write letters. The most amazing thing, however, was that if I began to whisper in his ear I soon managed to make him start talking. He answered all my questions pertinently; what, awake, he would have been careful to keep secret flowed from his lips. I believe that if a moon struck person has kept silent about a crime, you could get it out of him in that strange condition He who has a clear conscience, like we two, my dear Daniel, has, of course, nothing to fear. But listen, Daniel; you were certainly wanting, trying to go up into the observatory tower when you were scratching away at that walled-up door so horribly Did you want to go on with the work of old Roderich? Well, I shall get that out of you next time!'

As V. was speaking, the steward began trembling more and more; now his body was in the grip of convulsions, and he burst into a shrill, incomprehensible babbling. V. rang for the servants. Lamps were brought. The old man could not get up and was lifted like an automaton and carried to his bed. After almost an hour in this dreadful condition he fell into a deep sleep; when he awoke, he demanded wine to drink, and when this was brought him he sent out the servant who had brought it and locked himself in.

V. had really decided to try the experiment the moment he spoke of it to Daniel, though he had to admit to himself that Daniel, perhaps only now aware of his sleepwalking, would do all he could to avoid him and that any confession made in that state would be hard to build upon. Nevertheless, he went to the hall towards midnight, hoping that Daniel would sleepwalk in spite of himself. Soon there was a commotion in the courtyard; V. heard a window being broken, hurried down and, as he rushed along the corridors, was met by the stench of fumes which, he soon realized, were streaming out of the steward's room. Daniel was in the act of being carried out, stiff as death, to be laid in another room. One of the grooms – so the servants recounted – awakened by a strange muffled knocking, believed something had happened to the steward and was about to get up when the watchman in the courtyard cried: 'Fire! Fire! The steward's room is ablaze!'

At this cry, several other servants came running, but all efforts to break down the door were vain. They hurried into the yard, but the watchman had already broken the window of the room and had pulled down the burning curtains; a few jugs of water served to put out the flames. The steward was found unconscious on the floor in the middle of the room, still holding the candelabra which had set light to the curtains. The old man's eyebrows and hair were singed, and if the watchman had not noticed the fire he would have been burned to death. To their surprise, the servants found the door of his room secured by two recently fitted bolts which had not been there the previous evening; V., however, understood their purpose – the steward had wanted to make it impossible to sleepwalk out of the room.

The steward was seriously ill, he did not speak, he took little nourishment and he stared before him as if in anticipation of death. V. believed the old man would never get to his feet again. He had done everything he could for his protégé and had to await the result calmly; he now wanted to go back to K. His departure had been fixed for the following morning.

Late that evening he was packing his manuscripts when there fell into his hand a small packet which Baron Hubert had addressed to him with the inscription: 'To be read after the opening of my will.' V. could not understand how he had come to neglect this packet, and he was in the midst of opening it when the door opened and Daniel entered with quiet, ghostly steps He laid a black document case, which he was carrying under his arm, on the writing table; then, sinking to his knees with a deathly sigh, he grasped V.'s hands frantically and said, in a voice that seemed to come from the depths of the tomb: 'I do not want to die on the scaffold; He above judges'; he then rose with difficulty and much fearful gasping and left the room as he had come.

V. spent the night reading all that was contained in the black document case and in Hubert's packet, and what he read determined what he then did. As soon as he arrived in K. he visited the younger Baron Hubert, who received him disdainfully; the outcome of their ensuing discussion, however, was that the Baron declared before the court on the following day that he recognized the pretender to the entail as the legitimate son of Baron Wolfgang and consequently as the rightful heir He then drove quickly away; to his mother and sister, whom he left behind, he had written that they would probably never see him again.

Roderich was amazed at the turn events had taken, and begged V. to explain how this wonder had been brought about. V. put him off until after he had taken possession of the entail. The transfer of the estate was now further delayed by the court's demand for, in addition to Hubert's declaration, documentary proof of Roderich's legitimacy. V. offered him an apartment in Castle R., and added that Hubert's mother and sister, embarrassed by his sudden departure, would probably prefer to stay there too, rather than return to the noisy city. The delight with which Roderich accepted the notion of living under the same roof as the Baroness and her daughter was evidence of the deep impression the child Seraphine had made on him; within a few weeks he had gained Seraphine's love in return and her mother's assent to their marriage This was much too precipitate for V.; Roderich's legitimation as Lord of the Manor was still in doubt. Letters from Courland now interrupted the idyll· Hubert had not returned to his property there but had gone to Petersburg, where he had entered military service, and was now in the field against the Persians, with whom Russia had just commenced hostilities; this made it necessary for the Baroness and her daughter to depart for Courland, where disorder and confusion reigned Roderich, who already regarded himself as an adopted son, accompanied his beloved; and so it was that, when V also returned to K., the castle was deserted as before. The steward's illness became worse, and it was thought he would not recover; his duties were transferred to the old huntsman, Franz.

At last, after long delay, V. received the desired news from Switzerland. The priest who had officiated at Wolfgang's wedding had long since died, but an annotation in his hand had been discovered in the church register, to the effect that the person whom he had joined in holy wedlock in the name of Born with Mlle Julie de St Val had proved to him his legitimacy as Baron Wolfgang von R., the eldest son of Baron Roderich von R., of Castle R. Moreover, there were two witnesses to the marriage, a merchant in Geneva and an old French captain who lived in Lyons; Wolfgang had disclosed his identity to both of them, and their sworn statements confirmed the annotation in the church register. Nothing now stood in the way of the transfer of the estate, which was to take place the following autumn. Hubert had fallen in his first battle, and the property at Courland thus fell to Baroness Seraphine von R. It made a fine dowry for the overjoyed Roderich.

November had arrived when the Baroness and Roderich with his bride-to-be arrived in Castle R. The transfer of the estate followed, then Roderich's marriage to Seraphine. Many weeks passed in revelry, until at length the satiated guests departed – to the great delight of V., who did not want to take his leave of Castle R. without having initiated the new master into all the affairs relating to his new property. Since Daniel had appeared to him as a sleepwalker, V. had elected to sleep in old Roderich's bedroom, so as to be close by if there should be any more sleepwalking. It was thus in this apartment and the adjoining hall that the new Baron and V. met to transact their business. They were sitting there at the great table beside the blazing fire making their way through accounts and documents and oblivious to the muffled thundering of the sea, the shrieking of the gulls, the storm whistling through the castle and awakening evil echoes in the chimneys and narrow corridors. Suddenly a loud gust of wind resounded through the castle and the hall was filled with the light of the full moon. V. said merely: 'What terrible weather!'

The Baron, immersed in the prospect of wealth which had opened up before him, replied, as he turned over a leaf of the cash book with a satisfied smile: 'Indeed, very stormy.'

But now he started up in terror as the door of the hall sprang open and a white, ghostly figure came into view! It was Daniel – whom everyone supposed to be lying incapable of motion – again on his nocturnal wanderings. Dumbstruck, the Baron stared at the steward as he scratched away at the wall, groaning piteously. His face as white as death and his hair standing on end, the Baron jumped from his seat and approached the steward, crying loudly, so that the whole hall echoed: 'Daniel! Daniel! What are you doing here at this hour?'

The steward emitted the wailing howl that had burst from him on the occasion Wolfgang had offered him gold for his loyalty, and collapsed to the floor. V. called the servants; they lifted the steward, but all efforts to revive him were vain. Then the Baron cried, as if beside himself: 'Dear God, have I not heard that sleepwalkers may be on the threshold of death if one calls them by name? O wretch! I have killed the poor old man! I shall not know another moment's peace.'

When the servants had carried the body away and the hall was empty again, V. took the Baron by the hand and led him to the walled-up doorway. 'He who has just died at your feet, Baron Roderich,' he said, 'was the wicked murderer of your father.'

The Baron stared at him as if he were a ghost from Hell. V. continued: 'Now it is time to reveal the secret which burdened that wicked man and drove him to walk in his sleep. The Almighty Power has seen to it that the son has revenged the father's murder: the words you shouted in the sleepwalker's ear were the last spoken by your unhappy father.'

Trembling and unable to utter a word, the Baron sat beside V. as the latter told him of the contents of the package which Hubert had left behind. Hubert blamed himself, with expressions which were proof of the deepest regret, for the implacable hatred of his brother which had taken root in him from the moment old Roderich had established the entail; when Wolfgang had begun his courtship of Julie de St Val in Geneva, he believed he had acquired the means to destroy him. In collusion with Daniel, he sought to compel the old man to a decision which would reduce Wolfgang to despair. Old Roderich was obsessed with the idea of uniting his family with one of the oldest families in the kingdom: he believed he had read this union in the stars. He thus regarded Wolfgang's union with Julie as nothing less than a crime against the eternal powers, and every attempt to destroy it seemed to him justified. In this Hubert had seconded him. But Heaven had decreed that Wolfgang should prosper, and his actual marriage, and the birth of his son, remained a secret from Hubert. With the premonition of the nearness of death, there also came to old Roderich the premonition that Wolfgang had in fact united himself with the detested Julie; in a letter summoning him to Castle R. he had pronounced his son cursed if he did not destroy that union. It was this letter that Wolfgang burned beside his father's bier.

Roderich had written to Hubert that Wolfgang had married Julie, but that he would break up that union. Hubert took this for imagination and was not a little startled when Wolfgang himself not only confirmed the old man's suspicion but added that Julie had borne him a son and that very shortly he would inform her (who still held him to be a merchant) of his real standing. He intended to go to Geneva to fetch his beloved wife, but before he could do so death had claimed him. Hubert had kept silent as to the existence of a son and stolen the birthright for himself. But after a few years he began to feel regret. Shame prevented him from revealing his deceit, but he did not wish to take another penny from the rightful owner, made inquiries in Geneva and learned that Frau Born, inconsolable at the incomprehensible disappearance of her husband, had died, but that young Roderich Born was being brought up by a foster-father. To him, Hubert announced himself under an assumed name and forwarded sufficient money to raise the young Lord of the Manor in a fitting way.

How he had husbanded the income of the estate and how he had disposed of it in his will was already known. As for the death of his brother, Hubert wrote in such strange, enigmatic terms that it appeared likely he was at least indirectly responsible for it. The contents of the black document case had made all clear. It contained the treacherous correspondence between Hubert and Daniel; there was also a page which Daniel had written and signed: a terrible confession at which V. felt his whole being tremble. Hubert had come to Castle R. at Daniel's request; it was Daniel who had written to him telling him of the hundred and fifty thousand gold thalers. Within the steward there seethed a rage which had to discharge itself on the young man who had wanted to throw him out like a dog. He fanned the flames consuming the disappointed Hubert, and at meetings in the forest, in storm and snow, they agreed on Wolfgang's destruction.

'We must get rid of him,' Hubert had said, fingering his gun. 'Yes, we must get rid of him,' Daniel had agreed, 'but not like that.'

This inspired Hubert to dare greatly – he would murder the Baron, and no one would know of it; but when he at last received some money, he regretted the idea and intended to leave. Daniel himself had saddled the horse and led it from the stable, but when the Baron had made to mount it, Daniel had said in a scornful voice: 'The estate belongs to you, Baron Hubert, for its proud lord lies crushed in the tower's abyss. Perhaps you would now prefer to stay.'

Daniel had observed that, in his greed for gold, Wolfgang often rose at night, went to the door which formerly led to the tower and peered down with avaricious looks into the depths, which, he believed, concealed a great treasure. On the fateful night, Daniel had concealed himself behind the hall doors; as he heard the Baron open the door leading to the tower, he ran up behind him. The Baron, standing at the edge of the precipice, turned as he became aware of the presence of the mad servant in whose eyes murder was already gleaming and cried out in terror: 'Daniel! Daniel! What are you doing here at this hour?'

Daniel then shrieked wildly: 'Down with you, you mangy dog!' and hurled the Baron into the depths with a single blow.

Shattered by these revelations, the young Baron Roderich could find no peace in the castle where his father had been murdered. He lived on his property in Courland and went to Castle R. only in the autumn. Franz affirmed that Daniel still haunted the castle at the full moon and described the ghost just as he was when V. later saw and banished him. The discovery of these events, which shamed the memory of his father, had also driven the young Baron Hubert forth into the world.

Thus my great-uncle related all that had occurred. Then he took my hand and said very gently, his eyes filled with tears: 'Cousin, Cousin, even she, that gentle lady, has fallen victim to the evil power which resides in that place. Two days after we left Castle R. the Baron arranged a sleigh ride; he himself was driving with his wife, and as they were heading down the valley the horses, shying suddenly, bolted furiously away. "The old man, the old man is behind us!" the Baroness shrieked, and in that instant she was flung from the sleigh. She was found lifeless. She is dead. The Baron is inconsolable, and he too is near to dying. We shall never return there, Cousin.'

My uncle fell silent. Heartbroken, I took leave of him, and only the universal healer, Time, could soothe the pain in which I thought I should perish.

Years passed. V. had long been resting in his grave. I had left my homeland. The storm of battle blowing across Germany drove me to Petersburg. On my return, I was driving one dark summer night along the coast when I saw in the sky a great shining star. Approaching nearer, I saw that what I had taken for a star was a red flickering flame, though I did not understand how it could be so high in the sky.

'Coachman, whatever is that fire over there?' I asked.

'Oh,' he replied, 'that isn't a fire; that is the Castle R. lighthouse.'

Castle R.! As the coachman uttered the name, the image of those fateful autumn days sprang vividly to life within me. I saw the Baron, Seraphine, the strange old aunts; I saw myself, an infatuated youth, sighing like a furnace, with woeful ballad made to his mistress's eyebrow! Thus, moved by pain and a strange longing, I climbed out of the coach in the early morning at R., where it had stopped to take on mail. I recognized the house of the estate manager and asked after him.

The postal clerk took the pipe from his mouth and pushed back his nightcap. 'There is no estate manager here,' he said. 'This is a government office, and the officer is still asleep.'

On questioning further I learned that some sixteen years previously Baron Roderich von R., the last Lord of the Manor, had died without issue, and ownership had, in accordance with the terms of the entail, passed to the state. I went up to the castle. It lay in ruins. Many of its stones had been used to build the lighthouse, an old farmer assured me. He also had knowledge of the ghost: even now, he said, at the time of the full moon wailing could be heard from among the stones.

Poor, ill-advised Roderich! What evil power did you conjure up to poison in its first youth the race you thought to have planted for eternity?

Wandering Willie's Tale

Walter Scott

Ye maun have heard of Sir Robert Redgauntlet of that Ilk, who lived in these parts before the dear years. The country will lang mind him; and our fathers used to draw breath thick if ever they heard him named. He was out wi' the Hielandmen in Montrose's time; and again he was in the hills wi' Glencairn in the saxteen hundred and fifty-twa; and sae when King Charles the Second came in, wha was in sic favour as the Laird of Redgauntlet? He was knighted at Lonon court, wi' the King's ain sword; and being a red-hot prelatist, he came down here, rampauging like a lion, with commissions of lieutenancy (and of lunacy, for what I ken), to put down a' the Whigs and Covenanters in the country. Wild wark they made of it; for the Whigs were as dour as the Cavaliers were fierce, and it was which should first tire the other. Redgauntlet was aye for the strong hand; and his name is kend as wide in the country as Claverhouse's or Tam Dalyell's. Glen, nor dargle, nor mountain, nor cave, could hide the puir hill-folk when Redgauntlet was out with bugle and bloodhound after them, as if they had been sae mony deer. And troth when they fand them, they didna mak muckle mair ceremony than a Hielandman wi' a roebuck – It was just, 'Will ye tak the test?' – if not, 'Make ready – present – fire!' – and there lay the recusant.

Far and wide was Sir Robert hated and feared. Men thought he had a direct compact with Satan – that he was proof against steel – and that bullets happed aff his buff-coat like hailstanes from a hearth – that he had a mear that would turn a hare on the side of Carrifra-gawns – and muckle to the same purpose, of whilk mair anon. The best blessing they wared on him was, 'Deil scowp wi' Redgauntlet!' He wasna a bad maister to his ain folk, though, and was weel aneugh liked by his tenants; and as for the lackies and troopers that raid out wi' him to the persecutions, as the Whigs caa'd those killing times, they wad hae drunken themsells blind to his health at ony time.

Now you are to ken that my gudesire lived on Redgauntlet's grund – they ca' the place Primrose-Knowe. We had lived on the grund, and under the Redgauntlets, since the riding days, and lang before. It was a pleasant bit: and I think the air is callerer and fresher there than onywhere else in the country. It 's a' deserted now; and I sat on the broken door-cheek three days since, and was glad I couldna see the plight the place was in; but that 's a' wide o' the mark. There dwelt my gudesir, Steenie Steenson, a rambling, rattling chiel' he had been in his young days, and could play weel on the pipes; he was famous at *Hoopers and Girders* – a' Cumberland couldna touch him at *Jockie Lattin* – and he had the finest finger for the back-lilt between Berwick and Carlisle. The like o' Steenie wasna the sort that they made Whigs o'. And so he became a Tory, as they ca' it, which we now ca' Jacobites, just out of a kind of needcessity, that he might belang to some side or other. He had nae ill-will to the Whig bodies, and liked little to see the blude rin, though, being obliged to follow Sir Robert in hunting and hosting, watching and warding, he saw muckle mischief, and maybe did some, that he couldna avoid.

Now Steenie was a kind of favourite with his master, and kend a' the folks about the Castle, and was often sent for to play the pipes when they were at their merriment. Auld Dougal MacCallum, the butler, that had followed Sir Robert through gude and ill, thick and thin, pool and stream, was specially fond of the pipes, and aye gae my gudesir his gude word wi' the Laird; for Dougal could turn his master round his finger.

Weel, round came the Revolution, and it had like to have broken the hearts baith of Dougal and his master. But the change was not a'thegether sae great as they feared, and other folk thought for. The Whigs made an unco crawing what they wad do with their auld enemies, and in special wi' Sir Robert Redgauntlet. But there were ower mony great folks dipped in the same doings, to mak a spick and span new warld. So Parliament passed it a' ower easy; and Sir Robert, bating that he was held to hunting foxes instead of Covenanters, remained just the man he was. His revel was as loud, and his hall as well lighted, as ever it had been, though maybe he lacked the fines of the non-conformists, that used to come to stock his larder and cellar; for it is certain he began to be keener about the rents than his tenants used to find him before, and they behoved to be prompt to the rent-day, or else the Laird wasna pleased. And he was sic an awsome body, that naebody cared to anger him; for the oaths he swore, and the rage that he used to get into, and the looks that he put on, made men sometimes think him a devil incarnate.

Weel, my gudesire was nae manager – no that he was a very great misguider – but he hadna the saving gift, and he got twa terms' rent in arrear. He got the first brash at Whitsunday put ower wi' fair word and piping; but when Martinmas came, there was a summons from the grund-officer to come wi' the rent on a day preceese, or else Steenie behoved to flit. Sair wark he had to get the siller; but he was weel-freended, and at last he got the haill scraped thegether – a thousand merks – the maist of it was from a neighbour they caa'd Laurie Lapraik – a sly tod. Laurie had walth o' gear – could hunt wi the hound and rin wi' the hare – and be a Whig or Tory, saunt or sinner, as the wind stood. He was a professor in this Revolution warld, but he liked an orra sough of this warld, and a tune on the pipes weel aneugh at a by-time, and abune a', he thought he had gude security for the siller he lent my gudesire ower the stocking at Primrose-Knowe.

Away trots my gudesire to Redgauntlet Castle, wi' a heavy purse and a light heart, glad to be out of the Laird's danger. Weel, the first thing he learned at the Castle was, that Sir Robert had fretted himsell into a fit of the gout, because he did not appear before twelve o'clock. It wasna a'thegether for the sake of the money, Dougal thought; but because he didna like to part wi' my gudesire aff the grund. Dougal was glad to see Steenie, and brought him into the great oak parlour, and there sat the Laird his leesome lane, excepting that he had beside him a great, ill-favoured jackanape, that was a special pet of his; a cankered beast it was, and mony an ill-natured trick it played – ill to please it was, and easily angered – ran about the haill castle, chattering and yowling, and pinching, and biting folk, especially before ill-weather, or disturbances in the state. Sir Robert caa'd it Major Weir, after the warlock that was burnt; and few folk liked either the name or the conditions of the creature – they thought there was something in it by ordinar – and my gudesire was not just easy in his mind when the door shut on him, and he saw himself in the room wi' naebody but the Laird, Dougal MacCallum, and the Major, a thing that hadna chanced to him before.

Sir Robert sat, or, I should say, lay, in a great armed chair, wi' his grand velvet gown, and his feet on a cradle; for he had baith gout and gravel, and his face looked as gash and ghastly as Satan's. Major Weir sat opposite to him, in a red laced coat, and the Laird's wig on his head; and aye as Sir Robert girned wi' pain, the jackanape girned too, like a sheep's-head between a pair of tangs – an ill-faur'd, fearsome couple they were. The Laird's buff-coat was hung on a pin behind him, and his broadsword and his pistols within reach; for he keepit up the auld fashion of having the weapons ready, and a horse saddled day and night, just as he used to do when he was able to loup on horseback, and away after ony of the hill-folk he could get speerings of. Some said it was for fear of the Whigs taking vengeance, but I judge it was just his auld custom – he wasna gien to fear onything. The rental-book, wi' its black cover and brass clasps, was lying beside him; and a book of sculduddry sangs was put betwixt the leaves, to keep it open at the place where it bore evidence against the Goodman of Primrose-Knowe, as behind the hand with his mails and duties. Sir Robert gave my gudesire a look, as if he would have withered his heart in his bosom. Ye maun ken he had a way of bending his brows, that men saw the visible mark of a horse-shoe in his forehead, deep-dinted, as if it had been stamped there.

'Are ye come light-handed, ye son of a toom whistle?' said Sir Robert. 'Zounds! if you are –'

My gudesire, with as gude a countenance as he could put on, made a leg, and placed the bag of money on the table wi' a dash, like a man that does something clever. The Laird drew it to him hastily: 'Is it all here, Steenie, man?'

'Your honour will find it right,' said my gudesire.

'Here, Dougal,' said the Laird, 'gie Steenie a tass of brandy downstairs, till I count the siller and write the receipt.'

But they werena weel out of the room, when Sir Robert gied a yelloch that garr'd the Castle rock. Back ran Dougal – in flew the livery-men – yell on yell gied the Laird, ilk ane mair awfu' than the ither. My gudesire knew not whether to stand or flee, but he ventured back into the parlour, where a' was gaun hirdy-girdie – naebody to say 'come in', or 'gae out'. Terribly the Laird roared for cauld water to his feet, and wine to cool his throat; and hell, hell, hell, and its flames, was aye the word in his mouth. They brought him water, and when they plunged his swoln feet into the tub, he cried out it was burning; and folk say that it *did* bubble and sparkle like a seething caldron. He flung the cup at Dougal's head, and said he had given him blood instead of burgundy; and, sure aneugh, the lass washed clotted blood aff the carpet the neist day. The jackanape they caa'd Major Weir, it jibbered and cried as if it was mocking its master; my gudesire's head was like to turn – he forgot baith siller and receipt, and down stairs he banged; but as he ran, the shrieks came faint and fainter; there was a deep-drawn shivering groan, and word gaed through the Castle, that the Laird was dead.

Weel, away came my gudesire, wi' his finger in his mouth, and his best hope was, that Dougal had seen the money-bag, and heard the Laird speak of writing the receipt. The young Laird, now Sir John, came from Edinburgh, to see things put to rights. Sir John and his father never gree'd weel. Sir John had been bred an advocate, and afterwards sat in the last Scots Parliament and voted for the Union, having gotten, it was thought, a rug of the compensations – if his father could have come out of his grave, he would have brained him for it on his awn hearthstane. Some thought it was easier counting with the auld rough knight than the fair-spoken young ane – but mair of that anon.

Dougal MacCallum, poor body, neither grat nor graned, but gaed about the house looking like a corpse, but directing, as was his duty, a' the order of the grand funeral. Now, Dougal looked aye waur and waur when night was coming, and was aye the last to gang to his bed, whilk was in a little round just opposite the chamber of dais, whilk his master occupied while he was living, and where he now lay in state, as they caa'd it, weel-a-day! The night before the funeral, Dougal could keep his awn counsel nae langer; he cam doun with his proud spirit, and fairly asked auld Hutcheon to sit in his room with him for an hour. When they were in the round, Dougal took ae tass of brandy to himsell, and gave another to Hutcheon, and wished him all health, and lang life, and said that, for himsell, he wasna lang for this world; for that, every night since Sir Robert's death, his silver call had sounded from the state-chamber, just as it used to do at nights in his lifetime, to call Dougal to help to turn him in his bed. Dougal said, that being alone with the dead on that floor of the tower (for naebody cared to wake Sir Robert Redgauntlet like another corpse), he had never daured to answer the call, but that now his conscience checked him for neglecting his duty; for, 'though death breaks service,' said MacCallum, 'it shall never break my service to Sir Robert; and I will answer his next whistle, so be you will stand by me, Hutcheon.'

Hutcheon had nae will to the wark, but he had stood by Dougal in battle and broil, and he wad not fail him at this pinch; so down the carles sat ower a stoup of brandy, and Hutcheon, who was something of a clerk, would have read a chapter of the Bible; but Dougal would hear naething but a blaud of Davie Lindsay, whilk was the waur preparation.

When midnight came, and the house was quiet as the grave, sure aneugh the silver whistle sounded as sharp and shrill as if Sir Robert was blowing it, and up gat the twa auld serving-men, and tottered into the room where the dead man lay. Hutcheon saw aneugh at the first glance; for there were torches in the room, which showed him the foul fiend, in his ain shape, sitting on the Laird's coffin! Over he cowped as if he had been dead. He could not tell how lang he lay in a trance at the door, but when he gathered himself, he cried on his neighbour, and getting nae answer, raised the house, when Dougal was found lying dead within twa steps of the bed where his master's coffin was placed. As for the whistle, it was gaen anes and aye; but mony a time was it heard at the top of the house on the bartizan, and amang the auld chimneys and turrets, where the howlets have their nests. Sir John hushed the matter up, and the funeral passed over without mair bogle-wark.

But when a' was over, and the Laird was beginning to settle his affairs, every tenant was called up for his arrears, and my gudesire for the full sum that stood against him in the rental-book. Weel, away he trots to the Castle, to tell his story, and there he is introduced to Sir John, sitting in his father's chair, in deep mourning, with weepers and hanging cravat, and a small walking rapier by his side, instead of the auld broadsword, that had a hundred-weight of steel about it, what with blade, chape, and basket-hilt. I have heard their communing so often tauld ower, that I almost think I was there mysell, though I couldna be born at the time.

'I wuss ye joy, sir, of the head seat, and the white loaf, and the braid lairdship. Your father was a kind man to friends and followers; muckle grace to you, Sir John, to fill his shoon – his boots, I suld say, for he seldom wore shoon, unless it were muils when he had the gout.'

'Ay, Steenie,' quoth the Laird, sighing deeply and putting his napkin to his een, 'his was a sudden call, and he will be missed in the country; no time to set his house in order – weel prepared Godward, no doubt, which is the root of the matter – but left us behind a tangled hesp to wind, Steenie. – Hem! hem! We maun go to business, Steenie; much to do, and little time to do it in.'

Here he opened the fatal volume. I have heard of a thing they call Doomsday-book – I am clear it has been a rental of back-ganging tenants.

'Stephen,' said Sir John, still in the same soft, sleekit tone of voice, 'Stephen Stevenson, or Steenson, ye are down here for a year's rent behind the hand – due at last term.'

Stephen. 'Please your honour, Sir John, I paid it to your father.'

Sir John. 'Ye took a receipt then, doubtless, Stephen; and can produce it?'

Stephen. 'Indeed, I hadna time, an it like your honour; for nae sooner had I set doun the siller, and just as his honour Sir Robert, that 's gaen, drew it till him to count it, and write out the receipt, he was ta'en wi' the pains that removed him.'

'That was unlucky,' said Sir John, after a pause. 'But ye maybe paid it in the presence of somebody. I want but a *talis qualis* evidence, Stephen. I would go ower strictly to work with no poor man.'

Stephen. 'Troth, Sir John, there was naebody in the room but Dougal MacCallum the butler. But, as your honour kens, he has e'en followed his auld master.'

'Very unlucky again, Stephen,' said Sir John, without altering his voice a single note. 'The man to whom ye paid the money is dead – and the man who witnessed the payment is dead too – and the siller, which should have been to the fore, is neither seen nor heard tell of in the repositories. How am I to believe a' this?'

Stephen. 'I dinna ken, your honour; but there is a bit memorandum note of the very coins; for, God help me! I had to borrow out of twenty purses; and I am sure that ilka man there set down will take his grit oath for what purpose I borrowed the money.'

Sir John. 'I have little doubt ye *borrowed* the money, Steenie. It is the *payment* to my father that I want to have some proof of.'

Stephen. 'The siller maun be about the house, Sir John. And since your honour never got it, and his honour that was canna have ta'en it wi' him, maybe some of the family may have seen it.'

Sir John. 'We will examine the servants, Stephen; that is but reasonable.'

But lackey and lass, and page and groom, all denied stoutly that they had ever seen such a bag of money as my gudesire described. What was waur, he had unluckily not mentioned to any living soul of them his purpose of paying his rent. Ae quean had noticed something under his arm, but she took it for the pipes.

Sir John Redgauntlet ordered the servants out of the room, and then said to my gudesire: 'Now, Steenie, ye see you have fair play; and, as I have little doubt ye ken better where to find the siller than any other body, I beg, in fair terms, and for your own sake, that you will end this fasherie; for, Stephen, ye maun pay or flit.'

'The Lord forgie your opinion,' said Stephen, driven almost to his wit's end – 'I am an honest man.'

'So am I, Stephen,' said his honour; 'and so are all the folks in the house, I hope. But if there be a knave amongst us, it must be he that tells the story he cannot prove.' He paused, and then added, mair sternly, 'If I understand your trick, sir, you want to take advantage of some malicious reports concerning things in this family, and particularly respecting my father's sudden death, thereby to cheat me out of the money, and perhaps take away my character, by insinuating that I have received the rent I am demanding. – Where do you suppose this money to be? – I insist upon knowing.'

My gudesire saw everything look sae muckle against him, that he grew nearly desperate – however, he shifted from one foot to another, looked to every corner of the room, and made no answer.

'Speak out, sirrah,' said the Laird, assuming a look of his father's, a very particular ane, which he had when he was angry – it seemed as if the wrinkles of his frown made that selfsame fearful shape of a horse's shoe in the middle of his brow; – 'Speak out, sir! I *will* know your thoughts; – do you suppose that I have this money?'

'Far be it frae me to say so,' said Stephen.

'Do you charge any of my people with having taken it?'

'I wad be laith to charge them that may be innocent,' said my gudesire; 'and if there be any one that is guilty, I have nae proof.'

'Somewhere the money must be, if there is a word of truth in your story,' said Sir John; 'I ask where you think it is – and demand a correct answer?'

'In hell, if you *will* have my thoughts of it,' said my gudesire, driven to extremity – 'in hell! with your father, his jackanape, and his silver whistle.'

Down the stairs he ran (for the parlour was nae place for him after such a word), and he heard the Laird swearing blood and wounds behind him, as fast as ever did Sir Robert, and roaring for the bailie and the baron-officer.

Away rode my gudesire to his chief creditor (him they caa'd Laurie Lapraik) to try if he could make onything out of him; but when he tauld his story, he got but the warst word in his wame – thief, beggar, and dyvour, were the saftest terms; and to the boot of these hard terms, Laurie brought up the auld story of his dipping his hand in the blood of God's saunts, just as if a tenant could have helped riding with the Laird, and that a laid like Sir Robert Redgauntlet. My gudesire was, by this time, far beyond the bounds of patience, and, while he and Laurie were at deil speed the liars, he was wanchancie aneugh to abuse Lapraik's doctrine as weel as the man, and said things that garr'd folk's flesh grue that heard them; – he wasna just himsell, and he had lived wi' a wild set in his day.

At last they parted, and my gudesire was to ride home through the woods of Pitmurkie, that is a' fou of black firs, as they say. – I ken the wood, but the firs may be black or white for what I can tell. – At the entry of the wood there is a wild common, and on the edge of the common, a little lonely change-house, that was keepit then by an ostler-wife, they

suld hae caa'd her Tibbie Faw, and there puir Steenie cried for a mutchkin
of brandy, for he had had no refreshment the haill day. Tibbie was earnest
wi' him to take a bite of meat, but he couldna think o't, nor would he take
his foot out of the stirrup, and took off the brandy wholely at twa draughts,
and named a toast at each: the first was, the memory of Sir Robert
Redgauntlet, and might be never lie quiet in his grave till he had righted
his poor bond-tenant; and the second was, a health to Man's Enemy, if he
would but get him back the pock of siller, or tell him what came o't, for he
saw the haill world was like to regard him as a thief and a cheat, and he
took that waur than even the ruin of his house and hauld.

On he rode, little caring where. It was dark night turned, and the trees
made it yet darker, and he let the beast take its ain road through the wood;
when, all of a sudden, from tired and wearied that it was before, the nag
began to spring, and flee, and stend, that my gudesire could hardly keep
the saddle. – Upon the whilk, a horseman, suddenly riding up beside him,
said: 'That 's a mettle beast of yours, freend; will you sell him?' – So
saying, he touched the horse's neck with his riding-wand, and it fell into
its auld heigh-ho of a stumbling trot. 'But his spunk 's soon out of him, I
think,' continued the stranger, 'and that is like mony a man's courage,
that thinks he wad do great things till he come to the proof.'

My gudesire scarce listened to this, but spurred his horse, with, 'Gude
e'en to you, freend.'

But it 's like the stranger was ane that doesna lightly yield his point; for,
ride as Steenie liked, he was aye beside him at the selfsame pace. At last
my gudesire, Steenie Steenson, grew half angry; and, to say the truth, half
feared.

'What is it that ye want with me, freend?' he said. 'If ye be a robber, I
have nae money; if ye be a leal man, wanting company, I have nae heart
to mirth or speaking; and if ye want to ken the road, I scarce ken it mysell.'

'If you will tell me your grief,' said the stranger, 'I am one that, though
I have been sair miscaa'd in the world, am the only hand for helping my
freends.'

So my gudesire, to eas his ain heart, mair than from any hope of help,
told him the story from the beginning to end.

'It 's a hard pinch,' said the stranger; 'but I think I can help you.'

'If you could lend the money, sir, and take a lang day – I ken nae other
help on earth,' said my gudesire.

'But there may be some under the earth,' said the stranger. 'Come, I'll
be frank wi' you; I could lend you the money on bond, but you would
maybe scruple my terms. Now, I can tell you, that your auld Laird is

disturbed in his grave by your curses, and the wailing of your family, and if ye daur venture to go to see him, he will give you the receipt.'

My gudesire's hair stood on end at this proposal, but he thought his companion might be some humoursome chield that was trying to frighten him, and might end with lending him the money. Besides, he was bauld wi' brandy, and desperate wi' distress; and he said, he had courage to go to the gate of hell, and a step farther, for that receipt. – The stranger laughed.

Weel, they rode on through the thickest of the wood, when, all of a sudden, the horse stopped at the door of a great house; and, but that he knew the place was ten miles off, my father would have thought he was at Redgauntlet Castle. They rode into the outer courtyard, through the muckle faulding yetts, and aneath the auld portcullis; and the whole front of the house was lighted, and there were pipes and fiddles, and as much dancing and deray within as used to be in Sir Robert's house at Pace and Yule, and such high seasons. They lap off, and my gudesire, as seemed to him, fastened his horse to the very ring he had tied him to that morning, when he gaed to wait on the young Sir John.

'God!' said my gudesire, 'if Sir Robert's death be but a dream.'

He knocked at the ha' door just as he was wont, and his auld acquaintance, Dougal MacCallum – just after his wont, too – came to open the door, and said: 'Piper Steenie, are ye there, lad? Sir Robert has been crying for you.'

My gudesire was like a man in a dream – he looked for the stranger, but he was gane for the time. At last he just tried to say· 'Ha¹ Dougal Driveower, are ye living? I thought ye had been dead.'

'Never fash yoursell wi' me,' said Dougal, 'but look to yoursell; and see ye tak naething frae onybody here, neither meat, drink, or siller, except just the receipt that is your ain.'

So saying, he led the way out through halls and trances that were weel kend to my gudesire, and into the auld oak parlour; and there was as much singing of profane sangs, and birling of red wine, and speaking blasphemy and sculduddry, as had ever been in Redgauntlet Castle when it was at the blithest.

But, Lord take us in keeping! what a set of ghastly revellers they were that sat round that table! – My gudesire kend mony that had long before gane to their place, for often had he piped to the most part in the hall of Redgauntlet. There was the fierce Middleton, and the dissolute Rothes, and the crafty Lauderdale; and Dalyell, with his bald head and a beard to his girdle; and Earlshall, with Cameron's blude on his hand; and wild

Bonshaw, that tied blessed Mr Cargill's limbs till the blude sprang; and Dunbarton Douglas, the twice-turned traitor baith to country and king. There was the Bluidy Advocate MacKenyie, who, for his worldly wit and wisdom, had been to the rest as a god. And there was Claverhouse, as beautiful as when he lived, with his long, dark, curled locks, streaming down over his laced buff-coat, and his left hand always on his right spule-blade, to hide the wound that the silver bullet had made. He sat apart from them all, and looked at them with a melancholy, haughty countenance; while the rest hallooed, and sung, and laughed, that the room rang. But their smiles were fearfully contorted from time to time; and their laughter passed into such wild sounds, as made my gudesire's very nails grow blue, and chilled the marrow in his banes.

They that waited at the table were just the wicked serving-men and troopers, that had done their work and cruel bidding on earth. There was the Lang Lad of the Nethertown, that helped to take Argyle; and the Bishop's summoner, that they called the Deil's Rattle-bag; and the wicked guardsmen, in their laced coats; and the savage Highland Amorites, that shed blood like water; and many a proud serving-man, haughty of heart and bloody of hand, cringing to the rich, and making them wickeder than they would be; grinding the poor to powder, when the rich had broken them to fragments. And mony, mony mair were coming and ganging, a' as busy in their vocation as if they had been alive.

Sir Robert Redgauntlet, in the midst of a' this fearful riot, cried, wi' a voice like thunder, on Steenie Piper, to come to the board-head where he was sitting; his legs stretched out before him, and swathed up with flannel, with his holster pistols aside him, while the great broadsword rested against his chair, just as my gudesire had seen him the last time upon earth — the very cushion for the jackanape was close to him, but the creature itsell was not there — it wasna its hour, it 's likely; for he heard them say as he came forward, 'Is not the Major come yet?' And another answered: 'The jackanape will be here betimes the morn.' And when my gudesire came forward, Sir Robert, or his ghaist, or the deevil in his likeness, said: 'Weel, piper, hae ye settled wi' my son for the year's rent?'

With much ado my father gat breath to say, that Sir John would not settle without his honour's receipt.

'Ye shall hae that for a tune of the pipes, Steenie,' said the appearance of Sir Robert. 'Play us up *Weel hoddled, Luckie.*'

Now this was a tune my gudesire learned frae a warlock, that heard it when they were worshipping Satan at their meetings; and my gudesire had sometimes played it at the ranting suppers in Redgauntlet Castle, but never very willingly; and now he grew cauld at the very name of it, and said, for excuse, he hadna his pipes wi' him.

'MacCallum, ye limb of Beelzebub,' said the fearfu' Sir Robert, 'bring Steenie the pipes that I am keeping for him!'

MacCallum brought a pair of pipes might have served the piper of Donald of the Isles. But he gave my gudesire a nudge as he offered them; and looking secretly and closely, Steenie saw that the chanter was of steel, and heated to a white heat; so he had fair warning not to trust his fingers with it. So he excused himself again, and said, he was faint and frightened, and had not wind aneugh to fill the bag.

'Then ye maun eat and drink, Steenie,' said the figure; 'for we do little else here; and it's ill speaking between a fou man and a fasting.'

Now these were the very words that the bloody Earl of Douglas said to keep the king's messenger in hand, while he cut the head off MacLellan of Bombie, at the Threave Castle; and that put Steenie mair and mair on his guard. So he spoke up like a man, and said he came neither to eat, or drink, or make minstrelsy; but simply for his ain – to ken what was come o' the money he had paid, and to get a discharge for it; and he was so stout-hearted by this time, that he charged Sir Robert for conscience-sake – (he had no power to say the holy name) – and as he hoped for peace and rest, to spread no snares for him, but just to give him his ain.

The appearance gnashed its teeth and laughed, but it took from a large pocket-book the receipt, and handed it to Steenie. 'There is your receipt, ye pitiful cur; and for the money, my dog-whelp of a son may go look for it in the Cat's Cradle.'

My gudesire uttered mony thanks, and was about to retire, when Sir Robert roared aloud: 'Stop though, thou sack-doudling son of a whore! I am not done with thee. HERE we do nothing for nothing; and you must return on this very day twelvemonth, to pay your master the homage that you owe me for my protection.'

My father's tongue was loosed of a suddenty, and he said aloud: 'I refer mysell to God's pleasure, and not to yours.'

He had no sooner uttered the word than all was dark around him; and he sunk on the earth with such a sudden shock, that he lost both breath and sense.

How lang Steenie lay there, he could not tell; but when he came to himself, he was lying in the auld kirkyard of Redgauntlet parochine just at the door of the family aisle, and the scutcheon of the auld knight, Sir Robert, hanging over his head. There was a deep morning fog on grass and gravestane around him, and his horse was feeding quietly beside the minister's twa cows. Steenie would have thought the whole was a dream, but he had the receipt in his hand, fairly written and signed by the auld laird; only the last letters of his name were a little disorderly, written like one seized with sudden pain.

Sorely troubled in his mind, he left that dreary place, rode through the mist to Redgauntlet Castle, and with much ado he got speech of the Laird.

'Well, you dyvour bankrupt,' was the first word, 'have you brought me my rent?'

'No,' answered my gudesire, 'I have not; but I have brought your honour Sir Robert's receipt for it.'

'How, sirrah? – Sir Robert's receipt! – You told me he had not given you one.'

'Will your honour please to see if that bit line is right?'

Sir John looked at every line, and at every letter, with much attention; and at last, at the date, which my gudesire had not observed: '*From my appointed place*,' he read, '*this twenty-fifth of November*.' 'What! – That is yesterday! Villain, thou must have gone to hell for this!'

'I got it from your honour's father – whether he be in heaven or hell, I know not,' said Steenie.

'I will delate you for a warlock to the Privy Council!' said Sir John. 'I will send you to your master, the devil, with the help of a tar-barrel and a torch!'

'I intend to delate mysell to the Presbytery,' said Steenie, 'and tell them all I have seen last night, whilk are things fitter for them to judge of than a borrel man like me.'

Sir John paused, composed himsell, and desired to hear the full history; and my gudesire told it him from point to point, as I have told it you – word for word, neither more nor less.

Sir John was silent again for a long time, and at last he said, very composedly: 'Steenie, this story of yours concerns the honour of many a noble family besides mine; and if it be a leasing-making, to keep yourself out of my danger, the least you can expect is to have a red-hot iron driven through your tongue, and that will be as bad as scauding your fingers with a red-hot chanter. But yet it may be true, Steenie; and if the money cast up, I shall not know what to think of it. – But where shall we find the Cat's Cradle? There are cats enough about the old house, but I think they kitten without the ceremony of bed or cradle.'

'We were best ask Hutcheon,' said my gudesire; 'he kens a' the odd corners about as weel as – another serving-man that is now gane, and that I wad not like to name.'

Aweel, Hutcheon, when he was asked, told them, that a ruinous turret, lang disused, next to the clock-house, only accessible by a ladder, for the opening was on the outside, and far above the battlements, was called of old the Cat's Cradle.

'There will I go immediately,' said Sir John; and he took (with what purpose, heaven kens) one of his father's pistols from the hall-table, where they had lain since the night he died, and hastened to the battlements.

It was a dangerous place to climb, for the ladder was auld and frail, and wanted ane or twa rounds. However, up got Sir John, and entered at the turret door, where his body stopped the only little light that was in the bit turret. Something flees at him wi' a vengeance, maist dang him back ower – bang gaed the knight's pistol, and Hutcheon, that held the ladder, and my gudesire that stood beside him, hears a loud skelloch. A minute after, Sir John flings the body of the jackanape down to them, and cries that the siller is fund, and that they should come up and help him. And there was the bag of siller sure aneugh, and mony orra things besides, that had been missing for mony a day. And Sir John, when he had riped the turret weel, led my gudesire into the dining-parlour, and took him by the hand, and spoke kindly to him, and said he was sorry he should have doubted his word, and that he would hereafter be a good master to him, to make amends.

'And now, Steenie,' said Sir John, 'although this vision of yours tends, on the whole, to my father's credit, as an honest man, that he should, even after his death, desire to see justice done to a poor man like you, yet you are sensible that ill-dispositioned men might make bad constructions upon it, concerning his soul's health. So, I think, we had better lay the haill dirdum on that ill-deedie creature, Major Weir, and say naething about your dream in the wood of Pitmurkie. You had taken ower muckle brandy to be very certain about onything; and, Steenie, this receipt,' (his hand shook while he held it out,) – 'it's but a queer kind of document, and we will do best, I think, to put it quietly in the fire.'

'Od, but for as queer as it is, it 's a' the voucher I have for my rent,' said my gudesire, who was afraid, it may be, of losing the benefit of Sir Robert's discharge.

'I will bear the contents to your credit in the rental-book, and give you a discharge under my own hand,' said Sir John, 'and that on the spot. And, Steenie, if you can hold your tongue about this matter, you shall sit, from this term downward, at an easier rent.'

'Mony thanks to your honour,' said Steenie, who saw easily in what corner the wind was; 'doubtless I will be conformable to all your honour's

commands; only I would willingly speak wi' some powerful minister on
the subject, for I do not like the sort of soumons of appointment whilk
your honour's father –'

'Do not call the phantom my father!' said Sir John, interrupting him.

'Weel, then, the thing that was so like him,' said my gudesire; 'he spoke
of my coming back to him this time twelvemonth, and it 's a weight on my
conscience.'

'Aweel, then,' said Sir John, 'if you be so much distressed in mind, you
may speak to our minister of the parish; he is a douce man, regards the
honour of our family, and the mair that he may look for some patronage
from me.'

Wi' that, my gudesire readily agreed that the receipt should be burnt,
and the Laird threw it into the chimney with his ain hand. Burn it would
not for them, though; but away it flew up the lum, wi' a lang train of
sparks at its tail, and a hissing noise like a squib.

My gudesire gaed down to the manse, and the minister, when he had
heard the story said, it was his real opinion, that though my gudesire had
gaen very far in tampering with dangerous matters, yet, as he had refused
the devil's arles (for such was the offer of meat and drink), and had
refused to do homage by piping at his bidding, he hoped, that if he held
a circumspect walk hereafter, Satan could take little advantage by what
was come and gane. And, indeed, my gudesire, of his ain accord, long
forswore baith the pipes and the brandy – it was not even till the year was
out, and the fatal day passed, that he would so much as take the fiddle, or
drink usquebaugh or tippenny.

Sir John made up his story about the jackanape as he liked himsell; and
some believe till this day there was no more in the matter than the filching
nature of the brute. Indeed, ye 'll no hinder some to threap, that it was
nane o' the Auld Enemy that Dougal and my gudesire saw in the Laird's
room, but only that wanchancy creature, the Major, capering on the coffin;
and that, as to the blawing on the Laird's whistle that was heard after he
was dead, the filthy brute could do that as weel as the Laird himself, if no
better. But Heaven kens the truth, whilk first came out by the minister's
wife, after Sir John and her ain gudeman were baith in the moulds. And
then my gudesire, wha was failed in his limbs, but not in his judgment or
memory – at least nothing to speak of – was obliged to tell the real
narrative to his freends, for the credit of his good name. He might else
have been charged for a warlock.

The Queen of Spades

Alexander Pushkin

1

> When bleak was the weather
> They would meet together
> For cards – God forgive them!
> Some would win, others lost,
> And they chalked up the cost
> In bleak autumn weather
> When they met together.

There was a card party in the rooms of Narumov, an officer of the Horse Guards. The long winter night had passed unnoticed and it was after four in the morning when the company sat down to supper. Those who had won enjoyed their food; the others sat absent-mindedly in front of empty plates. But when the champagne appeared conversation became more lively and general.

'How did you fare, Surin?' Narumov asked.

'Oh I lost, as usual. I must confess, I have no luck: I stick to *mirandole*, never get excited, never lose my head, and yet I never win.'

'Do you mean to tell me you were not once tempted to back the red the whole evening? Your self-control amazes me.'

'But look at Hermann,' exclaimed one of the party, pointing to a young officer of the Engineers. 'Never held a card in his hands, never made a bet in his life, and yet he sits up till five in the morning watching us play.'

'Cards interest me very much,' said Hermann, 'but I am not in a position to risk the necessary in the hope of acquiring the superfluous.'

'Hermann is a German: he's careful, that's what that is!' remarked Tomsky. 'But if there is one person I can't understand it is my grandmother, Countess Anna Fedotovna.'

'Why is that?' the guests cried.

'I cannot conceive how it is that my grandmother does not play.'

'But surely there is nothing surprising in an old lady in her eighties not wanting to gamble?' said Narumov.

'Then you don't know about her?'

'No, nothing, absolutely nothing!'

'Well, listen then. I must tell you that some sixty years ago my grandmother went to Paris and was quite the rage there. People would run after her to catch a glimpse of *la Vénus moscovite*; Richelieu was at her beck and call, and grandmamma maintains that he very nearly blew his brains out because of her cruelty to him. In those days ladies used to play faro. One evening at the Court she lost a very considerable sum to the Duke of Orleans. When she got home she told my grandfather of her loss while removing the beauty spots from her face and untying her farthingale, and commanded him to pay her debt. My grandfather, so far as I remember, acted as a sort of major-domo to my grandmother. He feared her like fire; however, when he heard of such a frightful gambling loss he almost went out of his mind, fetched the bills they owed and pointed out to her that in six months they had spent half a million roubles and that in Paris they had neither their Moscow nor their Saratov estates upon which to draw, and flatly refused to pay. Grandmamma gave him a box on the ear and retired to bed without him as a sign of her displeasure. The following morning she sent for her husband, hoping that the simple punishment had had its effect, but she found him as obdurate as ever. For the first time in her life she went so far as to reason with him and explain, thinking to rouse his conscience and arguing with condescension, that there were debts and debts, and that a prince was different from a coach-builder. But it was not a bit of good – grandfather just would not hear of it. "Once and for all, no!" Grandmamma did not know what to do. Among her close acquaintances was a very remarkable man. You have heard of Count Saint-Germain, about whom so many marvellous stories are told. You know that he posed as the Wandering Jew and claimed to have discovered the elixir of life and the philosopher's stone, and so on. People laughed at him as a charlatan, and Casanova in his *Memoirs* says that he was a spy. Be that as it may, Saint-Germain, in spite of the mystery that surrounded him, had a most dignified appearance and was a very amiable person in society. Grandmamma is still to this day quite devoted to his memory and gets angry if anyone speaks of him with disrespect. Grandmamma knew that Saint-Germain had plenty of money at his disposal. She decided to appeal to him, and wrote a note asking him to come and see her immediately. The eccentric old man came at once and found her in terrible distress. She described in the blackest colours her husband's inhumanity, and ended by declaring that she laid all her hopes on his friendship and kindness. Saint-Germain pondered. "I could oblige you with the sum you want," he said, "but I know that you would not be easy until you had repaid me, and I should not like to involve you in fresh trouble. There is another way out – you could win it back."

' "But, my dear count," answered grandmamma, "I tell you I have no money at all."

' "That does not matter," Saint-Germain replied. "Listen now to what I am going to tell you."

'And he revealed to her a secret which all of us would give a great deal to know . . .'

The young gamblers redoubled their attention. Tomsky lit his pipe, puffed away for a moment and continued:

'That very evening grandmamma appeared at Versailles, at the *jeu de la reine*. The Duke of Orleans kept the bank. Grandmamma lightly excused herself for not having brought the money to pay off her debt, inventing some little story by way of explanation, and began to play against him. She selected three cards and played them one after the other: all three won, and grandmamma retrieved her loss completely.'

'Luck!' said one of the party.

'A fairy tale!' remarked Hermann.

'Marked cards, perhaps,' put in a third.

'I don't think so,' replied Tomsky impressively.

'What!' said Narumov. 'You have a grandmother who knows how to hit upon three lucky cards in succession, and you haven't learnt her secret yet?'

'That's the deuce of it!' Tomsky replied. 'She had four sons, one of whom was my father; all four were desperate gamblers, and yet she did not reveal her secret to a single one of them, though it would not have been a bad thing for them, or for me either. But listen to what my uncle, Count Ivan Ilyich, used to say, assuring me on his word of honour that it was true. Tchaplitsky – you know him, he died a pauper after squandering millions – as a young man once lost three hundred thousand roubles, to Zorich, if I remember rightly. He was in despair. Grandmamma was always very severe on the follies of young men, but somehow she took pity on Tchaplitsky. She gave him three cards, which he was to play one after the other, at the same time exacting from him a promise that he would never afterwards touch a card so long as he lived. Tchaplitsky went to Zorich's; they sat down to play. Tchaplitsky staked fifty thousand on his first card and won; doubled his stake and won; did the same again, won back his loss and ended up in pocket . . .

'But, I say, it's time to go to bed: it is a quarter to six already.'

And indeed dawn was breaking. The young men emptied their glasses and went home.

2

'Il paraît que monsieur est décidément pour les suivantes.'
'Que voulez-vous, madame? Elles sont plus fraîches.'

FROM A SOCIETY CONVERSATION

The old Countess X was seated before the looking-glass in her dressing-room. Three maids were standing round her. One held a pot of rouge, another a box of hairpins, and the third a tall cap with flame-coloured ribbons. The countess had not the slightest pretensions to beauty – it had faded long ago – but she still preserved all the habits of her youth, followed strictly the fashion of the seventies, and gave as much time and care to her toilette as she had sixty years before. A young girl whom she had brought up sat at an embroidery-frame by the window.

'Good morning, *grand'maman!*' said a young officer, coming into the room. '*Bonjour, Mademoiselle Lise. Grand'maman*, I have a favour to ask of you.'

'What is it, Paul?'

'I want you to let me introduce to you a friend of mine and bring him to your ball on Friday.'

'Bring him straight to the ball and introduce him to me then. Were you at the princess's last night?'

'Of course I was! It was most enjoyable: we danced until five in the morning. Mademoiselle Yeletsky looked enchanting!'

'Come, my dear! What is there enchanting about her? She isn't a patch on her grandmother, Princess Daria Petrovna. By the way, I expect Princess Daria Petrovna must have aged considerably?'

'How do you mean, aged?' Tomsky replied absentmindedly. 'She's been dead for the last seven years.'

The girl at the window raised her head and made a sign to the young man. He remembered that they concealed the deaths of her contemporaries from the old countess, and bit his lip. But the countess heard the news with the utmost indifference.

'Dead! I didn't know,' she said. 'We were maids of honour together, and as we were being presented the Empress . . .'

And for the hundredth time the countess repeated the story to her grandson.

'Well, Paul,' she said at the end; 'now help me to my feet. Lise, where is my snuff-box?'

And the countess went with her maids behind the screen to finish dressing. Tomsky was left *à deux* with the young girl.

'Who is it you want to introduce?' Lizaveta Ivanovna asked softly.

'Narumov. Do you know him?'

'No. Is he in the army?'

'Yes.'

'In the Engineers?'

'No, Horse Guards. What made you think he was in the Engineers?' The girl laughed and made no answer.

'Paul!' the countess called from behind the screen. 'Send me a new novel to read, only pray not one of those modern ones.'

'How do you mean, *grand'maman*?'

'I want a book in which the hero does not strangle either his father or his mother, and where there are no drowned corpses. I have a horror of drowned persons.'

'There aren't any novels of that sort nowadays. Wouldn't you like something in Russian?'

'Are there any Russian novels? . . . Send me something, my dear fellow, please send me something!'

'Excuse me, *grand'maman*: I must hurry . . . Goodbye, Lizaveta Ivanovna! I wonder, what made you think Narumov was in the Engineers?'

And Tomsky departed from the dressing-room.

Lizaveta Ivanovna was left alone. She abandoned her work and began to look out of the window. Soon, round the corner of a house on the other side of the street, a young officer appeared. Colour flooded her cheeks; she took up her work again, bending her head over her embroidery-frame. At that moment the countess came in, having finished dressing.

'Order the carriage, Lise,' she said, 'and let us go for a drive.'

Lizaveta Ivanovna rose from her embroidery-frame and began putting away her work.

'What is the matter with you, my child, are you deaf?' the countess cried. 'Be quick and order the carriage.'

'I will go at once,' the young girl answered quietly, and ran into the ante-room.

A servant came in and handed the countess a parcel of books from Prince Paul Alexandrovich.

'Good! Tell him I am much obliged,' said the countess. 'Lise, Lise, where are you off to?'

'To dress.'

'There is plenty of time, my dear. Sit down here. Open the first volume and read to me.'

The girl took the book and read a few lines.

'Louder!' said the countess. 'What is the matter with you, my dear? Have you lost your voice, or what? Wait a minute . . . Give me that footstool. A little closer. That will do!'

Lizaveta Ivanovna read two more pages. The countess yawned.

'Throw that book away,' she said. 'What nonsense it is! Send it back to Prince Paul with my thanks . . . What about the carriage?'

'The carriage is ready,' said Lizaveta Ivanovna, glancing out into the street.

'How is it you are not dressed?' the countess said. 'You always keep people waiting. It really is intolerable!'

Liza ran to her room. Hardly two minutes passed before the countess started ringing with all her might. Three maids rushed in at one door and a footman at the other.

'Why is it you don't come when you are called?' the countess said to them. 'Tell Lizaveta Ivanovna I am waiting.'

Lizaveta Ivanovna returned, wearing a hat and a pelisse.

'At last, my dear!' said the countess. 'Why the finery? What is it for? . . . For whose benefit? . . . And what is the weather like? Windy, isn't it?'

'No, your ladyship,' the footman answered, 'there is no wind at all.'

'You say anything that comes into your head! Open the window. Just as I thought: there is a wind, and a very cold one too! Dismiss the carriage. Lise, my child, we won't go out – you need not have dressed up after all.'

'And this is my life!' Lizaveta Ivanovna thought to herself.

Indeed, Lizaveta Ivanovna was a most unfortunate creature. 'Another's bread is bitter to the taste,' says Dante, 'and his staircase hard to climb'; and who should know the bitterness of dependence better than a poor orphan brought up by an old lady of quality? The countess was certainly not bad-hearted but she had all the caprices of a woman spoiled by society, she was stingy and coldly selfish, like all old people who have done with love and are out of touch with life around them. She took part in all the vanities of the fashionable world, dragged herself to balls, where she sat in a corner, rouged and attired after some bygone mode, like a misshapen but indispensable ornament of the ballroom. On their arrival the guests all went up to her and bowed low, as though in accordance with an old-established rite, and after that no one took any more notice of her. She received the whole town at her house, observing the strictest etiquette and not recognizing the faces of any of her guests. Her numerous servants, grown fat and grey in her entrance hall and the maids' quarters, did what they liked and vied with each other in robbing the decrepit old woman. Lizaveta Ivanovna was the household martyr. She poured out tea and was reprimanded for using too much sugar; she read novels aloud to the countess and was blamed for all the author's mistakes; she accompanied the countess on her drives and was answerable for the weather and the state of the roads. She was supposed to receive a salary, which was never paid in full and yet she was expected to be as well dressed as everyone else – that is, as very few indeed. In society she played the most pitiable role. Everybody knew her and nobody gave her any thought. At balls she danced only when someone was short of a partner, and the ladies would take her by the arm each time they wanted to go to the cloakroom to rearrange some detail of their toilette. She was sensitive and felt her position keenly, and looked about impatiently for a deliverer to come; but the young men, calculating in their empty-headed frivolity, honoured her with scant attention though Lizaveta Ivanovna was a hundred times more charming than the cold, brazen-faced heiresses they ran after. Many a time she crept away from the tedious, glittering drawing-room to go and weep in her humble little attic with its wallpaper screen, chest of drawers, small looking-glass and painted wooden bedstead, and where a tallow-candle burned dimly in a brass candlestick.

One morning, two days after the card party described at the beginning of this story and a week before the scene we have just witnessed – one morning Lizaveta Ivanovna, sitting at her embroidery-frame by the window, happened to glance out into the street and see a young Engineers officer standing stock-still gazing at her window. She lowered her head and went on with her work. Five minutes afterwards she looked out again – the young officer was still on the same spot. Not being in the habit of coquetting with passing officers, she looked out no more and went on sewing for a couple of hours without raising her head. Luncheon was announced. She got up to put away her embroidery-frame and, glancing casually into the street, saw the officer again. This seemed to her somewhat strange. After luncheon she went to the window with a certain feeling of uneasiness, but the officer was no longer there, and she forgot about him . . .

A day or so later, just as she was stepping into the carriage with the countess, she saw him again. He was standing right by the front door, his face hidden by his beaver collar; his dark eyes sparkled beneath his fur cap. Lizaveta Ivanovna felt alarmed, though she did not know why, and seated herself in the carriage, inexplicably agitated.

On returning home she ran to the window – the officer was standing in his accustomed place, his eyes fixed on her. She drew back, consumed with curiosity and excited by a feeling quite new to her.

Since then not a day had passed without the young man appearing at a certain hour beneath the windows of their house, and between him and her a sort of mute acquaintance was established. Sitting at her work she would sense his approach, and lifting her head she looked at him longer and longer every day. The young man seemed to be grateful to her for looking out: with the keen eyes of youth she saw the quick flush of his pale cheeks every time their glances met. By the end of a week she had smiled at him . . .

When Tomsky asked the countess's permission to introduce a friend of his the poor girl's heart beat violently. But hearing that Narumov was in the Horse Guards, not the Engineers, she regretted the indiscreet question by which she had betrayed her secret to the irresponsible Tomsky.

Hermann was the son of a German who had settled in Russia and who left him some small capital sum. Being firmly convinced that it was essential for him to make certain of his independence, Hermann did not touch even the interest on his income but lived on his pay, denying himself the slightest extravagance. But since he was reserved and ambitious his companions rarely had any opportunity for making fun of his extreme parsimony. He had strong passions and an ardent imagination, but strength of character preserved him from the customary mistakes of youth. Thus, for instance, though a gambler at heart he never touched cards, having decided that his means did not allow him (as he put it) 'to risk the necessary in the hope of acquiring the superfluous'. And yet he spent night after night at the card tables, watching with feverish anxiety the vicissitudes of the game.

The story of the three cards had made a powerful impression upon his imagination and it haunted his mind all night. 'Supposing,' he thought to himself the following evening as he wandered about Petersburg, 'supposing the old countess were to reveal her secret to me? Or tell me the three winning cards! Why shouldn't I try my luck? . . . Get introduced to her, win her favour – become her lover, perhaps. But all that would take time, and she is eighty-seven. She might be dead next week, or the day after tomorrow even! . . . And the story itself? Is it likely? No, economy, moderation and hard work are my three winning cards. With them I can treble my capital – increase it sevenfold and obtain for myself leisure and independence!' Musing thus, he found himself in one of the main streets of Petersburg, in front of a house of old-fashioned architecture. The street was lined with carriages which followed one another up to the lighted porch. Out of the carriages stepped now the shapely little foot of a young beauty, now a military boot with clinking spur, or a diplomat's striped stockings and buckled shoes. Fur coats and cloaks passed in rapid procession before the majestic-looking concierge. Hermann stopped.

'Whose house is that?' he asked a watchman in his box at the corner.

'The Countess X's,' the man told him. It was Tomsky's grandmother.

Hermann started. The strange story of the three cards came into his mind again. He began walking up and down past the house, thinking of its owner and her wonderful secret. It was late when he returned to his humble lodgings; he could not get to sleep for a long time, and when sleep did come he dreamed of cards, a green baize table, stacks of bank-notes and piles of gold. He played card after card, resolutely turning down the corners, winning all the time. He raked in the gold and stuffed his pockets with bank-notes. Waking late in the morning, he sighed over the loss of his fantastic wealth, and then, sallying forth to wander about the town again, once more found himself outside the countess's house. It was as though some supernatural force drew him there. He stopped and looked up at the windows. In one of them he saw a dark head bent over a book or some needlework. The head was raised. Hermann caught sight of a rosy face and a pair of black eyes. That moment decided his fate.

*

3

Vous m'écrivez, mon ange, des lettres de quatre pages plus vite que je ne puis les lire.

FROM A CORRESPONDENCE

Lizaveta Ivanovna had scarcely taken off her hat and mantle before the countess sent for her and again ordered the carriage. They went out to take their seats. Just as the two footmen were lifting the old lady and helping her through the carriage door Lizaveta Ivanovna saw her Engineers officer standing by the wheel. He seized her hand; before she had recovered from her alarm the young man had disappeared, leaving a letter between her fingers. She hid it in her glove, and for the rest of the drive neither saw nor heard anything. It was the countess's habit when they were out in the carriage to ask a constant stream of questions: 'Who was that we met?' – 'What bridge is this?' – 'What does that signboard say?' This time Lizaveta Ivanovna returned such random and irrelevant answers that the countess grew angry with her.

'What is the matter with you, my dear? Have you taken leave of your senses? Don't you hear me or understand what I say? . . . I speak distinctly enough, thank heaven, and am not in my dotage yet!'

Lizaveta Ivanovna paid no attention to her. When they returned home she ran up to her room and drew the letter out of her glove: it was unsealed. She read it. The letter contained a declaration of love: it was tender, respectful and had been copied word for word from a German novel. But Lizaveta Ivanovna did not know any German and she was delighted with it.

For all that, the letter troubled her greatly. For the first time in her life she was embarking upon secret and intimate relations with a young man. His boldness appalled her. She reproached herself for her imprudent behaviour, and did not know what to do: ought she to give up sitting at the window and by a show of indifference damp the young man's inclination to pursue her further? Should she return his letter to him? Or answer it coldly and firmly? There was nobody to whom she could turn for advice: she had neither female friend nor preceptor. Lizaveta Ivanovna decided to reply to the letter.

She sat down at her little writing-table, took pen and paper – and began to ponder. Several times she made a start and then tore the paper across: what she had written seemed to her either too indulgent or too harsh. At last she succeeded in composing a few lines with which she felt satisfied

'I am sure,' she wrote, 'that your intentions are honourable and that you had no wish to hurt me by any thoughtless conduct; but our acquaintance ought not to have begun in this manner. I return you your letter, and hope that in future I shall have no cause to complain of being shown a lack of respect which is undeserved.'

Next day, as soon as she saw Hermann approaching, Lizaveta Ivanovna got up from her embroidery-frame, went into the drawing-room, opened the little ventilating window and threw the letter into the street, trusting to the young officer's alertness. Hermann ran forward, picked the letter up and went into a confectioner's shop. Breaking the seal, he found his own letter and Lizaveta Ivanovna's reply. It was just what he had expected and he returned home engrossed in his plot.

Three days after this a sharp-eyed young person brought Lizaveta Ivanovna a note from a milliner's establishment. Lizaveta Ivanovna opened it uneasily, fearing it was a demand for money, and suddenly recognized Hermann's handwriting.

'You have made a mistake, my dear,' she said. 'This note is not for me.'

'Oh yes it is for you!' retorted the girl boldly, not troubling to conceal a knowing smile. 'Please read it.'

Lizaveta Ivanovna glanced at the letter. In it Hermann wanted her to meet him.

'Impossible!' she cried, alarmed at the request, at its coming so soon, and at the means employed to transmit it. 'I am sure this was not addressed to me.' And she tore the letter into fragments.

'If the letter was not for you, why did you tear it up?' said the girl. 'I would have returned it to the sender.'

'Be good enough, my dear,' said Lizaveta Ivanovna, flushing crimson at her remark, 'not to bring me any more letters. And tell the person who sent you that he ought to be ashamed . . .'

But Hermann did not give in. Every day Lizaveta Ivanovna received a letter from him by one means or another. They were no longer translated from the German. Hermann wrote them inspired by passion and in a style which was his own: they reflected both his inexorable desire and the disorder of an unbridled imagination. Lizaveta Ivanovna no longer thought of returning them: she drank them in eagerly and took to answering – and the notes she sent grew longer and more affectionate every hour. At last she threw out of the window to him the following letter:

There is a ball tonight at the Embassy. The countess will be there. We shall stay until about two o'clock. Here is an opportunity for you to see me alone. As soon as the countess is away the servants are sure to go to their quarters, leaving the concierge in the hall, but he usually retires to his lodge. Come at half past eleven. Walk straight up the stairs. If you meet anyone in the ante-room, ask if the countess is at home. They will say 'No,' but there will be no help for it – you will have to go away. But probably you will not meet anyone. The maids all sit together in the one room. Turn to the left out of the ante-room and keep straight on until you reach the countess's bedroom. In the bedroom, behind a screen, you will find two small doors: the one on the right leads into the study where the countess never goes; and the other on the left opens into a passage with a narrow winding staircase up to my room.

Hermann waited for the appointed hour like a tiger trembling for its prey. By ten o'clock in the evening he was already standing outside the countess's house. It was a frightful night: the wind howled, wet snow fell in big flakes; the street lamps burned dimly; the streets were deserted. From time to time a sledge drawn by a sorry-looking hack passed by, the driver on the watch for a belated fare. Hermann stood there without his great-coat, feeling neither the wind nor the snow. At last the countess's carriage was brought round. Hermann saw the old woman wrapped in sables being lifted into the vehicle by two footmen; then Liza in a light cloak, with natural flowers in her hair, flitted by. The carriage doors banged. The vehicle rolled heavily over the wet snow. The concierge closed the street-door. The lights in the windows went out. Hermann started to walk to and fro outside the deserted house; he went up to a street-lamp and glanced at his watch: it was twenty minutes past eleven. He stood still by the lamp-post, his eyes fixed on the hand of the watch. Precisely at half past eleven Hermann walked up the steps of the house and entered the brightly lit vestibule. The concierge was not there. Hermann ran up the stairs, opened the door of the ante-room and saw a footman asleep in a soiled, old-fashioned armchair by the side of a lamp. With a light, firm tread Hermann passed quickly by him. The ballroom and drawing-room were in darkness but the lamp in the ante-room shed a dim light into them. Hermann entered the bedroom. Ancient icons filled the icon-stand before which burned a golden lamp. Armchairs upholstered in faded damask and sofas with down cushions, the tassels of which had lost their gilt, were ranged with depressing symmetry round the walls hung with Chinese wallpaper. On one of the walls were two portraits painted in Paris by Madame Lebrun: the first of a stout, red-faced man of some forty years of age, in a light-green uniform with a star on his breast; the other – a beautiful young woman with an aquiline nose and a rose in the powdered hair drawn back over her temples. Every corner was crowded with porcelain shepherdesses, clocks made by the celebrated Leroy, little boxes, roulettes, fans and all the thousand and one playthings invented for ladies of fashion at the end of the last century together with Montgolfier's balloon and Mesmer's magnetism. Hermann stepped behind the screen. A small iron bedstead stood there; to the right was the door into the study – to the left, the other door into the passage. Hermann opened it and saw the narrow winding staircase leading to poor little Liza's room. But he turned about and went into the dark study.

The time passed slowly. Everything was quiet. The drawing-room clock struck twelve; the clocks in the other rooms chimed twelve, one after the other, and all was still again. Hermann stood leaning against the cold stove. He was quite calm: his heart beat evenly, like that of a man resolved upon a dangerous but inevitable undertaking. The clocks struck one, and then two, and he heard the distant rumble of a carriage. In spite of himself he was overcome with agitation. The carriage drove up to the house and stopped. He heard the clatter of the carriage-steps being lowered. In the house all was commotion. Servants ran to and fro, there was a confusion of voices, and lights appeared everywhere. Three ancient lady's maids bustled into the bedroom, followed by the countess who, half dead with fatigue, sank into a Voltaire armchair. Hermann watched through a crack in the door. Lizaveta Ivanovna passed close by him and he heard her footsteps hurrying up the stairs to her room. For a moment something akin to remorse assailed him but he quickly hardened his heart again.

The countess began undressing before the looking-glass. Her maids took off the cap trimmed with roses and lifted the powdered wig from her grey, closed-cropped head. Pins showered about her. The silver-trimmed yellow dress fell at her puffy feet. Hermann witnessed the hideous mysteries of her toilet; at last the countess put on bed jacket and night-cap, and in this attire, more suited to her age, she seemed less horrible and ugly.

Like most old people the countess suffered from sleeplessness. Having undressed, she sat down in a big armchair by the window and dismissed her maids. They took away the candles, leaving only the lamp before the icons to light the room. The countess sat there, her skin sallow with age, her flabby lips twitching, her body swaying to and fro. Her dim eyes were completely vacant and looking at her one might have imagined that the dreadful old woman was rocking her body not from choice but owing to some secret galvanic mechanism.

Suddenly an inexplicable change came over the deathlike face. The lips ceased to move, the eyes brightened: before the countess stood a strange young man.

'Do not be alarmed, for heaven's sake, do not be alarmed!' he said in a low, clear voice. 'I have no intention of doing you any harm, I have come to beg a favour of you.'

The old woman stared at him in silence, as if she had not heard. Hermann thought she must be deaf and bending down to her ear he repeated what he had just said. The old woman remained silent as before.

'You can ensure the happiness of my whole life,' Hermann went on, 'and at no cost to yourself. I know that you can name three cards in succession . . .'

Hermann stopped. The countess appeared to have grasped what he wanted and to be seeking words to frame her answer.

'It was a joke,' she said at last. 'I swear to you it was a joke.'

'No, madam,' Hermann retorted angrily. 'Remember Tchaplitsky, and how you enabled him to win back his loss.'

The countess was plainly perturbed. Her face expressed profound agitation; but soon she relapsed into her former impassivity.

'Can you not tell me those three winning cards?' Hermann went on.

The countess said nothing. Hermann continued:

'For whom would you keep your secret? For your grandsons? They are rich enough already: they don't appreciate the value of money. Your three cards would not help a spendthrift. A man who does not take care of his inheritance will die a beggar though all the demons of the world were at his command. I am not a spendthrift: I know the value of money. Your three cards would not be wasted on me. Well? . . .'

He paused, feverishly waiting for her reply. She was silent. Hermann fell on his knees.

'If your heart has ever known what it is to love, if you can remember the ecstasies of love, if you have ever smiled tenderly at the cry of your new-born son, if any human feeling has ever stirred in your breast, I appeal to you as wife, beloved one, mother – I implore you by all that is holy in life not to reject my prayer: tell me your secret. Of what use is it to you? Perhaps it is bound up with some terrible sin, with the loss of eternal salvation, with some bargain with the devil . . . Reflect – you are old: you have not much longer to live, and I am ready to take your sin upon my soul. Only tell me your secret. Remember that a man's happiness is in your hands; that not only I, but my children and my children's children will bless your memory and hold it sacred . . .'

The old woman answered not a word.

Hermann rose to his feet.

'You old hag!' he said, grinding his teeth. 'Then I will make you speak . . .'

With these words he drew a pistol from his pocket. At the sight of the pistol the countess for the second time showed signs of agitation. Her head shook and she raised a hand as though to protect herself from the shot . . . Then she fell back . . . and was still.

'Come, an end to this childish nonsense!' said Hermann, seizing her by the arm. 'I ask you for the last time – will you tell me those three cards? Yes or no?'

The countess made no answer. Hermann saw that she was dead.

4

7 mai 18—

Homme sans moeurs et sans religion!

FROM A CORRESPONDENCE

Lizaveta Ivanovna was sitting in her room, still in her ball dress, lost in thought. On returning home she had made haste to dismiss the sleepy maid who reluctantly offered to help her, saying that she would undress herself, and with trembling heart had gone to her own room, expecting to find Hermann and hoping that she would not find him. A glance convinced her he was not there, and she thanked fate for having prevented their meeting. She sat down without undressing and began to recall the circumstances that had led her so far in so short a time. It was not three weeks since she had first caught sight of the young man from the window – and yet she was carrying on a correspondence with him, and he had already succeeded in inducing her to agree to a nocturnal tryst! She knew his name only because he had signed some of his letters; she had never spoken to him, did not know the sound of his voice, had never heard him mentioned . . . until that evening. Strange to say, that very evening at the ball, Tomsky, piqued with the young Princess Pauline for flirting with somebody else instead of with him as she usually did, decided to revenge himself by a show of indifference. He asked Lizaveta Ivanovna to be his partner and danced the interminable mazurka with her. And all the time he kept teasing her about her partiality for officers of the Engineers, assuring her that he knew far more than she could suppose, and some of his sallies so found their mark that several times Lizaveta Ivanovna thought he must know her secret.

'Who told you all this?' she asked, laughing.

'A friend of someone you know,' Tomsky answered, 'a very remarkable person.'

'And who is this remarkable man?'

'His name is Hermann.'

Lizaveta Ivanova said nothing; but her hands and feet turned to ice.

'This Hermann,' continued Tomsky, 'is a truly romantic figure: he has the profile of a Napoleon and the soul of a Mephistopheles. I think there must be at least three crimes on his conscience. How pale you look!'

'I have a bad headache . . . Well, and what did this Hermann – or whatever his name is – tell you?'

'Hermann is very annoyed with his friend: he says that in his place he would act quite differently . . . I suspect in fact that Hermann has designs upon you himself; at any rate he listens to his friend's ecstatic exclamations with anything but indifference.'

'But where has he seen me?'

'In church, perhaps, or when you were out walking . . . heaven only knows! – in your own room maybe, while you were asleep, for there is nothing he –'

Three ladies coming up to invite Tomsky to choose between *'oubli ou regret?'* interrupted the conversation which had become so painfully interesting to Lizaveta Ivanovna.

The lady chosen by Tomsky was the Princess Pauline herself. She succeeded in effecting a reconciliation with him while they danced an extra turn and spun round once more before she was conducted to her chair. When he returned to his place neither Hermann nor Lizaveta Ivanovna was in Tomsky's thoughts. Lizaveta Ivanovna longed to resume the interrupted conversation but the mazurka came to an end and shortly afterwards the old countess took her departure.

Tomsky's words were nothing more than the usual smalltalk of the ballroom; but they sank deep into the girl's romantic heart. The portrait sketched by Tomsky resembled the picture she had herself drawn, and thanks to the novels of the day the commonplace figure both terrified and fascinated her. She sat there with her bare arms crossed and with her head, still adorned with flowers, sunk upon her naked bosom . . . Suddenly the door opened and Hermann came in . . . She shuddered.

'Where were you?' she asked in a frightened whisper.

'In the countess's bedroom,' Hermann answered. 'I have just left her. The countess is dead.'

'Merciful heavens! . . . what are you saying?'

'And I think,' added Hermann, 'that I am the cause of her death.'

Lizaveta darted a glance at him, and heard Tomsky's words echo in her soul: '. . . there must be at least three crimes on his conscience'. Hermann sat down in the window beside her and related all that had happened.

Lizaveta Ivanovna listened to him aghast. So all those passionate letters, those ardent pleas, the bold, determined pursuit had not been inspired by love! Money! – that was what his soul craved! It was not she who could satisfy his desires and make him happy! Poor child, she had been nothing but the blind tool of a thief, of the murderer of her aged benefactress! . . . She wept bitterly in a vain agony of repentance. Hermann watched in silence: he too was suffering torment; but neither the poor girl's tears nor her indescribable charm in her grief touched his hardened soul. He felt no pricking of conscience at the thought of the dead old woman. One thing only horrified him: the irreparable loss of the secret which was to have brought him wealth.

'You are a monster!' said Lizaveta Ivanovna at last.

'I did not mean her to die,' Hermann answered. 'My pistol was not loaded.'

Both were silent.

Morning came. Lizaveta Ivanovna blew out the candle which had burned down. A pale light illumined the room. She wiped her tear-stained eyes and looked up at Hermann: he was sitting on the window-sill with his arms folded, a menacing frown on his face. In this attitude he bore a remarkable likeness to the portrait of Napoleon. The likeness struck even Lizaveta Ivanovna.

'How shall I get you out of the house?' she said at last. 'I had thought of taking you down the street staircase but that means going through the bedroom, and I am afraid.'

'Tell me how to find this secret staircase – I will go alone.'

Lizaveta rose, took a key from the chest of drawers and gave it to Hermann with precise instructions. Hermann pressed her cold, unresponsive hand, kissed her bowed head and left her.

He walked down the winding stairway and entered the countess's bedroom again. The dead woman sat as though turned to stone. Her face wore a look of profound tranquillity. Hermann stood in front of her and gazed long and earnestly at her, as though trying to convince himself of the terrible truth. Then he went into the study, felt behind the tapestry for the door and began to descend the dark stairway, excited by strange emotions. 'Maybe some sixty years ago, at this very hour,' he thought, 'some happy youth – long since turned to dust – was stealing up this staircase into that very bedroom, in an embroidered tunic, his hair dressed *à l'oiseau royal*, pressing his three-cornered hat to his breast; and today the heart of his aged mistress has ceased to beat . . .'

At the bottom of the stairs Hermann saw a door which he opened with the same key, and found himself in a passage leading to the street.

5

That night the dead Baroness von W. appeared before me. She was all in white and said: 'How do you do, Mr Councillor?'

SWEDENBORG

Three days after that fatal night, at nine o'clock in the morning, Hermann repaired to the Convent of****, where the last respects were to be paid to the mortal remains of the dead countess. Though he felt no remorse he could not altogether stifle the voice of conscience which kept repeating to him: 'You are the old woman's murderer!' Having very little religious faith, he was exceedingly superstitious. Believing that the dead countess might exercise a malignant influence on his life, he decided to go to her funeral to beg and obtain her forgiveness.

The church was full. Hermann had difficulty in making his way through the crowd. The coffin rested on a rich catafalque beneath a canopy of velvet. The dead woman lay with her hands crossed on her breast, in a lace cap and a white satin robe. Around the bier stood the members of her household: servants in black clothes, with armorial ribbons on their shoulders and lighted candles in their hands; relatives in deep mourning – children, grandchildren and great-grandchildren. No one wept: tears would have been *une affectation*. The countess was so old that her death could not have taken anybody by surprise, and her family had long ceased to think of her as one of the living. A famous preacher delivered the funeral oration. In simple and touching phrases he described the peaceful passing of the saintly woman whose long life had been a quiet, touching preparation for a Christian end. 'The angel of death,' he declared, 'found her vigilant in devout meditation, awaiting the midnight coming of the bridegroom.' The service was concluded in melancholy decorum. First the relations went forward to bid farewell to the corpse. They were followed by a long procession of all those who had come to render their last homage to one who had for so many years been a participator in their frivolous amusements. After them came the members of the countess's household. The last of these was an old woman-retainer the same age as the deceased.

Two young girls supported her by the arms. She had not strength to prostrate herself – and she was the only one to shed tears as she kissed her mistress's cold hand. Hermann decided to approach the coffin after her. He knelt down on the cold stone strewed with branches of spruce-fir, and remained in that position for some minutes; at last he rose to his feet and, pale as the deceased herself, walked up the steps of the catafalque and bent over the corpse . . . At that moment it seemed to him that the dead woman darted a mocking look at him and winked her eye. Hermann drew back, missed his footing and crashed headlong to the floor. They picked him up. At the same time Lizaveta Ivanovna was carried out of the church in a swoon. This incident momentarily upset the solemnity of the mournful rite. There was a dull murmur among the congregation, and a tall thin man in the uniform of a court-chamberlain, a close relative of the deceased, whispered in the ear of an Englishman who was standing near him that the young officer was the natural son of the countess, to which the Englishman coldly replied, 'Oh?'

The whole of that day Hermann was strangely troubled. Repairing to a quiet little tavern to dine, he drank a great deal of wine, contrary to his habit, in the hope of stifling his inner agitation. But the wine only served to excite his imagination. Returning home, he threw himself on his bed without undressing, and fell heavily asleep.

It was night when he woke and the moon was shining into his room. He glanced at the time: it was a quarter to three. Sleep had left him; he sat on the bed and began thinking of the old countess's funeral.

Just then someone in the street looked in at him through the window and immediately walked on. Hermann paid no attention. A moment later he heard the door of his ante-room open. Hermann thought it was his orderly, drunk as usual, returning from some nocturnal excursion, but presently he heard an unfamiliar footstep: someone was softly shuffling along the floor in slippers. The door opened and a woman in white came in. Hermann mistook her for his old nurse and wondered what could have brought her at such an hour. But the woman in white glided across the room and stood before him – and Hermann recognized the countess!

'I have come to you against my will,' she said in a firm voice: 'but I am commanded to grant your request. The three, the seven and the ace will win for you if you play them in succession, provided that you do not stake more than one card in twenty-four hours and never play again as long as you live. I forgive you my death, on condition that you marry my ward, Lizaveta Ivanovna.'

With these words she turned softly, rustled to the door in her slippers, and disappeared. Hermann heard the street-door click and again saw someone peeping in at him through the window.

It was a long time before he could pull himself together and go into the next room. His orderly was asleep on the floor: Hermann had difficulty in waking him. The man was drunk as usual: there was no getting any sense out of him. The street-door was locked. Hermann returned to his room and, lighting a candle, wrote down all the details of his vision.

6

> 'Attendez!'
> 'How dare you say 'Attendez!' to me?'
> 'Your Excellency, I said "Attendez," sir.'

Two *idées fixes* cannot co-exist in the moral world any more than two physical bodies can occupy one and the same space. 'The three, the seven, the ace' soon drove all thought of the dead woman from Hermann's mind. 'Three, seven, ace' were perpetually in his head and on his lips. If he saw a young girl he would say, 'How graceful she is! A regular three of hearts!' Asked the time, he would reply, 'Five minutes to seven.' Every stout man reminded him of the ace. 'Three, seven, ace' haunted his dreams, assuming all sorts of shapes. The three blossomed before him like a luxuriant flower, the seven took the form of a Gothic portal, and aces became gigantic spiders. His whole attention was focused on one thought: how to make use of the secret which had cost him so dear. He began to consider resigning his commission in order to go and travel abroad. In the public gambling-houses in Paris he would compel fortune to give him his magical treasure. Chance spared him the trouble.

A circle of wealthy gamblers existed in Moscow, presided over by the celebrated Tchekalinsky, who had spent his life at the card-table and amassed millions, accepting promissory notes when he won and paying his losses in ready money. His long experience inspired the confidence of his fellow-players, while his open house, his famous chef and his gay and friendly manner secured for him the general respect of the public. He came to Petersburg. The young men of the capital flocked to his rooms, forsaking balls for cards and preferring the excitement of gambling to the seductions of flirting. Narumov brought Hermann to him.

They passed through a succession of magnificent rooms full of attentive servants. The place was crowded. Several generals and privy councillors were playing whist; young men smoking long pipes lounged about on sofas upholstered in damask. In the drawing-room some twenty gamblers jostled round a long table at which the master of the house was keeping bank. Tchekalinsky was a man of about sixty years of age and most dignified appearance; he had silvery-grey hair, a full, florid face with a kindly expression, and sparkling eyes which were always smiling. Narumov introduced Hermann. Shaking hands cordially, Tchekalinsky requested him not to stand on ceremony, and went on dealing.

The game continued for some while. On the table lay more than thirty cards. Tchekalinsky paused after each round to give the players time to arrange their cards and note their losses, listened courteously to their observations and more courteously still straightened the corner of a card that some careless hand had turned down. At last the game finished. Tchekalinsky shuffled the cards and prepared to deal again.

'Will you allow me to take a card?' said Hermann, stretching out his hand from behind a stout gentleman who was punting.

Tchekalinsky smiled and bowed graciously, in silent token of consent. Narumov laughingly congratulated Hermann on breaking his long abstention from cards and wished him a lucky start.

'There!' said Hermann, chalking some figures on the back of his card.

'How much?' asked the banker, screwing up his eyes. 'Excuse me, I cannot see.'

'Forty-seven thousand,' Hermann answered.

At these words every head was turned in a flash, and all eyes were fixed on Hermann.

'He has taken leave of his senses!' thought Narumov.

'Allow me to point out to you,' said Tchekalinsky with his unfailing smile, 'that you are playing rather high: nobody here has ever staked more than two hundred and seventy-five at a time.'

'Well?' returned Hermann. 'Do you accept my card or not?'

Tchekalinsky bowed with the same air of humble acquiescence.

'I only wanted to observe,' he said, 'that, being honoured with the confidence of my friends, I can only play against ready money. For my own part, of course, I am perfectly sure that your word is sufficient but for the sake of the rules of the game and our accounts I must request you to place the money on your card.'

Hermann took a bank-note from his pocket and handed it to Tchekalinsky, who after a cursory glance placed it on Hermann's card. He began to deal. On the right a nine turned up, and on the left a three.

'I win!' said Hermann, pointing to his card.

There was a murmur of astonishment among the company. Tchekalinsky frowned, but the smile quickly reappeared on his face.

'Would you like me to settle now?' he asked Hermann.

'If you please.'

Tchekalinsky took a number of bank-notes out of his pocket and paid there and then. Hermann picked up his money and left the table. Narumov could not believe his eyes. Hermann drank a glass of lemonade and departed home.

The following evening he appeared at Tchekalinsky's again. The host was dealing. Hermann walked up to the table; the players immediately made room for him. Tchekalinsky bowed graciously. Hermann waited for the next deal, took a card and placed on it his original forty-seven thousand together with his winnings of the day before. Tchekalinsky began to deal. A knave turned up on the right, a seven on the left.

Hermann showed his seven.

There was a general exclamation. Tchekalinsky was obviously disconcerted. He counted out ninety-four thousand and handed them to Hermann, who pocketed them in the coolest manner and instantly withdrew.

The next evening Hermann again made his appearance at the table. Everyone was expecting him; the generals and privy councillors left their whist to watch such extraordinary play. The young officers leaped up from their sofas and all the waiters collected in the drawing-room. Everyone pressed round Hermann. The other players left off punting, impatient to see what would happen. Hermann stood at the table, prepared to play alone against Tchekalinsky, who was pale but still smiling. Each broke the seal of a pack of cards. Tchekalinsky shuffled. Hermann took a card and covered it with a pile of bank-notes. It was like a duel. Deep silence reigned in the room.

Tchekalinsky began dealing; his hands trembled. A queen fell on the right, an ace on the left.

'Ace wins!' said Hermann, and showed his card.

'Your queen has lost,' said Tchekalinsky gently.

Hermann started: indeed, instead of an ace there lay before him the queen of spades. He could not believe his eyes or think how he could have made such a mistake.

At that moment it seemed to him that the queen of spades opened and closed her eye, and mocked him with a smile. He was struck by the extraordinary resemblance . . .

'The old woman!' he cried in terror.

Tchekalinsky gathered up his winnings. Hermann stood rooted to the spot. When he left the table everyone began talking at once.

'A fine game, that!' said the players.

Tchekalinsky shuffled the cards afresh and the game resumed as usual.

Conclusion

Hermann went out of his mind. He is now in room number 17 of the Obukhov Hospital. He returns no answer to questions put to him but mutters over and over again, with incredible rapidity: 'Three, seven, ace! Three, seven, queen!'

Lizaveta Ivanovna has married a very pleasant young man; he is in the civil service somewhere and has a good income. He is the son of the old countess's former steward. Lizaveta Ivanovna in her turn is bringing up a poor relative.

And Tomsky, who has been promoted to the rank of captain, has married the Princess Pauline.

The Old Nurse's Story

Elizabeth Gaskell

You know, my dears, that your mother was an orphan, and an only child; and I dare say you have heard that your grandfather was a clergyman up in Westmoreland, where I come from. I was just a girl in the village school, when, one day, your grandmother came in to ask the mistress if there was any scholar there who would do for a nursemaid; and mighty proud I was, I can tell ye, when the mistress called me up, and spoke to my being a good girl at my needle, and a steady honest girl, and one whose parents were very respectable, though they might be poor. I thought I should like nothing better than to serve the pretty young lady, who was blushing as deep as I was, as she spoke of the coming baby, and what I should have to do with it. However, I see you don't care so much for this part of my story, as for what you think is to come, so I'll tell you at once. I was engaged and settled at the parsonage before Miss Rosamond (that was the baby, who is now your mother) was born. To be sure, I had little enough to do with her when she came, for she was never out of her mother's arms, and slept by her all night long; and proud enough was I sometimes when missis trusted her to me. There never was such a baby before or since, though you've all of you been fine enough in your turns; but for sweet, winning ways, you've none of you come up to your mother. She took after her mother, who was a real lady born; a Miss Furnivall, a granddaughter of Lord Furnivall's in Northumberland. I believe she had neither brother nor sister, and had been brought up in my lord's family till she had married your grandfather, who was just a curate, son to a shopkeeper in Carlisle – but a clever, fine gentleman as ever was – and one who was a right-down hard worker in his parish, which was very wide, and scattered all abroad over the Westmoreland Fells. When your mother, little Miss Rosamond, was about four or five years old, both her parents died in a fortnight – one after the other. Ah! that was a sad time. My pretty young mistress and me was looking for another baby, when my master came home from one of his long rides, wet, and tired, and took the fever he died of; and then she never held up her head again, but just lived to see her dead baby; and have it laid on her breast before she sighed away her life. My mistress had asked me, on her death-bed, never to leave Miss Rosamond; but if she had never spoken a word, I would have gone with the little child to the end of the world.

The next thing, and before we had well stilled our sobs, the executors and guardians came to settle the affairs. They were my poor young mistress's own cousin, Lord Furnivall, and Mr Esthwaite, my master's brother, a shopkeeper in Manchester; not so well-to-do then as he was afterwards, and with a large family rising about him. Well! I don't know if it were their settling, or because of a letter my mistress wrote on her death-bed to her cousin, my lord; but somehow it was settled that Miss Rosamond and me were to go to Furnivall Manor House, in Northumberland, and my lord spoke as if it had been her mother's wish that she should live with his family, and as if he had no objections, for that one or two more or less could make no difference in so grand a household. So, though that was not the way in which I should have wished the coming of my bright and pretty pet to have been looked at – who was like a sunbeam in any family, be it never so grand – I was well pleased that all the folks in the Dale should stare and admire, when they heard I was going to be young lady's maid at my Lord Furnivall's at Furnivall Manor.

But I made a mistake in thinking we were to go and live where my lord did. It turned out that the family had left Furnivall Manor House fifty years or more. I could not hear that my poor young mistress had ever been there, though she had been brought up in the family; and I was sorry for that, for I should have liked Miss Rosamond's youth to have passed where her mother's had been.

My lord's gentleman, from whom I asked as many questions as I durst, said that the Manor House was at the foot of the Cumberland Fells, and a very grand place; that an old Miss Furnivall, a great-aunt of my lord's, lived there, with only a few servants; but that it was a very healthy place, and my lord had thought that it would suit Miss Rosamond very well for a few years, and that her being there might perhaps amuse his old aunt.

I was bidden by my lord to have Miss Rosamond's things ready by a certain day. He was a stern proud man, as they say all the Lords Furnivall were; and he never spoke a word more than was necessary. Folk did say he had loved my young mistress, but that, because she knew his father would object, she would never listen to him, and married Mr Esthwaite; but I don't know. He never married at any rate. But he never took much notice of Miss Rosamond; which I thought he might have done if he had cared for her dead mother. He sent his gentleman with us to the Manor House, telling him to join him at Newcastle that same evening; so there was no great length of time for him to make us known to all the strangers before he, too, shook us off; and we were left, two lonely young things (I was not eighteen), in the great old Manor House. It seems like yesterday that we drove there. We had left our own dear parsonage very early, and we had both cried as if our hearts would break, though we were travelling in my lord's carriage, which I thought so much of. And now it was long past noon on a September day, and we stopped to change horses for the last time at a little smoky town, all full of colliers and miners. Miss Rosamond had fallen asleep, but Mr Henry told me to waken her, that she might see the park and the Manor House as we drove up. I thought it rather a pity; but I did what he bade me, for fear he should complain of me to my lord. We had left all signs of a town, or even a village, and were then inside the gates of a large wild park – not like the parks here in the south, but with rocks, and the noise of running water, and gnarled thorn-trees, and old oaks, all white and peeled with age.

The road went up about two miles, and then we saw a great and stately house, with many trees close around it, so close that in some places their branches dragged against the walls when the wind blew; and some hung broken down; for no one seemed to take much charge of the place – to lop the wood, or to keep the moss-covered carriage-way in order. Only in front of the house all was clear. The great oval drive was without a weed; and neither tree nor creeper was allowed to grow over the long, many-win-dowed front; at both sides of which a wing projected, which were each the ends of other side fronts; for the house, although it was so desolate, was even grander than I expected. Behind it rose the Fells, which seemed unenclosed and bare enough; and on the left hand of the house, as you stood facing it, was a little, old-fashioned flower-garden, as I found out afterwards. A door opened out upon it from the west front; it had been scooped out of the thick dark wood for some old Lady Furnivall; but the branches of the great forest trees had grown and overshadowed it again, and there were very few flowers that would live there at that time.

When we drove up to the great front entrance and went into the hall I thought we should be lost – it was so large, and vast, and grand. There was a chandelier all of bronze, hung down from the middle of the ceiling; and

I had never seen one before, and looked at it all in amaze. Then, at one end of the hall, was a great fireplace, as large as the sides of the houses in my country, with massy andirons and dogs to hold the wood; and by it were heavy old-fashioned sofas. At the opposite end of the hall, to the left as you went in – on the western side – was an organ built into the wall, and so large that it filled up the best part of that end. Beyond it, on the same side, was a door; and opposite, on each side of the fireplace, were also doors leading to the east front; but those I never went through as long as I stayed in the house, so I can't tell you what lay beyond.

The afternoon was closing in, and the hall, which had no fire lighted in it, looked dark and gloomy, but we did not stay there a moment. The old servant, who had opened the door for us, bowed to Mr Henry, and took us in through the door at the further side of the great organ, and led us through several smaller halls and passages into the west drawing-room, where he said that Miss Furnivall was sitting. Poor little Miss Rosamond held very tight to me, as if she were scared and lost in that great place, and as for myself, I was not much better. The west drawing-room was very cheerful-looking, with a warm fire in it, and plenty of good, comfortable furniture about. Miss Furnivall was an old lady not far from eighty, I should think, but I do not know. She was thin and tall, and had a face as full of fine wrinkles as if they had been drawn all over it with a needle's point. Her eyes were very watchful, to make up, I suppose, for her being so deaf as to be obliged to use a trumpet. Sitting with her, working at the same great piece of tapestry, was Mrs Stark, her maid and companion, and almost as old as she was. She had lived with Miss Furnivall ever since they both were young, and now she seemed more like a friend than a servant; she looked so cold and grey, and stony, as if she had never loved or cared for anyone; and I don't suppose she did care for anyone, except her mistress; and, owing to the great deafness of the latter, Mrs Stark treated her very much as if she were a child. Mr Henry gave some message from my lord, and then he bowed good-bye to us all – taking no notice of my sweet little Miss Rosamond's outstretched hand – and left us standing there, being looked at by the two old ladies through their spectacles.

I was right glad when they rung for the old footman who had shown us in at first, and told him to take us to our rooms. So we went out of the great drawing-room, and into another sitting-room, and out of that, and then up a great flight of stairs, and along a broad gallery – which was something like a library, having books all down one side, and windows and writing-tables all down the other – till we came to our rooms, which I was not sorry to hear were just over the kitchens; for I began to think I should be lost in that wilderness of a house. There was an old nursery, that had been used for all the little lords and ladies long ago, with a pleasant fire burning in the grate, and the kettle boiling on the hob, and tea-things spread out on the table; and out of that room was the night-nursery, with a little crib for Miss Rosamond close to my bed. And old James called up Dorothy, his wife, to bid us welcome; and both he and she were so hospitable and kind, that by and by Miss Rosamond and me felt quite at home; and by the time tea was over, she was sitting on Dorothy's knee, and chatting away as fast as her little tongue could go. I soon found out that Dorothy was from Westmoreland, and that bound her and me together, as it were; and I would never wish to meet with kinder people than were old James and his wife. James had lived pretty nearly all his life in my lord's family, and thought there was no one so grand as they. He even looked down a little on his wife; because, till he had married her, she had never lived in any but a farmer's household. But he was very fond of her, as well he might be. They had one servant under them, to do all the rough work. Bessy they called her; and she and me, and James and Dorothy, with Miss Furnivall and Mrs Stark, made up the family; always remembering my sweet little Miss Rosamond! I used to wonder what they had done before she came, they thought so much of her now. Kitchen and drawing-room, it was all the same. The hard, sad Miss Furnivall, and the cold Mrs Stark, looked pleased when she came fluttering in like a bird, playing and pranking hither and thither, with a continual murmur, and pretty prattle of gladness. I am sure, they were sorry many a time when she flittered away into the kitchen, though they were too proud to ask her to stay with them, and were a little surprised at her taste; though to be sure, as Mrs Stark said, it was not to be wondered at, remembering what stock her father had come of. The great, old rambling house was a famous place for little Miss Rosamond. She made expeditions all over it, with me at her heels; all, except the east wing, which was never opened, and whither we never thought of going. But in the western and northern part was many a pleasant room; full of things that were curiosities to us, though they might not have been to people who had seen more. The windows were darkened by the sweeping boughs of the trees, and the ivy which had overgrown them: but, in the green gloom, we could manage to see old china jars and carved ivory boxes, and great heavy books, and, above all, the old pictures!

Once, I remember, my darling would have Dorothy go with us to tell us who they all were; for they were all portraits of some of my lord's family, though Dorothy could not tell us the names of every one. We had gone through most of the rooms, when we came to the old state drawing-room over the hall, and there was a picture of Miss Furnivall; or, as she was called in those days, Miss Grace, for she was the younger sister. Such a beauty she must have been! but with such a set, proud look, and such scorn looking out of her handsome eyes, with her eyebrows just a little raised, as if she wondered how anyone could have the impertinence to look at her; and her lip curled at us, as we stood there gazing. She had a dress on, the like of which I had never seen before, but it was all the fashion when she was young: a hat of some soft white stuff like beaver, pulled a little over her brows, and a beautiful plume of feathers sweeping round it on one side; and her gown of blue satin was open in front to a quilted white stomacher.

'Well, to be sure!' said I; when I had gazed my fill. 'Flesh is grass, they do say; but who would have thought that Miss Furnivall had been such an out-and-out beauty, to see her now?'

'Yes,' said Dorothy. 'Folks change sadly. But if what my master's father used to say was true, Miss Furnivall, the elder sister, was handsomer than Miss Grace. Her picture is here somewhere; but, if I show it you, you must never let on, even to James, that you have seen it. Can the little lady hold her tongue, think you?' asked she.

I was not so sure, for she was such a little sweet, bold, open-spoken child, so I set her to hide herself; and then I helped Dorothy to turn a great picture, that leaned with its face towards the wall, and was not hung up as the others were. To be sure, it beat Miss Grace for beauty; and, I think, for scornful pride, too, though in that matter it might be hard to choose. I could have looked at it an hour, but Dorothy seemed half frightened at having shown it to me, and hurried it back again, and bade me run and find Miss Rosamond, for that there were some ugly places about the house, where she should like ill for the child to go. I was a brave, high-spirited girl, and thought little of what the old woman said, for I liked hide-and-seek as well as any child in the parish; so off I ran to find my little one.

As winter drew on, and the days grew shorter, I was sometimes almost certain that I heard a noise as if some one was playing on the great organ in the hall. I did not hear it every evening; but, certainly, I did very often; usually when I was sitting with Miss Rosamond; after I had put her to bed, and keeping quite still and silent in the bedroom. Then I used to hear it booming and swelling away in the distance. The first night, when I went down to my supper, I asked Dorothy who had been playing music, and James said very shortly that I was a gowk to take the wind soughing among the trees for music: but I saw Dorothy look at him very fearfully, and Bessy, the kitchenmaid, said something beneath her breath, and went quite white.

I saw they did not like my question, so I held my peace till I was with Dorothy alone, when I knew I could get a good deal out of her. So, the next day, I watched my time, and I coaxed and asked her who it was that played the organ; for I knew that it was the organ and not the wind well enough, for all I had kept silence before James. But Dorothy had had her lesson, I'll warrant, and never a word could I get from her. So then I tried Bessy, though I had always held my head rather above her, as I was evened to James and Dorothy, and she was little better than their servant. So she said I must never, never tell; and if I ever told, I was never to say *she* had told me; but it was a very strange noise, and she had heard it many a'time, but most of all on winter nights, and before storms; and folks did say, it was the old lord playing on the great organ in the hall, just as he used to do when he was alive, but who the old lord was, or why he played, and why he played on stormy winter evenings in particular, she either could not or would not tell me. Well! I told you I had a brave heart; and I thought it was rather pleasant to have that grand music rolling about the house, let who would be the player; for now it rose above the great gusts of wind, and wailed and triumphed just like a living creature, and then it fell to a softness most complete; only it was always music, and tunes, so it was nonsense to call it the wind. I thought at first that it might be Miss Furnivall who played, unknown to Bessy; but, one day when I was in the hall by myself, I opened the organ and peeped all about it and around it, as I had done to the organ in Crosthwaite Church once before, and I saw it was all broken and destroyed inside, though it looked so brave and fine; and then, though it was noonday, my flesh began to creep a little, and I shut it up, and run away pretty quickly to my own bright nursery; and I did not like hearing the music for some time after that, any more than James and Dorothy did. All this time Miss Rosamond was making herself more and more beloved. The old ladies liked her to dine with them at their early dinner; James stood behind Miss Furnivall's chair, and I behind Miss Rosamond's all in state; and, after dinner, she would play about in a corner of the great drawing-room, as still as any mouse, while Miss Furnivall slept, and I had my dinner in the kitchen. But she was glad enough to come to me in the nursery afterwards; for, as she said, Miss Furnivall was so sad, and Mrs Stark so dull; but she and I were merry enough; and, by-and-by, I got not to care for that weird rolling music, which did one no harm, if we did not know where it came from.

That winter was very cold. In the middle of October the frosts began, and lasted many, many weeks. I remembered, one day at dinner, Miss Furnivall lifted up her sad, heavy eyes, and said to Mrs Stark, 'I am afraid we shall have a terrible winter,' in a strange kind of meaning way. But Mrs Stark pretended not to hear, and talked very loud of something else. My little lady and I did not care for the frost; not we! As long as it was dry we climbed up the steep brows, behind the house, and went up on the Fells, which were bleak, and bare enough, and there we ran races in the fresh, sharp air; and once we came down by a new path that took us past the two old gnarled holly-trees, which grew about halfway down by the east side of the house. But the days grew shorter and shorter; and the old lord, if it was he, played away more and more stormily and sadly on the great organ. One Sunday afternoon – it must have been towards the end of November – I asked Dorothy to take charge of little Missey when she came out of the drawing-room, after Miss Furnivall had had her nap; for it was too cold to take her with me to church, and yet I wanted to go. And Dorothy was glad enough to promise, and was so fond of the child that all seemed well; and Bessy and I set off very briskly, though the sky hung heavy and black over the white earth, as if the night had never fully gone away; and the air, though still, was very biting and keen.

'We shall have a fall of snow,' said Bessy to me. And sure enough, even while we were in church, it came down thick, in great large flakes, so thick it almost darkened the windows. It had stopped snowing before we came out, but it lay soft, thick and deep beneath our feet, as we tramped home. Before we got to the hall the moon rose, and I think it was lighter then – what with the moon, and what with the white dazzling snow – than it had been when we went to church, between two and three o'clock. I have not told you that Miss Furnivall and Mrs Stark never went to church: they used to read the prayers together, in their quiet gloomy way; they seemed to feel the Sunday very long without their tapestry-work to be busy at. So when I went to Dorothy in the kitchen, to fetch Miss Rosamond and take her upstairs with me, I did not much wonder when the old woman told me that the ladies had kept the child with them, and that she had never come to the kitchen, as I had bidden her, when she was tired of behaving pretty in the drawing-room. So I took off my things and went to find her, and bring her to her supper in the nursery. But when I went into the best drawing-room, there sat the two old ladies, very still and quiet, dropping out a word now and then, but looking as if nothing so bright and merry as Miss Rosamond had ever been near them. Still I thought she might be hiding from me; it was one of her pretty ways; and that she had persuaded them to look as if they knew nothing about her; so I went softly peeping under this sofa, and behind that chair, making believe I was sadly frightened at not finding her.

'What's the matter, Hester?' said Mrs Stark, sharply. I don't know if Miss Furnivall had seen me, for, as I told you, she was very deaf, and she sat quite still, idly staring into the fire, with her hopeless face. 'I'm only looking for my little Rosy-Posy,' replied I, still thinking that the child was there, and near me, though I could not see her.

'Miss Rosamond is not here,' said Mrs Stark. 'She went away more than an hour ago to find Dorothy.' And she too turned and went on looking into the fire.

My heart sank at this, and I began to wish I had never left my darling. I went back to Dorothy and told her. James was gone out for the day, but she and me and Bessy took lights and went up into the nursery first, and then we roamed over the great large house, calling and entreating Miss Rosamond to come out of her hiding-place, and not frighten us to death in that way. But there was no answer; no sound.

'Oh!' said I at last 'Can she have got into the east wing and hidden there?'

But Dorothy said it was not possible, for that she herself had never been in there; that the doors were always locked, and my lord's steward had the keys, she believed; at any rate, neither she nor James had ever seen them: so I said I would go back, and see if, after all, she was not hidden in the drawing-room, unknown to the old ladies; and if I found her there, I said, I would whip her well for the fright she had given me; but I never meant to do it. Well, I went back to the west drawing-room, and I told Mrs Stark we could not find her anywhere, and asked for leave to look all about the furniture there, for I thought now, that she might have fallen asleep in some warm hidden corner; but no! we looked, Miss Furnivall got up and looked, trembling all over, and she was nowhere there; then we set off again, everyone in the house, and looked in all the places we had searched before, but we could not find her. Miss Furnivall shivered and shook so much, that Mrs Stark took her back into the warm drawing-room; but not before they had made me promise to bring her to them when she was found. Well-a-day! I began to think she never would be found, when I bethought me to look out into the great front court, all covered with snow. I was upstairs when I looked out; but, it was such clear moonlight, I could see, quite plain, two little footprints, which might be traced from the hall door, and round the corner of the east wing. I don't know how I got down, but I tugged open the great, stiff hall door; and, throwing the skirt of my gown over my head for a cloak, I ran out. I turned the east corner, and there a black shadow fell on the snow; but when I came again into the moonlight, there were the little footmarks going up – up to the Fells. It was bitter cold;

so cold that the air almost took the skin off my face as I ran, but I ran on, crying to think how my poor little darling must be perished, and frightened. I was within sight of the holly-trees when I saw a shepherd coming down the hill, bearing something in his arms wrapped in his maud. He shouted to me, and asked me if I had lost a bairn; and, when I could not speak for crying, he bore towards me, and I saw my wee bairnie lying still, and white, and stiff, in his arms, as if she had been dead. He told me he had been up the Fells to gather in his sheep, before the deep cold of night came on, and that under the holly-trees (black marks on the hillside, where no other bush was for miles around) he had found my little lady – my lamb – my queen – my darling – stiff and cold, in the terrible sleep which is frost-begotten. Oh! the joy, and the tears of having her in my arms once again! for I would not let him carry her; but took her, maud and all, into my own arms, and held her near my own warm neck and heart, and felt the life stealing slowly back again into her little gentle limbs. But she was still insensible when we reached the hall, and I had no breath for speech. We went in by the kitchen door.

'Bring the warming-pan,' said I; and I carried her upstairs and began undressing her by the nursery fire, which Bessy had kept up. I called my little lammie all the sweet and playful names I could think of – even while my eyes were blinded by my tears; and at last, oh! at length she opened her large blue eyes. Then I put her into her warm bed, and sent Dorothy down to tell Miss Furnivall that all was well; and I made up my mind to sit by my darling's bedside the live-long night. She fell away into a soft sleep as soon as her pretty head had touched the pillow, and I watched by her till morning light; when she wakened up bright and clear – or so I thought at first – and, my dears, so I think now.

She said that she had fancied that she should like to go to Dorothy, for that both the old ladies were asleep, and it was very dull in the drawing-room; and that, as she was going through the west lobby, she saw the snow through the high window falling – falling – soft and steady; but she wanted to see it lying pretty and white on the ground; so she made her way into the great hall; and then, going to the window, she saw it bright and soft upon the drive; but while she stood there, she saw a little girl, not so old as she was, 'but so pretty,' said my darling, 'and this little girl beckoned to me to come out; and oh, she was so pretty and so sweet, I could not choose but go.' And then this other little girl had taken her by the hand, and side by side the two had gone round the east corner.

'Now you are a naughty little girl, and telling stories,' said I. 'What would your good mamma, that is in heaven, and never told a story in her life, say to her little Rosamond, if she heard her – and I dare say she does – telling stories!'

'Indeed, Hester,' sobbed out my child, 'I'm telling you true. Indeed I am.'

'Don't tell me!' said I, very stern. 'I tracked you by your footmarks through the snow; there were only yours to be seen: and if you had had a little girl to go hand-in-hand with you up the hill, don't you think the footprints would have gone along with yours?'

'I can't help it, dear, dear Hester,' said she, crying, 'if they did not; I never looked at her feet, but she held my hand fast and tight in her little one, and it was very, very cold. She took me up the Fell-path, up to the holly-trees; and there I saw a lady weeping and crying; but when she saw me, she hushed her weeping, and smiled very proud and grand, and took me on her knee, and began to lull me to sleep; and that's all, Hester – but that is true; and my dear mamma knows it is,' said she, crying. So I thought the child was in a fever, and pretended to believe her, as she went over her story – over and over again, and always the same. At last Dorothy knocked at the door with Miss Rosamond's breakfast; and she told me the old ladies were down in the eating parlour, and that they wanted to speak to me. They had both been into the night-nursery the evening before, but it was after Miss Rosamond was asleep; so they had only looked at her – not asked me any questions.

'I shall catch it,' thought I to myself, as I went along the north gallery. 'And yet,' I thought, taking courage, 'it was in their charge I left her; and it's they that's to blame for letting her steal away unknown and unwatched.' So I went in boldly, and told my story. I told it all to Miss Furnivall, shouting it close to her ear; but when I came to the mention of the other little girl out in the snow, coaxing and tempting her out, and willing her up to the grand and beautiful lady by the holly-tree, she threw her arms up – her old and withered arms – and cried aloud, 'Oh! Heaven, forgive! Have mercy!'

Mrs Stark took hold of her; roughly enough, I thought; but she was past Mrs Stark's management, and spoke to me, in a kind of wild warning and authority.

'Hester! keep her from that child! It will lure her to her death! That evil child! Tell her it is a wicked, naughty child.' Then Mrs Stark hurried me out of the room; where, indeed, I was glad enough to go; but Miss Furnivall kept shrieking out, 'Oh! have mercy! Wilt Thou never forgive! It is many a long year ago –'

I was very uneasy in my mind after that. I durst never leave Miss Rosamond, night or day, for fear lest she might slip off again, after some fancy or other; and all the more, because I thought I could make out that Miss Furnivall was crazy, from the odd ways about her; and I was afraid lest something of the same kind (which might be in the family, you know) hung over my darling. And the great frost never ceased all this time; and, whenever it was a more stormy night than usual, between the gusts, and through the wind, we heard the old lord playing on the great organ. But, old lord or not, wherever Miss Rosamond went, there I followed; for my love for her, pretty helpless orphan, was stronger than my fear for the grand and terrible sound. Besides, it rested with me to keep her cheerful and merry, as beseemed her age. So we played together, and wandered together, here and there, and everywhere; for I never dared to lose sight of her again in that large and rambling house. And so it happened, that one afternoon, not long before Christmas Day, we were playing together on the billiard-table in the great hall (not that we knew the right way of playing, but she liked to roll the smooth ivory balls with her pretty hands, and I liked to do whatever she did); and, by-and-by, without our noticing it, it grew dusk indoors, though it was still light in the open air, and I was thinking of taking her back into the nursery, when, all of a sudden, she cried out:

'Look, Hester! look! there is my poor little girl out in the snow!'

I turned towards the long narrow windows, and there, sure enough, I saw a little girl, less than my Miss Rosamond – dressed all unfit to be out-of-doors such a bitter night – crying, and beating against the window-panes, as if she wanted to be let in. She seemed to sob and wail, till Miss Rosamond could bear it no longer, and was flying to the door to open it, when, all of a sudden, and close upon us, the great organ pealed out so loud and thundering, it fairly made me tremble; and all the more, when I remembered me that, even in the stillness of that dead-cold weather, I had heard no sound of little battering hands upon the window-glass, although the Phantom Child had seemed to put forth all its force; and, although I had seen it wail and cry, no faintest touch of sound had fallen upon my ears. Whether I remembered all this at the very moment, I do not know; the great organ sound had so stunned me into terror; but this I know, I caught up Miss Rosamond before she got the hall-door opened, and clutched her, and carried her away, kicking and screaming into the large bright kitchen, where Dorothy and Agnes were busy with their mince-pies.

'What is the matter with my sweet one?' cried Dorothy, as I bore in Miss Rosamond, who was sobbing as if her heart would break.

'She won't let me open the door for my little girl to come in; and she'll die if she is out on the Fells all night. Cruel, naughty Hester,' she said, slapping me; but she might have struck harder, for I had seen a look of ghastly terror on Dorothy's face, which made my very blood run cold.

'Shut the back-kitchen door fast, and bolt it well,' said she to Bessy. She said no more; she gave me raisins and almonds to quiet Miss Rosamond: but she sobbed about the little girl in the snow, and would not touch any of the good things. I was thankful when she cried herself to sleep in bed. Then I stole down to the kitchen, and told Dorothy I had made up my mind. I would carry my darling back to my father's house in Applethwaite; where, if we lived humbly, we lived at peace. I said I had been frightened enough with the old lord's organ-playing; but now that I had seen for myself this little moaning child, all decked out as no child in the neighbourhood could be, beating and battering to get in, yet always without any sound or noise – with the dark wound on its right shoulder; and that Miss Rosamond had known it again for the phantom that had nearly lured her to her death (which Dorothy knew was true); I would stand it no longer.

I saw Dorothy change colour once or twice. When I had done, she told me she did not think I could take Miss Rosamond with me, for that she was my lord's ward, and I had no right over her; and she asked me, would I leave the child that I was so fond of, just for sounds and sights that could do me no harm; and that they had all had to get used to in their turns? I was all in a hot, trembling passion; and I said it was very well for her to talk, that knew what these sights and noises betokened, and that had, perhaps, had something to do with the Spectre Child while it was alive. And I taunted her so, that she told me all she knew, at last; and then I wished I had never been told, for it only made me more afraid than ever.

She said she had heard the tale from old neighbours, that were alive when she was first married; when folks used to come to the hall sometimes, before it had got such a bad name in the country-side: it might not be true, or it might, what she had been told.

The old lord was Miss Furnivall's father – Miss Grace, as Dorothy called her, for Miss Maude was the elder, and Miss Furnivall by rights. The old lord was eaten up with pride. Such a proud man was never seen or heard of; and his daughters were like him. No one was good enough to wed them, although they had choice enough; for they were the great beauties of their day, as I had seen by their portraits, where they hung in the state drawing-room. But, as the old saying is, 'Pride will have a fall'; and these two haughty beauties fell in love with the same man, and he no better than a foreign musician, whom their father had down from London to play music with him at the Manor House. For, above all things, next to his pride, the old lord loved music. He could play on nearly every instrument that ever was heard of; and it was a strange thing it did not soften him; but he was a fierce dour old man, and had broken his poor wife's heart with his cruelty, they said. He was mad after music, and would pay any money for it. So he got this foreigner to come; who made such beautiful music, that they said the very birds on the trees stopped their singing to listen. And, by degrees, this foreign gentleman got such a hold over the old lord, that nothing would serve him but that he must come every year; and it was he that had the great organ brought from Holland, and built up in the hall, where it stood now. He taught the old lord to play on it; but many and many a time, when Lord Furnivall was thinking of nothing but his fine organ, and his finer music, the dark foreigner was walking abroad in the woods with one of the young ladies; now Miss Maude, and then Miss Grace.

Miss Maude won the day and carried off the prize, such as it was; and he and she were married, all unknown to anyone; and before he made his next yearly visit, she had been confined of a little girl at a farm-house on the Moors, while her father and Miss Grace thought she was away at Doncaster Races. But though she was a wife and a mother, she was not a bit softened, but as haughty and as passionate as ever; and perhaps more so, for she was jealous of Miss Grace, to whom her foreign husband paid a deal of court – by way of blinding her – as he told his wife. But Miss Grace triumphed over Miss Maude, and Miss Maude grew fiercer and fiercer, both with her husband and with her sister; and the former – who could easily shake off what was disagreeable, and hide himself in foreign countries – went away a month before his usual time that summer, and half-threatened that he would never come back again. Meanwhile, the little girl was left at the farm-house, and her mother used to have her horse saddled and gallop wildly over the hills to see her once every week, at the very least – for where she loved, she loved; and where she hated, she hated. And the old lord went on playing – playing on his organ; and the servants thought the sweet music he made had soothed down his awful temper, of which (Dorothy said) some terrible tales could be told. He grew infirm too, and had to walk with a crutch; and his son – that was the present Lord Furnivall's father – was with the army in America, and the other son at sea; so Miss Maude had it pretty much her own way, and she and Miss Grace grew colder and bitterer to each other every day; till at last they hardly ever spoke, except when the old lord was by. The foreign musician came again the next summer, but it was for the last time; for they led him such a life with their jealousy and their passions, that he grew weary, and went away, and never was heard of again. And Miss Maude, who had always meant to have her marriage acknowledged when her father should be dead, was left now a deserted wife – whom nobody knew to have been married – with a child that she dared not own, although she loved it to distraction; living with a father whom she feared, and a sister whom she hated. When the next summer passed over and the dark foreigner never came, both Miss Maude and Miss Grace grew gloomy and sad; they had a haggard look about them, though they looked handsome as ever. But by-and-by Miss Maude brightened; for her father grew more and more infirm, and more than ever carried away by his music; and she and Miss Grace lived almost entirely apart, having separate rooms, the one on the west side, Miss Maude on the east – those very rooms which were now shut up. So she thought she might have her little girl with her, and no one need ever know except those who dared not speak about it, and were bound to believe that it was, as she said, a cottager's child she had taken a fancy to. All this, Dorothy said, was pretty well known; but what came afterwards no one knew, except Miss Grace, and Mrs Stark, who was even then her maid, and much more of a friend to her than ever her sister had been. But the servants supposed, from words that were dropped, that Miss Maude had triumphed over Miss Grace, and told her that all the time the dark foreigner had been mocking her with pretended love – he was her own husband; the colour left Miss Grace's cheek and lips that very day for ever, and she was heard to say many a time that sooner or later she would have her revenge; and Mrs Stark was for ever spying about the east rooms.

One fearful night, just after the New Year had come in, when the snow was lying thick and deep, and the flakes were still falling – fast enough to blind anyone who might be out and abroad – there was a great and violent noise heard, and the old lord's voice above all, cursing and swearing awfully, – and the cries of a little child, – and the proud defiance of a fierce woman, – and the sound of a blow, – and a dead stillness, – and moans and wailings dying away on the hillside! Then the old lord summoned all his servants, and told them, with terrible oaths, and words more terrible, that his daughter had disgraced herself, and that he had turned her out of doors – her, and her child – and that if ever they gave her help, – or food, – or shelter, – he prayed that they might never enter Heaven. And, all the while, Miss Grace stood by him, white and still as any stone; and when he had ended she heaved a great sigh, as much as to say her work was done, and her end was accomplished. But the old lord never touched his organ again, and died within the year; and no wonder! for, on the morrow of that wild and fearful night, the shepherds, coming down the Fell side, found

Miss Maude sitting, all crazy and smiling, under the holly-trees, nursing a dead child – with a terrible mark on its right shoulder. 'But that was not what killed it,' said Dorothy; 'it was the frost and the cold; every wild creature was in its hole, and every beast in its fold, while the child and its mother were turned out to wander on the Fells! And now you know all! and I wonder if you are less frightened now?'

I was more frightened than ever; but I said I was not. I wished Miss Rosamond and myself well out of that dreadful house for ever; but I would not leave her, and I dared not take her away. But oh! how I watched her, and guarded her! We bolted the doors, and shut the window-shutters fast, an hour or more before dark, rather than leave them open five minutes too late. But my little lady still heard the weird child crying and mourning; and not all we could do or say could keep her from wanting to go to her, and let her in from the cruel wind and the snow. All this time, I kept away from Miss Furnivall and Mrs Stark, as much as ever I could; for I feared them – I knew no good could be about them, with their grey hard faces, and their dreamy eyes, looking back into the ghastly years that were gone. But, even in my fear, I had a kind of pity – for Miss Furnivall, at least. Those gone down to the pit can hardly have a more hopeless look than that which was ever on her face. At last I even got so sorry for her – who never said a word but what was quite forced from her – that I prayed for her; and I taught Miss Rosamond to pray for one who had done a deadly sin; but often when she came to those words, she would listen, and start up from her knees, and say, 'I hear my little girl plaining and crying very sad – Oh! let her in, or she will die!'

One night – just after New Year's Day had come at last, and the long winter had taken a turn, as I hoped – I heard the west drawing-room bell ring three times, which was the signal for me. I would not leave Miss Rosamond alone, for all she was asleep – for the old lord had been playing wilder than ever – and I feared lest my darling should waken to hear the spectre child; see her I knew she could not. I had fastened the windows too well for that. So I took her out of her bed and wrapped her up in such outer clothes as were most handy, and carried her down to the drawing-room, where the old ladies sat at their tapestry-work as usual. They looked up when I came in, and Mrs Stark asked, quite astounded, 'Why did I bring Miss Rosamond there, out of her warm bed?' I had begun to whisper, 'Because I was afraid of her being tempted out while I was away, by the wild child in the snow,' when she stopped me short (with a glance at Miss Furnivall), and said Miss Furnivall wanted me to undo some work she had done wrong, and which neither of them could see to unpick. So I laid my pretty dear on the sofa, and sat down on a stool by them, and hardened my heart against them, as I heard the wind rising and howling.

Miss Rosamond slept on sound, for all the wind blew so; and Miss Furnivall said never a word, nor looked round when the gusts shook the windows. All at once she started up to her full height, and put up one hand, as if to bid us listen.

'I hear voices!' said she. 'I heard terrible screams – I hear my father's voice!'

Just at that moment my darling wakened with a sudden start: 'My little girl is crying, oh, how she is crying!' and she tried to get up and go to her, but she got her feet entangled in the blanket, and I caught her up; for my flesh had begun to creep at these noises, which they heard while we could catch no sound. In a minute or two the noises came, and gathered fast, and filled our ears; we, too, heard voices and screams, and no longer heard the winter's wind that raged abroad. Mrs Stark looked at me, and I at her, but we dared not speak. Suddenly Miss Furnivall went towards the door, out into the ante-room, through the west lobby, and opened the door into the great hall. Mrs Stark followed, and I durst not be left, though my heart almost stopped beating for fear. I wrapped my darling tight in my arms, and went out with them. In the hall the screams were louder than ever; they sounded to come from the east wing – nearer and nearer – close on the other side of the locked-up doors – close behind her. Then I noticed that the great bronze chandelier seemed all alight, though the hall was dim, and that a fire was blazing in the vast hearth-place, though it gave no heat; and I shuddered up with terror, and folded my darling closer to me. But as I did so, the east door shook, and she, suddenly struggling to get free from me, cried, 'Hester! I must go! My little girl is there; I hear her; she is coming! Hester, I must go!'

I held her tight with all my strength; with a set will, I held her. If I had died, my hands would have grasped her still, I was so resolved in my mind. Miss Furnivall stood listening, and paid no regard to my darling, who had got down to the ground, and whom I, upon my knees now, was holding with both my arms clasped round her neck; she still striving and crying to get free.

All at once the east door gave way with a thundering crash, as if torn in a violent passion, and there came into that broad and mysterious light, the figure of a tall old man, with grey hair and gleaming eyes. He drove before him, with many a relentless gesture of abhorrence, a stern and beautiful woman, with a little child clinging to her dress.

'Oh Hester! Hester!' cried Miss Rosamond. 'It's the lady! the lady below the holly-trees; and my little girl is with her. Hester! Hester! let me go to her; they are drawing me to them. I feel them – I feel them. I must go!'

Again she was almost convulsed by her efforts to get away; but I held her tighter and tighter, till I feared I should do her a hurt; but rather that than let her go towards those terrible phantoms. They passed along towards the great hall-door, where the winds howled and ravened for their prey; but before they reached that, the lady turned; and I could see that she defied the old man with a fierce and proud defiance; but then she quailed – and then she threw up her arms wildly and piteously to save her child – her little child – from a blow from his uplifted crutch.

And Miss Rosamond was torn as by a power stronger than mine, and writhed in my arms, and sobbed (for by this time the poor darling was growing faint).

'They want me to go with them on to the Fells – they are drawing me to them. Oh, my little girl! I would come, but cruel, wicked Hester holds me very tight.' But when she saw the uplifted crutch she swooned away, and I thanked God for it. Just at this moment – when the tall old man, his hair streaming as in the blast of a furnace, was going to strike the little shrinking child – Miss Furnivall, the old woman by my side, cried out, 'Oh, father! father! spare the little innocent child!' But just then I saw – we all saw – another phantom shape itself, and grow clear out of the blue and misty light that filled the hall; we had not seen her till now, for it was another lady who stood by the old man, with a look of relentless hate and triumphant scorn. That figure was very beautiful to look upon, with a soft white hat drawn down over the proud brows, and a red and curling lip. It was dressed in an open robe of blue satin. I had seen that figure before. It was the likeness of Miss Furnivall in her youth; and the terrible phantoms moved on, regardless of old Miss Furnivall's wild entreaty – and the uplifted crutch fell on the right shoulder of the little child, and the younger sister looked on, stony and deadly serene. But at that moment, the dim lights, and the fire that gave no heat, went out of themselves, and Miss Furnivall lay at our feet stricken down by the palsy – death-stricken.

Yes! she was carried to her bed that night never to rise again. She lay with her face to the wall, muttering low but muttering always: 'Alas! alas! what is done in youth can never be undone in age! What is done in youth can never be undone in age!'

The Open Door

Margaret Oliphant

I took the house of Brentwood on my return from India in 18—, for the temporary accommodation of my family, until I could find a permanent home for them. It had many advantages which made it peculiarly appropriate. It was within reach of Edinburgh, and my boy Roland, whose education had been considerably neglected, could go in and out to school, which was thought to be better for him than either leaving home altogether or staying there always with a tutor. The first of these expedients would have seemed preferable to me, the second commended itself to his mother. The doctor, like a judicious man, took the midway between. 'Put him on his pony, and let him ride into the High School every morning; it will do him all the good in the world,' Dr Simson said; 'and when it is bad weather there is the train.' His mother accepted this solution of the difficulty more easily than I could have hoped; and our pale-faced boy, who had never known anything more invigorating than Simla, began to encounter the brisk breezes of the North in the subdued severity of the month of May. Before the time of the vacation in July we had the satisfaction of seeing him begin to acquire something of the brown and ruddy complexion of his schoolfellows. The English system did not commend itself to Scotland in these days. There was no little Eton at Fettes; nor do I think, if there had been, that a genteel exotic of that class would have tempted either my wife or me. The lad was doubly precious to us, being the only one left us of many; and he was fragile in body, we believed, and deeply sensitive in mind. To keep him at home, and yet to send him to school – to combine the advantages of the two systems – seemed to be everything that could be desired. The two girls also found at Brentwood everything they wanted.

They were near enough to Edinburgh to have masters and lessons as many as they required for completing that never-ending education which the young people seem to require nowadays. Their mother married me when she was younger than Agatha, and I should like to see them improve upon their mother! I myself was then no more than twenty-five – an age at which I see the young fellows now groping about them, with no notion what they are going to do with their lives. However, I suppose every generation has a conceit of itself which elevates it, in its own opinion, above that which comes after it.

Brentwood stands on that fine and wealthy slope of country, one of the richest in Scotland, which lies between the Pentland Hills and the Firth. In clear weather you could see the blue gleam – like a bent bow, embracing the wealthy fields and scattered houses – of the great estuary on one side of you; and on the other the blue heights, not gigantic like those we had been used to, but just high enough for all the glories of the atmosphere, the play of clouds, and sweet reflections which give to a hilly country an interest and a charm which nothing else can emulate. Edinburgh, with its two lesser heights – the Castle and the Calton Hill – its spires and towers piercing through the smoke, and Arthur's Seat lying crouched behind, like a guardian no longer very needful, taking his repose beside the well-beloved charge, which is now, so to speak, able to take care of itself without him – lay at our right hand. From the lawn and the drawing-room windows we could see all these varieties of landscape. The colour was sometimes a little chilly, but sometimes, also, as animated and full of vicissitude as a drama. I was never tired of it. Its colour and freshness revived the eyes which had grown weary of arid plains and blazing skies. It was always cheery, and fresh, and full of repose.

The village of Brentwood lay almost under the house, on the other side of the deep little ravine, down which a stream – which ought to have been a lovely, wild, and frolicsome little river – flowed between its rocks and trees. The river, like so many in that district, had, however, in its earlier life been sacrificed to trade, and was grimy with paper-making. But this did not affect our pleasure in it so much as I have known it to affect other streams. Perhaps our water was more rapid – perhaps less clogged with dirt and refuse. Our side of the dell was charmingly *accidenté*, and clothed with fine trees, through which various paths wound down to the river-side and to the village bridge which crossed the stream. The village lay in the hollow, and climbed, with very prosaic houses, the other side. Village architecture does not flourish in Scotland. The blue slates and the grey stone are sworn foes to the picturesque; and though I do not, for my own part, dislike the interior of an old-fashioned pewed and galleried church, with its little family settlements on all sides, the square box outside, with its bit of a spire like a handle to lift it by, is not an improvement to the landscape. Still, a cluster of houses on differing elevations – with scraps of garden coming in between, a hedgerow with clothes laid out to dry, the opening of a street with its rural sociability, the women at their doors, the slow wagon lumbering along – gives a centre to the landscape. It was cheerful to look at, and convenient in a hundred ways. Within ourselves we had walks in plenty, the glen being always beautiful in all its phases, whether the woods were green in the spring or ruddy in the autumn. In the park which surrounded the house were the ruins of the former mansion of Brentwood, a much smaller and less important house than the solid Georgian edifice which we inhabited. The ruins were picturesque, however, and gave importance to the place. Even we, who were but temporary tenants, felt a vague pride in them, as if they somehow reflected a certain consequence upon ourselves. The old building had the remains of a tower, an indistinguishable mass of mason-work, overgrown with ivy, and the shells of walls attached to this were half filled up with soil. I had never examined it closely, I am ashamed to say. There was a large room, or what had been a large room, with the lower part of the windows still existing, on the principal floor, and underneath other windows, which were perfect, though half filled up with fallen soil, and waving with a wild growth of brambles and chance growths of all kinds. This was the oldest part of all. At a little distance were some very commonplace and disjointed fragments of the building, one of them suggesting a certain pathos by its very commonness and the complete wreck which it showed. This was the end of a low gable, a bit of grey wall, all encrusted with lichens, in which was a common doorway. Probably it had been a servants' entrance, a back door, or opening into what are called 'the offices' in Scotland. No offices remained to be entered – pantry and kitchen had all been swept out of being; but there stood the doorway open and vacant, free to all the winds, to the rabbits, and every wild creature. It struck my eye, the first time I went to Brentwood, like a melancholy comment upon a life that was over. A door that led to nothing – closed once perhaps with anxious care, bolted and guarded, now void of any meaning. It impressed me, I remember, from the first; so perhaps it may be said that my mind was prepared to attach to it an importance which nothing justified.

The summer was a very happy period of repose for us all. The warmth of Indian suns was still in our veins. It seemed to us that we could never have enough of the greenness, the dewiness, the freshness of the northern landscape. Even its mists were pleasant to us, taking all the fever out of us, and pouring in vigour and refreshment. In autumn we followed the fashion of the time, and went away for change which we did not in the least require. It was when the family had settled down for the winter, when the days were short and dark, and the rigorous reign of frost upon us, that the incidents occurred which alone could justify me in intruding upon the world my private affairs. These incidents were, however, of so curious a character, that I hope my inevitable references to my own family and pressing personal interests will meet with a general pardon.

I was absent in London when these events began. In London an old Indian plunges back into the interests with which all his previous life has been associated, and meets old friends at every step. I had been circulating among some half-dozen of these – enjoying the return to my former life in shadow, though I had been so thankful in substance to throw it aside – and had missed some of my home letters, what with going down from Friday to Monday to old Benbow's place in the country, and stopping on the way back to dine and sleep at Sellar's and to take a look into Cross's stables, which occupied another day. It is never safe to miss one's letters. In this transitory life, as the Prayer-book says, how can one ever be certain what is going to happen? All was well at home. I knew exactly (I thought) what they would have to say to me: 'The weather has been so fine, that Roland has not once gone by train, and he enjoys the ride beyond anything.' 'Dear papa, be sure that you don't forget anything, but bring us so-and-so and so-and-so' – a list as long as my arm. Dear girls and dearer mother! I would not for the world have forgotten their commissions, or lost their little letters, for all the Benbows and Crosses in the world.

But I was confident in my home-comfort and peacefulness. When I got back to my club, however, three or four letters were lying for me, upon some of which I noticed the 'immediate', 'urgent', which old-fashioned people and anxious people still believe will influence the post-office and quicken the speed of the mails. I was about to open one of these, when the club porter brought me two telegrams, one of which, he said, had arrived the night before. I opened, as was to be expected, the last first, and this was what I read: 'Why don't you come or answer? For God's sake, come. He is much worse.' This was a thunderbolt to fall upon a man's head who had one only son, and he the light of his eyes! The other telegram, which I opened with hands trembling so much that I lost time by my haste, was to much the same purport: 'No better; doctor afraid of brain-fever. Calls for you day and night. Let nothing detain you.' The first thing I did was to look up the timetables to see if there was any way of getting off sooner than by the night-train, though I knew well enough there was not; and then I read the letters, which furnished, alas! too clearly, all the details. They told me that the boy had been pale for some time, with a scared look. His mother had noticed it before I left home, but would not say anything to alarm me. This look had increased day by day; and soon it was observed that Roland came home at a wild gallop through the park, his pony panting and in foam, himself 'as white as a sheet', but with the perspiration streaming from his forehead. For a long time he had resisted all questioning, but at length had developed such strange changes of mood, showing a reluctance to go to school, a desire to be fetched in the carriage at night – which was a ridiculous piece of luxury – an unwillingness to go out into the grounds, and nervous starts at every sound, that his mother had insisted upon an explanation. When the boy – our boy Roland, who had never known what fear was – began to talk to her of voices he had heard in the park, and shadows that had appeared to him among the ruins, my wife promptly put him to bed and sent for Dr Simson – which, of course, was the only thing to do.

I hurried off that evening, as may be supposed, with an anxious heart. How I got through the hours before the starting of the train, I cannot tell. We must be thankful for the quickness of the railway when in anxiety; but to have thrown myself into a post-chaise as soon as horses could be put to, would have been a relief. I got to Edinburgh very early in the blackness of the winter morning, and scarcely dared look the man in the face at whom I gasped, 'What news?' My wife had sent the brougham for me, which I concluded, before the man spoke, was a bad sign. His answer was that stereotyped answer which leaves the imagination so wildly free – 'Just the same.' Just the same! What might that mean? The horses seemed to me to creep along the long, dark country road. As we dashed through the park, I thought I heard someone moaning among the trees, and clenched my fist at him (whoever he might be) with fury. Why had the fool of a woman at the gate allowed anyone to come in to disturb the quiet of the place? If I had not been in such hot haste to get home, I think I should have stopped the carriage and got out to see what tramp it was that had made an entrance, and chosen my grounds, of all places in the world – when my boy was ill! – to grumble and groan in. But I had no reason to complain of our slow pace here. The horses flew like lightning along the intervening path, and drew up at the door all panting, as if they had run a race. My wife stood waiting to receive me with a pale face, and a candle in her hand, which made her look paler still as the wind blew the flame about. 'He is sleeping,' she said in a whisper, as if her voice might wake him.

And I replied, when I could find my voice, also in a whisper, as though the jingling of the horses' furniture and the sound of their hoofs must not have been more dangerous. I stood on the steps with her a moment, almost afraid to go in, now that I was here; and it seemed to me that I saw without observing, if I may say so, that the horses were unwilling to turn round, though their stables lay that way, or that the men were unwilling. These things occurred to me afterwards, though at the moment I was not capable of anything but to ask questions and to hear the condition of the boy.

I looked at him from the door of his room, for we were afraid to go near, lest we should disturb that blessed sleep. It looked like actual sleep – not the lethargy into which my wife told me he would sometimes fall. She told me everything in the next room, which communicated with his, rising now and then and going to the door of communication; and in this there was much that was very startling and confusing to the mind. It appeared that ever since the winter began, since it was early dark and night had fallen before his return from school, he had been hearing voices among the ruins – at first only a groaning, he said, at which his pony was as much alarmed as he was, but by degrees a voice. The tears ran down my wife's cheeks as she described to me how he would start up in the night and cry out, 'Oh, mother, let me in! oh, mother, let me in!' with a pathos which rent her heart. And she sitting there all the time, only longing to do everything his heart could desire! But though she would try to soothe him, crying, 'You are at home, my darling. I am here. Don't you know me? Your mother is here,' he would only stare at her, and after a while spring up again with the same cry. At other times he would be quite reasonable, she said, asking eagerly when I was coming, but declaring that he must go with me as soon as I did so, 'to let them in'. 'The doctor thinks his nervous system must have received a shock,' my wife said. 'Oh, Henry, can it be that we have pushed him on too much with his work – a delicate boy like Roland? – and what is his work in comparison with his health? Even you would think little of honours or prizes if it hurt the boy's health.' Even I! as if I were an inhuman father sacrificing my child to my ambition. But I would not increase her trouble by taking any notice. After a while they persuaded me to lie down, to rest, and to eat – none of which things had been possible since I received their letters. The mere fact of being on the spot, of course, in itself was a great thing; and when I knew that I could be called in a moment, as soon as he was awake and wanted me, I felt capable, even in the dark, chill morning twilight, to snatch an hour or two's sleep. As it happened, I was so worn out with the strain of anxiety and he so quieted and consoled by knowing I had come, that I was not disturbed till the afternoon, when the twilight had again settled down. There was just daylight enough to see his face when I went to him: and what a change in a fortnight! He was paler and more worn, I thought, than even in those dreadful days in the plains before we left India. His hair seemed to me to have grown long and lank; his eyes were like blazing lights projecting out of his white face. He got hold of my hand in a cold and tremulous clutch, and waved to everybody to go away. 'Go away – even mother,' he said, 'go away.' This went to her heart, for she did not like that even I should have more of the boy's confidence than herself; but my wife has never been a woman to think of herself, and she left us alone. 'Are they all gone?' he said, eagerly. 'They would not let me speak. The doctor treated me as if I were a fool. You know I am not a fool, papa.'

'Yes, yes, my boy, I know; but you are ill, and quiet is so necessary. You are not only not a fool, Roland, but you are reasonable and understand. When you are ill you must deny yourself; you must not do everything that you might do being well.'

He waved his thin hand with a sort of indignation. 'Then, father, I am not ill,' he cried. 'Oh, I thought when you came you would not stop me – you would see the sense of it! What do you think is the matter with me? Simson is well enough, but he is only a doctor. What do you think is the matter with me? I am no more ill than you are. A doctor, of course, he thinks you are ill the moment he looks at you – that's what he's there for – and claps you into bed.'

'Which is the best place for you at present, my dear boy.'

'I made up my mind,' cried the little fellow, 'that I would stand it till you came home. I said to myself, I won't frighten mother and the girls. But now, father,' he cried, half jumping out of bed, 'it's not illness – it's a secret.'

His eyes shone so wildly, his face was so swept with strong feeling, that my heart sank within me. It could be nothing but fever that did it, and fever had been so fatal. I got him into my arms to put him back into bed. 'Roland,' I said, humouring the poor child, which I knew was the only way, 'if you are going to tell me this secret to do any good, you know you must be quite quiet, and not excite yourself. If you excite yourself, I must not let you speak.'

'Yes, father,' said the boy. He was quiet directly, like a man, as if he quite understood. When I had lain him back on his pillow, he looked up at me with that grateful sweet look with which children, when they are ill, break one's heart, the water coming into his eyes in his weakness. 'I was sure as soon as you were here you would know what to do,' he said.

'To be sure, my boy. Now keep quiet, and tell it all out like a man.' To think I was telling lies to my own child! for I did it only to humour him, thinking, poor little fellow, his brain was wrong.

'Yes, father. Father, there is someone in the park – someone that has been badly used.'

'Hush, my dear; you remember, there is to be no excitement. Well, who is this somebody, and who has been ill-using him? We will soon put a stop to that.'

'Ah,' cried Roland, 'but it is not so easy as you think. I don't know who it is. It is just a cry. Oh, if you could hear it! It gets into my head in my sleep. I heard it as clear – as clear; and they think that I am dreaming – or raving perhaps,' the boy said, with a sort of disdainful smile.

This look of his perplexed me; it was less like fever than I thought. 'Are you quite sure you have not dreamt it, Roland?' I said.

'Dreamt? – that!' He was springing up again when he suddenly bethought himself, and lay down flat with the same sort of smile on his face. 'The pony heard it too,' he said. 'She jumped as if she had been shot. If I had not grasped at the reins – for I was frightened, father –'

'No shame to you, my boy,' said I, though I scarcely knew why.

'If I hadn't held to her like a leech, she'd have pitched me over her head, and she never drew breath till we were at the door. Did the pony dream it?' he said, with a soft disdain, yet indulgence for my foolishness. Then he added slowly: 'It was only a cry the first time, and all the time before you went away. I wouldn't tell you, for it was so wretched to be frightened. I thought it might be a hare or a rabbit snared, and I went in the morning and looked, but there was nothing. It was after you went I heard it really first, and this is what he says.' He raised himself on his elbow close to me, and looked me in the face. ' "Oh, mother, let me in! oh, mother, let me in!" ' As he said the words a mist came over his face, the mouth quivered, the soft features all melted and changed, and when he had ended these pitiful words, dissolved in a shower of heavy tears.

Was it an hallucination? Was it the fever of the brain? Was it the disordered fancy caused by great bodily weakness? How could I tell? I thought it wisest to accept it as if it were all true.

'This is very touching, Roland,' I said.

'Oh, if you had just heard it, father! I said to myself, if father heard it he would do something; but mamma, you know, she's given over to Simson, and that fellow's a doctor, and never thinks of anything but clapping you into bed.'

'We must not blame Simson for being a doctor, Roland.'

'No, no,' said my boy, with delightful toleration and indulgence; 'oh, no; that's the good of him – that's what he's for; I know that. But you – you are different; you are just, father: and you'll do something – directly, papa, directly – this very night.'

'Surely,' I said. 'No doubt it is some little lost child.'

He gave me a sudden, swift look, investigating my face as though to see whether, after all, this was everything my eminence as 'father' came to – no more than that? Then he got hold of my shoulder, clutching it with his thin hand: 'Look here,' he said, with a quiver in his voice; 'suppose it wasn't – living at all!'

'My dear boy, how then could you have heard it?' I said.

He turned away from me with a pettish exclamation – 'As if you didn't know better than that!'

'Do you want to tell me it is a ghost?' I said.

Roland withdrew his hand; his countenance assumed an aspect of great dignity and gravity; a slight quiver remained about his lips. 'Whatever it was – you always said we were not to call names. It was something – in trouble. Oh, father, in terrible trouble!'

'But, my boy,' I said – I was at my wits' end – 'if it was a child that was lost, or any poor human creature – but, Roland, what do you want me to do?'

'I should know if I was you,' said the child, eagerly. 'That is what I always said to myself – Father will know. Oh, papa, papa, to have to face it night after night, in such terrible, terrible trouble! and never to be able to do it any good. I don't want to cry; it's like a baby, I know; but what can I do else? – out there all by itself in the ruin, and nobody to help it. I can't bear it, I can't bear it!' cried my generous boy. And in his weakness he burst out, after many attempts to restrain it, into a great childish fit of sobbing and tears.

I do not know that I ever was in a greater perplexity in my life; and afterwards, when I thought of it, there was something comic in it too. It is bad enough to find your child's mind possessed with the conviction that he has seen – or heard – a ghost. But that he should require you to go instantly and help that ghost, was the most bewildering experience that had ever come my way. I am a sober man myself, and not superstitious – at least any more than everybody is superstitious. Of course I do not believe in ghosts; but I don't deny, any more than other people, that there are stories which I cannot pretend to understand. My blood got a sort of chill in my veins at the idea that Roland should be a ghost-seer; for that generally means an hysterical temperament and weak health, and all that

men most hate and fear for their children. But that I should take up his
ghost and right its wrongs, and save it from its trouble, was such a mission
as was enough to confuse any man. I did my best to console my boy
without giving any promise of this astonishing kind; but he was too sharp
for me. He would have none of my caresses. With sobs breaking in at
intervals upon his voice, and the rain-drops hanging on his eyelids, he
yet returned to the charge.

'It will be there now – it will be there all the night. Oh, think, papa,
think, if it was me! I can't rest for thinking of it. Don't!' he cried, putting
away my hand – 'don't! You go and help it, and mother can take care of
me.'

'But, Roland, what can I do?'

My boy opened his eyes, which were large with weakness and fever,
and gave me a smile such, I think, as sick children only know the secret of.
'I was sure you would know as soon as you came. I always said – Father
will know: and mother,' he cried, with a softening of repose upon his face,
his limbs relaxing, his form sinking with a luxurious ease in his bed –
'mother can come and take care of me.'

I called her, and saw him turn to her with the complete dependence of
a child, and then I went away and left them, as perplexed a man as any in
Scotland. I must say, however, I had this consolation, that my mind was
greatly eased about Roland. He might be under an hallucination, but his
head was clear enough, and I did not think him so ill as everybody else
did. The girls were astonished even at the ease with which I took it. 'How
do you think he is?' they said in a breath, coming round me, laying hold
of me. 'Not half so ill as I expected,' I said; 'not very bad at all.' 'Oh, papa,
you are a darling,' cried Agatha, kissing me, and crying upon my shoulder;
while little Jeanie, who was as pale as Roland, clasped both her arms
round mine, and could not speak at all. I knew nothing about it, not half
so much as Simson: but they believed in me; they had a feeling that all
would go right now. God is very good to you when your children look to
you like that. It makes one humble, not proud. I was not worthy of it; and
then I recollected that I had to act the part of a father to Roland's ghost,
which made me almost laugh, though I might just as well have cried. It
was the strangest mission that ever was entrusted to mortal man.

It was then I remembered suddenly the looks of the men when they
turned to take the brougham to the stables in the dark that morning: they
had not liked it, and the horses had not liked it. I remembered that even
in my anxiety about Roland I had heard them tearing along the avenue
back to the stables, and had made a memorandum mentally that I must

speak of it. It seemed to me that the best thing I could do was go to the stables now and make a few inquiries. It is impossible to fathom the minds of rustics; there might be some devilry of practical joking, for anything I knew; or they might have some interest in getting up a bad reputation for the Brentwood avenue. It was getting dark by the time I went out, and nobody who knows the country will need to be told how black is the darkness of a November night under high laurel-bushes and yew-trees. I walked into the heart of the shrubberies two or three times, not seeing a step before me, till I came out upon the broader carriage-road, where the trees opened a little, and there was a faint grey glimmer of sky visible, under which the great limes and elms stood darkling like ghosts; but it grew black again as I approached the corner where the ruins lay. Both eyes and ears were on the alert, as may be supposed; but I could see nothing in the absolute gloom, and, so far as I can recollect, I heard nothing. Nevertheless there came a strong impression upon me that somebody was there. It is a sensation which most people have felt. I have seen when it has been strong enough to awake me out of sleep, the sense of someone looking at me. I suppose my imagination had been affected by Roland's story; and the mystery of the darkness is always full of suggestions. I stamped my feet violently on the gravel to rouse myself, and called out sharply, 'Who's there?' Nobody answered, nor did I expect anyone to answer, but the impression had been made. I was so foolish that I did not like to look back, but went sideways, keeping an eye on the gloom behind. It was with great relief that I spied the light in the stables, making a sort of oasis in the darkness. I walked very quickly into the midst of that lighted and cheerful place, and thought the clank of the groom's pail one of the pleasantest sounds I had ever heard. The coachman was the head of this little colony, and it was to his house I went to pursue my investigations. He was a native of the district, and had taken care of the place in the absence of the family for years; it was impossible but that he must know everything that was going on, and all the traditions of the place. The men, I could see, eyed me anxiously when I thus appeared at such an hour among them, and followed me with their eyes to Jarvis's house, where he lived alone with his old wife, their children being all married and out in the world. Mrs Jarvis met me with anxious questions. How was the poor young gentleman? but the others knew, I could see by their faces, that not even this was the foremost thing in my mind.

'Noises? – ou ay, there'll be noises – the wind in the trees, and the water soughing down the glen. As for tramps, Cornel, no, there's little o' that kind o' cattle about here; and Merran at the gate's a careful body.' Jarvis moved about with some embarrassment from one leg to another as he spoke. He kept in the shade, and did not look at me more than he could help. Evidently his mind was perturbed, and he had reasons for keeping his own counsel. His wife sat by, giving him a quick look now and then, but saying nothing. The kitchen was very snug and warm and bright – as different as could be from the chill and mystery of the night outside.

'I think you are trifling with me, Jarvis,' I said.

'Triflin', Cornel? no me. What would I trifle for? If the deevil himself was in the auld hoose, I have no interest in't one way or another –'

'Sandy, hold your peace!' cried his wife, imperatively.

'And what am I to hold my peace for, wi' the Cornel standing there asking a' thae questions? I'm saying, if the deevil himsel –'

'And I'm telling ye hold your peace!' cried the woman, in great excitement. 'Dark November weather and lang nichts, and us that ken a' we ken. How daur ye name – a name that shouldna be spoken?' She threw down her stocking and got up, also in great agitation. 'I tell't ye you never could keep it. It's no a thing that will hide; and the haill toun kens as weel as you or me. Tell the Cornel straight out – or see, I'll do it. I dinna hold wi' your secrets: and a secret that the haill toun kens!' She snapped her fingers with an air of large disdain. As for Jarvis, ruddy and big as he was, he shrank to nothing before this decided woman. He repeated to her two or three times her own adjuration, 'Hold your peace!' then, suddenly changing his tone, cried out, 'Tell him then, confound ye! I'll wash my hands o't. If a' the ghosts in Scotland were in the auld hoose, is that ony concern o' mine?'

After this I elicited without much difficulty the whole story. In the opinion of the Jarvises, and of everybody about, the certainty that the place was haunted was beyond all doubt. As Sandy and his wife warmed to the tale, one tripping up another in their eagerness to tell everything, it gradually developed as distinct a superstition as I ever heard, and not without poetry and pathos. How long it was since the voice had been heard first, nobody could tell with certainty. Jarvis's opinion was that his father, who had been coachman at Brentwood before him, had never heard anything about it, and that the whole thing had arisen within the last ten years, since the complete dismantling of the old house: which was a wonderfully modern date for a tale so well authenticated. According to these witnesses, and to several whom I questioned afterwards, and who were all in perfect agreement, it was only in the months of November and December that 'the visitation' occurred. During these months, the darkest of the year, scarcely a night passed without the recurrence of these inexplicable cries. Nothing, it was said, had ever been seen – at least nothing that could be identified. Some people, bolder or more imaginative than the others, had seen the darkness moving, Mrs Jarvis said, with unconscious poetry. It began when night fell and continued, at intervals, till day broke. Very often it was only an inarticulate cry and moaning, but sometimes the words which had taken possession of my poor boy's fancy had been distinctly audible – 'Oh, mother, let me in!' The Jarvises were not aware that there had ever been any investigation into it. The estate of Brentwood had lapsed into the hands of a distant branch of the family, who had lived but little there; and of the many people who had taken it, as I had done, few had remained through two Decembers. And nobody had taken the trouble to make a very close examination into the facts. 'No, no,' Jarvis said, shaking his head, 'No, no, Cornel. Wha wad set themsels up for a laughin'-stock to a' the country-side, making a wark about a ghost? Naebody believes in ghosts. It bid to be the wind in the trees, the last gentleman said, or some effec' o' the water wrastlin' among the rocks. He said it was a' quite easy explained: but he gave up the hoose. And when you cam, Cornel, we were awfu' anxious you should never hear. What for should I have spoiled the bargain and hairmed the property for nothing?'

'Do you call my child's life nothing?' I said in the trouble of the moment, unable to restrain myself. 'And instead of telling this all to me, you have told it to him – to a delicate boy, a child unable to sift evidence, or judge for himself, a tender-hearted young creature –'

I was walking about the room with an anger all the hotter that I felt it to be most likely quite unjust. My heart was full of bitterness against the stolid retainers of a family who were content to risk other people's children and comfort rather than let the house lie empty. If I had been warned I might have taken precautions, or left the place, or sent Roland away, a hundred things which now I could not do; and here I was with my boy in a brain-fever, and his life, the most precious life on earth, hanging in the balance, dependent on whether or not I could get to the reason of a commonplace ghost-story! I paced about in high wrath, not seeing what I was to do; for, to take Roland away, even if he were able to travel, would not settle his agitated mind; and I feared even that a scientific explanation of refracted sound, or reverberation, or any other of the easy certainties with which we elder men are silenced, would have very little effect upon the boy.

'Cornel,' said Jarvis, solemnly, 'and *she'll* bear me witness – the young gentleman never heard a word from me – no, nor from either groom or gardener; I'll gie ye my word for that. In the first place, he's no lad that invites ye to talk. There are some that are, and some that arena. Some will draw ye on, till ye've tellt them a' the clatter of the toun, and a' ye ken, and while mair. But Maister Roland, his mind's fu' of his books. He's aye civil and kind, and a fine lad; but no that sort. And ye see it's for a' our interest, Cornel, that you should stay at Brentwood. I took it upon mysel to pass the word – "No a syllable to Maister Roland, nor to the young leddies – no a syllable." The women-servants, that have little reason to be out at night, ken little or nothing about it. And some think it grand to have a ghost so long as they're no in the way of coming across it. If you had been tellt the story to begin with, maybe ye would have thought so yourself.'

This was true enough, though it did not throw any light upon my perplexity. If we had heard of it to start with, it is possible that all the family would have considered the possession of a ghost a distinct advantage. It is the fashion of the times. We never think what a risk it is to play with young imaginations, but cry out, in the fashionable jargon, 'A ghost! – nothing else was wanted to make it perfect.' I should not have been above this myself. I should have smiled, of course, at the idea of the ghost at all, but then to feel that it was mine would have pleased my vanity. Oh, yes, I claim no exemption. The girls would have been delighted. I could fancy their eagerness, their interest, and excitement. No; if we had been told, it would have done no good – we should have made the bargain all the more eagerly, the fools that we are. 'And there has been no attempt to investigate it,' I said, 'to see what it really is?'

'Eh, Cornel,' said the coachman's wife, 'wha would investigate, as ye call it, a thing that nobody believes in? Ye would be the laughing-stock of a' the country-side, as my man says.'

'But you believe in it,' I said, turning upon her hastily. The woman was taken by surprise. She made a step backward out of my way.

'Lord, Cornel, how ye frichten a body! Me! – there's awful strange things in this world. An unlearned person doesna ken what to think. But the minister and the gentry they just laugh in your face. Inquire into the thing that is not! Na, na, we just let it be.'

'Come with me, Jarvis,' I said, hastily, 'and we'll make an attempt at least. Say nothing to the men or to anybody. I'll come back after dinner, and we'll make a serious attempt to see what it is, if it is anything. If I hear it – which I doubt – you may be sure I shall never rest till I make it out. Be ready for me about ten o'clock.'

'Me, Cornel!' Jarvis said, in a faint voice. I had not been looking at him in my own preoccupation, but when I did so, I found that the greatest

change had come over the fat and ruddy coachman. 'Me, Cornel!' he
repeated, wiping the perspiration from his brow. His ruddy face hung in
flabby folds, his knees knocked together, his voice seemed half extinguished in his throat. Then he began to rub his hands and smile upon me
in a deprecating, imbecile way. 'There's nothing I wouldna do to pleasure
ye, Cornel,' taking a step farther back. 'I'm sure *she* kens I've aye said I
never had to do with a mair fair, weelspoken gentleman –' Here Jarvis
came to a pause, again looking at me, rubbing his hands.

'Well?' I said.

'But eh, sir!' he went on, with the same imbecile yet insinuating smile,
'if ye'll reflect that I am no used to my feet. With a horse atween my legs,
or the reins in my hand, I'm maybe nae worse than other men; but on fit,
Cornel – It's no the – bogles; – but I've been cavalry, ye see,' with a little
hoarse laugh, 'a' my life. To face a thing ye didna understan' – on your
feet, Cornel.'

'Well, sir if *I* do it,' said I tartly, 'why shouldn't you?'

'Eh, Cornel, there's an awful' difference. In the first place, ye tramp
about the haill country-side, and think naething of it; but a walk tires me
mair than a hunard miles' drive: and then yer'e a gentleman, and do your
ain pleasure; and you're no so ould as me; and it's for your ain bairn, ye
see, Cornel; and then –'

'He believes in it, Cornel, and you dinna believe in it,' the woman said.

'Will you come with me?' I said, turning to her.

She jumped back, upsetting her chair in her bewilderment. 'Me!' with
a scream, and then fell into a sort of hysterical laugh. 'I wouldna say but
what I would go; but what would the folk say to hear of Cornel Mortimer
with an auld silly woman at his heels?'

The suggestion made me laugh too, though I had little inclination for it.
'I'm sorry you have so little spirit, Jarvis,' I said. 'I must find someone else,
I suppose.'

Jarvis, touched by this, began to remonstrate, but I cut him short. My
butler was a soldier who had been with me in India, and was not supposed
to fear anything – man or devil – certainly not the former; and I felt that I
was losing time. The Jarvises were too thankful to get rid of me. They
attended me to the door with the most anxious courtesies. Outside, the
two grooms stood close by, a little confused by my sudden exit. I don't
know if perhaps they had been listening – at least standing as near as
possible, to catch any scrap of the conversation. I waved my hand to them
as I went past, in answer to their salutations, and it was very apparent to
me that they also were glad to see me go.

And it will be thought very strange, but it would be weak not to add, that I myself, though bent on the investigation I have spoken of, pledged to Roland to carry it out, and feeling that my boy's health, perhaps his life, depended on the result of my inquiry – I felt the most unaccountable reluctance to pass these ruins on my way home. My curiosity was intense; and yet it was all my mind could do to pull my body along. I dare say the scientific people would describe it the other way, and attribute my cowardice to the state of my stomach. I went on; but if I had followed my impulse, I should have turned and bolted. Everything in me seemed to cry out against it; my heart thumped, my pulses all began, like sledge-hammers, beating against my ears and every sensitive part. It was very dark, as I have said; the old house, with its shapeless tower, loomed a heavy mass through the darkness, which was only not entirely so solid as itself. On the other hand, the great dark cedars of which we were so proud seemed to fill up the night. My foot strayed out of the path in my confusion and the gloom together, and I brought myself up with a cry as I felt myself knock against something solid. What was it? The contact with hard stone and lime, and prickly bramble-bushes restored me a little to myself. 'Oh, it's only the old gable,' I said aloud, with a little laugh to reassure myself. The rough feeling of the stones reconciled me. As I groped about thus, I shook off my visionary folly. What so easily explained as that I should have strayed from the path in the darkness? This brought me back to common existence, as if I had been shaken by a wise hand out of all the silliness of superstition. How silly it was, after all! What did it matter which path I took? I laughed again, this time with better heart – when suddenly, in a moment, the blood was chilled in my veins, a shiver stole along my spine, my faculties seemed to forsake me. Close by me at my side, at my feet, there was a sigh. No, not a groan, not a moaning, not anything so tangible – a perfectly soft, faint, inarticulate sigh. I sprang back, and my heart stopped beating. Mistaken! no, mistake was impossible. I heard it as clearly as I hear myself speak; a long, soft, weary sigh, as if drawn to the utmost, and emptying out a load of sadness that filled the breast. To hear this in the solitude, in the dark, in the night (though it was still early), had an effect which I cannot describe. I feel it now – something cold creeping over me, up into my hair, and down to my feet, which refused to move. I cried out, with a trembling voice. 'Who is there?' as I had done before – but there was no reply.

I got home I don't quite know how; but in my mind there was no longer any indifference as to the thing, whatever it was, that haunted these ruins. My scepticism disappeared like a mist. I was as firmly determined that

there was something as Roland was. I did not for a moment pretend to
myself that it was possible I could be deceived; there were movements
and noises which I understood all about, cracklings of small branches in
the frost, and little rolls of gravel on the path, such as have a very eerie
sound sometimes, and perplex you with wonder as to who has done it,
when there is no real mystery; but I assure you all these little movements of
Nature don't affect you one bit *when there is something*. I understood *them*.
I did not understand the sigh. That was not simple Nature; there was
meaning in it – feeling, the soul of a creature invisible. This is the thing
that human nature trembles at – a creature invisible, yet with sensations,
feelings, a power somehow of expressing itself. I had not the same sense
of unwillingness to turn my back upon the scene of the mystery which I
had experienced in going by the stables; but I almost ran home, impelled
by eagerness to get everything done that had to be done in order to apply
myself to finding it out. Bagley was in the hall as usual when I went in. He
was always there in the afternoon, always with the appearance of perfect
occupation, yet, so far as I knew, never doing anything. The door was
open, so that I hurried in without any pause, breathless; but the sight of
his calm regard, as he came to help me off with my overcoat, subdued me
in a moment. Anything out of the way, anything incomprehensible, faded
to nothing in the presence of Bagley. You saw and wondered how he was
made: the parting of his hair, the tie of his white neckcloth, the fit of his
trousers, all perfect as works of art; but you could see how they were done,
which makes all the difference. I flung myself upon him, so to speak,
without waiting to note the extreme unlikeness of the man to anything of
the kind I meant. 'Bagley,' I said, 'I want you to come out with me tonight
to watch for –'

'Poachers, Colonel,' he said, a gleam of pleasure running all over him.

'No, Bagley; a great deal worse,' I cried.

'Yes, Colonel; at what hour, sir?' the man said; but then I had not told
him what it was.

It was ten o'clock when we set out. All was perfectly quiet indoors. My
wife was with Roland, who had been quite calm, she said, and who
(though, no doubt, the fever must run its course) had been better since I
came. I told Bagley to put on a thick greatcoat over his evening coat, and
did the same myself – with strong boots; for the soil was like a sponge, or
worse. Talking to him, I almost forgot what we were going to do. It was
darker even than it had been before, and Bagley kept very close to me as
we went along. I had a small lantern in my hand, which gave us a partial
guidance. We had come to the corner where the path turns. On one side

was the bowling-green, which the girls had taken possession of for their croquet-ground – a wonderful enclosure surrounded by high hedges of holly, three hundred years old and more; on the other, the ruins. Both were black as night; but before we got so far, there was a little opening in which we could just discern the trees and the lighter line of the road. I thought it best to pause there and take breath. 'Bagley,' I said, 'there is something about these ruins I don't understand. It is there I am going. Keep your eyes open and your wits about you. Be ready to pounce upon any stranger you see – anything, man or woman. Don't hurt, but seize – anything you see.' 'Colonel,' said Bagley, with a little tremor in his breath, 'they do say there's things there – as is neither man nor woman.' There was no time for words. 'Are you game to follow me, my man? that's the question,' I said. Bagley fell in without a word, and saluted. I knew then I had nothing to fear.

We went, so far as I could guess, exactly as I had come when I heard that sigh. The darkness, however, was so complete that all marks, as of trees or paths, disappeared. One moment we felt our feet on the gravel, another sinking noiselessly into the slippery grass, that was all. I had shut up my lantern, not wishing to scare anyone, whoever it might be. Bagley followed, it seemed to me, exactly in my footsteps as I made my way, as I supposed, towards the mass of the ruined house. We seemed to take a long time groping along seeking this; the squash of the wet soil under our feet was the only thing that marked our progress. After a while I stood still to see, or rather feel, where we were. The darkness was very still, but no stiller than is usual in a winter's night. The sounds I have mentioned – the crackling of twigs, the roll of a pebble, the sound of some rustle in the dead leaves, or creeping creature on the grass – were audible when you listened, all mysterious enough when your mind is disengaged, but to me cheering now as signs of the livingness of Nature, even in the death of the frost. As we stood still there came up from the trees in the glen the prolonged hoot of an owl. Bagley started with alarm, being in a state of general nervousness, and not knowing what he was afraid of. But to me the sound was encouraging and pleasant, being so comprehensible. 'An owl,' I said, under my breath. 'Y–es, Colonel,' said Bagley, his teeth chattering. We stood still about five minutes, while it broke into the still brooding of the air, the sound widening out in circles, dying upon the darkness. This sound, which is not a cheerful one, made me almost gay. It was natural, and relieved the tension of the mind. I moved on with new courage, my nervous excitement calming down.

When all at once, quite suddenly, close to us, at our feet, there broke out a cry. I made a spring backwards in the first moment of surprise and horror, and in doing so came sharply against the same rough masonry and brambles that had struck me before. This new sound came upwards from the ground – a low, moaning, wailing voice, full of suffering and pain. The contrast between it and the hoot of the owl was indescribable; the one with a wholesome wildness and naturalness that hurt nobody – the other, a sound that made one's blood curdle, full of human misery. With a great deal of fumbling – for in spite of everything I could do to keep up my courage my hands shook – I managed to remove the slide of my lantern. The light leaped out like something living, and made the place visible in a moment. We were what would have been inside the ruined building had anything remained by the gable-wall which I have described. It was close to us, the vacant doorway in it going out straight into the blackness outside. The light showed the bit of wall, the ivy glistening upon it in clouds of dark green, the bramble-branches waving, and below, the open door – a door that led to nothing. It was from this the voice came which died out just at the light flashed upon this strange scene. There was a moment's silence, and then it broke forth again. The sound was so near, so penetrating, so pitiful, that, on the nervous start I gave, the light fell out of my hand. As I groped for it in the dark my hand was clutched by Bagley, who I think must have dropped upon his knees; but I was too much perturbed myself to think much of this. He clutched at me in the confusion of his terror, forgetting all his usual decorum. 'For God's sake, what is it, sir?' he gasped. If I yielded, there was evidently an end of both of us. 'I can't tell,' I said, 'any more than you; that's what we've got to find out: up, man, up!' I pulled him to his feet. 'Will you go round and examine the other side, or will you stay here with the lantern?' Bagley gasped at me with a face of horror. 'Can't we stay together, Colonel?' he said – his knees were trembling under him. I pushed him against the corner of the wall, and put the light into his hands. 'Stand fast till I come back; shake yourself together, man; let nothing pass you,' I said. The voice was within two or three feet of us, of that there could be no doubt.

I went myself to the other side of the wall, keeping close to it. The light shook in Bagley's hand, but, tremulous though it was, shone out through the vacant door, one oblong block of light marking all the crumbling corners and hanging masses of foliage. Was that something dark huddled in a heap by the side of it? I pushed forward across the light in the doorway, and fell upon it with my hands; but it was only a juniper-bush growing close against the wall. Meanwhile, the sight of my figure crossing the doorway had brought Bagley's nervous excitement to a height: he flew at me, gripping my shoulder. 'I've got him, Colonel!' I've got him!' he cried, with a voice of sudden exultation. He thought it was a man, and was at once relieved. But at that moment the voice burst forth again between us, at our feet – more close to us than any separate being could be. He dropped off from me, and fell against the wall, his jaw dropping as if he were dying. I suppose, at the same moment, he saw that it was me whom he had clutched. I, for my part, had scarcely more command of myself. I snatched the light out of his hand, and flashed it all about me wildly. Nothing – the juniper-bush which I thought I had never seen before, the heavy growth of the glistening ivy, the brambles waving. It was close to my ears now, crying, crying, pleading as if for life. Either I heard the same words Roland had heard, or else, in my excitement, his imagination got possession of mine. The voice went on, growing into distinct articulation, but wavering about, now from one point, now from another, as if the owner of it were moving slowly back and forward – 'Mother! mother!' and then an outburst of wailing. As my mind steadied, getting accustomed (as one's mind gets accustomed to anything), it seemed to me as if some uneasy, miserable creature was pacing up and down before a closed door. Sometimes – but that must have been excitement – I thought I heard a sound like knocking, and then another burst, 'Oh, mother! mother!' All this close, close to the space where I was standing with my lantern – now before me, now behind me: a creature restless, unhappy, moaning, crying, before the vacant doorway, which no one could either shut or open more.

'Do you hear it, Bagley? Do you hear what it is saying?' I cried, stepping in through the doorway. He was lying against the wall – his eyes glazed, half dead with terror. He made a motion of his lips as if to answer me, but no sounds came; then lifted his hand with a curious imperative movement as if ordering me to be silent and listen. And how long I did so I cannot tell. It began to have an interest, an exciting hold upon me, which I could not describe. It seemed to call up visibly a scene anyone could understand – a something shut out, restlessly wandering to and fro; sometimes the voice dropped, as if throwing itself down – sometimes wandered off a few paces, growing sharp and clear. 'Oh, mother, let me in! oh, mother, mother, let me in! oh, let me in!' Every word was clear to me. No wonder the boy had gone wild with pity. I tried to steady my mind upon Roland, upon his conviction that I could do something, but my head swam with the excitement, even when I partially overcame the terror. At last the words died away, and there was a sound of sobs and moaning. I cried out, 'In the name of God who are you?' with a kind of feeling in my mind that to use the name of God was profane, seeing that I did not believe in ghosts or anything supernatural; but I did it all the same, and waited, my heart giving a leap of terror lest there should be a reply. Why this should have been I cannot tell, but I had a feeling that if there was an answer it would be more than I could bear. But there was no answer; the moaning went on, and then, as if it had been real, the voice rose, a little higher again, the words recommenced, 'Oh, mother, let me in! oh, mother, let me in!' with an expression that was heartbreaking to hear.

As if it had been real! What do I mean by that? I suppose I got less alarmed as the thing went on. I began to recover the use of my senses – I seemed to explain it all to myself by saying that this had once happened, that it was a recollection of a real scene. Why there should have seemed something quite satisfactory and composing in this explanation I cannot tell, but so it was. I began to listen almost as if it had been a play, forgetting Bagley, who, I almost think, had fainted, leaning against the wall. I was startled out of this strange spectatorship that had fallen upon me by the sudden rush of something which made my heart jump once more, a large black figure in the doorway waving its arms. 'Come in! come in! come in!' it shouted out hoarsely at the top of a deep bass voice, and then poor Bagley fell down senseless across the threshold. He was less sophisticated than I – he had not been able to bear it any longer. I took him for something supernatural, as he took me, and it was some time before I awoke to the necessities of the moment. I remembered only after, that from the time I began to give my attention to the man, I heard the other voice no more. It was some time before I brought him to. It must have been a strange scene; the lantern making a luminous spot in the darkness, the man's white face lying on the black earth, I over him, doing what I could for him. Probably I should have been thought to be murdering him had anyone seen us. When at last I succeeded in pouring a little brandy down his throat he sat up and looked about him wildly. 'What's up?' he said; then recognizing me, tried to struggle to his feet with a faint 'Beg your pardon, Colonel.' I got him home as best I could, making him lean upon my arm. The great fellow was as weak as a child. Fortunately he did not for some time remember what had happened. From the time Bagley fell the voice had stopped, and all was still.

'You've got an epidemic in your house, Colonel,' Simson said to me next morning. 'What's the meaning of it all? Here's your butler raving about a voice. This will never do, you know; and so far as I can make out, you are in it too.'

'Yes, I am in it, doctor. I thought I had better speak to you. Of course you are treating Roland all right – but the boy is not raving, he is as sane as you or me. It's all true.'

'As sane as – I – or you. I never thought the boy insane. He's got cerebral excitement, fever. I don't know what you've got. There's something very queer about the look of your eyes.'

'Come,' said I, 'you can't put us all to bed, you know. You had better listen and hear the symptoms in full.'

The doctor shrugged his shoulders, but he listened to me patiently. He did not believe a word of the story, that was clear; but he heard it all from the beginning to end. 'My dear fellow,' he said, 'the boy told me just the same. It's an epidemic. When one person falls a victim to this sort of thing, it's as safe as can be – there's always two or three.'

'Then how do you account for it?' I said.

'Oh, account for it! – that's a different matter; there's no accounting for the freaks our brains are subject to. If it's delusion; if it's some trick of the echoes or the winds – some phonetic disturbance or other–'

'Come with me tonight, and judge for yourself,' I said.

Upon this he laughed aloud, then said, 'That's not such a bad idea; but it would ruin me for ever if it were known that John Simson was ghost-hunting.'

'There it is,' said I; 'you dart down on us who are unlearned with your phonetic disturbances, but you daren't examine what the thing really is for fear of being laughed at. That's science!'

'It's not science – it's common sense,' said the doctor. 'The thing has delusion on the front of it. It is encouraging an unwholesome tendency even to examine. What good could come of it? Even if I am convinced, I shouldn't believe.'

'I should have said so yesterday; and I don't want you to be convinced or to believe,' said I. 'If you prove it to be a delusion, I shall be very much obliged to you for one. Come; somebody must go with me.'

'You are cool,' said the doctor. 'You've disabled this poor fellow of yours, and made him – on that point – a lunatic for life; and now you want to disable me. But for once, I'll do it. To save appearance, if you'll give me a bed, I'll come over after my last rounds.'

It was agreed that I should meet him at the gate, and that we should visit the scene of last night's occurrences before we came to the house, so that nobody might be the wiser. It was scarcely possible to hope that the cause of Bagley's sudden illness should not somehow steal into the knowledge of the servants at least, and it was better that all should be done as quietly as possible. The day seemed to me a very long one. I had to spend a certain part of it with Roland, which was a terrible ordeal for me – for what could I say to the boy? The improvement continued, but he was still in a very precarious state, and the trembling vehemence with which he turned to me when his mother left the room filled me with alarm. 'Father!' he said, quietly. 'Yes, my boy; I am giving my best attention to it – all is being done that I can do. I have not come to any conclusion – yet. I am neglecting nothing you said,' I cried. What I could not do was to give his active mind any encouragement to dwell upon the mystery. It was a hard predicament, for some satisfaction had to be given him. He looked at me very wistfully, with the great blue eyes which shone so large and brilliant out of his white and worn face. 'You must trust me,' I said. 'Yes, father. Father understands,' he said to himself, as if to soothe some inward doubt. I left him as soon as I could. He was about the most precious thing I had on earth, and his health my first thought; but yet somehow, in the excitement of this other subject, I put that aside, and preferred not to dwell upon Roland, which was the most curious part of it all.

That night at eleven I met Simson at the gate. He had come by train, and I let him in gently myself. I had been so much absorbed in the coming experiment that I passed the ruins in going to meet him, almost without thought, if you can understand that. I had my lantern; and he showed me a coil of taper which he had ready for use. 'There is nothing like light,' he said, in his scoffing tone. It was a very still night, scarcely a sound, but not so dark. We could keep the path without difficulty as we went along. As we approached the spot we could hear a low moaning, broken occasionally by a bitter cry. 'Perhaps that is your voice,' said the doctor; 'I thought it must be something of the kind. That's a poor brute caught in some of these infernal traps of yours; you'll find it among the bushes somewhere.' I said nothing. I felt no particular fear, but a triumphant satisfaction in what was to follow. I led him to the spot where Bagley and I had stood on the previous night. All was silent as a winter night could be – so silent that we heard far off the sound of the horses in the stables, the shutting of a window at the house. Simson lighted his taper and went peering about, poking into all the corners. We looked like two conspirators lying in wait for some unfortunate traveller; but not a sound broke the quiet. The moaning had stopped before we came up; a star or two shone over us in the sky, looking down as if surprised at our strange proceedings. Dr Simson did nothing but utter subdued laughs under his breath. 'I thought as much,' he said. 'It is just the same with tables and all other kinds of ghostly apparatus; a sceptic's presence stops everything. When I am present nothing ever comes off. How long do you think it will be necessary to stay here? Oh, I don't complain; only, when *you* are satisfied, *I* am – quite.'

I will not deny that I was disappointed beyond measure by this result. It made me look like a credulous fool. It gave the doctor such a pull over me as nothing else could. I should point all his morals for years to come, and his materialism, his scepticism, would be increased behind endurance. 'It seems, indeed,' I said, 'that there is to be no—' 'Manifestation,' he said, laughing; 'that is what all the mediums say. No manifestation in consequence of the presence of an unbeliever.' His laugh sounded very uncomfortable to me in the silence; and it was now near midnight. But that laugh seemed the signal; before it died away the moaning we had heard before was resumed. It started from some distance off, and came towards us, nearer and nearer, like someone walking along and moaning to himself. There could be no idea now that it was a hare caught in a trap. The approach was slow, like that of a weak person with little halts and pauses. We heard it coming along the grass straight towards the vacant doorway. Simson had been a little startled by the first sound. He said hastily, 'That child has no business to be out so late.' But he felt, as well as I, that this was no child's voice. As it came nearer, he grew silent, and, going to the doorway with his taper, stood looking out towards the sound. The taper being unprotected blew about in the night air, though there was scarcely any wind. I threw the light of my lantern steady and white across the same space. It was a blaze of light in the midst of the blackness. A little icy thrill had gone over me at the first sound, but as it came close, I confess that my only feeling was satisfaction. The scoffer could scoff no more. The light touched his own face, and showed a very perplexed countenance. If he was afraid, he concealed it with great success, but he was perplexed. And then all that had happened on the previous night was enacted once more. It fell strangely upon me with a sense of repetition. Every cry, every sob, seemed the same as before. I listened almost without any emotion at all in my own person, thinking of its effect upon Simson. He maintained a very bold front on the whole. All that coming and going of the voice was, if our ears could be trusted, exactly in front of the vacant, blank doorway, blazing full of light, which caught and shone in the glistening leaves of the great hollies at a little distance. Not a rabbit could have crossed the turf without being seen – but there was nothing. After a time, Simson, with a certain caution and boldily reluctance, as it seemed to me, went out with his roll of taper into this space. His figure showed against the holly in full outline. Just at this moment the voice sank, as was its custom, and seemed to fling itself down at the door. Simson recoiled violently, as if someone had come up against him, then turned, and held his taper low as if examining something. 'Do you see anybody?' I cried in a whisper, feeling the chill of nervous panic steal over me at this action. 'It's nothing but a — confounded juniper-bush,' he said. This I knew very well to be nonsense, for the juniper-bush was on the other side. He went about after this round and round, poking his taper everywhere, then returned to me on the inner side of the wall. He scoffed no longer; his face was contracted and pale. 'How long does this go on?' he whispered to me, like a man who does not wish to interrupt someone who is speaking. I had become too much perturbed myself to remark whether the successions and changes of the voice were the same as last night. It suddenly went out in the air almost as he was speaking, with a soft reiterated sob dying away. If there had been anything to be seen, I should have said that the person was at that moment crouching on the ground close to the door.

We walked home very silent afterwards. It was only when we were in sight of the house that I said, 'What do you think of it?' 'I can't tell what to think of it,' he said, quickly. He took – though he was a very temperate man – not the claret I was going to offer him, but some brandy from the tray, and swallowed it almost undiluted. 'Mind you, I don't believe a word of it,' he said, when he had lighted his candle; 'but I can't tell what to think,' he turned round to add, when he was half-way upstairs.

All of this, however, did me no good with the solution of my problem. I was to help this weeping, sobbing thing, which was already to me as distinct a personality as anything I knew – or what should I say to Roland? It was on my heart that my boy would die if I could not find some way of helping this creature. You may be surprised that I should speak of it in this way. I did not know if it was man or woman; but I no more doubted that it was a soul in pain than I doubted my own being; and it was my business to soothe this pain – to deliver it, if that was possible. Was ever such a task given to an anxious father trembling for his only boy? I felt in my heart, fantastic as it may appear, that I must fulfil this somehow, or part with my child; and you may conceive that rather than do that I was ready to die. But even my dying would not have advanced me – unless by bringing me into the same world with that seeker at the door.

Next morning Simson was out before breakfast, and came in with evident signs of the damp grass on his boots, and a look of worry and weariness, which did not say much for the night he had passed. He improved a little after breakfast, and visited his two patients, for Bagley was still an invalid. I went out with him on his way to the train, to hear what he had to say about the boy. 'He is going on very well,' he said; 'there are no complications as yet. But mind you, that's not a boy to be trifled with, Mortimer. Not a word to him about last night.' I had to tell him then of my last interview with Roland, and of the impossible demand he had made upon me – by which, though he tried to laugh, he was much discomposed, as I could see. 'We must just perjure ourselves all round,' he said, 'and swear you exorcized it'; but the man was too kind-hearted to be satisfied with that. 'It's frightfully serious for you, Mortimer. I can't laugh as I should like to. I wish I saw a way out of it, for your sake. By the way,' he added shortly, 'didn't you notice that juniper-bush on the left-hand side?' 'There was one on the right hand of the door. I noticed you made that mistake last night.' 'Mistake!' he cried, with a curious low laugh, pulling up the collar of his coat as though he felt the cold, 'there's no juniper there this morning, left or right. Just go and see.' As he stepped into the train a few minutes after, he looked back upon me and beckoned me for a parting word. 'I'm coming back tonight,' he said.

I don't think I had any feeling about this as I turned away from that common bustle of the railway which made my private preoccupations feel so strangely out of date. There had been a distinct satisfaction in my mind before that his scepticism had been so entirely defeated. But the more serious part of the matter pressed upon me now. I went straight from the railway to the manse, which stood on a little plateau on the side of the river opposite to the woods of Brentwood. The minister was one of a class which is not so common in Scotland as it used to be. He was a man of good family, well educated in the Scotch way, strong in philosophy, not so strong in Greek, strongest of all in experience – a man who had 'come across', in the course of his life, most people of note that had ever been in Scotland – and who was said to be very sound in doctrine, without infringing the toleration with which old men, who are good men, are generally endowed. He was old-fashioned, perhaps he did not think so much about the troublous problems of theology as many of the young men, nor ask himself any hard questions about the Confession of Faith – but he understood human nature, which is perhaps better. He received me with a cordial welcome. 'Come away, Colonel Mortimer,' he said; 'I'm all the more glad to see you, that I feel it's a good sign for the boy. He's doing well? – God be praised – and the Lord bless him and keep him. He has many a poor body's prayers – and that can do nobody harm.'

'He will need them all, Dr Moncrieff,' I said, 'and your counsel too.' And I told him the story – more than I had told Simson. The old clergyman listened to me with many suppressed exclamations, and at the end the water stood in his eyes.

'That's just beautiful,' he said. 'I do not mind to have heard anything like it, it's as fine as Burns when he wished deliverance to one – that is prayed for in no kirk. Ay, ay! so he would have you console the poor lost spirit? God bless the boy! There's something more than common in that, Colonel Mortimer. And also the faith of him in his father! I would like to put that into a sermon.' Then the old gentleman gave me an alarmed look, and said, 'No, no, I was not meaning a sermon, but I must write it down for the *Children's Record.*' I saw the thought that passed through his mind. Either he thought, or he feared I would think, of a funeral sermon. You may believe this did not make me more cheerful.

I can scarcely say that Dr Moncrieff gave me any advice. How could anyone advise on such a subject? But he said, 'I think I'll come too. I'm an old man; I'm less liable to be frightened than those that are further off the world unseen. It behoves me to think of my own journey there. I've no cut-and-dried beliefs on the subject. I'll come too: and maybe at the moment the Lord will put into our heads what to do.'

This gave me a little comfort – more than Simson had given me. To be clear about the cause of it was not my grand desire. It was another thing that was in my mind – my boy. As for the poor soul at the open door, I had no more doubt, as I have said, of its existence than I had of my own. It was no ghost to me. I knew the creature, and it was in trouble. That was my feeling about it, as it was Roland's. To hear it first was a great shock to my nerves, but not now, a man will get accustomed to anything. But to do something for it was the great problem; how was I to be serviceable to a being that was invisible, that was mortal no longer? 'Maybe at the moment the Lord will put it into our heads.' That is very old-fashioned phraseology, and a week before, most likely, I should have smiled (though always with kindness) at Dr Moncrieff's credulity; but there was a great comfort, whether rational or otherwise I cannot say, in the mere sound of the words.

The road to the station and the village lay through the glen – not by the ruins; but though the sunshine and the fresh air, and the beauty of the trees, and the sound of water were all very soothing to the spirits, my mind was so full of my own subject that I could not refrain from turning to the right as I got to the top of the glen, and going straight to the place which I may call the scene of all my thoughts. It was lying full in the sunshine, like all the rest of the world. The ruined gable looked due east, and in the present aspect of the sun the light streamed down through the doorway as our lantern had done, throwing a flood of light upon the damp grass beyond. There was a strange suggestion in the open door – so futile, a kind of emblem of vanity – all free around – so that you could go where you pleased, and yet that semblance of an enclosure – that way of entrance, unnecessary, leading to nothing. And why any creature should pray and weep to get in – to nothing, or be kept out – by nothing! You could not dwell upon it, or it made your brain go round. I remembered, however, what Simson said about the juniper, with a little smile in my own mind as to the inaccuracy of recollection, which even a scientific man will be guilty of. I could see now the light of my lantern gleaming upon the wet glistening surface of the spiky leaves at the right hand – and he ready to go to the stake for it that it was the left! I went round to make sure. And then I saw what he had said. Right or left there was no juniper at all. I was confounded by this, though it was entirely a matter of detail: nothing at all: a bush of brambles waving, the grass growing up to the very walls. But after all, though it gave me a shock for a moment, what did that matter? There were marks as if a number of footsteps had been up and down in front of the door, but these might have been our steps, and all was bright, and peaceful, and still. I poked about the other ruin – the larger ruins of the old house – for some time, as I had done before. There were marks upon the grass here and there, I could not call them footsteps, all about; but that told for nothing one way or another. I had examined the ruined rooms closely the first day. They were half filled up with soil and debris, withered brackens and bramble – no refuge for anyone there. It vexed me that Jarvis should see me coming from that spot when he came up to me for his orders. I don't know whether my nocturnal expeditions had got wind among the servants. But there was a significant look in his face. Something in it I felt was like my own sensation when Simson in the midst of his scepticism was struck dumb. Jarvis felt satisfied that his veracity had been put beyond question. I never spoke to a servant of mine in such a peremptory tone before. I sent him away 'with a flee in his lug', as the man described it afterwards. Interference of any kind was intolerable to me at such a moment.

But what was strangest of all was, that I could not face Roland. I did not go up to his room as I would have naturally done at once. This the girls could not understand. They saw there was some mystery in it. 'Mother has gone to lie down,' Agatha said; 'he has had such a good night.' 'But he wants you so, papa!' cried little Jeanie, always with her two arms embracing mine in a pretty way she had. I was obliged to go at last – but what could I say? I could only kiss him, and tell him to keep still – that I was doing all I could. There is something mystical about the patience of a child. 'It will come all right, won't it father?' he said. 'God grant it may! I hope so, Roland.' 'Oh yes, it will come all right.' Perhaps he understood that in the midst of my anxiety I could not stay with him as I should have done otherwise. But the girls were more surprised than it is possible to describe. They looked at me with wondering eyes. 'If I were ill, papa, and you only stayed with me a moment, I should break my heart,' said Agatha. But the boy had a sympathetic feeling. He knew that of my own will I would not have done it. I shut myself up in the library, where I could not rest, but kept pacing up and down like a caged beast. What could I do? and if I could do nothing, what would become of my boy? These were the questions that, without ceasing, pursued each other through my mind.

Simson came out to dinner, and when the house was all still, and most of the servants in bed, we went out and met Dr Moncrieff, as he had appointed, at the head of the glen. Simson, for his part, was disposed to scoff at the divine. 'If there are to be any spells, you know, I'll cut the whole concern,' he said. I did not make him any reply. I had not invited him; he could go or come as he pleased. He was very talkative, far more than suited my humour, as we went on. 'One thing is certain, you know, there must be some human agency,' he said. 'It is all bosh about apparitions. I never have investigated the laws of sound to any great extent, and there's a great deal in ventriloquism that we don't know much about.' 'If it's the same to you,' I said, 'I wish you'd keep all that to yourself, Simson. It doesn't suit my state of mind.' 'Oh, I hope I know how to respect idiosyncrasy,' he said. The very tone of his voice irritated me beyond measure. These scientific fellows, I wonder people put up with them as they do, when you have no mind for their cold-blooded confidence. Dr Moncrieff met us about eleven o'clock, the same time as on the previous night. He was a large man, with a venerable countenance and white hair – old, but in full vigour, and thinking less of a cold night walk than many a younger man. He had his lantern as I had. We were fully provided with means of lighting the place, and we were all of us resolute men. We had a rapid consultation as we went up, and the result was that we divided to different posts. Dr Moncrieff remained inside the wall – if you can call that inside where there was no wall but one. Simson placed himself on the side next the ruins, so as to intercept any communication with the old house, which was what his mind was fixed upon. I was posted on the other side. To say that nothing could come near without being seen was self-evident. It had been so also on the previous night. Now, with our three lights in the midst of the darkness the whole place seemed illuminated. Dr Moncrieff's lantern, which was a large one, without any means of shutting up – an old-fashioned lantern with a pierced and ornamental top – shone steadily, the rays shooting out of it upward into the gloom. He placed it on the grass, where the middle of the room would have been. The usual effect of the light streaming out of the doorway was prevented by the illumination which Simson and I on either side supplied. With these differences, everything seemed as on the previous night.

And what occurred was exactly the same, with the same air of repetition, point for point, as I had formerly remarked. I declare that it seemed to me as if I were pushed against, put aside, by the owner of the voice as he paced up and down in his trouble – though these are perfectly futile words, seeing that the stream of light from my lantern, and that from Simson's taper, lay broad and clear, without a shadow, without the smallest break, across the entire breadth of the grass. I had ceased even to be alarmed, for my part. My heart was rent with pity and trouble – pity for the poor suffering human creature that moaned and pleaded so, and trouble for myself and my boy. God! if I could not find my help – and what help could I find? – Roland would die.

We were all perfectly still till the first outburst was exhausted, as I knew (by experience) it would be. Dr Moncrieff, to whom it was new, was quite motionless on the other side of the wall, as we were in our places. My heart had remained almost at its usual beating during the voice. I was used to it, it did not rouse all my pulses as it did at first. But just as it threw itself sobbing at the door (I cannot use other words), there suddenly came something which sent the blood coursing through my veins and my heart into my mouth. It was a voice inside the wall – the minister's well-known voice. I would have been prepared for it in any kind of adjuration, but I was not prepared for what I heard. It came out with a sort of stammering, as if too much moved for utterance. 'Willie, Willie! Oh, God preserve us! is it you?'

These simple words had an effect upon me that the voice of the invisible creature had ceased to have. I thought the old man, whom I had brought into this danger, had gone mad with terror. I made a dash round to the other side of the wall, half crazed myself with the thought. He was standing where I had left him, his shadow thrown vague and large upon the grass by the lantern which stood at his feet. I lifted my own light to see his face as I rushed forward. He was very pale, his eyes wet and glistening, his mouth quivering with parted lips. He neither saw nor heard me. We that had gone through this experience before, had crouched towards each other to get a little strength to bear it. But he was not even aware that I was there His whole being seemed absorbed in anxiety and tenderness. He held out his hands, which trembled, but it seemed to me with eagerness, not fear. He went on speaking all the time. 'Willie, if it is you – and it's you, if it is not a delusion of Satan – Willie, lad! why come ye here frighting them that know you not? Why came ye not to me?'

He seemed to wait for an answer. When his voice ceased, his countenance, every line moving, continued to speak. Simson gave me another terrible shock, stealing into the open doorway with his light, as much awe-stricken, as wildly curious, as I. But the minister resumed, without seeing Simson, speaking to someone else. His voice took a tone of expostulation—

'Is this right to come here? Your mother's gone with your name on her lips. Do you think she would ever close her door on her own lad? Do ye think the Lord will close the door, ye faint-hearted creature? No! – I forbid ye! I forbid ye!' cried the old man. The sobbing voice had begun to resume its cries. He made a step forward, calling out the last words in a voice of command. 'I forbid ye! Cry out no more to man. Go home, ye wandering spirit! Go home! Do you hear me – me that christened ye, that have struggled with ye, that have wrestled for ye with the Lord?' Here the loud tones of his voice sank into tenderness. 'And her too, poor woman! poor woman! her you are calling upon. She's no here. You'll find her with the Lord. Go there and seek her, not here. Do you hear me, lad? go after her there. He'll let you in, though it's late. Man, take heart! if you will lie and sob and greet, let it be at Heaven's gate, and no your poor mother's ruined door.'

He stopped to get his breath, and the voice had stopped, not as it had done before, when its time was exhausted and all its repetitions said, but with a sobbing catch in the breath as if over-ruled. Then the minister spoke again: 'Are you hearing me, Will? Oh, laddie, you've liked the beggarly elements all your days. Be done with them now. Go home to the Father – the Father! Are you hearing me?' Here the old man sank down upon his knees, his face raised upwards, his hands held up with a tremble in them, all white in the light in the midst of the darkness. I resisted as long as I could, though I cannot tell why – then I, too, dropped upon my knees. Simson all the time stood in the doorway, with an expression in his face such as words could not tell, his under-lip dropped, his eyes wild, staring. It seemed to be to him that image of blank ignorance and wonder, that we were praying. All the time the voice, with a low arrested sobbing, lay just where he was standing, as I thought.

'Lord,' the minister said – 'Lord, take him into Thy everlasting habitations. The mother he cries to is with Thee. Who can open to him but Thee? Lord, when is it too late for Thee, or what is too hard for Thee? Lord, let that woman there draw him inower! Let her draw him inower!'

I sprang forward to catch something in my arms that flung itself wildly within the door. The illusion was so strong that I never paused till I felt my forehead graze against the wall and my hands clutch the ground – for there was nobody there to save from falling, as in my foolishness I thought. Simson held out his hand to me to help me up. He was trembling and cold, his lower lip hanging, his speech almost inarticulate. 'It's gone,' he said, stammering – 'it's gone!' We leant upon each other for a moment, trembling so much, both of us, that the whole scene trembled as if it were going to dissolve and disappear, and yet as long as I live I will never forget it – the shining of the strange lights, the blackness all round, the kneeling figure with all the whiteness of the light concentrated on its white venerable head and uplifted hands. A strange solemn stillness seemed to close all round us. By intervals a single syllable, 'Lord! Lord!' came from the old minister's lips. He saw none of us, nor thought of us. I never knew how long we stood, like sentinels guarding him at his prayers, holding our lights in a confused dazed way, not knowing what we did. But at last he rose from his knees and, standing up at his full height, raised his arms, as the Scotch manner is at the end of a religious service, and solemnly gave the apostolic benediction – to what? to the silent earth, the dark woods, the wide breathing atmosphere – for we were but spectators gasping an Amen!

It seemed to me that it must be the middle of the night, as we all walked back. It was in reality very late. Dr Moncrieff put his arm into mine. He walked slowly, with an air of exhaustion. It was as if we were coming from a death-bed. Something hushed and solemnized the very air. There was that sense of relief in it which there always is at the end of a death-struggle. And Nature persistent, never daunted, came back in all of us, as we returned into the ways of life. We said nothing to each other, indeed, for a time, but when we got clear of the trees and reached the opening near the house, where we could see the sky, Dr Moncrieff himself was the first to speak. 'I must be going,' he said, 'it's very late, I'm afraid. I will go down the glen, as I came.'

'But not alone. I am going with you, doctor.'

'Well, I will not oppose it. I am an old man, and agitation wearies more than work. Yes, I'll be thankful of your arm. Tonight, Colonel, you've done me more good turns than one.'

I pressed his hand on my arm, not feeling able to speak. But Simson, who turned with us, and who had gone along all this time with his taper flaring, in entire unconsciousness, came to himself, apparently at the sound of our voices, and put out that wild little torch with a quick movement, as if of shame. 'Let me carry your lantern,' he said, 'it is heavy.' He recovered with a spring, and in a moment, from the awe-stricken spectator he had been, became himself, sceptical and cynical. 'I should like to ask you a question,' he said. 'Do you believe in Purgatory, Doctor? It's not in the tenets of the Church, so far as I know.'

'Sir,' said Dr Moncrieff, 'an old man like me is sometimes not very sure what he believes. There is just one thing I am certain of – and that is the loving-kindness of God.'

'But I thought that was in this life. I am no theologian–'

'Sir,' said the old man again, with a tremor in him which I could feel going over all his frame, 'if I saw a friend of mine within the gates of hell, I would not despair, but his Father would take him by the hand still – if he cried like *you*.'

'I allow it is very strange – very strange. I cannot see through it. That there must be human agency, I feel sure. Doctor, what made you decide upon the person and the name?'

The minister put out his hand with the impatience which a man might show if he were asked how he recognized his brother. 'Tuts!' he said, in familiar speech – then more solemnly, 'how should I not recognize a person that I know better – far better – than I know you?'

'Then you saw the man?'

Dr Moncrieff made no reply. He moved his hand again with a little impatient movement, and walked on, leaning heavily on my arm. And we went on for a long time without another word, threading the dark paths, which were steep and slippery with the damp of the winter. The air was very still – not more than enough to make a faint sighing in the branches, which mingled with the sound of the water to which we were descending. When we spoke again, it was about indifferent matters – about the height of the river, and the recent rains. We parted with the minister at his own door, where his old housekeeper appeared in great perturbation, waiting for him. 'Eh me, minister! the young gentleman will be worse?' she cried.

'Far from that – better. God bless him!' Dr Moncrieff said.

I think if Simson had begun again to me with his questions, I should have pitched him over the rocks as we returned up the glen, but he was silent, by a good inspiration. And the sky was clearer than it had been for many nights, shining high over the trees, with here and there a star faintly gleaming through the wilderness of dark and bare branches. The air, as I have said, was very soft in them, with a subdued and peaceful cadence. It was real, like every natural sound, and came to us like a hush of peace and relief. I thought there was a sound in it as of the breath of a sleeper, and it seemed clear to me that Roland must be sleeping, satisfied and calm. We went up to his room when we went in. There we found the complete hush of rest. My wife looked up out of a doze, and gave me a smile. 'I think he is a great deal better, but you are very late,' she said in a whisper, shading the light with her hand that the doctor might see his patient. The boy had got back something like his own colour. He woke as we stood all round his bed. His eyes had the happy half-awakened look of childhood, glad to shut again, yet pleased with the interruption and glimmer of light. I stooped over him and kissed his forehead, which was moist and cool. 'All is well, Roland,' I said. He looked up at me with a glance of pleasure, and took my hand and laid his cheek upon it, and so went to sleep.

For some nights after, I watched among the ruins, spending all the dark hours up to midnight patrolling about the bit of wall which was associated with so many emotions, but I heard nothing, and saw nothing beyond the quiet course of Nature, nor, so far as I am aware, has anything been heard again. Dr Moncrieff gave me the history of the youth, whom he never hesitated to name. I did not ask, as Simson did, how he recognized him. He had been a prodigal – weak, foolish, easily imposed upon, and 'led away', as people say. All that we had heard had passed actually in life, the doctor said. The young man had come home thus a day or two after his mother died – who was no more than the housekeeper in the old house – and, distracted with the news, had thrown himself down at the door and called upon her to let him in. The old man could scarcely speak of it for tears. To me it seemed as if – heaven help us, how little do we know about anything! – a scene like that might impress itself somehow upon the hidden heart of Nature. I do not pretend to know how, but the repetition had struck me at the time as, in its terrible strangeness and incomprehensibility, almost mechanical – as if the unseen actor could not exceed or vary, but was bound to re-enact the whole. One thing that struck me, however, greatly, was the likeness between the old minister and my boy in the manner of regarding those strange phenomena. Dr Moncrieff was not terrified, as I had been myself, and all the rest of us. It was no 'ghost', as I fear we all vulgarly considered it, to him but – a poor creature whom he knew under these conditions, just as he had known him in the flesh, having no doubt of his identity. And to Roland it was the same. This spirit in pain – if it was a spirit – this voice out of the unseen – was a poor fellow-creature in misery, to be succoured and helped out of his trouble, to my boy. He spoke to me quite frankly about it when he got better. 'I knew father would find some way,' he said. And this was when he was strong and well, and all idea that he would turn hysterical or become a seer of visions had happily passed away.

I must add one curious fact which does not seem to me to have any relation to the above, but which Simson made great use of, as the human agency which he was determined to find somehow. He had examined the ruins very closely at the time of these occurrences; but afterwards, when all was over, as we went casually about them one Sunday afternoon in the idleness of that unemployed day, Simson with his stick penetrated an old window which had been entirely blocked up with fallen soil. He jumped down into it in great excitement, and called to me to follow. There we found a little hole – for it was more a hole than a room – entirely hidden under the ivy ruins, in which there was some quantity of straw laid in a corner, as if someone had made a bed there, and some remains of crusts about the floor. Someone had lodged there, and not very long before, he made out; and that this unknown being was the author of all the mysterious sounds we heard he was convinced. 'I told you it was human agency,' he said, triumphantly. He forgets, I suppose, how he and I stood with our lights seeing nothing, while the space between us was audibly traversed by something that could speak, and sob, and suffer. There is no argument with men of this kind. He is ready to get up a laugh against me on this slender ground. 'I was puzzled myself – I could not make it out – but I always felt convinced human agency was at the bottom of it. And here it is – and a clever fellow he must have been,' the doctor says.

Bagley left my service as soon as he got well. He assured me it was no want of respect; but he could not stand 'them kind of things', and the man was so shaken and ghastly that I was glad to give him a present and let him go. For my own part, I made a point of staying out the time, two years, for which I had taken Brentwood; but I did not renew my tenancy. By that time we had settled, and found for ourselves a pleasant home of our own.

I must add that when the doctor defies me, I can always bring back gravity to his countenance, and a pause in his railing, when I remind him of the juniper-bush. To me that was a matter of little importance. I could believe I was mistaken. I did not care about it one way or other; but on his mind the effect was different. The miserable voice, the spirit in pain, he could think of as the result of ventriloquism, or reverberation, or – anything you please: an elaborate prolonged hoax executed somehow by the tramp that had found a lodging in the old tower. But the juniper-bush staggered him. Things have effects so different on the minds of different men.

Mr Justice Harbottle

Sheridan Le Fanu

1. The Judge's House

Thirty years ago, an elderly man, to whom I paid quarterly a small annuity charged on some property of mine, came on the quarterday to receive it. He was a dry, sad, quiet man, who had known better days, and had always maintained an unexceptionable character. No better authority could be imagined for a ghost story.

He told me one, though with a manifest reluctance; he was drawn into the narration by his choosing to explain what I should not have remarked, that he had called two days earlier than that week after the strict day of payment which he had usually allowed to elapse. His reason was a sudden determination to change his lodgings, and the consequent necessity of paying his rent a little before it was due.

He lodged in the dark street in Westminster, in a spacious old house, very warm, being wainscoted from top to bottom, and furnished with no undue abundance of windows, and those fitted with thick sashes and small panes.

This house was, as the bills upon the windows testified, offered to be sold or let. But no one seemed to care to look at it.

A thin matron, in rusty black silk, very taciturn, with large, steady, alarmed eyes, that seemed to look in your face, to read what you might have seen in the dark rooms and passages through which you had passed, was in charge of it, with a solitary 'maid-of-all-work' under her command. My poor friend had taken lodgings in this house, on account of their extraordinary cheapness. He had occupied them for nearly a year without the slightest disturbance, and was the only tenant, under rent, in the house. He had two rooms; a sitting-room, and a bedroom with a closet opening from it, in which he kept his books and papers locked up. He had gone to his bed, having also locked the outer door. Unable to sleep, he had lighted a candle, and after having read for a time, had laid the book beside him. He heard the old clock at the stair-head strike one; and very shortly after, to his alarm, he saw the closet-door, which he thought he had locked, open stealthily, and a slight dark man, particularly sinister, and somewhere about fifty, dressed in mourning of a very antique fashion, such a suit as we see in Hogarth, entered the room on tip-toe. He was followed by an elder man, stout, and blotched with scurvy, and whose features, fixed as a corpse's, were stamped with dreadful force with a character of sensuality and villainy.

This old man wore a flowered-silk dressing-gown and ruffles, and he remarked a gold ring on his finger, and on his head a cap of velvet, such as, in the days of perukes, gentlemen wore in undress.

This direful old man carried in his ringed and ruffled hand a coil of rope; and these two figures crossed the floor diagonally, passing the foot of his bed, from the closet-door at the farther end of the room, at the left, near the window, to the door opening upon the lobby, close to the bed's head, at his right.

He did not attempt to describe his sensations as these figures passed so near him. He merely said, that so far from sleeping in that room again, no consideration the world could offer would induce him so much as to enter it again alone, even in the daylight. He found both doors, that of the closet, and that of the room opening upon the lobby, in the morning fast locked, as he had left them before going to bed.

In answer to a question of mine, he said that neither appeared the least conscious of his presence. They did not seem to glide, but walked as living men do, but without any sound, and he felt a vibration on the floor as they crossed it. He so obviously suffered from speaking about the apparitions, that I asked him no more questions.

There were in his description, however, certain coincidences so very singular, as to induce me, by that very post, to write to a friend much my senior, then living in a remote part of England, for the information which I knew he could give me. He had himself more than once pointed out that old house to my attention, and told me, though very briefly, the strange story which I now asked him to give me in greater detail.

His answer satisfied me; and the following pages convey its substance.
Your letter (he wrote) tells me you desire some particulars about the

closing years of the life of Mr Justice Harbottle, one of the judges of the Court of Common Pleas. You refer, of course, to the extraordinary occurrences that made that period of his life long after a theme for 'winter tales' and metaphysical speculation. I happen to know perhaps more than any other man living of those mysterious particulars.

The old family mansion, when I revisited London, more than thirty years ago, I examined for the last time. During the years that have passed since then, I hear that improvement, with its preliminary demolitions, has been doing wonders for the quarter of Westminster in which it stood. If I were quite certain that the house had been taken down, I should have no difficulty about naming the street in which it stood. As what I have to tell, however, is not likely to improve its letting value, and as I should not care to get into trouble, I prefer being silent on that particular point.

How old the house was, I can't tell. People said it was built by Roger Harbottle, a Turkey merchant, in the reign of King James I. I am not a good opinion upon such questions; but having been in it, though in its forlorn and deserted state, I can tell you in a general way what it was like. It was built of dark-red brick, and the door and windows were faced with stone that had turned yellow by time. It receded some feet from the line of the other houses in the street; and it had a florid and fanciful rail of iron about the broad steps that invited your ascent to the hall-door, in which were fixed, under a file of lamps, among scrolls and twisted leaves, two immense 'extinguishers' like the conical caps of fairies, into which, in old times, the footmen used to thrust their flambeaux when their chairs or coaches had set down their great people, in the hall or at the steps, as the case might be. That hall is panelled up to the ceiling, and has a large fireplace. Two or three stately old rooms open from it at each side. The windows of these are tall, with many small panes. Passing through the arch at the back of the hall, you come upon the wide and heavy well-staircase. There is a back staircase also. The mansion is large, and has not as much light, by any means, in proportion to its extent, as modern houses enjoy. When I saw it, it had long been untenanted, and had the gloomy reputation beside of a haunted house. Cobwebs floated from the ceilings or spanned the corners of the cornices, and dust lay thick over everything. The windows were stained with the dust and rain of fifty years, and darkness had thus grown darker.

When I made it my first visit, it was in company with my father, when I was still a boy, in the year 1808. I was about twelve years old, and my imagination impressible, as it always is at that age. I looked about me with great awe. I was here in the very centre and scene of those occurrences

which I had heard recounted at the fireside at home, with so delightful a
horror.

My father was an old bachelor of nearly sixty when he married. He had,
when a child, seen Judge Harbottle on the bench in his robes and wig a
dozen times at least before his death, which took place in 1748, and his
appearance made a powerful and unpleasant impression, not only on his
imagination, but upon his nerves.

The Judge was at that time a man of some sixty-seven years. He had a
great mulberry-coloured face, a big, carbuncled nose, fierce eyes, and a
grim and brutal mouth. My father, who was young at the time, thought it
the most formidable face he had ever seen; for there were evidences of
intellectual power in the formation and lines of the forehead. His voice
was loud and harsh, and gave effect to the sarcasm which was his habitual
weapon on the bench.

This old gentleman had the reputation of being about the wickedest
man in England. Even on the bench he now and then showed his scorn of
opinion. He had carried cases his own way, it was said, in spite of counsel,
authorities, and even of juries, by a sort of cajolery, violence, and
bamboozling, that somehow confused and overpowered resistance. He
had never actually committed himself; he was too cunning to do that. He
had the character of being, however, a dangerous and unscrupulous judge;
but his character did not trouble him. The associates he chose for his
hours of relaxation cared as little as he did about it.

2. Mr Peters

One night during the session of 1746 this old Judge went down in his
chair to wait in one of the rooms of the House of Lords for the result of a
division in which he and his order were interested.

This over, he was about to return to his house close by, in his chair; but
the night had become so soft and fine that he changed his mind, sent it
home empty, and with two footmen, each with a flambeau, set out on foot
in preference. Gout had made him rather a slow pedestrian. It took him
some time to get through the two or three streets he had to pass before
reaching his house.

In one of those narrow streets of tall houses, perfectly silent at that hour,
he overtook, slowly as he was walking, a very singular-looking old
gentleman.

He had a bottle-green coat on, with a cape to it, and large stone buttons,
a broad-leafed low-crowned hat, from under which a big powdered wig

escaped; he stooped very much, and supported his bending knees with the aid of a crutch-handled cane, and so shuffled and tottered along painfully.

'I ask your pardon, sir,' said this old man in a very quavering voice, as the burly Judge came up with him, and he extended his hand feebly towards his arm.

Mr Justice Harbottle saw that the man was by no means poorly dressed, and his manner that of a gentleman.

The Judge stopped short, and said, in his harsh peremptory tones, 'Well, sir, how can I serve you?'

'Can you direct me to Judge Harbottle's house? I have some intelligence of the very last importance to communicate to him.'

'Can you tell it before witnesses?' asked the Judge.

'By no means; it must reach *his* ear only,' quavered the old man earnestly.

'If that be so, sir, you have only to accompany me a few steps farther to reach my house, and obtain a private audience; for I am Judge Harbottle.'

With this invitation the infirm gentleman in the white wig complied very readily; and in another minute the stranger stood in what was then termed the front parlour of the Judge's house, *tête-à-tête* with that shrewd and dangerous functionary.

He had to sit down, being very much exhausted, and unable for a little time to speak; and then he had a fit of coughing, and after that a fit of gasping; and thus two or three minutes passed, during which the Judge dropped his roquelaure on an armchair, and threw his cocked hat over that.

The venerable pedestrian in the white wig quickly recovered his voice. With closed doors they remained together for some time.

There were guests waiting in the drawing-rooms, and the sound of men's voices laughing, and then of a female voice singing to a harpsichord, were heard distinctly in the hall over the stairs; for old Judge Harbottle had arranged one of his dubious jollifications, such as might well make the hair of godly men's heads stand upright, for that night.

This old gentleman in the powdered white wig, that rested on his stooped shoulders, must have had something to say that interested the Judge very much; for he would not have parted on easy terms with the ten minutes and upwards which that conference filched from the sort of revelry in which he most delighted, and in which he was the roaring king, and in some sort the tyrant also, of his company.

The footman who showed the aged gentleman out observed that the

Judge's mulberry-coloured face, pimples and all, were bleached to a dingy yellow, and there was the abstraction of agitated thought in his manner, as he bid the stranger good night. The servant saw that the conversation had been of serious import, and that the Judge was frightened.

Instead of stumping upstairs forthwith to his scandalous hilarities, his profane company, and his great china bowl of punch – the identical bowl from which a bygone Bishop of London, good easy man, had baptized this Judge's grandfather, now clinking round the rim with silver ladles, and hung with scrolls of lemon peel – instead, I say, of stumping and clambering up the great staircase to the cavern of his Circean enchantment, he stood with his big nose flattened against the window-pane, watching the progress of the feeble old man, who clung stiffly to the iron rail as he got down, step by step, to the pavement.

The hall-door had hardly closed, when the old Judge was in the hall bawling hasty orders, with such stimulating expletives as old colonels under excitement sometimes indulge in nowadays, with a stamp or two of his big foot, and a waving of his clenched fist in the air. He commanded the footman to overtake the old gentleman in the white wig, to offer him his protection on his way home, and in no case to show his face again without having ascertained where he lodged, and who he was, and all about him.

'By— sirrah! if you fail me in this, you doff my livery tonight!'

Forth bounced the stalwart footman, with his heavy cane under his arm, and skipped down the steps, and looked up and down the street after the singular figure, so easy to recognize.

What were his adventures I shall not tell you just now.

The old man, in the conference to which he had been admitted in that stately panelled room, had just told the Judge a very strange story. He might be himself a conspirator; he might possibly be crazed; or possibly his whole story was straight and true.

The aged gentleman in the bottle-green coat, on finding himself alone with Mr Justice Harbottle, had become agitated. He said,

'There is, perhaps you are not aware, my lord, a prisoner in Shrewsbury jail, charged with having forged a bill of exchange for a hundred and twenty pounds, and his name is Lewis Pyneweck, a grocer of that town.'

'Is there?' says the Judge, who knew well that there was.

'Yes, my lord,' says the old man.

'Then you had better say nothing to affect this case. If you do, by— I'll commit you; for I'm to try it,' says the Judge, with his terrible look and tone.

'I am not going to do anything of the kind, my lord; of him or his case I know nothing, and care nothing. But a fact has come to my knowledge which it behoves you to well consider.'

'And what may that fact be?' inquired the Judge; 'I'm in haste, sir, and beg you will use dispatch.'

'It has come to my knowledge, my lord, that a secret tribunal is in process of formation, the object of which is to take cognizance of the conduct of the judges; and first, of *your* conduct, my lord: it is a wicked conspiracy.'

'Who are of it?' demands the Judge.

'I know not a single name as yet. I know but the fact, my lord; it is most certainly true.'

'I'll have you before the Privy Council, sir,' says the Judge.

'That is what I most desire; but not for a day or two, my lord.'

'And why so?'

'I have not as yet a single name, as I told your lordship; but I expect to have a list of the most forward men in it, and some other papers connected with the plot, in two or three days.'

'You said one or two just now.'

'About that time, my lord.'

'Is this a Jacobite plot?'

'In the main I think it is, my lord.'

'Why, then, it is political. I have tried no State prisoners, nor am like to try any such. How, then, doth it concern me?'

'From what I can gather, my lord, there are those in it who desire private revenges upon certain judges.'

'What do they call their cabal?'

'The High Court of Appeal, my lord.'

'Who are you sir? What is your name?'

'Hugh Peters, my lord.'

'That should be a Whig name?'

'It is, my lord.'

'Where do you lodge, Mr Peters?'

'In Thames Street, my lord, over against the sign of the Three Kings.'

'Three Kings? Take care one be not too many for you, Mr Peters! How come you, an honest Whig, as you say, to be privy to a Jacobite plot? Answer me that.'

'My lord, a person in whom I take an interest has been seduced to take a part in it; and being frightened at the unexpected wickedness of their plans, he is resolved to become an informer for the Crown.'

'He resolves like a wise man, sir. What does he say of the persons? Who are in the plot? Doth he know them?'

'Only two, my lord; but he will be introduced to the club in a few days, and he will then have a list, and more exact information of their plans, and above all of their oaths, and their hours and places of meeting, with which he wishes to be acquainted before they can have any suspicions of his intentions. And being so informed, to whom, think you, my lord, had he best go then?'

'To the king's attorney-general straight. But you say this concerns me, sir, in particular? How about this prisoner, Lewis Pyneweck? Is he one of them?'

'I can't tell, my lord; but for some reason, it is thought your lordship will be well advised if you try him not. For if you do, it is feared 'twill shorten your days.'

'So far as I can learn, Mr Peters, this business smells pretty strong of blood and treason. The king's attorney-general will know how to deal with it. When shall I see you again, sir?'

'If you give me leave, my lord, either before your lordship's court sits, or after it rises, tomorrow. I should like to come and tell your lordship what has passed.'

'Do so, Mr Peters, at nine o'clock tomorrow morning. And see you play me no trick, sir, in this matter; if you do, by —, sir, I'll lay you by the heels!'

'You need fear no trick from me, my lord; had I not wished to serve you, and acquit my own conscience, I never would have come all this way to talk with your lordship.'

'I'm willing to believe you, Mr Peters; I'm willing to believe you, sir.'

And upon this they parted.

'He has either painted his face, or he is consumedly sick,' thought the old Judge.

The light had shone more effectually upon his features as he turned to leave the room with a low bow, and they looked, he fancied, unnaturally chalky.

'D— him!' said the Judge ungraciously, as he began to scale the stairs: 'he has half-spoiled my supper.'

But if he had, no one but the Judge himself perceived it, and the evidence was all, as anyone might perceive, the other way.

3. Lewis Pyneweck

In the meantime, the footman dispatched in pursuit of Mr Peters speedily overtook that feeble gentleman. The old man stopped when he heard the sound of pursuing steps, but any alarms that may have crossed his mind seemed to disappear on his recognizing the livery. He very gratefully accepted the proffered assistance, and placed his tremulous arm within the servant's for support. They had not gone far, however, when the old man stopped suddenly, saying,

'Dear me! as I live, I have dropped it. You heard it fall. My eyes, I fear, won't serve me, and I'm unable to stoop low enough; but if *you* will look, you shall have half the find. It is a guinea; I carried it in my glove.'

The street was silent and deserted. The footman had hardly descended to what he termed his 'hunkers', and begun to search the pavement about the spot which the old man indicated, when Mr Peters, who seemed very much exhausted, and breathed with difficulty, struck him a violent blow, from above, over the back of the head with a heavy instrument, and then another; and leaving him bleeding and senseless in the gutter, ran like a lamplighter down a lane to the right, and was gone.

When, an hour later, the watchman brought the man in livery home, still stupid and covered with blood, Judge Harbottle cursed his servant roundly, swore he was drunk, threatened him with an indictment for taking bribes to betray his master, and cheered him with a perspective of the broad street leading from the Old Bailey to Tyburn, the cart's tail, and the hangman's lash.

Notwithstanding this demonstration, the Judge was pleased. It was a disguised 'affidavit man', or footpad, no doubt, who had been employed to frighten him. The trick had fallen through.

A 'court of appeal', such as the false Hugh Peters had indicated, with assassination for its sanction, would be an uncomfortable institution for a 'hanging judge' like the Honourable Justice Harbottle. That sarcastic and ferocious administrator of the criminal code of England, at that time a rather pharisaical, bloody, and heinous system of justice, had reasons of his own for choosing to try that very Lewis Pyneweck, on whose behalf this audacious trick was devised. Try him he would. No man living should take that morsel out of his mouth.

Of Lewis Pyneweck of course, so far as the outer world could see, he knew nothing. He would try him after his fashion, without fear, favour, or affection.

But did he not remember a certain thin man, dressed in mourning, in whose house, in Shrewsbury, the Judge's lodgings used to be, until a scandal of his ill-treating his wife came suddenly to light? A grocer with a demure look, a soft step, and a lean face as dark as mahogany, with a nose sharp and long, standing ever so little awry, and a pair of dark steady brown eyes under thinly-traced black brows – a man whose thin lips wore always a faint unpleasant smile.

Had not that scoundrel an account to settle with the Judge? had he not been troublesome lately? and was not his name Lewis Pyneweck, some time grocer in Shrewsbury, and now prisoner in the jail of that town?

The reader may take it, if he pleases, as a sign that Judge Harbottle was a good Christian, that he suffered nothing ever from remorse. That was undoubtedly true. He had nevertheless done this grocer, forger, what you will, some five or six years before, a grievous wrong; but it was not that, but a possible scandal, and possible complications, that troubled the learned Judge now.

Did he not, as a lawyer, know, that to bring a man from his shop to the dock, the chances must be at least ninety-nine out of a hundred that he is guilty?

A weak man like his learned brother Withershins was not a judge to keep the high-roads safe, and make crime tremble. Old Judge Harbottle was the man to make the evil-disposed quiver, and to refresh the world with showers of wicked blood, and thus save the innocent, to the refrain of the ancient saw he loved to quote:

> Foolish pity
> Ruins a city.

In hanging that fellow he could not be wrong. The eye of a man accustomed to look upon the dock could not fail to read 'villain' written sharp and clear in his plotting face. Of course he would try him, and no one else should.

A saucy-looking woman, still handsome, in a mob-cap gay with blue ribbons, in a saque of flowered silk, with lace and rings on, much too fine for the Judge's housekeeper, which nevertheless she was, peeped into his study next morning, and, seeing the Judge alone, stepped in.

'Here's another letter from him, come by the post this morning. Can't you do nothing for him?' she said wheedlingly, with her arm over his neck, and her delicate finger and thumb fiddling with the lobe of his purple ear.

'I'll try,' said Judge Harbottle, not raising his eyes from the paper he was reading.

'I knew you'd do what I asked you,' she said.

The Judge clapt his gouty claw over his heart, and made her an ironical bow.

'What,' she asked, 'will you do?'

'Hang him,' said the Judge with a chuckle.

'You don't mean to; no, you don't, my little man,' said she, surveying herself in a mirror on the wall.

'I'm d——d but I think you're falling in love with your husband at last!' said Judge Harbottle.

'I'm blest but I think you're growing jealous of him,' replied the lady with a laugh. 'But no; he was always a bad one to me; I've done with him long ago.'

'And he with you, by George! When he took your fortune and your spoons and your ear-rings, he had all he wanted of you. He drove you from his house; and when he discovered you had made yourself comfortable, and found a good situation, he'd have taken your guineas and your silver and your ear-rings over again, and then allowed you half a dozen years more to make a new harvest for his mill. You don't wish him good; if you say you do, you lie.'

She laughed a wicked saucy laugh, and gave the terrible Rhadamanthus a playful tap on the chops.

'He wants me to send him money to fee a counsellor,' she said, while her eyes wandered over the pictures on the wall, and back again to the looking-glass; and certainly she did not look as if his jeopardy troubled her very much.

'Confound his impudence, the *scoundrel*!' thundered the old Judge, throwing himself back in his chair, as he used to do *in furore* on the bench, and the lines of his mouth looked brutal, and his eyes ready to leap from their sockets. 'If you answer his letter from my house to please yourself, you'll write your next from somebody else's to please me. You understand, my pretty witch, I'll not be pestered. Come, no pouting; whimpering won't do. You don't care a brass farthing for the villain, body or soul. You came here but to make a row. You are one of Mother Carey's chickens; and where you come, the storm is up. Get you gone, baggage! get you *gone*!' he repeated with a stamp; for a knock at the hall-door made her instantaneous disappearance indispensable.

I need hardly say that the venerable Hugh Peters did not appear again. The Judge never mentioned him. But oddly enough, considering how he laughed to scorn the weak invention which he had blown into dust at the very first puff, his white-wigged visitor and the conference in the dark front parlour were often in his memory.

His shrewd eye told him that allowing for change of tints and such disguises as the playhouse affords every night, the features of this false old man, who had turned out too hard for his tall footman, were identical with those of Lewis Pyneweck.

Judge Harbottle made his registrar call upon the crown solicitor, and tell him that there was a man in town who bore a wonderful resemblance to a prisoner in Shrewsbury jail named Lewis Pyneweck, and to make inquiry through the post forthwith whether anyone was personating Pyneweck in prison, and whether he had thus or otherwise made his escape.

The prisoner was safe, however, and no question as to his identity.

4. Interruption in Court

In due time Judge Harbottle went circuit; and in due time the judges were in Shrewsbury. News travelled slowly in those days, and newspapers, like the wagons and stage-coaches, took matters easily. Mrs Pyneweck, in the Judge's house, with a diminished household – the greater part of the Judge's servants having gone with him, for he had given up riding circuit, and travelled in his coach in state – kept house rather solitarily at home.

In spite of quarrels, in spite of mutual injuries – some of them, inflicted by herself, enormous – in spite of a married life of spited bickerings – a life in which there seemed no love or liking or forbearance, for years – now that Pyneweck stood in near danger of death, something like remorse came suddenly upon her. She knew that in Shrewsbury were transacting the scenes which were to determine his fate. She knew she did not love him; but she could not have supposed, even a fortnight before, that the hour of suspense could have affected her so powerfully.

She knew the day on which the trial was expected to take place. She could not get it out of her head for a minute; she felt faint as it drew towards evening.

Two or three days passed; and then she knew that the trial must be over by this time. There were floods between London and Shrewsbury, and news was long delayed. She wished the flood would last for ever. It was dreadful waiting to hear; dreadful to know that the event was over, and that she could not hear till self-willed rivers subsided; dreadful to know that they must subside and the news come at last.

She had some vague trust in the Judge's good nature, and much in the resources of chance and accident. She had contrived to send the money he wanted. He would not be without legal advice and energetic and skilled support.

At last the news did come – a long arrear all in a gush: a letter from a female friend in Shrewsbury; a return of the sentences, sent up for the Judge; and most important, because most easily got at, being told with great aplomb and brevity, and long-deferred intelligence of the Shrewsbury Assizes in the *Morning Advertiser.* Like an impatient reader of a novel, who reads the last page first, she read with dizzy eyes the list of the executions.

Two were respited, seven were hanged; and in that capital catalogue was this line:

'Lewis Pyneweck – forgery.'

She had to read it half a dozen times over before she was sure she understood it. Here was the paragraph:

'Sentence, Death – 7.

'Executed accordingly, on Friday the 13th instant, to wit:

'Thomas Primer, *alias* Duck – highway robbery.

'Flora Guy – stealing to the value of 11s. 6d.

'Arthur Pounden – burglary.

'Matilda Mummery – riot.

'Lewis Pyneweck – forgery, bill of exchange.'

And when she reached this, she read it over and over, feeling very cold and sick.

This buxom housekeeper was known in the house as Mrs Carwell – Carwell being her maiden name, which she had resumed.

No one in the house except its master knew her history. Her introduction had been managed craftily. No one suspected that it had been concerted between her and the old reprobate in scarlet and ermine.

Flora Carwell ran up the stairs now, and snatched her little girl, hardly seven years of age, whom she met in the lobby, hurriedly up in her arms, and carried her into her bedroom, without well knowing what she was doing, and sat down, placing the child before her. She was not able to speak. She held the child before her, and looked in the little girl's wondering face, and burst into tears of horror.

She thought the Judge could have saved him. I daresay he could. For a time she was furious with him; and hugged and kissed her bewildered little girl, who returned her gaze with large round eyes.

That little girl had lost her father, and knew nothing of the matter. She had been always told that her father was dead long ago.

A woman, coarse, uneducated, vain, and violent, does not reason, or even feel, very distinctly; but in these tears of consternation were mingling a self-upbraiding. She felt afraid of that little child.

But Mrs Carwell was a person who lived not upon sentiment, but upon beef and pudding; she consoled herself with punch; she did not trouble herself long even with resentments; she was a gross and material person, and could not mourn over the irrevocable for more than a limited number of hours, even if she would.

Judge Harbottle was soon in London again. Except the gout, this savage old epicurean never knew a day's sickness. He laughed and coaxed and bullied away the young woman's faint upbraidings, and in a little time Lewis Pyneweck troubled her no more; and the Judge secretly chuckled over the perfectly fair removal of a bore, who might have grown little by little something very like a tyrant.

It was the lot of the judge whose adventures I am now recounting to try criminal cases at the Old Bailey shortly after his return. He had commenced his charge to the jury in a case of forgery, and was, after his wont, thundering dead against the prisoner, with many a hard aggravation and cynical gibe, when suddenly all died away in silence, and, instead of looking at the jury, the eloquent Judge was gaping at some person in the body of the court.

Among the persons of small importance who stand and listen at the sides was one tall enough to show with a little prominence; a slight mean figure, dressed in seedy black, lean and dark of visage. He had just handed a letter to the crier, before he caught the Judge's eye.

That Judge descried, to his amazement, the features of Lewis Pyneweck. He had the usual faint thin-lipped smile; and with his blue chin raised in air, and as it seemed quite unconscious of the distinguished notice he had attracted, he was stretching his low cravat with his crooked fingers, while he slowly turned his head from side to side – a process which enabled the Judge to see distinctly a stripe of swollen blue round his neck, which indicated, he thought, the grip of the rope.

This man, with a few others, had got a footing on a step, from which he could better see the court. He now stepped down, and the Judge lost sight of him.

His lordship signed energetically with his hand in the direction in which this man had vanished. He turned to the tipstaff. He first effort to speak ended in a gasp. He cleared his throat, and told the astounded official to arrest that man who had interrupted the court.

'He's but this moment gone down *there*. Bring him in custody before me, within ten minutes' time, or I'll strip your gown from your shoulders and fine the sheriff!' he thundered, while his eyes flashed round the court in search of the functionary.

Attorneys, counsellors, idle spectators, gazed in the direction in which Mr Justice Harbottle had shaken his gnarled old hand. They compared notes. Not one had seen anyone making a disturbance. They asked one another if the Judge was losing his head.

Nothing came of the search. His lordship concluded his charge a great deal more tamely; and when the jury retired, he stared round the court with a wandering mind, and looked as if he would not have given sixpence to see the prisoner hanged.

5. Caleb Searcher

The Judge had received the letter; had he known from whom it came, he would no doubt have read it instantaneously. As it was he simply read the direction:

> To the Honourable
> The Lord Justice
> Elijah Harbottle,
> One of his Majesty's Justices of
> the Honourable Court of Common Pleas.

It remained forgotten in his pocket till he reached home.

When he pulled out that and others from the capacious pocket of his coat, it had its turn, as he sat in his library in his thick silk dressing-gown; and then he found its contents to be a closely-written letter, in a clerk's hand, and an enclosure in 'secretary hand', as I believe the angular scrivinary of law-writings in those days was termed, engrossed on a bit of parchment about the size of this page. The letter said:

Mr Justice Harbottle, – My Lord,

I am ordered by the High Court of Appeal to acquaint your lordship, in order to your better preparing yourself for your trial, that a true bill hath been sent down, and the indictment lieth against your lordship for the murder of one Lewis Pyneweck of Shrewsbury, citizen, wrongfully executed for the forgery of a bill of exchange, on the —th day of — last, by reason of the wilful perversion of the evidence, and the undue pressure put upon the jury, together with the illegal admission of evidence by your lordship, well knowing the same to be illegal, by all which the promoter of the prosecution of the said indictment, before the High Court of Appeal, hath lost his life.

And the trial of the said indictment, I am further ordered to acquaint your lordship, is fixed for the 10th day of — next ensuing, by the right honourable the Lord Chief-Justice Twofold, of the court aforesaid, to wit, the High Court of Appeal, on which day it will most certainly take place. And I am further to acquaint your lordship, to prevent any surprise or miscarriage, that your case stands first for the said day, and that the said High Court of Appeal sits day and night, and never rises; and herewith, by order of the said court, I furnish your lordship with a copy (extract) of the record in this case, except of the indictment, whereof, notwithstanding, the substance and effect is supplied to your lordship in this Notice. And further I am to inform you, that in case the jury then to try your lordship should find you guilty, the right honourable the Lord Chief-Justice will, in passing sentence of death upon you, fix the day of execution for the 10th day of —, being one calendar month from the day of your trial.

It was signed by

CALEB SEARCHER
Officer of the Crown Solicitor in
the
Kingdom of Life and Death.

The Judge glanced through the parchment.

' 'Sblood! Do they think a man like me is to be bamboozled by their buffoonery?'

The Judge's coarse features were wrung into one of his sneers; but he was pale. Possibly, after all, there was a conspiracy on foot. It was queer. Did they mean to pistol him in his carriage? or did they only aim at frightening him?

Judge Harbottle had more than enough of animal courage. He was not afraid of highwaymen, and he had fought more than his share of duels, being a foul-mouthed advocate while he held briefs at the bar. No one questioned his fighting qualities. But with respect to this particular case of Pyneweck, he lived in a house of glass. Was there not his pretty, dark-eyed, over-dressed housekeeper, Mrs Flora Carwell? Very easy for people who knew Shrewsbury to identify Mrs Pyneweck, if once put upon the scent; and had he not stormed and worked hard in that case? Had he not made it hard sailing for the prisoner? Did he not know very well what the bar thought of it? It would be the worst scandal that ever blasted judge.

So much there was intimidating in the matter, but nothing more. The Judge was a little bit gloomy for a day or two after, and more testy with everyone than usual.

He locked up the papers; and about a week after he asked his housekeeper, one day, in the library:

'Had your husband never a brother?'

Mrs Carwell squalled on this sudden introduction of the funereal topic, and cried exemplary 'piggins full', as the Judge used pleasantly to say. But he was in no mood for trifling now, and he said sternly:

'Come, madam! this wearies me. Do it another time; and give me an answer to my question.' So she did.

Pyneweck had no brother living. He once had one; but he died in Jamaica.

'How do you know is he dead?' asked the Judge.

'Because he told me so.'

'Not the dead man?'

'Pyneweck told me so.'

'Is that all?' sneered the Judge.

He pondered this matter; and time went on. The Judge was growing a little morose, and less enjoying. The subject struck nearer to his thoughts than he fancied it could have done. But so it is with most undivulged vexations, and there was no one to whom he could tell this one.

It was now the ninth; and Mr Justice Harbottle was glad. He knew nothing would come of it. Still it bothered him; and tomorrow would see it well over.

[What of the paper I have cited? No one saw it during his life; no one, after his death. He spoke of it to Dr Hedstone; and what purported to be 'a copy', in the old Judge's handwriting, was found. The original was nowhere. Was it a copy of an illusion, incident to brain disease? Such is my belief.]

6. Arrested

Judge Harbottle went this night to the play at Drury Lane. He was one of those old fellows who care nothing for late hours, and occasionally knocking about in pursuit of pleasure. He had appointed with two cronies of Lincoln's Inn to come home in his coach with him to sup after the play.

They were not in his box, but were to meet him near the entrance, and to get into his carriage there; and Mr Justice Harbottle, who hated waiting, was looking a little impatiently from the window.

The Judge yawned.

He told the footman to watch for Counsellor Thavies and Counsellor Beller, who were coming; and, with another yawn, he laid his cocked hat on his knees, closed his eyes, leaned back in his corner, wrapped his mantle closer about him, and began to think of pretty Mrs Abington.

And being a man who could sleep like a sailor, at a moment's notice, he was thinking of taking a nap. Those fellows had no business to keep a judge waiting.

He heard their voices now. Those rake-hell counsellors were laughing, and bantering, and sparring after their wont. The carriage swayed and jerked, as one got in, and then again as the other followed. The door clapped, and the coach was now jogging and rumbling over the pavement. The Judge was a little bit sulky. He did not care to sit up and open his eyes. Let them suppose he was asleep. He heard them laugh with more malice than good-humour, he thought, as they observed it. He would give them a d—d hard knock or two when they got to his door, and till then he would counterfeit his nap.

The clocks were chiming twelve. Beller and Thavies were silent as tombstones. They were generally loquacious and merry rascals.

The Judge suddenly felt himself roughly seized and thrust from his corner into the middle of the seat, and opening his eyes, instantly he found himself between his two companions.

Before he could blurt out the oath that was at his lips, he saw that they were two strangers – evil-looking fellows, each with a pistol in his hand, and dressed like Bow Street officers.

The Judge clutched at the check-string. The coach pulled up. He stared about him. They were not among houses; but through the windows, under a broad moonlight, he saw a black moor stretching lifelessly from right to left, with rotting trees, pointing fantastic branches in the air, standing here and there in groups, as if they held up their arms and twigs like fingers, in horrible glee at the Judge's coming.

A footman came to the window. He knew his long face and sunken eyes. He knew it was Dingly Chuff, fifteen years ago a footman in his service, whom he had turned off at a moment's notice, in a burst of jealousy, and indicted for a missing spoon. The man had died in prison of the jail-fever.

The Judge drew back in utter amazement. His armed companions signed mutely; and they were again gliding over this unknown moor.

The bloated and gouty old man, in his horror, considered the question of resistance. But his athletic days were long over. This moor was a desert. There was no help to be had. He was in the hands of strange servants, even if his recognition turned out to be a delusion, and they were under the command of his captors. There was nothing for it but submission, for the present.

Suddenly the coach was brought nearly to a standstill so that the prisoner saw an ominous sight from the window.

It was a gigantic gallows beside the road; it stood three-sided, and from each of its three broad beams at top depended in chains some eight or ten bodies, from several of which the cere-clothes had dropped away, leaving the skeletons swinging lightly by their chains. A tall ladder reached to the summit of the structure, and on the peat beneath lay bones.

On top of the dark transverse beam facing the road, from which, as from the other two completing the triangle of death, dangled a row of these unfortunates in chains, a hangman, with a pipe in his mouth, much as we see him in the famous print of the 'Idle Apprentice', though here his perch was ever so much higher, was reclining at his ease and listlessly shying bones, from a little heap at his elbow, at the skeletons that hung round, bringing down now a rib or two, now a hand, now half a leg. A long-sighted man could have discerned that he was a dark fellow, lean; and from continually looking down on the earth from the elevation over which, in another sense, he always hung, his nose, his lips, his chin were pendulous and loose, and drawn down into a monstrous grotesque.

This fellow took his pipe from his mouth on seeing the coach, stood up, and cut some solemn capers high on his beam, and shook a new rope in the air, crying with a voice high and distant as the caw of a raven hovering over a gibbet, 'A rope for Judge Harbottle!'

The coach was now driving on at its old swift pace.

So high a gallows as that, the Judge had never, even in his most hilarious moments, dreamed of. He thought he must be raving. And the dead footman! He shook his ears and strained his eyelids; but if he was dreaming, he was unable to awake himself.

There was no good in threatening these scoundrels. A *brutum fulmen* might bring a real one on his head.

Any submission to get out of their hands; and then heaven and earth he would move to unearth and hunt them down.

Suddenly they drove round a corner of a vast white building, and under a *porte-cochère*.

7. Chief-Justice Twofold

The Judge found himself in a corridor lighted with dingy oil-lamps, the walls of bare stone; it looked like a passage in a prison. His guards placed him in the hands of other people. Here and there he saw bony and gigantic soldiers passing to and fro, with muskets over their shoulders. They looked straight before them, grinding their teeth, in bleak fury, with no noise but the clank of their shoes. He saw these by glimpses, round corners, and at the ends of passages, but he did not actually pass them by.

And now, passing under a narrow doorway, he found himself in the dock, confronting a judge in his scarlet robes, in a large courthouse. There was nothing to elevate this temple of Themis above its vulgar kind elsewhere. Dingy enough it looked, in spite of candles lighted in decent abundance. A case had just closed, and the last juror's back was seen escaping through the door in the wall of the jury-box. There were some dozen barristers, some fiddling with pen and ink, others buried in briefs, some beckoning, with the plumes of their pens, to their attorneys, of whom there were no lack; there were clerks to-ing and fro-ing, and the officers of the court, and the registrar, who was handing up a paper to the judge; and the tipstaff, who was presenting a note at the end of his wand to a king's counsel over the heads of the crowd between. If this was the High Court of Appeal, which never rose day or night, it might account for the pale and jaded aspect of everybody in it. An air of indescribable gloom hung upon the pallid features of all the people here; no one ever smiled; all looked more or less secretly suffering.

'The King against Elijah Harbottle!' shouted the officer.

'Is the appellant Lewis Pyneweck in court?' asked Chief-Justice Twofold, in a voice of thunder, that shook the woodwork of the court, and boomed down the corridors.

Up stood Pyneweck from his place at the table.

'Arraign the prisoner!' roared the Chief; and Judge Harbottle felt the panels of the dock round him, and the floor, and the rails quiver in the vibrations of that tremendous voice.

The prisoner, *in limine*, objected to this pretended court, as being a sham, and non-existent in point of law; and then, that, even if it were a court constituted by law (the Judge was growing dazed), it had not and could not have any jurisdiction to try him for his conduct on the bench.

Whereupon the chief-justice laughed suddenly, and everyone in court, turning round upon the prisoner, laughed also, till the laugh grew and roared all round like a deafening acclamation; he saw nothing but glittering eyes and teeth, a universal stare and grin; but though all the voices laughed, not a single face of all those that concentrated their gaze upon him looked like a laughing face. The mirth subsided as suddenly as it began.

The indictment was read. Judge Harbottle actually pleaded! He pleaded 'Not guilty'. A jury was sworn. The trial proceeded. Judge Harbottle was bewildered. This could not be real. He must be either mad, or *going* mad, he thought.

One thing could not fail to strike even him. This Chief-Justice Twofold, who was knocking him about at every turn with sneer and gibe, and roaring him down with his tremendous voice, was a dilated effigy of himself; an image of Mr Justice Harbottle, at least double his size, and with all his fierce colouring, and his ferocity of eye and visage, enhanced awfully.

Nothing the prisoner could argue, cite, or state was permitted to retard for a moment the march of the case towards its catastrophe.

The chief-justice seemed to feel his power over the jury, and to exult and riot in the display of it. He glared at them, he nodded to them; he seemed to have established an understanding with them. The lights were faint in that part of the court. The jurors were mere shadows, sitting in rows; the prisoner could see a dozen pairs of white eyes shining, coldly, out of the darkness; and whenever the judge in his charge, which was contemptuously brief, nodded and grinned and gibed, the prisoner could see, in the obscurity, by the dip of all these rows of eyes together, that the jury nodded in acquiescence.

And now the charge was over, the huge chief-justice leaned back panting and gloating on the prisoner. Everyone in the court turned about, and gazed with steadfast hatred on the man in the dock. From the jury-box where the twelve sworn brethren were whispering together, a sound in the general stillness like a prolonged 'hiss-s-s!' was heard, and then, in answer to the challenge of the officer, 'How say you, gentlemen of the jury, guilty or not guilty?' came in a melancholy voice the finding, 'Guilty.'

The place seemed to the eyes of the prisoner to grow gradually darker and darker, till he could discern nothing distinctly but the lumen of the eyes that were turned upon him from every bench and side and corner and gallery of the building. The prisoner doubtless thought that he had quite enough to say, and conclusive, why sentence of death should not be pronounced upon him; but the lord chief-justice puffed it contemptuously away, like so much smoke, and proceeded to pass sentence of death upon the prisoner, having named the 10th of the ensuing month for his execution.

Before he had recovered the stun of this ominous farce, in obedience to the mandate, 'Remove the prisoner,' he was led from the dock. The lamps seemed all to have gone out, and there were stoves and charcoal-fires here and there, that threw a faint crimson light on the walls of the corridors through which he passed. The stones that composed them looked now enormous, cracked and unhewn.

He came into a vaulted smithy, where two men, naked to the waist, with heads like bulls, round shoulders, and the arms of giants, were welding red-hot chains together with hammers that pelted like thunderbolts.

They looked on the prisoner with fierce red eyes, and rested on their hammers for a minute; and said the elder to his companion, 'Take out Elijah Harbottle's gyves'; and with a pincers he plucked the end which lay dazzling in the fire from the furnace.

'One end locks,' said he, taking the cool end of the iron in one hand, while with the grip of a vice he seized the leg of the Judge, and locked the ring round his ankle. 'The other,' he said with a grin, 'is welded.'

The iron band that was to form the ring for the other leg lay still red-hot upon the stone floor, with brilliant sparks sporting up and down its surface.

His companion in his gigantic hands seized the old Judge's other leg, and pressed his foot immovably to the stone floor; while his senior in a twinkling, with a masterly application of pincers and hammer, sped the glowing bar round his ankle so tight that the skin and sinews smoked and bubbled again, and old Judge Harbottle uttered a yell that seemed to chill the very stones, and make the iron chains quiver on the wall.

Chains, vaults, smiths, and smithy all vanished in a moment; but the pain continued. Mr Justice Harbottle was suffering torture all round the ankle on which the infernal smiths had just been operating.

His friends Thavies and Beller were startled by the Judge's roar in the midst of their elegant trifling about a marriage *à la mode* case which was going on. The Judge was in panic as well as pain. The street-lamps and the light of his own hall-door restored him.

'I'm very bad,' growled he between his teeth; 'my foot's blazing. Who was he that hurt my foot? 'Tis the gout – 'tis the gout!' he said, awaking completely. 'How many hours have we been coming from the playhouse? 'Sblood, what has happened on the way? I've slept half the night?'

There had been no hitch or delay, and they had driven home at a good pace.

The Judge, however, was in gout; he was feverish too; and the attack, though very short, was sharp; and when, in about a fortnight, it subsided, his ferocious joviality did not return. He could not get this dream, as he chose to call it, out of his head.

8. Somebody Has Got Into the House

People remarked that the Judge was in the vapours. His doctor said he should go for a fortnight to Buxton.

Whenever the Judge fell into a brown study, he was always conning over the terms of the sentence pronounced upon him in his vision – 'in one calendar month from the date of this day'; and then the usual form, 'and you shall be hanged by the neck till you are dead,' &c. 'That will be the 10th – I'm not much in the way of being hanged. I know what stuff dreams are, and I laugh at them; but this is continually in my thoughts, as if it forecast misfortune of some sort. I wish the day my dream gave me were passed and over. I wish I were well purged of my gout. I wish I were as I used to be. 'Tis nothing but vapours, nothing but a maggot.' The copy of the parchment and letter which had announced his trial with many a snort and sneer he would read over and over again, and the scenery and people of his dream would rise about him in places the most unlikely, and steal him in a moment from all that surrounded him into a world of shadows.

The Judge had lost his iron energy and banter. He was growing taciturn and morose. The Bar remarked the change, as well they might. His friends thought him ill. The doctor said he was troubled with hypochondria, and that his gout was still lurking in his system, and ordered him to that ancient haunt of crutches and chalk-stones, Buxton.

The Judge's spirits were very low; he was frightened about himself; and he described to his housekeeper, having sent for her to his study to drink a dish of tea, his strange dream in his drive home from Drury Lane playhouse. He was sinking into the state of nervous dejection in which men lose their faith in orthodox advice, and in despair consult quacks, astrologers, and nursery story-tellers. Could such a dream mean that he was to have a fit, and so die on the 10th? She did not think so. On the contrary, it was certain some good luck must happen on that day.

The Judge kindled; and for the first time for many days, he looked for a minute or two like himself, and he tapped her on the cheek with the hand that was not in flannel.

'Odsbud! odsheart! you dear rogue! I had forgot. There is young Tom – yellow Tom, my nephew, you know, lies sick at Harrogate, why shouldn't he go that day as well as another, and if he does, I get an estate by it? Why, lookee, I asked Dr Hedstone yesterday if I was like to take a fit any time, and he laughed, and swore I was the last man in town to go off that way.'

The Judge sent most of his servants down to Buxton to make his lodgings and all things comfortable for him. He was to follow in a day or two.

It was now the 9th; and the next day well over, he might laugh at his visions and auguries.

On the evening of the 9th, Dr Hedstone's footman knocked at the Judge's door. The doctor ran up the dusky stairs to the drawing-room. It was a March evening, near the hour of sunset, with an east wind whistling sharply through the chimney-stacks. A wood fire blazed cheerily on the hearth. And Judge Harbottle, in what was then called a brigadier-wig, with his red roquelaure on, helped the glowing effect of the darkened chamber, which looked red all over like a room on fire.

The Judge had his feet on a stool, and his huge grim purple face confronted the fire, and seemed to pant and swell, as the blaze alternately spread upward and collapsed. He had fallen again among his blue devils, and was thinking of retiring from the Bench, and of fifty other gloomy things.

But the doctor, who was an energetic son of Aesculapius, would listen to no croaking, told the Judge he was full of gout, and in his present condition no judge even of his own case, but promised him leave to pronounce on all those melancholy questions, a fortnight later.

In the meantime the Judge must be very careful. He was overcharged with gout, and he must not provoke an attack, till the waters of Buxton should do that office for him, in their own salutary way.

The doctor did not think him perhaps quite so well as he pretended, for he told him he wanted rest, and would be better if he went forthwith to his bed.

Mr Gerningham, his valet, assisted him, and gave him his drops; and the Judge told him to wait in his bedroom till he should go to sleep.

Three persons that night had specially odd stories to tell.

The housekeeper had got rid of the trouble of amusing her little girl at this anxious time by giving her leave to run about the sitting-rooms and look at the pictures and china, on the usual condition of touching nothing. It was not until the last gleam of sunset had for some time faded, and the twilight had so deepened that she could no longer discern the colours on the china figures on the chimneypiece or in the cabinets, that the child returned to the housekeeper's room to find her mother.

To her she related, after some prattle about the china, and the pictures, and the Judge's two grand wigs in the dressing-room off the library, an adventure of an extraordinary kind.

In the hall was placed, as was customary in those times, the sedan-chair which the master of the house occasionally used, covered with stamped leather; and studded with gilt nails, and with its red silk blinds down. In this case, the doors of this old-fashioned conveyance were locked, the windows up, and, as I said, the blinds down, but not so closely that the curious child could not peep underneath one of them, and see into the interior.

A parting beam from the setting sun, admitted through the window of a back room, shot obliquely through the open door, and lighting on the chair, shone with a dull transparency through the crimson blind.

To her surprise, the child saw in the shadow a thin man dressed in black seated in it; he had sharp dark features; his nose, she fancied, a little awry, and his brown eyes were looking straight before him; his hand was on his thigh, and he stirred no more than the waxen figure she had seen at Southwark fair.

A child is so often lectured for asking questions and on the propriety of silence, and the superior wisdom of its elders, that it accepts most things at last in good faith; and the little girl acquiesced respectfully in the occupation of the chair by this mahogany-faced person as being all right and proper.

It was not until she asked her mother who this man was, and observed her scared face as she questioned her more minutely upon the appearance of the stranger, that she began to understand that she had seen something unaccountable.

Mrs Carwell took the key of the chair from its nail over the footman's shelf, and led the child by the hand up to the hall, having a lighted candle in her other hand. She stopped at a distance from the chair, and placed the candlestick in the child's hand.

'Peep in, Margery, again, and try if there's anything there,' she whispered; 'hold the candle near the blind so as to throw its light through the curtain.'

The child peeped, this time with a very solemn face, and intimated at once that he was gone.

'Look again, and be sure,' urged her mother.

The little girl was quite certain; and Mrs Carwell, with her mob-cap of lace and cherry-coloured ribbons, and her dark brown hair, not yet powdered, over a very pale face, unlocked the door, looked in, and beheld emptiness.

'All a mistake, child, you see.'

'*There*, ma'am! See there! He's gone round the corner,' said the child.

'Where?' said Mrs Carwell, stepping backward a step.

'Into that room.'

'Tut, child! 'twas the shadow,' cried Mrs Carwell angrily, because she was frightened. 'I moved the candle.' But she clutched one of the poles of the chair, which leant against the wall in the corner, and pounded the floor furiously with one end of it, being afraid to pass the open door the child had pointed to.

The cook and two kitchen-maids came running upstairs, not knowing what to make of this unwonted alarm.

They all searched the room; but it was still and empty, and no sign of anyone's having been here.

Some people may suppose that the direction given to her thoughts by this odd little incident will account for a very strange illusion which Mrs Carwell herself experienced about two hours later.

9. The Judge Leaves His House

Mrs Flora Carwell was going up the great staircase with a posset for the Judge in a china bowl, on a little silver tray.

Across the top of the well-staircase there runs a massive oak rail; and, raising her eyes accidentally, she saw an extremely odd-looking stranger, slim and long, leaning carelessly over with a pipe between his finger and thumb. Nose, lips, and chin seemed all to droop downward into extraordinary length, as he leant his odd peering face over the banister. In his other hand he held a coil of rope, one end of which escaped from under his elbow and hung over the rail.

Mrs Carwell, who had no suspicion at the moment, that he was not a real person, and fancied that he was someone employed in cording the Judge's luggage, called to know what he was doing there.

Instead of answering, he turned about, and walked across the lobby, at about the same leisurely pace at which she was ascending, and entered a room, into which she followed him. It was an uncarpeted and unfurnished chamber. An open trunk lay upon the floor empty, and beside it the coil of rope; but except herself there was no one in the room.

Mrs Carwell was very much frightened, and now concluded that the child must have seen the same ghost that had just appeared to her. Perhaps, when she was able to think it over, it was a relief to believe so;

for the face, figure, and dress described by the child were awfully like Pyneweck; and this certainly was not he.

Very much scared and very hysterical, Mrs Carwell ran down to her room, afraid to look over her shoulder, and got some companions about her, and wept, and talked, and drank more than one cordial, and talked and wept again, and so on, until, in those early days, it was ten o'clock, and time to go to bed.

A scullery-maid remained up finishing some of her scouring and 'scalding' for some time after the other servants – who, as I said, were few in number – that night had got to their beds. This was a low-browed, broad-faced, intrepid wench with black hair, who did not 'vally a ghost not a button,' and treated the housekeeper's hysterics with measureless scorn.

The old house was quiet, now. It was near twelve o'clock, no sounds were audible except the muffled wailing of the wintry winds, piping high among the roofs and chimneys, or rumbling at intervals, in under gusts, through the narrow channels of the street.

The spacious solitudes of the kitchen level were awfully dark, and this sceptical kitchen-wench was the only person now up and about, in the house. She hummed tunes to herself, for a time; and then stopped and listened; and then resumed her work again. At last, she was destined to be more terrified than even was the housekeeper.

There was a back-kitchen in this house, and from this she heard, as if coming from below its foundations, a sound like heavy strokes that seemed to shake the earth beneath her feet. Sometimes a dozen in sequence, at regular intervals; sometimes fewer. She walked out softly into the passage, and was surprised to see a dusky glow issuing from this room, as if from a charcoal fire.

The room seemed thick with smoke.

Looking in, she very dimly beheld a monstrous figure, over a furnace, beating with a mighty hammer the rings and rivets of a chain.

The strokes, swift and heavy as they looked, sounded hollow and distant. The man stopped, and pointed to something on the floor, that, through the smoky haze, looked, she thought, like a dead body. She remarked no more; but the servants in the room close by, startled from their sleep by a hideous scream, found her in a swoon on the flags, close to the door, where she had just witnessed this ghastly vision.

Startled by the girl's incoherent asseverations that she had seen the Judge's corpse on the floor, two servants having first searched the lower part of the house, went rather frightened upstairs to inquire whether their master was well. They found him, not in his bed, but in his room. He had a table with candles burning at his bedside, and was getting on his clothes again; and he swore and cursed at them roundly in his old style, telling them that he had business, and that he would discharge on the spot any scoundrel who should dare to disturb him again.

So the invalid was left to his quietude.

In the morning it was rumoured here and there in the street that the Judge was dead. A servant was sent from the house three doors away, by Counsellor Traverse, to inquire at Judge Harbottle's hall-door.

The servant who opened it was pale and reserved, and would only say that the Judge was ill. He had had a dangerous accident; Dr Hedstone had been with him at seven o'clock in the morning.

There were averted looks, short answers, pale and frowning faces, and all the usual signs that there was a secret that sat heavily upon their minds, and the time for disclosing which had not yet come. That time would arrive when the coroner had arrived, and the mortal scandal that had befallen the house could be no longer hidden. For that morning Mr Justice Harbottle had been found hanging by the neck from the banister at the top of the great staircase, and quite dead.

There was not the smallest sign of any struggle or resistance. There had not been heard a cry or any other noise in the slightest degree indicative of violence. There was medical evidence to show that, in his atrabilious state, it was quite on the cards that he might have made away with himself. The jury found accordingly that it was a case of suicide. But to those who were acquainted with the strange story which Judge Harbottle had related to at least two persons, the fact that the catastrophe occurred on the morning of the 10th March seemed a startling coincidence.

A few days after, the pomp of a great funeral attended him to the grave; and so, in the language of scripture, 'the rich man died, and was buried.'

Le Horla

Guy de Maupassant

May 8th. A perfect day! I spent all the morning lying on the grass in front of my house under the huge plane-tree, which casts its shade over the whole building. I love this part of the country and I love living here, because my roots are here, those deep sensitive roots which bind a man to the spot where his ancestors were born and died. The way people think there, the food they eat, their habits, the local dishes and expressions, the accent of the peasants, the tang of the soil, the smell of the villages, the very scent of the air itself go to form this bond.

I love this house where I grew up. From my windows I can see the Seine flowing past my garden on the other side of the road, almost part of my property, the deep broad river running from Rouen to Havre, thronged with boats passing.

To the left in the distance lies Rouen, a vast blue-roofed town nestling under a host of pointed Gothic spires. There are too many to count, some slender, some broad-based, all dominated by the cast-iron flèche of the cathedral; they all have their bells, which peal in the clear air on fine mornings, so that I hear the soft metallic hum in the distance and the ringing note of the bronze wafted on the breeze, now loud, now faint, as the wind rises and falls.

It was a gorgeous morning today.

About eleven o'clock a long line of ships passed in front of my garden-gate, towed by a tug no bigger than a fly, puffing painfully and spitting out a thick cloud of smoke.

Behind two English schooners, whose red ensign fluttered in the breeze, came a splendid Brazilian three-master, all white, beautifully clean and shining. I took off my hat to her, I don't know why; she was such a magnificent sight.

May 12th. For the last few days I've been a little feverish; I've not been feeling quite the thing, or rather I've been a bit depressed.

What is the origin of those mysterious influences which change our happiness into depression and our good spirits into anxiety? It is as if the atmosphere was full of unseen, unknown powers whose proximity affects us. I wake up on top of the world, wanting to sing; I wonder why. Then after a short stroll along the river I come back, convinced that some bad news is awaiting me at home. I can't understand it. Have I caught a chill which has upset my nerves and caused this depression? Is it the shape of the clouds or the ever-changing play of light on the landscape that has induced my black mood? I don't know. Everything round us, all that passes before our eyes unregistered, all that affects us unknowingly, all our subconscious contacts, all that we see without perceiving has an immediate, surprising, unaccountable effect on us, on our physical organs, and through them on our minds and even on the heart itself.

The mystery of the invisible is quite incomprehensible; we cannot fathom it with our poor weak senses – our eyes which cannot distinguish either the infinitely small or the infinitely large, either the too near or the too distant, the denizens of a star or of a drop of water – or our ears which deceive us by transmitting sound-waves as musical notes. Our ears are magicians which perform the miracle of changing these waves into sound and so give birth to music, making harmony out of nature's meaningless flux. Our sense of smell is less keen than that of a dog and our palate can hardly recognize the age of a wine.

If only we had other organs to perform other miracles for us, how much more we could discover in the world around us!

May 16th. I'm definitely ill and last month I was so well! I've got a temperature or rather some feverish nerve complaint, which affects me mentally as much as physically. I can't get rid of this horrible sensation of impending danger, this anticipation of some imminent misfortune or approaching death, a presentiment which is the symptom of some unknown disease developing in the bloodstream and the body.

May 18th. I've just been to see my doctor, for I can't get any sleep. He found my pulse rapid, my eye dilated and my nerves on edge, but nothing to worry about. He prescribed shower-baths and a dose of potassium bromide.

May 25th. No change! My condition is certainly very disturbing. As evening approaches, an unaccountable anxiety seizes me, as if the darkness hid some terrible threat to my life. I hurry over my dinner and try to read, but I don't understand the words and I can hardly read the letters. Then I pace up and down my sitting-room, oppressed by a vague overmastering fear, fear of going to bed and sleeping.

About two in the morning I go to my bedroom and as soon as I get there I double-lock the door and bolt it . . . I'm terrified of something, I don't know what; I've never been nervous before. I open my cupboards and look under the bed – I listen and listen – for what? Isn't it strange that a little discomfort, perhaps something wrong with my circulation, a slight congestion, some quite trivial upset in the defective, delicate working of our physical mechanism has the power to turn the most cheerful of men into a melancholic, the bravest into a coward? Soon I get into bed and wait for sleep as one would wait for the hangman. I wait for sleep in a state of terror, my heart thumping and my limbs twitching. I shiver all over in spite of the warmth of the bed-clothes, till suddenly I fall asleep like a man plunging into a stagnant pool to drown himself. I am not conscious of the approach of sleep as I used to be; it is now a treacherous foe lurking near me, ready to pounce on me, close my eyes, and destroy me.

I sleep for some time, two or three hours; then a dream or rather a nightmare seizes me. I know quite well that I am in bed and asleep – I realize it and I can see myself; and I am conscious, too, of someone approaching me, looking at me, touching me; next he climbs on to the bed, kneels on my chest, seizes my throat and grips it with all his strength to strangle me.

I struggle, paralysed by the ghastly impotence which affects one in a dream; I try to scream but I can't; I try with all my might, panting with the effort, to turn over and throw off the being who is crushing and suffocating me – and I am powerless.

Suddenly I wake up in panic terror, dripping with sweat, and light a candle; there is no one there.

After this struggle, which is repeated every night, I go to sleep at last and sleep peacefully till morning.

June 2nd. My condition is worse. What *is* the matter with me? The bromide and the baths are doing no good. Today, exhausted as I was already, I went for a walk in the Forest of Roumare to tire myself out. I thought at first that the fresh air, so soft and cool, full of the scent of grass and leaves, was invigorating my blood and stimulating my heart. I chose a broad hunters' drive and presently turned towards La Bouille by a narrow track bordered by two rows of huge trees, which interposed a thick dark-green roof between me and the sky.

Suddenly I shivered; it was not the shiver caused by cold but the shiver of fright.

I quickened my pace, nervous at being alone in the wood, irrationally, foolishly terrified by the absolute solitude. I felt I was being followed, that someone was walking close behind me, touching me.

I swung round sharply but I was alone. Behind me I saw nothing but the broad straight drive, empty and towering, and in front too it stretched as far as I could see, frighteningly empty.

I closed my eyes, I don't know why, and began to spin round and round on one heel like a top; I nearly fell down. When I opened my eyes again, the trees were dancing and the ground heaving; I had to sit down. Then I forgot which way I had come – I lost my head completely and hadn't an idea. I started off to the right and found myself back in the drive which had brought me to the middle of the forest.

June 3rd. I've had a dreadful night! I'm going away for a week or two. A little trip will no doubt do me good.

July 2nd. I'm home again, cured! Moreover I've had a delightful holiday; I went to Mont-Saint-Michel, which I didn't know.

What a marvellous view it is, when one arrives at Avranches, as I did, towards evening! The town is on a hill and I drove to the public garden on the edge of the city. I uttered a cry of amazement. There in front of me as far as I could see stretched an immensely wide bay; its widely separated coasts disappeared in the misty distance. In the centre of this vast bay, which reflected the gold of a cloudless sky, rose the dark point of a strange rock, surrounded by the sands. The sun had just set and against the sky, still crimson, was silhouetted the outline of this fantastic rock crowned with its fantastic abbey.

Early next morning I walked towards it. The tide was out as it had been the evening before and, as I got nearer, I saw the astonishing building rearing up before me. After more than an hour's walk I reached the huge rock mass, on which stands the little town dominated by the great church. I climbed the steep narrow street and entered the most perfect Gothic abode ever designed for God on earth, a whole town in itself, full of low halls crushed beneath vaulted ceilings and lofty galleries supported on slender columns. I made my way into this immense granite jewel, airy as lace with its crown of towers and slim spires with winding stairs inside. These thrust up into the clear sky by day and the dark sky by night, their strange heads bristling with devils and gargoyles, fantastic animals and monstrous flowers, joined to each other by delicate carved arches.

When I reached the top, I said to the monk who was showing me round: 'You must be very happy here, Father!'

He answered: 'It's very windy, Sir.' We began to talk, as we watched the tide rising, racing across the sands and covering them as with a steel breastplate. The monk told me an endless series of old stories and legends of the place.

One of these impressed me greatly. Local people living on the rock insist that a voice can be heard at night on the sands, followed by the bleating of two goats, one loud and one faint. Sceptics assert that it is only the cry of sea-birds, which sometimes sounds like bleating, sometimes like human lamentations. But fishermen coming home late swear that they have met an old shepherd, wandering over the dunes between two tides round the isolated little town; his head is always hidden by his cloak and he walks in front leading a he-goat with a man's head and a nanny with a woman's; both have long white hair and talk all the time, abusing each other in an unknown tongue and then suddenly pausing to bleat with all their might.

I said to the monk: 'Do you believe this?'

He replied in a low voice: 'I don't know.'

I went on: 'If there existed on earth beings other than ourselves, surely we must have discovered them long ago; you and I must have seen them.'

He answered: 'Can we see the hundred-thousandth part of what exists? Take the wind, for example, the most powerful force in nature; it blows men over, destroys houses, uproots trees, raises the sea into mountainous waves, undermines cliffs, and drives great ships on to reefs; it kills, whistles, moans, roars. Have you ever seen it? Can you ever see it? But it exists all the same.'

I had no answer to this obvious argument; the man was a philosopher – or was he only unsophisticated? I wasn't quite sure which, but I fell silent; the same thought had often occurred to me.

July 3rd. I slept badly. There is certainly something here, which makes me feverish, for my coachman suffers from the same trouble. When I got home yesterday, I noticed him looking pale and I asked: 'What is the matter with you, John?'

'The fact is I can't sleep, Sir; it's the nights that get me down. Since you went away, Sir, there's been some sort of spell on me.'

The other servants, however, are perfectly well, but I'm afraid of another attack myself.

July 4th. I'm certainly worse again. My old nightmares are back. Last night I felt as if someone was lying on top of me, with his mouth on mine, draining my life away through my lips. Yes, he was sucking my life from my mouth like a leech. Presently he got up satiated and I woke up so bruised, so exhausted, so worn out that I couldn't move. Another day or two of this and I shall have to go away again.

July 5th. Is my reason going? What happened last night is so inexplicable that my brain is in a whirl when I think of it.

I had locked my bedroom door, as I do now every night; then, feeling thirsty, I drank half a tumbler of water and I happened to notice that my water-bottle was full right up to the stopper.

After that I went to bed and fell into one of my ghastly trances, out of which I was awoken some two hours later by a still more terrifying shock.

Imagine a man being murdered in his sleep, waking up with a knife in his lungs and the death-rattle in his throat, covered with blood, fighting for breath, at his last gasp, not knowing what has happened – well, I was like that.

Having at last recovered myself, I felt thirsty again; so I lit my candle and went to the table where my water-bottle stood. I picked it up and tilted it to fill my glass; no water came, it was empty, absolutely empty! At first I didn't understand; then I suddenly realized with such a shock that I had to sit down, or rather I collapsed on to a chair! A minute later I started up and looked all round, but immediately sat down again, dazed with amazement and terror in front of the empty bottle. I gazed fixedly at it, searching for some explanation. My hands were shaking. Someone had drunk the water! Who? It must have been me, of course; it could have been no one else! So I must be a sleep-walker; without knowing it, I must be living this mysterious double life, which makes us wonder if there are two personalities in us or if some alien being, unknown and invisible, enters into us, while we are unconscious, and controls our body, which must obey the intruder as it obeys us or even more implicitly.

No one can realize my ghastly agony of mind; no one can imagine the feelings of a man, perfectly sane and wide awake, in possession of all his faculties, gazing in panic terror at an empty water-bottle, from which a little water has disappeared, while he was asleep. I stayed there till dawn, not daring to go back to bed.

July 6th. I am going mad! Someone has emptied my water-bottle again tonight – or rather I must have drunk it myself. But is it really I, is it? Who else could it be? My God! I'm going mad – no one can save me!

July 10th. I've just carried out several experiments with astonishing results. I must be mad – or am I?

On July 6th, before going to bed, I put on my table wine, milk, water, bread, and some strawberries. Someone – that is, I – drank all the water and some of the milk; neither the wine nor the strawberries were touched.

On July 7th I tried the same experiment with the same result.

On July 8th I omitted the water and the milk, and nothing was touched.

Finally, on July 9th I put on my table only water and milk, carefully wrapping the bottles in white muslin and tying down the stoppers. Then I rubbed my lips, my beard and my hands with black lead and went to bed.

I fell into a deep sleep, followed presently by an agonizing awakening. I hadn't stirred; there was no black mark on my sheets. I hurried to the table. The wrappings round the bottles were not stained. I untied the string round the stoppers. All the water and all the milk had been drunk. Oh! my God!

I'm just starting for Paris.

July 12th. Paris. I must have been crazy these last few days! I must have been the victim of an overwrought imagination, unless I've been walking in my sleep or under the influence, observed but never explained, called suggestion. Anyhow my panic terror came very close to madness and twenty-four hours in Paris have been enough to put me right. Yesterday, after some shopping and a round of visits, which brought a breath of fresh air into my mind, I finished up the evening at the Comédie-Française. They were playing a piece by the younger Alexandre Dumas and his sprightly penetrating wit has completed my cure. It is certainly dangerous for those engaged in brain work to live alone; we need the society of people who think and talk. Alone for a long period, we fill the void with fantasies.

I made my way back to my hotel along the boulevards. In the midst of the bustling crowd I smiled at my last week's terrors and imaginations, when I had seriously believed that an invisible being was installed in my house. We are poor weak creatures, easily frightened and upset, when we have to face some trivial incident which we cannot explain.

Instead of drawing the obvious inference: 'I can't understand this, because I don't know its cause', we immediately imagine some terrifying mystery or supernatural power at work.

July 14th. The Festival of the Republic. I've been walking about the streets, where the crackers and flags afforded me childish amusement. All the same it's pretty futile to cultivate the holiday spirit on a fixed date by Government decree. The masses are like a flock of unintelligent sheep, sometimes stupidly patient, sometimes fiercely undisciplined. The order is given: 'Amuse yourselves', and they obey; next they are told: 'Go and fight your neighbour', and again they obey. They are bidden to vote for the Emperor, and they vote for him; the next order is: 'Vote for the Republic', and they do so.

Those who control them are equally foolish; but instead of obeying a human master, they are the slaves of principles, which must of necessity be senseless, sterile, and false, just because they are principles, that is, ideas held to be established and immutable in a world where nothing is certain – light and sound themselves are only illusions.

July 16th. I had an experience yesterday, which has upset me considerably.

I was dining at the house of my cousin, Madame Sablé, whose husband is in command of the 76th Light Infantry at Limoges. There were two other young married women at dinner, one the wife of a Dr Parent, a specialist on nervous complaints, who has devoted much attention to the extraordinary development of recent experiment in hypnotism and suggestion.

He gave us a long account of the amazing results obtained by English scientists and doctors of the Nancy school. What he asserted to be facts seemed to me so inexplicable that I roundly declared I didn't believe them.

'We are,' he insisted, 'on the eve of the discovery of one of nature's most important secrets, I mean, one of the most important for this world of ours; for she holds others, no doubt, equally important for the bodies in space. Ever since man has been able to think and express his thoughts in speech and writing, he has been aware of the close proximity of a mystery, which eludes his gross imperfect senses, and he has been trying to make up for the impotence of his physical organs by exercising his intelligence. While human intelligence was rudimentary, these unseen phenomena which haunted him merely produced commonplace terror. This is the origin of popular beliefs in the supernatural, stories of prowling spirits, fairies, gnomes, and ghosts.

'But since rather more than a century ago there have been hints of something new. Mesmer and a few others have blazed an unexpected trail and we have, especially in the last four or five years, reached amazing results.'

My cousin, who was as incredulous as I, smiled. Dr Parent said to her: 'Would you like me to try to put you to sleep, Madame?'

'Yes, I'm quite willing.'

She sat down in an armchair and he began to fix her with a fascinating gaze. I was suddenly conscious of a vague feeling of uneasiness; my heart thumped and my throat contracted. I saw Madame Sablé's eyes close; her mouth twitched and her breast heaved.

In ten minutes she was asleep.

'Go behind her,' said the doctor to me.

I took a seat behind her and he placed a visiting-card in her hand, saying: 'This is a looking-glass; what do you see in it?'

She replied: 'I see my cousin.'

'What is he doing?'

'He is curling his moustache.'

'And now what?'

'He is taking a photograph out of his pocket.'

'Whom is the photograph of?'

'Himself.'

She was right! And the photograph had only been delivered to me at my hotel that evening.

'What does he look like in the photograph?'

'He is standing up with his hat in his hand.'

So she could see in this card, this piece of white pasteboard, what she would have seen in a mirror.

The young women were frightened and cried: 'That's enough; stop!'

But the doctor gave her the order: 'You will get up at eight o'clock tomorrow morning and go to your cousin at his hotel; you will ask him for the loan of five thousand francs, which your husband has asked you for and which he will want from you, when he comes tomorrow.'

He then woke her up.

On my way back to my hotel I was thinking over this curious séance and I began to feel doubts, not indeed about my cousin's good faith, which was certain and entirely above suspicion – I had known her like a sister from childhood – but about a possible deception on the part of the doctor. Could he have been concealing in his hand a mirror, which he showed to the sleeping lady at the same time as the visiting-card? Professional conjurers do equally wonderful things.

I got back to the hotel and went to bed.

This morning about half past eight I was woken by my valet, who said: 'Madame Sablé is here and wants to speak to you urgently, Sir.' I hurried into my clothes and had her in.

She sat down in a great state of agitation, keeping her eyes on the ground, and said without raising her veil: 'My dear cousin, I've got a great favour to ask you.'

'What is it, my dear?'

'I hate asking you but I can't help it. I want, and I simply must have, five thousand francs.'

'You can't mean it!'

'Yes, I do, or rather my husband does, and he has asked me to get it.'

I was dumbfounded that I couldn't speak without stammering. I wondered if she wasn't in collusion with Dr Parent to pull my leg, if the whole thing was not a practical joke, carefully rehearsed and well carried out. But all my doubts disappeared, as I watched her more closely. She was trembling with anxiety, the request was so painful to her, and I realized she was on the verge of tears. I knew she was not hard up and I went on: 'Do you really mean he cannot put his hand on five thousand francs? Think a minute. Are you sure he wanted you to ask me for the money?'

She hesitated for a few seconds as if making a great effort to remember, before she replied: 'Yes . . . yes! I'm quite sure.'

'Did he write to you?'

She hesitated again, pondering. I guessed the agony of her thoughts. She didn't know; she only knew that she had got to borrow five thousand francs from me for her husband. She steeled herself to tell a lie. 'Yes, I had a letter from him.'

'When? You didn't mention it yesterday.'

'I only got the letter this morning.'

'Could you show it to me?'

'No, I couldn't . . . It was an intimate personal letter. Besides . . . I've . . . I've burnt it.'

'Your husband must have run into debt then.'

She hesitated again, before saying in a low voice: 'I don't know.'

I said brutally: 'The fact is, I can't lay my hand on five thousand francs at the moment, my dear cousin.'

She uttered an agonized cry: 'Oh! please, please, you must find them!'

She was working herself up into a state of violent excitement – she clasped her hands in an attitude of prayer. The tone of her voice changed; she was sobbing and stammering, tortured and dominated by the peremptory command she had received.

'Oh! I beg and beseech you . . . if you only knew what a state I'm in . . . I simply must have the money today!'

I took pity on her. 'You shall have it as soon as I can get it, I promise.'

'Oh! thank you! It *is* good of you!'

I went on: 'Do you recollect what happened at your house yesterday?'

'Yes!'

'Do you remember Dr Parent putting you to sleep?'

'Yes!'

'Well, he told you to come and borrow five thousand francs from me this morning, and you are obeying his suggestion at this moment.'

She thought for a minute and then replied: 'But it's my husband who wants them.'

For an hour I tried to convince her but without success. When she had gone, I hurried to the doctor's house; he was just going out. After listening to me with a smile, he said: 'Are you convinced now?'

'I can't help it.'

'Let's go to your cousin's house.'

She was already dozing in a deck-chair, dead beat. The doctor felt her pulse and fixed his gaze on her for some minutes, raising one hand towards her eyes, which gradually closed under the overmastering influence of this magnetic force.

When she was asleep, the doctor said: 'Your husband doesn't need the five thousand francs after all. So you will forget that you ever asked your cousin for the loan, and if he mentions the subject, you will not understand.'

After that he woke her up. I took my wallet out of my pocket: 'Here is what you asked for this morning, my dear cousin!'

She was so taken aback that I dared not press the matter. I tried to recall it to her mind but she vehemently denied it; she thought I was making fun of her and finally nearly got seriously annoyed.

Well, that's that! I'm back at the hotel, so upset that I couldn't eat any lunch.

July 19th. I've told the story to several people and they all laughed at me. I don't know what to think. A wise man doesn't commit himself.

July 20th. I've been to dine at Bougival and I spent the evening at the Boat Club's dance. Everything obviously depends on one's surroundings. It would be the height of folly to believe in the supernatural on the Île de la Grenouillère, but at the top of the Mont-Saint-Michel or in the Indies it's quite another thing. The influence of one's surroundings is frighteningly powerful. I shall go home next week.

July 30th. I got home yesterday. Everything is all right.

August 2nd. Nothing to report. The weather is gorgeous. I spend my time watching the Seine flowing past.

August 4th. Trouble among the servants. They assert that glasses are getting broken in the cupboards. The valet accuses the kitchenmaid, who in turn accuses the sewing-maid, who accuses the other two. Who is responsible? It would take a Solomon to decide!

August 6th. This time I'm not mad; I've got the evidence of my own eyes . . . I've seen . . . yes, I've seen . . . there's no longer any question, I've seen!

At two o'clock I was walking in my rose-garden in the blazing sun . . . under a pergola of autumn roses just coming into bloom.

As I paused to look at a bush of Géant des Batailles with three splendid blooms on it, I saw distinctly, quite close to me, the stem of one of the roses curve, as if an unseen hand had bent it; then it broke as if the hand had picked it. After that the flower rose in the air, following the curve which an arm would have described in raising it to the nose. There it remained suspended in the air all by itself, a terrifying splash of red not three yards from my eyes.

I made a desperate leap to seize it but there was nothing there; it had disappeared. This made me furious with myself; a rational sane man has no right to have hallucinations of this kind.

But was it really an hallucination? I turned to look for the stem and found it at once without difficulty, freshly broken off, between the two other roses still on the branch.

I went back to the house thoroughly upset; for I am now certain, as certain as that night follows day, that there is close to me an invisible being of some sort, who lives on milk and water, who can touch, handle, and move things; this means that he has a material body, though not perceptible to our senses, and that he lives in the house with me.

August 7th. I had a peaceful night. He drank the water in my bottle but did not disturb my sleep. I wonder if I am mad. As I was walking along the river just now in the bright sun, I began to doubt my sanity; it was not a vague uncertainty, such as I have felt recently, but a definite positive doubt. I have seen lunatics; I have known several, who remained intelligent, lucid, and perfectly rational on everything in life except one point. They talked quite sensibly, fluently, penetratingly, and then suddenly their brain would run on the reef of their madness, collapse, split asunder, and sink in the raging, terrifying sea of their insanity with its breakers, fogs, and squalls.

I should certainly consider myself mad, if I were not perfectly clear in the head and fully conscious of my condition, if I were not continually probing and analysing it with complete lucidity. In fact, I must be the rational victim of an hallucination. Some mysterious disturbance must be working in my brain, one of those which physiologists today are trying to trace and define.

This disturbance must have produced a deep fissure in my mind and in the logical processes of my thought. Phenomena of this kind occur in dreams, in which we are not surprised at the most wildly fantastic happenings, because our critical faculty and power of objective examination are dormant, while the imaginative mechanism is awake and active. It is conceivable that one of the hidden notes on the keyboard of my brain is out of action. As the result of an accident some men lose the power of remembering proper names or figures or merely dates. It is an established fact that all the organs of thought are localized in different cells of the brain; it is therefore not surprising that my ability to control the absurdity of certain hallucinations should for the time being be in abeyance.

These thoughts were running in my head as I walked by the riverside. The stream was shining in the sun and all the earth seemed to smile. As I looked at the scene around me, my heart overflowed with love for everything that has life, for the swallows whose speed of movement is a joy to the eye and for the rushes on the bank, whose rustling is music to the ear.

Gradually, however, an unaccountable uneasiness swept over me. Some indefinable influence seemed to be sapping my energy and will-power; I felt I could not go on and must return. I was conscious with an urgency that was positively painful that I must go home, the kind of feeling one has, when one has left the bedside of a dear friend and suddenly has a presentiment that he has got worse.

So I turned back unwillingly, sure that, when I got home, I should find some bad news, a letter or a telegram; but there was nothing. I was more disturbed and surprised than if I had had some new fantastic experience.

August 8th. I had a dreadful evening yesterday. Now there is no manifestation of his presence but I am conscious of him quite close, spying on me, watching, possessing, dominating me. When he conceals himself like this, I fear him more than when supernatural phenomena reveal his invisible constant presence. But my sleep has not been disturbed.

August 9th. Nothing to report, but I'm terrified.

August 10th. Still nothing. What will happen tomorrow?

August 11th. Again nothing; but I can't stay in the house with this haunting fear and these torturing thoughts. I shall go away.

August 12th. 10 p.m. All day I've been trying to go away but I couldn't. I wanted to exercise my freedom of action and do this easy simple thing – go out, get into my carriage and drive to Rouen – and I couldn't do it. Why?

August 13th. Certain diseases seem to cause a breakdown in the physical mechanism of the body; our energies flag, our muscles relax, our bones become soft like flesh and our flesh is as water. That is my mental condition at this moment, a state of unaccountable depression. I have no strength, no courage; I'm not my own master, I have no will-power; I can't even make up my own mind, someone makes it up for me and I merely obey.

August 14th. I'm finished! I'm possessed, under some alien control; yet, that is literally true. Someone dictates my every act, my every movement, my every thought. I count for nothing, I just look on like a trembling slave at what I do. I want to go out and I just can't – *he* won't let me; so I stay where I am, helpless, shaking, in the armchair, where he keeps me sitting. I only want to get up in order to prove that I can; but I can't do it – I'm riveted to my seat and my chair is clamped to the floor, so that no power on earth could raise us. Then suddenly I feel I simply must go out into the garden and pick some strawberries and eat them. O my God, my God! Is there a God? If there is a God, let him set me free and deliver me from this torment! O God, grant me pardon and grace! Pity me, save me! I'm suffering the pains of Hell – oh! the horror of it all!

August 15th. My poor cousin must, I'm sure, have been subjected to this kind of possession and outside domination, when she came to borrow the five thousand francs from me. She was under the control of some alien power that had entered into her, some external alien tyrant. Does it portend the end of the world? What is the nature of this controlling power, invisible, inexplicable, this supernatural intruder who is my master?

So invisible beings do exist! How is it that since the beginning of the world they have never before shown themselves in this unmistakable way? I have never read of any occurrence similar to the manifestations in my house. If only I could leave the house, go away and never return, it would be my salvation! But I can't do it.

August 16th. Today I managed to escape for two hours, like a prisoner who finds the door of his cell accidentally left unlocked. I suddenly felt I was free, that he had gone away. I ordered my carriage at once and drove to Rouen. It was pure joy to be able to give the order 'To Rouen!' and be obeyed.

I stopped in front of the Library and asked for the loan of Dr Hermann Herestauss's great work on the unknown inhabitants of the ancient and modern world. Then, as I got into my carriage, I meant to say 'To the station!' but instead I shouted – I did not speak in my usual voice, I shouted so loud that the passers-by turned round – 'Home!' and sank back on the seat in an agony of terror. He had found me and resumed his control.

August 17th. I've had a ghastly night but I really ought to be glad. I read till one o'clock. Hermann Herestauss, Doctor of Philosophy and Cosmology, gives an account of the manifestations of all the unseen beings who prowl round mankind or have been imagined in dreams. He describes their origin, their sphere of influence, and their power. But none of them is at all like the being who haunts me. It would seem that man, ever since he has had the power of thought, has had a terrified presentiment of some new being, stronger than himself, who is destined to replace him in the world; feeling him close and unable to guess the nature of this master, in his panic terror he has imagined a whole fantastic race of occult presences, vague phantoms born of his fear.

Well, after reading till one in the morning, I went and sat by my open window to cool my forehead and brain in the gentle night breeze. It was fine and warm. How I should have loved that night in the old days!

There was no moon. The stars were twinkling and winking against the dark backcloth of the sky. Who lives in those other worlds? What shapes, what creatures, what animals, what plants exist there? Perhaps the thinkers in those distant worlds have wider knowledge and greater powers than we. Can they see things of which we know nothing? Will one of them some day or other make his way through space and appear in our world to conquer it, as the Normans crossed the sea in old days to enslave weaker races?

We are so feeble, so defenceless, so ignorant, we human pygmies, who inhabit this ball of mud set in the oceans!

I dropped off to sleep in the cool evening breeze with these thoughts running in my head. After I had been asleep for about forty minutes, I opened my eyes again without moving, woken up by a vague feeling of uneasiness. At first I noticed nothing; but suddenly I saw a page of the book, which lay open on the table, turn of itself. Not a breath of air was coming in by the window. Dumbfounded, I waited. About four minutes later I saw – yes, I saw with my own eyes – another page rise and fall back on the previous page, as if a finger had turned it. My armchair was empty – or seemed so – but I knew *he* was there, sitting in my place, reading. With one wild leap, the leap of a furious beast eager to tear his trainer to pieces, I was across the room, mad to seize him and crush him to death. But, before I could reach my chair, it was knocked over backwards as if someone had tried to escape from me; the table rocked, the lamp fell to the ground and went out, and my window banged to, as if a burglar, surprised, had disappeared into the darkness, slamming the shutters behind him.

He had run away! He had actually been afraid of me! In that case . . .

tomorrow or the day after or some day . . . I shall succeed in getting hold of him and bearing him to the ground. Even dogs sometimes go for their masters and seize them by the throat.

August 18th. I've been thinking all day. Yes! I'll obey him, do as he wills, carry out his orders, behave like a humble, submissive coward. He is stronger than I am but my time will come.

August 19th. Now I know, I know the whole story. I've just read this in the *Science Review*: 'An unusual piece of news comes to us from Rio de Janeiro. An epidemic of insanity, like the infectious attacks of madness which affected Europe in the Middle Ages, is raging at this moment in the Province of São Paulo. The victims leave their homes, deserting their villages and abandoning their fields; they assert that they are pursued, possessed, driven like cattle by beings who are invisible but can be felt, like vampires who drain their vitality in their sleep and drink water and milk without apparently touching any other kind of food.

'Professor Don Pedro Henriquez, accompanied by several medical experts, has started for the Province of São Paulo, in order to study on the spot the origin and symptoms of this strange epidemic and suggest to the Emperor such measures as may seem suitable to restore those affected to sanity.'

Now I remember quite well that lovely Brazilian three-master, which passed under my windows on her way up the Seine on May 8th last. I thought it such a beautiful ship, so white and cheerful. This being was on board on his way from South America, where his like originate. And he caught sight of me! He noticed my house, which was as white as his ship, and he leapt ashore. Oh! my God!

Now I know, I can guess the truth. Man's dominion is a thing of the past! *He* has come, the being who was an object of fear to primitive races, whom anxious priests tried to exorcize, whom sorcerers called up at midnight without ever yet seeing him in visible form, to whom the temporary lords of creation attributed in imagination the shape, monstrous or attractive, of gnomes, spirits, fairies or goblins. After the vulgar ideas inspired by pre-historic fears, scientific research has clarified the outlines of man's presentiment. Mesmer guessed it and in the last ten years doctors have discovered the exact nature of this being's power before its manifestation. They have experimented with this weapon of the new lord of the world, the imposition of a dominant will on the human soul, which thus becomes its slave. To this power they have given the name of magnetism, hypnotism, suggestion, and what not. I have seen them playing with it like silly children playing with fire. Woe to us! Woe to mankind! He has come . . . what is his name? . . . He seems to be shouting it aloud, but I can't catch it . . . yes, he is shouting it and I can't hear . . . say it again! . . . Le Horla, I've got it at last . . . Le Horla . . . that's his name . . . Le Horla has come!

The eagle has killed the dove, the wolf has eaten the sheep, the lion has devoured the horned aurochs; man has slain the lion with arrow, sword or gunpowder. But Le Horla is destined to make of man what man has made of horse and bullock, his chattel, his servant, and his food, by the mere power of his will. Woe to mankind!

Nevertheless the beast sometimes revolts and destroys his tamer . . . that is my task. I shall succeed but first I must recognize him, touch him, see him! Experts say that an animal's eye differs from ours and cannot distinguish as we can; similarly my human sight cannot distinguish the new being dominating me.

Why is this? Ah! now I recall what the monk at Mont-Saint-Michel said: 'Can we see the hundred-thousandth part of what exists? Take the wind, for example, the most powerful force in nature; it blows men over, destroys houses, uproots trees, raises the sea into mountainous waves, undermines cliffs, drives great ships on to reefs. The wind kills, whistles, moans, roars. Have you ever seen it? Can you ever see it? But it exists all the same!'

I pursued this line of thought; my eye is so inefficient, so imperfect, that it cannot distinguish even a solid body, if it is transparent like glass. If an unsilvered glass bars my path, my eye allows me to dash myself against it, as a bird in a room dashes itself against the window pane; and there are many other things that deceive the eye and lead it astray. So it is in no way surprising that it should be unable to discern a strange body, through which light can pass.

A new being! Why not? Something of this sort was surely bound to come. Why should man be the last word? We cannot see this being as we can all the previous results of evolution. True, and the reason is that its nature is more perfect, its body finer and more finished than ours. We are so feeble, so clumsily made; we are hampered by organs easily tired and often strained like overcomplicated springs. The human body lives like a plant or an animal, laboriously drawing nourishment from the air and from vegetable and animal matter, a living mechanism subject to disease, mutilation, and decay, short of breath, badly controlled, easily deceived, unreliable; it is poorly though ingeniously constructed, a piece of work at once coarse and delicate, a blueprint for a being capable of developing into something noble and intelligent.

There are so few of us on the earth, even if we include all forms of animal life from the crustacea to man. Why should there not be a new form of life, once the period necessary for the evolution of a new species has elapsed?

Why not one more? Why not also a new type of tree, with immense blossoms, brilliantly coloured, scenting a whole country? Why not other elements besides earth, air, fire, and water? There are four, only four of them, from which mankind draws its sustenance. What a pitifully small number! Why not forty, four hundred, four thousand? How poor, mean, wretched everything is! Grudgingly given, poorly designed, clumsily built! Could there be anything more ungainly than an elephant or a hippopotamus, more awkward than a camel?

But look at the butterfly, you will say, a very flower with wings! Why, I can envisage one as big as a hundred globes, whose wings have a form, a beauty, a sheen, a movement that defy imagination. I can picture it, winging its way from star to star, refreshing and scenting everything with the gentle rhythmic breath of its passage. I can see the denizens of space watching its flight in ecstasy and delight.

What is the matter with me? It must be Le Horla, haunting me, putting these wild ideas into my head; he is in me, possessing my soul. I must kill him!

August 19th. I *shall* kill him. I've seen him! Yesterday evening I was sitting at my table, pretending to concentrate on writing. I knew he would come prowling round, quite close, so close that I should be able to touch and perhaps seize him. And then I should have the strength of despair; I should use my hands, knees, chest, head, teeth, to strangle, crush, bite, tear him to pieces.

I watched for him, all my senses at full stretch.

I had lit my two lamps and the eight candles on my chimney-piece, as if the illumination would help me to detect him.

Facing me stood my bed, an old oak four-poster; on my right was the chimney-piece, on my left the door, carefully shut – I had left it open for some time in order to entice him in. Behind me was a tall cupboard with a mirror, which I use every day for shaving and dressing; I always look at myself from head to foot every time I pass it.

To deceive him, I pretended to write, for he was watching me too. Suddenly I felt, I was quite certain, he was reading over my shoulder, almost touching me.

I leapt to my feet with hands outstretched and swung round so quickly that I nearly fell. It was as light as day and yet I could not see myself in the glass! It was blank, unshadowed, dim, like deep water but luminous. But there was no reflection of me, though I was straight in front of it. I saw the great mirror-glass clear from top to bottom. I gazed in terror, not daring to advance or move; I knew he was there, but that he would escape me again, this being whose invisible body had absorbed my reflection.

I was dumbfounded. Then suddenly I began to see myself mistily in the glass, as one sees an object dimly through water; and the water seemed to be shifting slowly from left to right, and my reflection was clearing from second to second. It was like the end of an eclipse. Whatever was obscuring my image seemed to possess no clear-cut outline but was a kind of opaque transparency, gradually clearing.

At last I could distinguish myself completely as usual in the glass.

I have seen him! The terror of it is still upon me and I am trembling all over.

August 20th. How am I going to kill him, as I can't get hold of him? Poison? But he would see me putting it into the water. Besides, would our poisons have any effect on his invisible body? No, I'm sure they would not. What can I do then?

August 21st. I've sent for a locksmith from Rouen and ordered iron shutters for my bedroom, the kind of thing that some flats in Paris have on the ground floor for fear of thieves. He will make me an iron door too. I pretended to be highly nervous but I don't care what he thinks of me.

September 10th. Rouen: Hôtel Continental. I've done it . . . I've done it . . . but is he dead? It was a ghastly sight!

Yesterday the locksmith finished my iron shutters and door; so I left everything open till midnight, though it was beginning to get chilly.

Suddenly I was aware with a feeling of wild triumph that he was there. I got up slowly and walked up and down for some time, so that he shouldn't become suspicious. Then I took off my boots and thrust my feet carelessly into my slippers; next I closed the shutters and strolled casually to the door and double-locked it. After that I went back to the window and padlocked it, slipping the key into my pocket.

All at once I felt he was moving about round me, that he was afraid and was willing me to open the room. I very nearly yielded but I didn't quite; and backing to the door, I opened it a crack, just sufficient to let me out backwards. I am tall, and my head reached to the lintel. I was sure he could not have got out and I shut him in by himself. Triumph! I had got him at last! Then I ran downstairs to my drawing-room, which was immediately under my bedroom, and seized my two lamps, spilling the oil on the carpet, the furniture, everywhere. After that I set fire to it and made my escape, double-locking the heavy front door.

I ran and hid in a clump of laurels at the far end of the garden. I waited for what seemed an age; everything was dark and silent, not a movement, not a breath of air, not a star visible; overhead masses of cloud, which I could not see but which weighed, oh! so heavily, on my consciousness.

I kept my eyes on the house, waiting. How long it seemed! I began to think that the fire must have gone out by itself or that *he* had put it out, when one of the downstairs windows blew out under the pressure of the heat and a great tongue of flame, red and yellow, ran up the white wall to the roof, gently enfolding it in a fiery embrace. The trees, the branches, and the leaves were suddenly lit up and seemed to shiver with fear. The birds woke up and a dog began to bark; it looked like dawn. Two other windows blew out and I could see that the whole ground floor of my house was a raging fiery furnace. But a cry, a woman's horrible shrill shriek, rang out in the night and two windows on the top floor were flung open. I had forgotten the servants; I could see their panic-stricken faces and their waving arms. Then, mad with horror, I began to run towards the village, screaming: 'Help! Help! Fire! Fire!' I met people already hurrying to the scene and went back with them to watch.

By this time the whole house was one dreadful, magnificent holocaust, a terrifying sight, lighting up everything all round, a bonfire in which human beings were being burnt alive; and *he*, my prisoner, the new being, the new lord of the world, Le Horla, was being burnt too.

Suddenly the whole roof collapsed inside the walls and a volcano of flame shot up to the sky.

Through all the windows open on the blaze I could see the fiery inferno and I thought of *him* there in this furnace, dead.

Dead? I wonder. Wasn't his body, through which light could pass, impervious perhaps to what destroys our bodies?

Suppose he isn't dead! It may be that only time can destroy his invisible terror. Why should his astral body be transparent and invisible, if he had cause to fear disease, wounds, weakness, premature dissolution?

Premature dissolution? That is the sole source of fear in man. Le Horla is the next development of evolution after man. After man, who may die any day, any hour, any minute, as a result of accident, has come a being who can only die at his appointed day, hour, minute, when he has reached the term of his existence.

No! There is no doubt, no doubt whatever, that he is not dead! So there is nothing left for me to do but to kill myself!

Sir Edmund Orme

Ƨ

Henry James

The statement appears to have been written, though the fragment is undated, long after the death of his wife, whom I take to have been one of the persons referred to. There is, however, nothing in the strange story to establish this point, now perhaps not of importance. When I took possession of his effects I found these pages, in a locked drawer, among papers relating to the unfortunate lady's too brief career – she died in childbirth a year after her marriage: letters, memoranda, accounts, faded photographs, cards of invitation. That's the only connection I can point to, and you may easily, and will probably, think it too extravagant to have had a palpable basis. I can't, I allow, vouch for his having intended it as a report of real occurrence – I can only vouch for his general veracity. In any case it was written for himself, not for others. I offer it to others – having full option – precisely because of its oddity. Let them, in respect to the form of the thing, bear in mind that it was written quite for himself. I've altered nothing but the names.

If there's a story in the matter I recognize the exact moment at which it began. This was on a soft still Sunday noon in November, just after church, on the sunny Parade. Brighton was full of people; it was the height of the season and the day was even more respectable than lovely – which helped to account for the multitude of walkers. The blue sea itself was decorous; it seemed to doze with a gentle snore – if that *be* decorum – while nature preached a sermon. After writing letters all the morning I had come out to take a look at it before luncheon. I leaned over the rail dividing the King's Road from the beach, and I think I had smoked a cigarette, when I became conscious of an intended joke in the shape of a light walking-stick laid across my shoulders. The idea, I found, had been thrown off by Teddy Bostwick of the Rifles and was intended as a contribution to talk. Our talk came off as we strolled together – he always took your arm to show you he forgave your obtuseness about his humour – and looked at the people, and bowed to some of them, and wondered who others were, and differed in opinion as to the prettiness of girls. About Charlotte Marden we agreed, however, as we saw her come towards us with her mother; and there surely could have been no one who wouldn't have concurred. The Brighton air used of old to make plain girls pretty and pretty girls prettier still – I don't know whether it works the spell now. The place was at any rate rare for complexions, and Miss Marden's was one that made people turn round. It made *us* stop, heaven knows – at least it was one of the things, for we already knew the ladies.

We turned with them, we joined them, we went where they were going. They were only going to the end and back – they had just come out of church. It was another manifestation of Teddy's humour that he got immediate possession of Charlotte, leaving me to walk with her mother. However, I wasn't unhappy; the girl was before me and I had her to talk about. We prolonged our walk; Mrs Marden kept me and presently said she was tired and must rest. We found a place on a sheltered bench – we gossiped as the people passed. It had already struck me, in this pair, that the resemblance between mother and daughter was wonderful even among such resemblances, all the more that it took so little account of a difference of nature. One often hears mature mothers spoken of as warnings – signposts, more or less discouraging, of the way daughters may go. But there was nothing deterrent in the idea that Charlotte should at fifty-five be as beautiful, even though it were conditioned on her being as pale and preoccupied, as Mrs Marden. At twenty-two she had a rosy blankness and was admirably handsome. Her head had the charming shape of her mother's and her features the same fine order. Then there were looks and movements and tones – moments when you could scarce say if it were aspect or sound – which, between the two appearances, referred and reminded.

These ladies had a small fortune and a cheerful little house at Brighton, full of portraits and tokens and trophies – stuffed animals on the top of bookcases and sallow varnished fish under glass – to which Mrs Marden professed herself attached by pious memories. Her husband had been 'ordered' there in ill-health, to spend the last years of his life, and she had already mentioned to me that it was a place in which she felt herself still under the protection of his goodness. His goodness appeared to have been great, and she sometimes seemed to defend it from vague innuendo. Some sense of protection, of an influence invoked and cherished, was evidently necessary to her; she had a dim wistfulness, a longing for security. She wanted friends and had a good many. She was kind to me on our first meeting, and I never suspected her of the vulgar purpose of 'making up' to me – a suspicion of course unduly frequent in conceited young men. It never struck me that she wanted me for her daughter, nor yet, like some unnatural mammas, for herself. It was as if they had had a common deep shy need and had been ready to say: 'Oh, be friendly to us and be trustful! Don't be afraid – you won't be expected to marry us.' 'Of course there's something about mamma: that's really what makes her such a dear!' Charlotte said to me, confidentially, at an early stage of our acquaintance. She worshipped her mother's appearance. It was the only thing she was vain of; she accepted the raised eyebrows as a charming ultimate fact. 'She looks as if she were waiting for the doctor, dear mamma,' she said on another occasion. 'Perhaps *you're* the doctor; do you think you are?' It appeared in the event that I had some healing power. At any rate when I learned, for she once dropped the remark, that Mrs Marden also held there was something 'awfully strange' about Charlotte, the relation of the two ladies couldn't but be interesting. It was happy enough, at bottom; each had the other so on her mind.

On the Parade the stream of strollers held its course, and Charlotte presently went by with Teddy Bostwick. She smiled and nodded and continued, but when she came back she stopped and spoke to us. Captain Bostwick positively declined to go in – he pronounced the occasion too jolly: might they therefore take another turn? Her mother dropped a 'Do as you like,' and the girl gave me an impertinent smile over her shoulder as they quitted us. Teddy looked at me with his glass in one eye, but I didn't mind that: it was only of Miss Marden I was thinking as I laughed to my companion. 'She's a bit of a coquette, you know.'

'Don't say that – don't say that!' Mrs Marden murmured.

'The nicest girls always are – just a little,' I was magnanimous enough to plead.

'Then why are they always punished?'

The intensity of the question startled me – it had come out in a vivid flash. Therefore I had to think a moment before I put to her: 'What do you know of their punishment?'

'Well – I was a bad girl myself.'

'And were you punished?'

'I carry it through life,' she said as she looked away from me. 'Ah!' she suddenly panted in the next breath, rising to her feet and staring at her daughter, who had reappeared again with Captain Bostwick. She stood a few seconds, the queerest expression in her face; then she sank on the seat again and I saw she had blushed crimson. Charlotte, who had noticed it all, came straight up to her and, taking her hand with quick tenderness, seated herself at her other side. The girl had turned pale – she gave her mother a fixed, scared look. Mrs Marden, who had had some shock that escaped our detection, recovered herself; that is, she sat quiet and inexpressive, gazing at the indifferent crowd, the sunny air, the slumbering sea. My eye happened to fall nevertheless on the interlocked hands of the two ladies, and I quickly guessed the grasp of the elder to be violent. Bostwick stood before them, wondering what was the matter and asking me from his little vacant disk if *I* knew; which led Charlotte to say to him after a moment and with a certain irritation: 'Don't stand there that way, Captain Bostwick. Go away – *please* go away.'

I got up at this, hoping Mrs Marden wasn't ill; but she at once begged we wouldn't leave them, that we would particularly stay and that we would presently come home to luncheon. She drew me down beside her and for a moment I felt her hand press my arm in a way that might have been an involuntary betrayal of distress and might have been a private signal. What she should have wished to point out to me I couldn't divine: perhaps she had seen in the crowd somebody or something abnormal. She explained to us in a few minutes that she was all right, that she was only liable to palpitations: they came as quickly as they went. It was time to move – a truth on which we acted. The incident was felt to be closed. Bostwick and I lunched with our sociable friends, and when I walked away with him he professed he had never seen creatures more completely to his taste.

Mrs Marden had made us promise to come back the next day to tea, and had exhorted us in general to come as often as we could. Yet the next day when, at five o'clock, I knocked at the door of the pretty house it was but to learn that the ladies had gone up to town. They had left a message for us with the butler: he was to say they had suddenly been called and much regretted it. They would be absent a few days. This was all I could extract from the dumb domestic. I went again three days later, but they were still away; and it was not till the end of a week that I got a note from Mrs Marden. 'We're back,' she wrote, 'do come and forgive us.' It was on this occasion, I remember – the occasion of my going just after getting the note – that she told me she had distinct intuitions. I don't know how many people there were in England at that time in that predicament, but there were very few who would have mentioned it; so that the announcement struck me as original, especially as her point was that some of these uncanny promptings were connected with myself. There were other people present – idle Brighton folk, old women with frightened eyes and irrelevant interjections – and I had too few minutes' talk with Charlotte; but the day after this I met them both at dinner and had the satisfaction of sitting next to Miss Marden. I recall this passage as the hour of its first fully coming over me that she was a beautiful liberal creature. I had seen her personality in glimpses and gleams, like a song sung in snatches, but now it was before me in a large rosy glow, as if it had been a full volume of sound. I heard the whole of the air, and it was sweet fresh music, which I was often to hum over.

After dinner I had a few words with Mrs Marden; it was at the time, late in the evening, when tea was handed about. A servant passed near us with a tray. I asked her if she would have a cup and, on her assenting, took one and offered it to her. She put out her hand for it and I gave it her, safely as I supposed; but as her fingers were about to secure it she started and faltered, so that both my frail vessel and its fine recipient dropped with a crash of porcelain and without, on the part of my companion, the usual woman's motion to save her dress. I stooped to pick up the fragments, and when I raised myself Mrs Marden was looking across the room at her daughter, who returned it with lips of cheer but anxious eyes. 'Dear mamma, what on earth *is* the matter with you?' the silent question seemed to say. Mrs Marden coloured just as she had done after her strange movement on the Parade the other week, and I was therefore surprised when she said to me with unexpected assurance: 'You should really have a steadier hand!' I had begun to stammer a defence of my hand when I noticed her eyes fixed on me with an intense appeal. It was ambiguous at first and only added to my confusion; then suddenly I understood as plainly as if she had murmured, 'Make believe it was you – make believe it was you.' The servant came back to take the morsels of the cup and wipe up the spilt tea, and while I was in the midst of making believe Mrs Marden abruptly brushed away from me and from her daughter's attention and went into another room. She gave no heed to the state of her dress.

I saw nothing more of either that evening, but the next morning, in the King's Road, I met the younger lady with a roll of music in her muff. She told me she had been a little way alone, to practise duets with a friend, and I asked her if she would go a little way farther in company. She gave me leave to attend her to her door, and as we stood before it I inquired if

I might go in. 'No, not today – I don't want you,' she said very straight, though not unamiably; while the words caused me to direct a wistful disconcerted gaze at one of the windows of the house. It fell on the white face of Mrs Marden, turned out at us from the drawing-room. She stood long enough to show it *was* she and not the apparition I had come near taking it for, and then she vanished before her daughter had observed her. The girl, during our walk, had said nothing about her. As I had been told they didn't want me I left them alone a little, after which certain hazards kept us still longer apart. I finally went up to London, and while there received a pressing invitation to come immediately down to Tranton, a pretty old place in Sussex belonging to a couple whose acquaintance I had lately made.

I went to Tranton from town, and on arriving found the Mardens, with a dozen other people, in the house. The first thing Mrs Marden said was, 'Will you forgive me?' and when I asked what I had to forgive, she answered, 'My throwing my tea over you.' I replied that it had gone over herself; whereupon she said, 'At any rate I was very rude – but some time I think you'll understand, and then you'll make allowances for me.' The first day I was there she dropped two or three of these references – she had already indulged in more than one – to the mystic initiation in store for me; so that I began, as the phrase is, to chaff her about it, to say I'd rather it were less wonderful and take it out at once. She answered that when it should come to me I'd have indeed to take it out – there would be little enough option. That it *would* come was privately clear to her, a deep presentiment, which was the only reason she had ever mentioned the matter. Didn't I remember she had spoken to me of intuitions? From the first of her seeing me she had been sure there were things I shouldn't escape knowing. Meanwhile there was nothing to do but wait and keep cool, not to be precipitate. She particularly wished not to become extravagantly nervous. And I was, above all, not to be nervous myself – one got used to everything. I returned that though I couldn't make out what she was talking of I was terribly frightened; the absence of a clue gave such a range to one's imagination. I exaggerated on purpose; for if Mrs Marden was mystifying I can scarcely say she was alarming. I couldn't imagine what she meant, but I wondered more than I shuddered. I might have said to myself that she was a little wrong in the upper storey; but that never occurred to me. She struck me as hopelessly right.

There were other girls in the house, but Charlotte the most charming; which was so generally allowed that she almost interfered with the slaughter of ground game. There were two or three men, and I was of the number, who actually preferred her to the society of the beaters. In short, she was recognized as a form of sport superior and exquisite. She was kind to all of us – she made us go out late and come in early. I don't know whether she flirted, but several other members of the party thought *they* did. Indeed as regards himself Teddy Bostwick, who had come over from Brighton, was visibly sure.

The third of these days was a Sunday, which determined a pretty walk to morning service over the fields. It was grey, windless weather, and the bell of the little old church that nestled in the hollow of the Sussex Down sounded near and domestic. We were a straggling procession in the mild damp air – which, as always at that season, gave one the feeling that after the trees were bare there was more of it, a larger sky – and I managed to fall a good way behind with Miss Marden. I remember entertaining, as we moved together over the turf, a strong impulse to say something intensely personal, something violent and important, important for *me* – such as that I had never seen her so lovely or that that particular moment was the sweetest of my life. But always, in youth, such words have been on the lips many times before they're spoken to any effect; and I had the sense, not that I didn't know her well enough – I cared little for that – but that she didn't sufficiently know *me*. In the church, a museum of old Tranton tombs and brasses, the big Tranton pew was full. Several of us were scattered, and I found a seat for Miss Marden, and another for myself beside it, at a distance from her mother and from most of our friends. There were two or three decent rustics on the bench, who moved in farther to make room for us, and I took my place first, to cut off my companion from our neighbours. After she was seated there was still a space left, which remained empty till service was about half over.

This at least was the moment of my noting that another person had entered and had taken the seat. When I remarked him he had apparently been for some minutes in the pew – had settled himself and put down his hat beside him and, with his hands crossed on the knob of his cane, was gazing before him at the altar. He was a pale young man in black and with the air of a gentleman. His presence slightly startled me, for Miss Marden hadn't attracted my attention to it by moving to make room for him. After a few minutes, observing that he had no prayer book, I reached across my neighbour and placed mine before him, on the ledge of the pew; a manoeuvre the motive of which was not unconnected with the possibility that, in my own destitution, Miss Marden would give me one side of *her* velvet volume to hold. The pretext, however, was destined to fail, for at the moment I offered him the book the intruder – whose intrusion I had so condoned – rose from his place without thanking me, stepped noiselessly out of the pew, which had no door, and, so discreetly as to attract no attention, passed down the centre of the church. A few minutes had sufficed for his devotions. His behaviour was unbecoming, his early departure even more than his late arrival; but he managed so quietly that we were not incommoded, and I found, on turning a little to look after him, that nobody was disturbed by his withdrawal. I only noticed, and with surprise, that Mrs Marden had been so affected by it as to rise, all involuntarily, in her place. She stared at him as he passed, but he passed very quickly, and she as quickly dropped down again, though not too soon to catch my eye across the church. Five minutes later I asked her daughter, in a low voice, if she would kindly pass me back my prayer book – I had waited to see if she would spontaneously perform the act. The girl restored this aid to devotion, but had been so far from troubling herself about it that she could say to me as she did so: 'Why on earth did you put it there?' I was on the point of answering her when she dropped on her knees, and at this I held my tongue. I had only been going to say: 'To be decently civil.'

After the benediction, as we were leaving our places, I was slightly surprised again to see that Mrs Marden, instead of going out with her companions, had come up the aisle to join us, having apparently something to say to her daughter. She said it, but in an instant I saw it had been a pretext – her real business was with me. She pushed Charlotte forward and suddenly breathed to me: 'Did you see him?'

'The gentleman who sat down here? How could I help seeing him?'

'Hush!' she said with the intensest excitement; 'don't *speak* to her – don't tell her!' She slipped her hand into my arm, to keep me near her, to keep me, it seemed, away from her daughter. The precaution was unnecessary, for Teddy Bostwick had already taken possession of Miss Marden, and as they passed out of church in front of me I saw one of the other men close up on her other hand. It appeared to be felt that I had had my turn. Mrs Marden released me as soon as we got out, but not before I saw she had needed my support. 'Don't speak to anyone – don't tell anyone!' she went on.

'I don't understand. Tell anyone what?'

'Why, that you saw him.'

'Surely they saw him for themselves.'

'Not one of them, not one of them.' She spoke with such passionate decision that I glanced at her – she was staring straight before her. But she felt the challenge of my eyes and stopped short, in the old brown timber porch of the church, with the others well in advance of us; where, looking at me now and in quite an extraordinary manner, 'You're the only person,' she said; 'the only person in the world.'

'But *you*, dear madam?'

'Oh, me – of course. That's my curse!' And with this she moved rapidly off to join the rest of our group. I hovered at its outskirts on the way home – I had such food for rumination. Whom had I seen and why was the apparition – it rose before my mind's eye all clear again – invisible to the others? If an exception had been made for Mrs Marden why did it constitute a curse, and why was I to share so questionable a boon? This appeal, carried on in my own locked breast, kept me doubtless quiet enough at luncheon. After that repast I went out on the old terrace to smoke a cigarette, but had only taken a turn or two when I caught Mrs Marden's moulded mask at the window of one of the rooms open to the crooked flags. It reminded me of the same flitting presence behind the pane at Brighton the day I met Charlotte and walked home with her. But this time my ambiguous friend didn't vanish; she tapped on the pane and motioned me to come in. She was in a queer little apartment, one of the many reception rooms of which the ground floor at Tranton consisted; it was known as the Indian room and had a style denominated Eastern – bamboo lounges, lacquered screens, lanterns with long fringes and strange idols in cabinets, objects not held to conduce to sociability. The place was little used, and when I went round to her we had it to ourselves. As soon as I appeared she said to me: 'Please tell me this – are you in love with my daughter?'

I really had a little to take my time. 'Before I answer your question will you kindly tell me what gives you the idea? I don't consider I've been very forward.'

Mrs Marden, contradicting me with her beautiful anxious eyes, gave me no satisfaction on the point I mentioned; she only went on strenuously: 'Did you say nothing to her on the way to church?'

'What makes you think I said anything?'

'Why, the fact that you saw him.'

'Saw whom, dear Mrs Marden?'

'Oh, you know,' she answered gravely, even a little reproachfully, as if I were trying to humiliate her by making her name the unnameable.

'Do you mean the gentleman who formed the subject of your strange statement in church – the one who came into the pew?'

'You saw him, you saw him!' she panted, with a strange mixture of dismay and relief.

'Of course I saw him, and so did you.'

'It didn't follow. Did you feel it to be inevitable?'

I was puzzled again. 'Inevitable?'

'That you *should* see him?'

'Certainly, since I'm not blind.'

'You might have been. Everyone else is.' I was wonderfully at sea and I frankly confessed it to my questioner, but the case wasn't improved by her presently exclaiming: 'I knew you would, from the moment you should be really in love with her! I knew it would be the test – what do I mean? – the proof.'

'Are there such strange bewilderments attached to that high state?' I smiled to ask.

'You can judge for yourself. You see him, you see him!' – she quite exulted in it. 'You'll see him again.'

'I've no objection, but I shall take more interest in him if you'll kindly tell me who he is.'

She avoided my eyes – then consciously met them. 'I'll tell you if you'll tell me first what you said on the way to church.'

'Has she told you I said anything?'

'Do I need that?' she asked with expression.

'Oh yes, I remember – your intuitions! But I'm sorry to see they're at fault this time; because I really said nothing to your daughter that was the least out of the way.'

'Are you very, very sure?'

'On my honour, Mrs Marden.'

'Then you consider you're not in love with her?'

'That's another affair!' I laughed.

'You are – you *are*! You wouldn't have seen him if you hadn't been.'

'Then who the deuce *is* he, madam?' – I pressed it with some irritation.

Yet she would still only question me back. 'Didn't you at least *want* to say something to her – didn't you come very near it?'

Well, this was more to the point; it justified the famous intuitions. 'Ah "near" it as much as you like – call it the turn of a hair, I don't know what kept me quiet.'

'That was quite enough,' said Mrs Marden. 'It isn't what you say that makes the difference; it's what you feel. *That's* what he goes by.'

I was annoyed at last by her reiterated reference to an identity yet to be established, and I clasped my hands with an air of supplication which covered much real impatience, a sharper curiosity and even the first short throbs of a certain sacred dread. 'I entreat you to tell me whom you're talking about.'

She threw up her arms, looking away from me, as if to shake off both reserve and responsibility. 'Sir Edmund Orme.'

'And who may Sir Edmund Orme be?'

At the moment I spoke she gave a start. 'Hush – here they come.' Then as following the direction of her eyes, I saw Charlotte, out on the terrace, by our own window, she added, with an intensity of warning: 'Don't notice him – *never!*'

The girl, who now had had her hands beside her eyes, peering into the room and smiling, signed to us through the glass to admit her; on which I went and opened the long window. Her mother turned away and she came in with a laughing challenge: 'What plot in the world are you two hatching here?' Some plan – I forget what – was in prospect for the afternoon, as to which Mrs Marden's participation or consent was solicited, my own adhesion being taken for granted; and she had been half over the place in her quest. I was flurried, seeing the elder woman was – when she turned round to meet her daughter she disguised it to extravagance, throwing herself on the girl's neck and embracing her – so that, to pass it off, I overdid my gallantry.

'I've been asking your mother for your hand.'

'Oh indeed, and has she given it?' Miss Marden gaily returned.

'She was just going to when you appeared there.'

'Well, it's only for a moment – I'll leave you free.'

'Do you like him, Charlotte?' Mrs Marden asked with a candour I scarcely expected.

'It's difficult to say *before* him, isn't it?' the charming creature went on, entering into the humour of the thing, but looking at me as if she scarce liked me at all.

She would have had to say it before another person as well, for at that moment there stepped into the room from the terrace – the window had been left open – a gentleman who had come into sight, at least into mine, only within the instant. Mrs Marden had said, 'Here *they* come,' but he appeared to have followed her daughter at a certain distance. I recognized him at once as the personage who had sat beside us in church. This time I saw him better, saw his face and his carriage were strange. I speak of him as a personage, because one felt, indescribably, as if a reigning prince had come into the room. He held himself with something of the grand air and as if he were different from his company. Yet he looked fixedly and gravely at me, till I wondered what he expected. Did he consider that I should bend my knee or kiss his hand? He turned his eyes in the same way on Mrs Marden, but she knew what to do. After the first agitation produced by his approach she took no notice of him whatever; it made me remember her passionate adjuration to me. I had to achieve a great effort to imitate her, for though I knew nothing about him but that he was Sir Edmund Orme, his presence acted as a strong appeal, almost as an oppression. He stood there without speaking – young, pale, handsome, clean-shaven, decorous, with extraordinary light-blue eyes and something old-fashioned, like a portrait of years ago, in his head and in his manner of wearing his hair. He was in complete mourning – one immediately took him for very well dressed – and he carried his hat in his hand. He looked again strangely hard at me, harder than anyone in the world had ever looked before; and I remember feeling rather cold and wishing he would say something. No silence had ever seemed to me so soundless. All this was of course an impression intensely rapid; but that it had consumed some instants was proved to me suddenly by the expression of countenance of Charlotte Marden, who stared from one of us to the other – he never looked at her, and she had no appearance of looking at him – and then broke out with: 'What on earth is the matter with you? You've such odd faces!' I felt the colour come back to mine, and when she went on in the same tone, 'One would think you had seen a ghost!' I was conscious I had turned very red. Sir Edmund Orme never blushed, and I was sure no embarrassment touched him. One had met people of that sort, but never anyone with so high an indifference.

'Don't be impertinent, and go and tell them all that I'll join them,' said Mrs Marden with much dignity but with a tremor of voice that I caught.

'And will you come – *you*?' the girl asked, turning away. I made no answer, taking the question somehow as meant for her companion. But he was more silent than I, and when she reached the door – she was going out that way – she stopped, her hand on the knob, and looked at me, repeating it. I assented, springing forward to open the door for her, and as she passed out she exclaimed to me mockingly: 'You haven't got your wits about you – you shan't have my hand!'

I closed the door and turned round to find that Sir Edmund Orme had during the moment my back was presented to him retired by the window. Mrs Marden stood there and we looked at each other long. It had only then – as the girl flitted away – come home to me that her daughter was unconscious of what had happened. It was *that*, oddly enough, that gave me a sudden sharp shake – not my own perception of our visitor, which felt quite natural. It made the fact vivid to me that she had been equally unaware of him in church, and the two facts together – now that they were over – set my heart more sensibly beating. I wiped my forehead, and Mrs

Marden broke out with a low distressful wail: 'Now you know my life – now you know my life!'

'In God's name who is he – *what* is he?'

'He's a man I wronged.'

'How did you wrong him?'

'Oh, awfully – years ago.'

'Years ago? Why, he's very young.'

'Young – young?' cried Mrs Marden. 'He was born before I was!'

'Then why does he look so?'

She came nearer to me, she laid her hand on my arm, and there was something in her face that made me shrink a little. 'Don't you understand – don't you *feel*?' she intensely put to me.

'I feel very queer?' I laughed; and I was conscious that my note betrayed it.

'He's dead!' said Mrs Marden from her white face.

'Dead?' I panted. 'Then that gentleman was—?' I couldn't even say a word.

'Call him what you like – there are twenty vulgar names. He's a perfect presence.'

'He's a splendid presence!' I cried. 'The place is haunted, *haunted*!' I exulted in the word as if it stood for all I had ever dreamt of.

'It isn't the place – more's the pity!' she instantly returned. 'That has nothing to do with it!'

'Then it's you, dear lady?' I said as if this were still better.

'No, nor me either – I wish it were!'

'Perhaps it's me,' I suggested with a sickly smile.

'It's nobody but my child – my innocent, innocent child!' And with this Mrs Marden broke down – she dropped into a chair and burst into tears. I stammered some question – I pressed on her some bewildered appeal, but she waved me off, unexpectedly and passionately. I persisted – couldn't I help her, couldn't I intervene? 'You *have* intervened,' she sobbed; 'you're *in* it, you're *in* it.'

'I'm very glad to be in anything so extraordinary,' I boldly declared.

'Glad or not, you can't get out of it.'

'I don't want to get out of it – it's too interesting.'

'I'm glad you like it!' She had turned from me, making haste to dry her eyes. 'And now go away.'

'But I want to know more about it.'

'You'll see all you want. Go away!'

'But I want to understand what I see.'

'How can you – when I don't understand myself?' she helplessly cried.

'We'll do so together – we'll make it out.'

At this she got up, doing what more she could to obliterate her tears. 'Yes, it will be better together – that's why I've liked you.'

'Oh, we'll see it through!' I returned.

'Then you must control yourself better.'

'I will, I will – with practice.'

'You'll get used to it,' said my friend in a tone I never forgot. 'But go and join them – I'll come in a moment.'

I passed out to the terrace and felt I had a part to play. So far from dreading another encounter with the 'perfect presence', as she had called it, I was affected altogether in the sense of pleasure. I desired a renewal of my luck: I opened myself wide to the impression; I went round the house as quickly as if I expected to overtake Sir Edmund Orme. I didn't overtake him just then, but the day wasn't to close without my recognizing that, as Mrs Marden had said, I should see all I wanted of him.

We took, or most us took, the collective sociable walk which, in the English country house, is – or was at that time – the consecrated pastime of Sunday afternoons. We were restricted to such a regulated ramble as the ladies were good for; the afternoons, moreover, were short, and by five o'clock we were restored to the fireside in the hall with a sense, on my part at least, that we might have done a little more for our tea. Mrs Marden had said she would join us, but she hadn't appeared; her daughter, who had seen her again before we went out, only explained that she was tired. She remained invisible all the afternoon, but this was a detail to which I gave as little heed as I had given to the circumstance of my not having Charlotte to myself, even for five minutes, during all our walk. I was too much taken up with another interest to care; I felt beneath my feet the threshold of the strange door, in my life, which had suddenly been thrown open and out of which came an air of a keenness I had never breathed and of a taste stronger than wine. I had heard all my days of apparitions, but it was a different thing to have seen one and to know that I should in all likelihood see it familiarly, as I might say, again. I was on the look-out for it as a pilot for the flash of a revolving light, and ready to generalize on the sinister subject, to answer for it to all and sundry that ghosts were much less alarming and much more amusing than was commonly supposed. There's no doubt that I was much uplifted. I couldn't get over the distinction conferred on me, the exception – in the way of mystic enlargement of vision – made in my favour. At the same time I think I did justice to Mrs Marden's absence – a commentary, when I came to think, on what she had said to me: 'Now you know my life.' She had probably been exposed to our hoverer for years, and, not having my firm fibre, had broken down under it. Her nerve was gone, though she had also been able to attest that in a degree, one got used to it. She had got used to breaking down.

Afternoon tea, when the dusk fell early, was a friendly hour at Tranton; the firelight played into the wide white last-century hall; sympathies almost confessed themselves, lingering together, before dressing, on deep sofas, in muddy boots, for last words after walks; and even solitary absorption in the third volume of a novel that was wanted by someone else seemed a form of geniality. I watched my moment and went over to Charlotte when I saw her about to withdraw. The ladies had left the place one by one, and after I had addressed myself to her particularly the three men who had been near gradually dispersed. We had a little vague talk – she might have been a good deal preoccupied, and heaven knows *I* was – after which she said she must go; she should be late for dinner. I proved to her by book that she had plenty of time, and she objected that she must at any rate go up to see her mother, who, she feared, was unwell.

'On the contrary, she's better than she has been for a long time – I'll guarantee that,' I said. 'She has found out she can have confidence in me, and that has done her good.' Miss Marden had dropped into her chair again. I was standing before her, and she looked up at me without a smile, with a dim distress in her beautiful eyes: not exactly as if I were hurting her, but as if she were no longer disposed to treat as a joke what had passed – whatever it was, it would give at the same time no ground for the extreme of solemnity – between her mother and myself. But I could answer her inquiry in all kindness and candour, for I was really conscious that the poor lady had put off a part of her burden on me and was proportionately relieved and eased. 'I'm sure she has slept all the afternoon as she hasn't slept for years,' I went on. 'You've only to ask her.'

Charlotte got up again. 'You make yourself out very useful.'

'You've a good quarter of an hour,' I said. 'Haven't I a right to talk to you a little this way, alone, when your mother has given me your hand?'

'And is it *your* mother who has given me yours? I'm much obliged to her, but I don't want it. I think our hands are not our mothers' – they happen to be our own!' laughed the girl.

'Sit down, sit down and let me tell you!' I pleaded.

I still stood there urgently, to see if she wouldn't oblige me. She cast about, looking vaguely this way and that, as if under a compulsion that was slightly painful. The empty hall was quiet – we heard the loud ticking of the great clock. Then she slowly sank down and I drew a chair close to her. This made me face round to the fire again, and with the movement I saw disconcertedly that we weren't alone. The next instant, more strangely than I can say, my discomposure, instead of increasing, dropped, for the person before the fire was Sir Edmund Orme. He stood there as I had seen him in the Indian room, looking at me with the expressionless attention that borrowed gravity from his sombre distinction. I knew so much more about him now that I had to check a movement of recognition, an acknowledgment of his presence. When once I was aware of it, and that it lasted, the sense that we had company, Charlotte and I, quitted me: it was impressed on me, on the contrary, that we were but the more markedly thrown together. No influence from our companion reached her, and I made a tremendous and very nearly successful effort to hide from her that my own sensibility was other and my nerves as tense as harp strings. I say 'very nearly', because she watched me an instant – while my words were arrested – in a way that made me fear she was going to say again, as she had said in the Indian room: 'What on earth is the matter with you?'

What the matter with me was I quickly told her, for the full knowledge of it rolled over me with the touching sight of her unconsciousness. It was touching that she became in the presence of this extraordinary portent. What was portended, danger or sorrow, bliss or bane, was a minor question; all I saw, as she sat there, was that, innocent and charming, she was close to horror, as she might have thought it, that happened to be veiled from her but that might at any moment be disclosed. I didn't mind it now, as I found – at least more than I could bear; but nothing was more possible than she should, and if it wasn't curious and interesting it might easily be appalling. If I didn't mind it for myself, I afterwards made out, this was largely because I was so taken up with the idea of protecting her. My heart, all at once, beat high with this view; I determined to do everything I could to keep her sense sealed. What I could do might have been all obscure to me if I hadn't, as the minutes lapsed, become more aware than of anything else that I loved her. The way to save her was to love her, and the way to love her was to tell her, now, and here, that I did so. Sir Edmund Orme didn't prevent me, especially as, after a moment, he turned his back to us and stood looking discreetly at the fire. At the end of another moment he leaned his head on his arm, against the chimneypiece, with an air of gradual dejection, like a spirit still more weary than discreet. Charlotte Marden rose with a start at what I said to her – she jumped up to escape it; but she took no offence: the feeling I expressed was too real. She only moved about the room with a deprecating murmur, and I was so busy following up any little advantage I might have obtained that I didn't notice in what manner Sir Edmund Orme disappeared. I only found his place presently vacant. This made no difference – he had been so small a hindrance; I only remember being suddenly struck with something inexorable in the sweet sad headshake Charlotte gave me.

'I don't ask for an answer now,' I said; 'I only want you to be sure – to know how much depends on it.'

'Oh, I don't want to give it to you now or ever!' she replied. 'I hate the subject, please – I wish one could be let alone.' And then, since I might have found something harsh in this irrepressible artless cry of beauty beset, she added quickly, vaguely, kindly, as she left the room: 'Thank you, thank you – thank you so very much!'

At dinner I was generous enough to be glad for her that, on the same side of the table with me, she hadn't me in range. Her mother was nearly opposite me, and just after we had sat down Mrs Marden gave me a long, deep look that expressed, and to the utmost, our strange communion. It meant of course 'She has told me,' but it meant other things beside. At any rate I know what my mute response to her conveyed: 'I've seen him again – I've seen him again!' This didn't prevent Mrs Marden from treating her neighbours with her usual scrupulous blandness. After dinner, when, in the drawing-room, the men joined the ladies and I went straight up to her to tell her how I wished we might have some quiet words, she said at once, in a low tone, looking down at her fan while she opened and shut it: 'He's here – he's here.'

'Here?' I looked round the room, but was disappointed.

'Look where *she* is,' said Mrs Marden just with the faintest asperity. Charlotte was in fact not in the main saloon, but in a smaller into which it opened and which was known as the morning-room. I took a few steps and saw her, through a doorway, upright in the middle of the room, talking with three gentlemen whose backs were practically turned to me. For a moment my quest seemed vain; then I knew one of the gentlemen – the middle one – could but be Sir Edmund Orme. This time it *was* surprising that the others didn't see him. Charlotte might have seemed absolutely to have her eyes on him and to be addressing him straight. She saw me after an instant, however, and immediately averted herself. I returned to her mother with a sharpened fear the girl might think I was watching *her*, which would be unjust. Mrs Marden had found a small sofa – a little apart – and I sat down beside her. There were some questions I had so wanted to go into that I wished we were once more in the Indian room. I presently gathered, however, that our privacy quite sufficed. We communicated so closely and completely now, and with such silent reciprocities, that it would in every circumstance be adequate.

'Oh yes, he's there,' I said; 'and at about a quarter-past seven he was in the hall.'

'I knew it at the time – and I was so glad!' she answered straight.

'So glad?'

'That it was your affair this time and not mine. It's a rest for me.'

'Did you sleep all the afternoon?' I then asked.

'As I haven't done for months. But how did you know that?'

'As *you* knew, I take it, that Sir Edmund was in the hall. We shall evidently each of us know things now – where the other's concerned.'

'Where *he's* concerned,' Mrs Marden amended. 'It's a blessing, the way you take it,' she added with a long mild sigh.

'I take it,' I at once returned, 'as a man who's in love with your daughter.'

'Of course – of course.' Intense as I now felt my desire for the girl to be I couldn't help laughing a little at the tone of these words; and it led my companion immediately to say: 'Otherwise you wouldn't have seen him.'

Well, I esteemed my privilege, but I saw an objection to this. 'Does everyone see him who's in love with her? If so, there would be dozens.'

'They're not in love with her as you are.'

I took this in and couldn't but accept it. 'I can of course only speak for myself – and I found a moment before dinner to do so.'

'She told me as soon as she saw me,' Mrs Marden replied.

'And have I any hope – any chance?'

'That you may have is what I long for, what I pray for.'

The sore sincerity of this touched me. 'Ah, how can I thank you enough?' I murmured.

'I believe it will all pass – if she only loves you,' the poor woman pursued.

'It will all pass?' I was a little at a loss.

'I mean we shall then be rid of him – shall never see him again.'

'Oh, if she loves me I don't care how often I see him!' I roundly returned.

'Ah, you take it better than *I* could,' said my companion. 'You've the happiness not to know – not to understand.'

'I don't indeed. What on earth does he want?'

'He wants to make me suffer.' She turned her wan face upon me with it, and I saw now for the first time, and saw well, how perfectly, if this had been our visitant's design, he had done his work. 'For what I did to him,' she explained.

'And what did you do to him?'

She gave me an unforgettable look. 'I killed him.' As I had seen him fifty yards off only five minutes before, the words gave me a start. 'Yes, I make you jump; be careful. He's there still, but he killed himself. I broke his heart – he thought me awfully bad. We were to have been married, but I broke it off – just at the last. I saw someone I liked better; I had no reason but that. It wasn't for interest or money or position or any of that baseness. All the good things were his. It was simply that I fell in love with Major Marden. When I saw *him* I felt I couldn't marry anyone else. I wasn't in love with Edmund Orme; my mother and my elder, my married sister, had brought it about. But he did love me and I knew – that is, almost knew! – how much! But I told him I didn't care – that I couldn't, that I wouldn't ever. I threw him over, and he took something, some abominable drug or draught that proved fatal. It was dreadful, it was horrible, he was found that way – he died in agony. I married Major Marden, but not for five years. I was happy, perfectly happy – time obliterates. But when my husband died I began to see him.'

I had listened intently, wondering. 'To see your husband?'

'Never, never – *that* way, thank God! To see *him* – and with Chartie, always with Chartie. The first time it nearly killed me – about seven years ago, when she first came out. Never when I'm by myself – only with her. Sometimes not for months, then every day for a week. I've tried everything to break the spell – doctors and *régimes* and climates; I've prayed to God on my knees. That day at Brighton, on the Parade with you, when you thought I was ill, that was the first for an age. And then in the evening, when I knocked my tea over you, and the day you were at the door with her and I saw you from the window – each time he was there.'

'I see, I see.' I was more thrilled than I could say. 'It's an apparition like another.'

'Like another? Have you ever seen another?' she cried.

'No, I mean the sort of thing one has heard of. It's tremendously interesting to encounter a case.'

'Do you call me a "case"?' my friend cried with exquisite resentment.

'I was thinking of myself.'

'Oh, you're the right one!' she went on. 'I was right when I trusted you.'

'I'm devoutly grateful you did; but what made you do it?' I asked.

'I had thought the whole thing out. I had had time to in those dreadful years while he was punishing me in my daughter.'

'Hardly that,' I objected, 'if Miss Marden never knew.'

'That has been my terror, that she *will*, from one occasion to another. I've an unspeakable dread of the effect on her.'

'She shan't, she shan't!' I engaged in such a tone that several people looked round. Mrs Marden made me rise, and our talk dropped for that evening. The next day I told her I must leave Tranton – it was neither comfortable nor considerate to remain as a rejected suitor. She was disconcerted, but accepted my reasons, only appealing to me with mournful eyes: 'You'll leave me alone then with my burden?' It was, of course, understood between us that for many weeks to come there would be no discretion in 'worrying poor Charlotte'; such were the terms in which, with odd feminine and maternal inconsistency, she alluded to an attitude on my part that she favoured. I was prepared to be heroically considerate, but I held that even this delicacy permitted me to say a word to Miss Marden before I went. I begged her after breakfast to take a turn with me on the terrace, and as she hesitated, looking at me distantly, I let her know it was only to ask her a question and to say good-bye – I was going away for *her*.

She came out with me and we passed slowly round the house three or four times. Nothing is finer than this great airy platform, from which every glance is a sweep of the country with the sea on the farthest edge. It might have been that as we passed the windows we were conspicuous to our friends in the house, who would make out sarcastically why I was so significantly bolting. But I didn't care; I only wondered if they mightn't really this time receive the impression of Sir Edmund Orme, who joined us on one of our turns and strolled slowly on the other side of Charlotte. Of what odd essence he was made I know not; I've no theory about him – leaving that to others – any more than about such or such another of my fellow mortals (and *his* law of being) as I have elbowed in life. He was as positive, as individual and ultimate a fact as any of these. Above all, he was, by every seeming, of as fine and as sensitive, of as thoroughly honourable, a mixture; so that I should no more have thought of taking a liberty, of practising an experiment, with him, of touching him, for instance, or of addressing him, since he set the example of silence, than I should have thought of committing any other social grossness. He had always, as I saw more fully later, the perfect propriety of his position – looked always arrayed and anointed, and carried himself ever, in each particular, exactly as the occasion demanded. He struck me as strange, incontestably, but somehow always struck me as right. I very soon came to attach an idea of beauty to his unrecognized presence, the beauty of an old story, of love and pain and death. What I ended by feeling was that he was on my side, watching over my interest, looking to it that no trick should be played me and that my heart at least shouldn't be broken. Oh, he had taken them seriously, his own wound and his own loss – he had certainly proved this in his day. If poor Mrs Marden, responsible for these things, had, as she told me, thought the case out, I also treated it to the finest analysis I could bring to bear. It was a case of retributive justice, of the visiting on the children of the sins of the mothers, since not of the fathers. This wretched mother was to pay, in suffering, for the suffering she had inflicted, and as the disposition to trifle with an honest man's just expectations might crop up again, to my detriment, in the child, the latter young person was to be studied and watched, so that *she* might be made to suffer should she do an equal wrong. She might emulate her parent by some play of characteristic perversity not less than she resembled her in charm; and if that impulse should be determined in her, if she should be caught, that is to say, in some breach of faith or some heartless act, her eyes would on the spot, by an insidious logic, be opened suddenly and unpitiedly to the 'perfect presence', which she would then have to work as she could into her conception of a young lady's universe. I had no great fear for her, because I hadn't felt her lead me on from vanity, and I knew that if I was disconcerted it was because I had myself gone too fast. We should have a good deal of ground to get over at least before I should be in a position to be sacrificed by her. She couldn't take back what she had given before she had given rather more. Whether I asked for more was indeed another matter, and the question I put to her on the terrace that morning was whether I might continue during the winter to come to Mrs Marden's house. I promised not to come too often and not to speak to her for three months of the issue I had raised the day before. She replied that I might do as I liked, and on this we parted.

I carried out the vow I had made her; I held my tongue for my three months. Unexpectedly to myself there were moments of this time when she did strike me as capable of missing my homage even though she might be indifferent to my happiness. I wanted so to make her like me that I became subtle and ingenious, wonderfully alert, patiently diplomatic. Sometimes I thought I had earned my reward, brought her to the point of saying: 'Well, well, you're the best of them all – you may speak to me now.' Then there was a greater blankness than ever in her beauty and on certain days a mocking light in her eyes, a light of which the meaning seemed to be: 'If you don't take care I *will* accept you, to have done with you the more effectually.' Mrs Marden was a great help to me simply by believing in me, and I valued her faith all the more that it continued even through a sudden intermission of the miracle that had been wrought for me. After our visit to Tranton Sir Edmund Orme gave us a holiday, and I confess it was at first a disappointment to me. I felt myself by so much less designated, less involved and connected – all with Charlotte I mean to say.

'Oh, don't cry till you're out of the wood,' was her mother's comment; 'he has let me off sometimes for six months. He'll break out again when you least expect it – he understands his game.' For her these weeks were happy, and she was wise enough not to talk about me to the girl. She was so good as to assure me I was taking the right line, that I looked as if I felt secure and that in the long run women give way to this. She had known them do it even when the man was a fool for that appearance, for that confidence – a fool indeed on any terms. For herself she felt it a good time, almost her best, a Saint Martin's summer of the soul. She was better than she had been for years, and had me to thank for it. The sense of visitation was light on her – she wasn't in anguish every time she looked round. Charlotte contradicted me repeatedly, but contradicted herself still more. That winter by the old Sussex sea was a wonder of mildness, and we often sat out in the sun. I walked up and down with my young woman, and Mrs Marden, sometimes on a bench, sometimes in a bath chair, waited for us and smiled at us as we passed. I always looked out for a sign in her face – 'He's with you, he's with you' (she would see him before I should), but nothing came; the season had brought us as well a sort of spiritual softness. Towards the end of April the air was so like June that, meeting my two friends one night at some Brighton sociability – an evening party with amateur music – I drew the younger unresistingly out upon a balcony to which a window in one of the rooms stood open. The night was close and thick, the stars dim, and below us under the cliff we heard the deep rumble of the tide. We listened to it a little and there came to us, mixed with it from within the house, the sound of a violin accompanied by a piano – a performance that had been our pretext for escaping.

'Do you like me a little better?' I broke out after a minute. 'Could you listen to me again?'

I had no sooner spoken than she laid her hand quickly, with a certain force, on my arm. 'Hush! – isn't there someone there?' She was looking into the gloom of the far end of the balcony. This balcony ran the whole width of the house, a width very great in the best of the old houses at Brighton. We were to some extent lighted by the open window behind us, but the other windows, curtained within, left the darkness undiminished, so that I made out but dimly the figure of a gentleman standing there and looking at us. He was in evening dress, like a guest – I saw the vague sheen of his white shirt and the pale oval of his face – and he might perfectly have been a guest who had stepped out in advance of us to take the air. Charlotte took him for one at first – then evidently, even in a few seconds, saw that the intensity of his gaze was unconventional. What else she saw I couldn't determine; I was too occupied with my own impression to do more than feel the quick contact of her uneasiness. My own impression was in fact the strongest of sensations, a sensation of horror; for what could the thing mean but that the girl at last *saw*? I heard her give a sudden, gasping 'Ah!' and move quickly into the house. It was only afterwards I knew that I myself had had a totally new emotion – my horror passing into anger and my anger into a stride along the balcony with a gesture of reprobation. The case was simplified to the vision of an adorable girl menaced and terrified. I advanced to vindicate her security, but I found nothing there to meet me. It was either all a mistake or Sir Edmund Orme had vanished.

I followed her at once, but there were symptoms of confusion in the drawing-room when I passed in. A lady had fainted, the music had stopped; there was a shuffling of chairs and a pressing forward. The lady was not Charlotte, as I feared, but Mrs Marden, who had suddenly been taken ill. I remember the relief with which I learned this, for to see Charlotte stricken would have been anguish, and her mother's condition gave a channel to her agitation. It was, or course, all a matter for the people of the house and for the ladies, and I could have no share in attending to my friends or in conducting them to their carriage. Mrs Marden revived and insisted on going home, after which I uneasily withdrew.

I called the next morning for better news and I learnt she was more at ease, but on my asking if Charlotte would see me the message sent down was an excuse. There was nothing for me to do all day but roam with a beating heart. Towards evening, however, I received a line in pencil, brought by hand – 'Please come; mother wishes you.' Five minutes later I was at the door again and ushered into the drawing-room. Mrs Marden lay on the sofa, and as soon as I looked at her I saw the shadow of death in her face. But the first thing she said was that she was better, ever so much better; her poor old fluttered heart had misbehaved again, but now was decently quiet. She gave me her hand and I bent over her, my eyes on her eyes, and in this way was able to read what she didn't speak – 'I'm really very ill, but appear to take what I say exactly as I say it.' Charlotte stood there beside her, looking not frightened now, but intensely grave, and meeting no look of my own. 'She has told me – she has told me!' her mother went on.

'She has told you?' I stared from one of them to the other, wondering if my friend meant that the girl had named to her the unexplained appearance on the balcony.

'That you spoke to her again – that you're admirably faithful.'

I felt a thrill of joy at this; it showed me that memory uppermost, and also that her daughter had wished to say the thing that would most soothe her, not the thing that would alarm her. Yet I was myself now sure, as sure as if Mrs Marden had told me, that she knew and had known at the moment what her daughter had seen. 'I spoke – I spoke, but she gave me no answer,' I said.

'She will now, won't you, Chartie? I want it so, I want it!' our companion murmured with ineffable wistfulness.

'You're very good to me' – Charlotte addressed me, seriously and sweetly, but with her eyes fixed on the carpet. There was something different in her, different from all the past. She had recognized something, she felt a coercion. I could see her uncontrollably tremble.

'Ah, if you would let me show you *how* good I can be!' I cried as I held out my hands' to her. As I uttered the words I was touched with the knowledge that something had happened. A form had constituted itself on the other side of the couch, and the form leaned over Mrs Marden. My whole being went forth into a mute prayer that Charlotte shouldn't see it and that I should be able to betray nothing. The impulse to glance towards her mother was even stronger then the involuntary movement of taking in Sir Edmund Orme; but I could resist even that, and Mrs Marden was perfectly still. Charlotte got up to give me her hand, and then – with the definite act – she dreadfully saw. She gave, with a shriek, one stare of dismay, and another sound, the wail of one of the lost, fell at the same instant on my ear. But I had already sprung towards the creature I loved, to cover her, to veil her face, and she had as passionately thrown herself into my arms. I held her there a moment – pressing her close, given up to her, feeling each of her throbs with my own and not knowing which was which; then all of a sudden, coldly, I was sure we were alone. She released herself. The figure beside the sofa had vanished, but Mrs Marden lay in her place with closed eyes, with something in her stillness that gave us both a fresh terror. Charlotte expressed it in the cry of 'Mother, mother!' with which she flung herself down. I fell on my knees beside her – Mrs Marden had passed away.

Was the sound I heard when Chartie shrieked – the other and still more tragic sound I mean – the despairing cry of the poor lady's death-shock or the articulate sob (it was like a waft from a great storm) of the exorcized and pacified spirit? Possibly the latter, for that was mercifully the last of Sir Edmund Orme.

Angeline, or the Haunted House

Emile Zola

1

Almost two years ago now, I found myself riding on my bicycle along a deserted country lane in the region of Orgeval, just north of Poissy, when I was greatly surprised by the sudden appearance, quite close to the road, of a large house. I alighted from my machine in order that I might see it more clearly. It stood there under the grey November sky, as the cold wind swept the fallen leaves, a brick-built house of no especial character in the middle of a vast garden filled with elderly trees. But what made it unusual, what, indeed, endowed it with a wild strangeness which set one's nerves on edge, was the awful state of abandon in which it had been left. And so it was, since one of the iron gates had broken from its hinges, and since a large board announced in paint which had been faded by the rains that the property was for sale, that I entered the garden, yielding to a curiosity which was tinged with apprehension.

The house must have been uninhabited for some thirty or forty years. Through the course of many winters, bricks had worked loose from the cornices and by the window-frames, allowing an invasion of moss and lichens. The walls were lined with cracks, like premature wrinkles, marking what was still a sound enough building but for which no one cared any longer. Below the front door the stone steps, broken by the frosts and guarded by nettles and brambles, seemed to present a threshold to desolation and death. But most of all, the atmosphere of melancholy emanated from those bare, glaucous windows, their curtains gone, their glass smashed by stones from passing children, which permitted a view into the sombre emptiness of the rooms, like the open eyes of a corpse whose soul has been extinguished. Around the house the vast garden was a scene of devastation. What once had been a flower-bed was now scarcely recognizable under the rampant growth of weeds, whole paths had been devoured by voracious plants, the shrubberies had reverted to the character of virgin forests: I was presented with an impression of wild vegetation such as one finds in an abandoned cemetery, and all, that day, under the damp shade of ancient trees whose last leaves were being carried off by the autumn wind crying its sad complaint.

For a long time I stood there surrounded by this wail of despair which seemed to come from all that I saw about me. My heart was heavy with a dull fear, a growing unease, yet I was held by a burning compassion, a need to know and sympathize with all I could feel around me of unhappiness and suffering. Then, having finally made my decision to leave, and having perceived beyond the way, in the fork of two roads, a sort of inn, a poor place where one could buy a drink, I went in, resolved to satisfy my curiosity by encouraging the local people to talk.

The only person I found there was an old woman, who served me a glass of beer with a great deal of complaining. She complained that she found herself here on this forgotten road, where not two cyclists a day would pass. She talked aimlessly, related the story of her life, revealed that she was known as 'mère Toussaint', that she had come from Vernon with her man in order to take over the inn, that at first things had not gone too badly, but that since she was widowed everything had gone from bad to worse. Finally, after this flood of words, when I started to ask her about the nearby house, she became suddenly more circumspect, regarding me with a suspicious eye, as if I were attempting to tear from her some awful secret.

'Oh, you mean "La Sauvagière", the haunted house, as they call it round here . . . I know nothing of that, Monsieur. That goes back before my time. I shall have been here just thirty years next Easter, and that all goes back nearly forty years. When we came out here the house was already more or less in the state you see it in now. Summers pass and winters pass and no one sees anything move in there, except for the occasional falling stone.'

'But,' I asked, 'why hasn't it been sold, since it is for sale?'

'Oh, why indeed? How should I know? . . . They talk about it enough . . .'

In the end, I must have gained her confidence, whereupon it was clear that she was only too anxious to recount to me what it was that people talked about. First she told me how not one of the girls from the village would dare to venture into the grounds of 'La Sauvagière' after dusk, because it was rumoured that some poor soul returned there by night to haunt it. When I expressed surprise that such a story should still be found credible so near to Paris, she shrugged her shoulders, endeavouring at first to appear composed, but before long revealing her unspoken terror.

'But consider the facts, Monsieur. Why has it never been sold? I have seen prospective purchasers come and go, but they always leave more quickly than they arrived, and not one has ever come back a second time. And I can tell you one thing for sure, if any visitor dares to venture inside that house extraordinary things happen: doors slam noisily of their own accord, as if some awful wind were blowing; cries, moans, and the sound of sobbing rise from the cellars; and if anyone dares to stay longer a heart-rending voice starts to call out again and again "Angeline! Angeline! Angeline!" in such an anguished tone as to chill the very marrow of your bones . . . What I am telling you are proven facts. No one will deny them.'

I assure you that my own emotions were beginning to stir, and a shiver ran down my spine.

'But who is this Angeline?'

'I can see, Monsieur, that you are determined to know the whole story, though I must tell you again that I really know nothing myself.'

Nevertheless, she proceeded eventually to tell me everything. Some forty years previously, in about 1858, just at the time when the victorious Second Empire was holding one celebration after another, Monsieur de G—, who held a post at the Tuileries Palace, lost his wife. He had by her a daughter, some ten years old, called Angeline, indescribably beautiful, and the living image of her mother. Two years later Monsieur de G— married again, and his second wife was another renowned beauty, the widow of a general. Apparently, following this second marriage a terrible jealousy grew up between Angeline and her stepmother: the one grief-stricken to see her mother already forgotten, her place in the family so quickly usurped by this outsider; the other obsessed to distraction by the idea of having constantly before her this living portrait of a woman she feared she could never cause to be forgotten. 'La Sauvagière' belonged to the new Madame de G—, and it was there, so the story went, that one evening, on seeing the father lovingly embrace his daughter, in her jealous rage she struck the little girl such a blow that the wretched child fell to the floor dead, her neck broken. The end of the story was gruesome. The distraught father consented to bury his daughter himself in one of the cellars of the house, in order to save the murderess. The body of the child remained hidden there for years, while the story was put about that she had gone away to an aunt's. Then, one day, the howling of a dog who was found feverishly scratching at the ground caused the crime to be discovered, although the scandal of the discovery was subsequently suppressed by the Tuileries authorities. Now both Monsieur and Madame de G——were dead, but Angeline still returned every night to answer the call of the pitiful voice which summoned her from that mysterious world beyond the darkness.

'No one will deny what I have told you,' concluded the old woman. 'It is all as true as I am standing here.'

I had listened to her account in awe, struck by its implausibility, yet captivated by the dark and violent singularity of the drama. I had heard of this Monsieur de G——. I think I had known that he had remarried and that a family tragedy had overtaken him. Was it then true? What a moving and tragic story, exposing human passion to the point of exasperated frenzy, the most awful crime of passion one could ever imagine: a little girl as beautiful as a summer's day, loved and cherished, struck down by her stepmother, and then buried by her father in the corner of a cellar! What exquisite horror! I wanted to hear more, to talk about it, but I asked myself, to what end? Why not depart with the flower of popular imagination, this terrifying tale?

As I remounted my bicycle I cast a last glance in the direction of 'La Sauvagière'. Night was falling, and the desolate house looked back at me through the lifeless eyes of its dull, empty windows, whilst the autumn wind sighed a lament among the decaying trees.

2

Why should that story have become fixed in my mind until it became an agonizing obsession? It is one of those intellectual mysteries which are difficult to account for. In vain I told myself that such myths are rife in the countryside, that this particular one could have no real interest for me personally. Despite it all, the dead child haunted my thoughts: sweet, tragic Angeline, summoned every night for forty years by a voice whimpering among the empty rooms of the abandoned house.

So, for the first two months of the winter, I set about doing some research. Obviously, if ever such a disappearance, such a dramatic happening, had been noised abroad, the newspapers of the time would surely have spoken of it. I searched through the collections in the National Library without success: there was not a line which could have been linked with such a story. Then I questioned people who might have known something at the time, employees of the Tuileries: none was able to give me a clear answer – all I obtained was contradictory information. In fact, I had all but abandoned any hope of finding out the truth, though I was still tormented by the mystery, when, one morning, fate guided me on to a new track.

Every two or three weeks, out of a feeling of comradeship, affection and admiration, it was my habit to visit the elderly poet V—, who died last April, aged seventy. For many years his legs had been paralysed, and he was restricted to an armchair in his little studio in the rue Assas, the window of which looked out on to the Luxembourg Gardens. He was coming to the end of a life of dreaming: he had lived by his imagination, and created for himself a fabulous palace, where, far from the real world, he had loved and suffered. Which of us does not recall his kind, delicate face, his white hair and childish curls, his pale blue eyes with their youthful innocence? It would be wrong to say that he never told the truth, but the fact is that he was for ever inventing, with the result that one never quite knew where reality ended for him and where illusion began. He was a charming old man, who had long since ceased to be part of everyday life, but whose conversation often touched me deeply as a vague, discreet revelation of the unknown.

Thus I found myself that day chatting with him by the window in his tiny room, warmed as always by a blazing fire. Outside, there was the severest of frosts, so that the Luxembourg Gardens presented a snow-white carpet, a vast horizon of immaculate purity. For some reason, I suddenly found myself telling him of 'La Sauvagière' and the story which still preoccupied me: the father's remarriage, the stepmother's evil jealousy of the little girl who was the living portrait of her mother, the clandestine burial in the cellar. He listened to me with the same tranquil smile he wore even when he was sad. There followed a silence; his pale blue eyes gazed into the far distance, across the white expanses of the Luxembourg Gardens, and the shadow of a vision, which emanated from him, seemed to shudder vaguely around him.

'I used to know Monsieur de G— very well,' he said slowly. 'I knew his first wife, a divinely beautiful woman; I knew his second wife also, whose beauty was every bit as dazzling; and I was passionately in love with them both, although I never revealed the fact. I also knew Angeline, who was even more lovely and whom any man would have worshipped on his knees . . . But things did not happen quite as you have said.'

I became very excited. Was it here, then, the unexpected truth I had despaired of ever knowing? Was I about to discover everything? At first I was only too ready to believe what he was about to tell me, and I replied,

'Oh my dear friend, what a service you will render me! at last my poor head will be eased. Tell me quickly, I must know everything.'

But he was not listening to me; he was still gazing distractedly into the distance. When at last he spoke, it was as if in a dream, as if he had created the beings and the things he evoked for me.

'Angeline, by the age of twelve years, already possessed a woman's power to love, with all its capacity to feel joy and pain. It was she who became insanely jealous of her father's new wife, whom she saw daily in his arms. She suffered at the sight of this terrible betrayal on the part of the new couple. It was no longer just her mother they were affronting, it was she herself who was being tortured, it was her heart that was wounded. Every night she heard her mother calling her from the grave; and one night, determined to be reunited with her, no longer able to stand the pain, already dying from an excess of love, this little girl of twelve years thrust a knife into her heart.'

I cried out, 'Good heavens! Can that really be?'

He went on without hearing me. 'Imagine with what terror, what horror, Monsieur and Madame de G— discovered Angeline the next morning in her bed, the knife plunged into her breast right up to the handle! They were due to leave for Italy the following day, and there was nobody left in the house other than an elderly maid who had brought up the child. In their panic that they might be accused of a crime, they had the old maid help them bury the young body; but they in fact buried it in a corner of the conservatory behind the house, at the foot of a giant orange tree. And there it was that it was found when, after the death of both parents, the old maid told her story.'

By this time some doubts had begun to enter my mind, and I looked at him anxiously, asking myself whether he was fabricating.

'But,' I asked, 'do you believe then that Angeline really could return again every night in order to answer the heart-rending cry of the mysterious voice which summons her?'

'Return again, my friend? Ah, but everyone returns again. Why shouldn't the soul of the poor child inhabit again the place in which she has both loved and suffered? If a voice is heard calling after her, then life has not yet begun again for her; but it will do, be assured of that, for everything begins again, love is never lost, nor beauty . . . Angeline! Angeline! Angeline! One day she will live again in the sun and the flowers.'

Decidedly, I was now neither convinced nor comforted. My old friend V—, the child poet, had done nothing but increase my discomposure. It was evident that he was fabricating. Yet, like all seers, perhaps he was able to divine the truth?

'You are sure that everything you have told me is the absolute truth?' I ventured to inquire with a laugh.

'Of course, it is the truth. Is not everything to do with the Infinite the truth?'

I was never to see him again, as shortly afterwards I was obliged to leave Paris. He remains in my mind, however, his pensive gaze lost on the white expanse of the Luxembourg Gardens, so calm in the certainty of his infinite dream, whereas I was still tortured by my desire to establish once and for all that elusive phenomenon, the truth.

3

A year and half went by. I had been obliged to travel. My life had been affected by many joys and many sorrows on the stormy seas which bear us all away to unknown shores. But again and again I would hear, at a certain hour, first far away, then entering my conscious mind, that desperate cry: 'Angeline! Angeline! Angeline!' And it would leave me trembling, full of new doubts, tortured by the need to know. I could not forget, and there is nothing worse for me than the hell of uncertainty.

I cannot say how it came about that one glorious June evening I found myself once more on my bicycle in the deserted lane by 'La Sauvagière'. Had I consciously wished to see it again? Or was it an instinct which had directed me to turn off the main road and return to these parts? It was close on eight o'clock, but at the end of one of the longest days of the year the sky was still brilliant with a triumphantly setting sun, without a cloud, an infinity of azure and gold. And how sweet and delicate the air was, how fine the scents of the trees and the grass, what a subtle delight the immense peacefulness of the fields!

As on the first occasion when I arrived before 'La Sauvagière', astonishment caused me to jump down from my machine. For a moment I hesitated: was this the same place? A fine new gate shone in the light of the setting sun, the garden walls had been restored, and the house, which I could barely perceive behind the trees, seemed to me to have regained the joyful gaiety of youth. Was this then the promised resurrection? Had Angeline returned to life in answer to that distant voice?

I was standing transfixed in the roadway when the sound of a shuffling gait behind me caused me to start. It was 'mère Toussaint' bringing home her cow from a neighbouring field.

'So they weren't afraid?' I asked, motioning towards the house.

She recognized me and halted her animal.

'Ah, Monsieur, there are those who would trample on God Himself. The house was bought over a year ago now. It was a painter that did it, the artist B——, and you know what these artists will do.'

Whereupon she moved her cow on, adding with a shake of the head, 'Well, we shall just have to wait and see what happens.'

The painter B——, that delicate, inventive artist who had portrayed so many delightful Parisiennes! I knew him slightly: we had shaken hands at the theatre, in exhibitions, places where one runs into people. Suddenly I was overcome by an irresistible desire to enter, to confess to him, to beg him to tell me what he knew of the truth about this 'Sauvagière', whose mystery obsessed me. And without further thought, without care for my dusty cyclist's attire, which custom is beginning to tolerate these days in any case, I wheeled my bicycle over to the mossy trunk of an old tree. At the clear sound of the bell, the lever of which had accidentally struck the gate, there appeared a servant to whom I gave my card and who bade me wait a moment in the garden.

My surprise increased when I looked around me. The façade of the house had been repaired: no more cracks, no dislodged bricks. The steps, garnished with roses, had become once again a threshold of joyous welcome. The living windows were now smiling, telling of the joy within, behind their white lace curtains. As for the garden, it had been cleared of its nettles and brambles, the flower-bed had reappeared like a gigantic scented bouquet, the ancient trees had acquired new youth in their peaceful old age, under the golden rain of the spring sunshine.

When the servant reappeared, he led me into a drawing-room, informing me that his master had gone off to the neighbouring village but would be back before long. I was ready to wait for hours. I passed the time examining the room in which I found myself: it was luxuriously furnished with thick carpets, and cretonne curtains which matched the massive sofa and deep armchairs. These hangings were so extensive that when dusk suddenly arrived it took me by surprise. Before long it was almost completely dark. I do not know how long I had to wait there. I had evidently been forgotten; not even a lamp was brought for me. Seated in the shadows I started to relive the whole tragic story, to lose myself in reverie. Had Angeline been murdered? Had she thrust a knife into her own heart? And I have to admit that in this haunted house, upon which darkness had fallen once again, I felt fear. What initially was not much more than a certain unease, a slight chill, proceeded to grow beyond all proportion into an irrational terror which froze my whole being.

At first it seemed to me that I could hear obscure sounds in the distance. They must be coming from the depths of the cellars: a vague moaning, stifled sobs, heavy, ghostly footsteps. Then whatever it was began to come up from below, to draw closer, until the whole house seemed in the darkness to be filled with a terrible distress. Suddenly the awful cry rang out, 'Angeline! Angeline! Angeline!', with such growing force that it seemed to me I felt a cold breath touch my face. One of the drawing-room doors opened noisily; Angeline entered, and crossed the room without seeing me. I recognized her in the dim light which had penetrated with her from the hall outside. It was indeed the dead child of twelve years, incredibly beautiful with her exquisite blonde hair upon her shoulders, dressed in white, the white of the earth from which she returned every night. She passed by in silence, abstracted, and disappeared through another door, while once again the voice called out, this time from further off, 'Angeline! Angeline! Angeline!' I was left there standing with sweat on my forehead, in a state of horror which caused every hair of my body to rise in the dreadful wind which emanated from the enigma.

Then, almost immediately, as the servant finally came in with a lamp, I was conscious that the artist B— was there, shaking my hand, and apologizing for having let me wait so long. Without any attempt to preserve my self-respect, I rushed into telling him my story. As I did so, I was still trembling. At first he listened to me with no little surprise, and then with great good humour he hastened to reassure me.

'My dear fellow, you were probably unaware of the fact that I am a cousin of the second Madame de G—. The poor woman! To be accused of the murder of that child whom she loved and mourned quite as much as the father! For there is only one part of the story which is true: the poor creature did indeed die here, not by her own hand, for heaven's sake, but of a sudden fever. The shock was so great that her parents, having conceived a horror of this house, never wished to return here. Which explains why it remained uninhabited for as long as they were alive. After their deaths there followed interminable legal procedures, which prevented its sale. I wanted it, having coveted it for many years; and I can assure you that we have never yet seen any ghosts here!'

The chill returned to me as I mumbled. 'But I have just seen Angeline, here, only a moment ago . . . That frightful voice was summoning her, and she passed by here, through this very room . . .'

He looked at me, alarmed, believing perhaps that I was losing my sanity. Then suddenly he laughed, the resounding laugh of a man who is happy.

'That was my daughter you saw just now. Her godfather was, in fact Monsieur de G—, who gave her the name Angeline as an act of devoted memory. Having no doubt been called by her mother, she must have passed through this room.'

Thereupon he opened the door himself and called out again, 'Angeline! Angeline! Angeline!'

The child returned, now alive, now vibrant with gaiety. It was she, with her white dress, her exquisite blonde hair upon her shoulders, so beautiful, so radiant with hope, that she was like the spring itself, bearing in the form of a bud the promise of love, the lasting happiness of life.

What a charming ghost was this new child, born again from the one who had died. Death had been conquered. My old friend, the poet V—, had not lied; nothing is ever lost for ever, everything begins again, both beauty and love. Their mothers call them, these little girls of today, these lovers of tomorrow, and they live again under the sun and among the flowers. The house had been haunted by the promise of this reawakening; today the house was once more youthful and happy in the rediscovered joy of eternal life.

The Moonlit Road

Ambrose Bierce

1. Statement of Joel Hetman, Jr

I am the most unfortunate of men. Rich, respected, fairly well educated and of sound health – with many other advantages usually valued by those having them and coveted by those who have them not – I sometimes think that I should be less unhappy if they had been denied me, for then the contrast between my outer and my inner life would not be continually demanding a painful attention. In the stress of privation and the need of effort I might sometimes forget the sombre secret ever baffling the conjecture that it compels.

I am the only child of Joel and Julia Hetman. The one was a well-to-do country gentleman, the other a beautiful and accomplished woman to whom he was passionately attached with what I now know to have been a jealous and exacting devotion. The family home was a few miles from Nashville, Tennessee, a large, irregularly built dwelling of no particular order of architecture, a little way off the road, in a park of trees and shrubbery.

At the time of which I write I was nineteen years old, a student at Yale. One day I received a telegram from my father of such urgency that in compliance with its unexplained demand I left at once for home. At the railway station in Nashville a distant relative awaited me to apprise me of the reason for my recall: my mother had been barbarously murdered – why and by whom none could conjecture, but the circumstances were these:

My father had gone to Nashville, intending to return the next afternoon.

Something prevented his accomplishing the business in hand, so he returned on the same night, arriving just before the dawn. In his testimony before the coroner he explained that having no latchkey and not caring to disturb the sleeping servants, he had, with no clearly defined intention, gone around to the rear of the house. As he turned an angle of the building, he heard a sound as of a door gently closed, and saw in the darkness, indistinctly, the figure of a man, which instantly disappeared among the trees of the lawn. A hasty pursuit and brief search of the grounds in the belief that the trespasser was someone secretly visiting a servant proving fruitless, he entered at the unlocked door and mounted the stairs to my mother's chamber. Its door was open, and stepping into black darkness he fell headlong over some heavy object on the floor. I may spare myself the details; it was my poor mother, dead of strangulation by human hands!

Nothing had been taken from the house, the servants had heard no sound, and excepting those terrible finger marks upon the dead woman's throat – dear God! that I might forget them! – no trace of the assassin was ever found.

I gave up my studies and remained with my father, who, naturally, was greatly changed. Always of a sedate, taciturn disposition, he now fell into so deep a dejection that nothing could hold his attention, yet anything – a footfall, the sudden closing of a door – aroused in him a fitful interest; one might have called it an apprehension. At any small surprise of the senses he would start visibly and sometimes turn pale, then relapse into a melancholy apathy deeper than before. I suppose he was what is called a 'nervous wreck'. As to me, I was younger then than now – there is much in that. Youth is Gilead, in which is balm for every wound. Ah, that I might again dwell in that enchanted land! Unacquainted with grief, I knew not how to appraise my bereavement; I could not rightly estimate the strength of the stroke.

One night, a few months after the dreadful event, my father and I walked home from the city. The full moon was about three hours above the eastern horizon; the entire countryside had the solemn stillness of a summer night; our footfalls and the ceaseless song of the katydids were the only sound aloof. Black shadows of bordering trees lay athwart the road, which, in the short reaches between, gleamed a ghostly white. As we approached the gate to our dwelling, whose front was in shadow, and in which no light shone, my father, suddenly stopped and clutched my arm, saying, hardly above his breath:

'God! God! what is that?'

'I hear nothing,' I replied.

'But see – see!' he said, pointing along the road, directly ahead.

I said: 'Nothing is there. Come, father, let us go in – you are ill.'

He had released my arm and was standing rigid and motionless in the centre of the illuminated roadway, staring like one bereft of sense. His face in the moonlight showed a pallor and fixity inexpressibly distressing. I pulled gently at his sleeve, but he had forgotten my existence. Presently he began to retire backward, step by step, never for an instant removing his eyes from what he saw, or thought he saw. I turned half round to follow, but stood irresolute. I do not recall any feeling of fear, unless a sudden chill was its physical manifestation. It seemed as if an icy wind had touched my face and enfolded my body from head to foot; I could feel the stir of it in my hair.

At that moment my attention was drawn to a light that suddenly streamed from an upper window of the house: one of the servants, awakened by what mysterious premonition of evil who can say, and in obedience to an impulse that she was never able to name, had lit a lamp. When I turned to look for my father he was gone, and in all the years that have passed no whisper of his fate has come across the borderland of conjecture from the realm of the unknown.

2. Statement of Caspar Grattan

Today I am said to live; tomorrow, here in this room, will lie a senseless shape of clay that all too long was I. If anyone lift the cloth from the face of that unpleasant thing it will be in gratification of a mere morbid curiosity. Some, doubtless, will go further and inquire, 'Who was he?' In this writing I supply the only answer that I am able to make – Caspar Grattan. Surely, that should be enough. The name has served my small need for more than twenty years of a life of unknown length. True, I gave it to myself, but lacking another I had the right. In this world one must have a name; it prevents confusion, even when it does not establish identity. Some, though, are known by numbers, which also seem inadequate distinctions.

One day, for illustration, I was passing along a street of a city, far from here, when I met two men in uniform, one of whom, half pausing and looking curiously into my face, said to his companion, 'That man looks like 767.' Something in the number seemed familiar and horrible. Moved by an uncontrollable impulse, I sprang into a side street and ran until I fell exhausted in a country lane.

I have never forgotten that number, and always it comes to memory attended by gibbering obscenity, peals of joyless laughter, the clang of iron doors. So I say a name, even if self-bestowed, is better than a number. In the register of the potter's field I shall soon have both. What wealth!

Of him who shall find this paper I must beg a little consideration. It is not the history of my life; the knowledge to write that is denied me. This is only a record of broken and apparently unrelated memories, some of them as distinct and sequent as brilliant beads upon a thread, others remote and strange, having the character of crimson dreams with interspaces blank and black — witch-fires glowing still and red in a great desolation.

Standing upon the shore of eternity, I turn for a last look landward over the course by which I came. There are twenty years of footprints fairly distinct, the impressions of bleeding feet. They lead through poverty and pain, devious and unsure, as of one staggering beneath a burden —

> Remote, unfriended, melancholy, slow.

Ah, the poet's prophecy of Me — how admirable, how dreadfully admirable!

Backward beyond the beginning of this *via dolorosa* — this epic of suffering with episodes of sin — I see nothing clearly; it comes out of a cloud. I know that it spans only twenty years, yet I am an old man.

One does not remember one's birth — one has to be told. But with me it was different; life came to me full-handed and dowered me with all my faculties and powers. Of a previous existence I know no more than others, for all have stammering intimations that may be memories and may be dreams. I know only that my first consciousness was of maturity in body and mind — a consciousness accepted without surprise or conjecture. I merely found myself walking in a forest, half-clad, footsore, unutterably weary and hungry. Seeing a farmhouse, I approached and asked for food, which was given me by one who inquired my name. I did not know, yet knew that all had names. Greatly embarrassed, I retreated, and night coming on, lay down in the forest and slept.

The next day I entered a large town which I shall not name. Nor shall I recount further incidents of the life that is now to end — a life of wandering, always and everywhere haunted by an overmastering sense of crime in punishment of wrong and of terror in punishment of crime. Let me see if I can reduce it to narrative.

I seem once to have lived near a great city, a prosperous planter, married to a woman whom I loved and distrusted. We had, it sometimes seems, one child, a youth of brilliant parts and promise. He is at all times a vague figure, never clearly drawn, frequently altogether out of the picture.

One luckless evening it occurred to me to test my wife's fidelity in a vulgar, commonplace way familiar to everyone who has acquaintance with the literature of fact and fiction. I went to the city, telling my wife that I should be absent until the following afternoon. But I returned before daybreak and went to the rear of the house, purposing to enter by a door with which I had secretly so tampered that it would seem to lock, yet not actually fasten. As I approached it, I heard it gently open and close, and saw a man steal away into the darkness. With murder in my heart, I sprang after him, but he had vanished without even the bad luck of identification. Sometimes now I cannot even persuade myself that it was a human being.

Crazed with jealousy and rage, blind and bestial with all the elemental passions of insulted manhood, I entered the house and sprang up the stairs to the door of my wife's chamber. It was closed, but having tampered with its lock also, I easily entered and despite the black darkness soon stood by the side of her bed. My groping hands told me that although disarranged it was unoccupied.

'She is below,' I thought, 'and terrified by my entrance has evaded me in the darkness of the hall.'

With the purpose of seeking her I turned to leave the room, but took a wrong direction – the right one! My foot struck her, cowering in a corner of the room. Instantly my hands were at her throat, stifling a shriek, my knees were upon her struggling body; and there in the darkness, without a word of accusation or reproach, I strangled her till she died!

There ends the dream. I have related it in the past tense, but the present would be the fitter form, for again and again the sombre tragedy re-enacts itself in my consciousness – over and over I lay the plan, I suffer the confirmation, I redress the wrong. Then all is blank; and afterwards the rains beat against the grimy window-panes, or the snows fall upon my scant attire, the wheels rattle in the squalid streets where my life lies in poverty and mean employment. If there is ever sunshine I do not recall it; if there are birds they do not sing.

There is another dream, another vision of the night. I stand among the shadows in a moonlit road. I am aware of another presence, but whose I cannot rightly determine. In the shadows of a great dwelling I catch the gleam of white garments; then the figure of a woman confronts me in the road – my murdered wife! There is death in the face; there are marks upon the throat. The eyes are fixed on mine with an infinite gravity which is not reproach, nor hate, nor menace, nor anything less terrible than recognition. Before this awful apparition I retreat in terror – a terror that is upon me as I write. I can no longer rightly shape the words. See! they –

Now I am calm, but truly there is no more to tell: the incident ends where it began – in darkness and in doubt.

Yes, I am again in control of myself: 'the captain of my soul'. But that is not respite; it is another stage and phase of expiation. My penance, constant in degree, is mutable in kind: one of its variants is tranquillity. After all, it is only a life-sentence. 'To Hell for life' – that is a foolish penalty: the culprit chooses the duration of his punishment. Today my term expires.

To each and all, the peace that was not mine.

3. Statement of the Late Julia Hetman, through the Medium Bayrolles

I had retired early and fallen almost immediately into a peaceful sleep, from which I awoke with that indefinable sense of peril which is, I think, a common experience in that other, earlier life. Of its unmeaning character, too, I was entirely persuaded, yet that did not banish it. My husband, Joel Hetman, was away from home; the servants slept in another part of the house. But these were familiar conditions; they had never before distressed me. Nevertheless, the strange terror grew so insupportable that conquering my reluctance to move I sat up and lit the lamp at my bedside. Contrary to my expectation this gave me no relief; the light seemed rather an added danger, for I reflected that it would shine out under the door, disclosing my presence to whatever evil thing might lurk outside. You that are still in the flesh, subject to horrors of the imagination, think what a monstrous fear that must be which seeks in darkness security from malevolent existences of the night. That is to spring to close quarters with an unseen enemy – the strategy of despair!

Extinguishing the lamp I pulled the bedclothing about my head and lay trembling and silent, unable to shriek, forgetful to pray. In this pitiable state I must have lain for what you call hours – with us there are no hours, there is no time.

At last it came – a soft, irregular sound of footfalls on the stairs! They were slow, hesitant, uncertain, as of something that did not see its way; to my disordered reason all the more terrifying for that, as the approach of some blind and mindless malevolence to which is no appeal. I even thought that I must have left the hall lamp burning and the groping of this creature proved it a monster of the night. This was foolish and inconsistent with my previous dread of the light, but what would you have? Fear has no brains; it is an idiot. The dismal witness that it bears and the cowardly counsel that it whispers are unrelated. We know this well, we who have passed into the Realm of Terror, who skulk in eternal dusk among the scenes of our former lives, invisible even to ourselves and one another, yet hiding forlorn in lonely places; yearning for speech with our loved ones, yet dumb, and as fearful of them as they of us. Sometimes the disability is removed, the law suspended: by the deathless power of love or hate we break the spell – we are seen by those whom we would warn, console, or punish. What form we seem to them to bear we know not; we know only that we terrify even those whom we most wish to comfort, and from whom we most crave tenderness and sympathy.

Forgive, I pray you, this inconsequent digression by what was once a woman. You who consult us in this imperfect way – you do not understand. You ask foolish questions about things unknown and things forbidden. Much that we know and could impart in our speech is meaningless in yours. We must communicate with you through a stammering intelligence in that small fraction of our language that you yourselves can speak. You think that we are of another world. No we have knowledge of no world but yours, though for us it holds no sunlight, no warmth, no music, no laughter, no song of birds, nor any companionship. O God! what a thing it is to be a ghost, cowering and shivering in an altered world, a prey to apprehension and despair!

No, I did not die of fright: the Thing turned and went away. I heard it go down the stairs, hurriedly, I thought, as if itself in sudden fear. Then I rose to call for help. Hardly had my shaking hand found the doorknob when – merciful heaven! – I heard it returning. Its footfalls as it remounted the stairs were rapid, heavy and loud; they shook the house. I fled to an angle of the wall and crouched upon the floor. I tried to pray. I tried to call the name of my dear husband. Then I heard the door thrown open. There was an interval of unconsciouness, and when I revived I felt a strangling clutch upon my throat – felt my arms feebly beating against something that bore me backwards – felt my tongue thrusting itself from beneath my teeth! And then I passed into this life.

No, I have no knowledge of what it was. The sum of what we knew at death is the measure of what we know afterward of all that went before. Of this existence we know many things, but no new light falls upon any page of that; in memory is written all of it that we can read. Here are no heights of truth overlooking the confused landscape of that dubitable domain. We still dwell in the Valley of the Shadow, lurk in its desolate places, peering from brambles and thickets at its mad, malign inhabitants. How should we have new knowledge of that fading past?

What I am about to relate happened on a night. We know when it is night, for then you retire to your houses and we can venture from our places of concealment to move unafraid about our old homes, to look in at the windows, even to enter and gaze upon your faces as you sleep. I had lingered long near the dwelling where I had been so cruelly changed to what I am, as we do while any that we love or hate remain. Vainly I had sought some method of manifestation, some way to make my continued existence and my great love and poignant pity understood by my husband and son. Always if they slept they would wake, or if in my desperation I dared approach them when they were awake, would turn towards me the terrible eyes of the living, frightening me by the glances that I sought from the purpose that I held.

On this night I had searched for them without success, fearing to find them; they were nowhere in the house, nor about the moonlit lawn. For, although the sun is lost to us forever, the moon, full-orbed or slender, remains to us. Sometimes it shines by night, sometimes by day, but always it rises and sets, as in that other life.

I left the lawn and moved in the white light and silence along the road, aimless and sorrowing. Suddenly I heard the voice of my poor husband in exclamations of astonishment, with that of my son in reassurance and dissuasion; and there by the shadow of a group of trees they stood – near, so near! Their faces were towards me, the eyes of the elder man fixed upon mine. He saw me – at last, at last, he saw me! In the consciousness of that, my terror fled as a cruel dream. The death-spell was broken: Love had conquered Law! Mad with exultation I shouted – I *must* have shouted, 'He sees, he sees: he will understand!' Then, controlling myself, I moved forward, smiling and consciously beautiful, to offer myself to his arms, to comfort him with endearments, and, with my son's hand in mine, to speak words that should restore the broken bonds between the living and the dead.

Alas! alas! his face went white with fear, his eyes were as those of a hunted animal. He backed away from me, as I advanced, and at last turned and fled into the wood – whither, it is not given to me to know.

To my poor boy, left doubly desolate, I have never been able to impart a sense of my presence. Soon he, too, must pass to this Life Invisible and be lost to me forever.

A Haunted Island

Algernon Blackwood

The following events occurred on a small island of isolated position in a large Canadian lake, to whose cool waters the inhabitants of Montreal and Toronto flee for rest and recreation in the hot months. It is only to be regretted that events of such peculiar interest to the genuine student of the psychical should be entirely uncorroborated. Such unfortunately, however, is the case.

Our own party of nearly twenty had returned to Montreal that very day, and I was left in solitary possession for a week or two longer, in order to accomplish some important 'reading' for the law which I had foolishly neglected during the summer.

It was late in September, and the big trout and maskinonge were stirring themselves in the depths of the lake, and beginning slowly to move up to the surface waters as the north winds and early frosts lowered their temperature. Already the maples were crimson and gold, and the wild laughter of the loons echoed in sheltered bays that never knew their strange cry in the summer.

With a whole island to oneself, a two-storey cottage, a canoe, and only the chipmunks, and the farmer's weekly visit with eggs and bread, to disturb one, the opportunities for hard reading might be very great. It all depends!

The rest of the party had gone off with many warnings to beware of Indians, and not to stay late enough to be the victim of a frost that thinks nothing of forty below zero. After they had gone, the loneliness of the situation made itself unpleasantly felt. There were no other islands within six or seven miles, and though the mainland forests lay a couple of miles behind me, they stretched for a very great distance unbroken by any signs of human habitation. But, though the island was completely deserted and silent, the rocks and trees that had echoed human laughter and voices almost every hour of the day for two months could not fail to retain some memories of it all; and I was not surprised to fancy I heard a shout or a cry as I passed from rock to rock, and more than once to imagine that I heard my own name called aloud.

In the cottage there were six tiny little bedrooms divided from one another by plain unvarnished partitions of pine. A wooden bedstead, a mattress, and a chair, stood in each room, but I only found two mirrors, and one of these was broken.

The boards creaked a good deal as I moved about, and the signs of occupation were so recent that I could hardly believe I was alone. I half expected to find someone left behind, still trying to crowd into a box more than it would hold. The door of one room was stiff, and refused for a moment to open, and it required very little persuasion to imagine someone was holding the handle on the inside, and that when it opened I should meet a pair of human eyes.

A thorough search of the floor led me to select as my own sleeping quarters a little room with a diminutive balcony over the verandah roof. The room was very small, but the bed was large, and had the best mattress of them all. It was situated directly over the sitting-room where I should live and do my 'reading', and the miniature window looked out to the rising sun. With the exception of a narrow path which led from the front door and verandah through the trees to the boat-landing, the island was densely covered with maples, hemlocks, and cedars. The trees gathered in round the cottage so closely that the slightest wind made the branches scrape the roof and tap the wooden walls. A few moments after sunset the darkness became impenetrable, and ten yards beyond the glare of the lamps that shone through the sitting-room windows – of which there were four – you could not see an inch before your nose, nor move a step without running up against a tree.

The rest of that day I spent moving my belongings from my tent to the sitting-room, taking stock of the contents of the larder, and chopping enough wood for the stove to last me for a week. After that, just before sunset, I went round the island a couple of times in my canoe for precaution's sake. I had never dreamed of doing this before, but when a man is alone he does things that never occur to him when he is one of a large party.

How lonely the island seemed when I landed again! The sun was down, and twilight is unknown in these northern regions. The darkness comes up at once. The canoe safely pulled up and turned over on her face, I groped my way up the little narrow pathway to the verandah. The six lamps were soon burning merrily in the front room; but in the kitchen, where I 'dined', the shadows were so gloomy, and the lamplight was so inadequate, that the stars could be seen peeping through the cracks between the rafters.

I turned in early that night. Though it was calm and there was no wind, the creaking of my bedstead and the musical gurgle of the water over the rocks below were not the only sounds that reached my ears. As I lay awake, the appalling emptiness of the house grew upon me. The corridors and vacant rooms seemed to echo innumerable footsteps, shufflings, the rustle of skirts, and a constant undertone of whispering. When sleep at length overtook me, the breathings and noises, however, passed gently to mingle with the voices of my dreams.

A week passed by, and the 'reading' progressed favourably. On the tenth day of my solitude, a strange thing happened. I awoke after a good night's sleep to find myself possessed with a marked repugnance for my room. The air seemed to stifle me. The more I tried to define the cause of this dislike, the more unreasonable it appeared. There was something about the room that made me afraid. Absurd as it seems, this feeling clung to me obstinately while dressing, and more than once I caught myself shivering, and conscious of an inclination to get out of the room as quickly as possible. The more I tried to laugh it away, the more real it became; and when at last I was dressed, and went out into the passage, and downstairs into the kitchen, it was with feelings of relief, such as I might imagine would accompany one's escape from the presence of a dangerous contagious disease.

While cooking my breakfast, I carefully recalled every night spent in the room, in the hope that I might in some way connect the dislike I now felt with some disagreeable incident that had occurred in it. But the only thing I could recall was one stormy night when I suddenly awoke and heard the boards creaking so loudly in the corridor that I was convinced there were people in the house. So certain was I of this, that I had descended the stairs, gun in hand, only to find the doors and windows securely fastened, and the mice and black-beetles in sole possession of the floor. This was certainly not sufficient to account for the strength of my feelings.

The morning hours I spent in steady reading; and when I broke off in the middle of the day for a swim and luncheon, I was very much surprised, if not a little alarmed, to find that my dislike for the room had, if anything, grown stronger. Going upstairs to get a book, I experienced the most marked aversion to entering the room, and while within I was conscious all the time of an uncomfortable feeling that was half uneasiness and half apprehension. The result of it was that, instead of reading, I spent the afternoon on the water paddling and fishing, and when I got home about sundown, brought with me half a dozen delicious black bass for the supper-table and the larder.

As sleep was an important matter to me at this time, I had decided that if my aversion to the room was so strongly marked on my return as it had been before, I would move my bed down into the sitting-room, and sleep there. This was, I argued, in no sense a concession to an absurd and fanciful fear, but simply a precaution to ensure a good night's sleep. A bad night involved the loss of the next day's reading – a loss I was not prepared to incur.

I accordingly moved my bed downstairs into a corner of the sitting-room facing the door, and was moreover uncommonly glad when the operation was completed, and the door of the bedroom closed finally upon the shadows, the silence, and the strange *fear* that shared the room with them.

The croaking stroke of the kitchen clock sounded the hour of eight as I finished washing up my few dishes, and closing the kitchen door behind me, passed into the front room. All the lamps were lit, and their reflectors, which I had polished up during the day, threw a blaze of light into the room.

Outside the night was still and warm. Not a breath of air was stirring; the waves were silent, the trees motionless, and heavy clouds hung like an oppressive curtain over the heavens. The darkness seemed to have rolled up with unusual swiftness, and not the faintest glow of colour remained to show where the sun had set. There was present in the atmosphere that ominous and overwhelming silence which so often precedes the most violent storms.

I sat down to my books with my brain unusually clear, and in my heart the pleasant satisfaction of knowing that five black bass were lying in the ice-house, and that tomorrow morning the old farmer would arrive with fresh bread and eggs. I was soon absorbed in my books.

As the night wore on the silence deepened. Even the chipmunks were still; and the boards of the floors and walls ceased creaking. I read on steadily till, from the gloomy shadows of the kitchen, came the hoarse sound of the clock striking nine. How loud the strokes sounded! They were like blows of a big hammer. I closed one book and opened another, feeling that I was just warming up to my work.

This, however, did not last long. I presently found that I was reading the same paragraphs over twice, simple paragraphs that did not require such effort. Then I noticed that my mind began to wander to other things, and the effort to recall my thoughts became harder with each digression. Concentration was growing momentarily more difficult. Presently I discovered that I had turned over two pages instead of one, and had not noticed my mistake until I was well down the page. This was becoming serious. What was the disturbing influence? It could not be physical fatigue. On the contrary, my mind was unusually alert, and in a more receptive condition than usual. I made a new and determined effort to read, and for a short time succeeded in giving my whole attention to my subject. But in a very few moments again I found myself leaning back in my chair, staring vacantly into space.

Something was evidently at work in my subconsciousness. There was something I had neglected to do. Perhaps the kitchen door and windows were not fastened. I accordingly went to see, and found that they were! The fire perhaps needed attention. I went in to see, and found that it was all right! I looked at the lamps, went upstairs into every bedroom in turn, and then went round the house, and even into the ice-house. Nothing was wrong; everything was in its place. Yet something *was* wrong! The conviction grew stronger and stronger within me.

When I at length settled down to my books again and tried to read, I became aware, for the first time, that the room seemed growing cold. Yet the day had been oppressively warm, and evening had brought no relief. The six big lamps, moreover, gave out heat enough to warm the room pleasantly. But a chilliness, that perhaps crept up from the lake, made itself felt in the room, and caused me to get up to close the glass door opening on to the verandah.

For a brief moment I stood looking out at the shaft of light that fell from the windows and shone some little distance down the pathway, and out for a few feet into the lake.

As I looked, I saw a canoe glide into the pathway of light, and immediately crossing it, pass out of sight again into the darkness. It was perhaps a hundred feet from the shore, and it moved swiftly.

I was surprised that a canoe should pass the island at that time of night, for all the summer visitors from the other side of the lake had gone home weeks before, and the island was a long way out of any line of water traffic.

My reading from this moment did not make very good progress, for somehow the picture of that canoe, gliding so dimly and swiftly across the narrow track of light on the black waters, silhouetted itself against the background of my mind with singular vividness. It kept coming between my eyes and the printed page. The more I thought about it the more surprised I became. It was of larger build than any I had seen during the past summer months, and was more like the old Indian war canoes with the high curving bows and stern and wide beam. The more I tried to read, the less success attended my efforts; and finally I closed my books and went out on the verandah to walk up and down a bit, and shake the chilliness out of my bones.

The night was perfectly still, and as dark as imaginable. I stumbled down the path to the little landing wharf, where the water made the very faintest of gurgling under the timbers. The sound of a big tree falling in the mainland forest, far across the lake, stirred echoes in the heavy air, like the first guns of a distant night attack. No other sound disturbed the stillness that reigned supreme.

As I stood upon the wharf in the broad splash of light that followed me from the sitting-room windows, I saw another canoe cross the pathway of uncertain light upon the water, and disappear at once into the impenetrable gloom that lay beyond. This time I saw more distinctly than before. It was like the former canoe, a big birch-bark, with high-crested bows and stern and broad beam. It was paddled by two Indians, of whom the one in the stern – the steerer – appeared to be a very large man. I could see this very plainly; and though the second canoe was much nearer the island than the first, I judged that they were both on their way home to the Government Reservation, which was situated some fifteen miles away upon the mainland.

I was wondering in my mind what could possibly bring any Indians down to this part of the lake at such an hour of the night, when a third canoe, of precisely similar build, and also occupied by two Indians, passed silently round the end of the wharf. This time the canoe was very much nearer shore, and it suddenly flashed into my mind that the three canoes were in reality one and the same, and that only one canoe was circling the island!

This was by no means a pleasant reflection, because, if it were the correct solution of the unusual appearance of the three canoes in this lonely part of the lake at so late an hour, the purpose of the two men could only reasonably be considered to be in some way connected with myself. I had never known of the Indians attempting any violence upon the settlers who shared the wild, inhospitable country with them; at the same time, it was not beyond the region of possibility to suppose . . . But then I did not care even to think of such hideous possibilities, and my imagination immediately sought relief in all manner of other solutions to the problem, which indeed came readily enough to my mind, but did not succeed in recommending themselves to my reason.

Meanwhile, by a sort of instinct, I stepped back out of the bright light in which I had hitherto been standing, and waited in the deep shadow of a rock to see if the canoe would again make its appearance. Here I could see, without being seen, and the precaution seemed a wise one.

After less than five minutes the canoe, as I had anticipated, made its fourth appearance. This time it was not twenty yards from the wharf, and I saw that the Indians meant to land. I recognized the two men as those who had passed before, and the steerer was certainly an immense fellow. It was unquestionably the same canoe. There could be no longer any doubt that for some purpose of their own the men had been going round and round the island for some time, waiting for an opportunity to land. I strained my eyes to follow them in the darkness, but the night had completely swallowed them up, and not even the faintest swish of the paddles reached my ears as the Indians plied their long and powerful strokes. The canoe would be round again in a few moments, and this time it was possible that the men might land. It was well to be prepared. I knew nothing of their intentions, and two to one (when the two are big Indians!) late at night on a lonely island was not exactly my idea of pleasant intercourse.

In a corner of the sitting-room, leaning up against the back wall, stood my Marlin rifle, with ten cartridges in the magazine and one lying snugly in the greased breech. There was just time to get up to the house and take up a position of defence in that corner. Without an instant's hesitation I ran up to the verandah, carefully picking my way among the trees, so as to avoid being seen in the light. Entering the room, I shut the door leading to the verandah, and as quickly as possible turned out every one of the six lamps. To be in a room so brilliantly lighted, where my every movement could be observed from outside, while I could see nothing but impenetrable darkness at every window, was by all laws of warfare an unnecessary concession to the enemy. And this enemy, if enemy it was to be, was far too wily and dangerous to be granted any such advantages.

I stood in the corner of the room with my back against the wall, and my hand on the cold rifle-barrel. The table, covered with my books, lay between me and the door, but for the first few minutes after the lights were out the darkness was so intense that nothing could be discerned at all. Then, very gradually, the outline of the room became visible, and the framework of the windows began to shape itself dimly before my eyes.

After a few minutes the door (its upper half of glass), and the two windows that looked out upon the front verandah, became specially distinct; and I was glad that this was so, because if the Indians came up to the house I should be able to see their approach, and gather something of their plans. Nor was I mistaken, for there presently came to my ears the peculiar hollow sound of a canoe landing and being carefully dragged up over the rocks. The paddles I distinctly heard being placed underneath, and the silence that ensued thereupon I rightly interpreted to mean that the Indians were stealthily approaching the house . . .

While it would be absurd to claim that I was not alarmed – even frightened – at the gravity of the situation and its possible outcome, I speak the whole truth when I say that I was not overwhelmingly afraid for myself. I was conscious that even at this stage of the night I was passing into a psychical condition in which my sensations seemed no longer normal. Physical fear at no time entered into the nature of my feelings; and though I kept my hand upon my rifle the greater part of the night, I was all the time conscious that its assistance could be of little avail against the terrors that I had to face. More than once I seemed to feel most curiously that I was in no real sense a part of the proceedings, nor actually involved in them, but that I was playing the part of a spectator – a spectator, moreover, on a psychic rather than on a material plane. Many of my sensations that night were too vague for definite description and analysis, but the main feeling that will stay with me to the end of my days is the awful horror of it all, and the miserable sensation that if the strain had lasted a little longer than was actually the case my mind must inevitably have given way.

Meanwhile I stood still in my corner, and waited patiently for what was to come. The house was as still as the grave, but the inarticulate voices of the night sang in my ears, and I seemed to hear the blood running in my veins and dancing in my pulses.

If the Indians came to the back of the house, they would find the kitchen door and window securely fastened. They could not get in there without making considerable noise, which I was bound to hear. The only mode of getting in was by means of the door that faced me, and I kept my eyes glued on that door without taking them off for the smallest fraction of a second.

My sight adapted itself every minute better to the darkness. I saw the table that nearly filled the room, and left only a narrow passage on each side. I could also make out the straight backs of the wooden chairs pressed up against it, and could even distinguish my papers and inkstand lying on the white oilcloth covering. I thought of the gay faces that had gathered round that table during the summer, and I longed for the sunlight as I had never longed for it before.

Less than three feet to my left the passage-way led to the kitchen, and the stairs leading to the bedrooms above commenced in this passage-way, but almost in the sitting-room itself. Through the windows I could see the dim motionless outlines of the trees: not a leaf stirred, not a branch moved.

A few moments of this awful silence, and then I was aware of a soft tread on the boards of the verandah, so stealthy that it seemed an impression directly on my brain rather than upon the nerves of hearing. Immediately afterwards a black figure darkened the glass door, and I perceived that a face was pressed against the upper panes. A shiver ran down my back, and my hair was conscious of a tendency to rise and stand at right angles to my head.

It was the figure of an Indian, broad-shouldered and immense; indeed, the largest figure of a man I have ever seen outside of a circus hall. By some power of light that seemed to generate itself in the brain, I saw the strong dark face with the aquiline nose and high cheek-bones flattened against the glass. The direction of the gaze I could not determine; but faint gleams of light as the big eyes rolled round and showed their whites, told me plainly that no corner of the room escaped their searching.

For what seemed fully five minutes the dark figure stood there, with the huge shoulders bent forward so as to bring the head down to the level of the glass; while behind him, though not nearly so large, the shadowy form of the other Indian swayed to and fro like a bent tree. While I waited in an agony of suspense and agitation for their next movement little currents of icy sensation ran up and down my spine and my heart seemed alternately to stop beating and then start off again with terrifying rapidity. They must have heard its thumping and the singing of the blood in my head! Moreover, I was conscious, as I felt a cold stream of perspiration trickle down my face, of a desire to scream, to shout, to bang the walls like a child, to make a noise, or do anything that would relieve the suspense and bring things to a speedy climax.

It was probably this inclination that led me to another discovery, for when I tried to bring my rifle from behind my back to raise it and have it pointed at the door ready to fire, I found that I was powerless to move.

The muscles, paralysed by this strange fear, refused to obey the will. Here indeed was a terrifying complication!

There was a faint sound of rattling at the brass knob, and the door was pushed open a couple of inches. A pause of a few seconds, and it was pushed open still further. Without a sound of footsteps that was appreciable to my ears, the two figures glided into the room, and the man behind gently closed the door after him.

They were alone with me between the four walls. Could they see me standing there, so still and straight in my corner? Had they, perhaps, already seen me? My blood surged and sang like the roll of drums in an orchestra; and though I did my best to suppress my breathing, it sounded like the rushing of wind through a pneumatic tube.

My suspense as to the next move was soon at an end – only, however, to give place to a new and keener alarm. The men had hitherto exchanged no words and no signs, but there were general indications of a movement across the room, and whichever way they went they would have to pass round the table. If they came my way they would have to pass within six inches of my person. While I was considering this very disagreeable possibility, I perceived that the smaller Indian (smaller by comparison) suddenly raised his arm and pointed to the ceiling. The other fellow raised his head and followed the direction of his companion's arm. I began to understand at last. They were going upstairs, and the room directly overhead to which they pointed had been until this night my bedroom. It was the room in which I had experienced that very morning so strange a sensation of fear, and but for which I should then have been lying asleep in the narrow bed against the window.

The Indians then began to move silently around the room; they were going upstairs, and they were coming round my side of the table. So stealthy were their movements that, but for the abnormally sensitive state of the nerves, I should never have heard them. As it was, their cat-like tread was distinctly audible. Like two monstrous black cats they came round the table towards me, and for the first time I perceived that the smaller of the two dragged something along the floor behind him. As it trailed along over the floor with a soft, sweeping sound, I somehow got the impression that it was a large dead thing with outstretched wings, or a large, spreading cedar branch. Whatever it was, I was unable to see it even in outline, and I was too terrified, even had I possessed the power over my muscles, to move my neck forward in the effort to determine its nature.

Nearer and nearer they came. The leader rested a giant hand upon the table as he moved. My lips were glued together, and the air seemed to burn in my nostrils. I tried to close my eyes, so that I might not see as they passed me; but my eyelids had stiffened, and refused to obey. Would they never get by me? Sensation seemed also to have left my legs, and it was as if I were standing on mere supports of wood or stone. Worse still, I was conscious that I was losing the power of balance, the power to stand upright, or even to lean backwards against the wall. Some force was drawing me forward, and a dizzy terror seized me that I should lose my balance, and topple forward against the Indians just as they were in the act of passing me.

Even moments drawn out into hours must come to an end some time, and almost before I knew it the figures had passed me and had their feet upon the lower step of the stairs leading to the upper bedrooms. There could not have been six inches between us, and yet I was conscious only of a current of cold air that followed them. They had not touched me, and I was convinced that they had not seen me. Even the trailing thing on the floor behind them had not touched my feet, as I had dreaded it would, and on such an occasion as this I was grateful even for the smallest mercies.

The absence of the Indians from my immediate neighbourhood brought little sense of relief. I stood shivering and shuddering in my corner, and, beyond being able to breathe more freely, I felt no whit less uncomfortable. Also, I was aware that a certain light, which, without apparent source or rays, had enabled me to follow their every gesture and movement, had gone out of the room with their departure. An unnatural darkness now filled the room, and pervaded its every corner so that I could barely make out the positions of the windows and the glass doors.

As I said before, my condition was evidently an abnormal one. The capacity for feeling surprise seemed, as in dreams, to be wholly absent. My senses recorded with unusual accuracy every smallest occurrence, but I was able to draw only the simplest deductions.

The Indians soon reached the top of the stairs, and there they halted for a moment. I had not the faintest clue as to their next movement. They appeared to hesitate. They were listening attentively. Then I heard one of them, who by the weight of his soft tread must have been the giant, cross the narrow corridor and enter the room directly overhead – my own little bedroom. But for the insistence of that unaccountable dread I had experienced there in the morning, I should at that very moment have been lying in the bed with the big Indian in the room standing beside me.

For the space of a hundred seconds there was silence, such as might

A Haunted Island

have existed before the birth of sound. It was followed by a long quivering shriek of terror, which rang out into the night, and ended in a short gulp before it had run its full course. At the same moment the other Indian left his place at the head of the stairs, and joined his companion in the bedroom. I heard the 'thing' trailing behind him along the floor. A thud followed, as of something heavy falling, and then all became as still and silent as before.

It was at this point that the atmosphere, surcharged all day with the electricity of a fierce storm, found relief in a dancing flash of brilliant lightning simultaneously with a crash of loudest thunder. For five seconds every article in the room was visible to me with amazing distinctness, and through the windows I saw the tree trunks standing in solemn rows. The thunder pealed and echoed across the lake and among the distant islands, and the flood-gates of heaven then opened and let out their rain in streaming torrents.

The drops fell with a swift rushing sound upon the still waters of the lake, which leaped up to meet them, and pattered with the rattle of shot on the leaves of the maples and the roof of the cottage. A moment later, and another flash, even more brilliant and of longer duration than the first, lit up the sky from zenith to horizon, and bathed the room momentarily in dazzling whiteness. I could see the rain glistening on the leaves and branches outside. The wind rose suddenly, and in less than a minute the storm that had been gathering all day burst forth in its full fury.

Above all the noisy voices of the elements, the slightest sounds in the room overhead made themselves heard, and in the few seconds of deep silence that followed the shriek of terror and pain I was aware that the movements had commenced again. The men were leaving the room and approaching the top of the stairs. A short pause, and they began to descend. Behind them, tumbling from step to step, I could hear that trailing 'thing' being dragged along. It had become ponderous!

I awaited their approach with a degree of calmness, almost of apathy, which was only explicable on the ground that after a certain point Nature applies her own anaesthetic, and a merciful condition of numbness supervenes. On they came, step by step, nearer and nearer, with the shuffling sound of the burden behind growing louder as they approached.

They were already half-way down the stairs when I was galvanized afresh into a condition of terror by the consideration of a new and horrible possibility. It was the reflection that if another vivid flash of lightning were to come when the shadowy procession was in the room, perhaps when it was actually passing in front of me, I should see everything in detail, and worse, be seen myself! I could only hold my breath and wait – wait while the minutes lengthened into hours, and the procession made its slow progress round the room.

The Indians had reached the foot of the staircase. The form of the huge leader loomed in the doorway of the passage, and the burden with an ominous thud had dropped from the last step to the floor. There was a moment's pause while I saw the Indian turn and stoop to assist his companion. Then the procession moved forward again, entered the room close on my left, and began to move slowly round my side of the table. The leader was already beyond me, and his companion, dragging on the floor behind him the burden, whose confused outline I could dimly make out, was exactly in front of me, when the cavalcade came to a dead halt. At the same moment, with the strange suddenness of thunderstorms, the splash of the rain ceased altogether, and the wind died away into utter silence.

For the space of five seconds my heart seemed to stop beating, and then the worst came. A double flash of lightning lit up the room and its contents with merciless vividness.

The huge Indian leader stood a few feet past me on my right. One leg was stretched forward in the act of taking a step. His immense shoulders were turned toward his companion, and in all their magnificent fierceness I saw the outline of his features. His gaze was directed upon the burden his companion was dragging along the floor; but his profile, with the big aquiline nose, high cheek-bone, straight black hair and bold chin, burnt itself in that brief instant into my brain, never again to fade.

Dwarfish, compared with this gigantic figure, appeared the proportions of the other Indian, who, within twelve inches of my face, was stooping over the thing he was dragging in a position that lent to his person the additional horror of deformity. And the burden, lying upon a sweeping cedar branch which he held and dragged by a long stem, was the body of a white man. The scalp had been neatly lifted, and blood lay in a broad smear upon the cheeks and forehead.

Then, for the first time that night, the terror that had paralysed my muscles and my will lifted its unholy spell from my soul. With a loud cry I stretched out my arms to seize the big Indian by the throat, and, grasping only air, tumbled forward unconscious upon the ground.

I had recognized the body, and *the face was my own!* . . .

It was bright daylight when a man's voice recalled me to consciousness. I was lying where I had fallen, and the farmer was standing in the room with the loaves of bread in his hands. The horror of the night was still in my heart, and as the bluff settler helped me to my feet and picked up the rifle which had fallen with me, with many questions and expressions of condolence, I imagine my brief replies were neither self-explanatory nor even intelligible.

That day, after a thorough and fruitless search of the house, I left the island, and went over to spend my last ten days with the farmer; and when the time came for me to leave, the necessary reading had been accomplished, and my nerves had completely recovered their balance.

On the day of my departure the farmer started early in his big boat with my belongings to row to the point, twelve miles distant, where a little steamer ran twice a week for the accommodation of hunters. Late in the afternoon I went off in another direction in my canoe, wishing to see the island once again, where I had been the victim of so strange an experience.

In due course I arrived there, and made a tour of the island. I also made a search of the little house, and it was not without a curious sensation in my heart that I entered the little upstairs bedroom. There seemed nothing unusual.

Just after I re-embarked, I saw a canoe gliding ahead of me around the curve of the island. A canoe was an unusual sight at this time of the year, and this one seemed to have sprung from nowhere. Altering my course a little, I watched it disappear around the next projecting point of rock. It had high curving bows, and there were two Indians in it. I lingered with some excitement, to see if it would appear again round the other side of the island; and in less than five minutes it came into view. There were less than two hundred yards between us, and the Indians, sitting on their haunches, were paddling swiftly in my direction.

I never paddled faster in my life than I did in those next few minutes. When I turned to look again, the Indians had altered their course, and were again circling the island.

The sun was sinking behind the forests on the mainland, and the crimson-coloured clouds of sunset were reflected in the waters of the lake, when I looked round for the last time, and saw the big bark canoe and its two dusky occupants still going round the island. Then the shadows deepened rapidly; the lake grew black, and the night wind blew its first breath in my face as I turned a corner, and a projecting bluff of rock hid from my view both island and canoe.

The Rose Garden

M. R. James

Mr and Mrs Anstruther were at breakfast in the parlour of Westfield Hall, in the county of Essex. They were arranging plans for the day.

'George,' said Mrs Anstruther, 'I think you had better take the car to Maldon and see if you can get any of those knitted things I was speaking about which would do for my stall at the bazaar.'

'Oh well, if you wish it, Mary, of course I can do that, but I had half arranged to play a round with Geoffrey Williamson this morning. The bazaar isn't till Thursday of next week, is it?'

'What has that to do with it, George? I should have thought you would have guessed that if I can't get the things I want in Maldon I shall have to write to all manner of shops in town: and they are certain to send something quite unsuitable in price or quality the first time. If you have actually made an appointment with Mr Williamson, you had better keep it, but I must say I think you might have let me know.'

'Oh no, no, it wasn't really an appointment. I quite see what you mean. I'll go. And what shall you do yourself?'

'Why, when the work of the house is arranged for, I must see about laying out my new rose garden. By the way, before you start for Maldon I wish you would just take Collins to look at the place I fixed upon. You know it, of course.'

'Well, I'm not quite sure that I do, Mary. Is it at the upper end, towards the village?'

'Good gracious, no, my dear George; I thought I had made that quite clear. No, it's that small clearing just off the shrubbery path that goes towards the church.'

'Oh yes, where we were saying there must have been a summer-house once: the place with the old seat and the posts. But do you think there's enough sun there?'

'My dear George, do allow me *some* common sense, and don't credit me with all your ideas about summer-houses. Yes, there will be plenty of sun when we have got rid of some of those box-bushes. I know what you are going to say, and I have as little wish as you to strip the place bare. All I want Collins to do is to clear away the old seats and the posts and things before I come out in an hour's time. And I hope you will manage to get off fairly soon. After luncheon I think I shall go on with my sketch of the church; and if you please you can go over to the links, or –'

'Ah, a good idea – very good! Yes, you finish that sketch, Mary, and I should be glad of a round.'

'I was going to say, you might call on the Bishop; but I suppose it is no use my making *any* suggestion. And now do be getting ready, or half the morning will be gone.'

Mr Anstruther's face, which had shown symptoms of lengthening, shortened itself again, and he hurried from the room, and was soon heard giving orders in the passage. Mrs Anstruther, a stately dame of some fifty summers, proceeded, after a second consideration of the morning's letters, to her housekeeping.

Within a few minutes Mr Anstruther had discovered Collins in the greenhouse, and they were on their way to the site of the projected rose garden. I do not know much about the conditions most suitable to these nurseries, but I am inclined to believe that Mrs Anstruther, though in the habit of describing herself as 'a great gardener', had not been well advised in the selection of a spot for the purpose. It was a small, dank clearing, bounded on one side by a path, and on the other by thick box-bushes, laurels, and other evergreens. The ground was almost bare of grass and dark of aspect. Remains of rustic seats and an old and corrugated oak post somewhere near the middle of the clearing had given rise to Mr Anstruther's conjecture that a summer-house had once stood there.

Clearly Collins had not been put in possession of his mistress's intentions with regard to this plot of ground: and when he learnt them from Mr Anstruther he displayed no enthusiasm.

'Of course I could clear them seats away soon enough,' he said. 'They aren't no ornament to the place, Mr Anstruther, and rotten too. Look 'ere, sir,' – and he broke off a large piece – 'rotten right through. Yes, clear them away, to be sure we can do that.'

'And the post,' said Mr Anstruther, 'that's got to go too.'

Collins advanced, and shook the post with both hands: then he rubbed his chin.

'That's firm in the ground, that post is,' he said. 'That's been there a number of years, Mr Anstruther. I doubt I shan't get that up not quite so soon as what I can do with them seats.'

'But your mistress specially wishes it to be got out of the way in an hour's time,' said Mr Anstruther.

Collins smiled and shook his head slowly. 'You'll excuse me, sir, but you feel of it for yourself. No, sir, no one can't do what's impossible to 'em, can they, sir? I could git that post up by after tea-time, sir, but that'll want a lot of digging. What you require, you see, sir, if you'll excuse me naming of it, you want the soil loosening round this post 'ere, and me and the boy we shall take a little time doing of that. But now, these 'ere seats,' said Collins, appearing to appropriate this portion of the scheme as due to his own resourcefulness, 'why, I can get the barrer round and 'ave them cleared away in, why less than an hour's time from now, if you'll permit of it. Only –'

'Only what, Collins?'

'Well now, ain't for me to go against orders no more than what it is for you yourself – or anyone else' (this was added somewhat hurriedly), 'but if you'll pardon me, sir, this ain't the place I should have picked out for no rose garden myself. Why look at them box and laurestinus, 'ow they reg'lar preclude the light from –'

'Ah yes, but we've got to get rid of some of them, of course.'

'Oh, indeed, get rid of them! Yes, to be sure, but – I beg your pardon, Mr Anstruther –'

'I'm sorry, Collins, but I must be getting on now. I hear the car at the door. Your mistress will explain exactly what she wishes. I'll tell her, then, that you can see your way to clearing away the seats at once, and the post this afternoon. Good morning.'

Collins was left rubbing his chin. Mrs Anstruther received the report with some discontent, but did not insist upon any change of plan.

By four o'clock that afternoon she had dismissed her husband to his golf, had dealt faithfully with Collins and with the other duties of the day, and, having sent a campstool and umbrella to the proper spot, had just settled down to her sketch of the church as seen from the shrubbery, when a maid came hurrying down the path to report that Miss Wilkins had called.

Miss Wilkins was one of the few remaining members of the family from whom the Anstruthers had bought the Westfield estate some few years back. She had been staying in the neighbourhood, and this was probably a farewell visit. 'Perhaps you could ask Miss Wilkins to join me here,' said Mrs Anstruther, and soon Miss Wilkins, a person of mature years, approached.

'Yes, I'm leaving the Ashes tomorrow, and I shall be able to tell my brother how tremendously you have improved the place. Of course he can't help regretting the old house just a little – as I do myself – but the garden is really delightful now.'

'I am so glad you can say so. But you mustn't think we've finished our improvements. Let me show you where I mean to put a rose garden. It's close by here.'

The details of the project were laid before Miss Wilkins at some length; but her thoughts were evidently elsewhere.

'Yes, delightful,' she said at last rather absently. 'But do you know, Mrs Anstruther, I'm afraid I was thinking of old times. I'm *very* glad to have seen just this spot again before you altered it. Frank and I had quite a romance about this place.'

'Yes?' said Mrs Anstruther smilingly; 'do tell me what it was. Something quaint and charming, I'm sure.'

'Not so very charming, but it has always seemed to me curious. Neither of us would ever be here alone when we were children, and I'm not sure that I should care about it now in certain moods. It is one of those things that can hardly be put into words – by me at least – and that sound rather foolish if they are not properly expressed. I can tell you after a fashion what it was that gave us – well, almost a horror of the place when we were alone. It was towards the evening of one very hot autumn day, when Frank had disappeared mysteriously about the grounds, and I was looking for him to fetch him to tea, and going down this path I suddenly saw him, not hiding in the bushes, as I rather expected, but sitting on the bench in the old summer-house – there was a wooden summer-house here, you know – up in the corner, asleep, but with such a dreadful look on his face that I really thought he must be ill or even dead. I rushed at him and shook him, and told him to wake up; and wake up he did, with a scream. I assure you the poor boy seemed almost beside himself with fright. He hurried me away to the house, and was in a terrible state all that night, hardly sleeping. Someone had to sit up with him, as far as I remember. He was better very soon, but for days I couldn't get him to say why he had been in such a condition. It came out at last that he had really been asleep and had had a very odd disjointed sort of dream. He never *saw* much of what was around him, but he *felt* the scenes most vividly. First he made out that he was standing in a large room with a number of people in it, and that someone was opposite to him who was "very powerful", and he was being asked questions which he felt to be very important, and, whenever he answered them, someone – either the person opposite to him, or someone else in the room – seemed to be, as he said, making something up against him. All the voices sounded to him very distant, but he remembered bits of the things that were said: "Where were you on the 19th of October?" and "Is this your handwriting?" and so on. I can see now, of course, that he was dreaming of some trial: but we were never allowed to see the papers, and it was odd that a boy of eight should have such a vivid idea of what went on in a court. All the time he felt, he said, the most intense anxiety and oppression and hopelessness (though I don't suppose he used such words as that to me). Then, after that, there was an interval in which he remembered being dreadfully restless and miserable, and then there came another sort of picture, when he was aware that he had come out of doors on a dark raw morning with a little snow about. It was in a street, or at any rate among houses, and he felt that there were numbers and numbers of people there too, and that he was taken up some creaking wooden steps and stood on a sort of platform, but the only thing he could actually see was a small fire burning somewhere near him. Someone who had been holding his arm left hold of it and went towards this fire, and then he said the fright he was in was worse than at any other part of his dream, and if I had not wakened him up he didn't know what would have become of him. A curious dream for a child to have, wasn't it? Well, so much for that. It must have been later in the year that Frank and I were here, and I was sitting in the arbour just about sunset. I noticed the sun was going down, and told Frank to run in and see if tea was ready while I finished a chapter in the book I was reading. Frank was away longer than I expected, and the light was going so fast that I had to bend over my book to make it out. All at once I became conscious that someone was whispering to me inside the arbour. The only words I could distinguish, or thought I could, were something like "Pull, pull. I'll push, you pull."

'I started up in something of a fright. The voice – it was little more than a whisper – sounded so hoarse and angry, and yet as if it came from a long, long way off – just as it had done in Frank's dream. But, though I was startled, I had enough courage to look round and try to make out where the sound came from. And – this sounds very foolish, I know, but still it is the fact – I made sure that it was strongest when I put my ear to an old post which was part of the end of the seat. I was so certain of this that I remember making some marks on the post – as deep as I could with the scissors out of my work-basket. I don't know why. I wonder, by the way, whether that isn't the very post itself . . . Well, yes, it might be: there *are* marks and scratches on it – but one can't be sure. Anyhow, it was just like that post you have there. My father got to know that both of us had had a fright in the arbour, and he went down there himself one evening after dinner, and the arbour was pulled down at very short notice. I recollect hearing my father talking about it to an old man who used to do odd jobs in the place, and the old man saying, "Don't you fear for that, sir: he's fast enough in there without no one don't take and let him out." But when I asked who it was, I could get no satisfactory answer. Possibly my father or mother might have told me more about it when I grew up, but, as you know, they both died when we were still quite children. I must say it has always seemed very odd to me, and I've often asked the older people in the village whether they knew of anything strange: but either they knew nothing or they wouldn't tell me. Dear, dear, how I have been boring you with my childish remembrances! but indeed that arbour did absorb our thoughts quite remarkably for a time. You can fancy, can't you, the kind of stories that we made up for ourselves. Well, dear Mrs Anstruther, I must be leaving you now. We shall meet in town this winter, I hope, shan't we?' etc., etc.

The seats and the post were cleared away and uprooted respectively by that evening. Late summer weather is proverbially treacherous, and during dinner-time Mrs Collins sent up to ask for a little brandy, because her husband had took a nasty chill and she was afraid he would not be able to do much next day.

Mrs Anstruther's morning reflections were not wholly placid. She was sure some roughs had got into the plantation during the night. 'And another thing, George: the moment that Collins is about again, you must tell him to do something about the owls. I never heard anything like them, and I'm positive one came and perched somewhere just outside our window. If it had come in I should have been out of my wits: it must have been a very large bird, from its voice. Didn't you hear it? No, of course not, you were sound asleep as usual. Still, I must say, George, you don't look as if your night had done you much good.'

'My dear, I feel as if another of the same would turn me silly. You have no idea of the dreams I had. I couldn't speak of them when I woke up, and if this room wasn't so bright and sunny I shouldn't care to think of them even now.'

'Well, really, George, that isn't very common with you, I must say. You must have – no, you only had what I had yesterday – unless you had tea at that wretched club house: did you?'

'No, no; nothing but a cup of tea and some bread and butter. I should really like to know how I came to put my dream together – as I suppose one does put one's dreams together from a lot of little things one has been seeing or reading. Look here, Mary, it was like this – if I shan't be boring you –'

'I *wish* to hear what it was, George. I will tell you when I have had enough.'

'All right. I must tell you that it wasn't like other nightmares in one way, because I didn't really *see* anyone who spoke to me or touched me, and yet I was most fearfully impressed with the reality of it all. First I was sitting, no, moving about, in an old-fashioned sort of panelled room. I remember there was a fireplace and a lot of burnt papers in it, and I was in a great state of anxiety about something. There was someone else – a servant, I suppose, because I remember saying to him, "Horses, as quick as you can," and then waiting a bit: and next I heard several people coming upstairs and a noise like spurs on a boarded floor, and then the door opened and whatever it was that I was expecting happened.'

'Yes, but what was that?'

'You see, I couldn't tell: it was the sort of shock that upsets you in a dream. You either wake up or else everything goes black. That was what happened to me. Then I was in a big dark-walled room, panelled, I think, like the other, and a number of people, and I was evidently –'

'Standing your trial, I suppose, George.'

'Goodness! yes, Mary, I was; but did you dream that too? How very odd!'

'No, no; I didn't get enough sleep for that. Go on, George, and I will tell you afterwards.'

'Yes; well, I *was* being tried, for my life, I've no doubt, from the state I was in. I had no one speaking for me, and somewhere there was a most fearful fellow – on the bench I should have said, only that he seemed to be pitching into me most unfairly, and twisting everything I said, and asking most abominable questions.'

'What about?'

'Why, dates when I was at particular places, and letters I was supposed to have written, and why I had destroyed some papers; and I recollect his laughing at answers I made in a way that quite daunted me. It doesn't sound much, but I can tell you, Mary, it was really appalling at the time. I am quite certain there was such a man once, and a most horrible villain he must have been. The things he said –'

'Thank you, I have no wish to hear them. I can go to the links any day myself. How did it end?'

'Oh, against me; *he* saw to that. I do wish, Mary, I could give you a notion of the strain that came after that, and seemed to me to last for days: waiting and waiting, and sometimes writing things I knew to be enormously important to me, and waiting for answers and none coming, and after that I came out –'

'Ah!'

'What makes you say that? Do you know what sort of thing I saw?'

'Was it a dark cold day, and snow in the streets, and a fire burning somewhere near you?'

'By George, it was! You *have* had the same nightmare! Really not? Well, it is the oddest thing! Yes; I've no doubt it was an execution for high treason. I know I was laid on straw and jolted along most wretchedly, and then had to go up some steps, and someone was holding my arm, and I remember seeing a bit of a ladder and hearing a sound of a lot of people. I really don't think I could bear now to go into a crowd of people and hear the noise they make talking. However, mercifully, I didn't get to the real business. The dream passed off with a sort of thunder inside my head. But, Mary –'

'I know what you are going to ask. I suppose this is an instance of a kind of thought-reading. Miss Wilkins called yesterday and told me of a dream her brother had as a child when they lived here, and something did no doubt make me think of that when I was awake last night listening to those horrible owls and those men talking and laughing in the shrubbery (by the way, I wish you would see if they have done any damage, and speak to the police about it); and so, I suppose, from my brain it must have got into yours while you were asleep. Curious, no doubt, and I am sorry it gave you such a bad night. You had better be as much in the fresh air as you can today.'

'Oh, it's all right now; but I think I *will* go over to the Lodge and see if I can get a game with any of them. And you?'

'I have enough to do for this morning; and this afternoon, if I am not interrupted, there is my drawing.'

'To be sure – I want to see that finished very much.'

No damage was discoverable in the shrubbery. Mr Anstruther surveyed with faint interest the site of the rose garden, where the uprooted post still lay, and the hole it had occupied remained unfilled. Collins, upon inquiry made, proved to be better, but quite unable to come to his work. He expressed, by the mouth of his wife, a hope that he hadn't done nothing wrong clearing away them things. Mrs Collins added that there was a lot of talking people in Westfield, and the hold ones was the worst: seemed to think everything of them having been in the parish longer than what other people had. But as to what they said no more could then be ascertained than that it had quite upset Collins, and was a lot of nonsense.

Recruited by lunch and a brief period of slumber, Mrs Anstruther settled herself comfortably upon her sketching chair in the path leading through the shrubbery to the side-gate of the churchyard. Trees and buildings were among her favourite subjects, and here she had good studies of both. She worked hard, and the drawing was becoming a really pleasant thing to look upon by the time that the wooded hills to the west had shut off the sun. Still she would have persevered, but the light changed rapidly, and it became obvious that the last touches must be added on the morrow. She rose and turned towards the house, pausing for a time to take delight in the limpid green western sky. Then she passed on between the dark box-bushes, and, at a point just before the path debouched on the lawn, she stopped once again and considered the quiet evening landscape, and made a mental note that that must be the tower of one of the Roothing churches that one caught on the sky-line. Then a bird (perhaps) rustled in the box-bush on her left, and she turned and started at seeing what at first she took to be a Fifth of November mask peeping out among the branches. She looked closer.

It was not a mask. It was a face – large, smooth, and pink. She remembers the minute drops of perspiration which were starting from its forehead: she remembers how the jaws were clean-shaven and the eyes shut. She remembers also, and with an accuracy which makes the thought intolerable to her, how the mouth was open and a single tooth appeared below the upper lip. As she looked the face receded into the darkness of the bush. The shelter of the house was gained and the door shut before she collapsed.

Mr and Mrs Anstruther had been for a week or more recruiting at Brighton before they received a circular from the Essex Archaeological Society, and a query as to whether they possessed certain historical portraits which it was desired to include in the forthcoming work on Essex Portraits, to be published under the Society's auspices. There was an accompanying letter from the Secretary which contained the following passage: 'We are specially anxious to know whether you possess the original of the engraving of which I enclose a photograph. It represents Sir — —, Lord Chief Justice under Charles II, who, as you doubtless know, retired after his disgrace to Westfield, and is supposed to have died there of remorse. It may interest you to hear that a curious entry has recently been found in the registers not of Westfield but of Priors Roothing to the effect that the parish was so much troubled after his death that the rector of Westfield summoned the parsons of all the Roothings to come and lay him; which they did. The entry ends by saying: "The stake is in a field adjoining to the churchyard of Westfield, on the west side." Perhaps you can let us know if any tradition to this effect is current in your parish.'

The incidents which the 'enclosed photograph' recalled were productive of a severe shock to Mrs Anstruther. It was decided that she must spend the winter abroad.

Mr Anstruther, when he went down to Westfield to make the necessary arrangements, not unnaturally told his story to the rector (an old gentleman), who showed little surprise:

'Really I had managed to piece out for myself very much what must have happened, partly from old people's talk and partly from what I saw in your grounds. Of course we have suffered to some extent also. Yes, it was bad at first: like owls, as you say, and men talking sometimes. One night it was in this garden, and at other times about several of the cottages. But lately there has been very little: I think it will die out. There is nothing in our registers except the entry of the burial, and what I for a long time took to be the family motto: but last time I looked at it I noticed that it was added in a later hand and had the initials of one of our rectors quite late in the seventeenth century, A. C. – Augustine Crompton. Here it is, you see – *quieta non movere*. I suppose – Well, it is rather hard to say exactly what I do suppose.'

The Return of Imray

Rudyard Kipling

Imray achieved the impossible. Without warning, for no conceivable motive, in his youth, at the threshold of his career, he chose to disappear from the world – which is to say, the little Indian station where he lived.

Upon a day he was alive, well, happy, and in great evidence among the billiard tables at his Club. Upon a morning he was not, and no manner of search could make sure where he might be. He had stepped out of his place; he had not appeared at his office at the proper time, and his dogcart was not upon the public roads. For these reasons, and because he was hampering, in a microscopical degree, the administration of the Indian Empire, that Empire paused for one microscopical moment to make inquiry into the fate of Imray. Ponds were dragged, wells were plumbed, telegrams were dispatched down the lines of railways and to the nearest seaport town – twelve hundred miles away; but Imray was not at the end of the drag-ropes nor the telegraph wires. He was gone, and his place knew him no more. Then the work of the great Indian Empire swept forward, because it could not be delayed, and Imray from being a man became a mystery – such a thing as men talk over at their tables in the Club for a month, and then forget utterly. His guns, horses, and carts were sold to the highest bidder. His superior officer wrote an altogether absurd letter to his mother, saying that Imray had unaccountably disappeared, and his bungalow stood empty.

After three or four months of the scorching hot weather had gone by, my friend Strickland, of the Police, saw fit to rent the bungalow from the native landlord. This was before he was engaged to Miss Youghal – an affair which has been described in another place – and while he was pursuing his investigations into native life. His own life was sufficiently peculiar, and men complained of his manners and customs. There was always food in his house, but there were no regular times for meals. He ate, standing up and walking about, whatever he might find at the sideboard, and this is not good for human beings. His domestic equipment was limited to six rifles, three shot-guns, five saddles, and a collection of stiff-jointed mahseer-rods, bigger and stronger than the largest salmon-rods. These occupied one-half of his bungalow, and the other half was given up to Strickland and his dog Tietjens – an enormous Rampur slut who devoured daily the rations of two men. She spoke to Strickland in a language of her own; and whenever, walking abroad, she saw things calculated to destroy the peace of Her Majesty the Queen-Empress, she returned to her master and laid information. Strickland would take steps at once, and the end of his labours was trouble and fine and imprisonment for other people. The natives believed that Tietjens was a familiar spirit, and treated her with the great reverence that is born of hate and fear. One room in the bungalow was set apart for her special use. She owned a bedstead, a blanket, and a drinking-trough, and if anyone came into Strickland's room at night her custom was to knock down the invader and give tongue till someone came with a light. Strickland owed his life to her when he was on the Frontier in search of a local murderer, who came in the grey dawn to send Strickland much farther than the Andaman Islands. Tietjens caught the man as he was crawling into Strickland's tent with a dagger between his teeth; and after his record of iniquity was established in the eyes of the law he was hanged. From that date Tietjens wore a collar of rough silver, and employed a monogram on her night blanket; and the blanket was of double woven Kashmir cloth, for she was a delicate dog.

Under no circumstances would she be separated from Strickland; and once, when he was ill with fever, made great trouble for the doctors, because she did not know how to help her master and would not allow another creature to attempt aid. Macarnaght, of the Indian Medical Service, beat her over her head with a gun-butt before she could understand that she must give room for those who could give quinine.

A short time after Strickland had taken Imray's bungalow, my business took me through that Station, and naturally, the Club quarters being full, I quartered myself upon Strickland. It was a desirable bungalow, eight-roomed and heavily thatched against any chance of leakage from rain. Under the pitch of the roof ran a ceiling-cloth which looked just as neat as a whitewashed ceiling. The landlord had repainted it when Strickland took the bungalow. Unless you knew how Indian bungalows were built you would never have suspected that above the cloth lay the dark three-cornered cavern of the roof, where the beams and the underside of the thatch harboured all manner of rats, bats, ants, and foul things.

Tietjens met me in the verandah with a bay like the boom of the bell of St Paul's, putting her paws on my shoulder to show she was glad to see me. Strickland had contrived to claw together a sort of meal which he called lunch, and immediately after it was finished went out about his business. I was left alone with Tietjens and my own affairs. The heat of the summer had broken up and turned to the warm damp of the rains. There was no motion in the heated air, but the rain fell like ramrods on the earth, and flung up a blue mist when it splashed back. The bamboo, and the custard apples, the poinsettias, and the mango trees in the garden stood still while the warm water lashed through them, and the frogs began to sing among the aloe hedges. A little before the light failed, and when the rain was at its worst, I sat in the back verandah and heard the water roar from the eaves, and scratched myself because I was covered with the thing called prickly heat. Tietjens came out with me and put her head in my lap and was very sorrowful; so I gave her biscuits when tea was ready, and I took tea in the back verandah on account of the little coolness found there. The rooms of the house were dark behind me. I could smell Strickland's saddlery and the oil on his guns, and I had no desire to sit among these things. My own servant came to me in the twilight, the muslin of his clothes clinging tightly to his drenched body, and told me that a gentleman had called and wished to see someone. Very much against my will, but only because of the darkness of the rooms, I went into the naked drawing-room, telling my man to bring the lights. There might or might not have been a caller waiting – it seemed to me that I saw a figure by one of the windows – but when the lights came there was nothing save the spikes of the rain without, and the smell of the drinking earth in my nostrils. I explained to my servant that he was no wiser than he ought to be, and went back to the verandah to talk to Tietjens. She had gone out into the wet, and I could hardly coax her back to me, even with biscuits with sugar tops. Strickland came home, dripping wet, just before dinner, and the first thing he said was:

'Has anyone called?'

I explained, with apologies, that my servant had summoned me into the drawing-room on a false alarm; or that some loafer had tried to call on Strickland, and thinking better of it, had fled after giving his name. Strickland ordered dinner, without comment, and since it was a real dinner with a white tablecloth attached, we sat down.

At nine o'clock Strickland wanted to go to bed, and I was tired too. Tietjens, who had been lying underneath the table, rose up, and swung into the least exposed verandah as soon as her master moved to his own room, which was next to the stately chamber set apart for Tietjens. If a mere wife had wished to sleep out of doors in that pelting rain it would not have mattered; but Tietjens was a dog, and therefore the better animal. I looked at Strickland, expecting to see him flay her with a whip. He smiled queerly, as a man would smile after telling some unpleasant domestic tragedy. 'She has done this ever since I moved in here,' said he. 'Let her go.'

The dog was Strickland's dog, so I said nothing, but I felt all that Strickland felt in being thus made light of. Tietjens encamped outside my bedroom window, and storm after storm came up, thundered on the thatch, and died away. The lightning spattered the sky as a thrown egg spatters a barn door, but the light was pale blue, not yellow; and, looking through my split bamboo blinds, I could see the great dog standing, not sleeping, in the verandah, the hackles alift on her back and her feet anchored as tensely as the drawn wire-rope of a suspension bridge. In the very short pauses of the thunder I tried to sleep, but it seemed that someone wanted me very urgently. He, whoever he was, was trying to call me by name, but his voice was no more than a husky whisper. The thunder ceased, and Tietjens went into the garden and howled at the low moon. Somebody tried to open my door, walked about and about through the house, and stood breathing heavily in the verandahs, and just when I was falling asleep I fancied that I heard a wild hammering and clamouring above my head or on the door.

I ran into Strickland's room and asked him whether he was ill, and had been calling me. He was lying on his bed half dressed, a pipe in his mouth. 'I thought you'd come,' he said. 'Have I been walking round the house recently?'

I explained that he had been tramping in the dining-room and the smoking-room and two or three other places, and he laughed and told me to go back to bed. I went back to bed and slept till the morning, but through all my mixed dreams I was sure I was doing someone an injustice in not attending to his wants. What those wants were I could not tell; but a fluttering, whispering, bolt-fumbling, lurking, loitering Someone was reproaching me for my slackness, and, half awake, I heard the howling of Tietjens in the garden and the threshing of the rain.

I lived in that house for two days. Strickland went to his office daily, leaving me alone for eight or ten hours with Tietjens for my only companion. As long as the full light lasted I was comfortable, and so was Tietjens; but in the twilight she and I moved into the back verandah and cuddled each other for company. We were alone in the house, but none the less it was much too fully occupied by a tenant with whom I did not wish to interfere. I never saw him, but I could see the curtains between the rooms quivering where he had just passed through; I could hear the chairs creaking as the bamboos sprung under a weight that had just quitted them; and I could feel when I went to get a book from the dining-room that somebody was waiting in the shadows of the front verandah till I should have gone away. Tietjens made the twilight more interesting by glaring into the darkened rooms with every hair erect, and following the motions of something that I could not see. She never entered the rooms, but her eyes moved interestedly: that was quite sufficient. Only when my servant came to trim the lamps and make all light and habitable she would come in with me and spend her time sitting on her haunches, watching an invisible extra man as he moved about behind my shoulder. Dogs are cheerful companions.

I explained to Strickland, gently as might be, that I would go over to the Club and find for myself quarters there. I admired his hospitality, was pleased with his guns and rods, but I did not much care for his house and its atmosphere. He heard me out to the end, and then smiled very wearily, but without contempt, for he is a man who understands things. 'Stay on,' he said, 'and see what this thing means. All you have talked about I have known since I took the bungalow. Stay on and wait. Tietjens has left me. Are you going too?'

I had seen him through one little affair, connected with a heathen idol, that had brought me to the doors of a lunatic asylum, and I had no desire to help him through further experiences. He was a man to whom unpleasantness arrived as do dinners to ordinary people.

Therefore I explained more clearly than ever that I liked him immensely, and would be happy to see him in the daytime; but that I did not care to sleep under his roof. This was after dinner, when Tietjens had gone out to lie in the verandah.

''Pon my soul, I don't wonder,' said Strickland, with his eyes on the ceiling-cloth. 'Look at that!'

The tails of two brown snakes were hanging between the cloth and the cornice of the wall. They threw long shadows in the lamp-light.

'If you are afraid of snakes, of course –' said Strickland.

I hate and fear snakes, because if you look into the eyes of any snake you will see that it knows all and more of the mystery of man's fall, and that it feels all the contempt that the Devil felt when Adam was evicted from Eden. Besides which its bite is generally fatal, and it twists up trouser legs.

'You ought to get your thatch overhauled,' I said. 'Give me a mahseer-rod, and we'll poke 'em down.'

'They'll hide among the roof-beams,' said Strickland. 'I can't stand snakes overhead. I'm going up into the roof. If I shake 'em down, stand by with a cleaning-rod and break their backs.'

I was not anxious to assist Strickland in his work, but I took the cleaning-rod and waited in the dining-room, while Strickland brought a gardener's ladder from the verandah, and set it against the side of the room. The snake-tails drew themselves up and disappeared. We could hear the dry rushing scuttle of long bodies running over the baggy ceiling-cloth. Strickland took a lamp with him, while I tried to make clear to him the danger of hunting roof-snakes between a ceiling-cloth and a thatch, apart from the deteriora-tion of property caused by ripping out ceiling-cloths.

'Nonsense!' said Strickland. 'They're sure to hide near the walls by the cloth. The bricks are too cold for 'em, and the heat of the room is just what they like.' He put his hand to the corner of the stuff and ripped it from the cornice. It gave with a great sound of tearing, and Strickland put his head through the opening into the dark of the angle of the roof-beams. I set my teeth and lifted the rod, for I had not the least knowledge of what might descend.

'H'm!' said Strickland, and his voice rolled and rumbled in the roof. 'There's room for another set of rooms up here, and, by Jove, someone is occupying 'em!'

'Snakes?' I said from below.

'No. It's a buffalo. Hand me up the two last joints of a mahseer-rod, and I'll prod it. It's lying on the main roof-beam.'

I handed up the rod.

'What a nest for owls and serpents! No wonder the snakes live here,' said Strickland, climbing farther into the roof. I could see his elbow thrusting with the rod. 'Come out of that, whoever you are! Heads below there! It's falling.'

I saw the ceiling-cloth nearly in the centre of the room sag with a shape that was pressing it downwards and downwards towards the lighted lamp on the table. I snatched the lamp out of danger and stood back. Then the cloth ripped out from the walls, tore, split, swayed, and shot down upon the table something that I dared not look at, till Strickland had slid down the ladder and was standing by my side.

He did not say much, being a man of few words; but he picked up the loose end of the tablecloth and threw it over the remnants on the table.

'It strikes me,' said he, putting down the lamp, 'our friend Imray has come back. Oh! you would, would you?'

There was a movement under the cloth, and a little snake wriggled out, to be back-broken by the butt of the mahseer-rod. I was sufficiently sick to make no remarks worth recording.

Strickland meditated, and helped himself to drinks. The arrangement under the cloth made no more signs of life.

'Is it Imray?' I said.

Strickland turned back the cloth for a moment, and looked.

'It is Imray,' he said; 'and his throat is cut from ear to ear.'

Then we spoke, both together and to ourselves: 'That's why he whispered about the house.'

Tietjens, in the garden, began to bay furiously. A little later her great nose heaved open the dining-room door.

She sniffed and was still. The tattered ceiling-cloth hung down almost to the level of the table, and there was hardly room to move away from the discovery.

Tietjens came in and sat down; her teeth bared under her lip and her forepaws planted. She looked at Strickland.

'It's a bad business, old lady,' said he. 'Men don't climb up into the roofs of their bungalows to die, and they don't fasten up the ceiling-cloth behind 'em. Let's think it out.'

'Let's think it out somewhere else,' I said.

'Excellent idea! Turn the lamps out. We'll get into my room.'

I did not turn the lamps out. I went into Strickland's room first, and allowed him to make the darkness. Then he followed me, and we lit tobacco and thought. Strickland thought. I smoked furiously, because I was afraid.

'Imray is back,' said Strickland. 'The question is – who killed Imray? Don't talk, I've a notion of my own. When I took this bungalow I took over most of Imray's servants. Imray was guileless and inoffensive, wasn't he?'

I agreed; though the heap under the cloth had looked neither one thing nor the other.

'If I call in all the servants they will stand fast in a crowd and lie like Aryans. What do you suggest?'

'Call 'em in one by one,' I said.

'They'll run away and give the news to all their fellows,' said Strickland.

'We must segregate 'em. Do you suppose your servant knows anything about it?'

'He may, for aught I know; but I don't think it's likely. He has only been here two or three days,' I answered. 'What's your notion?'

'I can't quite tell. How the dickens did the man get the wrong side of the ceiling-cloth?'

There was a heavy coughing outside Strickland's bedroom door. This showed that Bahadur Khan, his body servant, had waked from sleep and wished to put Strickland to bed.

'Come in,' said Strickland. 'It's a very warm night, isn't it?'

Bahadur Khan, a great, green-turbaned, six-foot Mohammedan, said that it was a very warm night; but that there was more rain pending, which, by his Honour's favour, would bring relief to the country.

'It will be so, if God pleases,' said Strickland, tugging off his boots. 'It is in my mind, Bahadur Khan, that I have worked thee remorselessly for many days – ever since that time when thou first camest into my service. What time was that?'

'Has the Heaven-born forgotten? It was when Imray Sahib went secretly to Europe without warning given; and I – even I – came into the honoured service of the protector of the poor.'

'And Imray Sahib went to Europe?'

'It is so said among those who were his servants.'

'And thou wilt take service with him when he returns?'

'Assuredly, Sahib. He was a good master, and cherished his dependants.'

'That is true. I am very tired, but I go buck-shooting tomorrow. Give me the little Sharp rifle that I use for black-buck; it is in the case yonder.'

The man stooped over the case; handed barrels, stock, and fore-end to Strickland, who fitted all together, yawning dolefully. Then he reached down to the gun-case, took a solid-drawn cartridge, and slipped it into the breech of the .360 Express.

'And Imray Sahib has gone to Europe secretly! That is very strange, Bahadur Khan, is it not?'

'What do I know of the ways of the white man, Heaven born?'

'Very little, truly. But thou shalt know more anon. It has reached me that Imray Sahib has returned from his so long journeyings, and that even now he lies in the next room, waiting his servant.'

'Sahib!'

The lamplights slid along the barrels of the rifle as they levelled themselves at Bahadur Khan's broad breast.

'Go and look!' said Strickland. 'Take a lamp. Thy master is tired, and he waits thee. Go!'

The man picked up a lamp, and went into the dining-room, Strickland following, and almost pushing him with the muzzle of the rifle. He looked for a moment at the black depths behind the ceiling-cloth; at the writhing snake under foot; and last, a grey glaze settling on his face, at the thing under the tablecloth.

'Hast thou seen?' said Strickland after a pause.

'I have seen. I am clay in the white man's hands. What does the Presence do?'

'Hang thee within the month. What else?'

'For killing him? Nay, Sahib, consider. Walking among us, his servants, he cast his eyes upon my child, who was four years old. Him he bewitched, and in ten days he died of the fever – my child!'

'What said Imray Sahib?'

'He said he was a handsome child, and patted him on the head; wherefore my child died. Wherefore I killed Imray Sahib in the twilight, when he had come back from office, and was sleeping. Wherefore I dragged him up into the roof-beams and made all fast behind him. The Heaven-born knows all things. I am the servant of the Heaven-born.'

Strickland looked at me above the rifle, and said, in the vernacular, 'Thou art witness to this saying? He has killed.'

Bahadur Khan stood ashen grey in the light of the one lamp. The need for justification came upon him very swiftly. 'I am trapped,' he said, 'but the offence was that man's. He cast an evil eye upon my child, and I killed and hid him. Only such as are served by devils,' he glared at Tietjens, couched stolidly before him, 'only such could know what I did.'

'It was clever. But thou shouldst have lashed him to the beam with a rope. Now, thou thyself wilt hang by a rope. Orderly!'

A drowsy policeman answered Strickland's call. He was followed by another, and Tietjens sat wondrous still.

'Take him to the police station,' said Strickland. 'There is a case toward.'

'Do I hang, then?' said Bahadur Khan, making no attempt to escape, and keeping his eyes on the ground.

'If the sun shines or the water runs – yes!' said Strickland.

Bahadur Khan stepped back one long pace, quivered, and stood still. The two policemen waited further orders.

'Go!' said Strickland.

'Nay; but I go very swiftly,' said Bahadur Khan. 'Look! I am even now a dead man.'

He lifted his foot, and to the little toe there clung the head of the half-killed snake, firm fixed in the agony of death.

'I come of land-holding stock,' said Bahadur Khan, rocking where he stood. 'It were a disgrace to me to go to the public scaffold: therefore I take this way. Be it remembered that the Sahib's shirts are correctly enumerated, and that there is an extra piece of soap in his wash-basin. My child was bewitched, and I slew the wizard. Why should you seek to slay me with the rope? My honour is saved, and – and – I die.'

At the end of an hour he died, as they die who are bitten by a little brown *karait*, and the policemen bore him and the thing under the tablecloth to their appointed places. All were needed to make clear the disappearance of Imray.

'This,' said Strickland, very calmly, as he climbed into bed, 'is called the nineteenth century. Did you hear what the man said?'

'I heard,' I answered. 'Imray made a mistake.'

'Simply and solely through not knowing the nature of the Oriental, and the coincidence of a little seasonal fever. Bahadur Khan had been with him for four years.'

I shuddered. My own servant had been with me for exactly that length of time. When I went over to my own room I found my man waiting, impassive as the copper head on a penny, to pull off my boots.

'What has befallen Bahadur Khan?' said I.

'He was bitten by a snake and died. The rest the Sahib knows,' was the answer.

'And how much of this matter hast thou known?'

'As much as might be gathered from One coming in in the twilight to seek satisfaction. Gently, Sahib. Let me pull off those boots.'

I had just settled to the sleep of exhaustion when I heard Strickland shouting from his side of the house –

'Tietjens has come back to her place!'

And so she had. The great deerhound was couched statelily on her own bedstead on her own blanket, while, in the next room, the idle, empty ceiling-cloth waggled as it trailed on the table.

My Adventure in Norfolk

A. J. Alan

I don't know how it is with you, but during February *my* wife generally says to me: 'Have you thought at all about what we are going to do for August? And, of course, I say 'No,' and then she begins looking through the advertisements of bungalows to let.

Well, this happened last year, as usual, and she eventually produced one that looked possible. It said: 'Norfolk – Hickling Broad – Furnished Bungalow – Garden – Garage, Boathouse,' and all the rest of it – Oh – *and* plate and linen. It also mentioned an exorbitant rent. I pointed out the bit about the rent, but my wife said: 'Yes, you'll have to go down and see the landlord, and get him to come down. They always do.' As a matter of fact, they always don't, but that's a detail.

Anyway, I wrote off to the landlord and asked if he could arrange for me to stay the night in the place to see what it was really like. He wrote back and said: 'Certainly,' and that he was engaging Mrs So-and-so to come in and 'oblige me', and make up the beds and so forth.

I tell you, we do things thoroughly in our family – I have to sleep in all the beds, and when I come home my wife counts the bruises and decides whether they will do or not.

At any rate, I arrived, in a blinding snowstorm, at about *the* most desolate spot on God's earth. I'd come to Potter Heigham by train, and been driven on – (it was a good five miles from the station). Fortunately, Mrs Selston, the old lady who was going to 'do' for me, was there, and she'd lighted a fire, and cooked me a steak, for which I was truly thankful.

I somehow think the cow, or whatever they get steaks off, had only died that morning. It was very – er – obstinate. While I dined, she talked to me.

She *would* tell me all about an operation her husband had just had. *All* about it. It was almost a lecture on surgery. The steak was rather under-done, and it sort of made me feel I was illustrating her lecture. Anyway, she put me clean off my dinner, and then departed for the night.

I explored the bungalow and just had a look outside. It was, of course, very dark, but not snowing quite so hard. The garage stood about fifteen yards from the back door. I walked round it but didn't go in. I also went down to the edge of the broad, and verified the boathouse. The whole place looked as though it might be all right in the summertime, but just then it made one wonder why people ever wanted to go to the North Pole.

Anyhow, I went indoors, and settled down by the fire. You've no idea how quiet it was; even the water-fowl had taken a night off – at least, they weren't working.

At a few minutes to eleven I heard the first noise there'd been since Mrs What's-her-name – Selston – had cleared out. It was the sound of a car. If it had gone straight by I probably shouldn't have noticed it at all, only it didn't go straight by; it seemed to stop farther up the road, before it got to the house. Even that didn't make much impression. After all, cars *do* stop.

It must have been five or ten minutes before it was borne in on me that it hadn't gone on again. So I got up and looked out of the window. It had left off snowing, and there was a glare through the gate that showed that there were headlamps somewhere just out of sight. I thought I might as well stroll out and investigate.

I found a fair-sized limousine pulled up in the middle of the road about twenty yards short of my gate. The light was rather blinding, but when I got close to it I found a girl with the bonnet open, tinkering with the engine. Quite an attractive young female, from what one could see, but she was so muffled up in furs that it was rather hard to tell.

I said:

'Er – good evening – anything I can do?'

She said she didn't know what was the matter. The engine had just stopped, and wouldn't start again. And it *had!* It wouldn't even turn, either with the self-starter or the handle. The whole thing was awfully hot, and I asked her whether there was any water in the radiator. She didn't see why there shouldn't be, there always had been. This didn't strike me as entirely conclusive. I said, we'd better put some in, and see what happened. She said, why not use snow? But I thought not. There was an idea at the back of my mind that there was some reason why it was unwise to use melted snow, and it wasn't until I arrived with a bucketful that I remem-bered what it was. Of course – goitre.

When I got back to her she'd got the radiator cap off, and inserted what a Danish friend of mine calls a 'funeral'. We poured a little water in . . . Luckily I'd warned her to stand clear. The first tablespoonful that went in came straight out again, red-hot, and blew the 'funeral' sky-high. We waited a few minutes until things had cooled down a bit, but it was no go. As fast as we poured water in it simply ran out again into the road underneath. It was quite evident that she'd been driving with the radiator bone dry, and that her engine had seized right up.

I told her so. She said:

'Does that mean I've got to stop here all night?'

I explained that it wasn't as bad as all that; that is, if she cared to accept the hospitality of my poor roof (and it *was* a poor roof – it let the wet in). But she wouldn't hear of it. By the by, she didn't know the – er – circumstances, so it wasn't that. No, she wanted to leave the car where it was and go on on foot.

I said:

'Don't be silly, it's miles to anywhere.'

However, at that moment we heard a car coming along the road, the same way as she'd come. We could see its lights, too, although it was a very long way off. You know how flat Norfolk is – you can see a terrific distance.

I said:

'There's the way out of all your troubles. This thing, whatever it is, will give you a tow to the nearest garage, or at any rate a lift to some hotel.'

One would have expected her to show some relief, but she didn't. I began to wonder what she jolly well *did* want. She wouldn't let me help her to stop where she was, and she didn't seem anxious for anyone to help her to go anywhere else.

She was quite peculiar about it. She gripped hold of my arm, and said: 'What do you think this is that's coming?'

I said:

'I'm sure I don't know, being a stranger in these parts, but it sounds like a lorry full of milk cans.'

I offered to lay her sixpence about it (this was before the betting tax came in). She'd have had to pay, too, because it *was* a lorry full of milk cans. The driver had to pull up because there wasn't room to get by.

He got down and asked if there was anything he could do to help. We explained the situation. He said he was going to Norwich, and was quite ready to give her a tow if she wanted it. However, she wouldn't do that, and it was finally decided to shove her car into my garage for the night, to be sent for next day, and the lorry was to take her along to Norwich.

Well, I managed to find the key of the garage, and the lorry-driver –

Williams, his name was – and I ran the car in and locked the door. This having been done – (ablative absolute) – I suggested that it was a very cold night. Williams agreed, and said he didn't mind if he did. So I took them both indoors and mixed them a stiff whisky and water each. There wasn't any soda. And, naturally, the whole thing had left *me* very cold, too. I hadn't an overcoat on.

Up to now I hadn't seriously considered the young woman. For one thing it had been dark, *and* there had been a seized engine to look at. Er – I'm afraid that's not a very gallant remark. What I mean is that to anyone with a mechanical mind a motor car in that condition is much more interesting than – er – well, it *is* very interesting – but why labour the point? However, in the sitting-room, in the lamplight, it was possible to get more of an idea. She was a little older than I'd thought, and her eyes were too close together.

Of course, she wasn't a – how shall I put it? Her manners weren't quite easy and she was careful with her English. *You* know. But that wasn't it. She treated us with a lack of friendliness which was – well, we'd done nothing to deserve it. There was a sort of vague hostility and suspicion, which seemed rather hard lines, considering. Also, she was so anxious to keep in the shadows that if I hadn't moved the lamp away she'd never have got near the fire at all.

And the way she hurried the wretched Williams over his drink was quite distressing; and foolish, too, as *he* was going to drive, but that was her – funnel. When he'd gone out to start up his engine I asked her if she was all right for money, and she apparently was. Then they started off, and I shut up the place and went upstairs.

There happened to be a local guide-book in my bedroom, with maps in it. I looked at these and couldn't help wondering where the girl in the car had come from; I mean my road seemed so very unimportant. The sort of road one might use if one wanted to avoid people. If one were driving a stolen car, for instance. This was quite a thrilling idea. I thought it might be worth while having another look at the car. So I once more unhooked the key from the kitchen dresser and sallied forth into the snow. It was as black as pitch, and so still that my candle hardly flickered. It wasn't a large garage, and the car nearly filled it. By the by, we'd backed it in so as to make it easier to tow it out again.

The engine I'd already seen, so I squeezed past along the wall and opened the door in the body part of the car. At least, I only turned the handle, and the door was pushed open from the inside and – something – fell out on me. It pushed me quite hard, and wedged me against the wall. It also knocked the candle out of my hand and left me in the dark – which was a bit of a nuisance. I wondered what on earth the thing was – barging into me like that – so I felt it, rather gingerly, and found it was a man – a dead man – with a moustache. He'd evidently been sitting propped up against the door. I managed to put him back, as decorously as possible, and shut the door again.

After a lot of grovelling about under the car I found the candle and lighted it, and opened the opposite door and switched on the little lamp in the roof – and then – oo-er!

Of course, I had to make some sort of examination. He was an extremely tall and thin individual. He must have been well over six feet three. He was dark and very cadaverous looking. In fact, I don't suppose he'd ever looked so cadaverous in his life. He was wearing a trench coat.

It wasn't difficult to tell what he'd died of. He'd been shot through the back. I found the hole just under the right scrofula, or scalpel – what is shoulder-blade, anyway? Oh, clavicle – stupid of me – well, that's where it was, and the bullet had evidently gone through into the lung. I say 'evidently', and leave it at that.

There were no papers in his pockets, and no tailor's name on his clothes, but there was a note-case, with nine pounds in it. Altogether a most unpleasant business. Of course, it doesn't do to question the workings of Providence, but one couldn't help wishing it hadn't happened. It was just a little mysterious, too – er – who had killed him? It wasn't likely that the girl had or she wouldn't have been joy-riding about the country with him; and if someone else had murdered him why hadn't she mentioned it? Anyway, she hadn't and she'd gone, so one couldn't do anything for the time being. No telephone, of course. I just locked up the garage and went to bed. That was two o'clock.

Next morning I woke early, for some reason or other, and it occurred to me as a good idea to go and have a look at things – by daylight, and before Mrs Selston turned up. So I did. The first thing that struck me was that it had snowed heavily during the night, because there were no wheel tracks or footprints, and the second was that I'd left the key in the garage door. I opened it and went in. The place was completely empty. No car, no body, no nothing. There was a patch of grease on the floor where I'd dropped the candle, otherwise there was nothing to show I'd been there before. One of two things must have happened: either some people had come along during the night and taken the car away, or else I'd fallen asleep in front of the fire and dreamt the whole thing.

Then I remembered the whisky glasses.

They should still be in the sitting-room. I went back to look, and they were, all three of them. So it *hadn't* been a dream and the car *had* been fetched away, but they must have been jolly quiet over it.

The girl had left her glass on the mantelpiece, and it showed several very clearly defined finger-marks. Some were mine, naturally, because I'd fetched the glass from the kitchen and poured out the drink for her, but hers, her finger-marks, were clean, and mine were oily, so it was quite easy to tell them apart. It isn't necessary to point out that this glass was very important. There'd evidently been a murder, or something of that kind, and the girl must have known all about it, even if she hadn't actually done it herself, so anything she had left in the way of evidence ought to be handed over to the police; and this was all she *had* left. So I packed it up with meticulous care in an old biscuit box out of the larder.

When Mrs Selston came, I settled up with her and came back to town. Oh, I called on the landlord on the way and told him I'd 'let him know' about the bungalow. Then I caught my train, and in due course drove straight to Scotland Yard. I went up and saw my friend there. I produced the glass and asked him if his people could identify the marks. He said, 'Probably not,' but he sent it down to the fingerprint department and asked me where it came from. I said: 'Never you mind; let's have the identification first.' He said: 'All right.'

They're awfully quick, these people – the clerk was back in three minutes with a file of papers. They knew the girl all right. They told me her name and showed me her photograph; not flattering. Quite an adventurous lady, from all accounts. In the early part of her career she'd done time twice for shoplifting, chiefly in the book department. Then she'd what they call 'taken up with' a member of one of those race gangs one sometimes hears about.

My pal went on to say that there'd been a fight between two of these gangs, in the course of which her friend had got shot. She'd managed to get him away in a car, but it had broken down somewhere in Norfolk. So she'd left it and the dead man in someone's garage, and had started off for Norwich in a lorry. Only she never got there. On the way the lorry skidded, and both she and the driver – a fellow called Williams – had been thrown out, and they'd rammed their heads against a brick wall, which everyone knows is a fatal thing to do. At least, it was in their case.

I said: 'Look here, it's all very well, but you simply can't know all this; there hasn't been time – it only happened last night.'

He said: 'Last night be blowed! It all happened in February 1919. The people you've described have been dead for years.'

I said: 'Oh!'

And to think that I might have stuck to that nine pounds!

The Inexperienced Ghost

🕯

H. G. Wells

The scene amidst which Clayton told his last story comes back very vividly to my mind. There he sat, for the greater part of the time, in the corner of the authentic settle by the spacious open fire, and Sanderson sat beside him smoking the Broseley clay that bore his name. There was Evans, and that marvel among actors, Wish, who is also a modest man. We had all come down to the Mermaid Club that Saturday morning, except Clayton, who had slept there overnight – which indeed gave him the opening of his story. We had golfed until golfing was invisible; we had dined, and we were in that mood of tranquil kindliness when men will suffer a story. When Clayton began to tell one, we naturally supposed he was lying. It may be that indeed he was lying – of that the reader will speedily be able to judge as well as I. He began, it is true, with an air of matter-of-fact anecdote, but that we thought was only the incurable artifice of the man.

'I say!' he remarked, after a long consideration of the upward rain of sparks from the log that Sanderson had thumped, 'you know I was alone here last night?'

'Except for the domestics,' said Wish.

'Who sleep in the other wing,' said Clayton. 'Yes. Well –' He pulled at his cigar for some little time as though he still hesitated about his confidence. Then he said, quite quietly, 'I caught a ghost!'

'Caught a ghost, did you?' said Sanderson. 'Where is it?'

And Evans, who admires Clayton immensely, and has been four weeks in America, shouted, '*Caught* a ghost, did you, Clayton? I'm glad of it! Tell us all about it right now.'

Clayton said he would in a minute, and asked him to shut the door.

He looked apologetically at me. 'There's no eavesdropping, of course, but we don't want to upset our very excellent service with any rumours of ghosts in the place. There's too much shadow and oak panelling to trifle with that. And this, you know, wasn't a regular ghost. I don't think it will come again – ever.'

'You mean to say you didn't keep it?' said Sanderson.

'I hadn't the heart to,' said Clayton.

And Sanderson said he was surprised.

We laughed, and Clayton looked aggrieved. 'I know,' he said, with the flicker of a smile, 'but the fact is it really *was* a ghost, and I'm as sure of it as I am that I am talking to you now. I'm not joking. I mean what I say.'

Sanderson drew deeply at his pipe, with one reddish eye on Clayton, and then emitted a thin jet of smoke more eloquent than many words.

Clayton ignored the comment. 'It is the strangest thing that has ever happened in my life. You know I never believed in ghosts or anything of the sort, before, ever; and then, you know, I bag one in a corner; and the whole business is in my hands.'

He meditated still more profoundly and produced and began to pierce a second cigar with a curious little stabber he affected.

'You talked to it?' asked Wish.

'For the space, probably, of an hour.'

'Chatty?' I said, joining the party of the sceptics.

'The poor devil was in trouble,' said Clayton, bowed over his cigar-end, and with the very faintest note of reproof.

'Sobbing?' someone asked.

Clayton heaved a realistic sigh at the memory. 'Good Lord!' he said; 'yes.' And then, 'Poor fellow! yes.'

'Where did you strike it?' asked Evans, in his best American accent.

'I never realized', said Clayton, ignoring him, 'the poor sort of thing a ghost might be,' and he hung us up again for a time, while he sought for matches in his pocket and lit and warmed to his cigar.

'I took an advantage,' he reflected at last.

We were none of us in a hurry. 'A character,' he said, 'remains just the same character for all that it's been disembodied. That's a thing we too often forget. People with a certain strength or fixity of purpose may have ghosts of a certain strength and fixity of purpose – most haunting ghosts, you know, must be as one-idea'd as monomaniacs, and as obstinate as mules, to come back again and again. This poor creature wasn't.' He suddenly looked up rather queerly, and his eye went round the room. 'I say it,' he said, 'in all kindliness, but that is the plain truth of the case. Even at the first glance he struck me as weak.'

He punctuated with the help of his cigar.

'I came upon him, you know, in the long passage. His back was towards me, and I saw him first. Right off I knew him for a ghost. He was transparent, and whitish; clean through his chest I could see the glimmer of the little window at the end. And not only his physique, but his attitude, struck me as being weak. He looked, you know, as though he didn't know in the slightest whatever he meant to do. One hand was on the panelling and the other fluttered to his mouth. Like – *so!*'

'What sort of physique?' said Sanderson.

'Lean. You know that sort of young man's neck that has two great flutings down the back, here and here – so! And a little, meanish head with scrubby hair and rather bad ears. Shoulders bad, narrower than the hips; turndown collar, readymade short jacket, trousers baggy and a little frayed at the heels. That's how he took me. I came very quietly up the staircase. I did not carry a light, you know – the candles are on the landing table, and there is that lamp – and I was in my list slippers, and I saw him as I came up. I stopped dead at that – taking him in. I wasn't a bit afraid. I think that in most of these affairs one is never nearly so afraid or excited as one imagines one would be. I was surprised and interested. I thought, "Good Lord! Here's a ghost at last! And I haven't believed for a moment in ghosts during the last five-and-twenty years." '

'Um,' said Wish.

'I suppose I wasn't on the landing a moment before he found out I was there. He turned on me sharply, and I saw the face of an immature young man, a weak nose, a scrubby little moustache, a feeble chin. So for an instant we stood – he looking over his shoulder at me – and regarded one another. Then he seemed to remember his high calling. He turned round, drew himself up, projected his face, raised his arms, spread his hands in approved ghost fashion – came towards me. As he did so his little jaw dropped, and he emitted a faint, drawn-out "Boo!" No, it wasn't – not a bit dreadful. I'd dined. I'd had a bottle of champagne, and, being all alone, perhaps two or three – perhaps even four or five – whiskies, so I was as solid as rocks, and no more frightened than if I'd been assailed by a frog. "Boo!" I said. "Nonsense. You don't belong to *this* place. What are you doing here?"

'I could see him wince. "Boo-oo!" he said.

' "Boo – be hanged! Are you a member?" I said; and just to show I didn't care a pin for him I stepped through a corner of him and made to light my candle. "Are you a member?" I repeated, looking at him sideways.

He moved a little so as to stand clear of me, and his bearing became crestfallen. "No," he said, in answer to the persistent interrogation of my eye; "I'm not a member – I'm a ghost."

' "Well, that doesn't give you the run of the Mermaid Club. Is there anyone you want to see, or anything of that sort?" And doing it as steadily as possible for fear that he should mistake the carelessness of whisky for the distraction of fear, I got my candle alight. I turned on him, holding it. "What are you doing here?" I said.

He dropped his hands and stopped his booing, and there he stood, abashed and awkward, the ghost of a weak, silly, aimless young man. "I'm haunting," he said.

' "You haven't any business to," I said in a quiet voice.

' "I'm a ghost," he said, as if in defence.

' "That may be, but you haven't any business to haunt here. This is a respectable private club; people often stop here with nursemaids and children, and, going about in the careless way you do, some poor little mite could easily come upon you, and be scared out of her wits. I suppose you didn't think of that?"

' "No, sir," he said, "I didn't."

' "You should have done. You haven't any claim on the place, have you? Weren't murdered here, or anything of that sort?"

' "None, sir; but I thought as it was old and oak panelled –"

' "That's no excuse." I regarded him firmly. "Your coming here is a mistake," I said, in a tone of friendly superiority. I feigned to see if I had my matches, and then looked up at him frankly. "If I were you I wouldn't wait for cock-crow – I'd vanish right away."

He looked embarrassed. "The fact *is*, sir –" he began.

' "I'd vanish," I said, driving it home.

' "The fact is, sir, that – somehow – I can't."

' "You *can't*?"

' "No, sir. There's something I've forgotten. I've been hanging about here since midnight last night, hiding in the cupboards of the empty bedrooms and things like that. I'm flurried. I've never come haunting before, and it seems to put me out."

' "Put you out?"

' "Yes, sir. I've tried to do it several times, and it doesn't come off. There's some little thing has slipped me, and I can't get back."

'That, you know, rather bowled me over. He looked at me in such an abject way that for the life of me I couldn't keep up quite the high hectoring vein I had adopted. "That's queer," I said, and as I spoke I fancied I heard someone moving about down below. "Come into my room and tell me more about it," I said. I didn't, of course, understand this, and I tried to take him by the arm. But, of course, you might as well have tried to take hold of a puff of smoke! I had forgotten my number, I think; anyhow, I remember going into several bedrooms – it was lucky I was the only soul in that wing – until I saw my traps. "Here we are," I said, and sat down in the armchair; "sit down and tell me all about it. It seems to me you have got yourself into a jolly awkward position, old chap."

'Well, he said he wouldn't sit down; he'd prefer to flit up and down the room if it was all the same to me. And so he did, and in a little while we were deep in a long and serious talk. And presently, you know, something of those whiskies and sodas evaporated out of me, and I began to realize just a little what a thundering rum and weird business it was that I was in. There he was semi-transparent – the proper conventional phantom, and noiseless except for his ghost of a voice – flitting to and fro in that nice, clean, chintz-hung old bedroom. You could see the gleam of the copper candlesticks through him, and the lights on the brass fender, and the corners of the framed engravings on the wall, and there he was telling me all about this wretched little life of his that had recently ended on earth. He hadn't a particularly honest face, you know, but being transparent, of course, he couldn't avoid telling the truth.'

'Eh?' said Wish, suddenly sitting up in his chair.

'What?' said Clayton.

'Being transparent – couldn't avoid telling the truth – I don't see it,' said Wish.

'I don't see it,' said Clayton, with inimitable assurance. 'But it *is* so, I can assure you nevertheless. I don't believe he got once a nail's breadth off the Bible truth. He told me how he had been killed – he went down into a London basement with a candle to look for a leakage of gas – and described himself as a senior English master in a London private school when that release occurred.'

'Poor wretch!' said I.

'That's what I thought, and the more he talked the more I thought it. There he was, purposeless in life and purposeless out of it. He talked of his father and mother and his schoolmaster, and all who had ever been anything to him in the world, meanly. He had been too sensitive, too nervous; none of them had ever valued him properly or understood him, he said. He had never had a real friend in the world, I think; he had never had a success. He had shirked games and failed examinations. "It's like that with some people," he said; "whenever I got into the examination-room or anywhere everything seemed to go." Engaged to be married of course – to another over-sensitive person, I suppose – when the indiscretion with the gas escape ended his affairs. "And where are you now?" I asked. "Not in –?"

'He wasn't clear on that point at all. The impression he gave me was of a sort of vague, intermediate state, a special reserve for souls too non-existent for anything so positive as either sin or virtue. *I* don't know. He was much too egotistical and unobservant to give me any clear idea of the kind of place, kind of country, there is on the Other Side of Things. Wher-ever he was, he seems to have fallen in with a set of kindred spirits: ghosts of weak Cockney young men, who were on a footing of Christian names, and among these there was certainly a lot of talk about "going haunting" and things like that. Yes – going haunting! They seemed to think "haunt-ing" a tremendous adventure, and most of them funked it all the time. And so primed, you know, he had come.'

'But really!' said Wish to the fire.

'These are the impressions he gave me, anyhow,' said Clayton, modestly. 'I may, of course, have been in a rather uncritical state, but that was the sort of background he gave to himself. He kept flitting up and down, with his thin voice going – talking, talking about his wretched self, and never a word of clear, firm statement from first to last. He was thinner and sillier and more pointless than if he had been real and alive. Only then, you know, he would not have been in my bedroom here – if he *had* been alive. I should have kicked him out.'

'Of course,' said Evans, 'there *are* poor mortals like that.'

'And there's just as much chance of their having ghosts as the rest of us,' I admitted.

'What gave a sort of point to him, you know, was the fact that he did seem within limits to have found himself out. The mess he had made of haunting had depressed him terribly. He had been told it would be a "lark": he had come expecting it to be a "lark", and here it was nothing but another failure added to his record! He proclaimed himself an utter out-and-out failure. He said, and I can quite believe it, that he had never tried to do anything all his life that he hadn't made a perfect mess of – and through all the wastes of eternity he never would. If he had had sympathy, perhaps – He paused at that, and stood regarding me. He remarked that, strange as it might seem to me, nobody, not anyone, ever, had given him the amount of sympathy I was doing now. I could see what he wanted straight away, and I determined to head him off at once. I may be a brute, you know, but being the Only Real Friend, the recipient of the confidences of one of these egotistical weaklings, ghost or body, is beyond my physical endurance. I got up briskly. "Don't you brood on these things too much," I said. "The thing you've got to do is to get out of this – get out of this sharp. You pull yourself together and try." "I can't," he said. "You try," I said, and try he did.'

'Try!' said Sanderson. 'How?'

'Passes,' said Clayton.

'Passes?'

'Complicated series of gestures and passes with the hands. That's how he had come in, and that's how he had to get out again. Lord! what a business I had!'

'But how could *any* series of passes –' I began.

'My dear man,' said Clayton, turning on me and putting a great emphasis on certain words, 'you want *everything* clear. I don't know *how*. All I know is that you *do* – that he did, anyhow, at least. After a fearful time, you know, he got his passes right and suddenly disappeared.'

'Did you,' said Sanderson slowly, 'observe the passes?'

'Yes,' said Clayton, and seemed to think. 'It was tremendously queer,' he said. 'There we were, I and this thin vague ghost, in that silent room, in this silent, empty inn, in this silent little Friday-night town. Not a sound except our voices and a faint panting he made when he swung. There was the bedroom candle, and one candle on the dressing-table alight, that was all – sometimes one or other would flare up into a tall, lean, astonished flame for a space. And queer things happened. "I can't," he said; "I shall never – !" And suddenly he sat down on a little chair at the foot of the bed and began to sob and sob. Lord! what a harrowing, whimpering thing he seemed!

' "You pull yourself together," I said, and tried to pat him on the back, and . . . my confounded hand went through him! By that time, you know, I wasn't nearly so – massive as I had been on the landing. I got the queerness of it full. I remember snatching back my hand out of him, as it were, with a little thrill, and walking over to the dressing-table. "You pull yourself together," I said to him, "and try." And in order to encourage and help him I began to try as well.'

'What!' said Sanderson, 'the passes?'

'Yes, the passes.'

'But –' I said, moved by an idea that eluded me for a space.

'This is interesting,' said Sanderson, with his finger in his pipe-bowl. 'You mean to say this ghost of yours gave away –'

'Did his level best to give away the whole confounded barrier? Yes.'

'He didn't,' said Wish; 'he couldn't. Or you'd have gone there too.'

'That's precisely it,' I said, finding my elusive idea put into words for me.

'That *is* precisely it,' said Clayton, with thoughtful eyes upon the fire.

For just a little while there was silence.

'And at last he did it?' said Sanderson.

'At last he did it. I had to keep him up to it hard, but he did it at last – rather suddenly. He despaired, we had a scene, and then he got up abruptly and asked me to go through the whole performance, slowly, so that he might see. "I believe," he said, "if I could see I should spot what was wrong at once." And he did. "*I* know," he said. "What do you know?" said I. "*I* know," he repeated. Then he said peevishly, "I can't do it, if you look at me – I really *can't*; it's been that, partly, all along. I'm such a nervous fellow that you put me out." Well, we had a bit of an argument. Naturally I wanted to see; but he was as obstinate as a mule, and suddenly I had come over as tired as a dog – he tired me out. "All right," I said, "*I* won't look at you," and turned towards the mirror, on the wardrobe, by the bed.

'He started off very fast. I tried to follow him by looking in the looking-glass, to see just what it was had hung fire. Round went his arms and his hands, so, and so, and so, and then with a rush came to the last gesture of all – you stand erect and open out your arms – and so, don't you know, he stood. And then he didn't! He didn't! He wasn't! I wheeled round from the looking-glass to him. There was nothing! I was alone with the flaring candles and a staggering mind. What had happened? Had anything happened? Had I been dreaming? . . . And then, with an absurd note of finality about it, the clock upon the landing discovered the moment was ripe for striking *one*. So! – Ping! And I was as grave and sober as a judge, with all my champagne and whisky gone into the vast serene. Feeling queer, you know – confoundedly *queer*! Queer! Good Lord!'

He regarded his cigar-ash for a moment. 'That's all that happened,' he said.

'And then you went to bed?' asked Evans.

'What else was there to do?'

I looked Wish in the eye. We wanted to scoff, and there was something, something perhaps in Clayton's voice and manner, that hampered our desire.

'And about these passes?' said Sanderson.

'I believe I could do them now.'

'Oh!' said Sanderson, and produced a penknife and set himself to grub the dottle out of the bowl of his clay.

'Why don't you do them now?' said Sanderson, shutting his penknife with a click.

'That's what I'm going to do,' said Clayton.

'They won't work,' said Evans.

'If they do –' I suggested.

'You know, I'd rather you didn't,' said Wish, stretching out his legs.

'Why?' asked Evans.

'I'd rather he didn't,' said Wish.

'But he hasn't got 'em right,' said Sanderson, plugging too much tobacco into his pipe.

'All the same, I'd rather he didn't,' said Wish.

We argued with Wish. He said that for Clayton to go through those gestures was like mocking a serious matter. 'But you don't believe –?' I said. Wish glanced at Clayton, who was staring into the fire, weighing something in his mind. 'I do – more than half, anyhow, I do,' said Wish.

'Clayton,' said I, 'you're too good a liar for us. Most of it was all right. But that disappearance . . . happened to be convincing. Tell us, it's a tale of cock and bull.'

He stood up without heeding me, took the middle of the hearthrug, and faced me. For a moment he regarded his feet thoughtfully, and then for all the rest of the time his eyes were on the opposite wall, with an intent expression. He raised his two hands slowly to the level of his eyes and so began . . .

Now, Sanderson is a Freemason, a member of the lodge of the Four Kings, which devotes itself so ably to the study and elucidation of all the mysteries of Masonry past and present, and among the students of this lodge Sanderson is by no means the least. He followed Clayton's motions with a singular interest in his reddish eye. 'That's not bad,' he said, when it was done. 'You really do, you know, put things together, Clayton, in a most amazing fashion. But there's one little detail out.'

'I know,' said Clayton. 'I believe I could tell you which.'

'Well?'

'This,' said Clayton, and did a queer little twist and writhing and thrust of the hands.

'Yes.'

'That, you know, was what *he* couldn't get right,' said Clayton. 'But how do *you* –?'

'Most of this business, and particularly how you invented it, I don't understand at all,' said Sanderson, 'but just that phase – I do.' He reflected. 'These happen to be a series of gestures – connected with a certain branch of esoteric Masonry – Probably you know. Or else – *How?*' He reflected still further. 'I do not see I can do any harm in telling you just the proper twist. After all, if you know, you know; if you don't, you don't.'

'I know nothing,' said Clayton, 'except what the poor devil let out last night.'

'Well, anyhow,' said Sanderson, and placed his churchwarden very carefully upon the shelf over the fireplace. Then very rapidly he gesticulated with his hands.

'So?' said Clayton, repeating.

'So,' said Sanderson, and took his pipe in hand again.

'Ah, *now*,' said Clayton, 'I can do the whole thing – right.'

He stood up before the waning fire and smiled at us all. But I think there was just a little hesitation in his smile. 'If I begin –' he said.

'I wouldn't begin,' said Wish.

'It's all right!' said Evans. 'Matter is indestructible. You don't think any jiggery-pokery of this sort is going to snatch Clayton into the world of shades. Not it! You may try, Clayton, so far as I'm concerned, until your arms drop off at the wrists.'

'I don't believe that,' said Wish, and stood up and put his arm on Clayton's shoulder. 'You've made me half believe in that story somehow, and I don't want to see the thing done.'

'Goodness!' said I, 'here's Wish frightened!'

'I am,' said Wish, with real or admirably feigned intensity. 'I believe that if he goes through these motions right he'll *go*.'

'He'll not do anything of the sort,' I cried. 'There's only one way out of this world for men, and Clayton is thirty years from that. Besides . . . And such a ghost! Do you think –?'

Wish interrupted me by moving. He walked out from among our chairs and stopped beside the table and stood there. 'Clayton,' he said, 'you're a fool.'

Clayton, with a humorous light in his eyes, smiled back at him. 'Wish,' he said, 'is right, and all you others are wrong. I shall go. I shall get to the end of these passes, and as the last swish whistles through the air, Presto! – this hearthrug will be vacant, the room will be blank amazement, and a respectably-dressed gentleman of fifteen stone will plump into the world of shades. I'm certain. So will you be. I decline to argue further. Let the thing be tried.'

'No,' said Wish, and made a step and ceased, and Clayton raised his hands once more to repeat the spirit's passing.

By that time, you know, we were all in a state of tension – largely because of the behaviour of Wish. We sat all of us with our eyes on Clayton – I, at least, with a sort of tight, stiff feeling about me as though from the back of my skull to the middle of my thighs my body had been changed to steel. And there, with a gravity that was imperturbably serene, Clayton bowed and swayed and waved his hands and arms before us. As he drew towards the end one piled up, one tingled in one's teeth. The last gesture, I have said, was to swing the arms out wide open, with the face held up. And when, at last, he swung out to this closing gesture I ceased even to breathe. It was ridiculous, of course, but you know that ghost-story feeling. It was after dinner in a queer, old, shadowy house. Would he, after all –?

There he stood for one stupendous moment, with his arms open and his upturned face, assured and bright, in the glare of the hanging lamp. We hung through that moment as if it were an age, and then came from all of us something that was half a sigh of infinite relief and half a reassuring 'No!' For visibly – he wasn't going. It was all nonsense. He had told an idle story, and carried it almost to conviction, that was all! . . . And then in that moment the face of Clayton changed.

It changed. It changed as a lit house changes when its lights are suddenly extinguished. His eyes were suddenly eyes that were fixed, his smile was frozen on his lips, and he stood there still. He stood there, very gently swaying.

That moment, too, was an age. And then, you know, chairs were scraping, things were falling, and we were all moving. His knees seemed to give, and he fell forward, and Evans rose and caught him in his arms . . .

It stunned us all. For a minute I suppose no one said a coherent thing. We believed it, yet could not believe it . . . I came out of a muddled stupefaction to find myself kneeling beside him, and his vest and shirt were torn open, and Sanderson's hand lay on his heart . . .

Well – the simple fact before us could very well wait our convenience; there was no hurry for us to comprehend. It lay there for an hour; it lies athwart my memory, black and amazing still, to this day. Clayton had, indeed, passed into the world that lies so near to and so far from our own, and he had gone thither by the only road that mortal man may take. But whether he did indeed pass there by that poor ghost's incantation, or whether he was stricken suddenly by apoplexy in the midst of an idle tale – as the coroner's jury would have us believe – is no matter for my judging; it is just one of those inexplicable riddles that must remain unsolved until the final solution of all things shall come. All I certainly know is that, in the very moment, in the very instant, of concluding those passes, he changed, and staggered, and fell down before us – dead!

The Room in the Tower

E. F. Benson

It is probable that everybody who is at all a constant dreamer has had at least one experience of an event or a sequence of circumstances which have come to his mind in sleep being subsequently realized in the material world. But, in my opinion, so far from this being a strange thing, it would be far odder if this fulfilment did not occasionally happen, since our dreams are, as a rule, concerned with people whom we know and places with which we are familiar, such as might very naturally occur in the awake and daylit world. True, these dreams are often broken into by some absurd and fantastic incident, which puts them out of court in regard to their subsequent fulfilment, but on the mere calculation of chances, it does not appear in the least unlikely that a dream imagined by anyone who dreams constantly should occasionally come true. Not long ago, for instance, I experienced such a fulfilment of a dream which seems to me in no way remarkable and to have no kind of psychical significance. The manner of it was as follows.

A certain friend of mine, living abroad, is amiable enough to write to me about once in a fortnight. Thus, when fourteen days or thereabout have elapsed since I last heard from him, my mind, probably, either consciously or subconsciously, is expectant of a letter from him. One night last week I dreamed that as I was going upstairs to dress for dinner I heard, as I often heard, the sound of the postman's knock on my front door, and diverted my direction downstairs instead. There, among other correspondence, was a letter from him. Thereafter the fantastic entered, for on opening it I found inside the ace of diamonds, and scribbled across it in his well-known handwriting, 'I am sending you this for safe custody, as you know it is running an unreasonable risk to keep aces in Italy.' The next evening I was just preparing to go upstairs to dress when I heard the postman's knock, and did precisely as I had done in my dream. There, among other letters, was one from my friend. Only it did not contain the ace of diamonds. Had it done so, I should have attached more weight to the matter, which, as it stands, seems to me a perfectly ordinary coincidence. No doubt I consciously or subconsciously expected a letter from him, and this suggested to me my dream. Similarly, the fact that my friend had not written to me for a fortnight suggested to him that he should do so. But occasionally it is not so easy to find such an explanation, and for the following story I can find no explanation at all. It came out of the dark, and into the dark it has gone again.

All my life I have been a habitual dreamer: the nights are few, that is to say, when I do not find on awaking in the morning that some mental experience has been mine, and sometimes, all night long, apparently, a series of the most dazzling adventures befall me. Almost without exception these adventures are pleasant, though often merely trivial. It is of an exception that I am going to speak.

It was when I was about sixteen that a certain dream first came to me, and this is how it befell. It opened with my being set down at the door of a big red-brick house, where, I understood, I was going to stay. The servant who opened the door told me that tea was going on in the garden, and led me through a low dark-panelled hall, with a large open fireplace, on to a cheerful green lawn set round with flower beds. There were grouped about the tea-table a small party of people, but they were all strangers to me except one, who was a school-fellow called Jack Stone, clearly the son of the house, and he introduced me to his mother and father and a couple of sisters. I was, I remember, somewhat astonished to find myself here, for the boy in question was scarcely known to me, and I rather disliked what I knew of him: moreover, he had left school nearly a year before. The afternoon was very hot, and an intolerable oppression reigned. On the far side of the lawn ran a red-brick wall, with an iron gate in its centre, outside which stood a walnut-tree. We sat in the shadow of the house opposite a row of long windows, inside which I could see a table with cloth laid, glimmering with glass and silver. This garden front of the house was very long, and at one end of it stood a tower of three storeys, which looked to me much older than the rest of the building.

Before long, Mrs Stone, who, like the rest of the party, had sat in absolute silence, said to me, 'Jack will show you your room: I have given you the room in the tower.'

Quite inexplicably my heart sank at her words. I felt as if I had known that I should have the room in the tower, and that it contained something dreadful and significant. Jack instantly got up, and I understood that I had to follow him. In silence we passed through the hall, and mounted a great oak staircase with many corners, and arrived at a small landing with two doors set in it. He pushed one of these open for me to enter, and without coming in himself, closed it behind me. Then I knew that my conjecture had been right: there was something awful in the room, and with the terror of nightmare growing swiftly and enveloping me, I awoke in a spasm of terror.

Now that dream or variations on it occurred to me intermittently for fifteen years. Most often it came in exactly this form, the arrival, the tea out on the lawn, the deadly silence succeeded by that one deadly sentence, the mounting with Jack Stone up to the room in the tower where horror dwelt, and it always came to a close in the nightmare of terror at that which was in the room, though I never saw what it was. At other times I experienced variations on this same theme. Occasionally, for instance, we would be sitting at dinner in the dining-room, into the windows of which I had looked on the first night when the dream of this house visited me, but wherever we were, there was the same silence, the same sense of dreadful oppression and foreboding. And the silence I knew would always be broken by Mrs Stone saying to me, 'Jack will show you your room: I have given you the room in the tower.' Upon which (this was invariable) I had to follow him up the oak staircase with many corners, and enter the place that I dreaded more and more each time that I visited it in sleep. Or, again, I would find myself playing cards still in silence in a drawing-room lit with immense chandeliers, that gave a blinding illumination. What the game was I have no idea; what I remember, with a sense of miserable anticipation, was that soon Mrs Stone would get up and say to me, 'Jack will show you your room: I have given you the room in the tower.' This drawing-room where we played cards was next to the dining-room, and, as I have said, was always brilliantly illuminated, whereas the rest of the house was full of dusk and shadows. And yet, how often, in spite of those bouquets of lights, have I not pored over the cards that were dealt to me, scarcely able for some reason to see them. Their designs, too, were strange: there were no red suits, but all were black, and among them there were certain cards which were black all over. I hated and dreaded those.

As this dream continued to recur, I got to know the greater part of the house. There was a smoking-room beyond the drawing-room, at the end of a passage with a green baize door. It was always very dark there, and as often as I went there I passed somebody whom I could not see in the doorway coming out. Curious developments, too, took place in the characters that peopled the dream as might happen to living persons. Mrs Stone, for instance, who, when I first saw her, had been black haired, became grey, and instead of rising briskly, as she had done at first when she said, 'Jack will show you your room: I have given you the room in the tower,' got up very feebly, as if the strength was leaving her limbs. Jack also grew up, and became a rather ill-looking young man, with a brown moustache, while one of the sisters ceased to appear, and I understood she was married.

Then it so happened that I was not visited by this dream for six months or more, and I began to hope, in such inexplicable dread did I hold it, that it had passed away for good. But one night after this interval I again found myself being shown out on to the lawn for tea, and Mrs Stone was not there, while the others were all dressed in black. At once I guessed the reason, and my heart leaped at the thought that perhaps this time I should not have to sleep in the room in the tower, and though we usually all sat in silence, on this occasion the sense of relief made me talk and laugh as I had never yet done. But even then matters were not altogether comfortable, for no one else spoke, but they all looked secretly at each other. And soon the foolish stream of my talk ran dry, and gradually an apprehension worse than anything I had previously known gained on me as the light slowly faded.

Suddenly a voice which I knew well broke the stillness, the voice of Mrs Stone, saying, 'Jack will show you your room: I have given you the room in the tower.' It seemed to come from near the gate in the red-brick wall that bounded the lawn, and looking up, I saw that the grass outside was sown thick with gravestones. A curious greyish light shone from them, and I could read the lettering on the grave nearest me, and it was, 'In evil memory of Julia Stone.' And as usual Jack got up, and again I followed him through the hall and up the staircase with many corners. On this occasion it was darker than usual, and when I passed into the room in the tower I could only just see the furniture, the position of which was already familiar to me. Also there was a dreadful odour of decay in the room, and I woke screaming.

The dream, with such variations and developments as I have mentioned, went on at intervals for fifteen years. Sometimes I would dream it two or three nights in succession; once, as I have said, there was an intermission of six months, but taking a reasonable average, I should say that I dreamed it quite as often as once in a month. It had, as is plain, something of nightmare about it, since it always ended in the same appalling terror, which so far from getting less, seemed to me to gather fresh fear every time that I experienced it. There was, too, a strange and dreadful consistency about it. The characters in it, as I have mentioned, got regularly older, death and marriage visited this silent family, and I never in the dream, after Mrs Stone had died, set eyes on her again. But it was always her voice that told me that the room in the tower was prepared for me, and whether we had tea out on the lawn, or the scene was laid in one of the rooms overlooking it, I could always see her gravestone standing just outside the iron gate. It was the same, too, with the married daughter; usually she was not present, but once or twice she returned again, in company with a man, whom I took to be her husband. He, too, like the rest of them, was always silent. But, owing to the constant repetition of the dream, I had ceased to attach, in my waking hours, any significance to it. I never met Jack Stone again during all those years, nor did I ever see a house that resembled this dark house of my dream. And then something happened.

I had been in London in this year, up till the end of July, and during the first week in August went down to stay with a friend in a house he had taken for the summer months, in the Ashdown Forest district of Sussex. I left London early, for John Clinton was to meet me at Forest Row Station, and we were going to spend the day golfing, and go to his house in the evening. He had his motor with him, and we set off, about five in the afternoon, after a thoroughly delightful day, for the drive, the distance being some ten miles. As it was still so early we did not have tea at the clubhouse, but waited till we should get home. As we drove, the weather, which up till then had been, though hot, deliciously fresh, seemed to me to alter in quality, and become very stagnant and oppressive, and I felt that indefinable sense of ominous apprehension that I am accustomed to before thunder. John, however, did not share my views, attributing my loss of lightness to the fact that I had lost both my matches. Events proved, however, that I was right, though I do not think that the thunderstorm that broke that night was the sole cause of my depression.

Our way lay through deep high-banked lanes, and before we had gone very far I fell asleep, and was only awakened by the stopping of the motor. And with a sudden thrill, partly of fear but chiefly of curiosity, I found myself standing in the doorway of my house of dream. We went, I half wondering whether or not I was dreaming still, through a low oak-panelled hall, and out on to the lawn, where tea was laid in the shadow of the house. It was set in flower beds, a red-brick wall, with a gate in it, bounded one side, and out beyond that was a space of rough grass with a walnut-tree. The façade of the house was very long, and at one end stood a three-storied tower, markedly older than the rest.

Here for the moment all resemblance to the repeated dream ceased. There was no silent and somehow terrible family, but a large assembly of exceedingly cheerful persons, all of whom were known to me. And in spite of the horror with which the dream itself had always filled me, I felt nothing of it now that the scene of it was thus reproduced before me. But I felt the intensest curiosity as to what was going to happen.

Tea pursued its cheerful course, and before long Mrs Clinton got up. And at that moment I think I knew what she was going to say. She spoke to me, and what she said was:

'Jack will show you your room: I have given you the room in the tower.'

At that, for half a second, the horror of the dream took hold of me again. But it quickly passed, and again I felt nothing more than the most intense curiosity. It was not very long before it was amply satisfied.

John turned to me.

'Right up at the top of the house,' he said, 'but I think you'll be comfortable. We're absolutely full up. Would you like to go and see it now? By Jove, I believe that you are right, and that we are going to have a thunderstorm. How dark it has become.'

I got up and followed him. We passed through the hall, and up the perfectly familiar staircase. Then he opened the door, and I went in. And at that moment sheer unreasoning terror again possessed me. I did not know for certain what I feared: I simply feared. Then like a sudden recollection, when one remembers a name which has long escaped the memory, I knew what I feared. I feared Mrs Stone, whose grave with the sinister inscription, 'In evil memory', I had so often seen in my dream, just beyond the lawn which lay below my window. And then once more the fear passed so completely that I wondered what there was to fear, and I found myself, sober and quiet and sane, in the room in the tower, the name of which I had so often heard in my dream, and the scene of which was so familiar.

I looked round it with a certain sense of proprietorship, and found that nothing had been changed from the dreaming nights in which I knew it so well. Just to the left of the door was the bed, lengthways along the wall, with the head of it in the angle. In a line with it was the fireplace and a small bookcase; opposite the door the outer wall was pierced by two lattice-paned windows, between which stood the dressing-table, while ranged along the fourth wall was the washing-stand and a big cupboard.

My luggage had already been unpacked, for the furniture of dressing and undressing lay orderly on the washstand and toilet-table, while my dinner clothes were spread out on the coverlet of the bed. And then, with a sudden start of unexplained dismay, I saw that there were two rather conspicuous objects which I had not seen before in my dreams: one a life-sized oil-painting of Mrs Stone, the other a black-and-white sketch of Jack Stone, representing him as he had appeared to me only a week before in the last of the series of these repeated dreams, a rather secret and evil-looking man of about thirty. His picture hung between the windows, looking straight across the room to the other portrait, which hung at the side of the bed. At that I looked next, and as I looked I felt once more the horror of nightmare seize me.

It represented Mrs Stone as I had seen her last in my dreams: old and withered and white haired. But in spite of the evident feebleness of body, a dreadful exuberance and vitality shone through the envelope of flesh, an exuberance wholly malign, a vitality that foamed and frothed with unimaginable evil. Evil beamed from the narrow, leering eyes; it laughed in the demon-like mouth. The whole face was instinct with some secret and appalling mirth; the hands, clasped together on the knee, seemed shaking with suppressed and nameless glee. Then I saw also that it was signed in the left-hand bottom corner, and wondering who the artist could be, I looked more closely, and read the inscription, 'Julia Stone by Julia Stone'.

There came a tap at the door, and John Clinton entered.

'Got everything you want?' he asked.

'Rather more than I want,' said I, pointing to the picture.

He laughed.

'Hard-featured old lady,' he said. 'By herself, too, I remember. Anyhow she can't have flattered herself much.'

'But don't you see?' said I. 'It's scarcely a human face at all. It's the face of some witch, of some devil.'

He looked at it more closely.

'Yes; it isn't very pleasant,' he said. 'Scarcely a bedside manner, eh? Yes; I can imagine getting the nightmare, if I went to sleep with that close by my bed. I'll have it taken down if you like.'

'I really wish you would,' I said.

He rang the bell, and with the help of a servant we detached the picture and carried it out on to the landing, and put it with its face to the wall.

'By Jove, the old lady is a weight,' said John, mopping his forehead. 'I wonder if she had something on her mind.'

The extraordinary weight of the picture had struck me too. I was about to reply, when I caught sight of my own hand. There was blood on it, in considerable quantities, covering the whole palm.

'I've cut myself somehow,' said I.

John gave a little startled exclamation.

'Why, I have too,' he said.

Simultaneously the footman took out his handkerchief and wiped his hand with it. I saw that there was blood also on his handkerchief.

John and I went back into the tower room and washed the blood off; but neither on his hand nor on mine was there the slightest trace of a scratch or cut. It seemed to me that, having ascertained this, we both, by a sort of tacit consent, did not allude to it again. Something in my case had dimly occurred to me that I did not wish to think about. It was but a conjecture, but I fancied that I knew the same thing had occurred to him.

The heat and oppression of the air, for the storm we had expected was still undischarged, increased very much after dinner, and for some time most of the party, among whom were John Clinton and myself, sat outside on the path bounding the lawn, where we had had tea. The night was absolutely dark, and no twinkle of star or moon ray could penetrate the pall of cloud that overset the sky. By degrees our assembly thinned, the women went up to bed, men dispersed to the smoking- or billiard-room, and by eleven o'clock my host and I were the only two left. All the evening I thought that he had something on his mind, and as soon as we were alone he spoke.

'The man who helped us with the picture had blood on his hand, too, did you notice?' he said. 'I asked him just now if he had cut himself, and he said he supposed he had, but that he could find no mark of it. Now where did that blood come from?'

By dint of telling myself that I was not going to think about it, I had succeeded in not doing so, and I did not want, especially just at bedtime, to be reminded of it.

'I don't know,' said I, 'and I don't really care so long as the picture of Mrs Julia Stone is not by my bed.'

He got up.

'But it's odd,' he said. 'Ha! Now you'll see another odd thing.'

A dog of his, an Irish terrier by breed, had come out of the house as we talked. The door behind us into the hall was open, and a bright oblong of light shone across the lawn to the iron gate which led on to the rough grass outside, where the walnut-tree stood. I saw that the dog had all his hackles up, bristling with rage and fright; his lips were curled back from his teeth, as if he was ready to spring at something, and he was growling to himself. He took not the slightest notice of his master or me, but stiffly and tensely walked across the grass to the iron gate. There he stood for a moment, looking through the bars and still growling. Then of a sudden his courage seemed to desert him: he gave one long howl, and scuttled back to the house with a curious crouching sort of movement.

'He does that half a dozen times a day,' said John. 'He sees something which he both hates and fears.'

I walked to the gate and looked over it. Something was moving on the grass outside, and soon a sound which I could not instantly identify came to my ears. Then I remembered what it was: it was the purring of a cat. I lit a match, and saw the purrer, a big blue Persian, walking round and round in a little circle just outside the gate, stepping high and ecstatically, with tail carried aloft like a banner. Its eyes were bright and shining, and every now and then it put its head down and sniffed at the grass.

I laughed.

'The end of that mystery, I am afraid,' I said. 'Here's a large cat having Walpurgis night all alone.'

'Yes, that's Darius,' said John. 'He spends half the day and all night there. But that's not the end of the dog mystery, for Toby and he are the best of friends, but the beginning of the cat mystery. What's the cat doing there? And why is Darius pleased, while Toby is terror-stricken?'

At that moment I remembered the rather horrible details of my dreams when I saw through the gate, just where the cat was now, the white tombstone with the sinister inscription. But before I could answer the rain began, as suddenly and heavily as if a tap had been turned on, and simultaneously the big cat squeezed through the bars of the gate, and came leaping across the lawn to the house for shelter. Then it sat in the doorway, looking out eagerly into the dark. It spat and struck at John with its paw, as he pushed it in, in order to close the door.

Somehow, with the portrait of Julia Stone in the passage outside, the room in the tower had absolutely no alarm for me, and as I went to bed, feeling very sleepy and heavy, I had nothing more than interest for the curious incident about our bleeding hands, and the conduct of the cat and dog. The last thing I looked at before I put out my light was the square empty space by my bed where the portrait had been. Here the paper was of its original full tint of dark red: over the rest of the walls it had faded. Then I blew out my candle and instantly fell asleep.

My awakening was equally instantaneous, and I sat bolt upright in bed under the impression that some bright light had been flashed in my face, though it was now absolutely pitch dark. I knew exactly where I was, in the room which I had dreaded in dreams, but no horror that I ever felt when asleep approached the fear that now invaded and froze my brain. Immediately after a peal of thunder crackled just above the house, but the probability that it was only a flash of lightning which awoke me gave no reassurance to my galloping heart. Something I knew was in the room with me, and instinctively I put out my right hand, which was nearest the wall, to keep it away. And my hand touched the edge of a picture-frame hanging close to me.

I sprang out of bed, upsetting the small table that stood by it, and I heard my watch, candle, and matches clatter on to the floor. But for the moment there was no need of light, for a blinding flash leaped out of the clouds, and showed me that by my bed again hung the picture of Mrs Stone. And instantly the room went into blackness again. But in that flash I saw another thing also, namely a figure that leaned over the end of my bed, watching me. It was dressed in some close-clinging white garment, spotted and stained with mould, and the face was that of the portrait.

Overhead the thunder cracked and roared, and when it ceased and the deathly stillness succeeded, I heard the rustle of movement coming nearer me, and, more horrible yet, perceived an odour of corruption and decay. And then a hand was laid on the side of my neck, and close beside my ear I heard quick-taken, eager breathing. Yet I knew that this thing, though it could be perceived by touch, by smell, by eye and by ear, was still not of this earth, but something that had passed out of the body and had power to make itself manifest. Then a voice, already familiar to me, spoke.

'I knew you would come to the room in the tower,' it said. 'I have been long waiting for you. At last you have come. Tonight I shall feast; before long we will feast together.'

And the quick breathing came closer to me; I could feel it on my neck.

At that the terror, which I think had paralysed me for the moment, gave way to the wild instinct of self-preservation. I hit wildly with both arms, kicking out at the same moment, and heard a little animal-squeal, and something soft dropped with a thud beside me. I took a couple of steps forward, nearly tripping up over whatever it was that lay there, and by the merest good luck found the handle of the door. In another second I ran out on the landing, and had banged the door behind me. Almost at the same moment I heard a door open somewhere below, and John Clinton, candle in hand, came running upstairs.

'What is it?' he said. 'I sleep just below you, and heard a noise as if – Good heavens, there's blood on your shoulder.'

I stood there, so he told me afterwards, swaying from side to side, white as a sheet, with the mark on my shoulder as if a hand covered with blood had been laid there.

'It's in there,' I said, pointing. 'She, you know. The portrait is in there, too, hanging up on the place we took it from.'

At that he laughed.

'My dear fellow, this is mere nightmare,' he said.

He pushed by me, and opened the door, I standing there simply inert with terror, unable to stop him, unable to move.

'Phew! What an awful smell,' he said.

Then there was silence; he had passed out of my sight behind the open door. Next moment he came out again, as white as myself, and instantly shut it.

'Yes, the portrait's there,' he said, 'and on the floor is a thing – a thing spotted with earth, like what they bury people in. Come away, quick, come away.'

How I got downstairs I hardly know. An awful shuddering and nausea of the spirit rather than of the flesh had seized me, and more than once he had to place my feet upon the steps, while every now and then he cast glances of terror and apprehension up the stairs. But in time we came to his dressing-room on the floor below, and there I told him what I have here described.

The sequel can be made short; indeed, some of my readers have perhaps already guessed what it was, if they remember that inexplicable affair of the churchyard at West Fawley, some eight years ago, where an attempt was made three times to bury the body of a certain woman who had committed suicide. On each occasion the coffin was found in the course of a few days again protruding from the ground. After the third attempt, in order that the thing should not be talked about, the body was buried elsewhere in unconsecrated ground. Where it was buried was just outside the iron gate of the garden belonging to the house where this woman had lived. She had committed suicide in a room at the top of the tower in that house. Her name was Julia Stone.

Subsequently the body was again secretly dug up, and the coffin was found to be full of blood.

One Who Saw

A. M. Burrage

There are certain people, often well enough liked, genial souls whom one is always glad to meet, who yet have the faculty of disappearing without being missed. Crutchley must have been one of them. It wasn't until his name was casually mentioned that evening at the Storgates' that most of us remembered that we hadn't seen him about for the last year or two. It was Mrs Storgate's effort at remembering, with the help of those nearest her at table, the guests at a certain birthday party of four years since that was the cause of Crutchley's name being mentioned. And no sooner had it been mentioned than we were all laughing, because most of us had asked one another in the same breath what had become of him.

It was Jack Price who was able to supply the information.

'For the last year or two,' he said, 'he's been living very quietly with his people in Norfolk. I heard from him only the other day.'

Mrs Storgate was interested.

'I wonder why he's chosen to efface himself,' she asked of nobody in particular. 'He was rather a lamb in his way. I used to adore that shiny black hair of his which always made me think of patent leather. I believe he owed half his invitations to his hair. I told him once that he dined out on it four nights a week.'

'It's as white as the ceiling now,' Price remarked.

Having spoken he seemed to regret it, and Mrs Storgate exclaimed:

'Oh, no! We're speaking of *Simon* Crutchley.'

'I mean Simon,' said Price unwillingly.

There was a faint stir of consternation, and then a woman's voice rose above the rustle and murmur.

'Oh, but it seems impossible. That sleek, blue-black hair of his! And he can't be more than thirty-five.'

Somebody said that he'd heard of people's hair going suddenly white like that after an illness. Price was asked if Simon Crutchley had been ill. The answer was Yes. A nervous breakdown? Well, it was something very like that.

A lady who turned night into day all the year round and was suspected of drinking at least as much as was good for her, sighed, and remarked that everybody nowadays suffered from nerves. Mrs Storgate said that Simon Crutchley's breakdown and the change in his appearance doubtless accounted for his having dropped out and hidden himself away in Norfolk. And then another conversational hare was started.

Instead of joining in the hunt I found myself in a brown study, playing with breadcrumbs. I had rather liked Crutchley, although he wasn't exactly one of my own kind. He was one of those quiet fellows who are said colloquially to require a lot of knowing. In social life he had always been a detached figure, standing a little aloof from his fellow-men and seeming to study them with an air of faint and inoffensive cynicism. He was a writing man, which may have accounted for his slight mannerisms, but he didn't belong to the precious, superior and rather detestable school. Everybody agreed that he was quite a good scout, and nobody troubled to read his books, which consisted mainly of historical essays.

I tried to imagine Simon Crutchley with white hair, and then I caught myself speculating on the cause of his illness or 'breakdown'. He was the last sort of fellow whom one would have expected to be knocked to pieces like that. So far from indulging in excesses he had always been something of an aesthete. He had a comfortable private income and he certainly didn't overwork. Indeed I remembered his once telling me that he took a comfortable two years over a book.

It would be hard for me to say now whether it was by accident or design that I left at the same time as Price. Our ways lay in the same direction, and while we were lingering in the hall, waiting for our hats and coats, we agreed to share a taxi. I lived in the Temple, he in John Street, Adelphi. 'I'll tell the man to drive down Villiers Street,' I said, 'and up into the Strand again by the Tivoli, and I can drop you on the way.'

In the taxi we talked about Crutchley. I began it, and I asked leading questions. Price, you see, was the only man who seemed to have heard anything of him lately, and he was now sufficiently evasive to pique my curiosity.

'It's a queer and rather terrible story,' he said at last. 'There's no secret about it, at least I'm not pledged in any way, but I don't think poor old Simon would have liked me to tell it publicly over the dinner-table. For one thing, nobody would believe it, and, for another, it's rather long. Besides, he didn't tell me quite all. There's one bit he couldn't – or wouldn't – tell. There was just one bit he couldn't bring himself to describe to me, and I don't suppose he'll ever manage to describe it to anybody, so nobody but himself will ever have an idea of the actual *sight* which sent him off his head for six months and turned his hair as white as a tablecloth.'

'Oh,' said I, 'then it was all through something he *saw*?'

Price nodded.

'So he says. I admit it's a pretty incredible sort of story – yet somehow Simon Crutchley isn't the sort to imagine things. And after all, something obviously did happen to him. I'll tell you his story if you like. The night's young. Come into my place and have a drink, if you will.'

I thanked him and said that I would. He turned towards me and let a hand fall on my knee.

'Mind you,' he said, 'this is Crutchley's own story. If you don't believe it I don't want you to go about thinking that I'm a liar. I'm not reponsible for the truth of it; I'm only just passing it on. In a way I hope it isn't true. It isn't comfortable to think that such things may happen – *do* happen.'

Twenty minutes later, when we were sitting in the snug little library in Price's flat he told me his story, or, rather, Crutchley's. This is it.

You know the sort of work Crutchley used to do? If you don't, you at least know Stevenson's 'Memories and Portraits', and Crutchley worked with that sort of material. His study of Margaret of Anjou, by the way, is considered a classic in certain highbrow circles.

You will remember that Joan of Arc was very much in the air two or three years back. It was before Bernard Shaw's play was produced, but her recent canonization had just reminded the world that she was perhaps the greatest woman in history. It may have been this revival of interest in her which decided Crutchley to make her the subject of one of his historical portraits. He'd already treated Villon and Abelard and Heloise, and as soon as he'd decided on St Joan he went over to France to work, so to say, on the spot.

Crutchley always did his job conscientiously, using his own deductive faculties only for bridging the gaps in straight history. He went first to Domrémy, where the Maid was born, followed the old trail of that fifteenth-century campaign across France, and of course his journey ended inevitably at Rouen, where English spite and French cowardice burned her in the market-place.

I don't know if you know Rouen? Tourists don't stay there very much. They visit, but they don't stay. They come and hurry round the cathedral, gape at the statue of Joan of Arc in the Place de la Pucelle, throw a victorious smile at Napoleon Buonaparte galloping his bronze horse on a pedestal in the square, and rush on to Paris or back to one of the Channel ports. Rouen being half-way between Paris and the coast the typical English tourist finds that he can 'do' the place without sleeping in it.

Crutchley liked Rouen. It suited him. It is much more sober and austere than most of the French towns. It goes to bed early, and you don't have sex flaunted before you wherever you look. You find there an atmosphere like that of our own cathedral cities, and there is a great deal more to see than ever the one-day tourist imagines. Crutchley decided to stay on in the town and finish there his paper on Joan of Arc.

He found an hotel practically undiscovered by English and Americans – l'Hôtel d'Avignon. It stands half-way down one of those narrow old-world streets, quite near the Gare de la Rue Jeanne d'Arc. A single tramline runs through the narrow street in front of its unpretentious façade, and to enter you must pass a narrow archway, and through a winter garden littered with tables and chairs to a somewhat impressive main entrance with statuary on either side of the great glass-panelled doors.

Crutchley found the place by accident on his first day and took *déjeuner* in the great tapestried *salle à manger*. The food was good, and he found that the chef had a gift for Sole Normande. Out of curiosity he asked to see some of the bedrooms.

It was a hotel where many ate but few slept. At that time of the year many rooms were vacant on the first floor. He followed a chambermaid up the first flight of stairs and looked out through a door which he found open at the top. To his surprise he found that it gave entrance to a garden on the same level. The hotel, parts of which were hundreds of years old, had been built on the face of a steep hill, and the little garden thus stood a storey above the level of the street in front.

This garden was sunk deep in a hollow square, with the walls of the hotel rising high all around it. Three rows of shuttered windows looked out upon an open space which never saw the sun. For that obvious reason there had been no attempt to grow flowers, but one or two ferns had sprung up and a few small tenacious plants had attached themselves to a rockery. The soil was covered with loose gravel, and in the middle there grew a great plane tree which thrust its crest above the roof-tops so that, as seen by the birds, it must have looked as if it were growing in a great lidless box. To imagine the complete quietude of the spot one has only to remember how an enclosed square in one of the Inns of Court shuts out the noise of traffic from some of the busiest streets in the world. It did not occur to Crutchley that there may be something unhealthy about an open space shut out entirely from the sun. Some decrepit garden seats were ranged around the borders, and the plane tree hid most of the sky, sheltering the little enclosure like a great umbrella. Crutchley told me that he mistook silence and deathly stillness for peace, and decided that here was the very spot for him to write his version of the story of Jeanne d'Arc.

He took a bedroom on the same level, whose high, shuttered windows looked out on to the still garden square; and next day he took a writing-pad and a fountain-pen to one of the faded green seats and tried to start work.

From what he told me it wasn't a very successful attempt. The unnatural silence of the place bred in him an indefinable restlessness. It seemed to him that he sat more in twilight than in shade. He knew that a fresh wind was blowing, but it won not the least responsive whisper from the garden. The ferns might have been water-plants in an aquarium, so still they were. Sunlight, which burnished the blue sky, struck through the leaves of the plane tree, but it painted only the top of one of the walls high above his head. Crutchley frankly admitted that the place got on his nerves, and that it was a relief to go out and hear the friendly noise of the trams, and see the people drinking outside cafés and the little boys fishing for roach among the barges on the banks of the Seine.

He made several attempts to work in the garden, but they were all fruitless, and he took to working in his bedroom. He confessed to me that, even in the afternoon, he felt that there was something uncanny about the place. There's nothing in that. Many people would have felt the same; and Crutchley, although he had no definite belief in the supernatural, had had one or two minor experiences in his lifetime – too trifling, he said, to be worth recording – but teasing enough in their way, and of great interest to himself. Yet he had always smiled politely when ardent spiritualists had told him that he was 'susceptible'. He began by feeling vaguely that there was something 'wrong', in the psychical sense, with the garden. It was like a faint, unseizable, but disagreeable odour. He told me that he did not let it trouble him greatly. He wanted to work, and when he found that 'it' would not let him work in the garden, he removed himself and his writing materials to his room.

Crutchley had been five days at the hotel when something strange happened. It was his custom to undress in the dark, because his windows were overlooked by a dozen others and, by first of all turning off the light, he was saved from drawing the great shutters. That night he was smoking while he undressed, and when he was in his pyjamas he went to one of the open windows to throw out the stub of his cigarette. Having done so he lingered, looking out.

The usual unnatural stillness brooded over the garden square, intensified now by the spell of the night. Somewhere in the sky the moon was shining, and a few stray silver beams dappled the top of the north wall. The plane tree stood like a living thing entranced. Not one of its lower branches stirred, and its leaves might have been carved out of jade. Just enough light filtered from the sky to make the features of the garden faintly visible. Crutchley looked where his cigarette had fallen and now lay like a glow-worm, and raised his eyes to one of the long green decrepit seats. With a faint unreasonable thrill and a cold tingling of the nostrils he realized that somebody was sitting there.

As his eyes grew more used to the darkness the huddled form took the shape of a woman. She sat with her head turned away, one arm thrown along the sloping back of the seat, and her face resting against it. He said that her attitude was one of extreme dejection, of abject and complete despair.

Crutchley, you must understand, couldn't see her at all clearly, although she was not a dozen yards distant. Her dress was dark, but he could make out none of its details save that something like a flimsy scarf or thick veil trailed over the shoulder nearest him. He stood watching her, pricked by a vague sense of pity and conscious that, if she looked up, he would hardly be visible to her beyond the window, and that, in any event, the still glowing stub of cigarette would explain his presence.

But she did not look up, she did not move at all while Crutchley stood watching. So still she was that it was hard for him to realize that she breathed. She seemed to have fallen completely under the spell of the garden in which nothing ever stirred, and the scene before Crutchley's eyes might have been a nocturnal picture painted in oils.

Of course he made a guess or two about her. At the sight of anything unusual one's subconscious mind immediately begins to speculate and to suggest theories. Here, thought Crutchley, was a woman with some great sorrow, who, before retiring to her room had come to sit in this quiet garden, and there, under the stars, had given way to her despair.

I don't know how long Crutchley stood there, but probably it wasn't for many seconds. Thought is swift and time is slow when one stands still watching a motionless scene. He owned that his curiosity was deeply intrigued, and it was intrigued in a somewhat unusual way. He found himself desiring less to know the reason of her despair than to see her face. He had a definite and urgent temptation to go out and look at her, to use force if necessary in turning her face so that he might look into her eyes.

If you knew Crutchley at all well you must know that he was something more than ordinarily conventional. He concerned himself not only with what a gentleman ought to do but with what a gentleman ought to think. Thus when he came to realize that he was not only spying upon a strange woman's grief, but actually feeling tempted to force himself upon her and stare into eyes which he guessed were blinded by tears, it was sufficient to tear him away from the window and send him padding across the floor to the high bed at the far end of the room.

But he made no effort to sleep. He lay listening, waiting for a sound from the other side of those windows. In that silence he knew he must hear the least sound outside. But for ten minutes he listened in vain, picturing to himself the woman still rigid in the same posture of despair.

Presently he could bear it no longer. He jumped out of bed and went once more to the window. He told himself that it was human pity which drove him there. He walked heavily on his bare feet and he coughed. He made as much noise as he was reasonably able to make, hoping that she would hear and bestir herself. But when he reached the open window and looked out the seat was empty.

Crutchley stared at the empty seat, not quite crediting the evidence of his eyes. You see, according to his account, she couldn't have touched that loose gravel with her foot without making a distinct sound and to re-enter the hotel she must have opened a door with creaking hinges and a noisy latch. Yet he had heard nothing, and the garden was empty. Next morning he even tried the experiment of walking on tiptoe across the garden to see if it could be done in utter silence, and he was satisfied that it could not. Even an old grey cat, which he found blinking on a window ledge, made the gravel clink under its pads when he called it to him to be stroked.

Well, he slept indifferently that night, and in the morning, when the chambermaid came in, he asked her who was the sad-looking lady whom he had seen sitting at night in the garden.

The chambermaid turned towards the window, and he saw a rapid movement of her right hand. It was done very quickly and surreptitiously, just the touch of a forefinger on her brow and a rapid fumbling of fingers at her breast, but he knew that she had made the Sign of the Cross.

'There is no lady staying in the house,' she said with her back towards him. 'Monsieur has been mistaken. Will Monsieur take coffee or the English tea?'

Crutchley knew very well what that girl's gesture meant. He had mentioned something which she held to be unholy, and the look on her face when she turned it once more in his direction warned him that it would be useless to question her. He had a pretty restless day, doing little or no work. You mustn't think that he already regarded the experience as a supernatural one, although he was quite well aware of what was in the mind of the chambermaid; but it was macabre, it belonged to the realm of the seemingly inexplicable which was no satisfaction to him to dismiss as merely 'queer'.

Crutchley spoke the French of the average educated Englishman, and the only other person in the house who spoke English was the head waiter, who had spent some years in London. His English was probably at least as good as Crutchley's French, and he enjoyed the opportunity of airing it. He was in appearance a true Norman, tall, dark, and distinguished looking. One sees his type in certain English families which can truthfully boast of Norman ancestry. It was at *déjeuner* when he approached Crutchley, and, having handed him the wine list, bent over him confidentially.

'Are you quite comfortable in your room, sir?' he ventured.

'Oh, quite, thank you,' Crutchley answered briefly.

'There is a very nice room in the front, sir. Quite so big, and then there is the sun. Perhaps you like it better, sir?'

'No, thanks,' said Crutchley, 'I shouldn't get a wink of sleep. You see, none of your motor-traffic seems to be equipped with silencers, and with trams, motor-horns, and market carts bumping over the cobbles I should never have any peace.

The waiter said no more, merely bowing, but he looked disappointed. He managed to convey by a look that he had Monsieur's welfare at heart, but that Monsieur doubtless knew best and must please himself.

'I believe I'm on the trail of something queer,' Crutchley thought. 'That chambermaid's been talking to Pierre. I wonder what's wrong or what they think is wrong.'

He re-opened the subject when the waiter returned to him with a half-bottle of white wine.

'Why do you wish me to change my room, Pierre?'

'I do not wish Monsieur to change his room if he is satisfied.'

'When I am not satisfied I say so. Why did you think I might not be?'

'I wish Monsieur to be more comfortable. There is no sun behind the house. It is better to be where the sun comes sometimes. Besides, I think Monsieur is one who sees.'

This seemed cryptic, but Crutchley let it go. Pierre had duties to attend to, and, besides, Crutchley did not feel inclined to discuss with the waiter the lady he had seen in the garden on the preceding night.

During the afternoon and evening he tried to work, but he fought only a series of losing battles against distraction. He was as incapable of concentration as a boy in love. He knew – and he was angry with himself because he knew – that he was eking out his patience until night came, in the hope of seeing once more that still figure of despair in the garden.

Of course, I don't pretend to understand the nature of the attraction, nor was Crutchley able to explain it to me. But he told me that he couldn't keep his thoughts off the face which had been turned away from him. Imagination drew for him a succession of pictures, all of an unearthly beauty, such pictures as he had never before conceived. His mind, over which he now seemed to have only an imperfect control, exercised its new creative faculty all that afternoon and evening. Long before the hour of dinner he had decided that if she came to the garden he must see her face and thus end this long torment of speculation.

He went to his room that night at eleven o'clock, and he did not undress, but sat and smoked in an armchair beside his bed. From that position he could only see through the window the lighted windows of other rooms across the square of garden shining through the leaves of the plane tree. Towards midnight the last lights died out and the last distant murmur of voices died away. Then he got up and went softly across the room.

Before he reached the window he knew instinctively that he would see her sitting in the same place and in the same attitude of woe, and his eagerness was mingled with an indescribable fear. He seemed to hear a cry of warning from the honest workaday world into which he had been born – a world which he now seemed strangely to be leaving. He said that it was like starting on a voyage, feeling no motion from the ship, and then being suddenly aware of a spreading space of water between the vessel and the quay.

That night the invisible moon threw stronger beams upon the top of the north wall, and the stars burned brighter in a clearer sky. There was a little more light in the well of the garden than there had been on the preceding night, and on the seat that figure of tragic desolation was limned more clearly. The pose, the arrangement of the woman's garments, were the same in every detail, from the least fold to the wisp of veil which fell over her right shoulder. For he now saw that it was a veil, and guessed that it covered the face which was still turned from him. He was shaken, dragged in opposite directions by unreasonable dread and still more unreasonable curiosity. And while he stood looking, the palms of his hands grew wet and his mouth grew dry.

He was wellnigh helpless. His spirit struggled within him like a caged bird, longing to fly to her. That still figure was magnetic in some mighty sense which he had never realized before. It was hypnotic without needing to use its eyes. And presently Crutchley spoke to it for the first time, whispering through the open window across the intervening space of gloom.

'Madame,' he pleaded, 'look at me.'

The figure did not more. It might have been cast in bronze or carved out of stone.

'Oh, Madame, he whispered, 'let me see your face!'

Still there was no sound nor movement, but in his heart he heard the answer.

'So, then, I must come to you,' he heard himself say softly; and he groped for the door of his room.

Outside, a little way down the corridor, was one of the doors leading into the enclosed garden. Crutchley had taken but a step or two when a figure loomed up before him, his nerves were jerked like a hooked fish, and he uttered an involuntary cry of fear. Then came the click of an electric light switch, a globe overhead sprang alight, and he found himself confronted by Pierre the head waiter. Pierre barred the way and he spoke sternly, almost menacingly.

'Where are you going, sir?'

'What the devil has that got to do with you?' Crutchley demanded fiercely.

'The devil, eh? *Bien*, Monsieur, I think perhaps he have something to do with it. You will have the goodness, please, to return to your room. No, not the room which you have left, sir – that is not a good room – but come with me and I shall show you another.'

The waiter was keeping him from her. Crutchley turned upon him with a gesture of ferocity.

'What do you mean by interfering with me? This is not a prison or an asylum. I am going into the garden for a breath of air before I go to sleep.'

'That, sir, is impossible,' the waiter answered him. 'The air of the garden is not good at night. Besides, the doors are locked and the patron have the keys.'

Crutchley stared at him for a moment in silent fury.

'You are insolent,' he said. 'Tomorrow I shall report you. Do you take me for a thief because I leave my room at midnight? Never mind! I can reach the garden from my window.'

In an instant the waiter had him by the arm, holding him powerless in a grip known to wrestlers.

'Monsieur,' he said in a voice grown softer and more respectful, 'the *bon Dieu* has sent me to save you. I have wait tonight because I know you must try to enter the garden. Have I your permission to enter your room with you and speak with you a little while?'

Crutchley laughed out in angry impotence.

'This is Bedlam,' he said. 'Oh, come, if you must.'

Back in his room, with the waiter treading close upon his heels, Crutchley went straight to the window and looked out. The seat was empty.

'I do not think that she is there,' said the waiter softly, 'because I am here and I do not see. Monsieur is one who sees, as I tell him this morning, but he will not see her when he is with one who does not see.'

Crutchley turned upon the man impatiently.

'What are you talking about?' he demanded. 'Who is she?'

'Who she is, I cannot say.' The waiter blessed himself with quick, nervous fingers. 'But who she *was* I can perhaps tell Monsieur.'

Crutchley understood, almost without surprise, but with a sudden clamouring of fear.

'Do you mean,' he asked, 'that she is what we call a ghost, an apparition—'

'It matters not what one calls her, Monsieur. She is here sometimes for certain who are able to see her. Monsieur wishes very much to see her face. Monsieur must not see it. There was one who look five years ago, and another perhaps seven, eight. The first he make die after two, three days; the other, he is still mad. That is why I come to save you, Monsieur.'

Crutchley was now entirely back in his own world. That hidden face had lost its fascination for him, and he felt only the primeval dread which has its roots deep down in every one of us. He sat down on the bed, trying to keep his lips from twitching, and let the waiter talk.

'You asked Yvonne this morning, sir, who is the lady in the garden. And Yvonne guess, and she come and tell me, for all of us know of her. Monsieur, it all happened a long time ago – perhaps fifty – sixty years. There was in this town a notary of the name Lebrun. And in a village half-way from here to Dieppe is a grand château in which there live a lady, *une jeune fille* with her father and her mother. And the lady was very beautiful but not very good, Monsieur.

'Well, M. Lebrun, he fall in love with her. I think she love him, too – better as all the others. So he make application for her hand, but she was aristocrat and he was bourgeois, and besides he had not very much money, so the application was refused! And they find her another husband whom she love not, and she find herself someone else, and there is divorce. And she have many lovers, for she was very beautiful, but not good. For ten years – more, perhaps – she use her beauty to make slaves of men. And one, he made kill himself because of her, but she did not mind. And all the time M. Lebrun stayed single, because he could not love another woman.

'But at last this lady, she have a dreadful accident. It is a lamp which blow up and hurt her face. In those days the surgeons did not know how to make new features. It was dreadful, Monsieur. She had been so lovely, and now she have nothing left except just the eyes. And she go about wearing a long thick veil, because she have become terrible to see. And her lovers, they no longer love, and she have no husband because she have been divorce.

'So M. Lebrun, he write to her father, and once more he make offer for her hand. And her father, he is willing, because now she is no longer very young, and she is terrible to see. But her father, he was a man of honour, and he insist that M. Lebrun must see her face before he decide if he still wish her in marriage. So a meeting is arrange and her father and her mother bring her to this hotel, and M. Lebrun he come to see them here.

'The lady come with them wearing her thick veil. She insist to see M. Lebrun alone, so she wait out there in the garden, and when he come they bring him to her.

'Monsieur, I do not know what her face was like, and nobody know what pass between him and her in that garden there. Love is not always what we think it. Perhaps M. Lebrun think all the time that his love go deeper than her beauty, and when he see her dreadful changed face he find out the truth. Perhaps when she put aside the veil she see that he flinch. I only say perhaps, because nobody know. But M. Lebrun he walk out alone, and the lady stay sitting on the seat. And presently her parents come, but she does not speak or move. And they find in her hand a little empty bottle, Monsieur . . .

'All her life she have live for love, for admiration, and M. Lebrun, he is the last of her lovers, and when he no longer love it is for her the end of everything. She have bring the bottle with her in case her last lover love her no more. That is all, Monsieur. It happen many years ago, and if there is more of the story one does not remember it today. And now perhaps Monsieur understands why it would be best for him to sleep tonight in a front room, and change his hotel tomorrow.'

Crutchley sat listening and staring. He felt faint and sick.

'But why does she – come back?' he managed to ask.

The head waiter shrugged his shoulders.

'How should we know, Monsieur? She is a thing of evil. When her face was lovely, while she live, she use it to destroy men. Now she still use it to destroy – but otherwise. She have some great evil power which draw those who can see her. They feel they must not rest until they have looked upon her face. And, Monsieur, that face is not good to look upon.'

I had listened all this while to Price's version of Crutchley's story without making any comment, but now he paused for so long that at last I said:

'Well, that can't be all.'

Price was filling a pipe with an air of preoccupation.

'No,' he said, 'it isn't quite all. I wish it were. Crutchley was scared, and he had the sense to change to a room in the front of the house, and to clear out altogether next day. He paid his bill, and made Pierre a good-sized present in money. Having done that, he found that he hadn't quite enough money to get home with, and he'd used his last letter of credit. So he telegraphed for more, meaning to catch the night boat from Havre.

'Well, you can guess what happened. The wired money order didn't arrive in time, and he was compelled to stay another night in Rouen. He went to another hotel.

'All that day he could think of nothing else but that immobile figure of despair which he had seen on the seat. I imagine that if you or I had seen something which we believed to be a ghost we should find difficulty in concentrating our minds on anything else for some while afterwards.

'The horror of the thing had a fascination for Crutchley, and when night fell he began to ask himself if she were still there, hiding her face in that dark and silent garden. And he began to ask himself: 'Why shouldn't I go and see? It could not harm me just to look once, and quickly, and from a distance.'

'He didn't realize that she was calling him, drawing him to her through the lighted streets. Well, he walked round to the Hôtel d'Avignon. People were still sitting at the little tables under the glass roof, but he did not see Pierre. He walked straight on and through the swing doors, as if he were still staying in the house, and nobody noticed him. He climbed the stairs and went to one of the doors which opened out into the high enclosed garden behind. He found it on the latch, opened it softly and looked out. Then he stood, staring in horror and fascination at that which was on the seat.

'He was lost then, and he knew it. The power was too strong for him. He went to her step by step, as powerless to hold himself back as a needle before a magnet or a moth before a flame. And he bent over her . . .

'And here is the part that Crutchley can't really describe. It was painful to see him straining and groping after words, as if he were trying to speak in some strange language. There aren't really any words, I suppose. But he told me that it wasn't just that – that there weren't any features left. It was something much worse and much more subtle than that. And – oh, something happened, I know, before his senses left him. Poor devil, he couldn't tell me. He's getting better, as I told you, but his nerves are still in shreds and he's got one or two peculiar aversions.'

'What are they?' I asked.

'He can't bear to be touched, or to hear anybody laugh.'

Afterward

Edith Wharton

1

'Oh there *is* one, of course, but you'll never know it.'

The assertion, laughingly flung out six months earlier in a bright June garden, came back to Mary Boyne with a new perception of its significance as she stood, in the December dusk, waiting for the lamps to be brought into the library.

The words had been spoken by their friend, Alida Stair, as they sat at tea on her lawn at Pangbourne, in reference to the very house of which the library in question was the central, the pivotal 'feature'. Mary Boyne and her husband, in quest of a country place in one of the southern or south-western counties, had, on their arrival in England, carried their problem straight to Alida Stair, who had successfully solved it in her own case; but it was not until they had rejected, almost capriciously, several practical and judicious suggestions that she threw out: 'Well, there's Lyng, in Dorsetshire. It belongs to Hugo's cousins, and you can get it for a song.'

The reason she gave for its being obtainable on these terms – its remoteness from a station, its lack of electric light, hot-water pipes, and other vulgar necessities – were exactly those pleading in its favour with two romantic Americans perversely in search of the economic drawbacks which were associated, in their tradition, with unusual architectural felicities.

'I should never believe I was living in an old house unless I was thoroughly uncomfortable,' Ned Boyne, the more extravagant of the two, had jocosely insisted: 'the least hint of "convenience" would make me think it had been bought out of an exhibition, with the pieces numbered, and set up again.' And they had proceeded to enumerate, with humorous precision, their various doubts and demands, refusing to believe that the house their cousin recommended was *really* Tudor till they learned it had no heating system, or that the village church was literally in the grounds till she assured them of the deplorable uncertainty of the water supply.

'It's too uncomfortable to be true!' Edward Boyne had continued to exult as the avowal of each disadvantage was successively wrung from her; but he had cut short his rhapsody to ask, with a relapse to distrust: 'And the ghost? You've been concealing from us the fact that there is no ghost!'

Mary, at the moment, had laughed with him, yet almost with her laugh, being possessed of several sets of independent perceptions, had been struck by a note of flatness in Alida's answering hilarity.

'Oh, Dorsetshire's full of ghosts, you know.'

'Yes, yes; but that won't do. I don't want to have to drive ten miles to see somebody else's ghost. I want one of my own on the premises. *Is* there a ghost at Lyng?'

His rejoinder had made Alida laugh again, and it was then that she had flung back tantalizingly: 'Oh, there *is* one, of course, but you'll never know it.'

'Never know it?' Boyne pulled her up. 'But what in the world constitutes a ghost except for the fact of its being known for one?'

'I can't say. But that's the story.'

'That there's a ghost, but that nobody knows it's a ghost?'

'Well – not till afterwards, at any rate.'

'Till afterwards?'

'Not till long afterwards.'

'But if it's once been identified as an unearthly visitant, why hasn't its *signalement* been handed down in the family? How has it managed to preserve its incognito?'

Alida could only shake her head. 'Don't ask me. But it has.'

'And then suddenly' – Mary spoke up as if from cavernous depths of divination – 'suddenly, long afterwards, one says to one's self *"That was it?"*'

She was startled at the sepulchral sound with which her question fell on the banter of the other two, and she saw the shadow of the same surprise flit across Alida's pupils. 'I suppose so. One just has to wait.'

'Oh, hang waiting!' Ned broke in. 'Life's too short for a ghost who can only be enjoyed in retrospect. Can't we do better than that, Mary?'

But it turned out that in the event they were not destined to, for within three months of their conversation with Mrs Stair they were settled at

Lyng, and the life they had yearned for, to the point of planning it in advance in all its daily details, had actually begun for them.

It was to sit, in the thick December dusk, by just such a wide-hooded fireplace, under just such black oak rafters, with the sense that beyond the mullioned panes the downs were darkened to a deeper solitude: it was for the ultimate indulgence of such sensations that Mary Boyne, abruptly exiled from New York by her husband's business, had endured for nearly fourteen years the soul-deadening ugliness of a Middle Western town, and that Boyne had ground on doggedly at his engineering, till, with a suddenness that still made her blink, the prodigious windfall of the Blue Star Mine had put them at a stroke in possession of life and the leisure to taste it. They had never for a moment meant their new state to be one of idleness; but they meant to give themselves only to harmonious activities. She had her vision of painting and gardening (against a background of grey walls), he dreamed of the production of his long-planned book on the 'Economic Basis of Culture'; and with such absorbing work ahead no existence could be too sequestered: they could not get far enough from the world, or plunge deep enough into the past.

Dorsetshire had attracted them from the first by an air of remoteness out of all proportion to its geographical position. But to the Boynes it was one of the ever-recurring wonders of the whole incredibly compressed island – a nest of counties, as they put it – that for the production of its effect so little of a given quality went so far: that so few miles made a distance, and so short a distance a difference.

'It's that,' Ned had once enthusiastically explained, 'that gives such depth to their effects, such relief to their contrasts. They've been able to lay the butter so thick on every delicious mouthful.'

The butter had certainly been laid on thick at Lyng; the old house hidden under a shoulder of the downs had almost all the finer marks of commerce with a protracted past. The mere fact that it was neither large nor exceptional made it, to the Boynes, abound the more completely in its special charm – the charm of having been for centuries a deep dim reservoir of life. The life had probably not been of the most vivid order: for long periods, no doubt, it had fallen as noiselessly into the past as the quiet drizzle of autumn fell, hour after hour, into the fish pond between the yews; but these backwaters of existence sometimes breed, in their sluggish depths, strange acuities of emotion, and Mary Boyne had felt from the first the mysterious air of intenser memories.

The feeling had never been stronger than on this particular afternoon when, waiting in the library for the lamps to come, she rose from her seat, and stood among the shadows of the hearth. Her husband had gone off, after luncheon, for one of his long tramps on the downs. She had noticed of late that he preferred to go alone; and, in the tried security of their personal relations, had been driven to conclude that his book was bothering him and that he needed the afternoons to turn over in solitude the problems left from the morning's work. Certainly the book was not going as smoothly as she had thought it would, and there were lines of perplexity between his eyes such as had never been there in his engineering days. He had often, then, looked fagged to the verge of illness, but the native demon of 'worry' had never branded his brow. Yet the few pages he had so far read to her – the introduction, and a summary of the opening chapter – showed a firm hold on his subject, and an increasing confidence in his powers.

The fact threw her into deeper perplexity, since, now that he had done with 'business' and its disturbing contingencies, the one other possible source of anxiety was eliminated. Unless it were his health, then? But physically he had gained since they had come to Dorsetshire, grown robuster, ruddier and fresher-eyed. It was only within the last week that she had felt in him the undefinable change which made her restless in his absence, and as tongue-tied in his presence as though it were *she* who had a secret to keep from him!

The thought that there *was* a secret somewhere between them struck her with a sudden rap of wonder, and she looked about her down the long room.

'Can it be the house?' she mused.

The room itself might have been full of secrets. They seemed to be piling themselves up, as evening fell, like the layers and layers of velvet shadow dropping from the low ceiling, the rows of books, the smoke-blurred sculpture of the hearth.

'Why – of course – the house is haunted!' she reflected.

The ghost – Alida's imperceptible ghost – after figuring largely in the banter of their first month or two at Lyng, had been gradually left aside as too ineffectual for imaginative use. Mary had, indeed, as became the tenant of a haunted house, made the customary inquiries among her rural neighbours, but, beyond a vague 'The du say so, Ma'am,' the villagers had nothing to impart. The elusive spectre had apparently never had sufficient identity for a legend to crystallize about it, and after a time the Boynes had set the matter down to their profit-and-loss account, agreeing that Lyng was one of the few houses good enough in itself to dispense with supernatural enhancements.

'And I suppose, poor ineffectual demon, that's why it beats its beautiful wings in vain in the void,' Mary had laughingly concluded.

'Or, rather,' Ned answered in the same strain, 'why, amid so much that's ghostly, it can never affirm its separate existence as *the* ghost!' And thereupon their invisible housemate had finally dropped out of their references which were numerous enough to make them soon unaware of the loss.

Now, as she stood on the hearth, the subject of their earlier curiosity revived in her with a new sense of its meaning – a sense gradually acquired through daily contact with the scene of the lurking mystery. It was the house itself, of course, that possessed the ghost-seeing faculty, that communed visually but secretly with its own past; if one could only get into close enough communion with the house, one might surprise its secret, and acquire the ghost-sight on one's own account. Perhaps, in his long hours in this very room, where she never trespassed till the afternoon, her husband *had* acquired it already, and was silently carrying about the weight of whatever it had revealed to him. Mary was too well versed in the code of the spectral world not to know that one would not talk about the ghosts one saw: to do so was almost as great a breach of taste as to name a lady in a club. But this explanation did not really satisfy her. 'What, after all, except for the fun of the shudder,' she reflected, 'would he really care for any of their old ghosts?' And thence she was thrown back once more on the fundamental dilemma: the fact that one's greater or less susceptibility to spectral influences had no particular bearing on the case, since, when one *did* see a ghost at Lyng, one did not know it.

'Not till long afterwards,' Alida Stair had said. Well, supposing Ned *had* seen one when they first came, and had known only within the last week what had happened to him? More and more under the spell of the hour, she threw back her thoughts to the early days of their tenancy, but at first only to recall a lively confusion of unpacking, settling, arranging of books, and calling to each other from remote corners of the house as, treasure after treasure, it revealed itself to them. It was in this particular connection that she presently recalled a certain soft afternoon of the previous October, when, passing from the first rapturous flurry of exploration to a detailed inspection of the old house, she had pressed (like a novel heroine) a panel that opened on a flight of corkscrew stairs leading to a flat ledge of the roof – the roof which, from below, seemed to slope away on all sides too abruptly for any but practised feet to scale.

The view from this hidden coign was enchanting, and she had flown down to snatch Ned from his papers and give him the freedom of her discovery. She remembered still how, standing at her side, he had passed

his arm about her while their gaze flew to the long tossed horizon-line of
the downs, and then dropped contentedly back to trace the arabesque
of yew hedges about the fish-pond, and the shadow of the cedar on the
lawn.

'And now the other way,' he had said, turning her about within his arm;
and closely pressed to him, she had absorbed, like some long satisfying
draught, the picture of the grey-walled court, the squat lions on the gates,
and the lime-avenue reaching up to the highroad under the downs.

It was just then, while they gazed and held each other, that she had felt
his arm relax, and heard a sharp 'Hullo!' that made her turn to glance at
him.

Distinctly, yes, she now recalled that she had seen, as she glanced, a
shadow of anxiety, of perplexity, rather, fall across his face; and, following
his eyes, had beheld the figure of a man – a man in loose greyish clothes,
as it appeared to her – who was sauntering down the lime-avenue to the
court with the doubtful gait of a stranger who seeks his way. Her short-
sighted eyes had given her but a blurred impression of slightness and
greyishness, with something foreign, or at least unlocal, in the cut of the
figure or its dress; but her husband had apparently seen more – seen
enough to make him push past her with a hasty 'Wait!' and dash down
the stairs without pausing to give her a hand.

A slight tendency to dizziness obliged her, after a provisional clutch at
the chimney against which they had been leaning, to follow him first more
cautiously; and when she had reached the landing she paused again, for
a less definite reason, leaning over the banister to strain her eyes through
the silence of the brown sun-flecked depths. She lingered there till, somewhere in those depths, she heard the closing of a door; then, mechanically
impelled, she went down the shallow flights of steps till she reached the
lower hall.

The front door stood open on the sunlight of the court, and hall and court
were empty. The library door was open, too, and after listening in vain for
any sound of voices within, she crossed the threshold, and found her
husband alone, vaguely fingering the papers on his desk.

He looked up, as if surprised at her entrance, but the shadow of anxiety
had passed from his face, leaving it even, as she fancied, a little brighter
and clearer than usual.

'What was it?' Who was it?' she asked.

'Who?' he repeated, with the surprise still all on his side.

'The man we saw coming towards the house.'

He seemed to reflect. 'The man? Why, I thought I saw Peters; I dashed after him to say a word about the stable drains, but he had disappeared before I could get down.'

'Disappeared? But he seemed to be walking so slowly when we saw him.'

Boyne shrugged his shoulders. 'So I thought; but he must have got up steam in the interval. What do you say to our trying a scramble up Meldon Steep before sunset?'

That was all. At the time the occurrence had been less than nothing, had, indeed, been immediately obliterated by the magic of their first vision from Meldon Steep, a height which they had dreamed of climbing ever since they had first seen its bare spine rising above the roof of Lyng. Doubtless it was the mere fact of the other incident's having occurred on the very day of their ascent to Meldon that had kept it stored away in the fold of memory from which it now emerged; for in itself it had no mark of the portentous. At the moment there could have been nothing more natural than that Ned should dash himself from the roof in the pursuit of dilatory tradesmen. It was the period when they were always on the watch for one or the other of the specialists employed about the place; always lying in wait for them, and rushing out at them with questions, reproaches or reminders. And certainly in the distance the grey figure had looked like Peters.

Yet now, as she reviewed the scene, she felt her husband's explanation of it to have been invalidated by the look of anxiety on his face. Why had the familiar appearance of Peters made him anxious? Why, above all, if it was of such prime necessity to confer with him on the subject of the stable drains, had the failure to find him produced such a look of relief? Mary could not say that any one of these questions had occurred to her at the time, yet, from the promptness with which they now marshalled themselves at her summons, she had a sense that they must all along have been there, waiting their hour.

2

Weary with her thoughts, she moved to the window. The library was now quite dark, and she was surprised to see how much faint light the outer world still held.

As she peered out into it across the court, a figure shaped itself far down the perspective of bare limes: it looked a mere blot of deeper grey in the greyness, and for an instant, as it moved towards her, her heart thumped to the thought 'It's the ghost!'

She had time, in that long instant, to feel suddenly that the man of whom, two months earlier, she had had a distant vision from the roof, was now, at his predestined hour, about to reveal himself as *not* having been Peters; and her spirit sank under the impending fear of the disclosure. But almost with the next tick of the clock the figure, gaining substance and character, showed itself even to her weak sight as her husband's; and she turned to meet him, as he entered, with the confession of her folly.

'It's really too absurd,' she laughed out, 'but I never *can* remember!'

'Remember what?' Boyne questioned as they drew together.

'That when one sees the Lyng ghost one never knows it.'

Her hand was on his sleeve, and he kept it there, but with no response in his gesture or in the lines of his preoccupied face.

'Did you think you'd seen it?' he asked, after an appreciable interval.

'Why, I actually took *you* for it, my dear, in my mad determination to spot it!'

'Me – just now?' His alarm dropped away, and he turned from her with a faint echo of her laugh. 'Really, dearest, you'd better give it up, if that's the best you can do.'

'Oh, yes, I give it up. Have *you*?' she asked, turning round on him abruptly.

The parlour-maid had entered with letters and a lamp, and the light struck up into Boyne's face as he bent above the tray she presented.

'Have *you*?' Mary perversely insisted, when the servant had disappeared on her errand of illumination.

'Have I what?' he rejoined absently, the light bringing out the sharp stamp of worry between his brows as he turned over the letters.

'Given up trying to see the ghost.' Her heart beat a little at the experiment she was making.

Her husband, laying his letters aside, moved away into the shadow of the hearth.

'I never tried,' he said, tearing open the wrapper of a newspaper.

'Well, of course,' Mary persisted, 'the exasperating thing is that there's no use trying, since one can't be sure till so long afterwards.'

He was unfolding the paper as if he had hardly heard her; but after a pause, during which the sheets rustled spasmodically between his hands, he looked up to ask, 'Have you any idea *how long*?'

Mary had sunk into a low chair beside the fireplace. From her seat she glanced over, startled, at her husband's profile, which was projected against the circle of lamplight.

'No; none. Have *you*?' she retorted, repeating her former phrase with an added stress of intention.

Boyne crumpled the paper into a bunch, and then, inconsequently, turned back with it towards the lamp.

'Lord, no! I only meant,' he explained, with a faint tinge of impatience, 'is there any legend, any tradition, as to that?'

'Not that I know of,' she answered; but the impulse to add, 'What makes you ask?' was checked by the reappearance of the parlour-maid, with tea and a second lamp.

With the dispersal of shadows, and the repetition of the daily domestic office, Mary Boyne felt herself less oppressed by that sense of something mutely imminent which had darkened her afternoon. For a few moments she gave herself to the details of her task, and when she looked up from it she was struck to the point of bewilderment by the change in her husband's face. He had seated himself near the farther lamp, and was absorbed in the perusal of his letters; but was it something he had found in them, or merely the shifting of her own point of view, that had restored his features to their normal aspect? The longer she looked the more definitely the change affirmed itself. The lines of tension had vanished, and such traces of fatigue as lingered were of the kind easily attributable to steady mental effort. He glanced up, as if drawn by her gaze, and met her eyes with a smile.

'I'm dying for my tea, you know; and here's a letter for you,' he said.

She took the letter he held out in exchange for the cup she proffered him, and, returning to her seat, broke the seal with the languid gesture of the reader whose interests are all enclosed in the circle of one cherished presence.

Her next conscious notion was that of starting to her feet, the letter falling to them as she rose, while she held out to her husband a newspaper clipping.

'Ned! What's this? What does it mean?'

He had risen at the same instant, almost as if hearing her cry before she uttered it; and for a perceptible space of time he and she studied each other, like adversaries watching for an advantage, across the space between her chair and his desk.

'What's what? You fairly made me jump!' Boyne said at length, moving towards her with a sudden half-exasperated laugh. The shadow of apprehension was on his face again, not now a look of fixed foreboding, but a shifting vigilance of lips and eyes that gave her the sense of his feeling himself invisibly surrounded.

Her hand shook so that she could hardly give him the clipping.

'This article – from the *Waukesha Sentinel* – that a man named Elwell has brought suit against you – that there was something wrong about the Blue Star Mine. I can't understand more than half.'

They continued to face each other as she spoke, and to her astonishment she saw that her words had the almost immediate effect of dissipating the strained watchfulness of his look.

'Oh, *that!*' He glanced down the printed slip, and then folded it with the gestures of one who handles something harmless and familiar. 'What's the matter with you this afternoon, Mary? I thought you'd got bad news.'

She stood before him with her undefinable terror subsiding slowly under the reassurance of his tone.

'You knew about this, then – it's all right?'

'Certainly I knew about it; and it's all right.'

'But what *is* it? I don't understand. What does this man accuse you of?'

'Pretty nearly every crime in the calendar.' Boyne had tossed the clipping down, and thrown himself into an armchair near the fire. 'Do you want to hear the story? It's not particularly interesting – just a squabble over interests in the Blue Star.'

'But who is this Elwell? I don't know the name.'

'Oh, he's a fellow I put into it – gave him a hand up. I told you all about him at the time.'

'I dare say. I must have forgotten.' Vainly she strained back among her memories. 'But if you helped him, why does he make this return?'

'Probably some shyster lawyer got hold of him and talked him over. It's all rather technical and complicated. I thought that kind of thing bored you.'

His wife felt a sting of compunction. Theoretically, she deprecated the American wife's detachment from her husband's professional interests, but in practice she had always found it difficult to fix her attention on Boyne's report of the transactions in which his varied interests involved him. Besides, she had felt during their years of exile, that, in a community where the amenities of living could be obtained only at the cost of efforts as arduous as her husband's professional labours, such brief leisure as he and she could command should be used as an escape from immediate preoccupations, a flight to the life they always dreamed of living. Once or twice, now that this new life had actually drawn its magic circle about them, she had asked herself if she had done right; but hitherto such conjectures had been no more than the retrospective excursions of an active fancy. Now, for the first time, it startled her a little to find how little she knew of the material foundation on which her happiness was built.

She glanced at her husband, and was again reassured by the composure of his face; yet she felt the need of more definite grounds for her reassurance.

'But doesn't this suit worry you? Why have you never spoken to me about it?'

He answered both questions at once. 'I didn't speak of it at first because it *did* worry me – annoyed me, rather. But it's all ancient history now. Your correspondent must have got hold of a back number of the *Sentinel*.'

She felt a quick thrill of relief. 'You mean it's over? He's lost his case?'

There was a just perceptible delay in Boyne's reply. 'The suit's been withdrawn – that's all.'

But she persisted, as if to exonerate herself from the inward charge of being too easily put off. 'Withdrawn it because he saw he had no chance?'

'Oh, he had no chance,' Boyne answered.

She was still struggling with a dimly felt perplexity at the back of her thoughts.

'How long ago was it withdrawn?'

He paused, as if with a slight return of his former uncertainty. 'I've just had the news now; but I've been expecting it.'

'Just now – in one of your letters?'

'Yes; in one of my letters.'

She made no answer, and was aware only, after a short interval of waiting, that he had risen, and, strolling across the room, had placed himself on the sofa at her side. She felt him, as he did so, pass an arm about her, she felt his hand seek hers and clasp it, and turning slowly, drawn by the warmth of his cheek, she met his smiling eyes.

'It's all right – it's all right?' she questioned, through the flood of her dissolving doubts; and 'I give you my word it was never righter!' he laughed back at her, holding her close.

3

One of the strangest things she was afterwards to recall out of all the next day's strangeness was the sudden and complete recovery of her sense of security.

It was in the air when she woke in her low-ceiled, dusky room; it went with her downstairs to the breakfast-table, flashed out at her from the fire, and reduplicated itself from the flanks of the urn and the sturdy flutings of the Georgian teapot. It was as if, in some roundabout way, all her diffused fears of the previous day, with their moment of sharp concentration about the newspaper article – as if this dim questioning of the future, and started return upon the past, had between them liquidated the arrears of some haunting moral obligation. If she had indeed been careless of her husband's affairs, it was, her new state seemed to prove, because her faith in him instinctively justified such carelessness; and his right to her faith had now affirmed itself in the very face of menace and suspicion. She had never seen him more untroubled, more naturally and unconsciously himself, than after the cross-examination to which she had subjected him: it was almost as if he had been aware of her doubts, and had wanted the air cleared as much as she did.

It was as clear, thank Heaven! as the bright outer light that surprised her almost with a touch of summer when she issued from the house for her daily round of the gardens. She had left Boyne at his desk, indulging herself, as she passed the library door, by a last peep at his quiet face, where he bent, pipe in mouth, above his papers; and now she had her own morning's task to perform. The task involved, on such charmed winter days, almost as much happy loitering about the different quarters of her demesne as if spring were already at work there. There were such endless possibilities still before her, such opportunities to bring out the latent graces of the old place, without a single irreverent touch of alteration, that the winter was all too short to plan what spring and autumn executed. And her recovered sense of safety gave, on this particular morning, a peculiar zest to her progress through the sweet still place. She went first to the kitchen-garden, where the espaliered pear-trees drew complicated patterns on the walls, and pigeons were fluttering and preening about the silvery-slated roof of their cot. There was something wrong about the piping of the hothouse, and she was expecting an authority from Dorchester, who was to drive out between trains and make a diagnosis of the boiler. But when she dipped into the damp heat of the greenhouses, among the spiced scents and waxy pinks and reds of old-fashioned exotics – even the flora of Lyng was in the note! – she learned that the great man had not arrived, and, the day being too rare to waste in an artificial atmosphere, she came out again and paced along the springy turf of the bowling green to the gardens behind the house. At their farther end rose a grass terrace, looking across the fish pond and yew hedges to the long house-front with its twisted chimneystacks and blue roof angles all drenched in the pale moisture of the air.

Seen thus, across the level tracery of the gardens, it sent her, from open windows and hospitably smoking chimneys, the look of some warm human presence, of a mind slowly ripened on a sunny wall of experience. She had never before had such a sense of her intimacy with it, such a conviction that its secrets were all beneficent, kept, as they said to children, 'for one's good', such a trust in its power to gather up her life and Ned's into the harmonious pattern of the long, long story it sat there weaving in the sun.

She heard steps behind her, and turned, expecting to see the gardener, accompanied by the engineer from Dorchester. But only one figure was in sight, that of a youngish slightly built man, who, for reasons she could not on the spot have given, did not remotely resemble her notion of an authority on hothouse boilers. The newcomer, on seeing her, lifted his hat, and paused with the air of a gentleman – perhaps a traveller – who wishes to make it known that his intrusion is involuntary. Lyng occasionally attracted the more cultivated traveller, and Mary half-expected to see the stranger dissemble a camera, or justify his presence by producing it. But he made no gesture of any sort, and after a moment she asked, in a tone responding to the courteous hesitation of his attitude: 'Is there anyone you wish to see?'

'I came to see Mr Boyne,' he answered. His intonation, rather than his accent, was faintly American, and Mary, at the note, looked at him more closely. The brim of his soft felt hat cast a shade on his face, which, thus obscured, wore to her short-sighted gaze a look of seriousness, as of a person arriving 'on business', and civilly but firmly aware of his rights.

Past experience had made her equally sensible to such claims; but she was jealous of her husband's morning hours, and doubtful of his having given anyone the right to intrude on them.

'Have you an appointment with my husband?' she asked.

The visitor hesitated, as if unprepared for the question.

'I think he expects me,' he replied.

It was Mary's turn to hesitate. 'You see this is his time for work: he never sees anyone in the morning.'

He looked at her a moment without answering; then, as if accepting her decision, he began to move away. As he turned, Mary saw him pause and glance up at the peaceful house-front. Something in his air suggested weariness and disappointment, the dejection of the traveller who has come from far off whose hours are limited by the timetable. It occurred to her that if this were the case her refusal might have made his errand vain, and a sense of compunction caused her to hasten after him.

'May I ask if you have come a long way?'

He gave her the same grave look. 'Yes – I have come a long way.'

'Then, if you'll go to the house, no doubt my husband will see you now. You'll find him in the library.'

She did not know why she had added the last phrase, except from a vague impulse to atone for her previous inhospitality. The visitor seemed about to express his thanks, but her attention was distracted by the approach of the gardener with a companion who bore all the marks of being the expert from Dorchester.

'This way,' she said, waving the stranger to the house; and an instant later she had forgotten him in the absorption of her meeting with the boilermaker.

The encounter led to such far-reaching results that the engineer ended by finding it expedient to ignore his train, and Mary was beguiled into spending the remainder of the morning in absorbed confabulation among the flower-pots. When the colloquy ended, she was surprised to find that it was nearly luncheon-time, and she half-expected, as she hurried back to the house, to see her husband coming out to meet her. But she found no one in the court but an under-gardener raking the gravel, and the hall, when she entered it, was so silent that she guessed Boyne to be still at work.

Not wishing to disturb him, she turned into the drawing-room, and there, at her writing-table, lost herself in renewed calculations of the outlay to which the morning's conference had pledged her. The fact that she could permit herself such follies had not yet lost its novelty; and somehow, in contrast to the vague fears of the previous days, it now seemed an element of her recovered security, of the sense that, as Ned had said, things in general had never been 'righter'.

She was still luxuriating in a lavish play of figures when the parlour-maid, from the threshold, roused her with an inquiry as to the expediency of serving luncheon. It was one of their jokes that Trimmle announced luncheon as if she were divulging a state secret, and Mary, intent upon her papers, merely murmured an absent-minded assent.

She felt Trimmle wavering doubtfully on the threshold, as if in rebuke of such unconsidered assent; then her retreating steps sounded down the passage, and Mary, pushing away her papers, crossed the hall – and went to the library door. It was still closed, and she wavered in her turn, disliking to disturb her husband, yet anxious that he should not exceed his usual measure of work. As she stood there, balancing her impulses, Trimmle returned with the announcement of luncheon, and Mary, thus impelled, opened the library door.

Boyne was not at his desk, and she peered about her, expecting to discover him before the bookshelves, somewhere down the length of the room; but her call brought no response, and gradually it became clear to her that he was not there.

She turned back to the parlour-maid.

'Mr Boyne must be upstairs. Please tell him that luncheon is ready.'

Trimmle appeared to hesitate between the obvious duty of obedience and an equally obvious conviction of the foolishness of the injunction laid on her. The struggle resulted in her saying: 'If you please, Madam, Mr Boyne's not upstairs.'

'Not in his room? Are you sure?'

'I'm sure, Madam.'

Mary consulted the clock. 'Where is he, then?'

'He's gone out,' Trimmle announced, with the superior air of one who has respectfully waited for the question that a well-ordered mind would have put first.

Mary's conjecture had been right, then. Boyne must have gone to the gardens to meet her, and since she had missed him, it was clear that he had taken the shorter way by the south door, instead of going round to the court. She crossed the hall to the french window opening directly on the yew garden, but the parlour-maid, after another moment of inner conflict, decided to bring out: 'Please, Madam, Mr Boyne didn't go that way.'

Mary turned back. 'Where *did* he go? And when?'

'He went out of the front door, up the drive, Madam.' It was a matter of principle with Trimmle never to answer more than one question at a time.

'Up the drive? At this hour?' Mary went to the door herself, and glanced across the court through the tunnel of bare limes. But its perspective was as empty as when she had scanned it on entering.

'Did Mr Boyne leave no message?'

Trimmle seemed to surrender herself to a last struggle with the forces of chaos.

'No, Madam. He just went out with the gentleman.'

'The gentleman? What gentleman?' Mary wheeled about, as if to front this new factor.

'The gentleman who called, Madam,' said Trimmle resignedly.

'When did a gentleman call? Do explain yourself, Trimmle!'

Only the fact that Mary was very hungry, and that she wanted to consult her husband about the greenhouses, would have caused her to lay so unusual an injunction on her attendant; and even now she was detached enough to note in Trimmle's eye the dawning defiance of the respectful subordinate who has been pressed too hard.

'I couldn't exactly say the hour, Madam, because I didn't let the gentleman in,' she replied, with an air of discreetly ignoring the irregularity of her mistress's course.

'You didn't let him in?'

'No, Madam. When the bell rang I was dressing, and Agnes –'

'Go and ask Agnes, then,' said Mary.

Trimmle still wore her look of patient magnanimity. 'Agnes would not know, Madam, for she had unfortunately burnt her hand in trimming the wick of the new lamp from town' – Trimmle, as Mary was aware, had always been opposed to the new lamp – 'and so Mrs Dockett sent the kitchen-maid instead.'

Mary looked again at the clock. 'It's after two! Go and ask the kitchen-maid if Mr Boyne left any word.'

She went into luncheon without waiting, and Trimmle presently brought her there the kitchen-maid's statement that the gentleman had called about eleven o'clock, and that Mr Boyne had gone out with him without leaving any message. The kitchen-maid did not even know the caller's name, for he had written it on a slip of paper, which he had folded and handed to her, with the injunction to deliver it at once to Mr Boyne.

Mary finished her luncheon, still wondering, and when it was over, and Trimmle had brought the coffee to the drawing-room, her wonder had deepened to a first tinge of disquietude. It was unlike Boyne to absent himself without explanation at so unwonted an hour, and the difficulty of identifying the visitor whose summons he had apparently obeyed made his disappearance the more unaccountable. Mary Boyne's experience as the wife of a busy engineer, subject to sudden calls and compelled to keep irregular hours, had trained her to the philosophic acceptance of surprises; but since Boyne's withdrawal from business he had adopted a Benedictine regularity of life. As if to make up for the dispersed and agitated years, with their 'stand-up' lunches, and dinners rattled down to the jolting of the dining-cars, he cultivated the last refinement of punctuality and monotony, discouraging his wife's fancy for the unexpected, and declaring that to a delicate taste there were infinite gradations of pleasure in the recurrences of habit.

Still, since no life can completely defend itself from the unforeseen, it was evident that all Boyne's precautions would sooner or later prove unavailing, and Mary concluded that he had cut short a tiresome visit by walking with his caller to the station, or at least accompanying him for part of the way.

This conclusion relieved her from further preoccupation, and she went out herself to take up her conference with the gardener. Thence she walked to the village post office, a mile or so away; and when she turned towards home the early twilight was setting in.

She had taken a footpath across the downs, and as Boyne, meanwhile, had probably returned from the station by the highroad, there was little likelihood of their meeting. She felt sure, however, of his having reached the house before her; so sure that, when she entered it herself, without even pausing to inquire of Trimmle, she made directly for the library. But the library was still empty, and with an unwonted exactness of visual memory she observed that the papers on her husband's desk lay precisely as they had lain when she had gone in to call him to luncheon.

Then of a sudden she was seized by a vague dread of the unknown. She had closed the door behind her on entering, and as she stood alone in the long silent room, her dread seemed to take shape and sound, to be there breathing and lurking among the shadows. Her short-sighted eyes strained through them, half-discerning an actual presence, something aloof, that watched and knew; and in the recoil from that intangible presence she threw herself on the bell-rope and gave it a sharp pull.

The sharp summons brought Trimmle in precipitately with a lamp, and Mary breathed again at this sobering reappearance of the usual.

'You may bring tea if Mr Boyne is in,' she said, to justify her ring.

'Very well, Madam. But Mr Boyne is not in,' said Trimmle, putting down the lamp.

'Not in? You mean he's come back and gone out again?'

'No, Madam. He's never been back.'

The dread stirred again, and Mary knew that now it had her fast.

'Not since he went out with – the gentleman?'

'Not since he went out with the gentleman.'

'But who *was* the gentleman?' Mary insisted, with the shrill note of someone trying to be heard through a confusion of noises.

'That I couldn't say, Madam.' Trimmle, standing there by the lamp, seemed suddenly to grow less round and rosy, as though eclipsed by the same creeping shade of apprehension.

'But the kitchen-maid knows – wasn't it the kitchen-maid who let him in?'

'She doesn't know either, Madam, for he wrote his name on a folded paper.'

Mary, through her agitation, was aware that they were both designating the unknown visitor by a vague pronoun, instead of the conventional formula which, till then, had kept their allusions within the bounds of conformity. And at the same moment her mind caught at the suggestion of the folded paper.

'But he must have a name! Where's the paper?'

She moved to the desk, and began to turn over the documents that littered it. The first that caught her eye was an unfinished letter in her husband's hand, with his pen lying across it, as though dropped there at a sudden summons.

'My dear Parvis' – who was Parvis? – 'I have just received your letter announcing Elwell's death, and while I suppose there is now no further risk of trouble, it might be safer –'

She tossed the sheet aside, and continued her search; but no folded paper was discoverable among the letters and pages of manuscript which had been swept together in a heap, as if by a hurried or a startled gesture.

'But the kitchen-maid *saw* him. Send her here,' she commanded, wondering at her dullness in not thinking sooner of so simple a solution.

Trimmle vanished in a flash, as if thankful to be out of the room, and when she reappeared, conducting the agitated underling, Mary had regained her self-possession, and had her questions ready.

The gentleman was a stranger, yes – that she understood. But what had he said? And above all, what had he looked like? The first question was easily enough answered, for the disconcerting reason that he had said so little – had merely asked for Mr Boyne, and, scribbling something on a bit of paper, had requested that it should at once be carried in to him.

'Then you don't know what he wrote? You're not sure it *was* his name?'

The kitchen-maid was not sure, but supposed it was, since he had written it in answer to her inquiry as to whom she should announce.

'And when you carried the paper in to Mr Boyne, what did he say?'

The kitchen-maid did not think that Mr Boyne had said anything, but she could not be sure, for just as he had handed him the paper and he was opening it, she had become aware that the visitor had followed her into the library, and she had slipped out, leaving the gentlemen together.

'But then, if you left them in the library, how do you know that they went out of the house?'

This question plunged the witness into a momentary inarticulateness, from which she was rescued by Trimmle, who, by means of ingenious circumlocutions, elicited the statement that before she could cross the hall to the back passage she had heard the two gentlemen behind her, and had seen them go out of the front door together.

'Then, if you saw the strange gentleman twice, you must be able to tell me what he looked like.'

But with this final challenge to her powers of expression it became clear that the limit of the kitchen-maid's endurance had been reached. The obligation of going to the front door to 'show in' a visitor was in itself so subversive of the fundamental order of things that it had thrown her faculties into hopeless disarray, and she could only stammer out, after various panting efforts: 'His hat, mum, was different-like, as you might say –'

'Different? How different?' Mary flashed out, her own mind, in the same instant, leaping back to an image left on it that morning, and then lost under layers of subsequent impressions.

'His hat had a wide brim, you mean? and his face was pale – a youngish face?' Mary pressed her, with a white-lipped intensity of interrogation. But if the kitchen-maid found any adequate answer to this challenge, it was swept away for her listener down the rushing current of her own convictions. The stranger – the stranger in the garden! Why had Mary not thought of him before? She needed no one now to tell her that it was he who had called for her husband and gone away with him. But who was he, and why had Boyne obeyed him?

4

It leaped out at her suddenly, like a grin out of the dark, that they had often called England so little – 'such a confoundedly hard place to get lost in'.

A confoundedly hard place to get lost in! That had been her husband's phrase. And now, with the whole machinery of official investigation sweeping its flashlights from shore to shore, and across the dividing straits; now, with Boyne's name blazing from the walls of every town and village, his portrait (how that wrung her!) hawked up and down the country like the image of a hunted criminal; now the little compact populous island, so policed, surveyed, and administered, revealed itself as a Sphinx-like guardian of abysmal mysteries, staring back into his wife's anguished eyes as if with the wicked joy of knowing something they would never know!

In the fortnight since Boyne's disappearance there had been no word of him, no trace of his movements. Even the usual misleading reports that raise expectancy in tortured bosoms had been few and fleeting. No one but the kitchen-maid had seen Boyne leave the house, and no one else had seen 'the gentleman' who accompanied him. All inquiries in the neighbourhood failed to elicit the memory of a stranger's presence that day in the neighbourhood of Lyng. And no one had met Edward Boyne, either alone or in company, in any of the neighbouring villages, or on the road across the downs, or at either of the local railway-stations. The sunny English noon had swallowed him as completely as if he had gone out into the Cimmerian night.

Mary, while every official means of investigation was working at its highest pressure, had ransacked her husband's papers for any trace of antecedent complications, of entanglements or obligations unknown to her, that might throw a ray into the darkness. But if any such had existed in the background of Boyne's life, they had vanished like the slip of paper on which the visitor had written his name. There remained no possible thread of guidance except – if it were indeed an exception – the letter which Boyne had apparently been in the act of writing when he received his mysterious summons. That letter, read and reread by his wife, and submitted by her to the police, yielded little enough to feed conjecture.

'I have just heard of Elwell's death, and while I suppose there is now no further risk of trouble, it might be safer –' That was all. The 'risk of trouble' was easily explained by the newspaper clipping which had apprised Mary of the suit brought against her husband by one of his associates in the Blue Star enterprise. The only new information conveyed by the letter was the fact of its showing Boyne, when he wrote it, to be still apprehensive of the results of the suit, though he had told his wife that it had been withdrawn, and though the letter proved that the plaintiff was dead. It took several days of cabling to fix the identity of the 'Parvis' to whom the fragment was addressed, but even after these inquiries had shown him to be a Waukesha lawyer, no new facts concerning the Elwell suit were elicited. He appeared to have had no direct concern in it, but to have been conversant with the facts merely as an acquaintance, and possible intermediary; and he declared himself unable to guess with what object Boyne intended to seek his assistance.

This negative information, sole fruit of the first fortnight's search, was not increased by a jot during the slow weeks that followed. Mary knew that the investigations were still being carried on, but she had a vague sense of their gradually slackening, as the actual march of time seemed to slacken. It was as though the days, flying horror-struck from the shrouded image of the one inscrutable day, gained assurance as the distance lengthened, till at last they fell back into their normal gait. And so with the human imaginations at work on the dark event. No doubt it occupied them still, but week by week and hour by hour it grew less absorbing, took up less space, was slowly but inevitably crowded out of the foreground of consciousness by the new problems perpetually bubbling up from the cloudy cauldron of human experience.

Even Mary Boyne's consciousness gradually felt the same lowering of velocity. It still swayed with the incessant oscillations of conjecture; but they were slower, more rhythmical in their beat. There were even moments of weariness when, like the victim of some poison which leaves the brain clear, but holds the body motionless, she saw herself domesticated with the Horror, accepting its perpetual presence as one of the fixed conditions of life.

These moments lengthened into hours and days, till she passed into a phase of stolid acquiescence. She watched the routine of daily life with the incurious eye of a savage on whom the meaningless processes of civilization make but the faintest impression. She had come to regard herself as part of the routine, a spoke of the wheel, revolving with its motion; she felt almost like the furniture of the room in which she sat, an insensate object to be dusted and pushed about with the chairs and tables. And this deepening apathy held her fast at Lyng, in spite of the entreaties of friends and the usual medical recommendation of 'change'. Her friends supposed that her refusal to move was inspired by the belief that her husband would one day return to the spot from which he had vanished, and a beautiful legend grew up about this imaginary state of waiting. But in reality she had no such belief: the depths of anguish enclosing her were no longer lighted by flashes of hope. She was sure that Boyne would never come back, that he had gone out of her sight as completely as if Death itself had waited that day on the threshold. She had even renounced, one by one, the various theories as to his disappearance which had been advanced by the press, the police, and her own agonized imagination. In sheer lassitude her mind turned from these alternatives of horror, and sank back into the blank fact that he was gone.

No, she would never know what had become of him – no one would ever know. But the house *knew*; the library in which she spent her long lonely evenings knew. For it was here that the last scene had been enacted, here that the stranger had come, and spoken the word which had caused Boyne to rise and follow him. The floor she trod had felt his tread; the books on the shelves had seen his face; and there were moments when the intense consciousness of the old dusky walls seemed about to break out into some audible revelation of their secret. But the revelation never came, and she knew it would never come. Lyng was not one of the garrulous old houses that betray the secrets entrusted to them. Its very legend proved that it had always been the mute accomplice, the incorruptible custodian, of the mysteries it had surprised. And Mary Boyne, sitting face to face with its silence, felt the futility of seeking to break it by any human means.

5

'I don't say it *wasn't* straight, and yet I don't say it *was* straight. It was business.'

Mary, at the words, lifted her head with a start, and looked intently at the speaker.

When, half an hour before, a card with 'Mr Parvis' on it had been brought up to her, she had been immediately aware that the name had been a part of her consciousness ever since she had read it at the head of Boyne's unfinished letter. In the library she had found awaiting her a small sallow man with a bald head and gold eyeglasses, and it sent a tremor through her to know that this was the person to whom her husband's last known thought had been directed.

Parvis, civilly, but without vain preamble – in the manner of a man who has his watch in his hand – had set forth the object of his visit. He had 'run over' to England on business, and finding himself in the neighbourhood of Dorchester, had not wished to leave it without paying his respects to Mrs Boyne; and without asking her, if the occasion offered, what she meant to do about Bob Elwell's family.

The words touched the spring of some obscure dread in Mary's bosom. Did her visitor, after all, know what Boyne had meant by his unfinished phrase? She asked for an elucidation of his question, and noticed at once that he seemed surprised at her continued ignorance of the subject. Was it possible that she really knew as little as she said?

'I know nothing – you must tell me,' she faltered out; and her visitor thereupon proceeded to unfold his story. It threw, even to her confused perceptions, and imperfectly initiated vision, a lurid glare on the whole hazy episode of the Blue Star Mine. Her husband had made his money in that brilliant speculation at the cost of 'getting ahead' of someone less alert to seize the chance; and the victim of his ingenuity was young Robert Elwell, who had 'put him on' to the Blue Star scheme.

Parvis, at Mary's first cry, had thrown her a sobering glance through his impartial glasses.

'Bob Elwell wasn't smart enough, that's all; if he had been, he might have turned round and served Boyne the same way. It's the kind of thing that happens every day in business. I guess it's what the scientists call the survival of the fittest – see?' said Mr Parvis, evidently pleased with the aptness of his analogy.

Mary felt a physical shrinking from the next question she tried to frame; it was as though the words on her lips had a taste that nauseated her.

'But then, you accuse my husband of doing something dishonourable?'

Mr Parvis surveyed the question dispassionately. 'Oh, no, I don't. I don't even say it wasn't straight.' He glanced up and down the long lines of books, as if one of them might have supplied him with the definition he sought. 'I don't say it *wasn't* straight, and yet I don't say it *was* straight. It was business.' After all, no definition in his category could be more comprehensive than that.

Mary sat staring at him with a look of terror. He seemed to her like the indifferent emissary of some evil power.

'But Mr Elwell's lawyers apparently did not take your view, since I suppose the suit was withdrawn by their advice.'

'Oh, yes; they knew he hadn't a leg to stand on, technically. It was when they advised him to withdraw the suit that he got desperate. You see, he'd borrowed most of the money he lost in the Blue Star, and he was up a tree. That's why he shot himself when they told him he had no show.'

The horror was sweeping over Mary in great deafening waves.

'He shot himself? He killed himself because of *that*?'

'Well, he didn't kill himself, exactly. He dragged on two months before he died.' Parvis emitted the statement as unemotionally as a gramophone grinding out its 'record'.

'You mean that he tried to kill himself, and failed? And tried again?'

'Oh, he didn't have to *try* again,' said Parvis grimly.

The sat opposite each other in silence, he swinging his eyeglasses thoughtfully about his finger, she, motionless, her arms stretched along her knees in an attitude of rigid tension.

'But if you knew all this,' she began at length, hardly able to force her voice above a whisper, 'how is it that when I wrote you at the time of my husband's disappearance you said you didn't understand the letter?'

Parvis received this without perceptible embarrassment: 'Why, I didn't understand it – strictly speaking. And it wasn't the time to talk about it, if I had. The Elwell business was settled when the suit was withdrawn. Nothing I could have told you would have helped you to find your husband.'

Mary continued to scrutinize him. 'Then why are you telling me now?'

Still Parvis did not hesitate. 'Well, to begin with, I supposed you knew more than you appear to – I mean about the circumstances of Elwell's death. And then people are talking of it now; the whole matter's been raked up again. And I thought if you didn't know you ought to.'

She remained silent, and he continued: 'You see, it's only come out lately what a bad state Elwell's affairs were in. His wife's a proud woman, and she fought on as long as she could, going to work, and taking sewing at home when she got too sick – something with the heart, I believe. But she had his mother to look after, and the children, and she broke down under it, and finally had to ask for help. That called attention to the case, and the papers took it up, and a subscription was started. Everybody out there liked Bob Elwell, and most of the prominent names in the place are down on the list, and people began to wonder why –'

Parvis broke off to fumble in an inner pocket. 'Here,' he continued, 'here's an account of the whole thing from the *Sentinel* – a little sensational, of course. But I guess you'd better look it over.'

He held out a newspaper to Mary, who unfolded it slowly, remembering, as she did so, the evening when, in that same room, the perusal of a clipping from the *Sentinel* had first shaken the depths of her security.

As she opened the paper, her eyes, shrinking from the glaring headlines, 'Widow of Boyne's Victim Forced to Appeal for Aid', ran down the column of text to two portraits inserted in it. The first was her husband's, taken from a photograph made the year they had come to England. It was the picture of him that she liked best, the one that stood on the writing-table upstairs in her bedroom. As the eyes in the photograph met hers, she felt it would be impossible to read what was said of him, and closed her lids with the sharpness of the pain.

'I thought if you felt disposed to put your name down –' she heard Parvis continue.

She opened her eyes with an effort, and they fell on the other portrait. It was that of a youngish man, slightly built, with features somewhat blurred by the shadow of a projecting hat-brim. Where had she seen that outline before? She stared at it confusedly, her heart hammering in her ears. Then she gave a cry.

'This is the man – the man who came for my husband!'

She heard Parvis start to his feet, and was dimly aware that she had slipped backwards into the corner of the sofa, and that he was bending above her in alarm. She straightened herself, and reached out for the paper, which she had dropped.

'It's the man! I should know him anywhere!' she persisted in a voice that sounded to her own ears like a scream.

Parvis's answer seemed to come to her from far off, down endless fog-muffled windings.

'Mrs Boyne, you're not very well. Shall I call somebody? Shall I get a glass of water?'

'No, no, no!' She threw herself towards him, her hand frantically clutching the newspaper. 'I tell you, it's the man! I *know* him! He spoke to me in the garden!'

Parvis took the journal from her, directing his glasses to the portrait. 'It can't be, Mrs Boyne. It's Robert Elwell.'

'Robert Elwell?' Her white stare seemed to travel into space. 'Then it was Robert Elwell who came for him.'

'Came for Boyne? The day he went away from here?' Parvis's voice dropped as hers rose. He bent over, laying a fraternal hand on her, as if to coax her gently back into her seat. 'Why, Elwell was dead! Don't you remember?'

Mary sat with her eyes fixed on the picture, unconscious of what he was saying.

'Don't you remember Boyne's unfinished letter to me – the one you found on his desk that day? It was written just after he'd heard of Elwell's death.' She noticed an odd shake in Parvis's unemotional voice. 'Surely you remember!' he urged.

Yes, she remembered: that was the profoundest horror of it. Elwell had died the day before her husband's disappearance; and this was Elwell's portrait; and it was the portrait of the man who had spoken to her in the garden. She lifted her head and looked slowly about the library. The library could have borne witness that it was also the portrait of the man who had come in that day to call Boyne from his unfinished letter. Through the misty surgings of her brain she heard the faint boom of half-forgotten words – words spoken by Alida Stair on the lawn at Pangbourne before Boyne and his wife had ever seen the house at Lyng, or had imagined that they might one day live there.

'This was the man who spoke to me,' she repeated.

She looked again at Parvis. He was trying to conceal his disturbance under what he probably imagined to be an expression of indulgent commiseration; but the edges of his lips were blue. 'He thinks me mad; but I'm not mad,' she reflected; and suddenly, there flashed upon her a way of justifying her strange affirmation.

She sat quiet, controlling the quiver of her lips, and waiting till she could trust her voice; then she said, looking straight at Parvis: 'Will you answer me one question, please? When was it that Robert Elwell tried to kill himself?'

'When – when?' Parvis stammered.

'Yes; the date. Please try to remember.'

She saw that he was growing still more afraid of her. 'I have a reason,' she insisted.

'Yes, yes. Only I can't remember. About two months before, I should say.'

'I want the date,' she repeated.

Parvis picked up the newspaper. 'We might see here,' he said, still humouring her. He ran his eyes down the page. 'Here it is. Last October – the –'

She caught the words from him. 'The 20th, wasn't it?' With a sharp look at her, he verified. 'Yes, the 20th. Then you *did* know?'

'I know now.' Her gaze continued to travel past him. 'Sunday, the 20th – that was the day he came here first.'

Parvis's voice was almost inaudible. 'Came *here* first?'

'Yes.'

'You saw him twice, then?'

'Yes, twice.' She just breathed it at him. 'He came first on the 20th of October. I remember the date because it was the day we went up Meldon Steep for the first time.' She felt a faint gasp of inward laughter at the thought that but for that she might have forgotten.

Parvis continued to scrutinize her, as if trying to intercept her gaze.

'We saw him from the roof,' she went on. 'He came down the lime-avenue towards the house. He was dressed just as he is in that picture. My husband saw him first. He was frightened, and ran down ahead of me; but there was no one there. He had vanished.'

'Elwell had vanished?' Parvis faltered.

'Yes.' Their two whispers seemed to grope for each other. 'I couldn't think what had happened. I see now. He *tried* to come then; but he wasn't dead enough – he couldn't reach us. He had to wait for two months to die; and then he came back again – and Ned went with him.'

She nodded at Parvis with the look of triumph of a child who has worked out a difficult puzzle. But suddenly she lifted her hands with a desperate gesture, pressing them to her temples.

'Oh, my God! I sent him to Ned – I told him where to go! I sent him to this room!' she screamed.

She felt the walls of books rush towards her, like inward falling ruins, and she heard Parvis, a long way off, through the ruins, crying to her, and struggling to get at her. But she was numb to his touch, she did not know what he was saying. Through the tumult she heard but one clear note, the voice of Alida Stair, speaking on the lawn at Pangbourne.

'You won't know till afterwards,' it said. 'You won't know till long, long afterwards.'

The Wardrobe

Thomas Mann

It was cloudy, cool, and half-dark when the Berlin–Rome express drew in at a middle-sized station on its way. Albrecht van der Qualen, solitary traveller in a first-class compartment with lace covers over the plush upholstery, roused himself and sat up. He felt a flat taste in his mouth, and in his body the none-too-agreeable sensations produced when the train comes to a stop after a long journey and we are aware of the cessation of rhythmic motion and conscious of calls and signals from without. It is like coming to oneself out of drunkenness or lethargy. Our nerves, suddenly deprived of the supporting rhythm, feel bewildered and forlorn. And this the more if we have just roused out of the heavy sleep one falls into in a train.

Albrecht van der Qualen stretched a little, moved to the window, and let down the pane. He looked along the train. Men were busy at the mail van, unloading and loading parcels. The engine gave out a series of sounds, it snorted and rumbled a bit, standing still, but only as a horse stands still, lifting its hoof, twitching its ears, and awaiting impatiently the signal to go on. A tall, stout woman in a long raincoat, with a face expressive of nothing but worry, was dragging a hundred-pound suitcase along the train, propelling it before her with pushes from one knee. She was saying nothing, but looking heated and distressed. Her upper lip stuck out, with little beads of sweat upon it – altogether she was a pathetic figure. 'You poor dear thing,' van der Qualen thought. 'If I could help you, soothe you, take you in – only for the sake of that upper lip. But each for himself, so things are arranged in life; and I stand here at this moment perfectly carefree, looking at you as I might at a beetle that has fallen on its back.'

It was half-dark in the station shed. Dawn or twilight – he did not know. He had slept, who could say whether for two, five, or twelve hours? He had sometimes slept for twenty-four, or even more, unbrokenly, an extraordinarily profound sleep. He wore a half-length dark-brown winter overcoat with a velvet collar. From his features it was hard to judge his age: one might actually hesitate between twenty-five and the end of the thirties. He had a yellowish skin, but his eyes were black like live coals and had deep shadows round them. These eyes boded nothing good. Several doctors, speaking frankly as man to man, had not given him many more months. His dark hair was smoothly parted on one side.

In Berlin – although Berlin had not been the beginning of his journey – he had climbed into the train just as it was moving off – incidentally with his red leather hand-bag. He had gone to sleep and now at waking felt himself so completely absolved from time that a sense of refreshment streamed through him. He rejoiced in the knowledge that at the end of the thin gold chain he wore round his neck there was only a little medallion in his waistcoat pocket. He did not like to be aware of the hour or of the day of the week, and moreover he had no truck with the calendars. Some time ago he had lost the habit of knowing the day of the month or even the month of the year. Everything must be in the air – so he put it in his mind, and the phrase was comprehensive though rather vague. He was seldom or never disturbed in this programme, as he took pains to keep all upsetting knowledge at a distance from him. After all, was it not enough for him to know more or less what season it was? 'It is more or less autumn,' he thought, gazing out into the damp and gloomy train shed. 'More I do not know. Do I even know where I am?'

His satisfaction at this thought amounted to a thrill of pleasure. No, he did not know where he was! Was he still in Germany? Beyond a doubt. In North Germany? That remained to be seen. While his eyes were still heavy with sleep the window of his compartment had glided past an illuminated sign; it probably had the name of the station on it, but not the picture of a single letter had been transmitted to his brain. In still dazed condition he had heard the conductor call the name two or three times, but not a syllable had he grasped. But out there in a twilight of which he knew not so much as whether it was morning or evening lay a strange place, an unknown town. Albrecht van der Qualen took his felt hat out of the rack, seized his red leather hand-bag, the strap of which secured a red and white silk and wool plaid into which was rolled an umbrella with a silver crook – and although his ticket was labelled Florence, he left the compartment and the train, walked along the shed, deposited his luggage at the cloakroom, lighted a cigar, thrust his hands – he carried neither stick nor umbrella – into his overcoat pockets, and left the station.

Outside in the damp, gloomy, and nearly empty square five or six hackney coachmen were snapping their whips, and a man with braided cap and long cloak in which he huddled shivering inquired politely: *'Hotel zum braven Mann?'* Van der Qualen thanked him politely and held on his way. The people whom he met had their coat-collars turned up; he put his up too, nestled his chin into the velvet, smoked, and went his way, not slowly and not too fast.

He passed along a low wall and an old gate with two massive towers; he crossed a bridge with statues on the railings and saw the water rolling slow and turbid below. A long wooden boat, ancient and crumbling, came by, sculled a man with a long pole in the stern. Van der Qualen stood for a while leaning over the rail of the bridge. 'Here,' he said to himself, 'is a river; here is *the* river. It is nice to think that I call it that because I do not know its name.' Then he went on.

He walked straight on for a little, on the pavement of a street which was neither very narrow nor very broad; then he turned off to the left. It was evening. The electric arc-lights came on, flickered, glowed, sputtered, and then illuminated the gloom. The shops were closing. 'So we may say that it is in every respect autumn,' thought van der Qualen, proceeding along the wet black pavement. He wore no galoshes, but his boots were very thick-soled, durable, and firm, and withal not lacking in elegance.

He held to the left. Men moved past him, they hurried on their business or coming from it. 'And I move with them,' he thought, 'and am as alone and as strange as probably no man has ever been before. I have no business and no goal. I have not even a stick to lean upon. More remote, freer, more detached, no one can be, I owe nothing to anybody, nobody owes anything to me. God has never held out His hand over me, He knows me not at all. Honest unhappiness without charity is a good thing; a man can say to himself: I owe God nothing.'

He soon came to the edge of the town. Probably he had slanted across it at about the middle. He found himself on a broad suburban street with trees and villas, turned to his right, passed three or four cross-streets almost like village lanes, lighted only by lanterns, and came to a stop in a somewhat wider one before a wooden door next to a commonplace house painted a dingy yellow, which had nevertheless the striking feature of very convex and quite opaque plate-glass windows. But on the door was a sign: 'In this house on the third floor there are rooms to let.' 'Ah!' he remarked; tossed away the end of his cigar, passed through the door along a boarding which formed the dividing line between two properties, and then turned left through the door of the house itself. A shabby grey runner ran across the entry. He covered it in two steps and began to mount the simple wooden stair.

The doors to the several apartments were very modest too; they had white glass panes with woven wire over them and on some of them were name-plates. The landings were lighted by oil lamps. On the third storey, the top one, for the attic came next, were entrances right and left, simple brown doors without name-plates. Van der Qualen pulled the brass bell in the middle. It rang, but there was no sign from within. He knocked left. No answer. He knocked right. He heard light steps within, very long, like strides, and the door opened.

A woman stood there, a lady, tall, lean, and old. She wore a cap with a large pale-lilac bow and an old-fashioned, faded black gown. She had a sunken birdlike face and on her brow there was an eruption, a sort of fungus growth. It was rather repulsive.

'Good evening,' said van der Qualen. 'The rooms?'

The old lady nodded; she nodded and smiled slowly, without a word, understandingly, and with her beautiful long white hand made a slow, languid, and elegant gesture towards the next, the left-hand door. Then she retired and appeared again with a key. 'Look,' he thought, standing behind her as she unlocked the door; 'you are like some kind of banshee, a figure out of Hoffmann, madam.' She took the oil lamp from its hook and ushered him in.

It was a small, low-ceiled room with a brown floor. Its walls were covered with straw-coloured matting. There was a window at the back in the right-hand wall, shrouded in long, thin white muslin folds. A white door also on the right led into the next room. This room was pathetically bare, with staring white walls, against which three straw chairs, painted pink, stood out like strawberries from whipped cream. A wardrobe, a washing-stand with a mirror . . . The bed, a mammoth mahogany piece, stood free in the middle of the room.

'Have you any objections?' asked the old woman, and passed her lovely long, white hand lightly over the fungus growth on her forehead. It was as though she had said that by accident because she could not think for the moment of a more ordinary phrase. For she added at once: '– so to speak?'

'No, I have no objections,' said van der Qualen. 'The rooms are rather cleverly furnished. I will take them. I'd like to have somebody fetch my luggage from the station, here is the ticket. You will be kind enough to make up the bed and give me some water. I'll take the house key now, and the key to the apartment . . . I'd like a couple of towels. I'll wash up and go into the city for supper and come back later.'

He drew a nickel case out of his pocket, took out some soap, and began to wash his face and hands, looking as he did so through the convex window-panes far down over the muddy, gas-lit suburban streets, over the arc-lights and the villas. As he dried his hands he went over to the wardrobe. It was a square one, varnished brown, rather shaky, with a simple curved top. It stood in the centre of the right-hand wall exactly in the niche of a second white door, which of course led into the rooms to which the main and middle door on the landing gave access. 'Here is something in the world that is well arranged,' thought van der Qualen. 'This wardrobe fits into the door niche as though it were made for it.' He opened the wardrobe door. It was entirely empty, with several rows of hooks in the ceiling; but it proved to have no back, being closed behind by a piece of rough, common grey burlap, fastened by nails or tacks at the four corners.

Van der Qualen closed the wardrobe door, took his hat, turned up the collar of his coat once more, put out the candle, and set forth. As he went through the front room he thought to hear mingled with the sound of his own steps a sort of ringing in the other room: a soft, clear, metallic sound – but perhaps he was mistaken. As though a gold ring were to fall into a silver basin, he thought, as he locked the outer door. He went down the steps and out of the gate and took the way to the town.

In a busy street he entered a lighted restaurant and sat down at one of the front tables, turning his back to all the world. He ate a *soupe aux fines herbes* with croûtons, a steak with a poached egg, a compote and wine, a small piece of green gorgonzola and half a pear. While he paid and put on his coat he took a few puffs from a Russian cigarette, then lighted a cigar and went out. He strolled for a while, found his homeward route into the suburb, and went leisurely back.

The house with the plate-glass windows lay quite dark and silent when van der Qualen opened the house door and mounted the dim stair. He lighted himself with matches as he went, and opened the left-hand brown door in the third storey. He laid hat and overcoat on the divan, lighted the lamp on the big writing-table, and found there his hand-bag as well as the plaid and umbrella. He unrolled the plaid and got a bottle of cognac, then a little glass and took a sip now and then as he sat in the armchair finishing his cigar. 'How fortunate, after all,' thought he, 'that there is cognac in the world!' Then he went into the bedroom, where he lighted the candle on the night-table, put out the light in the other room, and began to undress. Piece by piece he put down his good, unobtrusive grey suit on the red chair beside the bed; but then as he loosened his braces he remembered his hat and overcoat, which still lay on the couch. He fetched them into the bedroom and opened the wardrobe . . . He took a step backwards and reached behind him to clutch one of the large dark-red mahogany balls which ornamented the bedposts. The room, with its four white walls, from which the three pink chairs stood out like strawberries from whipped cream, lay in the unstable light of the candle. But the wardrobe over there was open and it was not empty. Somebody was standing in it, a creature so lovely that Albrecht van der Qualen's heart stood still a moment and then in long, deep, quiet throbs resumed its beating. She was quite nude and one of her slender arms reached up to crook a forefinger round one of the hooks in the ceiling of the wardrobe. Long waves of brown hair rested on the childlike shoulders – they breathed that charm to which the only answer is a sob. The candlelight was mirrored in her narrow black eyes. Her mouth was a little large, but it had an expression as sweet as the lips of sleep when after long days of pain they kiss our brow. Her ankles nestled and her slender limbs clung to one another.

Albrecht van der Qualen rubbed one hand over his eyes and stared . . . and he saw that down in the right corner the sacking was loosened from the back of the wardrobe. 'What –' said he . . . 'won't you come in – or how should I put it – out? Have a little glass of cognac? Half a glass?' But he expected no answer to this and he got none. Her narrow, shining eyes, so very black that they seemed bottomless and inexpressive – they were directed upon him, but aimlessly and somewhat blurred, as though they did not see him.

'Shall I tell you a story?' she said suddenly in a low, husky voice.

'Tell me a story,' he answered. He had sunk down in a sitting posture on the edge of the bed, his overcoat lay across his knees with his folded hands resting upon it. His mouth stood a little open, his eyes half-closed. But the blood pulsated warm and mildly through his body and there was a gentle singing in his ears. She had let herself down in the cupboard and embraced a drawn-up knee with her slender arms, while the other leg stretched out before her. Her little breasts were pressed together by her upper arm, and the light gleamed on the skin of her flexed knee. She talked . . . talked in a soft voice, while the candle-flame performed its noiseless dance.

Two walked on the heath and her head lay on his shoulder. There was a perfume from all growing things, but the evening mist already rose from the ground. So it began. And often it was in verse, rhyming in that incomparably sweet and flowing way that comes to us now and again in the half-slumber of fever. But it ended badly; a sad ending: the two holding each other indissolubly embraced and, while their lips rest on each other, one stabbing the other above the waist with a broad knife – and not without good cause. So it ended. And then she stood up with an infinitely sweet and modest gesture, lifted the grey sacking at the right-hand corner – and was no more there.

From now on he found her every evening in the wardrobe and listened to her stories – how many evenings? How many days, weeks, or months did he remain in this house and in this city? It would profit nobody to know. Who would care for a miserable statistic? And we are aware that Albrecht van der Qualen had been told by several physicians that he had but a few months to live. She told him stories. They were sad stories, without relief; but they rested like a sweet burden upon the heart and made it beat longer and more blissfully. Often he forgot himself. His blood swelled up in him, he stretched out his hands to her, and she did not resist him. But then for several evenings he did not find her in the wardrobe, and when she came back she did not tell him anything for several evenings and then by degrees resumed, until he again forgot himself.

How long it lasted – who knows? Who even knows whether Albrecht van der Qualen actually awoke on that grey afternoon and went into the unknown city; whether he did not remain asleep in his first-class carriage and let the Berlin–Rome express bear him swiftly over the mountains? Would any of us care to take the responsibility of giving a definite answer? It is all uncertain. 'Everything must be in the air . . .'

The Buick Saloon

Ann Bridge

To Mrs James St George Bernard Bowlby it seemed almost providential that she should recover from the series of illnesses which had perforce kept her in England, at the precise moment when Bowlby was promoted from being No. 2 to being No. 1 in the Grand Oriental Bank in Peking. Her improved health and his improved circumstances made it obvious that now at last she should join him, and she wrote to suggest it. Bowlby, of course, agreed, and out she came. He went down to meet her in Shanghai, but business having called him farther still, to Hong Kong, Mrs Bowlby proceeded to Peking alone, and took up her quarters in the big, ugly, grey-brick house over the bank in Legation Street. She tried, as many managers' wives had tried before her, to do her best with the solid mahogany and green leather furniture provided by the bank, wondering the while how Bowlby, so dependent always on the feminine touch on his life and surroundings, had endured the lesser solidities of the sub-manager's house alone for so long. She bought silks and black-wood and scroll paintings. She also bought a car. 'You'll need a car, and you'd better have a saloon, because of the dust,' Bowlby had said.

People who come to Peking without motors of their own seldom buy new ones. There are always second-hand cars going, from many sources; the leavings of transferred diplomatists, the jetsam of financial ventures, the sediment of conferences. So one morning Mrs Bowlby went down with Thompson, the new No. 2 in the bank, to Maxon's garage in the Nan Shih Tzu to choose her car. After much conversation with the Canadian manager they pitched on a Buick saloon. It was a Buick of the type which is practically standard in the Far East, and had been entirely repainted outside, a respectable dark blue; the inside had been newly done up in a pleasant soft grey which appealed to Mrs Bowlby. The manager was loud in its praises. The suspension was excellent. ('You want that on these roads, Mrs Bowlby.') The driver and his colleague sat outside. ('Much better, Mr Thompson. If these fellows have been eating garlic – they shouldn't, but do –') Thompson knew they did, and agreed heartily. Mrs Bowlby, new to such transactions, wanted to know whom the car had belonged to. The manager was firmly vague. This was not a commission sale – he had bought the car when the owner left. Very good people – 'from the Quarter'. This fully satisfied Thompson, who knew that only Europeans live (above the rose, anyhow) in the Legation Quarter of Peking.

So the Buick saloon was bought. Thompson, having heard at the club that the late Grand Oriental chauffeur drank petrol, did not re-engage him with the rest of the servants according to custom, but secured instead for Mrs Bowlby the chauffeur of a departing manager of the Banque Franco-Belge. By the time Bowlby returned from Hong Kong the chauffeur and his colleagues had been fitted out with khaki livery for winter, with white for summer – in either case with trim gold cuff-and-hat-bands – and Mrs Bowlby, in her blue saloon, had settled down to pay her calls.

In Peking the newcomer calls first; a curious and discouraging system. It is an ordeal even to the hardened. Mrs Bowlby was not hardened; she was a small, shy, frail woman, who wore grey by preference, and looked grey – eyes, hair, and skin. She had no idea of asserting herself; if she had things in her – subtleties, delicacies – she did not wear them outside; she did not impose herself. She hated the calls. But as she was also extremely conscientious, day after day, trying to fortify herself by the sight of the two khaki-and-gold figures in front of her exhaling their possible garlic to the outer air beyond the glass partition, she called. She called on the diplomats' wives in the Quarter; she called on 'the Salt' (officials of the Salt Gabelle); she called on the Customs – English, Italian, American, and French; she called on the Posts – French, Italian, American, and English. The annual displacement of pasteboard in Peking must amount to many tons, and in this useful work Mrs Bowlby, alone in the grey interior of her car, faithfully took her share. She carried with her a little list on which, with the help of her Number One Boy (as much a permanent fixture in the bank house, almost, as the doors and windows), she had written out the styles, titles and addresses of the ladies she wished to visit. The late chauffeur of the Banque Franco-Belge spoke excellent French; so did Mrs Bowlby – it was one of her few accomplishments; but as no Chinese can or will master European names, the Europeans needs must learn and use the peculiar versions current among them. 'Ta Ch'in chai T'ai-t'ai, Turkuo-fu,' read out Mrs Bowlby when she wished to call on the wife of the German minister. 'Oui, Madame!' said Shwang. 'Péi T'ai-t'pai, Kung Hsien Hutung,' read out Mrs Bowlby when visiting Mrs Bray, the doctor's wife; but when she wished to call on Mrs Bennett, the wife of the commandant of the English Guard, and Mrs Baines, the chaplain's wife, she found that they were both Péi T'ai-t'ai too – which led to confusion.

It began towards the end of the first week. Possibly it was her absorption in the lists and the Chinese names that prevented her from noticing it sooner, but at the end of that week Mrs Bowlby would have sworn that she heard French spoken beside her as she drove about. Once, a little later, as she was driving down the rue Marco Polo to fetch her husband from the club, a voice said: 'C'est lui!' in an underbreath, eagerly – or so she thought. The windows were lowered, and Mrs Bowlby put it down to the servants in front. But it persisted. More than once she thought she heard a soft sigh. 'Nerves!' thought Mrs Bowlby – her nerves were always a menace, and Peking, she knew, was bad for them.

She went on saying 'nerves' for two or three more days; then, one afternoon, she changed her mind. She was driving along the Ta Chiang an Chieh, the great thoroughfare running east and west outside the Legation Quarter, where the trams ring and clang past the scarlet walls and golden roofs of the Forbidden City, and long lines of camels, coming in with coal from the country as they have come for centuries, cross the road between the Dodges and Daimlers of the new China. It was a soft, brilliant afternoon in April, and the cinder track along the Glacis of the Quarter was thronged with riders; polo had begun, and as the car neared Hatamen Street she caught a glimpse of the white and scarlet figures through the drifting dust on her right. At the corner of the Hatamen the car stopped; a string of camels was passing up to the great gateway, and she had to wait.

She sat back in the car, glad of the pause; she was unusually moved by the loveliness of the day, by the beauty and strangeness of the scene, by the whole magic of spring in Peking. She was going later to watch the polo, a terrifying game; she wished Jim didn't play. Suddenly, across her idle thoughts, a voice beside her spoke clearly: 'Au revoir!' it said, 'mon très-cher. Ne tombes pas, je t'en prie.' And as the car moved forward behind the last of the camels, soft and unmistakable there came a sigh, and the words 'Ce polo! Quel sport affreux! Dieu, que je le déteste!' in a passionate undertone.

'That *wasn't* the chauffeur!' was what Mrs Bowlby found herself saying.

The front windows were up. And besides, that low, rather husky voice, the cultivated and clear accent, could not be confounded for a moment with Shwang's guttural French. And besides, what chauffeur would talk like that? The thing was ridiculous. 'And it *wasn't* nerves this time,' said Mrs Bowlby, her thoughts running this way and that round the pheno- menon. 'She did say it.' 'Then it was she who said: "C'est lui!" before –' she said almost triumphantly, a moment later.

Curiously, though she was puzzled and startled, she realized presently that she was not in the least frightened. That someone with a beautiful voice should speak French in her car was absurd and impossible, but it wasn't alarming. In her timid way Mrs Bowlby rather prided herself on her common sense, and as she shopped and called she considered this extraordinary occurrence from all the common sense points of view that she could think of, but it remained a baffling and obstinate fact. Before her drive was over she found herself wishing simply to hear the voice again. It was ridiculous, but she did. And she had her wish. As the car turned into Legation Street an hour later she saw that it was too late to go to the polo; the last chukka was over, and the players were leaving the ground, over which dust still hung in the low brilliant light, in cars and rickshas. As she passed the gate the voice spoke again – almost in front of her, this time, as though the speaker were leaning forward to the window. 'Le voilà!' it said – and then, quite loudly, 'Jacques!' Mrs Bowlby almost leaned out of the window herself, to look for whoever was being summoned – as she sat back, conscious of her folly, she heard again beside her, quite low: 'Il ne m'a pas vue.'

There was no mistake about it. It was broad daylight; there she was in her car, bowling along Legation Street – past the Belgian bank, past the German Legation; rickshaws skimming in front of her, Madame de Réan bowing to her. And just as clear and certain as all these things had been this woman's voice, calling to 'Jacques', whoever he was – terrified lest he should fall at polo, hating the game for his sake. What a lovely voice it was! Who was she, Mrs Bowlby wondered, and what and who was Jacques? 'Mon très-cher!' she had called him – a delicious expression. It belonged to the day and the place – it was near to her own mood as she had sat at the corner of the Hatamen and noticed the spring, and hated the polo too for Jim's sake. She would have liked to call Jim 'mon très-cher', only he would have been so surprised.

The thought of Bowlby brought her up with a round turn. What would he say to this affair? Instantly, though she prolonged the discussion with herself for form's sake, she knew that she was not going to tell him. Not yet, anyhow. Bowlby had not been very satisfied with her choice of a car as it was – he said it was too big and too expensive to run. Besides, there was the question of her nerves. If he failed to hear the voice too she would be in a terribly difficult position. But there was more to it than that. She had a faint sense that she had been eavesdropping, however involuntarily. She had no right to give away even a voice which said 'mon très-cher' in that tone.

This feeling grew upon her in the days that followed. The voice that haunted the Buick became of almost daily occurrence, furnishing a curious secret background to her social routine of calls and 'At Homes'. It spoke always in French, always to or about 'Jacques' – a person, whoever he was, greatly loved. Sometimes it was clear to Mrs Bowlby that she was hearing only half of a conversation between the two, as one does at the telephone. The man's voice she never heard, but, as at the telephone, she could often guess at what he said. Much of the speech was trivial enough; arrangements for meetings at lunches, at the polo; for week-end parties at Pao-ma-chang in the temple of this person or that. This was more eerie than anything else to Mrs Bowlby – the hearing of plans concerned with people she knew, 'Alors, dimanche prochain, chez les Milne.' Meeting 'les Milne' soon after, she would stare at them uneasily, as though by looking long enough she might find about them some trace of the presence which was more familiar to her than their own. Her voice was making ghosts of the living. But whether plans, or snatches of talk about people or ponies, there came always, sooner or later, the undernote of tenderness, now hesitant, now frank – the close concern, the monopolizing happiness of a woman in love.

It puzzled Mrs Bowlby that the car should only register, as it were, the woman's voice. But then the whole affair bristled with puzzles. Why did Bowlby hear nothing? For he did not – she would have realized her worst fears if she *had* told him. She remembered always the first time that the voice spoke when he was with her. They were going to a Thé Dansant at the Peking Hotel, a farewell party for some minister. As the car swung out of the Jade Canal Road, past the policemen who stand with fixed bayonets at the edge of the Glacis, the voice began suddenly, as it so often did, in French: 'Then I leave thee now – thou wilt send back the car?' And as they lurched across the tramlines towards the huge European building and pulled up, it went on: 'But tonight, one will dance, *n'est-ce pas?*'

'Goodness, what a crowd!' said Bowlby. 'This is going to be simply awful. Don't let's stay long. Will half an hour be enough, do you think?'

Mrs Bowlby stared at him without answering. Was it possible? She nearly gave herself away in the shock of astonishment. 'What's the matter?' said Bowlby. 'What are you looking at?'

Bowlby had not heard a word!

She noticed other things. There were certain places where the voice 'came through', so to speak, more clearly and regularly than elsewhere. Intermittent fragments, sometimes unintelligible, occurred anywhere. But she came to know where to expect to hear most. Near the polo ground, for instance, which she hardly ever passed without hearing some expression of anxiety or pride. She often went to the polo, for Jim was a keen and brilliant player; but it was a horror while he played, and this feeling was a sort of link, it seemed to her, between her and her unseen companion. More and more, too, she heard it near the Hatamen and the hu-t'ungs or alleys to the east of it. Mrs Bowlby liked the East City. It lies rather in a backwater, between the crowded noisy thoroughfare of Hatamen Street, with its trams, dust, cars, and camels, and the silent angle of the Tartar Wall, rising above the low one-story houses. A good many Europeans live there, and she was always glad when a call took her that way, through the narrow hu-t'ungs where the car lurched over heaps of rubbish or skidded in the deep dust, and rickshaws pulled aside into gateways to let her pass. Many of these lanes end vaguely in big open spaces, where pigs root among the refuse and little boys wander about, singing long monotonous songs with a curious jerky rhythm in their high nasal voices. Sometimes, as she waited before a scarlet door, a flute-player out of sight would begin to play, and the thin sweet melody filled the sunny air between the blank grey walls. Flowering trees showed here and there above them; coppersmiths plied their trade on the steps of carved marble gateways; dogs and beggars sunned themselves under the white and scarlet walls of temple courtyards. Here, more than anywhere else, the voice spoke clearly, freely, continuously, the rounded French syllables falling on the air from nowhere, now high, light, and merry, with teasing words and inflection, now sinking into low murmurs of rapturous happiness. At such times Mrs Bowlby sat wholly absorbed in listening, drawn by the lovely voice into a world not her own and held fascinated by the spell of this passionate adventure. Happy as she was with Bowlby, her life with him had never known anything like this. He had never wanted, and she had never dared to use, the endearments lavished by the late owner of the Buick saloon on her Jacques.

She heard enough to follow the course of the affair pretty closely. They met when they could in public, but somewhere in the Chinese City there was clearly a meeting-place of their own – 'notre petit asile'. And gradually

this haven began to take shape in Mrs Bowlby's mind. Joyous references
were made to various features of it. Tomorrow they would drink tea on
the stone table under 'our great white pine'. There was the fishpond
shaped like a shamrock where one of the goldfish died – 'pourtant en
Irlande cela porte bonheur, le trèfle, n'est-ce pas?' The parapet of this
pond broke away and had to be repaired, and 'Jacques' made some sort of
inscription in the damp mortar, for the voice thrilled softly one day as it
murmured: 'Maintenant il se lit là pour toujours, ton amour!' And all
through that enchanted spring, first the lilac bushes perfumed the hours
spent beneath the pine, and then the acacias that stood in a square round
the shamrock pond. Still more that life and hers seemed to Mrs Bowlby
strangely mingled; her own lilacs bloomed and scented the courtyard
behind the grey bank building, and one day as they drove to lunch in the
British Legation she drew Jim's attention to the scent of the acacias, which
drowned the whole compound in perfume. But Bowlby said, with a sort
of shiver, that he hated the smell; and he swore at the chauffeur in French,
which he spoke even better than his wife.

The desire grew on Mrs Bowlby to know more of her pair, who and
what they were and how their story ended. But it seemed wholly
impossible to find out. Her reticences made her quite unequal to setting
anyone on to question the people at the garage again. And then one day,
accidentally, the clue was given to her. She had been calling at one of the
houses in the French Legation; the two house servants, in blue and silver
gowns, stood respectfully on the steps; her footman held open the door of
the car for her. As she seated herself the voice said in a clear tone of
command: 'Deux cent trente, Por Hua Shan Hut'ung!' Acting on an
impulse which surprised her, Mrs Bowlby repeated the order: 'Deux cent
trente, Por Hua Shan Hut'ung,' she said. Shwang's colleague bowed and
shut the door. But she caught sight, as she spoke, of the faces of the two
servants on the steps. Was it imagination? Surely not. She would have
sworn that a flicker of some emotion – surprise, and recollection – had
appeared for a moment on their sealed and impassive countenances. In
Peking the servants in Legation houses are commonly handed on from
employer to employer, like the furniture, and the fact struck on her with
sudden conviction – they had heard those words before!

Her heart rose with excitement as the car swung out of the compound
into Legation Street. Where was it going? She had no idea where the Por
Hua Shan Hut'ung was. Was she about to get a stage nearer to the solution
of the mystery at last? At the Hatamen the Buick turned south along the
Glacis. So far so good. They left the Hatamen, bumped into the Suchow

Hut'ung, followed on down the Tung Tsung Pu Hut'ung right into the heart of the East City. Her breath came fast. It must be right. Now they were skirting the edge of one of the rubbish-strewn open spaces, and the East Wall rose close ahead of them. They turned left, parallel with it; turned right again towards it; stopped. Shwang beckoned to a pancake-seller who was rolling out his wares in a doorway, and a colloquy in Chinese ensued. They went on slowly then, down a lane between high walls which ended at the Wall's very foot, and pulled up some hundred yards short of it before a high scarlet door, whose rows of golden knobs in fives betokened the former dwelling of some Chinese of rank.

It was only when Liu came to open the door and held out his cotton-gloved hand for her cards that Mrs Bowlby realized that she had no idea what she was going to do. She could not call on a voice! She summoned Shwang, Liu's French was not his strong point. 'Ask,' she said to Shwang, 'who lives here – the T'ai-t'ai's name.' Shwang rang the bell. There was a long pause. Shwang rang again. There came a sound of shuffling feet inside; creaking on its hinges the door opened, and the head of an old Chinaman, thinly bearded and topped with a little black cap, appeared in the crack. A conversation followed, and then Shwang returned to the car.

'The house is empty,' he said. 'Ask him who lived there last,' said Mrs Bowlby. Another and longer conversation followed, but at last Shwang came to the window with the information that a foreign T'ai-t'ai, 'Fa-kuo T'ai-t'ai' (French lady), he thought, had lived there, but she had gone away. With that Mrs Bowlby had to be content. It was something. It might be much. The car had moved on towards the Wall, seeking a place to turn, when an idea struck her. Telling Shwang to wait, she got out, and glanced along the foot of the Wall in both directions. Yes! Some two hundred yards from where she stood one of those huge ramps, used in former times to ride or drive up on to the summit of the Wall, descended into the dusty strip of waste land at its foot. She hurried towards it, nervously, picking her way between the rough fallen lumps of stone and heaps of rubbish; she was afraid that the servants would regard her action as strange, and that when she reached the foot of the ramp she might not be able to get up it. Since Boxer times the top of the Tartar Wall is forbidden as a promenade, save for a short strip just above the Legation Quarter, and the ramps are stoutly closed at the foot, theoretically. But in China theory and practice do not always correspond, Mrs Bowlby knew; and as she hurried, she hoped.

Her hope was justified. Though a solid wooden barrier closed the foot of the ramp, a few feet higher up a little bolt-hole, large enough to admit a goat or a small man, had been picked away in the masonry of the parapet. Mrs Bowlby scrambled through and found herself on the cobbled slope of the ramp; panting a little, she walked up it on to the Wall. The great flagged top, broad enough for two motor-lorries to drive abreast, stretched away to left and right; a thick undergrowth of thorny bushes had sprung up between the flags, and through them wound a little path, manifestly used by goats and goat-herds. Below her Peking lay spread out – a city turned by the trees which grow in every courtyard into the semblance of a green wood, out of which rose the immense golden roofs of the Forbidden City; beyond it, far away, the faint mauve line of the Western Hills hung on the sky.

But Mrs Bowlby had no eyes for the unparalleled view. Peeping cautiously through the battlements she located the Buick saloon, shining incongruously neat and modern in its squalid and deserted surroundings; by it she took her bearings, and moved with a beating heart along the little path between the thorns. Hoopoes flew out in front of her, calling their sweet note, and perched again, raising and lowering their crests; she never heeded them, nor her torn silk stockings. Now she was above the car; yes, there was the lane up which they had come, and the wall beyond it was the wall of that house! She could see the doorkeeper, doll-like below her, still standing in his scarlet doorway, watching the car curiously. The garden wall stretched up close to the foot of the City Wall itself, so that, as she came abreast of it, the whole compound – the house, with its manifold courtyards, and the formal garden – lay spread out at her feet with the minute perfection of a child's toy farm on the floor.

Mrs Bowlby stood looking down at it. A dream-like sense of unreality came over her, greater than any yet caused even by her impossible voice. A magnificent white pine, trunk and branches gleaming as if whitewashed among its dark needles, rose out of the garden, and below it stood a round stone table among groups of lilacs. Just as the voice had described it! Close by, separated from the pine garden by a wall pierced with a fan-shaped doorway, was another with a goldfish pond like a shamrock, and round it stood a square pleached alley of acacias. Flowers in great tubs bloomed everywhere. Here was the very setting of her lovers' secret idyll; silent, sunny, sweet, it lay under the brooding protection of the Tartar Wall. Here she was indeed near to the heart of her mystery, Mrs Bowlby felt, as she leaned on the stone parapet, looking down at the deserted garden. A strange fancy came to her that she would have liked to bring Jim here, and people it once again. But she and Jim, she reflected with a little sigh, were staid married people, with no need of a secret haven hidden away in the East City. And with the thought of Jim the claims of everyday life reasserted themselves. She must go – and with a last glance at the garden she hastened back to the car.

During the next day or so Mrs Bowlby brooded over her new discovery and all that had led to it. Everything – the place where the address had been given by the voice, the flicker of recognition on the faces of the servants at the house in the French Legation, that fact of the doorkeeper in the East City having mentioned a Fa-kuo T'ai-t'ai as his late employer – pointed to one thing, that the former owner of the Buick saloon had lived in the house where she had first called on that momentous afternoon. More than ever, the thing took hold of her – having penetrated the secret of the voice so far, she felt that she must follow it further yet. Timid or not, she must brace herself to ask some questions.

At a dinner a few nights later she found herself seated next to Mr van Adam. Mr van Adam was an elderly American, the doyen of Peking society, who had seen everything and known everyone since before Boxer days – a walking memory and a mine of social information. Mrs Bowlby determined to apply to him. She displayed unwonted craft. She spoke of Legation compounds in general and of the French compound in particular; she praised the garden of the house where she had called. And then: 'Who lived there before the Vernets came?' she asked, and waited eagerly for the answer. Mr van Adam eyed her a little curiously, she thought, but replied that it was a certain Count d'Ardennes. 'Was he married?' Mrs Bowlby next inquired. Oh, yes, he was married right enough – but the usual reminiscent flow of anecdote seemed to fail Mr van Adam in this case. Struggling against a vague sense of difficulty, of a hitch somewhere, Mrs Bowlby pushed on nevertheless to an inquiry as to what the Countess d'Ardennes was like. 'A siren!' Mr van Adam replied briefly – adding, 'Lovely creature, though, as ever stepped.'

He edged away rather from the subject, or so it seemed to Mrs Bowlby, but she nerved herself to another question – 'Had they a car?' Mr van Adam fairly stared at that; then he broke into a laugh. 'Car? Why, yes – she went everywhere in a yellow Buick – we used to call it "the canary".' The talk drifted off on to cars in general, and Mrs Bowlby let it drift; she was revolving in her mind the form of her last question. Her curiosity must look odd, she reflected nervously; it was all more difficult, somehow, than she had expected. Her craft was failing her – she could not think of a good excuse for further questions that would not run the risk of betraying her secret. There must have been a scandal – there *would* have been, of course; but Mrs Bowlby was not of the order of women who in Peking ask

coolly at the dinner-table: 'And what was *her* scandal?' At dessert, in
desperation, she put it hurriedly, badly: 'When did the d'Ardennes leave?'

Mr van Adam paused before he answered: 'Oh, going on for a year ago,
now. She was ill, they said – looked it, anyway – and went back to France.
He was transferred to Bangkok soon after, but I don't know if she's gone
out to him again. The East didn't suit her.' 'Oh, poor thing!' murmured
Mrs Bowlby, softly and sincerely, her heart full of pity for the woman with
the lovely voice and the lovely name, whose failing health had severed her
from her Jacques. Not even love such as hers could control this wretched
feeble body, reflected Mrs Bowlby, whom few places suited. The ladies
rose, and too absorbed in her reflections to pay any further attention to Mr
van Adam, she rose and went with them.

At this stage Mrs Bowlby went to Pei-t'ai-ho for the summer. Peking,
with a temperature of over 100 degrees in the shade, is no place for
delicate women in July and August. Cars are not allowed on the sandy
roads of the pleasant straggling seaside resort, and missionaries and
diplomatists alike are obliged to fall back on rickshaws and donkeys as a
means of locomotion. So the Buick saloon was left in Peking with Jim,
who came down for long weekends as often as he could. Thus separated
from her car, and in changed surroundings, Mrs Bowlby endeavoured to
take stock of the whole affair dispassionately. Get away from it she could
not. Bathing, idling on the hot sunny beach, walking through the green
paths bordered with maize and kaoliang, sitting out in the blessedly cool
dark after dinner, she found herself as much absorbed as ever in this
personality whose secret life she so strangely shared. Curiously enough,
she felt no wish to ask any more questions of any one. With her knowledge
of Madame d'Ardennes's name the sense of eavesdropping had returned
in full force. One thing struck her as a little odd: that if there *had* been a
scandal she should not have heard of it – in Peking, where scandals were
innumerable, and treated with startling openness and frank disregard.
Perhaps she had been mistaken, though, in Mr van Adam's attitude, and
there had not been one. Or – the illumination came to her belated and
suddenly – hadn't Mr van Adam's son in the Customs, who went home
last year, been called Jack? He had! and Mrs Bowlby shuddered at the
thought of her clumsiness. She could not have chosen a worse person for
her inquiries.

Another thing, at Pei-t'ai-ho, she realized with a certain astonishment
– that she had not been perceptibly shocked by this intrigue. Mrs Bowlby
had always believed herself to hold thoroughly conventional British views
on marriage; the late owner of the Buick saloon clearly had not, yet Mrs

Bowlby had never thought of censuring her. She had even been a little resentful of Mr van Adam's calling her a 'siren'. Sirens were cold-hearted creatures, who lured men frivolously to their doom; her voice was not the voice of a siren. Mrs Bowlby was all on the side of her voice. Didn't such love justify itself, argued Mrs Bowlby, awake at last to her own moral failure to condemn another, or very nearly? Perhaps, she caught herself thinking, if people knew as much about all love-affairs as she knew about this one, they would be less censorious.

Mrs Bowlby stayed late at Pei-t'ai-ho, well on into September, till the breezes blew chilly off the sea, the green paths had faded to a dusty yellow, and the maize and kaoliang were being cut. When she returned to Peking she was at once very busy – calling begins all over again after the seaside holiday, and she spent hours in the Buick saloon leaving cards. The voice was with her again, as before. But something had overshadowed the blissful happiness of the spring days; there was an undertone of distress, of foreboding, often in the conversations. What exactly caused it she could not make out. But it increased, and one day half-way through October, driving in the East City, the voice dropped away into a burst of passionate sobbing. This distressed Mrs Bowlby extraordinarily. It was a strange and terrible thing to sit in the car with those low, heart-broken sounds at her side. She almost put out her arms to take and comfort the unhappy creature – but there was only empty air, and the empty seat, with her bag, her book and her little calling list. Obeying one of those sudden impulses which the voice alone seemed to call out in her, she abandoned her calls and told Shwang to drive to the Por Hua Shan Hut'ung. As they neared it the sobs beside her ceased, and murmured apologies for being *un peu énervée* followed.

When she reached the house Mrs Bowlby got out, and again climbed the ramp on to the Tartar Wall. The thorns and bushes between the battlements were brown and sere, and no hoopoes flew and fluted among them. She reached the spot where she could look down into the gardens. The lilacs were bare now, as her own were; the tubs of flowers were gone, and heaps of leaves had drifted round the feet of the acacias – only the white pine stood up, stately and untouched by the general decay. A deep melancholy took hold of Mrs Bowlby; already shaken by the sobs in the car, the desolation of this deserted autumn garden weighed with an intense oppression on her spirit. She turned away, slowly, and slowly descended to the Buick. The sense of impending misfortune had seized on her too; something, she vaguely felt, had come to an end in that garden.

As she was about to get into the car another impulse moved her. She felt an overmastering desire to enter that garden and see its features from close at hand. The oppression still hung over her, and she felt that a visit to the garden might in some way resolve it. She looked in her purse and found a five-dollar note. Handing it to the startled Shwang, 'Give that,' said Mrs Bowlby, 'to the k'ai-men-ti, and tell him I wish to walk in the garden of that house.' Shwang bowed; rang the bell; conversed; Mrs Bowlby waited, trembling with impatience, till the clinching argument of the note was at last produced, and the old man whom she had seen before beckoned to her to enter.

She followed him through several courtyards. It was a rambling Chinese house, little modernized; the blind paper lattice of the windows looked blankly on to the miniature lakes and rocky landscapes in the open courts. Finally they passed through a round doorway into the garden below the Tartar Wall, and bowing, the old custodian stood aside to let her walk alone.

Before her rose the white pine, and she strolled towards it, and sitting down on a marble bench beside the round stone table, gazed about her. Beautiful even in its decay, melancholy, serene, the garden lay under the battlements which cut the pale autumn sky behind her. And here the owner of the voice had sat, hidden and secure, her lover beside her! A sudden burst of tears surprised Mrs Bowlby. Cruel life, she thought, which parts dear lovers. Had *she* too sat here alone? A sharp unexpected sense of her own solitude drove Mrs Bowlby up from her seat. This visit was a mistake; her oppression was not lightened; to have sat in this place seemed somehow to have involved herself in the disaster and misery of that parted pair. She wandered on, through the fan-shaped doorway, and came to a halt beside the goldfish pond. Staring at it through her tears, she noticed the repair to the coping of which the voice had spoken, where 'Jacques' had made an inscription in the damp mortar. She moved round to the place where it still showed white against the grey surface, murmuring, 'Maintenant il se lit là pour toujours, ton amour!' – the phrase of the voice had stayed rooted in her mind. Stooping down, she read the inscription, scratched out neatly and carefully with a penknife in the fine plaster:

> Douce sépulture, mon coeur dans ton coeur,
> Doux paradis, mon âme dans ton âme.

And below two sets of initials:

A. de A.
de
J. StG. B. B.

The verse touched Mrs Bowlby to fresh tears, and it was actually a moment or two before she focused her attention on the initials. When she did, she started back as though a serpent had stung her, and shut her eyes and stood still. Then with a curious blind movement she opened her bag and took out one of her own cards, and laid it on the coping beside the inscription, as if to compare them. *Mrs J. St G. B. Bowlby* – the fine black letters stared up at her, uncompromising and clear, from the white oblong, beside the capitals cut in the plaster. There could be no mistake. Her mystery was solved at last, but it seemed as if she could not take it in. 'Jim?' murmured Mrs Bowlby to herself, as if puzzled – and then 'Jacques?' Slowly, while she stood there, all the connections and verifications unrolled themselves backwards in her mind with devastating certainty and force. Her sentiment, her intuition on the wall had been terribly right – something *had* come to an end in that garden that day. Standing by the shamrock pond, with the first waves of an engulfing desolation sweeping over her, hardly conscious of her words, she whispered: 'Pourtant cela porte bonheur, le trèfle, n'est-ce pas?'

And with that second question from the voice she seemed at last to wake from the sort of stupor in which she had stood. Intolerable! She must hear no more. Passing back, almost running, into the pine garden, she beckoned to the old k'ai-men-ti to take her out. He led her again, bowing, through the courtyards to the great gateway. Through the open red and gold doors she saw the Buick saloon, dark and shiny, standing as she had so often, and with what pleasure, seen it stand before how many doors? She stopped and looked round her almost wildly – behind her the garden, before her the Buick! Liu caught sight of her, and flew to hold open the door. But Mrs Bowlby did not get in. She made Shwang call a rickshaw, and when it came ordered him to direct the coolie to take her to the bank house. Shwang, exercising the respectful supervision which Chinese servants are wont to bestow on their employers, reminded her that she was to go to the polo to pick up the lao-yé, Bowlby. Before his astonished eyes his mistress shuddered visibly from head to foot. 'The bank! The bank!' she repeated, with a sort of desperate impatience.

Standing before his scarlet door, lighting his little black and silver pipe, the old k'ai-men-ti watched them go. First the rickshaw, with a small drooping grey figure in it, lurched down the dusty hu-t'ung, and after it, empty, bumped the Buick saloon.

The Tower

Marghanita Laski

The road begins to rise in a series of gentle curves, passing through pleasing groves of olives and vines. 5 km. on the left is the fork for Florence. To the right may be seen the Tower of Sacrifice (470 steps) built in 1535 by Niccolo di Ferramano; superstitious fear left the tower intact when, in 1549, the surrounding village was completely destroyed . . .

Triumphantly Caroline lifted her finger from the fine italic type. There was nothing to mar the success of this afternoon. Not only had she taken the car out alone for the first time, driving unerringly on the right-hand side of the road, but what she had achieved was not a simple drive but a cultural excursion. She had taken the Italian guide-book Neville was always urging on her, and hesitantly, haltingly, she had managed to piece out enough of the language to choose a route that took in four well-thought-of frescoes, two universally-admired campaniles, and one wooden crucifix in a village church quite a long way from the main road. It was not, after all, such a bad thing that a British Council meeting had kept Neville in Florence. True, he was certain to know all about the campaniles and the frescoes, but there was just a chance that he hadn't discovered the crucifix, and how gratifying if she could, at last, have something of her own to contribute to his constantly accumulating hoard of culture.

But could she add still more? There was at least another hour of daylight, and it wouldn't take more than thirty-five minutes to get back to the flat in Florence. Perhaps there would just be time to add this tower to her dutiful collection? What was it called? She bent to the guide-book again, carefully tracing the text with her finger to be sure she was translating it correctly, word by word.

But this time her moving finger stopped abruptly at the name of Niccolo di Ferramano. There had risen in her mind a picture – no, not a picture, a portrait – of a thin white face with deep-set black eyes that stared intently into hers. Why a portrait? she asked, and then she remembered.

It had been about three months ago, just after they were married, when Neville had first brought her to Florence. He himself had already lived there for two years, and during that time had been at least as concerned to accumulate Tuscan culture for himself as to disseminate English culture to the Italians. What more natural than that he should wish to share – perhaps even to show off – his discoveries to his young wife?

Caroline had come out to Italy with the idea that when she had worked through one or two galleries and made a few trips – say to Assisi and Siena – she would have done her duty as a British Council wife, and could then settle down to examining the Florentine shops, which everyone had told her were too marvellous for words. But Neville had been contemptuous of her programme. 'You can see the stuff in the galleries at any time,' he had said, 'but I'd like you to start with the pieces that the ordinary tourist doesn't see,' and of course Caroline couldn't possibly let herself be classed as an ordinary tourist. She had been proud to accompany Neville to castles and palaces privately owned to which his work gave him entry, and there to gaze with what she hoped was pleasure on the undiscovered Raphael, the Titian that had hung on the same wall ever since it was painted, the Giotto fresco under which the family that had originally commissioned it still said their prayers.

It had been on one of these pilgrimages that she had seen the face of the young man with the black eyes. They had made a long slow drive over narrow ill-made roads and at last had come to a castle on the top of a hill. The family was, to Neville's disappointment, away, but the housekeeper remembered him and led them to a long gallery lined with five centuries of family portraits.

Though she could not have admitted it even to herself, Caroline had become almost anaesthetized to Italian art. Dutifully she had followed Neville along the gallery, listening politely while in his light well-bred voice he had told her intimate anecdotes of history, and involuntarily she had let her eyes wander round the room, glancing anywhere but at the particular portrait of Neville's immediate dissertation.

It was thus that her eye was caught by a face on the other side of the room, and forgetting what was due to politeness she caught her husband's arm and demanded, 'Neville, who's that girl over there?'

But he was pleased with her. He said, 'Ah, I'm glad you picked that one out. It's generally thought to be the best thing in the collection – a Bronzino, of course,' and they went over to look at it.

The picture was painted in rich pale colours, a green curtain, a blue dress, a young face with calm brown eyes under plaits of honey-gold hair. Caroline read out the name under the picture – *Giovanna di Ferramano, 1531–1549.* That was the year the village was destroyed, she remembered now, sitting in the car by the roadside, but then she had exclaimed, 'Neville, she was only eighteen when she died.'

'They married young in those days,' Neville commented, and Caroline said in surprise, 'Oh, was she married?' It had been the radiantly virginal character of the face that had caught at her inattention.

'Yes, she was married,' Neville answered, and added, 'Look at the portrait beside her. It's Bronzino again. What do you think of it?'

And this was when Caroline had seen the pale young man. There were no clear light colours in this picture. There was only the whiteness of the face, the blackness of the eyes, the hair, the clothes, and the glint of gold letters on the pile of books on which the young man rested his hand. Underneath this picture was written *Portrait of an Unknown Gentleman.*

'Do you mean he's her husband?' Caroline asked. 'Surely they'd know if he was, instead of calling him an Unknown Gentleman?'

'He's Niccolo di Ferramano all right,' said Neville. 'I've seen another portrait of him somewhere, and it's not a face one would forget, but,' he added reluctantly, because he hated to admit ignorance, 'there's apparently some queer scandal about him, and though they don't turn his picture out, they won't even mention his name. Last time I was here, the old Count himself took me through the gallery. I asked him about little Giovanna and her husband.' He laughed uneasily. 'Mind you, my Italian was far from perfect at that time, but it was horribly clear that I shouldn't have asked.' 'But what did he *say*?' Caroline demanded. 'I've tried to remember,' said Neville. 'For some reason it stuck in my mind. He said either "She was lost" or "She was damned", but which word it was I can never be sure. The portrait of Niccolo he just ignored altogether.'

'What was wrong with Niccolo, I wonder?' mused Caroline, and Neville answered, 'I don't know but I can guess. Do you notice the lettering on those books up there, under his hand? It's all in Hebrew or Arabic. Undoubtedly the unmentionable Niccolo dabbled in Black Magic.'

Caroline shivered. 'I don't like him,' she said. 'Let's look at Giovanna again,' and they had moved back to the first portrait, and Neville had said casually, 'Do you know, she's rather like you.'

'I've just got time to look at the tower,' Caroline now said aloud, and she put the guide-book back in the pigeon-hole under the dashboard, and drove carefully along the gentle curves until she came to the fork for Florence on the left.

On the top of a little hill to the right stood a tall round tower. There was no other building in sight. In a land where every available piece of ground is cultivated, there was no cultivated ground around this tower. On the left was the fork for Florence: on the right a rough track led up to the top of the hill.

Caroline knew that she wanted to take the fork to the left, to Florence and home and Neville and – said an urgent voice inside her – for safety. This voice so much shocked her that she got out of the car and began to trudge up the dusty track towards the tower.

After all, I may not come this way again, she argued; it seems silly to miss the chance of seeing it when I've already got a reason for being interested. I'm only just going to have a quick look – and she glanced at the setting sun, telling herself that she would indeed have to be quick if she were to get back to Florence before dark.

And now she had climbed the hill and was standing in front of the tower. It was built of narrow red bricks, and only thin slits pierced its surface right up to the top where Caroline could see some kind of narrow platform encircling it. Before her was an arched doorway. I'm just going to have a quick look, she assured herself again, and then she walked in.

She was in an empty room with a low arched ceiling. A narrow stone staircase clung to the wall and circled round the room to disappear through a hole in the ceiling.

'There ought to be a wonderful view at the top,' said Caroline firmly to herself, and she laid her hand on the rusty rail and started to climb, and as she climbed, she counted.

'– thirty-nine, forty, forty-one,' she said, and with the forty-first step she came through the ceiling and saw over her head, far far above, the deep blue evening sky, a small circle of blue framed in a narrowing shaft round which the narrow staircase spiralled. There was no inner wall; only the rusty railing protected the climber on the inside.

'– eighty-three, eighty-four –' counted Caroline. The sky above her was losing its colour and she wondered why the narrow slit windows in the wall had all been so placed that they spiralled round the staircase too high for anyone climbing it to see through them.

'It's getting dark very quickly,' said Caroline at the hundred-and-fiftieth step. 'I know what the tower is like now. It would be much more sensible to give up and go home.'

At the two-hundred-and-sixty-ninth step, her hand, moving forward on the railing, met only empty space. For an interminable second she shivered, pressing back to the hard brick on the other side. Then hesitantly she groped forwards, upwards, and at last her fingers met the rusty rail again, and again she climbed.

But now the breaks in the rail became more and more frequent. Sometimes she had to climb several steps with her left shoulder pressed tightly to the brick wall before her searching hand could find the tenuous rusty comfort again.

At the three-hundred-and-seventy-fifth step, the rail, as her moving hand clutched it, crumpled away under her fingers. 'I'd better just go by the wall,' she told herself, and now her left hand traced the rough brick as she climbed up and up.

'Four-hundred-and-twenty-two, four-hundred-and-twenty-three,' counted Caroline with part of her brain. 'I really ought to go down now,' said another part, 'I wish – oh, I want to go down now –' but she could not. 'It would be so silly to give up,' she told herself, desperately trying to rationalize what drove her on. 'Just because one's afraid –' and then she had to stifle that thought too, and there was nothing left in her brain but the steadily mounting tally of the steps.

'– four-hundred-and-seventy!' said Caroline aloud with explosive relief, and then she stopped abruptly because the steps had stopped too. There was nothing ahead but a piece of broken railing barring her way, and the sky drained now of all its colour, was still some twenty feet above her head.

'But how idiotic,' she said to the air. 'The whole thing's absolutely pointless,' and then the fingers of her left hand, exploring the wall beside her, met not brick but wood.

She turned to see what it was, and there in the wall, level with the top step, was a small wooden door. 'So it does go somewhere after all,' she said, and she fumbled with the rusty handle. The door pushed open and she stepped through.

She was on a narrow stone platform about a yard wide. It seemed to encircle the tower. The platform sloped downwards away from the tower and its stones were smooth and very shiny – and this was all she noticed before she looked beyond the stones and down.

She was immeasurably, unbelievably high and alone and the ground below was a world away. It was not credible, not possible that she should be so far from the ground. All her being was suddenly absorbed in the single impulse to hurl herself from the sloping platform. 'I cannot go down any other way,' she said, and then she heard what she said and stepped back, frenziedly clutching the soft rotten wood of the doorway with hands sodden with sweat. There is no other way, said the voice in her brain, there is no other way.

'This is vertigo,' said Caroline. 'I've only got to close my eyes and keep still for a minute and it will pass off. It's bound to pass off. I've never had it before but I know what it is and it's vertigo.' She closed her eyes and kept very still and felt the cold sweat running down her body.

'I should be all right now,' she said at last, and carefully she stepped back through the doorway on to the four-hundred-and-seventieth step and pulled the door shut before her. She looked up at the sky, swiftly darkening with night. Then, for the first time, she looked down into the shaft of the tower, down to the narrow unprotected staircase spiralling round and round and round, and disappearing into the dark. She said – she screamed – 'I can't go down.'

She stood still on the top step, staring downwards, and slowly the last light faded from the tower. She could not move. It was not possible that she should dare to go down, step by step down the unprotected stairs into the dark below. It would be much easier to fall, said the voice in her head, to take one step to the left and fall and it would all be over. You cannot climb down.

She began to cry, shuddering with the pain of her sobs. It could not be true that she had brought herself to this peril, that there could be no safety for her unless she could climb down the menacing stairs. The reality *must* be that she was safe at home with Neville – but this was the reality and here were the stairs; at last she stopped crying and said 'Now I shall go down.'

'One!' she counted and, her right hand tearing at the brick wall, she moved first one and then the other foot down to the second step. 'Two!' she counted, and then she thought of the depth below her and stood still, stupefied with terror. The stone beneath her feet, the brick against her hand were too frail protections for her exposed body. They could not save her from the voice that repeated that it would be easier to fall. Abruptly she sat down on the step.

'Two,' she counted again, and spreading both her hands tightly against the step on each side of her, she swung her body off the second step, down on to the third. 'Three,' she counted, then 'four' then 'five', pressing closer and closer into the wall, away from the empty drop on the other side.

At the twenty-first step she said, 'I think I can do it now.' She slid her right hand up the rough wall and slowly stood upright. Then with the other hand she reached for the railing it was now too dark to see, but it was not there.

For timeless time she stood there, knowing nothing but fear. 'Twenty-one,' she said, 'twenty-one,' over and over again, but she could not step on to the twenty-second stair.

Something brushed her face. She knew it was a bat, not a hand, that touched her but still it was horror beyond conceivable horror, and it was this horror, without any sense of moving from dread to safety, that at last impelled her down the stairs.

'Twenty-three, twenty-four, twenty-five –' she counted, and around her the air was full of whispering skin-stretched wings. If one of them should touch her again, she must fall. 'Twenty-six, twenty-seven, twenty-eight –' The skin of her right hand was torn and hot with blood, for she would never lift it from the wall, only press it slowly down and force her rigid legs to move from the knowledge of each step to the peril of the next.

So Caroline came down the dark tower She could not think. She could know nothing but fear. Only her brain remorselessly recorded the tally. 'Five hundred and one,' it counted, 'five hundred and two – and three and four –'

Footsteps in the Snow

Mario Soldati

It was the last straw that broke the camel's back. Just before lunchtime he had come back to the hotel and gone up to his room. His wife was in the bathroom, combing her hair – she had not locked herself in as she usually did. And so he thought it was all right to go in. But she shouted at him with hate, yes, real hate in her voice:

'Do you mind closing the door please?'

He closed the door, went out of the room, left the hotel.

It was still snowing.

While he lunched in the old restaurant with all its gilt decoration, mirrors, and stained glass, he gazed out at the snow falling against the dark russet background of Palazzo Carignano. The snow, lying on the baroque cornices, the window mouldings, the pattern of oblique lines and ornaments, repeated, retraced inevitably and precisely the light strokes of Guarini's pen when in his first rapid sketches he pictured the façade of the palace. Similarly, Gioberti, in the centre of the square, was limned in snow only on the shoulders, and arms, the folds of his frock-coat, around his head. It seemed no longer a monument but an impression of a monument dashed off by a De Pisis with a few brush-strokes of white paint. It appeared beautiful even though it wasn't.

The snow simplified everything like a great designer.

He thought of his father who, whenever he quarrelled with his mother, lunched out – always or nearly always in that same restaurant where he was now for like reasons and which in his father's time looked exactly the same in every detail as it was today and had been 130 years before. 130 plus 40 = 170!

He thought of his father's life and then he thought of his own, so different and yet in a way so similar. Wasn't there a woman in existence then with whom life might at least be tolerable?

One after the other, he thought of all the women who had preceded his wife. He tried to be objective. One after the other, he dismissed them. They were no better than his wife. They were just the same. The only difference, the slight preference that he was tempted to allow the others lay merely in the fact that he had not married *them* whereas he had married *her*. If he had married any one of the others she would have immediately become quite as tiresome – he was sure of it.

He might as well have saved time and stopped at the first – he told himself, heaving a deep sigh. But who was the first?

Who was the very first he had been with when this absurd and inevitable idea of marriage flashed through his mind?

It was a long reverie, long, slow, uncertain, delving back into the distant, forgotten past, back to his adolescent days. And meanwhile his eyes almost independently and as if indulging in some pleasant, lethargic and silly optical exercise, stared fascinated at the snow which was falling gently and steadily against the dark backdrop of Palazzo Carignano, the dense flakes, however, following ever-changing courses and taking ever-changing shapes – great fleeting arabesques forming and disintegrating before the eye could catch them.

A long reverie. It was impossible to remember them all. Too many years had passed. But the first? Who was the first?

The first, without any doubt, had been Lina.

A little bit older than him, perhaps. Blonde, tall, strong but at the same time rosy, soft-skinned, vital, open-minded, intelligent and most tender A Turin girl, too. A bank-clerk.

They had carried on a flirtation – our countryfolk would say 'they had spoken to each other' – all spring, from March to June or July, no longer. Everything was fine. He had been happy. Happier than with any other woman later on in life. If only he had known! If only he had even suspected! But Lina had been sudden, complete, gratuitous happiness . . . Why couldn't this boon be repeated at least once more? He had his whole life before him! And so he had left her.

It had been he – there was no doubt about this, either – he and not she had been the one to break it off. But why?

For nothing at all. Just like that. Summer was coming. Holidays were in the air – a good excuse He, middle class, she, on the other hand, a working girl. But that was not why he had broken it off. He had broken it off simply because he was twenty, still without a degree and no job in sight – how could he possibly think seriously of marriage?

Yet he had thought of it – when one night in the park of an old villa, then a few kilometres outside the city, today overtaken by a suburb.

Embracing Lina, he had felt a completely different sensation from what he had experienced with all the others. Anyway until then they had been few.

Sitting on the grass, amid the scent of a great magnolia, in almost total darkness, he could still see her red lips, her strong, gleaming white teeth and above all her big, blue eyes. She was the first real woman in his life. A being so similar to himself and yet so profoundly different. The creature he was holding close, melting into one with her, obeying in a natural yet mysterious way the finest and highest instinct. Due to the simple fact that he was no longer embracing himself but another person, he seemed to be embracing the infinite.

In the grounds of the old villa, that May night, he clasped the infinite tightly to him, beneath his lips, in his hands.

Then why let it slip away? Why not live together, always, till death did them part.

Why not marry Lina?

And he thought about it, yes, he had thought about it. But at once, or almost at once, he had dismissed the idea as sheer folly.

Now, thirty years later, he knew that it might have been the wise thing to do – or at least an act of folly no greater than the one he eventually committed.

It would really have been just as well!

With all these reflections it was getting late. After lunch he had sat motionless looking out at the snow. For how long? He was roused by the timid voice of a waiter presenting the bill. The great glittering gold dining-room was completely empty. There at the other end he recognized two gentlemen in overcoats and hats as the owner and the senior waiter – they were obviously waiting for him to go before leaving themselves.

He looked at the time. It was almost five o'clock. So that was why the façade of Palazzo Carignano was no longer reddish but black. Night was near He paid up and went out.

He strolled aimlessly along under the arcades. When he felt tired he would turn into a café – that was it. But to go back to the hotel and see his wife again – no, not yet.

He strolled under the arcades, desperate yet happy at the same time. Outside, it was still snowing. He remembered reading in a Touring Club guide that Turin has fourteen kilometres of arcades. What other town in the world can offer such a civilized amenity? Bologna, maybe? Padua? But they are not tall, airy and modern like these!

So he walked on and on and it had been dark for some time when he finally found himself at the corner of Corso Vinzaglio and Corso Vittorio which from his childhood days had always seemed to him the boundary of nineteenth-century bourgeois Turin. That corner, to be exact, where the arcades of the two main streets meet after a journey of fourteen kilometres across the city and up the gentle slope on which it is built from the banks of the Po. Beyond the corner was the last stretch of Corso Vittorio, dreary for lack of arcades – here were the Prison, Borgo San Paolo, workers, factories, the cruel future.

He smiled at that old idea. The future is always cruel. It is by nature. Now, after so many years, he no longer felt that gulf between the bourgeois and the working-class city, the nineteenth and the twentieth century. That old corner of Corso Vinzaglio and Corso Vittorio stretching like a jetty out into the sea, the night and the future was no longer a jetty, no longer the farthest limit. The sea, facing him, had become dry land. The future had become the present. And bourgeois Turin willingly accepted the embraces of working-class Turin, her glory, riches and defence.

But, for anyone, bourgeois or working class, on a snowy winter's night like that, strolling aimlessly along the arcades, trying to ease some private grief, the corner of Corso Vinzaglio and Corso Vittorio was still a natural spot to pause.

How often during that one far-off spring of their love, had he stopped right there at night with Lina, before turning to *rebrousser chemin*!

Just at the corner he saw that a taxi was parked in the rank by the pavement.

Should he go back to the hotel? And face that bitch?

He felt a tightening round his heart.

But what was he to do then?

During the long walk through the arcades, in the confusion of memories and daydreams that seemed to fall and flow, dancing and intertwining like snowflakes, a favourite image returned persistently, a sweet, lovely, consoling image: the park at the old villa, that night in May, Lina's face beneath his kisses.

'Taxi' – he called with sudden resolve. And, climbing in, he told the driver the name of what so many years before had been a village separated from the city and was now a small suburb.

When he arrived, it had stopped snowing. He left the taxi in the square of the village, still unchanged with its low houses and their large doorways and thick buttressed walls: old country houses and farm cottages huddling together. But already, beyond the snow-laden roofs, and no more than two hundred metres in the direction of Turin, there were to be seen towering, geometrical, chequered by a thousand lighted windows and balconies, the first joint-owned buildings, houses under mortgage, workers' and clerks' ugly blocks of flats.

There was a café still open. He offered the driver a drink and asked him to wait there. He would not be long.

The villa was only a few steps away: two hundred metres, just off the square. He remembered. The gate suddenly appeared in a lane of the old village. From there on, the lane became a country road sloping down to the nearby river Dora and flanked on one side for some distance by the boundary wall of the villa. He recalled a holy-water stoup a few metres past the gate, a holy-water stoup or a votive shrine almost against the wall: and a gap in the wall blocked by a large thicket and hidden, in any case, by the shrine. The park was very big; the villa, eighteenth-century and usually unoccupied except in autumn for the holiday season.

Perhaps today everything had changed. Perhaps the gap was no longer there. So many years! No matter, if nothing else he had to see that old wall again which – at least so it seemed today – had embraced the nearest moment to truth in his whole life . . . To truth or to happiness? Both. He confused the two.

Naturally, it was not so easy. Simply crossing the square, and following the lane as far as the gate – it was quite a little undertaking. He sank up to his calves in the soft, fresh snow as he was not wearing suitable shoes. The lane was deserted and dim. Old lamps with enamelled shades, widely spaced out at the corners of the houses, shone like gems in the cold, pure night air. If it had not been for the music, songs, laughter, bawling and applause coming from the television sets in the houses as he passed by, he might have been walking through a forsaken village. The voices and sounds, either because of the thickness of the walls or the deep snow that covered everything, were strangely muffled as if swathed in cotton-wool.

Soon they died away. All he could hear was his own heavy breathing and the light crunch of each step as he planted his foot in the snow, followed by a splutter as it dropped about when he raised his foot again.

There was the gate. Behind him lay the village and the city. Facing, just the villa and the open countryside. If he paused a moment and held his breath, he could sense it from the silence. And in that silence, now almost absolute, as soon as he set off again, the sound of his footsteps in the snow seemed deafening.

The shrine was there. Old, peeling, dilapidated. Now it seemed unlikely that they would have bothered to repair the gap. But suppose they had?

He struggled up the bank. Up over the snow: and the snow, sliding away in lumps, carried him down again. By putting on his gloves and grasping a crumbling cornice which separated the base of the shrine from the actual niche containing the figure of the Madonna or Saint, he finally made it: there was the grating but no light burning inside; he couldn't see or remember.

The snow had covered in a single mass both thicket and wall. To discover a gap you had to know of its existence.

No, it had not been repaired: and all that snow, by covering it, made it easier to get across.

When he reached an avenue in the park, he stopped, his heart pounding, and once more listened to the silence: but now for a long, long time, as if in depth.

The air was still, clear and chilly. Nearby, the only sounds were the occasional cracking of boughs as they broke beneath the weight of fresh snow and the muffled thuds that followed: and, Lord knows why, the thuds and cracks had a kind of live, tortured quality. Far away the whistle of a train, shunting maybe in the station at Alpignano: the rumble of a lorry over towards Pianezza, on the road the other side of the Dora.

As he stood motionless in the middle of the avenue, listening to all these sounds, far and near, his eyes gradually became accustomed to the gloom. Or maybe it was the snow itself shedding light. Apart from some black, mysterious shadows under the thickest clumps of evergreens – pines, cedars, magnolias, holm-oaks – everything seemed to him as bright as day: but without the colours.

He began to move forward, slowly. Here and there among the trees he could make out flower-beds: great circles and ovals where the snow was convex in shape and appeared to be deeper. He noticed at regular intervals along both sides of the avenue oblong mounds from the top of which emerged the curved backs of iron park-benches. Then a frozen fountain, a stone bust.

And above all he noticed away to the right through the delicate clear tracery of naked trees, in a space left by the evergreens, the great grey front of the villa.

He was not so far away now. Another hundred metres and he would be there. There, among the flower-beds, the hedges and the trees, in that open space in front of the villa, in that parterre at whose edge, beneath the great magnolia, he thought he embraced the infinite: Lina!

As he gazed at the façade of the villa and began to make out the outlines of the windows, the little rococo portico, the iron balconies, he suddenly stopped, terrified by a natural enough thought but which until then – maybe because of the magic of memories or the spell of time and place – had not crossed his mind: what if there was someone at the villa?

He knew that during the war and for a long time after the war it had been lived in or at any rate occupied by a number of evacuee families all the year round, winter included. They heated the great rooms with stoves, cooked in the fireplaces: in short, they made the best of it.

Now suppose just one of those families was still there?

Or what if there was a caretaker, a gardener?

In that case, though, there would very probably be a dog. And by now, after more than five minutes since he had climbed over the wall and walked through the park, the dog would have barked or at least growled behind a door if they had it shut in. But, though he strained his ears, he could hear nothing.

True, he remembered hearing about some particularly intelligent and ferocious watch-dogs which, without stirring, allow the thief or intruder to enter the grounds they guard: they let him almost reach the house: then they take him by surprise and leap at his legs or throat.

Afraid? Was he afraid? By natural association of ideas he remembered his wife. What was there fiercer to fear? And smiling at himself, he walked on.

He reached the villa. Ten metres farther and he stood in the centre of the wide empty space in front of the house. Here the brightness of the snow was still more intense. He looked up at the sky as if looking for the moon and the stars. But it was overcast – uniform, high, grey cloud: but with a touch of white, surely a reflection from the snow.

Where was the big magnolia tree?

It was there. There on the left. Enormous, solid, veneered in white and black. Its lowest branches, snow-laden, bent down to within a metre of the ground: beneath you could glimpse a sort of vast, deep, pitch-dark cavern. It was there in that cavern that he had brushed true happiness for the first and last time in his life.

As he looked at the cavern, all at once with a start he seemed to remember a certain sentence that Lina had said to him: and on hearing it he had felt a sudden urge to weep, shout, go berserk: to run away with Lina to America or Australia, just the two of them, married and ready to make a fresh start, far from all that had been their reality till then. The effect had been so strong that immediately afterwards he had felt afraid. He had tried to forget that sentence: soon, after a few weeks, he had tried to forget Lina, too. And he had succeeded: but only for thirty years.

Now Lina was there. Alive, there, with him. And the sentence? . . . the sentence?

He closed his eyes in an attempt to remember, to remember it exactly, word for word. He closed his eyes, clasped his hand over them and half-turned with his back to the magnolia: this, too, was to help him think, to avoid the temptation of looking at the magnolia until he remembered the exact expression: for the magnolia which fascinated him, white, black, oppressive, mysterious, would distract him.

Well, Lina, at a certain moment slipping from his embrace, had looked straight at him with her laughing blue eyes, spoken his name and softly whispered, almost breathed on his face:

'What would your mother say if she saw you here?'

That was it, he was sure: in his whole life he could remember nothing more beautiful.

He heard the sound of a light footstep in the snow: then more steps that came up behind him. He shivered: it was terror yet at the same time something akin to pleasure. He felt that he must turn around, but he didn't have the courage. Maybe by turning around he would see. Oh, it was worth the effort, no doubt. But fear was stronger.

Now the steps stopped terribly near, perhaps less than a metre behind him. He seemed to feel an icy-cold breath on the nape of the neck. The wind?

He felt his eyes suddenly filling with tears. Have pity! Forgive me! – he wanted to cry out. Not pity or forgiveness because he believed even at that crucial moment that he had wronged Lina by leaving her: but pity and forgiveness for no particular reason, simply because he was afraid. And Lina? Where was Lina now? He had never heard of her since, that was that: and there was no reason to think that . . .

A rustling, a quick, gossamer light tread, then a creaking, a crack, a thud. As if the person who had approached him in the snow had stopped behind him, almost near enough to touch him, had abruptly turned and run away. Or maybe it was merely his imagination: the only real sounds were the crack and the final thud: another branch, like so many breaking beneath the weight of the snow. Perhaps a magnolia branch, this time; that was just the direction from which the sound had come.

He turned to see.

He turned and saw in the snow, in a direct line between him and the magnolia, the fresh, clear prints of two small feet, a woman's: footprints that came up to him from the magnolia and then went back to the tree.

He first impulse, of course, was to run to the magnolia. But he couldn't. He felt that his legs wouldn't support him.

The second impulse was to shout.

Meanwhile, a snowflake fell, then another: a moment and it had started to snow again.

As soon as he felt strong enough, he called:

'Who is it? Who's there?'

But his voice died away, echoless, in the air blanketed by the snow which was now falling heavily.

Why did he lack the courage to follow those little footprints up to the magnolia?

In a few minutes the snow would obliterate them and he would never know: he would lose, together with the proof that it was not a hallucination and that the footprints were real, the last opportunity of knowing.

But perhaps that was exactly his intention. He didn't want to know. He was afraid of knowing.

At a run, sinking deep in the snow, stumbling, falling, plunging on somehow, he crossed the deserted park to the gap in the wall: he clambered over and did not stop until he reached the village square and saw the small, distant, green shape of his taxi bathed in golden light, outside the café where he had left it.

The Wind

Ray Bradbury

The phone rang at five-thirty that evening. It was December, and long since dark as Thompson picked up the phone.

'Hello.'

'Hello, *Herb*?'

'Oh, it's you, Allin.'

'Is your wife home, Herb?'

'Sure. Why?'

'Damn it.'

Herb Thompson held the receiver quietly. 'What's up? You sound funny.'

'I wanted you to come over tonight.'

'We're having company.'

'I wanted you to spend the night. When's your wife going away?'

'That's next week,' said Thompson. 'She'll be in Ohio for about nine days. Her mother's sick. I'll come over then.'

'I wish you could come over tonight.'

'Wish I could. Company and all, my wife'd kill me.'

'I wish you could come over.'

'What's it? the wind again?'

'Oh, no. No.'

'Is it the wind?' asked Thompson.

The voice on the phone hesitated. 'Yeah. Yeah, it's the wind.'

'It's a clear night, there's not much wind.'

'There's enough. It comes in the window and blows the curtains a little bit. Just enough to tell me.'

'Look, why don't you come and spend the night here?' said Herb Thompson looking around the lighted hall.

'Oh, no. It's too late for that. It might catch me on the way over. It's a damned long distance. I wouldn't dare, but thanks, anyway. It's thirty miles, but thanks.'

'Take a sleeping-tablet.'

'I've been standing in the door for the past hour, Herb. I can see it building up in the west. There are some clouds there and I saw one of them kind of rip apart. There's a wind coming, all right.'

'Well, you just take a nice sleeping-tablet. And call me any time you want to call. Later this evening if you want.'

'Any time?' said the voice on the phone.

'Sure.'

'I'll do that, but I wish you could come out. Yet I wouldn't want you hurt. You're my best friend and I wouldn't want that. Maybe it's best I face this thing alone. I'm sorry I bother you.'

'Hell, what's a friend for? Tell you what you do, sit down and get some writing done this evening,' said Herb Thompson, shifting from one foot to the other in the hall. 'You'll forget about the Himalayas and the Valley of the Winds and this preoccupation of yours with storms and hurricanes. Get another chapter done on your next travel book.'

'I might do that. Maybe I will, I don't know. Maybe I will. I might do that. Thanks a lot for letting me bother you.'

'Thanks, hell. Get off the line, now, you. My wife's calling me to dinner.'

Herb Thompson hung up.

He went and sat down at the supper table and his wife sat across from him. 'Was that Allin?' she asked. He nodded. 'Him and his winds that blow up and winds that blow down and winds that blow hot and blow cold,' she said, handing him his plate heaped with food.

'He did have a time in the Himalayas, during the war,' said Herb Thompson.

'You don't believe what he said about that valley, do you?'

'It makes a good story.'

'Climbing around, climbing up things. Why do men climb mountains and scare themselves?'

'It was snowing,' said Herb Thompson.

'Was it?'

'And raining and hailing and blowing all at once, in that valley. Allin's told me a dozen times. He tells it well. He was up pretty high. Clouds, and all. The valley made a noise.'

'I *bet* it did,' she said.

'Like a lot of winds instead of just one. Winds from all over the world.' He took a bite. 'So says Allin.'

'He shouldn't have gone there and looked, in the first place,' she said. 'You go poking around and first thing you know you get ideas. Winds start getting angry at you for intruding, and they follow you.'

'Don't joke, he's my best friend,' snapped Herb Thompson.

'It's all so silly!'

'Nevertheless he's been through a lot. That storm in Bombay, later, and the typhoon off New Guinea two months after that. And that time, in Cornwall.'

'I have no sympathy for a man who continually runs into wind storms and hurricanes, and then gets a persecution complex because of it.'

The phone rang just then.

'Don't answer it,' she said.

'Maybe it's important.'

'It's only Allin again.'

They sat there and the phone rang nine times and they didn't answer. Finally, it quieted. They finished dinner. Out in the kitchen, the window curtains gently moved in the small breeze from a slightly opened window.

The phone rang again.

'I can't let it ring,' he said, and answered it. 'Oh, hello, Allin.'

'Herb! It's here! It got here!'

'You're too near the phone, back up a little.'

'I stood in the open door and waited for it. I saw it coming down the highway, shaking all the trees, one by one, until it shook the trees just outside the house and it dived down toward the door and I slammed the door in its face!'

Thompson didn't say anything. He couldn't think of anything to say, his wife was watching him in the hall door.

'How interesting,' he said, at last.

'It's all round the house, Herb. I can't get out now, I can't do anything. But I fooled it, I let it think it had me, and just as it came down to get me I slammed and locked the door! I was ready for it, I've been getting ready for weeks.'

'Have you, now; tell me about it, Allin, old man.' Herb Thompson played it jovially into the phone, while his wife looked on and his neck began to sweat.

'It began six weeks ago . . .'

'Oh, yes? Well, well.'

'. . . I thought I had it licked. I thought it had given up following and trying to get me. But it was just waiting. Six weeks ago I heard the wind laughing and whispering around the corners of my house, out here. Just for an hour or so, not very long, not very loud. Then it went away.'

Thompson nodded into the phone. 'Glad to hear it, glad to hear it.' His wife stared at him.

'It came back, the next night. It slammed the shutters and kicked sparks out of the chimney. It came back five nights in a row, a little stronger each time. When I opened the front door, it came in at me and tried to pull me out, but it wasn't strong enough. Tonight it *is.*'

'Glad to hear you're feeling better,' said Thompson.

'I'm not better, what's wrong with you? Is your wife listening to us?'

'Yes.'

'Oh, I see. I know I sound like a fool.'

'Not at all. Go on.'

Thompson's wife went back into the kitchen. He relaxed. He sat down on a little chair near the phone. 'Go on, Allin, get it out of you, you'll sleep better.'

'It's all around the house now, like a great big vacuum machine nuzzling at all the gables. It's knocking the trees around.'

'That's funny, there's no wind *here*, Allin.'

'Of course not, it doesn't care about you, only about me.'

'I guess that's one way to explain it.'

'It's a killer, Herb, the biggest damnedest prehistoric killer that ever hunted prey. A big sniffling hound, trying to smell me out, find me. It pushes its big cold nose up to the house, taking air, and when it finds me in the parlour it drives its pressure there, and when I'm in the kitchen it goes there. It's trying to get in the windows, now, but I had them reinforced and I put new hinges on the doors, and bolts. It's a strong house. They built them strong in the old days. I've got all the lights in the house on, now. The house is all lighted up, bright. The wind followed me from room to room, looking through all the windows, when I switched them on. Oh!'

'What's wrong?'

'It just snatched off the front screen door!'

'I wish you'd come over here and spend the night, Allin.'

'I can't! God, I can't leave the house. I can't do anything. I know this wind. Lord, it's big and it's clever. I tried to light a cigarette a moment ago, and a little draught sucked the match out. The wind likes to play games, it likes to taunt me, it's taking its time with me; it's got all night.

And now! God, right now, one of my old travel books, on the library table, I wish you could see it. A little breeze from God knows what small hole in the house, the little breeze is – blowing the pages one by one. I wish you could see it. There's my introduction. Do you remember the introduction to my book on Tibet, Herb?'

'Yes.'

'This book is dedicated to those who lost the game of elements, written by one who has seen, but who has always escaped.'

'Yes, I remember.'

'The lights have gone out!'

The phone crackled.

'The power lines just went down. Are you there, Herb?'

'I still hear you.'

'The wind doesn't like all that light in my house, it tore the power lines down. The telephone will probably go next. Oh, it's a real party, me and the wind, I tell you! Just a second.'

'Allin?' A silence. Herb leaned against the mouthpiece. His wife glanced in from the kitchen. Herb Thompson waited. 'Allin?'

'I'm back,' said the voice on the phone. 'There was a draught from the door and I shoved some wadding under it to keep it from blowing on my feet. I'm glad you didn't come out after all, Herb, I wouldn't want you in this mess. There! It just broke one of the living-room windows and a regular gale is in the house, knocking pictures off the wall! Do you hear it?'

Herb Thompson listened. There was a wild sirening on the phone and a whistling and banging. Allin shouted over it. 'Do you hear it?'

Herb Thompson swallowed drily. 'I hear it.'

'It wants me alive, Herb. It doesn't dare knock the house down in one fell blow. That'd kill me. It wants me alive, so it can pull me apart, finger by finger. It wants what's inside me. My mind, my brain. It wants my life-power, my psychic force, my ego. It wants intellect.'

'My wife's calling me, Allin. I have to go wipe the dishes.'

'It's a big cloud of vapours, winds from all over the world. The same wind that ripped the Celebes a year ago, the same pampero that killed in Argentina, the typhoon that fed on Hawaii, the hurricane that knocked the coast of Africa early this year. It's part of all those storms I escaped. It followed me from the Himalayas because it didn't want me to know what I know about the Valley of the Winds where it gathers and plans its destruction. Something, a long time ago, gave it a start in the direction of life. I know its feeding grounds, I know where it is born and where parts of it expire. For that reason, it hates me; and my books that tell how to defeat it. It doesn't want me preaching any more. It wants to incorporate me into its huge body, to give it knowledge. It wants me on its own side!'

'I have to hang up, Allin, my wife –'

'What?' A pause, the blowing of the wind in the phone, distantly. 'What did you say?'

'Call me back in about an hour, Allin.'

He hung up.

He went out to wipe the dishes. His wife looked at him and he looked at the dishes, rubbing them with a towel.

'What's it like out tonight?' he said.

'Nice. Not very chilly. Stars,' she said. 'Why?'

'Nothing.'

The phone rang three times in the next hour. At eight o'clock the company arrived, Stoddard and his wife. They sat around until eight-thirty talking and then got out and set up the card table and began to play Gin.

Herb Thompson shuffled the cards over and over, with a clittering, shuttering effect and clapped them out, one at a time before the three other players. Talk went back and forth. He lit a cigar and made it into a fine grey ash at the tip, and adjusted his cards in his hand and on occasion lifted his head and listened. There was no sound outside the house. His wife saw him do this, and he cut it out immediately, and discarded a Jack of Clubs.

He puffed slowly on his cigar and they all talked quietly with occasional small eruptions of laughter, and the clock in the hall sweetly chimed nine o'clock.

'Here we all are,' said Herb Thompson, taking his cigar out and looking at it reflectively. 'And life is sure funny.'

'Eh?' said Mr Stoddard.

'Nothing, except here we are, living our lives, and some place else on earth a billion other people live their lives.'

'That's a rather obvious statement.'

'Life,' he put his cigar back in his lips, 'is a lonely thing. Even with married people. Sometimes when you're in a person's arms you feel a million miles away from them.'

'I like *that*,' said his wife.

'I didn't mean it that way,' he explained, not with haste; because he felt no guilt, he took his time. 'I mean we all believe what we believe and live our own little lives while other people live entirely different ones. I mean, we sit here in this room while a thousand people are dying. Some of cancer, some of pneumonia, some of tuberculosis. I imagine someone in the United States is dying right now in a wrecked car.'

'This isn't very stimulating conversation,' said his wife.

'I mean to say, we all live and don't think about how other people think or live their lives or die. We wait until death comes *to* us. What I mean is here we sit, on our self-assured butt-bones, while, thirty miles away, in a big old house, completely surrounded by night and God-knows-what, one of the finest guys who ever lived is –'

'Herb!'

He puffed and chewed on his cigar and stared blindly at his cards. 'Sorry.' He blinked rapidly and bit his cigar. 'Is it my turn?'

'It's your turn.'

The playing went around the table, with a flittering of cards, murmurs, conversation. Herb Thompson sank lower into his chair and began to look ill.

The phone rang. Thompson jumped and ran to it and jerked it off the hook.

'Herb! I've been calling and calling. What's it like at your house, Herb?'

'What do you mean, what's it like?'

'Has the company come?'

'Hell, yes, it has –'

'Are you talking and laughing and playing cards?'

'Christ, yes, but what has that got to do with –'

'Are you smoking your ten-cent cigar?'

'God damn it, yes, but . . .'

'Swell,' said the voice on the phone. 'That sure is swell. I wish I could be there. I wish I didn't know the things I know. I wish lots of things.'

'Are you all right?'

'So far, so good. I'm locked in the kitchen now. Part of the front wall of the house blew in. But I planned my retreat. When the kitchen door gives, I'm heading for the cellar. If I'm lucky I may hold out there until morning. It'll have to tear the whole damned house down to get to me, and the cellar floor is pretty solid. I have a shovel and I may dig – deeper . . .'

It sounded like a lot of other voices on the phone.

'What's *that*?' Herb Thompson demanded, cold, shivering.

'That?' asked the voice on the phone. 'Those are the voices of twelve thousand killed in a typhoon, seven thousand killed by a hurricane, three thousand buried by a cyclone. Am I boring you? That's what the wind is. It's a lot of people dead. The wind killed them, took their minds to give itself intelligence. It took all their voices and made them into one voice. All those millions of people killed in the past ten thousand years, tortured and run from continent to continent on the backs and in the bellies of monsoons and whirlwinds. Oh Christ, what a poem you could write about it!'

The phone echoed and rang with voices and shouts and whinings.

'Come on back, Herb,' called his wife from the card table.

'That's how the wind gets more intelligent each year, it adds to itself, body by body, life by life, death by death.'

'We're waiting for you, Herb,' called his wife.

'Damn it!' He turned, almost snarling. 'Wait just a moment, won't you!' Back to the phone. 'Allin, if you want me to come out there now, I will! I should have come earlier . . .'

'Wouldn't think of it. This is a grudge fight, wouldn't do to have you in it now. I'd better hang up. The kitchen door looks bad; I'll have to get in the cellar.'

'Call me back, later?'

'Maybe, if I'm lucky. I don't think I'll make it. I slipped away and escaped so many times, but I think it has me now. I hope I haven't bothered you too much, Herb.'

'You haven't bothered anyone, damn it. Call me back.'

'I'll try . . .'

Herb Thompson went back to the card game. His wife glared at him. 'How's Allin, your friend?' she asked. 'Is he sober?'

'He's never taken a drink in his life,' said Thompson, sullenly, sitting down. 'I should have gone out there hours ago.'

'But he's called every night for six weeks and you've been out there at least ten nights to stay with him and nothing was wrong.'

'He needs help. He might hurt himself.'

'You were just out there, two nights ago, you can't always be running after him.'

'First thing in the morning I'll move him into a sanatorium. Didn't want to. He seems so reasonable otherwise.'

At ten-thirty coffee was served. Herb Thompson drank his slowly, looking at the phone. I wonder if he's in the cellar now, he thought.

Herb Thompson walked to the phone, called long-distance, gave the number.

'I'm sorry,' said the operator. 'The lines are down in that district. When the lines are repaired, we will put your call through.'

'Then the telephone lines *are* down!' cried Thompson. He let the phone drop. Turning, he slammed open the closet door, pulled out his coat. 'Oh Lord,' he said. 'Oh, Lord, Lord,' he said to his amazed guests and his wife with the coffee urn in her hand. 'Herb!' she cried. 'I've got to get out there!' he said, slipping into his coat.

There was a soft, faint stirring at the door.

Everybody in the room tensed and straightened up.

'Who could that be?' asked his wife.

The soft stirring was repeated, very quietly.

Thompson hurried down the hall where he stopped, alert.

Outside, faintly, he heard laughter.

'I'll be damned,' said Thompson. He put his hand on the doorknob, pleasantly shocked and relieved. 'I'd know that laugh anywhere. It's Allin. He came on over in his car, after all. Couldn't wait until morning to tell me his confounded stories.' Thompson smiled weakly. 'Probably brought some friends with him. Sounds like a lot of other . . .'

He opened the front door.

The porch was empty.

Thompson showed no surprise; his face grew amused and sly. He laughed. 'Allin? None of your tricks now! Come on.' He switched on the porch-light and peered out and around. 'Where are you, Allin? Come on, now.'

A breeze blew into his face.

Thompson waited a moment, suddenly chilled to his marrow. He stepped out on the porch and looked uneasily, and very carefully, about.

A sudden wind caught and whipped his coat flaps, dishevelled his hair. He thought he heard laughter again. The wind rounded the house and was a pressure everywhere at once, and then, storming for a full minute, passed on.

The wind died down, sad, mourning in the high trees, passing away; going back out to the sea, to the Celebes, to the Ivory Coast, to Sumatra and Cape Horn, to Cornwall and the Philippines. Fading, fading, fading.

Thompson stood there, cold. He went in and closed the door and leaned against it, and didn't move, eyes closed.

'What's wrong . . .?' asked his wife.

Exorcizing Baldassare

Edward Hyams

A few years ago some friends of mine called Robbie-Blackthorne came to England from the United States where he had been managing the American head-office of the British Rare Metals Export Consortium. Robbie-Blackthorne is English and he was recalled to become Deputy Managing Director in London. His wife's a Virginian; she is very pretty, slender, tall, lively, dark, involved in everything that is going on, and I am allowed to be in love with her. They started looking for a country house; I should explain that James Robbie-Blackthorne's income is something over £20,000 a year and that Bernice has money of her own; they could afford to buy the house they wanted instead of being obliged, like the rest of us, to pretend to want the house they could afford. They found it in Sussex, a white jewel on a wooded hillside, standing in a hundred-acre park. It had been built by William Kent to designs drawn by him and Lord Burlington based on the plans for Vivaldi's Villa Scarabini on Lake Como. I do not think that in all England there is a more beautiful house of its really very convenient size. It had, however, a sinister incident in its career, an incident almost Gothic and very much at odds with its clear and smiling face, its Renaissance good sense. I went with James and Bernice to look at it, and the agent, a pleasant and well-bred man in his fifties with a remarkable gift for telling a story, told us this one as we moved from room to splendid room, from one beautiful prospect to another.

It seems that the house had not long been completed when its owner and builder, Sir Henry Waterperry, had invited to stay with him a half-English Italian whom he had met and admired during his Grand Tour, Count Baldassare Baldassar. The Count was to advise on the finishing of the moulded ceilings which were being made – they are now a great treasure of course – by a family of Florentine plasterers whom Waterperry had imported for the purpose; they were a father and two sons, and the daughter who cooked and kept house for them. These Florentines were accommodated in a wing of the house not yet prepared for proper occupation, with a few pieces of necessary furniture. Baldassare, whom the agent described as a notorious womanizer even in that age of unashamed lust, seduced the plasterer's very pretty daughter, a girl of sixteen; 'seduced' is a polite way of putting it; it was, in fact, a brutal rape carried out with the help of the Count's two body-servants, Austrians from Merano and men of the vilest antecedents.

The plasterer and his sons were not of the class which, at that time, made a necessary connection between the virginity of a daughter or sister with the honour of the family, whatever that may mean. But the girl's virginity had considerable value in the marriage market even among artisans; moreover, the father and his sons all loved the girl. After she had told them what had happened to her, which was not until she found herself pregnant, the three men chose a night to make the Count's two servants blind drunk on brandy and at one in the morning made their way to Baldassare's bedroom. There they gagged and bound him while he was still struggling out of a drunken sleep, for he had adopted the English custom of drinking too much at dinner; fastened one end of a rope round his neck and the other to a bolt screwed into the floorboards; then threw him out of the window. They later drew the body back into the room, carried it out into the grounds and, having weighted it with stones, sank it in the ornamental lake which had recently been completed in imitation of Mr Hoare's new lake at Stourhead. Before doing so, however, they cut off the Count's nose and ears, and on the following day – the agent pointed to the ceiling-moulding in the great saloon as he told us this part – they moulded these organs into the plaster of their work, to form the nose and ears of the life-size reclining Jupiter which is the central motif of the ceiling design. The Count's disappearance caused no serious alarm for some weeks; his life had been full of such escapades, and it was assumed that he was off with a woman or a boy. By the time that his body, released by the nibbling of the giant carp with which the lake had been stocked, floated to the surface in a very dilapidated condition, the plasterers, well-paid and well-thanked, were back in Florence.

But this was only the introduction to a story which Bernice had listened to, enchanted; and as we passed from the saloon into the long gallery with its Tuscan mosaic floor, the agent, halting, continued. He said that the first manifestation of Count Baldassare's uneasy phantom was recorded in 1813 when Castlereagh was staying with the Waterperrys on his way to Vienna and had the misfortune to encounter the ghost walking the gallery – an atrocious spectacle, earless, noseless and with the neck stretched like a turkey's at a poulterer's. Castlereagh stood his ground and the thing vanished through the wall beside him, between a portrait of Sir Bingham Waterperry and one of his mother, the Lady Elizabeth. The manifestation had since been regular and it was accompanied by a rather disagreeable shriek or cry for help uttered only once and of which Castlereagh, in his account of the experience which appears as an ironical postscriptum in a letter to Metternich now in the British Museum, says nothing. The agent went on to say, with some emphasis, that these phenomena were not malignant; there was, for example, no such tradition as afflicted Mereworth Castle until it was exorcized, of misfortune dogging the owners. There was by no means a curse on the house; on the contrary, it had, for over a century, had a very happy history.

'A ghost! Oh, James, we positively must have this house.' Thus Bernice; James was willing but the asking-price struck him as too high; and he was a good deal taken aback when his first offer, a more realistic figure, was flatly refused. He was even more surprised when, having advanced the ghost and the scream as serious faults in the property, almost as bad as inefficient drains or a leaking roof and therefore proper as bargaining points, he was told that, on the contrary, the ghost and the scream were valuable amenities, justifying the high price demanded. The agent told him, 'I will be perfectly candid with you, sir. It is precisely because of this interesting and harmless haunting that we are confident, indeed certain, of getting our price.'

James, who was as fond of his wife as of his money, or almost, paid.

I first saw and heard the manifestations when I stayed with the Robbie-Blackthornes during the Christmas of 1962. James had been out all afternoon, rough shooting over his small estate; it was just before that winter's heavy snowfalls began. He had come in and was taking a bath. Bernice and I were beside the great fire of cedar logs in the saloon, she sewing (she does exquisite *petit-point*) while I read an Italian novel which a publisher had asked me to translate. We had a transistor radio on the low table between us, playing French pop songs very softly, and the only other sound was the crackle and hiss of the fire.

Then we heard it, the most hideous, heart-shaking cry, half-scream, half-howl, that I have ever heard in my life, cut off abruptly after about three seconds. It brought me, shaking, to my feet. I looked at Bernice; her hands were still, her face sheet-white. But she was not a coward and a moment later she was rising and saying, 'Come on. You'd better see it. We'll just have time.'

Side by side we raced up the wide, shallow staircase, perhaps the most perfectly proportioned in England, to the gallery. It was not quite dark, for there is a system of low-intensity concealed lighting which is switched on, electronically, at dusk. By the time we were on the spot Baldassare's ghost was half-way along its customary walk from the end of the gallery where it emerged from the life-sized portrait of Bernice's grandmother, Helen Jefferson, to the point where the John portrait of Robbie-Blackthorne's father hung, at which point the ghost invariably faded into or passed through the wall.

The first thing I noticed, for I had my wits about me and I do not believe in ghosts, was a very curious variation in intensity of the appearance; that is to say, at one moment the thing was quite sharp and clear; at the next rather foggy and faded; the sharp and clear appearance coincided with intervals of bare, white enamelled wall; the less clear tones, with pictures, as if these were showing through the ghost and so confusing one's sight of it. The figure I saw was that of a slender and elegant male of about fifty, dressed in black breeches and coat, silk stockings and buckled shoes; he wore no sword; and as far as I could see he was not wearing a wig, but his own hair cut and curled in the Roman style later fashionable in England. The face, quite clearly seen when the thing was opposite a bare patch of wall, was an atrocity – noseless, earless, the neck grotesquely stretched, the eyes starting horribly from their sockets.

We stood and watched this horror until, at what I was told was the usual place, it disappeared. I should add that, albeit a disbeliever, this was the only time in my life when I experienced that curious disturbance of the scalp by fear, described in the phrase, 'My hair stood on end.' I had caught hold of Bernice's hand and could feel that she was shaking. When Count Baldassare, or whatever it was, had vanished, we returned to the saloon without exchanging a word. I put more logs on the fire and we drew close to it. Bernice, crouched in her chair, dropped her lovely face into her cupped hands and said, 'Oh, Edward, I've been such a fool, such a God-damned fool.'

I could think of nothing to say to that but, 'Not you, sweetheart,' and she went on, 'I thought it would be fun. But I can't stand it. At first I didn't mind. I still don't mind seeing him, poor creature; much. It does make the house more interesting. But that yell. It was much quieter at first. Much lower. I didn't mind it, nor did the servants. But now we can't keep any. It gets louder and louder, more and more hideous. I can't live with it; I can't, I can't . . .'

'How often does it happen?'

'You can never tell. Sometimes several nights in succession; sometimes not for weeks. And hardly ever in the summer.'

'Ever in the daytime?'

'Twice, last winter.'

James came in then. He was in a dressing-gown, half-dressed; his eyes went straight to Bernice and he looked worried. He said, 'Ring for drinks, honey,' and to me, 'Well, you've heard our friend?'

'And seen him.'

'What do you think?'

'I try not to. Not yet.'

The servant came in with the drinks tray, and when we were all served James said, 'I confess I'm worried.'

'You? That does surprise me.'

'Why? Oh, I'm not afraid of the thing, whatever it is, but . . .' He hesitated and I said, 'Well, but . . . ?'

'I don't like having the whole rational basis of my life, my thinking, my ideas about the way things are, overthrown and turned inside out. Yet I can't deny the evidence of my own sense, or Bernice's. I don't believe in ghosts, Edward; but he's here, isn't he?'

'Something is, I agree.'

'Have you any suggestions?'

'Yes, James. Follow the logic of the situation. Your own philosophy won't work here; use the one that's appropriate, accept the terms of that kind of thinking which doesn't deny the reality of ghosts; and act accordingly.'

'Meaning what, in practice?'

'Call in an exorcist.'

'My dear chap, this isn't darkest Africa. Where the hell do you think I'm to get one?'

'Across the road at the vicarage. Your parish priest is an exorcist, it's part of his qualifications.'

'Are you serious? Well I'm damned. The things one doesn't know.'

The vicar carried out that exorcism with thoroughness and relish. It did not work, nor had I really expected that it would although it had to be tried because there are recorded and well-authenticated cases where it has worked, just as there are unquestionable cases of people getting their warts removed by charms. I suspect that the reason is the same in both cases; the ghosts, like the warts, are what, in the horrible jargon of medical psychology, are called psychosomatic phenomena. The man who has warts, the man who sees a ghost, has made them himself out of some kind of nervous distress. Set his mind, his nerves, at rest by convincing him, if only by a sufficiently confident assertion accompanied by some hocus-pocus, that the warts, or the ghost, will go away, and go away they will.

But I never really believed that Count Baldassare was a psychosomatic phenomenon. Bernice might, by her own nervous state, have persuaded James and even the servants to see and to hear him; but not me, because although I was under her influence in the sense that I was more or less in love with her, I did not live in the same house with her. I was not under the same kind of pressure from her fear as were James and her servants. Moreover, without saying anything to either of them on the following night, when Baldassare walked again, I recorded his scream on the little tape-recorder I use for interviewing and I never yet heard of a tape-recorder with neuroses.

I must cast back for a moment; although as I've told you James readily assented, in his wife's presence, to try exorcism, he modified that attitude considerably when we were alone together later. He said, 'We shall have to go through with it now, but I'd just as soon you'd minded your own damn business and kept your mouth shut. Are you still hopeful of getting Bernice away from me?'

'You never can tell, James. And why do you object, anyway? Do you mean that you think exorcism is all nonsense?'

'That isn't what I mean. No. Look, do you really think it might work?'

'I only know that it worked at other places. Mereworth Castle, for example.'

'Right. Suppose it works here? Know what that'll mean? It will knock anything up to ten thousand pounds off the price of the property. It's worth at least that in publicity, if we wanted to sell. Actually, we don't. But you know my position. If the rest of the Board take it into their heads that I've got to go to Moscow or Peking for three or four years, I'd want to sell. And I should drop a packet owing to your damned officious interference.'

'James,' I said, 'you make me sick. Where do you get this very nice Madeira, by the way?'

'I shan't tell you. And what the hell do you mean? I make you sick?'

'You saw the state Bernice is in, poor sweet. I'd say her peace of mind was worth ten thousand, or a hundred thousand come to that.'

'Then it's as well she's married to me and not you, isn't it?'

'A dirty crack, James. But there are other means than money of helping her.'

'Spoken like a lover. Or, forgive me, a would-be lover. Look, leave it alone, will you? I know Bernice. She'll get used to it.'

'If I can help it, she won't have to.'

I was able to take my first step in psychic research when I discovered that Bernice, having been trained in somewhat Victorian notions by her Cabot mother, still kept a diary as a sort of semi-religious duty. In this she had recorded the dates and times of every one of Baldassare's manifestations since she and James had moved into the house. I asked her for a list of these and I began to study them. Even that small beginning brought her a comfort which was my first reward.

I started trying to find some kind of pattern, some system or series in the appearance of the ghost. There was nothing of the kind; the figures were random, there was not a trace of what I may call mathematical sense in them. What did strike me, though, was the enormously greater frequency of winter over autumn, summer or spring manifestations; and that led me to study the factor of time more closely. I then discovered something else; that this winter predominance was paralleled by a similarly numerical superiority of night over day appearances. Daytime manifestations were so rare as to be negligible. And there was one other thing; the great majority of the manifestations occurred in the small hours, at about dawn. Now this was odd, for it is a well-known fact that ghosts do, and indeed are, constrained to vanish with the dawn.

– 'My hour,' says the ghost of Hamlet's father,

> 'My hour is almost come,
> When I to sulphurous and tormenting flames
> Must render up myself.'

And that hour was, as is usual in such cases, cock-crow. But Baldassare, and this made me smell a very odd rat indeed, preferred to appear at the very moment when others of his kind were disappearing. A careful analysis of the figures showed clearly that he had, moreover, a very decided preference for the small hours of mid January over all other seasons and times.

Oddly enough it was the introduction of a book on the cultivation of less hardy flowering shrubs – I was helping Bernice to replant part of her gardens – which gave me the clue to the interpretation of this curious fact. January is, in Britain, the coldest month of the year and its small hours the coldest time. I went up to London, sought the help of a most agreeable man at the Meteorological Office and established that whenever, even on the two summer occasions, our Count had walked at times outside this special favourite season, the weather had been quite exceptionally cold. In fact there was what scientists call a 'critical' temperature for his appearances. Now this made no sense at all, or so it seemed to me. After all, in life he had been a Neapolitan, not an Eskimo. This time it was Bernice who, unwittingly, gave me a clue which did not appear as such for some time; I admit I was slow on the uptake on that occasion; when I showed and explained the very odd results I was getting, she said, 'Honey, how very odd. You might think that poor Baldassare was thermostatically controlled.'

And so, of course, he was; but I must not run ahead of myself. I took three days of thinking in circles before I saw the point which Bernice had, unwittingly, made, but when that happened I wasted no time. I got a step-ladder from the kitchens and a very powerful electric hand-lantern from the garage, and having made some rough calculations I went over the section of the wall and ceiling of the gallery with a thoroughness and care I did not know myself capable of, but then I'd do anything for Bernice.

It took me just three hours to find what I was looking for; it was in a rather bad seventeenth-century Dutch portrait of Sir Amyas Waterperry which had been left in the house because it was part of the wall-panelling and which depicted him with a leash of those Irish wolf-hounds with which he had hunted three Cromwellian spies among his tenants to death. The pupil of this portrait's left eye was a glass lens; the bared teeth of one hound constituted a small grating.

I said nothing to the household; I was soon in the attics, but it then took me half an hour to penetrate the camouflage – crates, old furniture, and some stacked, rejected paintings of no interest – which had been used to conceal the beautifully made Japanese self-swivelling projector, a tape-recorder, amplifier and loudspeaker, the latter just behind the hound's mouth in the picture; a very large battery of dry cells in one of the crates; and a roof thermostat. For the layman there was no clue to the provenance of all this gear. But not for nothing had I been a radar officer in the last year of the war; the capacitors in the amplifier which I dismantled were made by only one firm in Britain. I disconnected the batteries to exorcize Baldassare, put one of those capacitors in my pocket, returned step-ladder, torch and tools to the kitchen quarters, found Bernice in her new conservatory, and told her I had to go to Leicester for a day or two. She lent me her DB4 so that I was able to keep up a nice steady hundred and twenty on the motorway.

I did not beat about the bush with the Managing Director of the firm I was in Leicester to see. I told him, briefly, what had been happening and what I had discovered. At first he was inclined to laugh his head off, but he changed his manner when I told him, with a great deal of conviction, that if he would not give me the name of the customer to whom those capacitors had been supplied – the one I produced bore a series number – I would take much pleasure in involving his firm in some of the dirtiest and most expensive litigation of its long and, owing to patent problems, litigious career. One hour later, after a quick lunch at his expense, I was on the motorway again and much amused at the effrontery which had dictated the name of the firm I was bound to see; Messrs Manifestations Ltd, of Clerkenwell.

Before I reached Clerkenwell I stopped at a post office in the suburbs and telephoned James in his Leadenhall Street office. I told him enough to exasperate him and violently to stimulate his curiosity; not enough to satisfy him. This made certain that he would drop the business, important or otherwise, which he was engaged on and join me at the offices of Messrs Manifestations Ltd. He was there before me, for I had the usual trouble in parking the car. A hint on a card got us straight in to the Managing Director of Manifestations. He turned out to be a charming, youngish man wearing beautifully made high camp clothes with a manner to match, and he never batted an eyelid, unless slightly flirtatiously at James, who is very good-looking, when I described my discovery for James's benefit as well as his. Only when I came to the increasing loudness and frightfulness of Baldassare's dying scream did he raise an eyebrow and flick a lever on the office intercom to summon a subordinate who turned out to be foreman of the electrical workshops.

'Oh, Ronald, sorry to bother you, but we have a complaint about the automatic volume control on job number four thousand and seven oblique stroke sixty-two.'

'And that doesn't surprise me, sir. I told the Board those German variable resistances weren't man enough for our work, but would they listen? No, they were cheap and that was all they thought of. If I've said it once I've said it fifty times, the dearest is the cheapest in the long run and always will be . . .'

'Now, Ronald, don't be tiresome. The point is, what can we do about it?'

'I can send a fitter down in a day or two and replace the component. But the job's out of the guarantee period and it'll have to be paid for and what's the client going to say?'

I cut in on the technical chit-chat. 'Just a minute. There's no question of repairing the apparatus. This ghost has got to stop walking, see? You can take your damned gear out of the house. And moreover we want an explanation of this outrage and it had better be a good one.'

At that it was James's turn; he said to me, 'How many times do I have to ask you to stop this officious interference in my business?' And to the other men, 'An explanation, yes. But as to removing the apparatus, certainly not. One thing though, can you fit me a small manual switch, so that I can control the ghost?'

'Yes, sir, we are often asked for that. It will cost you about four pounds,' the engineer said; and, at a nod from his boss, left us.

'Come on,' I said, tapping the desk. 'Explanation.'

'My dear, it's surely self-evident. A good haunted house, especially a historic house, or an old rectory, or even a good nineteenth-century Gothic place, is worth far more money than one without a ghost. The apparatus in Mr Robbie-Blackthorne's place was put in on a contract for the last of the Waterperrys, Sir Gosham, before he sold out and went to New Zealand. For the stories to go with the ghost, you know, we employ some of the best-known writers in the world. No names, no pack-drill, dearie, but how do you suppose some of them live at six thousand a year on the kind of books they write? As for the rest, it's mere technology. Mind you, my dears, it's a very very old business. Oh, not my firm, I founded that when I came down from Oxford where, as you'll have guessed, I took a first in Greats. No, I mean the idea; it used to be called 'working the oracle' and the only difference is that the priests of Delphi and the Sybil of Cumae didn't have our electronic advantages . . .'

I turned to James and I said, 'For Bernice's sake, whom we both love, I implore you to get rid of this thing.'

'Rubbish,' he said. 'As this gentleman has made clear, there's nothing like a ghost to keep the value up.'

The Manifestations man cut in, 'My dears, as Sir Gosham Waterperry would say – such a *butch*, my dears – you're too right. Do you realize that no less than four of our customers have sold otherwise unsaleable properties, but *white elephants*, my dears, to the Society for Spiritualist Research.'

'Why the thermostat?' I asked.

'Nobody, however psychic, wants a ghost walking and shrieking all the time, dearie. And the right time is deep winter and old night. So cold makes a good switch. Of course, one gets cold nights in other seasons, but by and large . . .'

'I get it. Well, whatever Mr Robbie-Blackthorne here may say, his wife may have other ideas, and if she has I warn you I'm going to prosecute.'

'You can't, ducky. There's no law against what we shall call practical joking.'

'It can't be legal to exploit it for profit.'

'No idea, but that's not our pigeon, is it? That would be the agent, or his principal. Prosecute away, dearie, it won't hurt us and it'll cost you the eyes out of your head if I know anything about lawyers; and I do, my father was one and he left me half a million.'

He was right, at that.

When dearest Bernice had the whole story she said, 'I think James has been perfectly beastly. I might just as well have married an American. You've been my angel, my guardian angel. Darling, I'll divorce him and you shall marry me.'

I was a good deal taken aback. I said, 'Oh, sweetheart,' and took her in my arms. But I couldn't see why I should sacrifice the intense pleasure of being in love for the sake of marrying her; and the very next day an important assignment took me to San Francisco . . . for nearly a year.

When I returned I found that Robbie-Blackthorne was being moved by his firm to Hong Kong for four years. Baldassare has started to walk again.

The Leaf-Sweeper

Muriel Spark

Behind the town hall there is a wooded parkland which, towards the end of November, begins to draw a thin blue cloud right into itself; and as a rule the park floats in this haze until mid-February. I pass every day, and see Johnnie Geddes in the heart of this mist, sweeping up the leaves. Now and again he stops, and jerking his long head erect, looks indignantly at the pile of leaves, as if it ought not to be there; then he sweeps on. This business of leaf-sweeping he learnt during the years he spent in the asylum; it was the job they always gave him to do; and when he was discharged the town council gave him the leaves to sweep. But the indignant movement of the head comes naturally to him, for this has been one of his habits since he was the most promising and buoyant and vociferous graduate of his year. He looks much older than he is, for it is not quite twenty years ago that Johnnie founded the Society for the Abolition of Christmas.

Johnnie was living with his aunt then. I was at school, and in the Christmas holidays Miss Geddes gave me her nephew's pamphlet, *How to Grow Rich at Christmas*. It sounded very likely, but it turned out that you grow rich at Christmas by doing away with Christmas, and so pondered Johnnie's pamphlet no further.

But it was only his first attempt. He had, within the next three years, founded his society of Abolitionists. His new book, *Abolish Christmas or We Die*, was in great demand at the public library, and my turn for it came at last. Johnnie was really convincing, this time, and most people were completely won over until after they had closed the book. I got an old copy for sixpence the other day, and despite the lapse of time it still proves conclusively that Christmas is a national crime. Johnnie demonstrates that every human unit in the kingdom faces inevitable starvation within a period inversely proportional to that in which one in every six industrial-productivity units, if you see what he means, stops producing toys to fill the stockings of the educational-intake units. He cites appalling statistics to show that 1·024 per cent of the time squandered each Christmas in reckless shopping and thoughtless churchgoing brings the nation closer to its doom by five years. A few readers protested, but Johnnie was able to demolish their muddled arguments, and meanwhile the Society for the Abolition of Christmas increased. But Johnnie was troubled. Not only did Christmas rage throughout the kingdom as usual that year, but he had private information that many of the Society's members had broken the Oath of Abstention.

He decided, then, to strike at the very roots of Christmas. Johnnie gave up his job on the Drainage Supply Board; he gave up all his prospects, and, financed by a few supporters, retreated for two years to study the roots of Christmas. Then, all jubilant, Johnnie produced his next and last book, in which he established, either that Christmas was an invention of the Early Fathers to propitiate the pagans, or it was invented by the pagans to placate the Early Fathers, I forget which. Against the advice of his friends, Johnnie entitled it *Christmas and Christianity*. It sold eighteen copies. Johnnie never really recovered from this; and it happened, about that time, that the girl he was engaged to, an ardent Abolitionist, sent him a pullover she had knitted, for Christmas; he sent it back, enclosing a copy of the Society's rules, and she sent back the ring. But in any case, during Johnnie's absence, the Society had been undermined by a moderate faction. These moderates finally became more moderate, and the whole thing broke up.

Soon after this, I left the district, and it was some years before I saw Johnnie again. One Sunday afternoon in summer, I was idling among the crowds who were gathered to hear the speakers at Hyde Park. One little crowd surrounded a man who bore a banner marked 'Crusade against Christmas'; his voice was frightening; it carried an unusually long way. This was Johnnie. A man in the crowd told me Johnnie was there every Sunday, very violent about Christmas, and that he would soon be taken up for insulting language. As I saw in the papers, he was soon taken up for insulting language. And a few months later I heard that poor Johnnie was in a mental home, because he had Christmas on the brain and couldn't stop shouting about it.

After that I forgot all about him until three years ago, in December, I went to live near the town where Johnnie had spent his youth. On the afternoon of Christmas Eve I was walking with a friend, noticing what had changed in my absence, and what hadn't. We passed a long, large house, once famous for its armoury, and I saw that the iron gates were wide open.

'They used to be kept shut,' I said.

'That's an asylum now,' said my friend; 'they let the mild cases work in the grounds, and leave the gates open to give them a feeling of freedom.'

'But,' said my friend, 'they lock everything inside. Door after door. The lift as well; they keep it locked.'

While my friend was chattering, I stood in the gateway and looked in. Just beyond the gate was a great bare elm tree. There I saw a man in brown corduroys, sweeping up the leaves. Poor soul, he was shouting about Christmas.

'That's Johnnie Geddes,' I said. 'Has he been here all these years?'

'Yes,' said my friend as we walked on. 'I believe he gets worse at this time of year.'

'Does his aunt see him?'

'Yes. And she sees nobody else.'

We were, in fact, approaching the house where Miss Geddes lived. I suggested we call on her. I had known her well.

'No fear,' said my friend.

I decided to go in, all the same, and my friend walked on to the town.

Miss Geddes had changed, more than the landscape. She had been a solemn, calm woman, and now she moved about quickly, and gave short agitated smiles. She took me to her sitting-room, and as she opened the door she called to someone inside.

'Johnnie, see who's come to see us!'

A man, dressed in a dark suit, was standing on a chair, fixing holly behind a picture. He jumped down.

'Happy Christmas,' he said. 'A Happy and a Merry Christmas indeed. I do hope,' he said, 'you're going to stay for tea, as we've got a delightful Christmas cake, and at this season of goodwill I would be cheered indeed if you could see how charmingly it's decorated; it has "Happy Christmas" in red icing, and then there's a robin and . . .'

'Johnnie,' said Miss Geddes, 'you're forgetting the carols.'

'The carols,' he said. He lifted a gramophone record from a pile and put it on. It was *The Holly and the Ivy*.

'It's *The Holly and the Ivy*,' said Miss Geddes. 'Can't we have something else? We had that all morning.'

'It is sublime,' he said, beaming from his chair, and holding up his hand for silence.

While Miss Geddes went to fetch the tea, and he sat absorbed in his carol, I watched him. He was so like Johnnie, that if I hadn't seen poor Johnnie a few moments before, sweeping up the asylum leaves, I would have thought he really was Johnnie. Miss Geddes returned with the tray, and while he rose to put on another record, he said something that startled me.

'I saw you in the crowd that Sunday when I was speaking at Hyde Park.'

'What a memory you have!' said Miss Geddes.

'It must be ten years ago,' he said.

'My nephew has altered his opinion of Christmas,' she explained. 'He always comes home for Christmas now, and don't we have a jolly time, Johnnie?'

'Rather!' he said. 'Oh, let me cut the cake.'

He was very excited about the cake. With a flourish he dug a large knife into the side. The knife slipped, and I saw it run deep into his finger. Miss Geddes did not move. He wrenched his cut finger away, and went on slicing the cake.

'Isn't it bleeding?' I said.

He held up his hand. I could see the deep cut, but there was no blood.

Deliberately, and perhaps desperately, I turned to Miss Geddes.

'That house up the road,' I said, 'I see it's a mental home now. I passed it this afternoon.'

'Johnnie,' said Miss Geddes, as one who knows the game is up, 'go and fetch the mince-pies.'

He went, whistling a carol.

'You passed the asylum,' said Miss Geddes wearily.

'Yes,' I said.

'And you saw Johnnie sweeping up the leaves.'

'Yes.'

We could still hear the whistling of the carol.

'Who is *he*?' I said.

'That's Johnnie's ghost,' she said. 'He comes home every Christmas.'

'But,' she said, 'I don't like him. I can't bear him any longer, and I'm going away tomorrow. I don't want Johnnie's ghost, I want Johnnie in flesh and blood.'

I shuddered, thinking of the cut finger that could not bleed. And I left, before Johnnie's ghost returned with the mince-pies.

Next day, as I had arranged to join a family who lived in the town, I started walking over about noon. Because of the light mist, I didn't see at first who it was approaching. It was a man, waving his arm to me. It turned out to be Johnnie's ghost.

'Happy Christmas. What do you think,' said Johnnie's ghost, 'my aunt has gone to London. Fancy, on Christmas Day, and I thought she was at church, and here I am without anyone to spend a jolly Christmas with, and, of course, I forgive her, as it's the season of goodwill, but I'm glad to see you, because now I can come with you, wherever it is you're going, and we can all have a Happy . . .'

'Go away,' I said, and walked on.

It sounds hard. But perhaps you don't know how repulsive and loath-some is the ghost of a living man. The ghosts of the dead may be all right, but the ghost of mad Johnnie gave me the creeps.

'Clear off,' I said.

He continued walking beside me. 'As it's the time of goodwill, I make allowances for your tone,' he said. 'But I'm coming.'

We had reached the asylum gates, and there, in the grounds, I saw Johnnie sweeping the leaves. I suppose it was his way of going on strike, working on Christmas Day. He was making a noise about Christmas.

On a sudden impulse I said to Johnny's ghost, 'You want company?'

'Certainly,' he replied. 'It's the season of . . .'

'Then you shall have it,' I said.

I stood in the gateway. 'Oh, Johnny,' I called.

He looked up.

'I've brought your ghost to see you, Johnnie.'

'Well, well,' said Johnnie, advancing to meet his ghost, 'Just imagine it!'

'Happy Christmas,' said Johnnie's ghost.

'Oh, really?' said Johnnie.

I left them to it. And when I looked back, wondering if they would come to blows, I saw that Johnnie's ghost was sweeping the leaves as well. They seemed to be arguing at the same time. But it was still misty, and really, I can't say whether, when I looked a second time, there were two men or one man sweeping the leaves.

Johnnie began to improve in the New Year. At least, he stopped shouting about Christmas, and then he never mentioned it at all; in a few months, when he had almost stopped saying anything, they discharged him.

The town council gave him the leaves of the park to sweep. He seldom speaks, and recognizes nobody. I see him every day at the late end of the year, working within the mist. Sometimes, if there is a sudden gust, he jerks his head up to watch a few leaves falling behind him, as if amazed that they are undeniably there, although, by rights, the falling of leaves should be stopped.

'Dear Ghost . . .'

Fielden Hughes

This is a true story. There is not much point in inventing ghost stories. Anyone can do it. It is rather like playing a game whose rules one has made up without telling anyone else what they are. They have to be accepted, but if there *is* a ghostly world, it must have its own rules and laws, which can only be observed and reported as if that world were any other field of scientific inquiry.

Another point worth making about this story – or as I prefer to think of it – this report. It has none of the trappings of a ghost story of traditional kind: no midnight hours, no dark corners, no weird noises; nothing in fact to help it at all in the way of spectral stage props. On the contrary, the events I am going to report took place in the glorious blaze of the most marvellous summer in living memory – the summer of 1921.

It was so wonderful that you might adapt a famous saying to its splendour: 'Good was it in that summer to be alive: but to be young was very heaven.' There are plenty of people still alive who will recall its apparently endless procession of golden days: its unclouded nacreous dawns, its magnificent noons of blue and gold, its days sinking into warm noble evenings full of the promise of another day of the kind of summer one dreams about but seldom gets. It stretched – that peerless summer – from an ecstatic spring to an autumn like an aristocrat bowing himself out at the end of a golden age, a perfect regime. It justified by itself the mere fact of having been alive in its time.

It was qualified for that 'very heaven', for I was only twenty-one. I celebrated my birthday in its October, and I recall smiling to myself at the idea which occurred to my mind on that day. The world, I reflected, as I saw the imperial decorations on the trees, leaves holding themselves poised between the cool green of the summer and the burning colours of the autumn, reluctant to let the summer go, rejoicing in the colour carnival of the autumn, was an opulent father to my coming-of-age.

At the end of July, I was to begin a six weeks' holiday, from which you may guess my profession; and the way I resolved to spend it will tell you what my second profession was. I made up my mind to find some quiet country town and pass the six weeks in writing a novel. I settled on the place for my work in ways that suit me best. There is a little East Anglian town which I will disguise by calling it Crome Stratford. Its real name is even more attractive to me; and let me say now that the altering of a few names will be the only liberty I shall take with the truth; and that only to cover the risk that there may still be people about who may remember me even after nearly forty-five years.

I was living at this time with my parents at Taunton, and they – knowing well my ways – were not even mildly inquiring when I packed a suitcase and went off saying I would write when I had found out where I was going. I had never been to Crome Stratford. I had read its name and made my own fantasy of its character, which was itself an apéritif of the spirit.

Everything was up to exciting expectation. The little hot train, with its two coaches and its tank engine, puffed through a deep cutting and pulling up, panting agreeably, at a pretty station whose name-board actually announced that it was Crome Stratford. The time was a few minutes before four in the afternoon, and all non-human things drowsed pleasantly in the heat. I was the only passenger to alight, and so the driver had nothing to do but lean on the side of his engine and watch me with a slow kindly interest. The station-master himself, in peaked gold-braided cap and frock-coat, took my ticket, waving the train off with his free hand, assisted by the guard with green flag. The train gave a heave to pick up its load, the guard swung expertly aboard, and the engine moved under the bridge and towards the exciting tracery and lace of the trees on each side of the cutting beyond.

Now I was free to consult the station-master, and he looked smilingly at me as if he knew I would. I told him that I proposed to make a stay in the town and asked if he had any suggestions where I might put up.

'Well,' he said, 'there's the Bell Inn. That's if you don't mind a bit of jollification on market days and Saturday nights.'

I said that as my stay was to be a fairly long one, I would prefer private accommodation. He had an expressive face. It now lit up with a smile that said he had the answer. His arm went out towards the bridge.

'You go out of the station,' he said, as if it were all settled, 'and over the bridge. You'll see four houses in a row. They're called Sevastopol Terrace. Call at Number 2 and ask for Mrs Wane. Tell her I sent you – Mr Jolbury – and I think you'll find she'll fix you up.'

Sevastopol Terrace consisted of four red-brick cottages without elegance of any sort. They could not have been more ordinary if the architect had entered a competition for the most mediocre dwellings. They stood silent in the sunshine, their name the only imaginative thing about them, the road with its trees the only sight worth looking at. At my knock, the door opened and there stood Mrs Wane, a small sandy-haired woman with a snub nose, blue eyes, hard-working hands and a shapeless grey dress. We went into a dead front room, seldom used, with uneasy chairs, a sofa, a very small piano with a fretworked front panel behind which was stretched faded red silk. Its yellow keys grinned up silently at the ceiling. Over the fireplace, its grate stuffed with orange tissue paper, there was the enlarged photograph of a man in khaki; he was dark, with a full moustache, and an expression of slight astonishment on his face. I made a satisfactory deal with Mrs Wane, who showed me my bedroom at the back of the house, and, on learning of my literary purpose, said there was a writing-table I could have. Finally, she said that tea would be ready in five minutes. Would I have it with her? Miss Jannison would not be in till after five. I said I would drink tea and, as I thought was expected, have meals with the ladies.

Miss Jannison turned out to be a woman about fifty, stout, with a large ginger chignon, as it was then called, and a kindly infectious laugh. She was employed in the office of a local solicitor, and I took her to be that combination of qualities labelled a 'treasure' – that is to say, one who offered for a small salary total devotion and identification with her employer's interests, and a willingness to use her extensive knowledge of the minutiae of the practice to do any job from copying to getting the tea.

Nothing could have been more ordinary, reassuring or humble. We three met daily for the evening meal and were soon on excellent terms, each in the role assumed by each or attributed by the others. Mrs Wane proved an excellent cook, a firm head of the household – saying for example at ten sharp each night, 'Well, I'm off to bed. Those who are silly enough to stay up can and welcome, I'm sure.' At week-ends we saw more of each other. All our meals on Sunday we took together, and tea on

Sundays was something of a ceremonial, being served by Mrs Wane to us and herself in that dead little front room.

The blue and cloudless days went by, and that novel did not get itself under way. The weather and the countryside conspired to prevent it. Often after breakfast, I would go off for the day – to sleepy ancient Bury St Edmunds or to the bookshops of Ipswich. A few pages began to take form, often to be torn up in that mood Doctor Johnson speaks of when he says, 'If you think well of what you wrote at night, tear it up in the morning.'

But quite soon after I had become a lodger at Mrs Wane's, the shadow of a strange uneasiness began to make itself manifest in my mind. I cannot possibly locate its advent in relation to my arrival. Like the beginnings, in the physical realm, of a headache that is far as yet from being a pain, I must have ignored it. I doubt if I can even recollect, in that dim grey dawn of psychic discomfort, the order of the symptoms – if I may use so diagnostic a word for what was at first only the smallest interference with my mental euphoria.

I should make it abundantly clear to the reader that I am what my friends delight to call an 'extrovert'. I am not neurotic and not particularly imaginative in the context of fear. But I think that the very first sign I had that all was not quite well with me was the realization that I *was afraid of something*. Afraid in a way that I had never experienced before, or, for that matter, since this time.

Now no man in his senses can merely say, even to himself, 'I am afraid. That's what is the matter with me. I am afraid.' The question he puts to himself – for he could not confide such a thing to anyone while he hoped to be regarded as sane – the question is, 'Afraid of what?' And that was just the question I could not answer.

I began to be two persons. One of them was this creature who as he went about the house was irrationally afraid. The other was the 'me' I knew so well, as you know yourself, detachedly seeing this state of affairs, and watching the unmistakable behaviour of a quietly frightened person. It was not only an odd state of affairs. It was, in its own secret way, horrible.

I wish it was acceptable in ordinary terms to give these two selves of mine separate names, for separate identities they were. I wish even more that some quantitative terms were permissible, so that I could report – quite truly, in stark fact, that somewhere in my consciousness there was a *small* area of awareness of a frightening character, surrounded by the large sturdy commonplace self which arranged eating and drinking, conversation and observation of the sunlit everyday world. I must repeat that this glorious summer weather made fear seem the more *outré* and irrational. Put quite simply, the lovely golden light, like a great friendly angel in nurse's uniform, was saying to that little frightened me, 'What on earth is there to be frightened of? I'll leave the sun turned on for you if you're really frightened.'

So I watched the behaviour of my fear. Perhaps the first thing I can now recall as significant was my absolute inability to stay in that little house alone. Mrs Wane and Miss Jannison, who had become close friends over the years, used to take a walk before supper every evening. They would go out about six and return an hour later. This hour was one of revelation to me. It was a time when, with the house to myself, I could have written in peace and quiet. It was a useful one from every point of view. The day was drawing to a close. I had the benefit of a pricking conscience, having spent a great part of the day in some excursion on the pretext, perhaps, of thinking out the next chapter. Now, if any, was the time to reap the harvest of thought and get it into the storage barn of my paper. But when the two women had gone out, *I dared not stay in the house alone.* No; say rather IT did not dare to stay alone. When I saw them in the lobby by the front door, pulling on their decent lace gloves ready to go, I felt a strange warning – no: not warning; words are such poor servants of meaning: say a queer slight dislocation of inner vision, accompanied by this vague fear, and by my impatient repudiation of its need. For all this latter feeling, before they could close the door behind them, leaving me with the secret cold fingers of the house, I was out of the back door and in the little garden with a book, there to stay till I heard the sounds of their return, their feminine voices, Miss Jannison's steps on the stairs ascending to her bedroom, the joyous chink of crockery in the kitchen as Mrs Wane made the first moves towards supper. Then IT would lie down within me, and I would enter the house, making the commonplace remarks and using the trite humour which were in themselves as consoling and composing as the noise of the crockery.

I cannot remember precisely when the next phenomenon occurred: a sign much less equivocal than the nameless fear that possessed me at the times and on the occasions I have described. All I am sure of is that I have not reversed in memory cause and effect, though when I recount this next thing, it may appear that if I have not carried out a reversal, then the world of which I am speaking does so for reasons we cannot know.

This new phenomenon is easy and simple to state. Its effect on me is not. It is simply that I became certain that I was being followed by *something* down the stairs whenever I had been up to my room. In the morning, when I came down to breakfast, or when I had been to my room during the day to get something I needed, pen, wallet, whatever – always this deep conviction that something followed. In the splendid light of day, in that unspeakably commonplace house, at any hour, those feet coming down just behind my own. I did not hear them, you understand. I did not hear anything. *There was nothing to hear.* It would have been better if there had been. If I could have turned round, hearing them, and hoped – nay, been certain of seeing something, everything would have been normal, of this world, in my flesh and senses. However horrible, it would have been *outside me.* Outside me, not terribly inside. For this I could analyse – that the fear and the impression of being followed were in some hideous way an invasion of me from what sources I could not tell. I could not repel them. I could not understand them. I could not exclude or evade them. They were a part of me, as alien as some dread disease, yet as much and as inextricably a part of a new and unwanted me as that.

I began to watch my two companions for any sign that they knew what was going on in the house or in me: to discern in them any evidence that they had passed through this dreadful introduction to the real presence of the house and were deliberately keeping silent about it so as not – could they be so evil? – to turn away a member of the household whose presence was certainly profitable, possibly entertaining, and above all, maybe a kind of vicarious security.

There was no such sign, no such evidence. That part of me which was capable of objective observation and inference could see nothing to support ideas like that. They were, it was staringly obvious, precisely what they seemed. A plain little widow, ekeing out her modest means by taking in lodgers and doing her honest best to give them value for their money; and an equally plain spinster of the most sensible kind whose work and her residence in this house were her life; as sane as a toothbrush, and as unromantic.

I knew of course that Mrs Wane was a widow; and I knew that the exceptionally plain soldier in the picture was her deceased husband. One Sunday after the ceremonial tea, Mrs Wane, in conversation, had used him as a time-peg, as people do. She was putting the tea-things together to take them out to the kitchen and was at that moment holding what I privately thought to be a very ugly metal teapot. Miss Jannison nodded at it.

'I always liked that teapot,' she said.

'Yes. It is nice,' agreed Mrs Wane. 'Sidney and me bought it on his last leave.'

From this remark, I concluded that Sidney Wane had been killed in action, a conclusion justified neither by the premisses nor in the fact, as we shall see.

Mrs Wane took out a tray loaded with tea-things, and came back into the room to get the admired teapot. She was looking thoughtful. Not looking at me, she addressed a question to me by name.

'Do you believe in premonitions?' she asked.

'No,' I replied in the half-jocular way that was supposed to be part of my role in the house, 'I can't say I do. At any rate, I've never had one that was worth having.'

She was at the door when I thought to say:

'Do you believe in premonitions, Mrs Wane?'

She did not speak; only nodded her head, looking very serious.

'Tell me about it,' I said.

Now she shook her head.

'I'd rather not,' she replied very finally. 'It's a painful subject,' on which she went out and closed the door behind her. Wondering why she should raise a painful subject herself, I immediately turned to Miss Jannison with the obvious question. It was answered gravely and directly.

'She often thinks about that on Sundays,' she said. 'Two years ago, on a Sunday, she had a premonition of something awful all day. Her husband, who went into business when he came out of the army, used to get up first and go off to work. That Monday morning, when Mrs Wane came downstairs, she found him in the kitchen. He had hanged himself there.'

A horrible inner warmth flooded me for an instant, to be succeeded by a chill equally terrible. On the instant, my mind was filled with some foreign emotion like an injection of a compound of dread, piercing vision and a shrinking from the immediate future. I would not, I dared not allow this feeling to crystallize in words even in the outraged privacy of my mind. Through what seemed to me to be its swirl, I addressed Miss Jannison. I could manage only one word, the answer to which I both needed and dreaded.

'Why?' I asked her.

She was sitting on the sofa, the hard, ordinary uncomfortable sofa. I photographed her then, and can see her now in the stillness of memory. She had some needlework in her hands, and her head was bowed over it. She answered in a tone as commonplace as all her surroundings; as impersonal as the sunshine that lay dimly golden on the blind drawn to protect the absurd furniture in the room.

'There had to be an inquest, of course,' she said. 'But nothing definite came out of it. He had no troubles – money or drink or anything like that.'

I felt a strange violence – a kind of anger rising inside me.

'There must have been a reason,' I said with a violence that matched my feeling. 'There had to be. Tell me what it was.'

Miss Jannison looked up at me momentarily, but without surprise. She actually bit off a piece of thread before she replied.

'Well,' she said, 'if you ask me – it's only my opinion, of course . . .'

I could have struck her with my fist, poor thing. I was not angry with her. I was as afraid as a poisonous snake and as dangerous.

'I am asking you,' I said, controlling myself with terrible difficulty.

She put down her needlework and rose.

'Excuse me,' she said, 'I must go and help Mrs Wane with the washing-up.'

I stood up too, directly in her path to the door.

'The reason,' I said. 'Tell me the reason.'

When it came, her reply fitted with everything about that place: the furniture, the red brick, the teapot, the stilted, stiff unnatural photograph of the dead man over the mantelpiece.

'I reckon,' she said, 'that like a lot of other men, he couldn't settle down to ordinary life after his time in the army. It wasn't the same any more. Whatever makes you like life had gone out of it. He never liked being a soldier, but when he got back home, he didn't like that either. Some fellows managed better than he did to put up with it. He couldn't. He used to brood a lot. You could hardly get a word out of him some days.'

I stared first at the photograph of Sidney Wane and then at Miss Jannison.

'Do you mean,' I asked solemnly, 'that he killed himself because he was bored?'

Miss Jannison moved to the door and put her head on the knob.

'I wouldn't say bored,' she replied. 'Say lost. There was a lot like that when they came back. Killed in inaction, you might say.'

She went out of the room and closed the door. The little house was deathly still in the afternoon sunshine, except that from the kitchen came the sound of the pots being washed up. I felt as if those small sounds were coming from another world, homely and ordinary, and as if I, alone in the room with that photograph, were in a strange half-world, with nothing clear, nothing understood except the voices of the unease and fear of my spirit.

I moved close to the photograph and stared at the dead face in it. He stared with the same cold intensity not at me but past me. It was horrible: the stillness of the face, those eyes fixed on some object of vision beyond me or my glance. His hair was close-cropped beneath his hat with its badge of the Suffolk Regiment. The peak of the cap came down almost to the bridge of his nose, hiding his forehead. The military clothing, cap and tunic, sat unnaturally upon him, like a dinner-jacket on a ploughboy. Nothing fitted with either his body, his temperament or his final act. Now that I knew what that act had been, he was dressed for me in the horror of the grotesque. My eyes moved involuntarily to his neck, and I turned away alike from the photograph and the dreadful images which I violently extruded from my mind.

The door opened and the two women came into the room. Mrs Wane, as if she bore in her patient serving hands the golden evening, as she had an hour before borne in the tea-things, spoke briskly.

'Now,' she said. 'How shall we spend the evening? Is anyone for church? Or a walk? Or shall we have a hand of cards?'

Hardly were the words out of her mouth before, with the suddenness of a pistol shot, the photograph of her husband fell, shattering its glass in the hearth.

'Oh, dear,' said Miss Jannison, looking troubled. 'Look at that.'

In the rigidity of my mind, assuming a terrible cause and effect, I was astounded at Mrs Wane's reaction. She pursed her mouth with an effect of complacency and went to the hearth to pick up the pieces.

'It's the cord,' she said, holding a piece up for our inspection. 'I knew it would go one of these days. Get me a dustpan and brush, Miss Jannison. I'll soon clear this mess up.'

'Yes. All right,' replied Miss Jannison. 'But I'm sorry that happened. Now you'll have to have it framed. The frame's broken too.'

With a matter-of-fact little air, Mrs Wane shook her head as she stooped there.

'I shan't do that,' she replied. 'I never really liked that photograph. I only put it up there to please Sidney. I like to remember him the way he was before he went into the army. I shall just put it away somewhere.'

Now I knew that we were not three in that house, but four. The women and I passed the evening in reading and conversation. We had supper together, and the lovely day outside sank away into twilight and then into darkness. At ten o'clock, Mrs Wane made her usual remark about going to bed, and Miss Jannison followed her immediately. The only artificial light in the house was by means of paraffin lamps and candles. They lit their candles and went upstairs.

'You'll lock up before you go to bed, won't you?' said Mrs Wane to me from the stairs.

When they had gone, I opened the front door and stood in the road under the stars. The soft air stirred very gently and the leaves of the trees opposite rustled. Somebody passed along in the sweet darkness and wished me good night as I stood silently there. I gazed up at the sky, drew in breaths of the fragrant summer air, and felt the wide lovely sanity of the world. Only I knew what there was in that little house standing behind me in its shadows. For a few brief moments I lingered in my love of the beautiful clean universe around me, and then turned and went in. The situation had taken a new turn. I did not know what to expect. I did not know what to expect *from myself*. I was on guard against new fears. As if everything were made of the thinnest glass, I closed the door and slowly, very slowly, locked the door against the wholesomeness outside, the stars, the space, the trees, the wide world. I lit my candle on its table in the little lobby and then put out the lamp in that dreadful little front room. As I did so, I glanced fearfully at the space where the photograph had been, a space cleaner than its surrounding wall. I went slowly upstairs, each creak sending a chill down my spine, the sudden bark of a dog outside giving my viscera a terrible tug. I closed my bedroom door abruptly, as if enclosing the room against an evil inundation. But, in bed, I realized that my feelings had undergone a change. They were less tense, as a man's may be when he knows something which before was a mystery. I did not expect sleep, and so it came, swiftly and dreamlessly, so that I woke to another bright morning, the lovely erected on a foundation of the ordinary, symbolized by the smell of bacon cooking below. The touch of water as I washed, the bright dancing gleaming fluid so much of this world: the smell of shaving-cream and toothpaste offering the banal comfort and security of an advertisement; and the knowledge, now absorbed, that the household was four, not three.

As I prepared for the day, made my toilet and dressed, my mind was busy with the problem of what I was to do about the situation: for I was as convinced of its reality as I was of the reality of the sunlit world outside. It may well seem odd that I have not mentioned, even that I had not thought of, the obvious step of getting out, incontinent. All I had to do, in my bedroom there, was to pack my bag, then eat my breakfast, pay my bill and go. There were trains running through the lovely vital healthy land.

There were people everywhere as secure and usual as a butcher in his white apron or a baker in his white hat. I thought of it now, and knew in a second that I should not do this: that the idea had come to me late for reasons other than my will and decision. *I knew I had to stay in that house.* With my reason, in that morning hour, I told myself that I was involved in a fascinating thing; fearful certainly, but fascinating. I reminded myself that I knew all, and that there was no reason why I should not stay out my time and write as I intended. But even as I so reflected, I realized that these were not in the usual sense my thoughts. I knew, with a kind of resignation, *that my thinking was being done for me.* The story was not at an end.

That August day was perfect, with the freshness of a virgin among sophisticated women. It beckoned and promised. The light was tender and young, and the smallest breeze excited and charmed the skin. Smoking an after-breakfast cigarette in the little back garden, while Miss Jannison called good-bye and Mrs Wane chinked and splashed over the washing-up, I decided that this was a day to be spent at the seaside. I told Mrs Wane of my intention, which she applauded, and away I went to the station *en route* for Lowestoft. I reached there about half past eleven, and settled with my newspaper in a deckchair. Next to me was an empty chair: not empty long. About noon, it was occupied by a middle-aged woman, who soon made occasion to talk to me. At first her talk was of passing matters – the crowds, the heat, the place. Then quite suddenly she said something so to the point that I did not react against it being so personal.

'You're troubled about something, aren't you?' she said very gently.

As if the question had demanded a truthful answer like an inquiry about a train time, I replied without demur.

'Yes,' I said. 'I am.'

'Will you tell me what it is?' she asked.

I stirred myself in my chair to take a good look at her. She must have been about fifty. She wore gold-rimmed spectacles and a hat so absurd as to enhance the impression she gave of honesty and kindliness. On an impulse – or was it? – I decided to tell her, certain that she would not think the whole story ridiculous. She listened intently till I had done.

'May I tell you what I think?' she asked then.

'Certainly,' I replied. 'I'd like to hear.'

'It's quite clear to me,' she said. 'I believe in spirits or ghosts or whatever name you like to give to the part of us that you now know exists when the body has fallen away. That poor spirit was driven to his terrible deed by distress that was very real to him, however silly you or anybody else may think it to have been. Afterwards, in the clear vision that death brings with it, he saw how wrong he had been, how cruel to that kind little woman. He's trying to tell her that, and he can't leave the house till he has done it. He's in touch with you to be his messenger. You know that now, but you're refusing the message. You mustn't, my dear. You must take it and set the poor ghost free.'

A chill of my former fear fell upon me.

'I can't do that,' I said. 'I won't. I can't leave the place. Let his message – if there is one – be carried some other way.'

She surveyed me as if I had been a recalcitrant servant. Her blue eyes twinkled through her gold-rimmed glasses.

'You told me that you didn't dare to stay in the house when the others had gone for their walk.'

'That's right,' I said. 'Daren't is the right word. And I daren't now.'

'That's just the time when he was trying hardest to get his message to you. You must stay in the house and give him his chance. I doubt if he'll leave you till you do. Maybe you're his only chance.'

I looked hard at her.

'How do you know all this?' I asked.

She gathered up her handbag and magazine, and rose to her feet. She looked down at me, smiling.

'Your way,' she replied. 'Experience. Now I must go home to lunch. How strange I should come to you this morning.'

I did not reply, but my tongue did.

'Not strange. Quite natural.'

'Good,' she said. 'Very very good.'

Then she was gone, walking against the sun so that I could hardly see her departure.

I reached Crome Stratford about ten past six that evening. When I got into the house, it was empty and silent. The two women had gone for their evening walk. I felt a strong inclination to walk right through the house. In the front room, I stared at the empty place over the mantel where the photograph had been, and at the drawn blind. I went up to my bedroom and picked up my writing-pad and envelopes. I was paying little attention to the very things I was arranging: the pad and envelopes to write some letters: so be it. Then, almost like a somnambulist, I walked slowly down the stairs and went into the spotless silent kitchen where he . . .

I sat at the table and spread my papers before me – the letters requiring reply, my notepaper and envelopes. I took out my fountain pen. The little kitchen had the peace of a Dutch interior. The evening sun pouring across the window put it half in gold, half in oblique shadow. Everything was in a kind of attendant order, left by Mrs Wane's housewifely care: the crockery on the dresser, the gleaming cooking range, the dustless surfaces. The place shone quietly with her care, and on the mantelpiece stood a cheap little alarm clock that ticked loudly in the evening stillness. There was not even a sound from the outside world. Half my mind was on the letters I intended to write: half on the ranging furtive thought of where his body had hung. Behind me – in front of me . . . where? I sighed impatiently and opened my writing-pad. Once writing, I finished four or five letters. Nothing happened and nothing broke the silence except the voice of the clock and the faint sense of my pen moving over the paper. The window was open a little at the top, and occasionally the curtains stirred in a passing soundless breeze. The shadows in the room moved solemnly with the sun and the light imperceptibly faded: no – not faded – began to give up some of its brightness to the coming night. I put each letter in its envelope as I finished it, and wrote the address. Lulled by the total lack of event, I found myself for the first time free of fear. My eyes felt heavy and my limbs agreeably weary from the warmth and the day's excursion. I was relaxed, my own man again. I moved into that half slumber that one gets in church at sermon time on a hot evening: one hears the voice and some of the words, but the impressions are jumbled, the sense of location displaced. Then something happened that turned me into a thing of fear. My whole body was a prison of terror. I uttered a sound like the futile cry of a man in a nightmare. I struggled to shout at the dark terrors that flapped about my mind and put them to flight. I thought I saw something – a limp form – unnaturally hanging in the room in front of me. Almost at once I knew what had torn me out of my half-sleep. It was the closing of the front door as the women came in from their walk. The kitchen door opened and Mrs Wane came in, still wearing her hat, pulling off her gloves. She glanced at the letters on the table and gave an approving smile.

'Been doing your correspondence?' she said. 'What a good man. Now off you go while I make the supper.'

I picked up my letters and went with them to the little table in the lobby where the night candles stood ready. It was our custom to leave letters there, and when the postman called with the delivery in the morning, Mrs Wane would give them to him to take to the post office.

That night at supper, which we ate in the kitchen, I was in very high spirits, living up to my reputation as a wit and an amusing fellow. Miss Jannison responded to my mood, giggling and rejoining as if the occasion was some sort of strange birthday party. My happiness was mysterious and irrational. I felt as though the events I have related were from a book I had read, already almost forgotten, and in any case of no real significance: as if, indeed, they had in some queer way been erased. But Mrs Wane did not join in our gaiety. She made some pretence of doing so, but her smiles were not spontaneous. It was as if she had something on her mind other than what was going on around her. Miss Jannison, amid her giggles, noticed it. She looked at one moment closely at her friend.

'Are you all right, dear?' she asked.

With a false brightness, Mrs Wane replied, 'Quite all right. Why shouldn't I be?'

Miss Jannison nodded, unconvinced.

'I thought maybe you had one of your headaches. The sun, perhaps.'

'No, no. I'm all right. Just a bit tired maybe. I think I'll go to bed shortly after supper,' replied Mrs Wane.

'You do that,' said Miss Jannison. 'We'll wash up, won't we?' – looking at me. I nodded, glancing at Mrs Wane. She had lost her usual air of common-sense acceptance of life, her manner of being able to manage everything efficiently. She looked like – what could it be? – like someone who had mislaid a possession and was trying to remember where it might be. It was not that she was tired or headachey: she was going to bed because she needed to be alone to think about whatever it was that preoccupied her. When the meal was over, she rose.

'Well, if you won't mind excusing me,' she began.

'Not at all,' replied Miss Jannison in a motherly tone. 'Away you go and have a good rest.'

Next morning, I was having breakfast when I heard the postman knock at the door. I heard him speaking to Mrs Wane. I heard her close the door on his departure; but she did not immediately return to the kitchen where I sat at breakfast, as she usually did. I was reading the paper, which I had propped up against that teapot, and it did just occur to me that she was a long time in the lobby. There was no sound at all. Then she came in and spoke to me. I looked up at her. Her face, with its snub nose and its sandy hair, was as pale as death; and its homely smiling expression had given place to a mask such as I had never seen on a human countenance. It had a terrible dignity of sadness, a piercing accusation like an angel with a sword, and a dreadful quietness. She held out to me a letter. The envelope and notepaper were mine. It was addressed to someone called Mags.

'How did you know he called me Mags?' she asked, the only movement in her face her lips.

I did not need to ask any question. She had found this letter among my mail on the little table when she gave the rest to the postman.

'I didn't know,' I replied in the same dead tone.

'No. I never told you. Read the letter.'

I did not want to read it. I shook my head.

'Read it,' she said, in a voice there was no disobeying.

I took out the piece of my own notepaper and read the few words written on it.

> Mags dear,
>   Forgive me. Forgive me.

'That's not my writing,' I said in a whisper.

'It's his,' she said, still with an expression that set us in a world in which no two human beings ever spoke to one another. 'But you wrote it. I found it with your letters. He came to you last night, didn't he?'

'I don't know. I didn't know.'

'I knew as soon as I came in. The house was empty.'

I said no word, but I knew it was true.

'He stayed with me until you came. He was here. I knew he was always here. I didn't think anyone else would ever know. But you knew and he came to you. And now he's gone for ever.'

She took the letter from my hands and burst into loud and bitter weeping.

Sonata for Harp and Bicycle

Joan Aiken

'No one is allowed to remain in the building after five p.m.,' Mr Manaby told his new assistant, showing him into the little room that was like the inside of an egg carton.

'Why not?'

'Directorial policy,' said Mr Manaby. But that was not the real reason.

Gaunt and sooty, Grimes Buildings lurched up the side of a hill towards Clerkenwell. Every little office within its dim and crumbling exterior owned one tiny crumb of light – such was the proud boast of the architect – but towards evening the crumbs were collected, absorbed and demolished as by an immense vacuum cleaner, and yielded to an uncontrollable mass of dark that came tumbling in through windows and doors to take their place. Darkness infested the building like a flight of bats returning willingly to roost.

'Wash hands, please. Wash hands, please,' the intercom began to bawl in the passage at four-forty-five. Without much need of prompting the staff hustled like lemmings along the corridors to the green and blue-tiled washrooms that mocked the encroaching dusk with an illusion of cheerfulness.

'All papers into cases, please,' the Tannoy warned, five minutes later. 'Look at your desks, ladies and gentlemen. Any documents left lying about? Kindly put them away. Desks must be left clear and tidy. Drawers must be shut.'

A multitudinous shuffling, a rustling as of innumerable bluebottles might have been heard by the attentive ear after this injunction, as the employees of Moreton Wold and Company thrust their papers into briefcases, clipped statistical abstracts together and slammed them into filing cabinets; dropped discarded copy into wastepaper baskets. Two minutes later, and not a desk throughout Grimes Buildings bore more than its customary coating of dust.

'Hats and coats on, please. Hats and coats on, please. Did you bring an umbrella? Have you left any shopping on the floor?'

At three minutes to five the home-going throng was in the lifts and on the stairs; a clattering staccato-voiced flood momentarily darkened the great double doors of the building, and then as the first faint notes of St Paul's came echoing faintly on the frosty air, to be picked up near at hand by the louder chime of St Biddulph's on the Wall, the entire premises of Moreton Wold stood empty.

'But why is it?' Jason Ashgrove, the new copywriter, asked his secretary. 'Why are the staff herded out so fast in the evenings? Not that I'm against it, mind you, I think it's an admirable idea in many ways, but there is the liberty of the individual to be considered, don't you think?'

'Hush!' Miss Golden, casting a glance towards the door, held up her felt-tip in warning or reproof. 'You mustn't ask that sort of question. When you are taken on to the Established Staff you'll be told. Not before.'

'But I want to know now,' said Jason in discontent. 'Do you know?'

'Yes I do,' Miss Golden answered tantalizingly. 'Come on, or we shan't have done the Oat Crisp layout by a quarter to.' And she stared firmly down at the copy in front of her, lips folded, candyfloss hair falling over her face, lashes hiding eyes like peridots, a girl with a secret.

Jason was annoyed. He rapped out a couple of rude and witty rhymes which Miss Golden let pass in a withering silence.

'What do you want for Christmas, Miss Golden? Sherry? Fudge? Bath cubes?'

'I want to go away with a clear conscience about Oat Crisps,' Miss Golden retorted. It was not true; what she chiefly wanted was Mr Jason Ashgrove, but he had not realized this yet.

'Come on, don't be a tease! I'm sure you haven't been on the Established Staff all that long,' he coaxed her. 'What happens when one is taken on, anyway? Does the Managing Director have us up for a confidential chat? Or are we given a little book called The Awful Secret of Grimes Buildings?'

Miss Golden wasn't telling. She opened her desk drawer and took out a white towel and a cake of rosy soap.

'Wash hands, please! Wash hands, please!'

Jason was frustrated. 'You'll be sorry,' he said. 'I shall do something desperate.'

'Oh no, you mustn't!' Her eyes were large with fright. She ran from the room and was back within a couple of minutes, still drying her hands.

'If I took you out to dinner, wouldn't you give me just a tiny hint?'

Side by side Miss Golden and Mr Ashgrove ran along the green-floored corridors, battled down the white marble stairs, among the hundred other employees from the tenth floor, and the nine hundred from the floors below.

He saw her lips move as she said something, but in the clatter of two thousand feet the words were lost.

'. . . f-f-fire-escape,' he heard, as they came into the momentary hush of the coir-carpeted entrance hall. And '. . . it's to do with a bicycle. A bicycle and a harp.'

'I don't understand.'

Now they were in the street, chilly with the winter-dusk smells of celery on barrows, of swept-up leaves heaped in faraway parks, and cold layers of dew sinking among the withered evening primroses in the building sites. London lay about them wreathed in twilit mystery and fading against the barred and smoky sky. Like a ninth wave the sound of traffic overtook and swallowed them.

'Please tell me!'

But, shaking her head, she stepped on to a scarlet home-bound bus and was borne away from him.

Jason stood undecided on the pavement, with the crowds dividing round him as round the pier of a bridge. He scratched his head and looked about him for guidance.

An ambulance clanged, a taxi screeched, a drill stuttered, a siren wailed on the river, a door slammed, a van hooted, and close beside his ear a bicycle bell tinkled its tiny warning.

A bicycle, she had said. A bicycle and a harp.

Jason turned and stared at Grimes Buildings.

Somewhere, he knew, there was a back way in, a service entrance. He walked slowly past the main doors, with their tubs of snowy chrysanthemums, and on up Glass Street. A tiny furtive wedge of darkness beckoned him, a snicket, a hacket, an alley carved into the thickness of the building. It was so narrow that at any moment, it seemed, the over-topping walls would come together and squeeze it out of existence.

Walking as softly as an Indian, Jason passed through it, slid by a file of dustbins, and found the foot of the fire-escape. Iron treads rose into the mist, like an illustration to a Gothic fairytale.

He began to climb.

When he had mounted to the ninth storey he paused for breath. It was a lonely place. The lighting consisted of a dim bulb at the foot of every flight. A well of gloom sank beneath him. The cold fingers of the wind nagged and fluttered at the edges of his jacket, and he pulled the string of the fire-door and edged inside.

Grimes Buildings were triangular, with the street forming the base of the triangle, and the fire-escape the point. Jason could see two long passages coming towards him, meeting at an acute angle where he stood. He started down the left-hand one, tiptoeing in the cave-like silence. Nowhere was there any sound, except for the faraway drip of a tap. No night watchman would stay in the building; none was needed. No precautions were taken. Burglars gave the place a wide berth.

Jason opened a door at random; then another. Offices lay everywhere about him, empty and forbidding. Some held lipstick-stained tissues, spilt powder, and orange-peel; others were still foggy with cigarette smoke. Here was a director's suite of rooms – a desk like half an acre of frozen lake, inch-thick carpet, roses, and the smell of cigars. Here was a conference room with scattered squares of doodled blotting-paper. All equally empty.

He was not sure when he first began to notice the bell. Telephone, he thought at first, and then he remembered that all the outside lines were disconnected at five. And this bell, anyway, had not the regularity of a telephone's double ring: there was a tinkle, and then silence: a long ring, and then silence: a whole volley of rings together, and then silence.

Jason stood listening, and fear knocked against his ribs and shortened his breath. He knew that he must move or be paralysed by it. He ran up a flight of stairs and found himself with two more endless green corridors beckoning him like a pair of dividers.

Another sound now: a waft of ice-thin notes, riffling up an arpeggio like a flurry of sleet. Far away down the passage it echoed. Jason ran in pursuit, but as he ran the music receded. He circled the building, but it always outdistanced him, and when he came back to the stairs, he heard it fading away on to the storey below.

He hesitated, and as he did so, heard once more the bell: the bicycle bell. It was approaching him fast, bearing down on him, urgent, menacing. He could hear the pedals, almost see the shimmer of an invisible wheel. Absurdly, he was reminded of the insistent clamour of an ice-cream vendor, summoning children on a sultry Sunday afternoon.

There was a little fireman's alcove beside him, with buckets and pumps.

He hurled himself into it. The bell stopped beside him, and then there was a moment while his heart tried to shake itself loose in his chest. He was looking into two eyes carved out of expressionless air; he was held by two hands knotted together out of the width of dark.

'Daisy? Daisy?' came the whisper. 'Is that you, Daisy? Have you come to give me your answer?'

Jason tried to speak, but no words came.

'It's *not* Daisy! Who are you?' The sibilants were full of threat. 'You can't stay here! This is private property.'

He was thrust along the corridor. It was like being pushed by a whirlwind – the fire-door opened ahead of him without a touch, and he was on the openwork platform, clutching the slender rail. Still the hands would not let him go.

'How about it?' the whisper mocked him. 'How about jumping? It's an easy death compared with some.'

Jason looked down into the smoky void. The darkness nodded to him like a familiar.

'You wouldn't be much loss, would you? What have you got to live for?'

Miss Golden, Jason thought. She would miss me. And the syllables Berenice Golden lingered in the air like a chime. Drawing on some unknown deposit of courage he shook himself loose from the holding hands, and ran down the fire-escape without looking back.

Next morning when Miss Golden, crisp, fragrant and punctual, shut the door of Room 92 behind her, she stopped short by the hat-pegs with a horrified gasp.

'Mr *Ashgrove*! Your *hair*!'

'It makes me look very distinguished, don't you think?' he said.

It did indeed have this effect, for his Byronic dark cut had changed to a stippled silver.

'How did it happen? You've not –' her voice sank to a whisper – '*You've not been in Grimes Buildings after dark?*'

'What if I have?'

'Have you?'

'Miss Golden – Berenice,' he said earnestly. 'Who was Daisy? I can see that you know. Tell me her story.'

'Did you see him?' she asked faintly.

'Him?'

'William Heron – the Wailing Watchman. Oh,' she exclaimed in terror. 'I can see that you must have. Then you are doomed – doomed!'

'If I'm doomed,' said Jason, 'let's have coffee and you tell me all about it.'

'It all happened over fifty years ago,' said Berenice, as she spooned out coffee powder with distracted extravagance. 'Heron was the night watchman in this building, patrolling the corridors from dusk to dawn every night on his bicycle. He fell in love with a Miss Bell who taught the harp. She rented a room – this room – and gave lessons in it. She began to reciprocate his love, and they used to share a picnic supper every night at eleven, and she'd stay on a while to keep him company. It was an idyll, among the fire-buckets and the furnace-pipes.

'On Christmas Eve he had summoned up the courage to propose to her. The day before he had told her that he was going to ask her a very important question. Next night he came to the Buildings with a huge bunch of roses and a bottle of wine. But Miss Bell never turned up.

'The explanation was simple. Miss Bell, of course, had been losing a lot of sleep through her nocturnal romance, as she gave lessons all day, and so she used to take a nap in her music-room between seven and ten every evening, to save going home. In order to make sure that she would wake up, she persuaded her father, a distant relation of Graham Bell who shared some of the more famous Bell's mechanical ingenuity, to install an alarm device, a kind of telephone, in her room, which called her every evening at ten. She was far too modest and shy to let Heron know that she spent those hours actually in the building, and to give him the chance of waking her himself.

'Alas! On this important evening the gadget failed and she never woke up. Telephones were in their infancy at that time, you must remember.

'Heron waited and waited. At last, mad with grief and jealousy, having rung up her home and discovered that she was not there, he concluded that she had rejected him, ran to the fire-escape, and cast himself off it, holding the roses and the bottle of wine. He jumped from the tenth floor.

'Daisy did not long survive him, but pined away soon after; since that day their ghosts have haunted Grimes Buildings, he vainly patrolling the corridors on his bicycle in search of her, she playing her harp in the small room she rented. *But they never meet.* And anyone who meets the ghost of William Heron will himself within five days leap down from the same fatal fire-escape.'

She gazed at him with tragic eyes.

'In that case we mustn't lose a minute,' said Jason and he enveloped her in an embrace as prolonged as it was ardent. Looking down at the gossamer hair sprayed across his shoulder, he added, 'Just the same, it is a preposterous situation. Firstly, I have no intention of jumping off the fire-escape –' here, however, he repressed a shudder as he remembered the cold, clutching hands of the evening before – 'And secondly, I find it quite nonsensical that those two inefficient ghosts have spent fifty years in this building without coming across each other. We must remedy the matter, Berenice. We must not begrudge our new-found happiness to others.'

He gave her another kiss so impassioned that the electric typewriter against which they were leaning began chattering to itself in a frenzy of enthusiasm.

'This very evening,' he went on, looking at his watch, 'we will put matters right for that unhappy couple, and then, if I really have only five more days to live, which I don't for one moment believe, we will proceed to spend them together, my bewitching Berenice, in the most advantageous manner possible.'

She nodded, spellbound.

'Can you work a switchboard?' She nodded again. 'My love, you are perfection itself. Meet me in the switchboard room, then, at ten this evening. I would say, have dinner with me, but I shall need to make one or two purchases and see an old R A F friend. You will be safe from Heron's curse in the switchboard room if he always keeps to the corridors.'

'I would rather meet him and die with you,' she murmured.

'My angel, I hope that won't be necessary. Now,' he said sighing, 'I suppose we should get down to our day's work.' Strangely enough, the copy they wrote that day, although engendered from such agitated minds, sold more packets of Oat Crisps than any other advertising matter before or since.

That evening when Jason entered Grimes Buildings he was carrying two bottles of wine, two bunches of red roses, and a large canvas-covered bundle. Miss Golden, who had concealed herself in the telephone exchange before the offices closed for the night, gazed at these things with interest.

'Now,' said Jason after he had greeted her, 'I want you first of all to ring our own extension.'

'No one will reply, surely?'

'I think *she* will reply.'

Sure enough, when Berenice rang extension 170 a faint, sleepy voice, distant and yet clear, whispered, 'Hullo?'

'Is that Miss Bell?'

'. . . Yes.'

Berenice went a little pale. Her eyes sought Jason's and, prompted by him, she said formally, 'Switchboard here, Miss Bell, your ten o'clock call.'

'Thank you,' whispered the telephone.

'Excellent,' Jason remarked, as Miss Golden replaced the receiver with a trembling hand. He unfastened his package and slipped its straps over his shoulders. 'Now, plug in the intercom.'

Berenice did so, and then announced, loudly and clearly, 'Attention. Night watchman on duty, please. Night watchman on duty. You have an urgent summons to Room 92. You have an urgent summons to Room 92.'

Her voice echoed and reverberated through the empty corridors, then the Tannoy coughed itself to silence.

'Now we must run. You take the roses, sweetheart, and I'll carry the bottles.'

Together they raced up eight flights of stairs and along the green corridor to Room 92. As they neared the door a burst of music met them – harp music swelling out, sweet and triumphant. Jason took one of the bunches of roses from Berenice, opened the door a little way, and gently deposited the flowers, with the bottle, inside the door. As he closed it again Berenice said breathlessly, 'Did you see anything?'

'No,' he said. 'The room was too full of music.'

His eyes were shining.

They stood hand in hand, reluctant to move away, waiting for they hardly knew what. Suddenly the door flew open again. Neither Berenice nor Jason, afterwards, cared to speak of what they saw then, but each was left with a memory, bright as the picture on a Salvador Dali calendar, of a bicycle bearing on its saddle a harp, a bottle of wine, and a bouquet of red roses, sweeping improbably down the corridor and far, far away.

'We can go now,' said Jason. He led Berenice to the fire-door, tucking the other bottle of Mâcon into his jacket pocket. A black wind from the north whistled beneath, as they stood on the openwork iron platform, looking down.

'We don't want our evening to be spoilt by the thought of that curse hanging over us,' he said, 'so this is the practical thing to do. Hang on to the roses.' And holding his love firmly, Jason pulled the ripcord of his RAF friend's parachute and leapt off the fire-escape.

A bridal shower of rose petals adorned the descent of Miss Golden, who was possibly the only girl to be kissed in mid-air in the district of Clerkenwell at ten minutes to midnight on Christmas Eve.

Come and Get Me

Elizabeth Walter

After the death of General Derby, VC, in his eighty-sixth year the house was put up for sale. The General's wife had died some years earlier and his son in the war, so there was no one to inherit. Plas Aderyn was put on the market and found no takers. No one was entirely surprised.

The house (nineteenth-century) was large by any standards. In later years most of it had been shut off. It stood in ample wooded grounds and the woods were encroaching to a point where they threatened to engulf the house. The banks of rhododendrons bordering the drive had spilled over to create a tunnel of gloom; in places weeds smothered the gravel; everything was rank and overgrown. 'Needs a fortune spending on the grounds,' was the unanimous verdict. And that was before you got to the house.

'Commanding extensive views over the Elan Valley reservoirs', said the estate agent's circular with perfect truth. The view from the front windows was probably the finest in all Radnorshire. Not for nothing did the overgrown drive wind uphill. Yet the same chance that had given Plas Aderyn its spectacular panorama had in a sense condemned it to death, for the village which had once served its needs and supplied its labour lay drowned at the bottom of the lake. The nearest centre – and that a small one – was now some miles away. The house stood in awesome isolation in a region not thickly populated at best.

So there was good reason for the place to stay on the market, despite a not-too-recent photograph in *Country Life* which gave prospective purchasers no idea of what was meant by 'nine miles from Rhayader' in terms of rural solitude. Soon even the estate agent virtually forgot the existence of Plas Aderyn. A winter gale blew his 'for sale' notice down. Unless you caught a glimpse of it from the other side of the valley, when it still looked singularly impressive, it might as well have sunk with its village beneath the lake.

It was precisely such a glimpse which brought Lieutenant Michael Hodges and three men to Plas Aderyn on a warm May afternoon. Army units were holding manoeuvres in the area whose object was a defence of the dams against an imaginary enemy driving northwards. Hodges, having caught sight of the house and learned in the village that it was empty, had secured permission to set up an observation post in the grounds, the only stipulation being that he should cause no damage. As his commanding officer reminded him, 'This isn't the real thing.'

Hodges was not an imaginative young man, despite the seriousness with which he played military games. Nevertheless, as his Army Land-Rover turned into the overgrown driveway, he felt a momentary unease. If this were for real, he thought, he would be proceeding with extreme caution, expecting an ambush or boobytrap at every turn. In fact it was more like jungle warfare than an exercise taking place in the Welsh hills. He was almost surprised that the only natives appeared to be birds and squirrels, so unused to man that they were unafraid. The whole wood resounded with birdsong. It was one of the loudest and most tuneful avian concerts that Hodges or any of the others had ever heard.

'You can see why they called it Plas Aderyn, can't you, sir?' said Corporal Miller as they stopped at the foot of the terrace in front of the house.

'No,' Hodges said, 'I can't. You tell me.'

'Plas Aderyn means place of the bird.'

'How'd you find that out?' asked one of the privates.

'A little bird told me,' Miller said with a wink. It was well known that the corporal had been out with a local girl the previous evening, so the others did not press the point.

Meanwhile Lieutenant Hodges had quickly reconnoitred and decided to set up his observation post where the Land-Rover had stopped, and where a balustrade, still with a worn urn or two in position, marked the limit of once-cultivated ground. The terrace immediately below the house was slightly higher, but he had ascertained that the view was no better and, as he said, there was less chance of causing damage where they were. He did not specify what damage might result from their presence to a house whose ground-floor windows were already broken and boarded up. Instead, he concentrated on giving orders with unaccustomed officiousness, causing his men to glance at one another in surprise. They could not know that as he neared the house their officer had had an overwhelming desire to run away. If every window had been bristling with machine-guns, he could not have felt a greater reluctance to approach. That there was no reason for this fear had merely made it all the more terrifying. Lieutenant Hodges was not accustomed to nerves. Even now, safely back on the lower terrace, he was uneasy. He busied himself checking positions on a map.

It was Corporal Miller who put into words the anxiety Hodges was sup-pressing, though the corporal's voice was cheerful enough as he said brightly, with the air of one intent on making an intelligent observation, 'Sir, d'you notice how the birds have stopped?'

Lieutenant Hodges made pretence of listening. So it wasn't his imag-ination after all. There really was a curious waiting stillness.

He said briskly, 'It's probably the time of day.'

No one was naturalist enough to contradict him. The two privates were already kneeling with field glasses clamped to their eyes, resting their elbows on the balustrade as they surveyed the road along the lake's farther side. It was as well, since they might otherwise have dropped the glasses when the silence was shattered by a laugh, a terrible, shrill ha-ha-ha that was human but maniac, and seemed to come from everywhere at once.

'It's all right, it's only a woodpecker,' Hodges said to the three white faces turned towards him, well knowing it to be a lie.

As if in mockery, the laugh came again, this time from behind them. They swung round as one man.

The house gazed vacantly back at them with a deceptively innocent air. Hodges was reminded of the childhood game of statues. Had it been creep-ing up on them while their backs were turned? Then he abused himself inwardly for a fool. What had got into him? Could a house move forward of its own free will? Even before the echoes of the laugh had finished bouncing back and forth across the valley, he was striving to get a grip on himself. The echoes, of course, explained the ubiquity of the laughter, but they did not imply more than one man. Some village simpleton, even perhaps a schoolboy, was playing tricks on them.

Drawing his revolver from its holster and wishing that for the man-oeuvres they had not been issued only with blanks (not that he wanted to shoot anyone, but it would have been a source of confidence to know that he could), Hodges started to move towards the house, motioning the others to follow him. The distance seemed suddenly vast. His every nerve was tense as he waited for the next burst of laughter. Worse still, he had no idea what he was going to do next. Lead, he thought, I couldn't even lead men to their destruction, though I may be doing exactly that; for with every step he felt the old nameless horror: he did not want to go near the house.

It was Corporal Miller who saved him, by clutching his arm and pointing with a shaking hand. 'Look, sir, there's someone at the window. The place is inhabited. There must be some mistake.'

Hodges looked and saw he was pointing at a first-floor window directly above the front door. A white blur moved, vanished, reappeared. He ordered one of the privates to take a look through the glasses while the rest of them came to a halt.

'It's a man, sir,' the private reported, 'a young man with very dark hair. I can't see no more because of the angle and the window being so small. And he keeps ducking out of sight like he was in a punch-and-judy show. I don't think he wants to be seen.'

'He's probably trespassing, like us, and doesn't want to be prosecuted,' Hodges was saying when the maniac laugh rang out again. This time there was no mistaking its source: the man at the window was laughing his head off, except that no normal being ever laughed like that.

'He's escaped from some loony-bin,' Corporal Miller suggested. 'He's on the run and holed up here.'

It seemed the likeliest explanation. The little group halted uncertainly.

'We'll report it to the police,' Hodges said, trying not to let his relief sound evident. 'We don't want to get too near. You never know how it might affect a chap as far gone as he is. We don't want him throwing himself down.'

The man was leaning so far out that this seemed a distinct possibility.

'Careful!' Hodges shouted. 'You'll fall!'

The man looked directly at them for an instant, then waved his arms violently.

'Come and get me!' he shouted. 'Come and get me! I'm here. What are you waiting for?'

Suddenly, as though seized by unseen hands, he vanished. The window was nothing but an empty square. The silence was so intense it was as if he had been gagged in mid-sentence, or even mid-syllable.

The men looked at Hodges uneasily. 'Well, what d'you make of that, sir?' one of them asked.

Hodges said, 'I think he's an epileptic. He must have had a fit.'

'Perhaps he's got shut in there, sir,' Corporal Miller suggested. 'D'you think we ought to go and see?'

'Yes,' Hodges said, wishing Miller had not made the suggestion. He led the way forward resolutely.

The front door was locked, barred and padlocked, the windows on each side boarded up. The lieutenant tested them, but everything was nailed securely. There was no obvious means of getting in. Nor was there sign that anyone had tried to. The dead years' mouldering leaves lay undisturbed, blown by past winds into piles along the terrace and rotted down by many seasons' rains.

'Place gives you the creeps, don't it?' someone said. Hodges did not contradict him, but merely ordered, 'Let's go round and try the back.'

The drive curved round the house to outhouses and stables, presenting the same spectacle of decay. A conservatory, mostly glassless, seemed to offer a means of entrance. Hodges climbed gingerly in. A bird flew out in alarm and in one corner there was a scuttling, but the door leading to the house was locked.

'Perhaps he shinned up a drainpipe,' suggested one of the men who had not yet spoken. He put his hand on one to demonstrate. A rusted iron support clattered down, narrowly missing him, and the pipe leaned outwards from the wall of the house.

'I don't think so,' Hodges said quickly. 'Let's go back to the front and shout.'

They called loud and long, but there was no answer.

Miller suggested, 'Perhaps he's dead.'

'Dead long ago,' Hodges said before he could stop himself.

White faces looked at him. 'Cor, sir, d'you mean a ghost?'

'Of course not.' Hodges denied it quickly. 'Only I don't see how he got in. Unless he got on the roof and broke in that way.' He looked speculatively at the trees. There was no immediate overhang, no branch convenient to a window.

'Come on,' he said. 'One last shout, then we'll go.'

The echoes volleyed their voices to and fro across the valley, but the silence remained absolute. Nor was it broken as they returned to the Land-Rover, for no one had a word to say. In silence they piled in. In silence Corporal Miller started the engine, and in silence they drove away.

Lieutenant Hodges did not report the incident, he merely stated that Plas Aderyn had proved unsuitable as an observation post; but during the two days they remained stationed in the district he made some inquiries of his own. The general-store-cum-post-office proved the best source of information because he could go in there alone, whereas in the pub he risked making a fool of himself in front of his brother officers, which he naturally wished to avoid. The news that Hodges had seen a ghost, or even that he thought he had seen one, was not the kind he wanted to get around.

But if ghost it was, it was a recent one, he argued. There had been nothing unusual about the dress, nothing to suggest that the young man was not of their own time, even if not of their world. And Mr Thomas who kept the general store was very willing to tell the lieutenant what he knew. Yes, it was seven or eight years or thereabouts since old General Derby had passed on, a fine gentleman he was, and his wife a real lady, he took her death very hardly, and such a pity about his son.

'What about his son?' Hodges asked, his ears pricking.

'He died, sir. During the war.'

'Tell me about it,' Hodges invited.

Mr Thomas did not hesitate, merely pausing to serve ice-cream to two small girls and some corn-plasters to a woman with bunions the size of eggs.

'Ever so good they are,' he assured Hodges. 'We sell a lot of them here. You want to keep some handy yourself, sir, for when you're marching. I first discovered them during the war.'

'Of course,' Hodges said, 'you were in it.'

'Three and a half years and for two of them I was overseas. Never came back on leave once in all that time, sir. Quite missed the old place, I did.'

'But you came back,' Hodges reminded him, 'which is more than young Derby did.'

'Oh, he wasn't killed in action. He was home on leave when it happened. Drowned he was. In the lake. Accident, they said. Missed his way in the darkness. But you hear so many tales.'

'What did you hear?' Hodges persisted.

'Well, sir, I was away, like, when it happened. But some said it was suicide.'

'Who did?'

'My dad did, for one. He gave him a lift up from the station – the railway was still operating then – and my dad had had to go down to fetch a delivery. He had the store then, you see. He saw Captain Derby get off the train as if he was sleep-walking and start up the road for home. He had no luggage, and he was in battledress. Looked as if he hadn't shaved for two days. It was a pouring wet July evening – must have been in 'forty-four – so my dad offered him a lift as far as the village and he was glad enough to accept. Not that he had a word to say for himself, just sat there like a sack of potatoes. We heard later he was on leave from Normandy, and my

Come and Get Me

dad reckoned he was dead beat. He had to drop him in the village – there wasn't the petrol to go on, and it's another two miles to Plas Aderyn, but he must have made it all right. Two days later his father reported him missing. Said he couldn't settle and had gone out for a walk at night and never come back. He had the whole village searching, and they found where he'd gone down the bank into the lake. Of course it was hushed up a bit – no one wanted to hurt the old General, and it was bad enough the body never being found. But you can understand why there began to be rumours of suicide. Battle fatigue, I think they said it was. Some officers came down to see the General and it was all very hush-hush – but you know how these things get around. I only heard it from my dad, who had to give evidence at the inquest; he couldn't get over the way the Captain looked that night when he drove him up from the station. Talked about it to the end of his days, he did.'

'Didn't anyone else see Captain Derby while he was home on that last leave?'

'Only the people at Plas Aderyn.'

'Who was there besides the General and his wife?'

'The General's batman – Taylor, his name was. Oh, and old Olwen, of course. Servants were always hard to come by, with the place being so isolated. During the war they had to shut most of it up.'

'Are Taylor and old Olwen still alive?'

'Taylor I couldn't tell you. A few years later he came into money and moved away. Quite a large sum it was, though it was too bad it meant he left his old master. But I dare say the General could no longer afford his pay.'

'Why, were they poor?'

'The old man didn't leave anything except the house and some sticks of furniture. There was barely enough to pay the small legacy he left old Olwen.'

'Hardly a businessman.'

'No, he wasn't,' Mr Thomas said, glancing round his shop and reflecting that he was. 'They were well enough off when he came. He had his pension, mind, he wasn't starving, but everyone was very surprised. Didn't leave as much as I shall, I shouldn't wonder.' He smiled, self-satisfied.

'What about old Olwen, as you call her?' Hodges persisted.

'Olwen Roberts lives with her daughter now. But she is not good in the upper storey. You will not get anything out of her.'

'Is she very old?'

'Past eighty, but she is senile. Go and see for yourself, if you wish. Number two, Gwynfa Villas, just past the chapel. Mrs Hughes, her daughter is.'

When Hodges called on the pretext of being a distant relative of General Derby's, Mrs Hughes looked at him doubtfully.

'You're very welcome to come in, sir, but Mother's memory's not all it might be. I doubt she'll understand what you want.'

Old Olwen sat, a shapeless bundle, her jaws working ceaselessly. She did not look up when they entered, not even when her daughter said, 'Mother, there's a gentleman to see you.' Instead, Hodges found himself transfixed by the beady black eye of an African grey parrot on a perch beside her. He exclaimed aloud. 'You don't see many of those.'

'He belonged to the General,' Mrs Hughes explained proudly. 'We took him over when the old man died. Couldn't leave you to starve, could we, Polly? A wonderful talker he is, too.'

'Nuts,' said the parrot distinctly.

'Not again, you greedy bird.'

'Nuts. You're nuts,' the parrot insisted.

Mrs Hughes said proudly, 'Isn't he a clever boy?'

'They live to a great age, don't they?' Hodges said. 'Is this one old?' He congratulated himself on having avoided a gender, since there seemed some doubt about the parrot's sex.

'The vet says he's fifty,' Polly's owner answered.

'Did General Derby have him long?'

'Since just before the war, Mr Taylor once told me – the General's batman he was.'

'Taylor, where are my dress studs?' the parrot demanded in a completely different voice.

'That's the General,' Mrs Hughes whispered as if in the presence of genius. 'He imitates all of them – we know what they sounded like.'

'Who was the "nuts"?' Hodges asked, also in a whisper.

'That was Taylor.'

'Does he ever imitate General Derby's son?'

'No, because he hardly ever heard him. Captain Derby was away at the war, you see.'

'And does he imitate your mother?'

'Oh yes. It makes me feel quite queer at times. It's her as she used to be. Sometimes I could swear she'd recovered, but when I come in it's only Polly here.'

'It must be most peculiar,' Hodges agreed sympathetically. 'Rather like hearing a ghost.'

'Yes, there they are dead and gone and that parrot will say, "Thank you, Olwen, that will do nicely," just like Mrs Derby used to say. They were good people, very generous to Mother. It's a shame such a tragedy had to happen to them.'

'You mean their son's death?'

'Yes, dreadful to think of him lying at the bottom of the lake.'

'You won't fish him out of the lake,' old Olwen said suddenly. 'He was never in it.'

'Now, Mother, you know that's not true.'

The small shapeless bundle relapsed into silence. Mrs Hughes looked at the lieutenant expressively.

'You see how it is,' she whispered.

'You're nuts,' the parrot said rudely.

Discomfited, Lieutenant Hodges took his leave.

A year later the unit was back in the Elan Valley for more manoeuvres, this time against an imaginary enemy striking southwards. No enemy would have done such a thing, but that merely added to the make-believe atmosphere. This was playing at soldiers on the grand scale. Plas Aderyn was still standing and still empty, but Lieutenant Hodges was relieved to find that he was posted at one of the lower lakes, to hold the road that ran like a dividing line between two levels, where the numbing thunder of the dam, unending, drove everything else out of mind.

So he was not best pleased when someone said to him in the mess that evening, 'Hear you saw a ghost up here last year.'

Of course he should have known the men would talk and the story get around, yet he was unprepared for it. 'I don't know about a ghost,' he said shortly. 'We encountered some village idiot hanging round an old house.'

He gave a brief account of the events at Plas Aderyn, saying nothing about the house being securely locked. 'He was getting excited,' he concluded, 'and I thought it best to come away before we frightened him. You never know what half-wits like that will do.'

'Nothing very ghostly about that,' the inquirer said in disappointment. 'I was expecting a headless lady at the least.'

'Where did all this take place?' a quiet voice demanded.

Hodges looked up to meet the gaze of Colonel Anstruther.

Several officers from other units had been invited to observe the man-oeuvres. Anstruther was one of these. He was a legendary figure, his war service one long record of decorations and citations, and one of the youngest officers to achieve a full colonelcy. It seemed unlikely that this query was motivated by anything other than politeness.

'Plas Aderyn, sir,' Hodges said.

'Isn't that General Derby's old home?'

'I believe it is, sir.'

'And now you claim it's got a ghost?'

The grey eyes were amused and disbelieving.

'I don't claim anything,' Hodges said.

'Very wise. There are so many possible interpretations. The supernatural should always be our last resort.'

Hodges agreed with him, though in this case, where he had exhausted all natural explanations, the supernatural was all that remained. Fortunately for him, the talk turned to other channels, and it was only later, after the meal had been cleared away and the company had dispersed for the evening, that Anstruther sought him out.

The Colonel came to the point at once. 'Tell me what really happened at Plas Aderyn, Lieutenant,' he commanded, drawing up a chair. 'I'm sure there's more to it than you told us. Aha, I see from your face that I'm right.'

Nothing loath, the Lieutenant went over everything from the beginning. His superior listened without saying a word.

'What do you make of it, sir?' Hodges asked when the silence had prolonged itself into what felt like eternity. 'Do you believe in ghosts?'

'I don't know,' Colonel Anstruther said slowly, 'but if I did I could believe there'd be one here. I used to know the Derbys,' he added in explanation. 'That was why I was interested, of course.'

'Did you know their son, sir?'

The Colonel gave him a sharp glance. 'Very well. He and I were at Sandhurst together. Now tell me why you asked.'

'Only because I understand there was some question of suicide when he was drowned in the lake while on leave from Normandy, although I understand an open verdict was returned.'

'Jack Derby committed suicide all right.' The Colonel spoke with absolute conviction. 'It was the most sensible thing he could do. He was not on leave; he'd run away from the battlefield. For cowardice in the face of the enemy, he would have been court-martialled and shot.'

'Poor devil,' Hodges said involuntarily.

'Poor devil indeed. I don't believe Jack Derby was a coward. He'd kept up magnificently until then. It's just that when you're in an exposed position, with no hope of relief or reinforcement and being constantly pounded by the enemy's guns, most of us would walk out if we thought we could get away with it. The trouble was that Jack Derby did. What made it all the worse was that he was the son of a general, and a general who'd won the VC. General Derby wasn't equipped to understand what Jack had been through. It wouldn't surprise me if he hadn't suggested the lake.'

'But that would be murder!'

'No more so than putting a man against a wall and pumping lead into him. At least Jack avoided that disgrace, which would certainly have killed his father. But it can't have been an easy decision. On the whole I'm not surprised to hear he's a ghost.'

'The old woman who used to work there,' Hodges said hesitantly, 'maintains he's not in the lake.'

'What?'

'Yes, sir. Of course she's senile. I dare say she was getting confused.'

Colonel Anstruther showed a trace of excitement. 'Where is she? Is she still alive?'

'I don't know, sir. I saw her last year in the village. I can easily find out, if you like.'

'Do that,' the Colonel said. 'I'd like to see her. I'm going to lay Jack Derby's ghost. When a man's dead he has the right to sleep easy. And so have the rest of us.'

Old Olwen was still alive. She seemed the same in every detail when the two officers were ushered in, a hunched grey bundle sitting over a coal fire despite the warmth of May.

'Mother feels the cold,' Mrs Hughes explained unnecessarily. 'And of course poor Polly does too.'

The parrot, who had been dozing on his perch, opened his eyes at their coming. Grey, wrinkled, reptilian eyelids rolled up over his round black eyes.

'Good morning,' Colonel Anstruther said cheerily, approaching the old woman with a professional bedside air. 'You used to know some friends of mine, the Derbys. I thought you could tell me how they were.'

Silence.

'The Derbys at Plas Aderyn,' he prompted.

Old Olwen said suddenly, 'They're all dead.'

'Fancy that now!' Mrs Hughes exclaimed delightedly. 'Mother understood what you said.'

Anstruther shot her a warning glance. 'Do you remember Jack Derby?' he asked gently.

The old woman's eyes were blank. Behind her, the parrot clawed his way to one end of his perch, then the other.

'Excited he is,' Mrs Hughes informed them. 'Come, Polly, be a good boy.'

The parrot let out an ear-splitting screech that caused both officers to start nervously.

'Who's he imitating?' Hodges asked.

'No one, sir. That's just his parrot language.'

'Sounds pretty bad to me.'

'You blackmailing hound,' the parrot said distinctly, in what Hodges recognized as General Derby's voice.

Anstruther turned pale. 'My God! It's uncanny. I could have sworn the old boy was in this room.'

'He often says it, sir,' Mrs Hughes apologized. 'No matter who's here. Embarrassing it is.'

'You're nuts,' the parrot said.

'You're nuts,' old Olwen echoed.

Anstruther said, 'I should be if I had to live with that.'

'That's the General's batman, sir. Taylor,' Lieutenant Hodges explained.

'I know. I knew Taylor. But imagine the old General having to live with the fellow everlastingly saying that.'

Anstruther drew up a chair and took old Olwen's hand in his strong one. 'Tell me about the time Jack Derby died.'

The filmed moist eyes rested on his for a moment, then swivelled away, blank.

'It was summer, wasn't it?' Anstruther persisted. 'He came home unexpectedly on leave. He went out for a walk one night and didn't come back. They found where he'd fallen into the lake.'

Silence.

'Olwen, you may clear away.' Mrs Derby's gracious tones came clearly.

'Yes, madam,' Olwen said.

The Colonel tugged gently at her hand. 'You remember Jack Derby, don't you – Jack who was drowned in the lake?'

'He came back,' she said.

'Yes, I know. He took part in the Normandy landings and then he came back on leave. Tell me what happened, Olwen. I'm perfectly sure you know.'

'I used to take his meals. Up all those stairs. I was out of breath, I can tell you.'

Mrs Hughes said, 'Fancy her remembering that!'

'You liked him, didn't you?'

'You blackmailing hound,' the parrot repeated.

Anstruther looked strained. 'Could we move him out?'

'It's your uniforms, sir,' Mrs Hughes said soothingly. 'They get him excited, see. He hasn't seen them for years.' She turned to Hodges. 'You were in civvies when you called last year.'

'Quite right. I was. But we can hardly do a quick-change. Should we come back again some other day?' This last was to Anstruther, who said quickly, 'Who's to say it wouldn't be exactly the same?'

'The same as before, sir, will do nicely,' the parrot said obsequiously. 'I wouldn't want anything to happen to Captain Jack.'

It gave another ear-splitting screech, and old Olwen said, 'It's none of our business, Taylor. I won't go along with you.'

'You're nuts.'

'Nuts in May,' Hodges said, joking. The non-sequiturs were getting him down. He did not feel the same desire as Anstruther to lay Jack Derby's ghost, for time had blurred the terror he had felt as he approached Plas Aderyn. If Jack Derby had yielded to the fear all men feel in the face of danger, he was neither sympathetic nor shocked. It had happened before he was born. In a sense he himself had run away from that laugh –

And suddenly the laugh was all around him, a terrible maniac sound, as the parrot reared up on its perch, wings flapping, while shriek after shriek came from its open beak.

'Come and get me, ha-ha-ha! Come and get me!'

In the sudden silence old Olwen said quite distinctly, 'That was Captain Jack.'

Colonel Anstruther recovered first. He put a hand on old Olwen's shoulder, almost visibly restraining himself from shaking her.

'What do you mean – that was Captain Jack?' he demanded. Hodges was surprised by the hoarseness of his voice.

The old woman shrank away from him. 'I heard him,' she said, and began to cry.

'Now you've upset her,' Mrs Hughes said reproachfully. It was impossible to tell whether she was accusing the Colonel or the bird. She pushed past and put her arms round her mother. 'There now, dear, it's all right.'

'Mrs Hughes,' Hodges interrupted urgently, 'do you ever let that bird out?'

'Let him out?' She stared at him stupidly.

'I mean, is he allowed to fly?'

'Oh no. He mightn't come back, might he?'

'Could he – has he ever escaped?'

'No. We had a special chain put on him. But the General used to let him fly about the house.'

'Are you sure he didn't get out?' Lieutenant Hodges persisted. 'Just before I came to see you last year?'

If only that could be the explanation! But Mrs Hughes was already shaking her head. 'We take him outside sometimes in the summer, but we don't let him off his chain.'

'No good, Hodges. That would have been too easy an answer.' Colonel Anstruther looked suddenly tired. Old Olwen continued to whimper, and the parrot had become a bundle of ragged grey feathers hunched miserably in the middle of his perch. It was as though all three had been diminished by the bird's outburst and could never be the same again. Hodges felt the prickling of goose-flesh. He was unashamedly relieved when the Colonel stood up to go.

Outside, Anstruther hesitated.

'Where to now, sir?' Hodges asked.

'There's no need for you to come,' the Colonel said, 'but I'm going up to Plas Aderyn. I want to get to the bottom of this.'

Hodges's heart sank, but he said dutifully, 'I'll come with you.'

Anstruther looked at him keenly. 'I tell you, there's no need. Jack Derby was a good friend of mine. Besides, I've always felt guilty about him. It was my evidence that convicted him.'

'I didn't know it ever came to a court-martial, sir.'

'It didn't, but I was responsible for his arrest. Unfortunately, in the confusion he escaped – after all, it was a major battle – and made his way back here. It wasn't too difficult after D-Day; officers were to and fro across the Channel all the time. And by the time the military police got here to arrest him, he was lying at the bottom of the lake.'

'Mr Thomas in the general store mentioned something about some soldiers coming.'

'Well, now you know why they came. Naturally, the affair was hushed up in the circumstances. Jack was dead, and there was his father to think of. If it had got out, it would have sent the General round the bend. He was one of the old school: die at your post even if it's pointless, if that's what you've been ordered to do. To use your common sense was to besmirch your honour. I've often wondered if he knew.'

'About his son, you mean?'

'Yes. Did Jack tell him? It would have taken some guts if he did. Funny, when you think that Jack was accused of cowardice. Perhaps you understand now why I think the General may have suggested the lake.'

'I begin to, sir. The equivalent of presenting his son with a loaded pistol.'

'Exactly. Jack may have felt he had good reason to come back and haunt. So I'm going up to Plas Aderyn to see if I can help him.'

Hodges said, 'I'll come too.'

Nothing had changed at Plas Aderyn. It was quintessentially the same. The rhododendrons bordering the driveway might have been fractionally higher; there might have been another slate or two off the roof. One of the urns on the balustrade of the lower terrace had toppled over and lay spilling something more like dust than earth across the flags. As they parked the car a squirrel darted away, chattering shrilly, but no birdsong rang in the woods.

The old uneasiness settled upon Hodges like the weight of a heavy coat. He glanced at Colonel Anstruther, who was looking about him with frank curiosity.

'I expect it's changed since you saw it, sir.'

'I never did see it,' Anstruther answered. 'I wasn't in the habit of visiting Jack's home. It must have been a magnificent place once. Pity it had to go to rack and ruin. Let's go and take a look inside.'

Hodges followed, uncertain of how to account for his own reluctance and quite unable to tell Anstruther how he felt. The Colonel was striding boldly forward, as if he were an expected guest. His feet crunched confidently on the gravel. Over-confidently? Were his shoulders too square-set? Hodges dismissed such notions as part of his own disturbed imaginings. After all, he was keeping pace with the Colonel and not exactly hanging back.

By silent consent they ignored the main doorway under its portico and went round to the back of the house.

'Everything's locked, sir,' Hodges volunteered. 'I tried the doors and windows when I was here last year.'

'Then we'll just have to break in, shan't we?' Anstruther said testily. 'Most of the glass has gone in the larder window. Help me knock out the rest and see if you can squeeze through.'

The Lieutenant was much smaller and lighter than the Colonel; it was common sense that he should go first. Nevertheless, Hodges regretted his lack of bulk and inches. What might be waiting for him when he got inside?'

Nothing was, of course, though he heard mice scamper and detected movement in the dust-swathed cobwebs where spiders lurked. He turned to Anstruther. 'I'll see if I can unbolt the kitchen door, sir. That would be the best way for you to come in.'

The bolts resisted him at first, and when he mastered them they squeaked resentment at their long deprivation of oil. He stepped out to join the Colonel, and as he did so the air was darkened by beating wings. Great black flapping wings that folded and settled about the body of an enormous carrion crow, who perched on an outhouse not half a dozen yards distant and said interrogatively 'Caw?'

'Caw yourself!' Hodges answered in relieved reflex. The crow wouldn't do them any harm. And it was not unfitting that it should preside over what was literally 'the place of the bird'.

'Ugly brute, isn't he?' said the Colonel. 'Bet he's had his share of newborn lambs.'

Hodges looked at the cruel heavy beak distastefully. He had momentarily forgotten that, for all its name, the carrion crow did not always wait for death.

'Caw!' the bird said derisively.

'Perhaps, sir,' Hodges suggested, 'we'd better get inside.'

The Colonel led the way through the stone-flagged kitchen towards the hall. Hodges was surprised by the gloom. What with boarded-up or shuttered windows, encroaching trees and dirt-encrusted panes, very little light entered Plas Aderyn and what there was was grey. There was no trace of the sunlight they had left outside; it was as though the sun had never shone in these high rooms with their elaborate plaster-work ceilings, although the house faced south-west. Nor was Hodges prepared for the smell, a decaying, musty odour that seemed to cling to everything.

'Dry rot here all right,' the Colonel observed.

As if in confirmation, his foot went through the tread of the bottom stair. The wood did not snap, it gave almost with a sigh of protest, enveloping the Colonel's shoe in a cloud of feathery, spore-laden dust.

'Careful, Hodges,' the Colonel warned. 'Doesn't look as though these stairs will bear us. Keep well away from the centre of the treads.'

'Better let me go first, sir,' Hodges suggested. 'If it bears me, it ought to be all right for you.'

He led the way, keeping to the outside edge and walking gently as he gripped the banister-rail. Behind him he could hear the Colonel, who was breathing hard as if short of wind.

The first-floor landing, a replica of the hall beneath it, seemed to have innumerable doors, all now standing open upon the rotting rooms within.

Yet Hodges felt himself drawn as if by instinct to the right one – the room above the porch from which he had seen the figure wave. It was a square room, not as big as the master-bedrooms, with dressing-rooms that lay to either side of it. The glass in its sash-window was broken and rain and leaves had flooded in. The mess in the grate suggested that jackdaws had nested in the chimney, and a closer look revealed the body of a bird. Hodges felt the hairs on the back of his neck prickle. He had an overwhelming urge to get out. He glanced nervously behind him as though afraid the door might move suddenly upon its hinges and trap him for evermore. But no. It remained unbudging and wide open and Colonel Anstruther was attentively examining the door.

He looked up as Hodges turned towards him. 'The owners of this place didn't intend to be disturbed by nocturnal prowlers. Ever seen such a massive lock on a bedroom door?'

The lock would have done service for a strong-room. It was surprisingly strong, a kind of double mortice which shot two steel bolts into the jamb. The door would have given at the hinges before such a lock would burst.

Anstruther was looking about with interest. 'Odd that it's only on this one door.' He walked across to one of the master-bedrooms. 'The others have normal locks. They must have kept the family jewels in this room. Come on, let's see if they've left any there for us.'

Hodges could do nothing but follow the Colonel, but his every nerve cried 'Don't!' The square room had an inexplicable atmosphere of terror; all he wanted was to get out. It was as though the walls were closing in on him, the ceiling pressing down from above, the trees massing together outside the windows to prevent any escape by that means. While Anstruther stood still in the middle of the room and stared around him, he walked over to the window and gazed out. He could just glimpse the sunlit terrace like something in another world.

Anstruther joined him. 'Must have been lovely once. See what a good view you get of the driveway. No one could sneak up on you unawares. You can see the turn-in from the road and the stretch below the lower terrace. Gave you plenty of time to get the red carpet out.'

'You can see the lake too,' Hodges said involuntarily.

Anstruther nodded. 'So you can. That is, you could if the bars would let you.'

'Bars?'

'This window used to be barred.'

The Colonel ran his hand down the window-frame which clearly bore the marks of sockets which had once held bars in place.

Hodges shivered. 'It must have been like a prison, with that lock on the door as well.'

The distress which oppressed him, he realized, was very much like what a prisoner must feel: the caged hopelessness; the resentment of injustice; frustration and self-loathing; envy of all who had the freedom to come and go. He imagined himself sitting at the window, eyes fixed on the empty drive, for in its last years Plas Aderyn could have had few visitors; even a delivery van would have been an event. Then suddenly someone comes, strangers come, a chance of rescue; one leaped up and waved one's arms about: 'Here I am. Come and get me. Come and get me!'

'Steady on, old boy,' the Colonel said.

Hodges looked down at the restraining hand. Had he really waved his arms and shouted? Was it his own voice he had heard? Or was it the cry of madness or despair recreated by a parrot from the lips of a man long dead?

White-faced, he shook off Anstruther's hand. 'My God, sir, this room *was* a prison. It's where they used to keep Captain Jack.'

'Jack Derby? Who kept him? What's got into you? You know he was drowned in the lake.'

The Colonel's questions came like a hail of bullets, but Hodges was too excited to reply.

'Old Olwen said he didn't drown. She used to bring his meals up. And the parrot heard him often enough.'

Anstruther shook him. 'Will you kindly explain what you're talking about? You sound beside yourself.'

'No.' Hodges pointed to the door, where a line of bruised wood showed at shoulder-height. 'The poor devil must have beaten his hands to pulp with his hammering. And only his gaolers to hear.'

'And who were his gaolers?'

'Why, his parents, Taylor the batman, old Olwen.'

Anstruther looked shaken. 'I don't know what you mean.'

'Let's go outside, sir, if you don't mind.'

Anstruther led the way.

On the landing Lieutenant Hodges regained a little of his composure.

'I can't prove it,' he began, 'but Jack Derby's body was never recovered from the lake and old Olwen swore he wasn't in it. Yet he's never been seen again. So what happened to him when he came home accused of cowardice, with the military police hard on his heels? Obviously death was the neatest solution. But suppose Jack Derby wasn't willing to die? You mentioned that his father would have taken his disgrace hard and might have suggested the lake as an honourable alternative to court-martial. But what if Jack wouldn't agree? The disgrace would become public and the family name be sullied. Sooner than have that, I think his father locked him up.'

Anstruther said shakily, 'It's possible. General Derby was a determined and autocratic man. But what happened in the end? Where *is* Jack?' He glanced round – nervously, it seemed.

'I think he went mad,' Hodges said. 'You remember the parrot mimicking Taylor? "You're nuts," he kept saying, "You're nuts." Shut up here, year in, year out, seeing no one but those four, and with that insistent suggestion – if you weren't mad to start with, you'd probably end up that way.'

'It doesn't seem possible,' Anstruther said, 'that they should keep Jack here in secret for – what is it? Years, you say?'

'He was believed dead and there were only the four of them. Nobody came to the house. Or if they did, well, that window commands a good view of the driveway. Jack could be silenced while visitors were here.'

Hodges had a disturbing vision of that wildly waving figure swept from the window as if felled by a sudden blow. Mr Thomas had described the ex-batman as a big fellow . . . And no one had seen Jack's corpse.

For corpse there was, Hodges was convinced of it. Jack Derby was no longer alive. He could almost fix the date of his death if he knew when the ex-batman had departed . . .

He turned to Anstruther. 'I'll tell you something else.'

Anstruther looked at him in mute inquiry. He seemed suddenly to have shrunk.

'Taylor extorted money from the General as the price of his silence,' Hodges said. 'You heard what the General called him, over and over again: "You blackmailing hound". After Jack's death, Taylor quit with most of the General's fortune. We know he came into money and the General died nearly broke.'

'If he's still alive . . .'

'You could prove nothing. It would be a waste of time to try.'

There was a sheen of sweat on Anstruther's face. He said thickly, 'Let's get out of here.'

Hodges was only too eager to comply. Once again he led the way down the rotten staircase, the Colonel treading at his heels. The isolation, the emptiness, the silence, these were getting on his nerves. It was as if the atmosphere of unhappiness that clung to Plas Aderyn was seeping into his soul.

In the hall a single shaft of sunlight had found its way between the shutter-boards. It pointed like a finger up the staircase in the direction from which they had come.

The Colonel mopped his face. 'I don't know about you, Hodges, but I've had enough horrors for one day. I need time to think over what you've said, to get adjusted –'

And then above them they heard the laugh.

There was no mistaking it. Even though the Colonel had only heard it reproduced by the parrot, he knew it at once for what it was. But now it rang out immediately above them, from the empty room at the top of the stairs.

'Come and get me, ha-ha-ha! Come and get me!'

The maniac shrieks went on.

White-faced, Anstruther and Hodges stared at each other; then, with one accord, turned for the door.

'Don't go. Come and get me, Anstruther. Why don't you? I'm up here.'

The Colonel stopped, transfixed. His eyes sought Hodges. Hodges had also stopped.

'There's someone there,' the Colonel whispered.

'There can't be,' Hodges said.

They both knew the room was empty. There was nowhere anyone could have hid. If in another room they would have heard him crossing the landing above them. But still the voice went on.

'Come up here, Anstruther. Come and get me.'

The Colonel took a step towards the stairs.

'Don't go, sir,' Hodges protested.

The Colonel seemed not to have heard.

'That's right,' the voice cried, as if its possessor could see them, 'since you should be here instead of me.'

The Colonel stopped again. His face was ashen. 'What do you mean?' he cried.

The voice seemed exultant at being answered. 'Don't tell me you've forgotten,' it called. 'How you turned tail and walked the other way in a battle and I went after you and brought you back. We could have hushed it up, I wouldn't have split on you, but you didn't trust me enough for that. You arranged things, staged some witnesses, and accused me of cowardice.'

'Why, you –'

'Liar, is it? All right, come and get me. Come and see what it's like up here, behind locked doors and barred windows where I spent the rest of my youth.'

'Jack, I didn't mean –'

'You meant me to be shot. A neat, quick ending, and no risk of my betraying you. When I escaped you were worried, until you heard I'd drowned myself. I wish now I had. My father suggested it, because he thought only of the family name. But I wouldn't agree. I didn't see why I should die when I was innocent. So he condemned me to a living death up here.'

'No! It's not true.' Anstruther's voice sounded strangled.

'It's as true as I stand here. Come and get me, Anstruther. Come and get me. I've waited for you long enough.'

Anstruther was clinging to the newel-post.

'It's no use,' the voice went on. 'All your honours and your medals can't save you. Your courage was founded on a lie. I know you tried to expiate, but while you expiated I rotted here. Was that right? Was that just? Was that honourable, Anstruther? Is that how an officer and a gentleman behaves? Come up and face me man to man, and see if you recognize me. After all these years I've changed.'

Like a man in a dream, Anstruther let go the newel-post, squared his shoulders and faced the stairs.

'Sir!' Hodges called, not knowing what to say, what to make of these fantastic accusations.

Anstruther took no heed. As if on ceremonial parade, he mounted the staircase, head held high and hand where his sword-hilt should have been. Hodges stood watching the stiff back, hearing the steady footsteps, until everything suddenly disappeared in a crash of splintered wood and dust.

He thought he heard Anstruther cry out, he thought he heard Captain Jack's laughter, but he was sure of nothing but the great hole which gaped half way up the staircase where the rotten timbers had given way.

There was no sound now but the last patter of falling debris. With infinite caution Hodges approached and leaned over, clinging to the banisters, which still seemed firm enough.

Through the dust and the splintered timbers he saw Anstruther lying, his body unnaturally still. But there was something else, something lying beneath him; a glimpse of khaki; a scatter of buttons, tarnished gilt. As the dust subsided, whiteness gleamed. There were fingers. Forearms. Surely that was a skull, still with a lock of dark hair clinging to it. An officer's swagger-stick.

Hodges gazed, faint with horror, fighting against vertigo, to where in the cellars below Plas Aderyn the broken-necked body of Colonel Anstruther lay clasped in the skeleton arms of Captain Jack.

the peat fire in a blaze, sees that there is enough

Andrina

George Mackay Brown

Andrina comes to see me every afternoon in winter, just before it gets dark. She lights my lamp, sets the peat fire in a blaze, sees that there is enough water in my bucket that stands on the wall niche. If I have a cold (which isn't often, I'm a tough old seaman) she fusses a little, puts an extra peat or two on the fire, fills a stone hot-water bottle, puts an old thick jersey about my shoulders.

That good Andrina – as soon as she has gone, after her occasional ministrations to keep pleurisy or pneumonia away – I throw the jersey from my shoulders and mix myself a toddy, whisky and hot water and sugar. The hot water bottle in the bed will be cold long before I climb into it, round about midnight: having read my few chapters of Conrad.

Towards the end of February last year I did get a very bad cold, the worst for years. I woke up, shuddering, one morning, and crawled between fire and cupboard, gasping like a fish out of water, to get a breakfast ready. (Not that I had an appetite.) There was a stone lodged somewhere in my right lung, that blocked my breath.

I forced down a few tasteless mouthfuls, and drank hot ugly tea. There was nothing to do after that but get back to bed with my book. Reading was no pleasure either – my head was a block of pulsing wood.

'Well,' I thought, 'Andrina'll be here in five or six hours' time. She won't be able to do much for me. This cold, or flu, or whatever it is, will run its course. Still, it'll cheer me to see the girl.'

Andrina did not come that afternoon. I expected her with the first cluster of shadows: the slow lift of the latch, the low greeting, the 'tut-tut' of sweet disapproval at some of the things she saw as soon as the lamp was burning ... I was, though, in that strange fatalistic mood that sometimes accompanies a fever, when a man doesn't really care what happens. If the house was to go on fire, he might think, 'What's this, flames?' and try to save himself: but it wouldn't horrify or thrill him.

I accepted that afternoon, when the window was blackness at last with a first salting of stars, that for some reason or another Andrina couldn't come. I fell asleep again.

I woke up. A grey light at the window. My throat was dry – there was a fire in my face – my head was more throbbingly wooden than ever. I got up, my feet flashing with cold pain on the stone floor, drank a cup of water, and climbed back into bed. My teeth actually clacked and chattered in my head for five minutes or more – a thing I had only read about before.

I slept again, and woke up just as the winter sun was making brief stained glass of sea and sky. It was, again, Andrina's time. Today there were things she could do for me: get aspirin from the shop, surround my greyness with three or four very hot bottles, mix the strongest toddy in the world. A few words from her would be like a bell-buoy to a sailor in a hopeless fog. She did not come.

She did not come again on the third afternoon.

I woke, tremblingly, like a ghost in a hollow stone. It was black night. Wind soughed in the chimney. There was, from time to time, spatters of rain against the window. It was the longest night of my life. I experienced, over again, some of the dull and sordid events of my life; one certain episode was repeated again and again like an ancient gramophone record being put on time after time, and a rusty needle scuttling over worn wax. The shameful images broke and melted at last into sleep. Love had been killed but many ghosts had been awakened.

When I woke up I heard, for the first time in four days, the sound of a voice. It was Stanley the postman speaking to the dog of Bighouse. 'There now, isn't that loud big words to say so early? It's just a letter for Minnie, a drapery catalogue. There's a good boy, go and tell Minnie I have a love letter for her ... Is that you, Minnie? I thought old Ben here was going to tear me in pieces then. Yes, Minnie, a fine morning, it is that ...'

I have never liked that postman – a servile lickspittle to anyone he thinks is of consequence in the island – but that morning he came past my window like a messenger of light. He opened the door without knocking (I am a person of small consequence). He said, 'Letter from a long distance, skipper.' He put the letter on the chair nearest the door. I was shaping my mouth to say, 'I'm not very well. I wonder . . .' If words did come out of my mouth, they must have been whispers, a ghost appeal. He looked at the dead fire and the closed window. He said, 'Phew! It's fuggy in here, skipper. You want to get some fresh air . . .' Then he went, closing the door behind him. (He would not, as I had briefly hoped, be taking word to Andrina, or the doctor down in the village.)

I imagined, until I drowsed again, Captain Scott writing his few last words in the Antarctic tent.

In a day or two, of course, I was as right as rain; a tough old salt like me isn't killed off that easily.

But there was a sense of desolation on me. It was as if I had been betrayed – deliberately kicked when I was down. I came almost to the verge of self-pity. Why had my friend left me in my bad time?

Then good sense asserted itself. 'Torvald, you old fraud,' I said to myself. 'What claim have you got, anyway, on a winsome twenty-year-old? None at all. Look at it this way, man – you've had a whole winter of her kindness and consideration. She brought a lamp into your dark time: ever since the Harvest Home when (like a fool) you had too much whisky and she supported you home and rolled you unconscious into bed . . . Well, for some reason or another, Andrina hasn't been able to come these last few days. I'll find out, today, the reason.'

It was high time for me to get to the village. There was not a crust or scraping of butter or jam in the cupboard. The shop was also the post office – I had to draw two weeks' pension. I promised myself a pint or two in the pub, to wash the last of that sickness out of me.

It struck me, as I trudged those two miles, that I knew nothing about Andrina at all. I had never asked, and she had said nothing. What was her father? Had she sisters and brothers? Even the district of the island where she lived had never cropped up in our talks. It was sufficient that she came every evening, soon after sunset, and performed her quiet ministrations, and lingered awhile; and left a peace behind – a sense that everything in the house was pure, as if it had stood with open doors and windows at the heart of a clean summer wind.

Yet the girl had never done, all last winter, asking me questions about myself – all the good and bad and exciting things that had happened to me. Of course I told her this and that. Old men love to make their past vivid and significant, to stand in relation to a few trivial events in as fair and bold a light as possible. To add spice to those bits of autobiography, I let on to have been a reckless wild daring lad – a known and somewhat feared figure in many a port from Hong Kong to Durban to San Francisco. I presented to her a character somewhere between Captain Cook and Captain Hook.

And the girl loved those pieces of mingled fiction and fact; turning the wick of my lamp down a little to make everything more mysterious, stirring the peats into new flowers of flame . . .

One story I did not tell her completely. It is the episode in my life that hurts me whenever I think of it (which is rarely, for that time is locked up and the key dropped deep in the Atlantic: but it haunted me – as I hinted – during my recent illness).

On her last evening at my fireside I did, I know, let drop a hint or two to Andrina – a few half-ashamed half-boastful fragments. Suddenly, before I had finished – as if she could foresee and suffer the end – she had put a white look and cold kiss on my cheek, and gone out at the door; as it turned out, for the last time.

Hurt or not, I will mention it here and now. You who look and listen are not Andrina – to you it will seem a tale of crude country manners: a mingling of innocence and heartlessness.

In the island, fifty years ago, a young man and a young woman came together. They had known each other all their lives up to then, of course – they had sat in the school room together – but on one particular day in early summer this boy from one croft and this girl from another distant croft looked at each other with new eyes.

After the midsummer dance in the barn of the big house, they walked together across the hill through the lingering enchantment of twilight – it is never dark then – and came to the rocks and the sand and sea just as the sun was rising. For an hour and more they lingered, tranced creatures indeed, beside those bright sighings and swirlings. Far in the north-east the springs of day were beginning to surge up.

It was a tale soaked in the light of a single brief summer. The boy and the girl lived, it seemed, on each other's heartbeats. Their parents' crofts were miles apart, but they contrived to meet, as if by accident, most days; at the crossroads, in the village shop, on the side of the hill. But really these places were too earthy and open – there were too many windows – their feet drew secretly night after night to the beach with its bird-cries, its cave, its changing waters. There no one disturbed their communings – the shy touches of hand and mouth – the words that were nonsense but that became in his mouth sometimes a sweet mysterious music – 'Sigrid'.

The boy – his future, once this idyll of a summer was ended, was to go to the university in Aberdeen and there study to be a man of security and position and some leisure – an estate his crofting ancestors had never known.

No such door was to open for Sigrid – she was bound to the few family acres – the digging of peat – the making of butter and cheese. But for a short time only. Her place would be beside the young man with whom she shared her breath and heartbeats, once he had gained his teacher's certificate. They walked day after day beside the shining beckoning waters.

But one evening, at the cave, towards the end of that summer, when the corn was taking a first burnish, she had something urgent to tell him – a tremulous perilous secret thing. And at once the summertime spell was broken. He shook his head. He looked away. He looked at her again as if she were some slut who had insulted him. She put out her hand to him, her mouth trembling. He thrust her away. He turned. He ran up the beach and along the sand-track to the road above; and the ripening fields gathered him soon and hid him from her.

And the girl was left alone at the mouth of the cave, with the burden of a greater more desolate mystery on her.

The young man did not go to any seat of higher learning. That same day he was at the emigration agents in Hamnavoe, asking for an urgent immediate passage to Canada or Australia or South Africa – anywhere.

Thereafter the tale became complicated and more cruel and pathetic still. The girl followed him as best she could to his transatlantic refuge a month or so later; only to discover that the bird had flown. He had signed on a ship bound for furthest ports, as an ordinary seaman: so she was told, and she was more utterly lost than ever.

That rootlessness, for the next half century, was to be his life: making salt circles about the globe, with no secure footage anywhere. To be sure, he studied his navigation manuals, he rose at last to be a ship's officer, and more. The barren years became a burden to him. There is a time, when white hairs come, to turn one's back on long and practised skills and arts, that have long since lost their savours. This the sailor did, and he set his course homeward to his island; hoping that fifty winters might have scabbed over an old wound.

And so it was, or seemed to be. A few remembered him vaguely. The name of a certain vanished woman – who must be elderly, like himself, now – he never mentioned, nor did he ever hear it uttered. Her parents' croft was a ruin, a ruckle of stones on the side of the hill. He climbed up to it one day and looked at it coldly. No sweet ghost lingered at the end of the house, waiting for a twilight summons – 'Sigrid . . .'

*

I got my pension cashed, and a basket full of provisions, in the village shop. Tina Stewart the postmistress knew everybody and everything; all the shifting subtle web of relationship in the island. I tried devious approaches with her. What was new or strange in the island? Had anyone been taken suddenly ill? Had anybody – a young woman, for example – had to leave the island suddenly, for whatever reason? The hawk eye of Miss Stewart regarded me long and hard. No, said she, she had never known the island quieter. Nobody had come or gone. 'Only yourself, Captain Torvald, has been bedridden, I hear. You better take good care of yourself, you all alone up there. There's still a greyness in your face . . .' I said I was sorry to take her time up. Somebody had mentioned a name – Andrina – to me, in a certain connection. It was a matter of no importance. Could Miss Stewart, however, tell me which farm or croft this Andrina came from?

Tina looked at me a long while, then shook her head. There was nobody of that name – woman or girl or child – in the island; and there never had been, to her certain knowledge.

I paid for my messages, with trembling fingers, and left.

I felt the need of a drink. At the bar counter stood Isaac Irving the landlord. Two fishermen stood at the far end, next the fire, drinking their pints and playing dominoes.

I said, after the third whisky, 'Look, Isaac, I suppose the whole island knows that Andrina – that girl – has been coming all winter up to my place, to do a bit of cleaning and washing and cooking for me. She hasn't been for a week now and more. Do you know if there's anything the matter with her?' (What I dreaded to hear was that Andrina had suddenly fallen in love; her little rockpools of charity and kindness drowned in that huge incoming flood; and cloistered herself against the time of her wedding.)

Isaac looked at me as if I was out of my mind. 'A young woman,' said he. 'A young woman up at your house? A home help, is she? I didn't know you had a home help. How many whiskies did you have before you came here, skipper, eh?' And he winked at the two grinning fishermen over by the fire.

I drank down my fourth whisky and prepared to go.

'Sorry, skipper,' Isaac Irving called after me. 'I think you must have imagined that girl, whatever her name is, when the fever was on you. Sometimes that happens. The only women I saw when I had the flu were hags and witches. You're lucky, skipper – a honey like Andrina!'

I was utterly bewildered. Isaac Irving knows the island and its people, if anything, even better than Tina Stewart. And he is a kindly man, not given to making fools of the lost and the delusion-ridden.

*

Going home, March airs were moving over the island. The sky, almost overnight, was taller and bluer. Daffodils trumpeted, silently the entry of spring from ditches here and there. A young lamb danced, all four feet in the air at once.

I found, lying on the table, unopened, the letter that had been delivered three mornings ago. There was an Australian postmark. It had been posted in late October.

'I followed your young flight from Selskay half round the world, and at last stopped here in Tasmania, knowing that it was useless for me to go any farther. I have kept a silence too, because I had such regard for you that I did not want you to suffer as I had, in many ways, over the years. We are both old, maybe I am writing this in vain, for you might never have returned to Selskay; or you might be dust or salt. I think, if you are still alive and (it may be) lonely, that what I will write might gladden you, though the end of it is sadness, like so much of life. Of your child – our child – I do not say anything, because you did not wish to acknowledge her. But that child had, in her turn, a daughter, and I think I have seen such sweetness but rarely. I thank you that you, in a sense (though unwillingly), gave that light and goodness to my age. She would have been a lamp in your winter, too, for often I spoke to her about you and that long-gone summer we shared, which was, to me at least, such a wonder. I told her nothing of the end of that time, that you and some others thought to be shameful. I told her only things that came sweetly from my mouth. And she would say, often, "I wish I knew that grandfather of mine. Gran, do you think he's lonely? I think he would be glad of somebody to make him a pot of tea and see to his fire. Some day I'm going to Scotland and I'm going to knock on his door, wherever he lives, and I'll do things for him. Did you love him very much, gran? He must be a good person, that old sailor, ever to have been loved by you. I *will* see him. I'll hear the old stories from his own mouth. Most of all, of course, the love story – for you, gran, tell me nothing about that . . ." I am writing this letter, Bill, to tell you that this can never now be. Our granddaughter Andrina died last week, suddenly, in the first stirrings of spring . . .'

Later, over the fire, I thought of the brightness and burgeoning and dew that visitant had brought across the threshold of my latest winter, night after night; and of how she had always come with the first shadows and the first star; but there, where she was dust, a new time was brightening earth and sea.

The Axe

Penelope Fitzgerald

. . . You will recall that when the planned redundancies became necessary as the result of the discouraging trading figures shown by this small firm – in contrast, so I gather from the Company reports, with several of your other enterprises – you personally deputed to me the task of 'speaking' to those who were to be asked to leave. It was suggested to me that if they were asked to resign in order to avoid the unpleasantness of being given their cards, it might be unnecessary for the firm to offer any compensation. Having glanced personally through my staff sheets, you underlined the names of four people, the first being that of my clerical assistant, W. S. Singlebury. Your actual words to me were that he seemed fairly old and could probably be frightened into taking a powder. You were speaking to me in your 'democratic' style.

From this point on I feel able to write more freely, it being well understood, at office-managerial level, that you do not read more than the first two sentences of any given report. You believe that anything which cannot be put into two sentences is not worth attending to, a piece of wisdom which you usually attribute to the late Lord Beaverbrook.

As I question whether you have ever seen Singlebury, with whom this report is mainly concerned, it may be helpful to describe him. He worked for the Company for many more years than myself, and his attendance record was excellent. On Mondays, Wednesdays and Fridays, he wore a blue suit and a green knitted garment with a front zip. On Tuesdays and Thursdays he wore a pair of grey trousers of man-made material which he called 'my flannels', and a fawn cardigan. The cardigan was omitted in summer. He had, however, one distinguishing feature, very light blue eyes, with a defensive expression, as though apologizing for something which he felt guilty about, but could not put right. The fact is that he was getting old. Getting old is, of course, a crime of which we grow more guilty every day.

Singlebury had no wife or dependants, and was by no means a communicative man. His room is, or was, a kind of cubby-hole adjoining mine – you have to go through it to get into my room – and it was always kept very neat. About his 'things' he did show some mild emotion. They had to be ranged in a certain pattern in respect to his in and out trays, and Singlebury stayed behind for two or three minutes every evening to do this. He also managed to retain every year the complimentary desk calendar sent to us by Dino's, the Italian café on the corner. Singlebury was in fact the only one of my personnel who was always quite certain of the date. To this too his attitude was apologetic. His phrase was, 'I'm afraid it's Tuesday.'

His work, as was freely admitted, was his life, but the nature of his duties – though they included the post-book and the addressograph – were rather hard to define, having grown round him with the years. I can only say that after he left, I was surprised myself to discover how much he had had to do.

Oddly connected in my mind with the matter of the redundancies is the irritation of the damp in the office this summer and the peculiar smell (not the ordinary smell of damp), emphasized by the sudden appearance of representatives of a firm of damp eliminators who had not been sent for by me, nor is there any record of my having done so. These people simply vanished at the end of the day and have not returned. Another firm, to whom I applied as a result of frequent complaints by the female staff, have answered my letters but have so far failed to call.

Singlebury remained unaffected by the smell. Joining, very much against his usual habit, in one of the too frequent discussions of the subject, he said that he knew what it was; it was the smell of disappointment. For an awkward moment I thought he must have found out by some means that he was going to be asked to go, but he went on to explain that in 1942 the whole building had been requisitioned by the Admiralty and that relatives had been allowed to wait or queue there in the hope of getting news of those missing at sea. The repeated disappointment of these women, Singlebury said, must have permeated the building like a corrosive gas. All this was very unlike him. I make it a point not to encourage anything morbid. Singlebury was quite insistent, and added, as though by way of proof, that the lino in the corridors was Admiralty issue and had not been renewed since 1942 either. I was astonished to realize that he had been working in the building for so many years before the present tenancy. I realized that he must be considerably older than he had given us to understand. This, of course, will mean that there are wrong entries on his cards.

The actual notification to the redundant staff passed off rather better, in a way, than I had anticipated. By that time everyone in the office seemed inexplicably conversant with the details, and several of them in fact had gone far beyond their terms of reference, young Patel, for instance, who openly admits that he will be leaving us as soon as he can get a better job, taking me aside and telling me that to such a man as Singlebury dismissal would be like death. Dismissal is not the right word, I said. But death is, Patel replied. Singlebury himself, however, took it very quietly. Even when I raised the question of the Company's Early Retirement pension scheme, which I could not pretend was over-generous, he said very little. He was generally felt to be in a state of shock. The two girls whom you asked me to speak to were quite unaffected, having already found themselves employment as hostesses at the Dolphinarium near here. Mrs Horrocks, of Filing, on the other hand, *did* protest, and was so offensive on the question of severance pay that I was obliged to agree to refer it to a higher level. I consider this as one of the hardest day's work that I have ever done for the Company.

Just before his month's notice (if we are to call it that) was up, Singlebury, to my great surprise, asked me to come home with him one evening for a meal. In all the past years the idea of his having a home, still less asking anyone back to it, had never arisen, and I did not at all want to go there now. I felt sure, too, that he would want to reopen the matter of compensation, and only a quite unjustified feeling of guilt made me accept. We took an Underground together after work, travelling in the late rush-hour to Clapham North, and walked some distance in the rain. His place, when we eventually got to it, seemed particularly inconvenient, the entrance being through a small cleaner's shop. It consisted of one room and a shared toilet on the half-landing. The room itself was tidy, arranged, so it struck me, much on the lines of his cubby-hole, but the window was shut and it was oppressively stuffy. This is where I bury myself, said Singlebury.

There were no cooking arrangements and he left me there while he went down to fetch us something ready to eat from the Steakorama next to the cleaners. In his absence I took the opportunity to examine his room, though of course not in an inquisitive or prying manner. I was struck by the fact that none of his small store of stationery had been brought home from the office. He returned with two steaks wrapped in aluminium foil, evidently a special treat in my honour, and afterwards he went out on to the landing and made cocoa, a drink which I had not tasted for more than thirty years. The evening dragged rather. In the course of conversation it turned out that Singlebury was fond of reading. There were in fact several issues of a colour-printed encyclopaedia which he had been collecting as it came out, but unfortunately it had ceased publication after the seventh part. Reading is my hobby, he said. I pointed out that a hobby was rather something that one did with one's hands or in the open air – a relief from the work of the brain. Oh, I don't accept that distinction, Singlebury said. The mind and the body are the same. Well, one cannot deny the connection, I replied. Fear, for example, releases adrenalin, which directly affects the nerves. I don't mean connection, I mean identity, Singlebury said, the mind is the blood. Nonsense, I said, you might just as well tell me that the blood is the mind. It stands to reason that the blood can't think.

I was right, after all, in thinking that he would refer to the matter of the redundancy. This was not until he was seeing me off at the bus-stop, when for a moment he turned his grey, exposed-looking face away from me and said that he did not see how he could manage if he really had to go. He stood there like someone who has 'tried to give satisfaction' – he even used this phrase, saying that if the expression were not redolent of a bygone age, he would like to feel he had given satisfaction. Fortunately we had not long to wait for the 45 bus.

At the expiry of the month the staff gave a small tea-party for those who were leaving. I cannot describe this occasion as a success.

The following Monday I missed Singlebury as a familiar presence and also, as mentioned above, because I had never quite realized how much work he had been taking upon himself. As a direct consequence of losing him I found myself having to stay late – not altogether unwillingly, since although following general instructions I have discouraged overtime, the extra pay in my own case would be instrumental in making ends meet. Meanwhile Singlebury's desk had not been cleared – that is, of the trays, pencil-sharpener and complimentary calendar which were, of course, office property. The feeling that he would come back – not like Mrs Horrocks, who has rung up and called round incessantly – but simply come back to work out of habit and through not knowing what else to do, was very strong, without being openly mentioned. I myself half expected and dreaded it, and I had mentally prepared two or three lines of argument in order to persuade him, if he *did* come, not to try it again. Nothing happened, however, and on the Thursday I personally removed the 'things' from the cubby-hole into my own room.

Meanwhile in order to dispel certain quite unfounded rumours I thought it best to issue a notice for general circulation, pointing out that if Mr Singlebury should turn out to have taken any unwise step, and if in consequence any inquiry should be necessary, we should be the first to hear about it from the police. I dictated this to our only permanent typist, who immediately said, oh, he would never do that. He would never cause any unpleasantness like bringing police into the place, he'd do all he could to avoid that. I did not encourage any further discussion, but I asked my wife, who is very used to social work, to call round at Singlebury's place in Clapham North and find out how he was. She did not have very much luck. The people in the cleaner's shop knew, or thought they knew, that he was away, but they had not been sufficiently interested to ask where he was going.

On Friday young Patel said he would be leaving, as the damp and the smell were affecting his health. The damp is certainly not drying out in this seasonably warm weather.

I also, as you know, received another invitation on the Friday, at very short notice, in fact no notice at all; I was told to come to your house in Suffolk Park Gardens that evening for drinks. I was not unduly elated, having been asked once before after I had done rather an awkward small job for you. In our Company, justice has not only not to be done, but it must be seen not to be done. The food was quite nice; it came from your Caterers Grade 3. I spent most of the evening talking to Ted Hollow, one of the area sales-managers. I did not expect to be introduced to your wife, nor was I. Towards the end of the evening you spoke to me for three minutes in the small room with a green marble floor and matching wallpaper leading to the ground-floor toilets. You asked me if everything was all right, to which I replied, all right for whom? You said that nobody's fault was nobody's funeral. I said that I had tried to give satisfaction. Passing on towards the washbasins, you told me with seeming cordiality to be careful and watch it when I had had mixed drinks.

I would describe my feeling at this point as resentment, and I cannot identify exactly the moment when it passed into unease. I do know that I was acutely uneasy as I crossed the hall and saw two of your domestic staff, a man and a woman, holding my coat, which I had left in the lobby, and apparently trying to brush it. Your domestic staff all appear to be of foreign extraction and I personally feel sorry for them and do not grudge them a smile at the oddly assorted guests. Then I saw they were not smiling at my coat but that they seemed to be examining their fingers and looking at me earnestly and silently, and the collar or shoulders of my coat was covered with blood. As I came up to them, although they were still both absolutely silent, the illusion or impression passed, and I put on my coat and left the house in what I hope was a normal manner.

I now come to the present time. The feeling of uneasiness which I have described as making itself felt in your house has not diminished during this past weekend, and partly to take my mind off it and partly for the reasons I have given, I decided to work overtime again tonight, Monday the 23rd. This was in spite of the fact that the damp smell had become almost a stench, as of something putrid, which must have affected my nerves to some extent, because when I went out to get something to eat at Dino's I left the lights on, both in my own office, and in the entrance hall. I mean that for the first time since I began to work for the Company I left them on deliberately. As I walked to the corner I looked back and saw the two solitary lights looking somewhat forlorn in contrast to the glitter of the Arab-American Mutual Loan Corporation opposite. After my meal I felt absolutely reluctant to go back to the building, and wished then that I had not given way to the impulse to leave the lights on, but since I had done so and they must be turned off, I had no choice.

As I stood in the empty hallway I could hear the numerous creakings, settlings and faint tickings of an old building, possibly associated with the plumbing system. The lifts for reasons of economy do not operate after 6.30 p.m., so I began to walk up the stairs. After one flight I felt a strong creeping tension in the nerves of the back such as any of us feel when there is danger from behind; one might say that the body was thinking for itself on these occasions. I did not look round, but simply continued upwards as rapidly as I could. At the third floor I paused, and could hear footsteps coming patiently up behind me. This was not a surprise; I had been expecting them all evening.

Just at the door of my own office, or rather of the cubby-hole, for I have to pass through that, I turned, and saw at the end of the dim corridor what I had also expected, Singlebury, advancing towards me with his unmistakable shuffling step. My first reaction was a kind of bewilderment as to why he, who had been such an excellent timekeeper, so regular day by day, should become a creature of the night. He was wearing the blue suit. This I could make out by its familiar outline, but it was not till he came halfway down the corridor towards me, and reached the patch of light falling through the window from the street, that I saw that he was not himself – I mean that his head was nodding or rather swivelling irregularly from side to side. It crossed my mind that Singlebury was drunk. I had never known him drunk or indeed seen him take anything to drink, even at the office Christmas party, but one cannot estimate the effect that trouble will have upon a man. I began to think what steps I should take in this situation. I turned on the light in his cubby-hole as I went through and waited at the entrance of my own office. As he appeared in the outer doorway I saw that I had not been correct about the reason for the odd movement of the head. The throat was cut from ear to ear so that the head was nearly severed from the shoulders. It was this which had given the impression of nodding, or rather, lolling. As he walked into his cubby-hole Singlebury raised both hands and tried to steady the head as though conscious that something was wrong. The eyes were thickly filmed over, as one sees in the carcasses in a butcher's shop.

I shut and locked my door, and not wishing to give way to nausea, or to lose all control of myself, I sat down at my desk. My work was waiting for me as I had left it – it was the file on the matter of the damp elimination – and, there not being anything else to do, I tried to look through it. On the other side of the door I could hear Singlebury sit down also, and then try the drawers of the table, evidently looking for the 'things' without which he could not start work. After the drawers had been tried, one after another, several times, there was almost total silence.

The present position is that I am locked in my office and would not, no matter what you offered me, indeed I could not, go out through the cubby-hole and pass what is sitting at the desk. The early cleaners will not be here for seven hours and forty-five minutes. I have passed the time so far as best I could in writing this report. One consideration strikes me. If what I have next door is a visitant which should not be walking but buried in the earth, then its wound cannot bleed, and there will be no stream of blood moving slowly under the whole width of the communicating door. However I am sitting at the moment with my back to the door, so that, without turning round, I have no means of telling whether it has done so or not.

The Game of Dice

Alain Danielou

'Let's begin,' said Jay Prakash as soon as the lamps were lighted. They sat together and drew lots. On the eve of the spring festival it is the custom to play games of chance. Jay Prakash had gathered some of his college friends for this night of gamblings. Barefoot servants brought betel in silver boxes, mango, sherbet, cigarettes. Lalit was breathing the warm fragrance that mounted from the garden, enjoying the luxury of the cushions, the richness of the light. He was playing absentmindedly, and cast the die beyond the square of felt. Jay Prakash protested: 'Pay attention to the game!'

Lalit made an effort to overcome the intoxication he felt from this big house, its carpets, its balconies, its chandeliers. He tried to play properly, but his luck was out. He very soon lost all he had and wanted to quit. Jay Prakash said with annoyance:

'What a rotten player you are!'

'I've lost all I have, I don't want to play. Go on without me, my luck's against me.'

'What nonsense! I'll advance you what you need: we're not playing for big stakes. Don't be such a miser.'

Without replying, Lalit went on with the game, but his bad luck continued. He looked so downcast that the others laughed at him. He ended up by laughing himself.

By daybreak Lalit was deeply in debt to Jay Prakash. He went out into the dewy garden, softly pushed the gate and stepped into the deserted street. He hesitated a moment, then set off very quickly in the opposite direction from the college hostel.

A few days later Jay Prakash was getting ready to go back to college. They told him that a young woman wished to speak with him. He came out into the gallery about the garden and saw a girl plainly dressed, with the red mark of a married woman in the parting of her hair. He made out that she was the wife of Lalit. 'He has left us,' she told him, 'and we don't know where he has gone. Here is a letter he has addressed to you.'

She sat down on the ground and wept. Jay Prakash seized the letter and read:

Jay Prakash, God in His goodness has given me parents who are very poor. Out of vanity I have always tried to hide it. With great effort and hardship they have supported me at college. All they possess would not suffice to pay my poor debt to you. I cannot bear my disgrace. I am going away forever. Good-bye.

Jay Prakash tried to question the young woman, but she knew nothing and he had to let her go, humble, abandoned, shaken by her sobbing.

Jay Prakash was an old friend of Lalit's. He thought of the cruelty of his sarcasm, the stupidity of his jokes, and determined to do all he could to find his friend, retrieve this disaster. He swore to put off his own marriage until he had brought back Lalit to his wife.

He sent out agents in every direction to look for him But in spite of all his efforts months went by and still there was no trace. Two years later the girl died.

Few people nowadays remember this story. But, faithful to his vow, Jay Prakash has never married. The sad events of his youth seem to have influenced the whole course of his life. It is not that he had lived sad or miserable or that he often thinks of them. But it seems that his heart is always in quest of something he can never find.

Years passed, then other years.

For some years Jay Prakash has been living in a dilapidated house overlooking the river.

The pearly light that plays upon the rippling waters has become for him a companion that embodies all the joy and beauty and sweetness that he cannot find within himself. In the early morning the sound of prayers, of songs, of ritual ablutions awakens him like a babbling of familiar birds. His eyes languish upon naked bodies, brilliant robes. He amuses himself watching children's games, the old men's beards, the long hair of ascetics who leave their forest solitudes, sometimes, on pilgrimage to the holy city. All this peaceful and happy life sustains a world of dream where strange fragrances of beauty drift in the rainbow haze that lolls upon the waters.

Jay Prakash thought that this world of dream must rest on some deep and wonderful reality whose harmony was reflected in the beauty of colour and of form. For a long time he sought in the writings of mystics and the philosophers the solid base beneath the appearances that enchant us. But he could not find there anything to fill his empty heart.

Every day he heard the pilgrims crying, with the obscure faith of a millennial love: 'O Ganga, our Mother,' before they plunged into the sacred waters. Day after day it met his ear, their tenderness for the wide, slow river, whose silent, unperceptible caress undermines the crumbling steps of palaces. Little by little it stirred in his heart a chord long muted which now day by day became more sensitive. Little by little Jay Prakash discovered his strange love for this mysterious river which, people said, had come down from heaven: it was the source of all this prosperous life, this ample beauty. He understood that he could cast into its waters the burden of a tenderness without object that was weighing down his soul. The city and its palaces, the flowering gardens, golden bodies, songs, mist and prayers were but the ornaments of the divine stream. It was towards this river, now, that the impetuous torrent of his heart was flooding. It was this river that linked him with his soul, the river that brought him a message of peace. In thought he mounted to its far-off source, the very gate of heaven.

His love for the sacred river gradually filled with sweetness the monotonous days of approaching age. An ambition slowly took form in him and every day it gathered strength. It was to journey up the river to the holy and mysterious spot where, leaving heaven, Ganga appears upon the earth. It was as it were a strange call that every wave, every ripple, every eddy of the current incessantly repeated in his heart. This desire grew so strong that one day, feeling himself old and ill, he decided to leave without delay to go and pay homage, before he left this world, at the source of the sacred river.

Jay Prakash made the journey half unconscious with ecstasy. He did not notice the trains, the porters, the crowd. The difficulties he met in his pilgrimage only made more precious still the light and joy he bore within himself as if within a shrine. He got down at the little station at the foot of the mountains from where the narrow pilgrim road starts out from Badrinath.

He set off alone, on foot, by the path that follows the river – now a joyous torrent. All along the way pious souls have built rest-houses where travellers may find shelter for the night. The way was deserted. At rare intervals he met a few belated pilgrims coming down. Seeing the old man hurrying along the path, they said to him: '*Aré*, father, the season is over. The passes will soon be blocked with snow. Go back home and come again in spring.'

But Jay Prakash knew there would be no more spring for him: the deep insistence of his soul dragged his failing frame towards the cradle of his love, unconscious of fatigue and cold.

And so after long stages he arrived one day within sight of the great cliff of ice that he had wished to see, and then to die.

Now that there rose before him the goal almost attained, a caravan approached and soon passed near to him – porters carrying bells and gongs and silver vessels. They were the priests of the temple of Ganga who, leaving the source, were coming down for the winter, as they do every year. No human being could stay in these icy solitudes during the cold. Some of the priests came up to the lost man, determined to make him turn back with them. They were going along the road closing one after another the pilgrims' rest-houses. But Jay Prakash would not turn back. This journey would be his last, what matter? Obeying the call of his soul he had come to prostrate himself before the sacred fount and he would certainly not return without having accomplished his vow and prayed in the temple. He begged one of the priests to return with him and unlock the door a moment. But they would not listen. He promised them all he possessed. Nothing would move them. They had put the Goddess to sleep for the winter, they said: the door once closed could not be opened again until the spring. The sky began to threaten. Unable to convince the obstinate man, they continued on their way.

Towards evening, exhausted, Jay Prakash reached the great temple that is built at the very edge of the sacred source. He made the ritual circumambulation, vainly shook the heavy door, and then, overwhelmed, fell down upon the steps resolved to die.

How long he lay there unconscious he could not have said. But it seemed to him that a strange well-being suddenly arose in him; a warmth, a calm enveloped him like a caress. Was it already death? But a firm hand pressed upon his shoulder, a voice was calling him. Lifting his head, Jay Prakash saw an ascetic, almost nude, with long bushy hair and an iron girdle, a trident in his hand. His face was hollowed, but his body had the adolescent softness that yogis keep their whole life through.

'You can't stay here at night, elder brother,' he said: 'come with me and tomorrow you will decide what you want to do.'

The last light of day outlined the heavy clouds: their menacing shadow overhung the narrow valley where there leapt an icy wind. Jay Prakash let himself be dragged along by the ascetic. They climbed the steep slope by a narrow path until, under a rock, appeared the entrance to a cave. Within, before a little shrine, an oil lamp was burning; dry grass served for a bed. The ascetic made him sit down and shared with him his evening meal, balls of raw flour kneaded with water. He seemed to possess no covering, though the cold was already keen. But to warm Jay Prakash he lit a little fire near the entrance. Then, sitting on the ground beside him, he said:

'Elder brother, the winter night is long: let us play to pass the time.'

He threw down dice and set out fifteen white and fifteen black pebbles for counters. The sight of dice made Jay Prakash shudder. He had never touched them since that unfortunate night so long ago. He was about to refuse when his eyes met the fixed gaze of the ascetic. Subdued, he bent his head. He hardly remembered the rules of the game, he felt heavy with sleep. Still, for fear of offending his host he must play at least one round.

The ascetic had extraordinary skill and daring and Jay Prakash was very soon caught by the excitement of the game. One round followed another. He had forgotten fatigue and sleepiness, the bitter night outside. A sort of intoxication seized him as the black and white pebbles went on changing hands. The ascetic lost speedily, but when he had only one counter left his luck changed and he won everything back, till Jay Prakash in his turn had only a single pebble. Then he began to lose again.

The fire had gone out. Jay Prakash noticed that the flame of the lamp never wavered but shone unmoving like a star. He wanted to point out this detail to his host but, lost in the game, he paid no attention, and Jay Prakash himself, trying to overcome the regular swing of luck that carried the pebbles just to one side of the game and then to the other, forgot all but the game.

Day had dawned without their noticing it. It was the ascetic's turn to win and for the sixth time since they had begun to play he was steadily taking back the pebbles Jay Prakash had piled up. Soon there were only five, then four, then three, two, only one. Would fortune change her mind? No: this time she abandoned Jay Prakash and the ascetic took his last counter. He got up then, smiled, and motioning Jay Prakash towards the light outside, held out to him something wrapped in a bit of silk.

'The sky seems to have cleared. Go down, elder brother, to the temple and place my offering on the steps.'

Jay Prakash felt no fatigue from his sleepless night; he was, on the contrary, rested and refreshed. He went out. The clouds had cleared away, a warm breeze came up from the valley.

Going down the steep slope, he noticed that the ground which had seemed hard and bare in the evening gloom was covered with grass and flowers. As he was about to reach the temple he saw a group approaching and recognized the priests he had met the evening before. He went up to them in surprise.

'Have you forgotten something? Will you open the temple a moment so that I may fulfil my vow?'

The priests did not seem to recognize him and looked at him in astonishment. One of them said:

'In a moment, Grandfather, the temple will be open for all; today is the Feast of Spring.'

Jay Prakash went up to the threshold and untied the rag of silk to place the ascetic's offering on the steps. It was one of the pebbles that had served as counters for the game. Then Jay Prakash saw that it was engraved and read the single word 'Lalit'.

He ran towards the ascetic's cave. But the slope was smooth and bare. There was neither cave nor path.

The July Ghost

A. S. Byatt

'I think I must move out of where I'm living,' he said. 'I have this problem with my landlady.'

He picked a long, bright hair off the back of her dress, so deftly that the act seemed simply considerate. He had been skilful at balancing glass, plate and cutlery, too. He had a look of dignified misery, like a dejected hawk. She was interested.

'What sort of problem? Amatory, financial, or domestic?'

'None of those, really. Well, not financial.'

He turned the hair on his finger, examining it intently, not meeting her eye.

'Not financial. Can you tell me? I might know somewhere you could stay. I know a lot of people.'

'You would.' He smiled shyly. 'It's not an easy problem to describe. There's just the two of us. I occupy the attics. Mostly.'

He came to a stop. He was obviously reserved and secretive. But he was telling her something. This is usually attractive.

'Mostly?' Encouraging him.

'Oh, it's not like *that*. Well, not . . . Shall we sit down?'

They moved across the party, which was a big party, on a hot day. He stopped and found a bottle and filled her glass. He had not needed to ask what she was drinking. They sat side by side on a sofa: he admired the brilliant poppies bold on her emerald dress, and her pretty sandals. She had come to London for the summer to work in the British Museum. She could really have managed with microfilm in Tucson for what little manuscript research was needed, but there was a dragging love affair to end. There is an age at which, however desperately happy one is in stolen moments, days, or weekends with one's married professor, one either prises him loose or cuts and runs. She had had a stab at both, and now considered she had successfully cut and run. So it was nice to be immediately appreciated. Problems are capable of solution. She said as much to him, turning her soft face to his ravaged one, swinging the long bright hair. It had begun a year ago, he told her in a rush, at another party actually; he had met this woman, the landlady in question, and had made, not immediately, a kind of *faux pas*, he now saw, and she had been very decent, all things considered, and so . . .

He had said, 'I think I must move out of where I'm living.' He had been quite wild, had nearly not come to the party, but could not go on drinking alone. The woman had considered him coolly and asked, 'Why?' One could not, he said, go on in a place where one had once been blissfully happy, and was now miserable, however convenient the place. Convenient, that was, for work, and friends, and things that seemed, as he mentioned them, ashy and insubstantial compared to the memory and the hope of opening the door and finding Anne outside it, laughing and breathless, waiting to be told what he had read, or thought, or eaten, or felt that day. Someone I loved left, he told the woman. Reticent on that occasion too, he bit back the flurry of sentences about the total unexpectedness of it, the arriving back and finding only an envelope on a clean table, and spaces in the bookshelves, the record stack, the kitchen cupboard. It must have been planned for weeks, she must have been thinking it out while he rolled on her, while she poured wine for him, while . . . No, no. Vituperation is undignified and in this case what he felt was lower and worse than rage: just pure, child-like loss. 'One ought not to mind places,' he said to the woman. 'But one does,' she had said. 'I know.'

She had suggested to him that he could come and be her lodger, then; she had, she said, a lot of spare space going to waste, and her husband wasn't there much. 'We've not had a lot to say to each other, lately.' He could be quite self-contained, there was a kitchen and bathroom in the attics; she wouldn't bother him. There was a large garden. It was possibly this that decided him: it was very hot, central London, the time of year when a man feels he would give anything to live in a room opening on to grass and trees, not a high flat in a dusty street. And if Anne came back, the door would be locked and mortice-locked. He could stop thinking about Anne coming back. That was a decisive move: Anne thought he wasn't decisive. He would live without Anne.

*

For some weeks after he moved in he had seen very little of the woman. They met on the stairs, and once she came up, on a hot Sunday, to tell him he must feel free to use the garden. He had offered to do some weeding and mowing and she had accepted. That was the weekend her husband came back, driving furiously up to the front door, running in, and calling in the empty hall, 'Imogen, Imogen!' To which she had replied, uncharacteristically by screaming hysterically. There was nothing in her husband, Noel's, appearance to warrant this reaction; their lodger, peering over the banister at the sound, had seen their upturned faces in the stairwell and watched hers settle into its usual prim and placid expression as he did so. Seeing Noel, a balding, fluffy-templed, stooping thirty-five or so, shabby corduroy suit, cotton polo neck, he realized he was now able to guess her age, as he had not been. She was a very neat woman, faded blonde, her hair in a knot on the back of her head, her legs long and slender, her eyes downcast. Mild was not quite the right word for her, though. She explained then that she had screamed because Noel had come home unexpectedly and startled her: she was sorry. It seemed a reasonable explanation. The extraordinary vehemence of the screaming was probably an echo in the stairwell. Noel seemed wholly downcast by it, all the same.

He had kept out of the way, that weekend, taking the stairs two at a time and lightly, feeling a little aggrieved, looking out of his kitchen window into the lovely, overgrown garden, that they were lurking indoors, wasting all the summer sun. At Sunday lunch-time he had heard the husband, Noel, shouting on the stairs.

'I can't go on, if you go on like that. I've done my best, I've tried to get through. Nothing will shift you, will it, you won't *try*, will you, you just go on and on. Well, I have my life to live, you can't throw a life away . . . can you?'

He had crept out again on to the dark upper landing and seen her standing, half-way down the stairs, quite still, watching Noel wave his arms and roar, or almost roar, with a look of impassive patience, as though this nuisance must pass off. Noel swallowed and gasped; he turned his face up to her and said plaintively,

'You do see I can't stand it?' I'll be in touch, shall I? You must want . . . you must need . . . you must . . .'

She didn't speak.

'If you need anything, you know where to get me.'

'Yes.'

'Oh, well . . .' said Noel, and went to the door. She watched him, from

the stairs, until it was shut, and then came up again, step by step, as
though it was an effort, a little, and went on coming past her bedroom, to
his landing, to come in and ask him, entirely naturally, please to use the
garden if he wanted to, and please not to mind marital rows. She was sure
he understood . . . things were difficult . . . Noel wouldn't be back for
some time. He was a journalist: his work took him away a lot. Just as well.
She committed herself to the 'just as well'. She was a very economical
speaker.

So he took to sitting in the garden. It was a lovely place: a huge, hidden,
walled south London garden, with old fruit trees at the end, a wildly
waving disorderly buddleia, curving beds full of old roses, and a lawn of
overgrown, dense rye-grass. Over the wall at the foot was the Common,
with a footpath running behind all the gardens. She came out to the shed
and helped him to assemble and oil the lawnmower, standing on the little
path under the apple branches while he cut an experimental serpentine
across her hay. Over the wall came the high sound of children's voices,
and the thunk and thud of a football. He asked her how to raise the blades:
he was not mechanically minded.

'The children get quite noisy,' she said. 'And dogs. I hope they don't
bother you. There aren't many safe places for children, round here.'

He replied truthfully that he never heard sounds that didn't concern
him, when he was concentrating. When he'd got the lawn into shape, he
was going to sit on it and do a lot of reading, try to get his mind in trim
again, to write a paper on Hardy's poems, on their curiously archaic
vocabulary.

'It isn't very far to the road on the other side, really,' she said. 'It just
seems to be. The Common is an illusion of space, really. Just a spur of
brambles and gorse-bushes and bits of football pitch between two fast
four-laned main roads. I hate London commons.'

'There's a lovely smell, though, from the gorse and the wet grass. It's a
pleasant illusion.'

'No illusions are pleasant,' she said, decisively, and went in. He
wondered what she did with her time: apart from little shopping
expeditions she seemed to be always in the house. He was sure that when
he'd met her she'd been introduced as having some profession: vaguely
literary, vaguely academic, like everyone he knew. Perhaps she wrote
poetry in her north-facing living-room. He had no idea what it would be
like. Women generally wrote emotional poetry, much nicer than men, as
Kingsley Amis has stated, but she seemed, despite her placid stillness, too

spare and too fierce – grim? – for that. He remembered the screaming. Perhaps she wrote Plath-like chants of violence. He didn't think that quite fitted the bill, either. Perhaps she was a freelance radio journalist. He didn't bother to ask anyone who might be a common acquaintance. During the whole year, he explained to the American at the party, he hadn't actually *discussed* her with anyone. Of course he wouldn't, she agreed vaguely and warmly. She knew he wouldn't. He didn't see why he shouldn't, in fact, but went on, for the time, with his narrative.

They had got to know each other a little better over the next few weeks, at least on the level of borrowing tea, or even sharing pots of it. The weather had got hotter. He had found an old-fashioned deck-chair, with faded striped canvas, in the shed, and had brushed it over and brought it out on to his mown lawn, where he sat writing a little, reading a little, getting up and pulling up a tuft of couch grass. He had been wrong about the children not bothering him: there was a succession of incursions by all sizes of children looking for all sizes of balls, which bounced to his feet, or crashed in the shrubs, or vanished in the herbaceous border, black and white footballs, beach-balls with concentric circles of primary colours, acid yellow tennis balls. The children came over the wall: black faces, brown faces, floppy long hair, shaven heads, respectable dotted sun-hats and camouflaged cotton army hats from Milletts. They came over easily, as though they were used to it, sandals, training shoes, a few bare toes, grubby sunburned legs, cotton skirts, jeans, football shorts. Sometimes, perched on the top, they saw him and gestured at the balls; one or two asked permission. Sometimes he threw a ball back, but was apt to knock down a few knobby little unripe apples or pears. There was a gate in the wall, under the fringing trees, which he once tried to open, spending time on rusty bolts only to discover that the lock was new and secure, and the key not in it.

The boy sitting in the tree did not seem to be looking for a ball. He was in a fork of the tree nearest the gate, swinging his legs, doing something to a knot in a frayed end of rope that was attached to the branch he sat on. He wore blue jeans and training shoes, and a brilliant tee shirt, striped in the colours of the spectrum, arranged in the right order, which the man on the grass found visually pleasing. He had rather long blond hair, falling over his eyes, so that his face was obscured.

'Hey, you. Do you think you ought to be up there? It might not be safe.'

The boy looked up, grinned, and vanished monkey-like over the wall. He had a nice, frank grin, friendly, not cheeky.

He was there again, the next day, leaning back in the crook of the tree, arms crossed. He had on the same shirt and jeans. The man watched him, expecting him to move again, but he sat, immobile, smiling down pleasantly, and then staring up at the sky. The man read a little, looked up, saw him still there, and said.

'Have you lost anything?'

The child did not reply: after a moment he climbed down a little, swung along the branch hand over hand, dropped to the ground, raised an arm in salute, and was up over the usual route over the wall.

Two days later he was lying on his stomach on the edge of the lawn, out of the shade, this time in a white tee shirt with a pattern of blue ships and water-lines on it, his bare feet and legs stretched in the sun. He was chewing a grass stem, and studying the earth, as though watching for insects. The man said 'Hi, there,' and the boy looked up, met his look with intensely blue eyes under long lashes, smiled with the same complete warmth and openness, and returned his look to the earth.

He felt reluctant to inform on the boy, who seemed so harmless and considerate: but when he met him walking out of the kitchen door, spoke to him, and got no answer but the gentle smile before the boy ran off towards the wall, he wondered if he should speak to his landlady. So he asked her, did she mind the children coming in the garden. She said no, children must look for balls, that was part of being children. He persisted – they sat there, too, and he had met one coming out of the house. He hadn't seemed to be doing any harm, the boy, but you couldn't tell. He thought she should know.

He was probably a friend of her son's, she said. She looked at him kindly and explained. Her son had run off the Common with some other children, two years ago, in the summer, in July, and had been killed on the road. More or less instantly, she had added drily, as though calculating that just *enough* information would preclude the need for further questions. He said he was sorry, very sorry, feeling to blame, which was ridiculous, and a little injured, because he had not known about her son, and might inadvertently have made a fool of himself with some casual reference whose ignorance would be embarrassing.

What was the boy like, she said. The one in the house? 'I don't – talk to his friends. I find it painful. It could be Timmy, or Martin. They might have lost something, or want . . .'

He described the boy. Blond, about ten at a guess, he was not very good at children's ages, very blue eyes, slightly built, with a rainbow-striped tee shirt and blue jeans, mostly though not always – oh, and those football practice shoes, black and green. And the other tee shirt, with the ships and wavy lines. And an extraordinarily nice smile. A really *warm* smile. A nice-looking boy.

He was used to her being silent. But this silence went on and on and on. She was just staring into the garden. After a time, she said, in her precise conversational tone,

'The only thing I want, the only thing I want at all in this world, is to see that boy.'

She stared at the garden and he stared with her, until the grass began to dance with empty light, and the edges of the shrubbery wavered. For a brief moment he shared the strain of not seeing the boy. Then she gave a little sigh, sat down, neatly, as always, and passed out at his feet.

After this she became, for her, voluble. He didn't move after she fainted, but sat patiently by her, until she stirred and sat up; then he fetched her some water, and would have gone away, but she talked.

'I'm too rational to see ghosts, I'm not someone who would see anything there was to see, I don't believe in an after-life. I don't see how anyone can, I always found a kind of satisfaction for myself in the idea that one just came to an end, to a sliced-off stop. But that was myself; I didn't think *he* – not *he* – I thought ghosts were what people *wanted* to see, or were afraid to see . . . and after he died, and best hope I had, it sounds silly, was that I would go mad enough so that instead of waiting every day for him to come home from school and rattle the letter-box I might actually have the illusion of seeing or hearing him come in. Because I can't stop my body and mind waiting, every day, every day, I can't let go. And his bedroom, sometimes at night I go in, I think I might just for a moment forget he *wasn't* in there sleeping, I think I would pay almost anything – anything at all – for a moment of seeing him like I used to. In his pyjamas, with his – his – his hair . . . ruffled, and, his . . . you said, his . . . that *smile*.

'When it happened, they got Noel, and Noel came in and shouted my name, like he did the other day, that's why I screamed, because it – seemed the same – and then they said, he is dead, and I thought coolly, *is* dead, that will go on and on and on till the end of time, it's a continuous present tense, one thinks the most ridiculous things, there I was thinking about grammar, the verb to be, when it ends to be dead . . . And then I came out into the garden, and I half saw, in my mind's eye, a kind of ghost of his face, just the eyes and hair, coming towards me – like every day waiting for him to come home, the way you think of your son, with such pleasure, when he's – not there – and I – I thought – no, I won't *see* him, because he is dead, and I won't dream about him because he is dead, I'll be rational and practical and continue to live because one must, and there was Noel . . .

'I got it wrong, you see, I was so *sensible*, and then I was so shocked because I couldn't get to want anything – I couldn't *talk* to Noel – I – I – made Noel take away, destroy, all the photos, I – didn't dream, you can will not to dream, I didn't . . . visit a grave, flowers, there isn't any point. I was so sensible. Only my body wouldn't stop waiting and all it wants is to – see that boy. *That* boy. That boy you – saw.'

He did not say that he might have seen another boy, maybe even a boy who had been given the tee shirts and jeans afterwards. He did not say, though the idea crossed his mind, that maybe what he had seen was some kind of impression from her terrible desire to see a boy where nothing was. The boy had had nothing terrible, no aura of pain about him: he had been, his memory insisted, such a pleasant, courteous, self-contained boy, with his own purposes. And in fact the woman herself almost immediately raised the possibility that what he had seen was what she desired to see, a kind of mix-up of radio waves, like when you overheard police messages on the radio, or got BBC 1 on a switch that said ITV. She was thinking fast, and went on almost immediately to say that perhaps his sense of loss, his loss of Anne, which was what had led her to feel she could bear his presence in her house, was what had brought them – dare she say – near enough, for their wavelengths, to mingle, perhaps, had made him susceptible . . . You mean, he had said, we are a kind of emotional vacuum, between us, that must be filled. Something like that, she had said, and had added, 'But I don't believe in ghosts.'

Anne, he thought, could not be a ghost, because she was elsewhere, with someone else, doing for someone else those little things she had done so gaily for him, tasty little suppers, bits of research, a sudden vase of unusual flowers, a new bold shirt, unlike his own cautious taste, but suiting him, suiting him. In a sense, Anne was worse lost because voluntarily absent, an absence that could not be loved because love was at an end, for Anne.

'I don't suppose you will, now,' the woman was saying. 'I think talking would probably stop any – mixing of messages, if that's what it is, don't you? But – if – *if* he comes again' – and here for the first time her eyes were full of tears – 'if – you must promise, you will *tell* me, you must promise.'

He had promised, easily enough, because he was fairly sure she was right, the boy would not be seen again. But the next day he was on the lawn, nearer than ever, sitting on the grass beside the deck-chair, his arms clasping his bent, warm brown knees, the thick, pale hair glittering in the sun. He was wearing a football shirt, this time, Chelsea's colours. Sitting down in the deck-chair, the man could have put out a hand and touched him, but did not: it was not, it seemed, a possible gesture to make. But the boy looked up and smiled, with a pleasant complicity, as though they now understood each other very well. The man tried speech: he said, 'It's nice to see you again,' and the boy nodded acknowledgement of this remark, without speaking himself. This was the beginning of communication between them, or what the man supposed to be communication. He did not think of fetching the woman. He became aware that he was in some strange way *enjoying the boy's company*. His pleasant stillness – and he sat there all morning, occasionally lying back on the grass, occasionally staring thoughtfully at the house – was calming and comfortable. The man did quite a lot of work – wrote about three reasonable pages on Hardy's original air-blue gown – and looked up now and then to make sure the boy was still there and happy.

He went to report to the woman – as he had after all promised to do – that evening. She had obviously been waiting and hoping – her unnatural calm had given way to agitated pacing, and her eyes were dark and deeper in. At this point in the story he found in himself a necessity to bowdlerize for the sympathetic American, as he had indeed already begun to do. He had mentioned only a child who had 'seemed like' the woman's lost son, and he now ceased to mention the child at all, as an actor in the story, with the result that what the American woman heard was a tale of how he, the man, had become increasingly involved in the woman's solitary grief, how their two losses had become a kind of *folie à deux* from which he could not extricate himself. What follows is not what he told the American girl, though it may be clear at which points the bowdlerized version coincided with what he really believed to have happened. There was a sense he could not at first analyse that it was improper to talk about the boy – not because he might not be believed; that did not come into it; but because something dreadful might happen.

'He sat on the lawn all morning. In a football shirt.'

'Chelsea?'

'Chelsea.'

'What did he do? Does he look happy? Did he speak?' Her desire to know was terrible.

'He doesn't speak. He didn't move much. He seemed – very calm. He stayed a long time.'

'This is terrible. This is ludicrous. There *is no boy*.'

'No. But I saw him.'

'Why you?'

'I don't know.' A pause. 'I do *like* him.'

'He is – was – a most likeable boy.'

Some days later he saw the boy running along the landing in the evening, wearing what might have been pyjamas, in peacock towelling, or might have been a track suit. Pyjamas, the woman stated confidently, when he told her: his new pyjamas. With white ribbed cuffs, weren't they? and a white polo neck? He corroborated this, watching her cry – she cried more easily now – finding her anxiety and disturbance very hard to bear. But it never occurred to him that it was possible to break his promise to tell her when he saw the boy. That was another curious imperative from some undefined authority.

They discussed clothes. If there were ghosts, how could they appear in clothes long burned, or rotted, or worn away by other people? You could imagine, they agreed, that something of a person might linger – as the Tibetans and others believe the soul lingers near the body before setting out on its long journey. But clothes? And in this case so many clothes? I must be seeing your memories, he told her, and she nodded fiercely, compressing her lips, agreeing that this was likely, adding, 'I am too rational to go mad, so I seem to be putting it on you.'

He tried a joke. 'That isn't very kind to me, to infer that madness comes more easily to me.'

'No, sensitivity. I am insensible. I was always a bit like that, and this made it worse. I am the *last* person to see any ghost that was trying to haunt me.'

'We agreed it was your memories I saw.'

'Yes. We agree. That's rational. As rational as we can be, considering.'

All the same, the brilliance of the boy's blue regard, his gravely smiling salutation in the garden next morning, did not seem like anyone's tortured memories of earlier happiness. The man spoke to him directly then:

'Is there anything I can *do* for you? Anything you want? Can I help you?'

The boy seemed to puzzle about this for a while, inclining his head as though hearing was difficult. Then he nodded, quickly and perhaps

urgently, turned, and ran into the house, looking back to make sure he was followed. The man entered the living-room through the french windows, behind the running boy, who stopped for a moment in the centre of the room, with the man blinking behind him at the sudden transition from sunlight to comparative dark. The woman was sitting in an armchair, looking at nothing there. She often sat like that. She looked up, across the boy, at the man, and the boy, his face for the first time anxious, met the man's eyes again, asking, before he went out into the house.

'What is it? What is it? Have you seen him again? Why are you . . .?'

'He came in here. He went – out through the door.'

'I didn't see him.'

'No.'

'Did he – oh, this is so *silly* – did he see me?'

He could not remember. He told the only truth he knew.

'He brought me in here.'

'Oh, what can I do, what am I going to *do*? If I killed myself – I have thought of that – but the idea that I should be with him is an illusion I . . . this silly situation is the nearest I shall ever get. To him. He was *in here with me*?'

'Yes.'

And she was crying again. Out in the garden he could see the boy, swinging agile on the apple branch.

He was not quite sure, looking back, when he had thought he had realized what the boy had wanted him to do. This was also at the party, his worst piece of what he called bowdlerization, though in some sense it was clearly the opposite of bowdlerization. He told the American girl that he had come to the conclusion that it was the woman herself who had wanted it, though there was in fact, throughout, no sign of her wanting anything except to see the boy, as she said. The boy, bolder and more frequent, had appeared several nights running on the landing, wandering in and out of bathrooms and bedrooms, restlessly, a little agitated, questing almost, until it had 'come to' the man that what he required was to be re-engendered, for him, the man, to give to his mother another child, into which he could peacefully vanish. The idea was so clear that it was like another imperative, though he did not have the courage to ask the child to confirm it. Possibly this was out of delicacy – the child was too young to be talked to about sex. Possibly there were other reasons. Possibly he was mistaken: the situation was making him hysterical, he felt action of

some kind was required and must be possible. He could not spend the rest of the summer, the rest of his life, describing non-existent tee shirts and blond smiles.

He could think of no sensible way of embarking on his venture, so in the end simply walked into her bedroom one night. She was lying there, reading; when she saw him her instinctive gesture was to hide, not her bare arms and throat, but her book. She seemed, in fact, quite unsurprised to see his pyjamaed figure, and, after she had recovered her coolness, brought out the book definitely and laid it on the bedspread.

'My new taste in illegitimate literature. I keep them in a box under the bed.'

Ena Twigg, Medium. The Infinite Hive. The Spirit World. Is There Life After Death?

'Pathetic,' she proffered.

He sat down delicately on the bed.

'Please, don't grieve so. Please, let yourself be comforted. Please . . .'

He put an arm round her. She shuddered. He pulled her closer. He asked why she had had only the one son, and she seemed to understand the purport of his question, for she tried, angular and chilly, to lean on him a little, she became apparently compliant. 'No real reason,' she assured him, no material reason. Just her husband's profession and lack of inclination: that covered it.

'Perhaps,' he suggested, 'if she would be comforted a little, perhaps she could hope, perhaps . . .'

For comfort then, she said, dolefully, and lay back, pushing Ena Twigg off the bed with one fierce gesture, then lying placidly. He got in beside her, put his arms round her, kissed her cold cheek, thought of Anne, of what was never to be again. Come on, he said to the woman, you must live, you must try to live, let us hold each other for comfort.

She hissed at him 'Don't *talk*' between clenched teeth, so he stroked her lightly, over her nightdress, breasts and buttocks and long stiff legs, composed like an effigy on an Elizabethan tomb. She allowed this, trembling slightly, and then trembling violently: he took this to be a sign of some mixture of pleasure and pain, of the return of life to stone. He put a hand between her legs and she moved them heavily apart; he heaved himself over her and pushed, unsuccessfully. She was contorted and locked tight: frigid, he thought grimly, was not the word. *Rigor mortis*, his mind said to him, before she began to scream.

He was ridiculously cross about this. He jumped away and said quite

rudely 'Shut up,' and then ungraciously 'I'm sorry.' She stopped screaming as suddenly as she had begun and made one of her painstaking economical explanations.

'Sex and death don't go. I can't afford to let go of my grip on myself. I hoped. What you hoped. It was a bad idea. I apologize.'

'Oh, never mind,' he said and rushed out again on to the landing, feeling foolish and almost in tears for warm, lovely Anne.

The child was on the landing, waiting. When the man saw him, he looked questioning, and then turned his face against the wall and leant there, rigid, his shoulders hunched, his hair hiding his expression. There was a similarity between woman and child. The man felt, for the first time, almost uncharitable towards the boy, and then felt something else.

'Look, I'm sorry. I tried. I did try. Please turn round.'

Uncompromising, rigid, clenched back view.

'Oh well,' said the man, and went into his bedroom.

So now, he said to the American woman at the party, I feel a fool, I feel embarrassed, I feel we are hurting, not helping each other, I feel it isn't a refuge. Of course you feel that, she said, of course you're right – it was temporarily necessary, it helped both of you, but you've got to live your life. Yes, he said, I've done my best, I've tried to get through, I have my life to live. Look, she said, I want to help, I really do, I have these wonderful friends I'm renting this flat from, why don't you come, just for a few days, just for a break, why don't you? They're real sympathetic people, you'd like them, I like them, you could get your emotions kind of straightened out. She'd probably be glad to see the back of you, she must feel as bad as you do, she's got to relate to her situation in her own way in the end. We all have.

He said he would think about it. He knew he had elected to tell the sympathetic American because he had sensed she would be – would offer – a way out. He had to get out. He took her home from the party and went back to his house and landlady without seeing her into her flat. They both knew that this reticence was promising – that he hadn't come in then, because he meant to come later. Her warmth and readiness were like sunshine, she was open. He did not know what to say to the woman.

In fact, she made it easy for him: she asked, briskly, if he now found it perhaps uncomfortable to stay, and he replied that he had felt he should move on, he was of so little use ... Very well, she had agreed, and had

added crisply that it had to be better for everyone if 'all this' came to an
end. He remembered the firmness with which she had told him that no
illusions were pleasant. She was strong: too strong for her own good. It
would take years to wear away that stony, closed, simply surviving
insensibility. It was not his job. He would go. All the same, he felt bad.

He got out his suitcases and put some things in them. He went down to
the garden, nervously, and put away the deck-chair. The garden was
empty. There were no voices over the wall. The silence was thick and
deadening. He wondered, knowing he would not see the boy again, if
anyone else would do so, or if, now he was gone, no one would describe
a tee shirt, a sandal, a smile, seen, remembered, or desired. He went slowly
up to his room again.

The boy was sitting on his suitcase, arms crossed, face frowning and
serious. He held the man's look for a long moment, and then the man
went and sat on his bed. The boy continued to sit. The man found himself
speaking.

'You do see I have to go? I've tried to get through. I can't get through.
I'm no use to you, am I?'

The boy remained immobile, his head on one side, considering. The
man stood up and walked towards him.

'Please. Let me go. What are we, in this house? A man and a woman
and a child, and none of us can get through. You can't want that?'

He went as close as he dared. He had, he thought, the intention of
putting his hand on or through the child. But could not bring himself to
feel there was no boy. So he stood, and repeated,

'I can't get through. Do you want me to stay?'

Upon which, as he stood helplessly there, the boy turned on him again
the brilliant, open, confiding, beautiful desired smile.